ISBN 978-0-276-44282-7

www.readersdigest.co.uk

The Reader's Digest Association Limited, 11 Westferry Circus, Canary Wharf, London E14 4HE

and in Canada
www.rd.ca

The Reader's Digest Association (Canada) ULC, 1100 René-Lévesque Blvd. West, Montréal,
Québec, H3B 5H5 Canada

# of love & life

Three novels selected and condensed
by **Reader's Digest**

The Reader's Digest Association Limited, London, Montreal

CONTENTS

*It's the
Little
Things*

ERICA JAMES

How I came to write It's the Little Things . . .

*My sons and I were staying on Phuket when
the Boxing Day tsunami happened in 2004
and I suspected that one day I would write
about it. However, it wasn't until the spring of
2007 that I felt the time was right to do so. I
didn't want to write a book about the actual
event itself, more a story about how lives could
be changed as a result of such an ordeal.
We humans have an astonishing ability to
survive the seemingly insurmountable, not to
mention the little things . . .*

Chapter One

DR CHLOE HENNESSEY had long since mastered the art of maintaining a perfectly neutral expression.

'Exactly how much bigger do you want to be, Chelsea?' she asked.

Chelsea Savage put her hands in front of her chest—a chest that looked to be about the same size as Chloe's—but before she could open her mouth, her mother piped up, 'She wants to be a 34GG.' A stout, blousily dressed woman in her forties, Mrs Savage worked behind the bar at the Fox and Feathers and was well known for her ability to stamp on any potential bar-room brawls. She was also known for starting a few brawls in her time and more than lived up to her name. Not for nothing was she nicknamed The Pit Bull at the surgery.

'And you are currently what size, Chelsea?' Chloe asked her patient.

'She's a 34A,' chimed in Mrs Savage. 'And it's making her depressed. She's a right pain at times, let me tell you. Always mooching about the place with a face on her like a wet Sunday in Bridlington.'

Chloe kept her gaze deliberately on the sixteen-year-old girl before her. 'Are you depressed, Chelsea?' she probed.

Chelsea nodded. 'Now and then, yeah.'

'The thing is,' Mrs Savage butted in again, 'if she's going to make it as a model, she'll have to have them made bigger.'

Even since Chelsea had been crowned Eastbury's May Queen last year Mrs Savage had bragged that her daughter was going to be famous; that she would be on the front of every magazine and tabloid.

'If I'm not mistaken, Mrs Savage,' Chloe said patiently, 'most catwalk models don't have a double-G cup size. Quite the reverse, in fact.'

'I'm not talking about those zero-sized airheads who can't keep a meal down them,' the woman said. 'Chelsea's going to be a glamour model.' She smiled proudly at her daughter. 'Isn't that right, love?'

Chelsea nodded and twiddled with her earring. 'So what do you think, Doctor? Can I have the surgery? For free, like.'

'It's a little more complicated than that, Chelsea. You see, you are only sixteen and we have to decide whether you really—'

The Pit Bull raised a hand. 'Whoa there! End of. Absolutely end of. I know my rights. If Chelsea's not happy with her body and it's causing her mental anguish, then she's entitled to have implants on the NHS. Now, give us the forms we need to sign and we'll be on our way. And no offence, but you could do with some implants yourself. With a decent pair of hooters, you might not spend so many nights on your own.'

Great, thought Chloe. All those years of training, hard slog and sleepless nights only to wind up being trashed and told how to do my job.

With afternoon surgery over, and only running a few minutes late for her home visits, Chloe slipped out unnoticed to the car park at the back of the building before the practice manager could collar her. It was Chloe's first day back after a week away skiing in Austria, but she didn't doubt Karen could find something to nag her about. Usually it was her timekeeping. She spent far too long with the patients, she was frequently warned. At the age of thirty-seven, Chloe was the youngest doctor at Eastbury Surgery, and was perhaps, as the other doctors regularly teased her, still the most idealistic. The practice had doubled in the last ten years owing to the expansion of the Cheshire village, sitting as it was within a commutable distance of Manchester.

Her first home visit on Lark Lane was only a five-minute drive away. Ron Tuttle lived in one of the original sandstone farm workers' cottages. There had been a Tuttle living on Lark Lane for more than a hundred and seventy years. But not for much longer unless Ron—the last in the line of Tuttles—took better care of himself.

She parked on the road outside his cottage and, case in hand, walked up the short path that was lined with King Alfred daffodils. She gave the door knocker a loud rap and adopted her most robust bedside manner. Anything less would be deemed as patronising.

Minutes passed and she risked another go at the tarnished knocker. 'I heard you the first time,' came an angry shout from inside. The door opened. 'Who do you think I am, Roger-flipping-Bannister?'

'Roger Who?'

'First man to run a mile in less than four minutes. Don't you know nothing, girl?'

'I know plenty. Now, can I come in or do you want me to examine your prostate here on the step?'

'Mother Teresa's love child, that's you!' he roared.

'That's an improvement on a fortnight ago when I was Harold Shipman's love child. These sweet endearments of yours will have to stop, you know, or people will talk.'

The old man's eyes glinted with a smile and, leaning heavily on his walking stick, he stood aside to let her in. Closing the door after her, he said, 'I never had this trouble with your father. How is he?'

'Making hay with Mum. They're hardly ever at home these days. They're like a couple of kids.'

'What would you rather they were doing? Sitting miserably at home waiting to die? Anyhow, give the doc my regards when you do see him next. Cup of tea before we get down to business?'

'Thank you, but another time, perhaps.'

Ron Tuttle sniffed. 'Your father always had time for a brew.'

With the last of her visits completed, Chloe decided to nip home for an hour before evening surgery. A few of the patients she had seen that afternoon were elderly, and much of what they'd had to say to her had been gilded with nostalgic references to The Great Dr Hennessey Senior, who had retired five years ago. Chloe had no problem accepting that her father was a hard act to follow, or that she would always be compared with him. Or that some people couldn't take her seriously because they remembered her as a child tearing round the village on her bike with her brother, Nick. Her father's own testimony spurred her on. These same patients, who now claimed he could do no wrong, had once upon a time complained that he was nothing but a smooth-talking upstart who didn't know a bunion from a green-stick fracture.

Chloe had never intended to move back home to Eastbury, but then she'd never intended to very nearly lose her life and the man she'd thought she would marry. When that had happened, throwing her life into turmoil, the pull of her childhood roots had seemed the answer to her crisis and, as if by magic, everything had slipped into place.

A new GP was needed at Eastbury Surgery and Pocket House, an end-of-terrace cottage facing the village green came on the market. It was a stone's throw from her parents, as well as her closest friends, Dan and Sally. And by Easter 2005, almost four months after surviving one of the world's worst natural disasters, she'd moved from Nottingham back to Cheshire and her life had taken on a degree of normality again. As had Dan's and Sally's lives, for they, on holiday with Chloe and Paul, had also been caught up in the Boxing Day tsunami.

She locked her car and walked round to the back of the cottage. It was a beautiful March afternoon, and her small garden was teeming with new life. The magnolia tree, the forsythia bushes and the camellias basking in the late afternoon sun against the stone wall of the garage were all in full flower. This was her favourite time of the year, when, against all the odds, hope sprang eternally. She let herself in and walked through to the conservatory that she'd had built onto the kitchen.

With only forty-five minutes before she had to be back at work for evening surgery, she made herself a cup of coffee and checked her answering machine. There was a message was from her mother, reminding her that it was Dad's birthday on Friday.

'He's insisting on trying out the new recipes he learned during that cookery weekend, so be warned. See you Friday.'

The next message was from her father. 'Just to say I'm under orders from your mother to cook her favourite seafood risotto for dinner on Saturday. See you at seven.'

Her parents, Jennifer and Graham, ran the Ministry of Misinformation. They did it effortlessly and to great effect; the one rarely knew what the other was up to.

The last message was from—

Chloe backed away from the machine as if it was about to explode. Hearing that voice—*his* voice—her insides churned.

'Hi, Chloe, it's Paul. Yes, I know, this is probably the last voice on earth you expected to hear again. The thing is . . . Oh, hell, I didn't think it would be so hard to do this—look, I don't suppose there's any chance we could get together for a chat, could we? You can contact me on my mobile. My number is—'

But Paul—*That man! That snake in the grass!*—as her mother had renamed him—had taken so long with his message, he'd run out of space on her machine. He hadn't rung back to give her the number either. He'd probably assumed that she'd received his message in full.

Which she had, loud and clear, three weeks after they had flown home to Nottingham after that disastrous holiday on Phuket. While she was off work with her leg in plaster, a fractured collar bone and numerous cuts and bruises, he'd announced that he didn't love her any more.

'Surviving the tsunami has brought it home to me that we only get one chance in this life,' he'd said.

It turned out he'd been having an affair for goodness knows how long and coming so close to his own demise had helped him to make up his mind who he really wanted to be with. Now, three years and three months later, Paul Stratton wanted to get together for a drink and a chat. Did he really think she'd agree to meet him?

It was hair-washing night at Corner Cottage.

Neither Dan nor his son Marcus enjoyed the experience: Marcus hated getting the soapy water in his eyes and Dan hated to see his son cry. Leaning over the side of the bath, with a frog-shaped plastic watering can in his left hand and his young son's head resting against his right, Dan said, as he always did, 'I promise I won't let you go. Now close your eyes and tilt your head back. Ready?'

Marcus screwed his eyes up and braced himself. 'Cold!' he squealed as the water cascaded over his baby-soft hair. 'Mr Squeaky! Mr Squeaky!'

Dan reached for the flannel—called Mr Squeaky because Dan had once made a squeaky noise with it when he wrung it out—and gave it to Marcus, who covered his eyes with it. Dan refilled the watering can and rinsed away the last remaining bubbles.

'Job done, buddy,' Dan said with a salute. 'Another dangerous mission accomplished. Tomorrow we airlift in back-up troops and form an assault on your toenails. It's hazardous work, but we're a crack team and more than up for it.'

Marcus looked doubtfully at his toes. He then smiled and offered the flannel to Dan. 'Make him squeak.'

Dan happily obliged and then suggested it was time to pull out the plug. Marcus scrambled to his feet.

The smell and touch of his freshly washed, pyjama-clad son never failed to remind Dan that from the very first moment he had held Marcus his whole being had undergone a dramatic change. Even now, as he thought of that day when he sat in the chair beside Sally's hospital bed with Marcus lying peacefully in his arms, Dan could recall how happy he had felt. And yes, he had cried. He could have put it down to relief and exhaustion—Sally had, after all, just gone through thirty-six hours of excruciating labour—but it was so much more than that.

He had been overwhelmed by the miracle that was the birth of his child. It was something he still felt now. And never more so than when it was his son's bedtime. Two and a half years old, Marcus loved bedtime.

He had a finely tuned ritual of lining up his army of cuddly toys along the edge of his bed against the wall, and saving the places either side of him for his extra-special henchmen—Rory Bear and Rumpus Red Bear—before sitting bolt upright with his arms round the two large bears eagerly waiting for Dan to read to him.

Tonight, as they settled into the delights of the relentlessly Hungry Caterpillar, Dan thought of Sally. It was a quarter to seven and she probably wouldn't be home for another hour. She worked too hard. Yet he could never say that to her. Not when he perceived himself as having got the better end of the deal and occasionally felt guilty about it.

If somebody had told him that Sally would end up being the bread-winner of the family and he would become a house husband, he would have laughed in their face. You have to be joking. Nonetheless here he was, a thirty-nine-year-old Domestic God—as Chloe called him—who enjoyed nothing more than spending his days painting, making pizzas, ambling down to the duck pond, and generally having fun. There hadn't been a single day when he'd regretted stepping back from his career at a major league accountancy firm.

Of course, Dan couldn't very well bang on to Sally about how much fun he was having, just as there were other things he couldn't admit to her either. He would never be able to explain to Sally how vulnerable fatherhood made him feel. It had come as a huge shock to him to learn that something as pure and simple as his love for Marcus, coupled with the innate need to protect him from the world, ensured that he was an easy target for anguish. If surviving the tsunami had made him realise how fleeting the nature of life was, being a father had honed that knowledge to a lethal sharpness.

But none of this he shared with Sally. Nor did he tell her that he still occasionally woke in the middle of the night with his heart pounding and his brain terrifyingly wired to the events of that Boxing Day just over three years ago. The nightmare had recently changed, though. For a long time it had been the same dream, a crystal clear replay of what had happened—the awesome, unstoppable power of the water, the deafening roar of it, the screams, and his failure. But now the dream had taken on a new and far more disturbing slant. A slant that had him stumbling breathlessly out of bed and pushing open the door of his son's room to make sure he was all right. What if he could never shake off the nightmare and the guilt that lay behind it? He'd been hailed a hero at the time because he'd saved the life of a five-year-old girl, but what of her brother, the small boy he hadn't been able to save?

'Daddy read now.'

'Sorry,' Dan said. 'I was miles away.'

Nudging at the book on his lap, Marcus smiled. It was a smile that had the ability to stir a great tenderness in Dan. To make everything seem all right. He hung onto it.

With the meter running on her fee, Sally Oliver made neat and precise notes on her legal pad. As a partner at the firm of McKenzie Stuart, she headed up a department that dealt with high-value, high-profile divorce settlements.

Adamson v. *Adamson* had all the hallmarks of a long-haul flight to hell and back. Julia and Murray Adamson would ensure that this case would run and run. Sadly, Sally had seen it all before.

'Experience tells me this is going to cost me, right?'

Sally put down her pen and looked directly at her client, Murray Adamson. A self-made man, he had built up a kitchen-and-bathroom-fitting empire and then sold it in the late 1990s for a killing. He now diversified with small start-up businesses. His private life wasn't such a model of success. He was fifty-one years old and newly separated from wife number two after she'd discovered he'd been cheating on her in the same way he'd cheated on wife number one.

'Yes,' Sally said frankly. 'This will be expensive. But obviously, I'll do my best to minimise the extent of the damage.'

'And you're probably thinking, Stupid man, ink barely dry on his last settlement and here he is again. Doesn't he learn?'

'You don't pay me to think like that.'

'But it's what's going through your head, isn't it?'

No, she thought. What's going through my head is I should never have agreed to meet you after normal office hours. She said, 'Statistics show that second marriages have a greater failure rate than first marriages.'

He gave her one of his super-strength smiles. 'I know it's no excuse,' he said, 'but I don't seem able to resist the charms of a beautiful woman. I guess I'm just a hapless romantic.'

She looked pointedly at her watch. 'Well, I have all the information I need for now,' she said. 'When I hear from the other side, I'll be in touch. Don't hesitate to ring if there's anything you want to discuss.'

'I appreciate you sparing the time for me, Sally. It means a lot.'

She tried not to flinch. She hated male clients calling her by her Christian name. She watched him uncross his legs and stand up. She stood up too and started putting her desk in order, despite there not being a thing out of place. According to Chloe she was obsessively tidy and should have therapy for it. Chloe often joked that she should be forced to live in a house that had never been cleaned or tidied, that a dose of healthy squalor would get things in perspective for her. Little did Chloe know that that was exactly what Sally had grown up with. It was why she needed her surroundings to be so clean and uncluttered.

'Can I tempt you into a drink?'

'I'm sorry,' Sally said. 'If I'm any later getting home I'll have a furious husband to placate. He's probably scraping a ruined meal into the bin as we speak.'

'Sounds like an offer of dinner would be nearer the mark in that case.'

A knock at the door saved Sally from having to respond and Tom McKenzie came in. 'Oh, sorry, Sally,' he said affably, 'I didn't know you had anyone here with you.'

'That's all right,' she said, 'your timing's perfect; we've just finished.'

The two men acknowledged each other with a hearty exchange. Murray Adamson was a highly valued client.

'May I have a quick word before you head off home?' Tom asked Sally.

'Of course. Let me just see Mr Adamson out.'

Leading the way, Sally walked him briskly towards the deserted reception area and summoned a lift. While they waited, Murray Adamson offered his hand to her. 'I'll wait to hear from you, then.'

'Yes, I'll be in touch just as soon as I have anything to report,' she said.

The distant hum of a vacuum cleaner starting up coincided with the arrival of the lift and before the doors had even closed on her client she had moved away. Retracing her steps to her office, she worked the muscles of her shoulders. She was tired. She'd been awake since crazy o'clock after Marcus had woken in the night, wanting a drink.

She found Tom perched on her desk, reading her notes. 'It says here, in your scarily neat script, that the man's a serial womaniser and deserves to lose every penny of his ill-gotten gains.'

Sally smiled. 'It says no such thing. Did you really want a word?'

'Of course not. Bill told me who you had coming in and since that particular client's reputation goes before him, I decided to hang about and make myself useful.'

Sally had suspected as much. As senior partners, both Bill and Tom were fifteen years older than her and Tom was absurdly chivalrous by nature. 'I am old enough to look after myself, you know,' she said. 'But if it gives you a warm, fuzzy feeling inside, your timing really was perfect. He'd just asked me out for the obligatory drink.'

'I heard dinner mentioned.'

She laughed. 'Just how long did you have your ear pressed up against my door?'

'Long enough to know when the cavalry's required. Now, go home before your husband calls the police and reports you as missing.'

The advantage of leaving so late was that the traffic out of Manchester was minimal; within no time she was on the M6. She may have physically distanced herself from work, but mentally it was always with her. She loved her job. It was who she was. It defined her. But to confess that she found work easier than being at home with her son was only slightly less of a crime in certain quarters than if she'd been hanging about school gates supplying drugs to ten-year-olds.

Some would call her heartless. Her mother for one. 'No one will ever love you,' she had flung at Sally when she was a teenager, 'for the simple reason you have a stone where your heart should be.'

When Dan had first told her he loved her, Sally's initial thought had been, 'See, Mum, someone does love me! You were wrong!'

She'd met Dan at Chloe's twenty-eighth birthday party in Nottingham, where Chloe was living at the time. Sally had travelled up from London for the weekend, accompanied by her new boyfriend. Dan had arrived at the party with Chloe's brother, but it wasn't until she had gone out to the kitchen to help Chloe organise the food that they met properly. He had been on his own, grating cheese.

'Hi,' he'd said, 'if you're looking for Chloe, she's upstairs changing. Some idiot spilled red wine down her dress. I'm Dan, by the way.'

'I'm Sally,' she said.

'I know exactly who you are,' he'd replied. 'You're Chloe's best friend from her university days here in Nottingham.'

'I see you have an advantage over me; I know nothing about you.'

This was a lie. She'd heard a great deal about Dan Oliver over the last few months. He worked for the same firm of accountants as Chloe's older brother, Nick. Chloe had said he was extremely good looking and an initial impression confirmed this as being true. He was tall, well over six feet, with short dark hair. He had dark, engaging eyes and an equally engaging smile. The downside was that he was wearing faded brown cords, a green and white check shirt and a fawn pullover. He looked the epitome of Home Counties chic. Not her type at all. But Chloe had said he was smart and ambitious, which was just her type.

'Really?' he said. 'You've heard nothing about me at all? Not a single word? I'm crushed. I would have hoped, at the very least, Chloe would have told you about my stunning good looks and what a catch I am. Please make my day and tell me you're here alone.'

'My new boyfriend's here with me.'

'Can you ditch him?'

There was something so persuasively forceful and proprietorial about him, Sally did as he asked.

A month after they'd met, Dan was moved to his firm's Manchester office and they embarked on a long-distance relationship. They did that for two years and then Sally moved north to be with him. Work colleagues thought she was mad and accused her of throwing away her promising career by moving to Manchester. Others said that it probably didn't matter in the long run, as she and Dan would end up marrying and starting a family, so why not throw in the towel sooner rather than later?

However, starting a family wasn't something either of them was keen to rush into. She had never been happier and the thought of introducing a third party to their relationship frightened her. She loved Dan so very much, she didn't trust herself to love a child as well.

As an adult, the two most spontaneous things she had done in her life were falling in love with Dan and conceiving Marcus. Everything else had been precisely worked out. But extreme circumstances can cause a person to act out of character, and Sally knew that their survival of the devastating events of the Boxing Day tsunami in Thailand caused her and Dan to make the most life-changing decision of their lives. They did it that very night in the immediate aftermath of the disaster. In the darkness of the hotel room they'd been moved to—their old room had been destroyed—they'd clung to each other in exhausted and tearful shock. Whether it was from relief or a need to distract themselves from the horror of what they'd experienced, they'd begun to make love.

'We can't,' she'd said. 'I don't have my—'

He'd shushed her with a kiss. 'Let's make a baby,' he'd whispered, 'otherwise none of this makes any sense.'

Sally was ten minutes from home when her mobile rang from its cradle on the dashboard. Caller ID told her who it was and she answered the call with a smile. 'Hi, Chloe,' she said. 'How was your holiday?'

'It was fantastic. We had perfect snow conditions. I can't tell you how much I wish I was back there right now.'

'Not a good first day back at work, I presume?'

'You presume correctly,' Chloe said. 'Now, prepare to be amazed.

Guess who left a message for me on my answering machine. None other than Paul.'

'You're kidding me! What the hell did he have to say for himself?'

'He wants to meet up.'

'He can want it, but you won't agree, will you?'

'Of course not.'

They talked some more, promised to get together soon and then rang off just as Sally drove past the sign for Eastbury. Her very first sighting of the village had been during the Easter holidays in her first year at Nottingham. By then she and Chloe had become firm friends and Chloe had invited her to stay for the weekend. Even now Sally could remember how clean and bright and unreal everything had felt to her. The sun had shone from a blue sky, daffodils had been in full bloom on the green, ducks had been quacking on the pond, people on horseback had trotted by on the road and, most unreal of all, Chloe's parents had been so easy-going and welcoming—the complete opposite to what Sally was used to. She had vowed that this was just the kind of place where she would one day live.

And here she was, she thought, as she pulled onto the drive of Corner Cottage and parked. She looked up at the house. Its solid, Victorian demeanour had always appealed to her and its ample five bedrooms, two bathrooms, conservatory and half-acre of garden had been everything and more she could have wished for in a home. It still gave her a secret thrill knowing that she owned such a house.

It was Chloe's day off. She spent the morning dealing with the paperwork that had piled up while she'd been away. Her reward for such virtuous behaviour was to treat herself to an unhurried session at the gym. The ridiculously named 'Rejoovin' was a luxurious health and fitness centre at Cartwright Hall, the local hotel. It was a ten-minute drive away and Chloe went there as often as time permitted.

She'd jogged six miles on the treadmill, listening to Snow Patrol on her iPod, when she caught sight of somebody familiar coming out of the men's changing room. He spotted her at the same time and gave her a friendly smile. Just her luck that the best-looking guy she'd set eyes on in a long while had to keep seeing her when the sweat was pouring off her and her face was a most unattractive shade of beetroot.

He'd started coming here the week before she'd gone away on holiday. He was the fittest guy here. He had a strong swimmer's body with broad shoulders, neat waist and long legs. He looked exceptionally good in a pair of shorts and thank the Lord he wasn't wearing one of those awful wife-beater vests, but a normal, loose-fitting T-shirt. Nor was he one of those vain types who strutted cockily about the gym.

She'd vowed she'd never go out with a vain man again. She'd had enough of that with Paul. She thought of Sally's advice on the phone the other day when she'd explained about Paul ringing her. 'Don't even bother replying to him,' she had said. Not that Chloe could, when she didn't have his number.

But would she have called him? She wanted to say that her answer would be no, yet she suspected she wouldn't be able to resist the temptation to speak to him again, to prove to him, and maybe to herself, that she had indeed moved on. But that wasn't entirely the truth. Oh, yes, she'd moved on, but she was still angry. It was an anger that burned deep within her. It filled that space in her where once there had been a tiny life just beginning to take form and shape.

They'd been together since her twenty-eighth birthday. A friend had brought him along to her party and within seconds of being introduced someone had knocked his arm and he'd spilled a glass of red wine down her front. He'd sent her an apologetic bunch of flowers the following day, along with his telephone number. 'When you've forgiven me,' he'd written, 'perhaps you'd let me take you shopping so I can buy you a new dress to replace the one I ruined. Then afterwards we could go out for dinner with you wearing it.' Smooth as it was, what girl could have resisted such an offer?

She and Paul quickly slipped into the pattern of being a couple. Within ten months he'd moved in with her and Chloe's mother was beginning to crack jokes about being too young to be a grandmother. But Chloe hadn't been fooled. She'd known that her mother was itching to get her hands on a grandchild. Had things been different, she would have got her wish, for Paul's parting gesture, unbeknown to him, was to leave Chloe pregnant. It had been a short-lived pregnancy, though, and Chloe had told no one about it. Not her parents, not even Dan and Sally.

There had been signs before Paul's departure that perhaps all was not well, but Chloe had ignored the warning signs—the extra workload that kept him late at the office, the half-hearted interest in going out. She had convinced herself that he was just working too hard. Equally, she'd convinced herself that their Christmas and New Year holiday to Phuket with Dan and Sally was going to result in a proposal from him.

All Christmas Day she had waited for Paul to get down on one knee and present her with a ring. At bedtime she had spent longer in the bathroom than normal, sure that he was in the bedroom mustering his courage to propose. But when she had finally emerged from the bathroom, she found him asleep. She'd been so disappointed but concluded that maybe he was waiting for New Year's Eve. She'd slid into bed beside him and kissed his cheek.

Usually a heavy sleeper, she woke several times in the night from the same dream, that she was on an aeroplane and being rocked by turbulence. When she roused herself fully and seeing that Paul was still sleeping soundly, she decided to go and use the hotel gym. When she entered the gym, she saw that Dan had beaten her to it and was already pounding away on the treadmill. She'd just warmed up when all of a sudden the world had turned upside-down and she was being crushed.

Back in the present, she gave a small start, realising the treadmill next to her was now occupied. It was the good-looking man with the great body, and he was speaking to her. Surprise made her lose her rhythm and she stumbled. She reached out to the safety bar to keep from falling over, then took off her headphones.

'Sorry,' he apologised, 'I didn't mean to interrupt you. I just wanted to say hi, and that I missed seeing you last week. I hope you weren't ill?'

'I was away on a skiing holiday,' she said. 'Do you ski?'

'Not as often as I'd like these days. I was in Austria for the New Year.'

'That's where I've just come back from.'

'Really? Where were you?'

'Obergurgl. Do you know it?'

He gave her a dazzling smile. A smile so bright it could light up half the country. It had to be adding dangerously to his carbon footprint. 'That's exactly where I was,' he said. 'What a coincidence.'

She dabbed at her face with her towel, surreptitiously clocking his left hand. No ring. Unless, of course, he was married but didn't wear one. Not that his marital status had anything to do with her. They were talking. *Just* talking. He is not chatting you up, she told herself firmly. Remember the rule: if you fancy him on first sight, you can't have him.

The rule had been set in place because when Paul had left her, she'd set out ruthlessly to find a replacement. It still shamed her when she thought of the disastrous rebound relationships she'd hurled herself into. Eventually, she'd come to her senses, understanding that it wasn't Paul she wanted to replace, but the baby she had lost.

The man with the high-wattage smile was now running at the same speed as her, their pace evenly matched. She liked the look of his thick, black, curly hair bouncing on the top of his head. Very sexy.

Without doubt, Laurel House was one of the most attractive properties in the village. Built in the early nineteenth century of classic Cheshire sandstone, and with its nearest neighbour being the squat Norman church of St Andrew, it provided endless opportunities for water-colourists and photographers hoping to capture the essence of idyllic village charm.

Out of habit Chloe went round to the back of the house. She heard Jennifer and Graham Hennessey before she saw them.

Her mother's voice, shrill and defensive, cut through the cool evening air. 'There's no need to jump down my throat. All I was saying was that you tend to have a heavy hand when it comes to seasoning.'

Oh, hello, Chloe. You're early.'

'No, Dad, I'm on time. What are you doing up that ladder when you're supposed to be cooking your birthday dinner?'

'I said exactly the same thing to him myself not ten minutes ago. But no, he insisted on cleaning our bedroom windowsill. He's quite mad.'

'I wouldn't have to if the window cleaner had done a half-decent job of it in the first place.'

Chloe's father clambered down the ladder with a bucket of water and a sponge. He kissed her cheek. 'You look well,' he said.

'You too. Happy Birthday!' She held out the present she'd brought for him. 'Seeing as you've got your hands full, shall I take it inside for you?'

'Yes, come and help me put the finishing touches to supper.'

'Keep him away from the salt!' Mum called after them. 'My blood pressure's shooting off the chart as it is.'

'I've told you a million times, there's absolutely nothing wrong with your blood pressure.'

Chloe laughed. 'Be quiet you two, or I'll have to send for the hyper-bole police.'

Ever since Dad had retired he had assumed responsibility for all cook-ing at Laurel House. After a few false starts—a curry that nearly took the enamel off their teeth—he'd soon got the hang of it and relished showing off his growing prowess.

Looking at her parents now as they sat in the dining room with the evening sun pouring in through the window, Chloe thought how, for all their silly bickering, she envied them their marriage. After more than forty years together they were still happy. Their days were filled with visits to National Trust properties, gardens, galleries and evening classes. Then there were the weekends away and the holidays abroad.

'If I tell you something, Mum, will you promise not to overreact,' Chloe said, while her father was cutting her a slice of lemon tart.

'I've never overreacted in my life,' said her mother indignantly.

Dad snorted. But before they could sidetrack the conversation, Chloe said, 'While I was away, Paul left a message on my answering machine.'

'And what did that man, that snake in the grass, want?' Mum's voice was low and tightly controlled.

'He wants to meet up for a chat.'

'Do you think you will?'

'Of course she won't, Graham! She's got far more sense than that.'

'Actually,' said Chloe, 'if he hadn't got cut off before leaving me his number, I think I would have called him. What harm would it do?'

It was difficult to gauge who was more shocked, Chloe's parents or Chloe herself. It was all very well thinking such a thought, but saying it out loud was a different matter altogether.

Chapter Two

DAN HAD LEARNED very quickly that dealing with the hierarchy of Eastbury village's nursery mafia was not so different to locking horns with an office full of Machiavellian careerists. The trick was to keep well away from troublemakers. To this end, he ensured that for the three mornings a week when Marcus attended nursery, they arrived with seconds to spare; time enough only for Marcus to shrug off his coat and give Dan a hurried kiss goodbye.

The pick-up was timed with equal SAS-like precision. Get it wrong and Dan could easily be accosted by one of the Mumzillas. The ones to watch were Diane Davenport, Annette Bayley and Sandra McPhearson, or Lardy McFierce as Dan thought of her. She was a bossy-boots who had no qualms when it came to bullying people into doing her bidding.

Thank goodness he had such a great ally in Rosie Peach. She was married to Dave, the local builder, and their son, Charlie, was Marcus's best friend. Rosie was as determined as Dan was to keep a healthy distance between her and the Mumzillas.

Before Marcus had progressed to nursery, there had been a brief period of Mother-and-Toddlering to get through and when Dan had rolled up with Marcus for his first session in the village hall, the reaction towards him had been divided. Those who knew him had treated him as nothing more than a novelty in their midst. But those who didn't know him were wary.

Nobody had ever come right out and said it to their faces, but both Dan and Sally knew that the general consensus in the village was that they had some kind of weird metropolitan marriage going on. It annoyed Sally. 'Plenty of couples do what we do,' she said. 'Role reversal is hardly pioneering stuff.'

It was exactly what he'd told her when her maternity leave had been coming to an end. Their original plan had been that when Sally returned to work, they would employ a nanny to look after Marcus. But the reality of leaving his son with someone else appalled Dan. Had Sally not been so desperate to return to work, he might have hinted that she stay home with Marcus. But that was out of the question.

In the months after Marcus's birth, Sally had suffered a debilitating period of postnatal depression. Dan had been powerless to help her, other than on a wholly practical level. He'd taken paternity leave and assumed the lion's share of care for Marcus. It was during this time that he'd begun to think it simply wasn't in him to trust anybody else with his son. The next logical thought had been for him to suggest to Sally that he should take a long-term break from his career and be at home with Marcus. They looked at it every which way until eventually they decided there was only one way to find out; they would give it a go.

Once the decision had been made and Sally knew exactly when she'd be returning to work, her depression lifted. It was all the evidence Dan needed to know that they were doing the right thing.

As Dan unlocked the back door at Corner Cottage that afternoon he could hear the telephone ringing. It took him a moment to recognise who was at the other end. He hadn't heard from Andy Hope in a long time. They'd been at Durham University together and had kept in touch sporadically over the years. 'Andy, how are you?'

'I'm fine. But I wish I was calling under better circumstances. Do you remember Derek Lockley?'

Dan could picture Derek quite clearly. Del Boy, they used to call him. Thin, wiry bloke, ran the university rock-climbing club. 'I remember him well,' Dan said. 'What's he up to these days?'

'I'm sorry to be the bearer of bad news, but he's dead. He committed suicide. His family's already held the funeral, a small private affair, but there's to be a memorial service for him. I'm ringing round the old gang to see who can go. I think we should, don't you?'

Shocked, Dan agreed straight away that he'd make sure he could attend. It didn't seem right to indulge in any trivial what-are-you-doing-now? banter after that, and with the date of the memorial service written on the kitchen calendar, Dan rang off.

To Dan's knowledge, Derek was the first of his contemporaries to die. It was a chilling thought.

Two weeks after receiving Paul's message on her answering machine, Chloe came home from evening surgery to find he'd left her another. This time he'd managed to include his mobile number.

She pressed the replay button and listened to his voice again. 'Hi, Chloe, Paul here. Knowing how unreliable these machines can be, I'm assuming you didn't get my last message. Anyway, I'd really like to see you. So how about it?' He then went on to give his number.

She wrote it down and went upstairs to gather her gym things. An hour on the treadmill would give her some thinking time. She needed to plan how she was going to respond.

The gym was busy, and there, already on the treadmill next to the one she always used, was He of the Dark Curly Hair. Despite having run alongside each other on several occasions now, they'd never got beyond the pleasantries that most people exchanged when working out and so she still didn't even know his name.

He gave her a friendly smile as she approached. 'Hi,' he said. 'I thought you weren't joining us tonight. Good day?'

'Not bad,' she said, keying in her running programme on the machine and setting off with a gentle warm-up jog. 'How about you?'

'Busy. Crazily so. Fortunately it's my day off tomorrow.'

'Snap,' she said. 'Mine too.'

'Doing anything special?'

'Nothing planned. You?'

'No plans yet.'

When he didn't say anything else, she increased her speed and wondered what kind of work he did. But no way would she ask him. That was a big no-no. Moreover it might give out the wrong signal. Ask too many questions and he'd assume she was coming onto him. Being single at her age was a minefield. It was so easy to be viewed as a predator. A desperate predator whose body clock was demanding to have her eggs fertilised *NOW!* The thought made her think of Paul, which in turn sent a direct message to her legs to run faster.

Out of the corner of her eye she was aware that He of the Dark Curly Hair was slowing his speed now.

'I was wondering,' he said, 'given that you mentioned you had no plans for tomorrow, whether you might be free to have lunch with me? Or maybe you'd rather play safe and settle for a drink only?'

It was the thoughtful politeness of his invitation that she found so appealing.

Four days had passed since Andy Hope had telephoned with the news about Derek Lockley's death and Dan hadn't slept properly since. Every night he kept being jarred awake by the same horrific dream. He'd even cried out last night and woken Sally.

'What is it?' she'd asked. 'Are you feeling unwell?'

'It's nothing,' he'd said. 'I'll just get a glass of water. Go back to sleep.'

Powerless to stop himself he went and checked on Marcus. He was fast asleep, his face nestled into the furry belly of one of his teddies.

Not wanting to go back to bed, Dan went downstairs to make himself a drink. While he waited for the kettle to boil he stared at his reflection in the window. What was happening to him? Why, after all this time, was he still dreaming of something that had happened more than three years ago? Not only that, why couldn't he share what he was going through with Sally? What was holding him back?

Oh, he knew what was holding him back all right. It was because he was ashamed of the gut-wrenching fear he still carried around with him. He felt diminished by it. Less of a man. Certainly not the man Sally and Marcus needed. Or the man his father had brought him up to be.

Dan's father came from hardy Gloucestershire stock that looked danger square in the eye and ordered it to bugger off, or else! And Glynis Oliver, Dan's mother, came of similar plucky stock. Little wonder then that Dan had always felt that he didn't quite live up to expectation. His biggest act of defiance had been to marry Sally. To say that Sally was not quite the wife Ronald and Glynis Oliver had had in mind for their son and heir, would be a huge understatement. Yet, despite it all—her council-estate upbringing, her comprehensive and redbrick university education—they politely accepted Sally into the fold. Not surprisingly, his parents had been horrified at the prospect of Dan taking time out from his career to look after Marcus.

The night of Boxing Day 2004, when Dan had eventually found a telephone that worked and called home to his parents to let them know he and Sally were all right, Ronald and Glynis's reaction had been predictably muted. 'Right,' his father had said, 'jolly good. Yes. Well done. Looks pretty ropy there from the pictures we've seen on the news. Shall I pass you over to your mother?'

Pretty ropy. Yeah, that about summed up the situation. That's what you get when an undersea earthquake releases energy equivalent to thousands of Hiroshima-sized atomic bombs and triggers a series of tsunamis that wipe out the lives of nigh on a quarter of a million people. He shuddered at the thought of all those deaths. In particular, the death of one small boy who had been the same age as Marcus was now.

'Dan?'

He spun round. Sally was standing in the doorway, her turquoise silk dressing gown belted loosely round her waist. Her short, dark hair was attractively tousled, giving her face a vulnerable softness.

'I'm sorry,' he said, thinking how lovely she looked in the half-light. 'Did I wake you?'

'Not really. Work things on my mind. You know what I'm like; I can't fully let go.' She came over to him.

He put his arm round her. I know the feeling, he thought, wishing he had something as commonplace as work on his mind.

It was a beautifully sunny day. A perfect day for having lunch with a good-looking man. A man whose name Chloe still didn't know.

Incredibly, they'd parted last night at the gym without having exchanged this all-important piece of information about each other. They'd got as far as establishing where and when they'd meet, when he'd reached into his running shorts' pocket and pulled out a mobile phone—he must have had it switched to silent and vibrate mode because she certainly hadn't heard it. He'd put it to his ear and stepped off the treadmill. 'Tomorrow,' he'd mouthed at her, and then he was gone, off like a rocket towards the changing rooms. Only bad news could have had provoked such a reaction, she'd concluded. Or perhaps he was a fireman and had got the call to go tearing off to the fire station?

Now, as she gave her appearance one last check in the mirror—her long blonde hair was satisfyingly sleek and shiny and her blue eyes enhanced with a light touch of mascara—she selfishly hoped that whatever bad news he had been on the receiving end of wouldn't prevent him meeting her for lunch.

Not that this lunch was going to be anything special, she told herself, gathering up her bag and keys and imagining what he might look like in proper clothes. It would be just two gym buddies having a bite to eat together on their day off.

Jeans. She'd bet a king's ransom that he'd look great in jeans, the denim all nicely moulded to those taut muscular thighs of his . . .

No, it was nothing to get too excited about.

With an open-necked shirt revealing a glimpse of chest hair . . .

Definitely nothing to get ahead of oneself over and think where it might lead. Absolutely no need at all.

She arrived at the Bells of Peover exactly on time and after a quick scan of the pub's interior went back outside, deciding it was warm enough to sit at one of the tables that offered a good view of the church directly opposite. OK, so he wasn't here yet. No need to panic. No need to think she'd been stood up.

Ten minutes later, and studying the menu with intense concentration, she was still reassuring herself with the same advice.

Twenty minutes later, after being asked for the second time if she was ready to order, she sipped her glass of tomato juice and tried hard not to look like a pathetic loser who had been stood up. She rummaged in her bag in search of the most face-saving device known to mankind— you were never alone with a mobile phone in your hand!

She'd made two phone calls last night; one to Paul and then one to Sally. She hadn't mentioned anything about Paul to her friend, but she had told her all about He of the Dark Curly Hair. Appalling situation, she texted, I think I've been stood up! Please advise.

Sally's response came back almost at once: The rat! No worries. We'll track him down and make him pay!

Smiling to herself, Chloe felt a shadow fall across her. She glanced up, straight into the handsome face of her date.

'I'm so unbelievably sorry,' he said. 'Are you very angry with me?'

Angry, she thought, taking in the whole of his stunning six-feet-plus frame. How could anyone be angry with someone who looked so head-turningly good? The jeans were just as she'd pictured, as was the open-necked shirt—it was a blue and white check affair that was doing ridiculous things to his sky-blue eyes.

'I swear I'm not always so unreliable,' he said when she hadn't replied, 'but something came up that I had to deal with and, being the idiot I am, I hadn't thought to get a contact number yesterday. May I?'

She moved her bag from the wooden bench seat so he could sit down next to her. 'It's not only phone numbers we should have exchanged,' she said. 'I don't even know your name.'

He smiled. 'I realised that oversight when I left you last night.' He held out his hand. 'Let's do this properly. My name's Seth Hawthorne and I'm really pleased you didn't leave before I got here.'

'Hello, Seth,' she said, taking his hand. 'I'm Chloe Hennessey.'

'Are you ready to order now?' The waitress was back again.

'I think we need a little longer,' Chloe said, passing Seth the menu.

'No, I already know what I want,' he said. 'You first, Chloe.'

'I'll have the ploughman's and a small glass of Chardonnay.'

'Ditto on the ploughman's. And I'll have a Budweiser, please.'

'We seem to have similar tastes in quite a few things,' he said when they were alone. But then he cringed. 'I'm sorry, that sounded like the lamest of chat-up lines, didn't it? Can you pretend I never said it?'

'Pretend you never said what?'

He smiled. 'Thanks. And thanks for waiting for me.'

'It was a close-run thing. Five minutes more and you wouldn't have found me here. My best friend and I were texting each other and deciding what we'd do to punish you for standing me up.'

'Ah, and what conclusion had you reached?'

'Luckily for you, you appeared in the nick of time.'

Their food and drinks arrived and after a brief flurry of activity they were alone again. 'You left the gym in such a hurry last night,' she said. 'Was everything OK?'

His expression became serious. 'Yes, sorry about that, but I had to go.'

'That's OK,' she said lightly, wishing he'd expand. 'I had this sudden picture of you being a fireman and having to dash heroically off to the fire station for an emergency.'

'A fireman, that's a new one on me. Do you think I look like one?'

'You have the right build.'

'Ah, so a case of if the stereotype fits? Should I take that as a compliment? I know women have a bit of a thing about firemen.'

'If I'm honest, I don't understand the attraction. I'm not into uniforms and an excess of bare-chested posing for calendars.'

'And your sort would be?'

'Any man who can make me laugh,' she said.

'In that case, knock, knock?'

'Who's there?'

'A very short man who can't reach the bell.'

She laughed. 'That's terrible.'

'I know. So tell me what you do when you're not at the gym and making me feel totally inadequate. You can run some, can't you?'

'I'm a GP, just as my father was. He's retired now and I work at the practice where he worked for many years.'

'And where's that?'

'Where I live, in Eastbury. How about you? We've established you don't put out fires for a living, so what do you do?'

'What do you think I do?' He was smiling, yet there was something behind that smile. Was he teasing her? Or was he testing her? Rooting out any hidden prejudices she might have.

'I don't think you're a teacher,' she said, deciding to play along. 'Teachers have enough holiday allowance as it is without having a mid-week day off as well.'

'I could be a supply teacher. But I'm not, so that's one guess gone. Four left.'

'Hey, you never said there was a limit on guesses. Give me a clue.'

He picked up a stick of celery from his plate and waved the leafy end of it at her. 'Smart girl like you, you don't need any clues.'

Her competitive spirit roused, she put her mind fully to the matter. 'Accountant,' she said.

'Three guesses left. And I'll rule out law and medicine for you.'

'Mm . . . you run your own business? Something in computers? IT?'

'No, I work for a big organisation. That's two guesses left.'

'Got it! You're a policeman.'

'One guess left.'

A buzzing noise went off from inside Chloe's handbag.

'That's probably your friend wanting to know if I had the decency to turn up. I'll leave you to answer it while I go in search of the facilities.'

Chloe watched him walk away, then flipped open her mobile. Well? Sally had texted. Has he arrived or do I buy a staple gun on way home?

He's here. All OK, Chloe quickly tapped in. Speak tonight!

Not home till late, came back Sally's reply. Speak tomorrow.

Chloe returned her mobile to her bag, disappointed. She couldn't remember when she'd last spent an evening gossiping with Sally.

'What's the verdict, then? Has your friend forgiven me?'

'A staple gun was mentioned,' Chloe said, as Seth resumed his seat next to her. 'But you'll be glad to know I've held her off.'

'She sounds like a good friend, someone who cares about you.'

'You're right. Sally and I have known each other since university. Her husband, Dan, is also a good friend. The three of us are very close.

Especially so since—' Chloe stopped herself short. Why go into all that? It was hardly an appropriate subject to discuss on a first date.

'Since what?' he asked, turning to face her.

'It's nothing. Really.' She reached for her glass of wine and took a sip.

'Is that my cue to back off?' he asked.

'It might be better if you did. It would be a shame to spoil such a pleasant lunch by getting too serious. I wouldn't want you to get the wrong idea about me, that I'm a world-class misery.'

'I'd rather know the real you by discussing what's important to you.'

It could have sounded an appallingly cheesy line, but his tone was soft and sincere. She studied his expression for any sign of artifice.

'Perhaps you're doing yourself a disservice,' he pressed, 'as well as underestimating what might be of interest to me.'

Bingo! 'I've worked it out. Human behaviour's your thing. You're a psychologist, aren't you? A therapist?'

'And that,' he said, mimicking the noise of a game-show hooter, 'was your last guess. Sloppy work, seeing as we'd already ruled out medicine.'

She smiled. 'Look, it's no big deal. The reason Dan, Sally and I are especially close is because we shared an extreme situation.'

'What was it?'

'We were spending Christmas on Phuket and got caught up in the Boxing Day tsunami.'

'How caught up?'

'We thought we were going to die.'

He stared at her thoughtfully. 'That sounds like a seriously major big deal to me. And not something you can easily shake off. If ever.'

'The part of it I know I'll never forget is how Dan and I tried to save this little boy—' She stopped herself short. 'I'm sorry,' she said. 'But I did warn you that I'd end up depressing you.'

'Please don't apologise. What happened to the little boy?'

'He died.'

'But at least you tried to save him. That's what's important in a situation like that.'

'I don't think Dan would agree with you.'

'I'm sorry, I didn't mean to trivialise what you'd gone through. Tell me what happened.'

'It started for Dan and me when we were in the hotel gym. We were the only ones in there and when the first wave hit, the building collapsed around us like a pack of cards. When the water started to recede, taking us with it, we desperately held on to each other. Then we were thrown against a tree and we clung to it for all we were worth.

'When the water had receded to a safe distance, we let go and then a woman who ran the hotel crèche came running and screaming to us for help. The crèche had been destroyed and somewhere in the wreckage were her two children—she'd brought them to work with her that morning, something she'd never done before. By now I knew I'd broken my leg and was as good as useless, but Dan was brilliant. He found one of the children and got her out, but the other, the little girl's brother, was stuck further under the rubble. We needed more help but the hotel had been badly hit and there was chaos all around us.

'Then everyone started to yell that another wave was coming. People were running and climbing up onto roofs, trees, anything that had survived the first wave. Even the mother, whose son we were trying to save, had run for safety. It was clear that the second wave was bigger and more powerful than the first and I tried to drag Dan away, but he wouldn't listen. He was convinced he could free the boy. Amazingly, he did; he managed to shift the slab of concrete that had the boy pinned beneath it, but it was too late. The wave hit us with such a force, we were smashed against God knows what.

'Dan was devastated that he hadn't been able to save that little boy. The child's body was found washed up on the shore the next day. He was so young, about the same age as Dan and Sally's son is now.' She reached for her drink. 'Are you sure you're not some kind of a therapist? This is the most I've said about what happened in ages.'

He shook his head. 'People say I'm a good listener. What about Sally? Where was she when the waves hit?'

'It was awful for her. And Paul.'

'Paul?'

'He was my boyfriend at the time. They were both still fast asleep in bed when the first wave hit. They woke to the sound of crashing glass. Both Sally and Paul said it was as if they'd suddenly been thrown inside a washing machine. At least I had Dan with me when that first wave came in; they were both on their own. Even though they weren't badly hurt, just really shaken up with superficial cuts and bruises, I often think it must have been worse for them because they were alone.'

'Well, then,' she said in a forced upbeat voice, 'now that I've thoroughly spoiled the moment, say something to cheer us both up.'

He took a moment before speaking. 'I don't know whether it would cheer you up, but I know it would me. Can I see you again? And not just at the gym?'

The Easter weekend was not going well for Sally.

It was Saturday morning, she had a thumping headache and, while she was happy that Dan had driven to the supermarket to do the shopping, she was not quite so pleased that he'd left Marcus behind with the promise that she would take him to feed the ducks. As a result, for the last ten minutes Marcus had been waddling excitedly about the kitchen wearing a pair of yellow Marigold gloves on his feet and quacking loudly.

'We'll go in a minute,' she told him. 'Mummy's just got something very important to do. I know!' she said brightly, 'why don't you watch one of your favourite DVDs?'

As if sensing he was being conned, Marcus considered her proposition. 'With a dink and bicksies?' he bargained.

'Yes, with a drink and biscuits,' she corrected him.

Once she had him set up in the playroom, happily watching *Finding Nemo* and still wearing his Marigolds, she went into the study and switched on her laptop. She'd promised Dan she wouldn't work this weekend, but this wasn't really work; it was an article for the Law Society's *Gazette*.

She hadn't even got as far as opening the relevant document when the telephone rang on the desk. It was her brother, Terry.

'Thought you might like to know,' he said gruffly and without preamble, 'Mum's been told she needs her hip replacing.'

'Is she in a lot of pain?'

'What the bleeding hell do you think? The doc's told her she's to go on a waiting list and we all know what that means. She'll be dead and buried before she sees hide nor hair of a new hip.'

'Why have you rung me, Terry?' she asked, knowing all too well why he had. The only time Terry or her mother phoned was when they were in need of something. There was always some urgent financial crisis that only Sally could solve and they knew they could always rely on her, for the simple fact they knew the hold they had over her. Basically, she paid Terry and her mother to keep out of her life. They were an untidy reminder of the person she had once been.

'We thought you would want to help,' Terry said in answer to her question. 'It is our mum, when all's said and done. Family is family.'

'What are you asking me specifically, Terry?'

'That's you all over, isn't it? You like to make us beg, don't you?'

'You want me to pay for her to go privately, is that it?' she asked.

'Oh, Brain of Britain finally gets it!'

'There's no need for sarcasm, Terry. Exactly how long has the doctor told Mum she'll have to wait if she has the operation done on the NHS?'

'I don't know specifics. Probably more than a year is likely.'

Sally had no idea what the cost of a private operation would be, but she guessed it would be more than she could hide from Dan. In the past she had underplayed the money she had handed over to her family, but this amount would be nigh on impossible to conceal.

'It's probably best if I talk it over with Mum,' Sally said, thinking that she wouldn't put it beyond her family to pull a fast one on her. She bent down to her briefcase for her diary and flicked through the pages. 'Tell Mum I could manage a visit next weekend.'

The call didn't go on for much longer. It was nearly a year since Sally had last seen her mother. The visits over to Hull were not happy occasions and were best kept to a minimum.

She put her diary away and returned her attention to her laptop. She was so absorbed in what she was doing, she didn't hear Dan arrive back. She only knew he was home when she heard him say, 'I thought you weren't doing any work this weekend?'

'This doesn't count as work,' she said. 'Do you remember me mentioning I was asked to do a piece for the Law Society's *Gazette*, it's—'

'How long have you been here, *not working*?' he interrupted her.

She caught the uncharacteristic sharpness in his voice and looked away from the screen to where Dan was standing in the doorway. 'No more than a few minutes,' she said.

He frowned and she knew he didn't believe her.

'OK, a bit longer than a few minutes,' she conceded.

Still he didn't say anything. Then he turned his back on her and disappeared. I should go after him, she thought. But she didn't. Why should she have to apologise for what she was doing? Didn't he understand how important it was to her? It was all right for him, he had nothing more pressing to do than—

She stopped herself from going any further.

Minutes later she heard Marcus's shrill voice calling out to her—'Bye Mummy!'—followed by the sound of the back door slamming. She went to the window that overlooked the front garden. Dan appeared from round the side of the house with Marcus sitting on his shoulders. She could see a clear plastic bag of crumbled bread in Marcus's hands. *Damn!* She'd forgotten all about those bloody ducks.

She went back to her desk and laptop, but try as she might, she couldn't concentrate. She saved the document and then switched off the laptop. Rattled, she considered Dan's reaction to her working. She would have preferred it if they'd had an all-out blazing row, but that wasn't Dan's style He went quiet. Not a sulking, brooding quiet, but a stiff-upper-lip quiet. She knew it was the way he'd been brought up. In contrast, she'd been raised in an environment where it was a matter of honour to fight one's corner. When she'd left Hull to go to university in Nottingham, she'd realised the street fighter in her would have to be tamed. Discreet manipulation was her new modus operandi.

But now and again the old Sally Wilson wanted to break out and scream like a fishwife. This was one such moment. She wanted to yell at Dan and tell him never, *ever*, to turn his back on her again. The closest she had come to showing her true colours and really letting rip had been in the months after Marcus was born

Postnatal depression was not something she had remotely prepared herself for. What a shock she'd had. She'd been unable to get out of bed some days, lying there in tears, her body too leaden to move.

Chloe had been so kind and caring with her, and in the end she had gently taken Sally in her arms one day and explained that she was suffering from postnatal depression and that it was time to do something about it. By getting it out in the open, Sally had hoped that the worst would be over. She was wrong. Things got a lot worse before they got better.

Poor Dan would come home from work most days to be confronted by a demon from hell. When she wasn't having a go at him she was bawling her eyes out because she'd spent the day trying to soothe a fractious Marcus. Naturally, the second Dan lifted Marcus out of his cot and lay him on his shoulder, the screaming stopped and Marcus fell asleep, exhausted. 'How did you do that?' Sally would demand of Dan, both grateful and furious. 'Show me what you did!'

During those desperate weeks and months, Dan's patience was endless and when he took extended paternity leave to help her she wept for days on end with shame and relief. Thinking now how good Dan had been with her, Sally felt guilty for thinking badly of him earlier.

To make amends, she decided to make lunch. They'd have a proper lunch in the conservatory with a bottle of wine and napkins. Hopefully Dan would see it as a peace offering and forgive her.

Her good intentions were all for nothing. Dan and Marcus returned with fish and chips from the chip shop in the village. 'It was Marcus's suggestion,' Dan said. 'Sorry if we've spoiled your plans.'

'You don't sound particularly sorry,' Sally responded. She switched off the pan of water she was heating for the pasta.

'What's that supposed to mean?'

'Chips! Chips!' Bouncing on his toes, Marcus was grinning broadly.

'Marcus,' Sally said sharply, 'I've told you before not to interrupt.'

'I want my chips! Chips, chips, *CHIPS*! Yum, yum, yum in my *TUM*!'

'Please, Marcus, I'm talking to Daddy right now.'

'Hey, big guy, why don't you go and wash your hands and then we'll have our chips? How does that sound?'

When they were alone, Sally was seething with frustration. 'You never back me up.'

'I do, you just don't realise it.'

'Maybe I need more of it from you.'

He looked at her steadily. 'Ever thought that Marcus and I might need more from you? That it would be a real novelty for us to have the best of you at the weekend and not the dregs?'

Marcus chose that moment to reappear and for the rest of the day they didn't have time to themselves. Yet, when Marcus went to bed and it looked like they would have a chance to clear the air, Sally retreated to the study to work on her article. She knew hiding from Dan wasn't the answer, but she didn't trust herself not to retaliate and lose her temper over his absurd accusation.

It was nearly midnight when she finally switched off her laptop and went upstairs to bed. Dan was already asleep. Having this unresolved ill feeling between them didn't bode well for tomorrow.

Not when Dan's parents were arriving to stay for the next two days.

Normally Chloe wouldn't dream of driving the short distance to Corner Cottage, but in true Bank Holiday Monday fashion a relentless downpour of rain had started in the night and it was showing no sign of letting up. She parked behind Dan's parents' car and sprinted up the driveway to the front door where Sally was waiting for her.

'Your parents are already here,' Sally said, 'and they're doing sterling service. Graham's helping Dan in the kitchen and Jennifer's keeping the conversation going with Ronald and Glynis. She's a star.'

Chloe laughed. 'Don't, whatever you do, tell her that or it'll go to her head. Hello, my best little boy in all the world, how are you?'

Marcus had materialised in the hall behind his mother. Smiling, he held out a small bowl of gherkins to Chloe. 'Mm . . . lovely,' she said, helping herself to one, at the same time kissing Marcus on the cheek.

'They're my favebit,' Marcus said, stuffing three into his mouth at once.

'*Favourite*,' Sally corrected as he shot off towards the kitchen.

'He seems on fine form,' Chloe said.

Sally sighed. 'He's mischief incarnate, ignoring everything I say and showing off horribly. He's been like it since yesterday when Dan's parents arrived. They gave him the biggest Easter egg imaginable and have been encouraging him to eat it behind my back at every opportunity. He's as high as a kite on sugar overload.'

'How long are they staying?'

'Only until tomorrow morning, thank God. Come on, let's get you a drink. I'm two ahead of you already.'

'**M**y compliments to the chef,' Chloe's mother said. 'This lamb is delicious, Dan. What have you done to it to achieve such perfection?'

'It couldn't be easier; I just marinated it overnight in red wine and juniper berries.'

Glynis turned to Sally. 'You're a very lucky girl having a husband who can cook so marvellously.'

'I am indeed,' Sally said quietly, exchanging a look with Chloe.

It was a look Chloe knew of old. She had endured many such occasions with Dan's parents and knew the best way to get through them was to nod and smile. It had to be said, though, as irritating as the Oliver seniors were, they were marginally less offensive than Sally's family. She had only met Kath Wilson once—at Dan and Sally's wedding—but in Chloe's opinion, she was an outstandingly poisonous piece of work.

'Of course, you know what they say, don't you?' Jennifer said. 'Behind every successful man there's an astonished woman.'

Everyone laughed, including Marcus. His mouth wide open, he gave everyone a ringside view of the mushy remains of a half-chewed potato.

'That's enough, Marcus,' Sally said.

Marcus ignored her and continued to laugh, his head tipped back.

'I said that's enough, Marcus.' Sally's tone was sharp and raised. 'Dan, can't you make him stop? I might as well not be here the way he's carrying on. He won't do a single thing I ask of him.'

Chloe put a hand on Marcus's shoulder. 'Basic rules of comedy, Marcus: perfect timing and always leave them wanting more. Eat up, or there might not by any pudding for you.'

He instantly fell silent and lowered his cutlery. He stared up at Chloe, his face adorably anxious. 'Will be more choxy egg for me?' he asked.

'Later,' Dan said from the head of the table. 'For now, let's see if you can finish what's on your plate.'

'And then choxy?'

'Yes, but only if you've been very good. Can you do that?'

Marcus nodded and began shovelling peas into his mouth.

'Marcus—'

'Seconds for anyone?' Dan asked, cutting Sally off.

Disaster just about averted, Chloe waited for Dan to carve her some more lamb. An all-out battle of wills between Sally and Marcus would be the icing on the cake on what was turning into a dreadful way to spend the day. Only now did she realise that Dan and Sally had scarcely exchanged more than a few words throughout the meal. Whatever was going on, she hoped Marcus wouldn't get caught in any crossfire.

Since the day he'd been born, Marcus had been extremely dear to Chloe. Sometimes, when she held him, he soothed the dull, pulsing ache of the child she'd lost. At other times he made the pain more acute, reminding her cruelly that her own child would have been more or less the same age as he was.

'Still no man in your life, Chloe?'

Oh, God, not that old cookie. 'No, Glynis,' she said cheerfully, 'I'm afraid not. I'm a huge disappointment to everyone, I know. Spinsterhood beckons ever more surely.'

'Rubbish, darling. A spinster is an unclaimed treasure, that's all.'

Chloe raised her glass to her ever-supportive father. 'Thanks, Dad.'

Before coming here, she'd made her parents promise—Dan and Sally, too—that they wouldn't refer to her lunch date with Seth. She'd told them about it the previous night. The last thing she wanted was for Ronald and Glynis to interrogate her about him. Sadly, she and Seth hadn't been able to get together again since that day, owing to him being busy in the run-up to Easter, but he'd promised to call tonight.

'Better not to leave it too late, though,' Glynis prattled on. 'It would be a shame for you to miss out on a family, wouldn't it? Still, you'll always have your career.'

'Come on, Mum, give Chloe a break, will you?'

'A break,' Glynis repeated, looking at Dan as if he'd slapped her. 'I'm sure I don't know what you mean, Daniel.'

Dan reached over and topped up his mother's glass. 'Tell us about your next jaunt away, Jennifer. Is it Rome you're going to?'

'More wine this end of the table, Dan,' Sally said, bringing her empty glass down with a clumsy hand. 'We're running dry. And, Marcus, will you please stop scraping your plate.'

'No, we're going to Florence. Graham's found this charming little hotel on the Internet. Do you use the net much, Glynis?'

'Goodness me, no!' From the disgusted expression on Glynis's face anyone would think she'd just been asked if she used a vibrator.

The conversation rumbled on. As did Sally's wine consumption, Chloe noticed. She seemed morose and self-absorbed and, to put it bluntly, well on the road to being drunk. What had got into her?

When everyone had finished eating, Chloe pushed back her seat. She had decided to get Sally alone. 'Dan,' she said, 'since you did all the cooking, Sally and I will clear away.'

'Good idea, Chloe,' Sally muttered, up on her feet and swaying slightly. 'I thought you'd never ask.'

Out in the kitchen, Chloe put the kettle on, then manoeuvred Sally into a chair. She made the strongest cup of coffee she could get away with, added cold water to cool it down and took it to the table where her friend was sitting with her head in her hands.

'Drink this,' she said. 'Doctor's orders.'

'You're cross with me, aren't you?' Sally said.

'No, I'm not.'

'Liar. You're having a miserable time here.'

'Not as miserable as the time you're obviously having. What's wrong? Have you and Dan had an argument?'

'Why do you ask that?'

'Because you've barely exchanged a civil word with each other, and that's really not like you two. Drink your coffee.'

'But it's revolting.'

'So is getting drunk at our age.'

Sally winced. 'You could try and dress it up to sound less sordid.'

'You would have seen through any attempt at that. Do you want to tell me what you and Dan have argued about?'

'We haven't argued. That's the problem. You know as well as I do that with Dan it's always a case of what he *doesn't* say. He wears that bloody stoic silence of his like a suit of armour. Nothing gets through it.'

'So what *isn't* he saying?'

'I think he resents the amount of time I devote to work.'

'Is he worried that perhaps Marcus isn't seeing enough of you?' Chloe asked, treading warily. 'Is that the problem, do you think?'

'I spend as much time as I can with Marcus,' Sally said defensively.

'I know you do.'

'You're not suggesting that that's why Marcus has been difficult with me recently, are you?'

'Has he been difficult with you?'

Sally sighed heavily. 'You saw what he was like earlier. He ignores everything I say and does everything Dan asks him to do.' She slumped back into the chair. 'If you really want to know, I'm tired of being made to feel the bad cop to Dan's good cop.'

'Oh, Sally, it's just a phase. Children can be devious little monkeys. They know instinctively how to play off one parent against another to get what they want. Trust me, boys always grow up to be devoted to their mothers. Now, finish that coffee, while I dig out the desserts.'

With the volume pumped up, Seth was listening to Arcade Fire. Was there a finer band around at the moment? He didn't think so. When 'Intervention' came to an end, he switched off the music. He went downstairs, made himself a cup of coffee and when he came back up to the spare room that doubled as an office, he marshalled his thoughts firmly into line. 'Right,' he said out loud. 'Work.'

For Seth it was irrelevant that it was a bank holiday; for him it had been as busy as any other day and he'd spent most of it applying himself to the backlog of papers that had been accumulating on his desk.

The trouble with his job was that it was almost impossible not to be on duty 24/7. He'd been in Crantsford as Owen's assistant for six months now and the time had flown by. Regrettably, Owen was not the most helpful of bosses. Widowed last year, and close to retirement, he was more than ready to wind down and Seth had become resigned to having dumped on him anything Owen didn't want to do.

Two hours passed and then, as a reward for his industry, Seth went downstairs again and helped himself to a beer from the fridge.

He drank it straight from the bottle, leaning back against the worktop. Only then did he allow himself his real reward: to think of Chloe. He had to ration very strictly the amount of time he spent thinking about her, because whenever he did he got completely distracted and ended up grinning like an idiot. He was doing it now. But what man wouldn't? She was lovely, every perfect, well-toned, streamlined inch of her.

But all it took to wipe the idiotic grin from his face was one thought. He hadn't actually lied to Chloe, yet nor had he been completely candid with her. He wanted her to get to know the real him before her opinion was tainted by prejudice.

All he had to do was judge when it was the right moment to tell Chloe the truth, and hope that she'd take it well.

He checked the time: nine fifteen. Time to make that promised call.

Chapter Three

SALLY WOKE UP the next morning determined to be in a better mood. She slid carefully out of bed, not wanting to disturb Dan. The rest of the house was perfectly quiet. But then it was only half past five. In the shower, she told herself she had nothing to feel guilty about. It had been a simple mistake of drinking more than was sensible. There was nothing to feel bad about in claiming a headache and going to bed the minute Chloe and her parents had left.

It was probably as well that she'd fallen asleep the moment her head had hit the pillow because surely Dan's stoicism could only stretch so far. Had she been awake when he joined her in bed, he would have been bound to ask her what the hell she thought she'd been playing at.

With everyone still sleeping, she quietly left the house and drove to work. With hardly any traffic on the roads, she was in Manchester and at her desk by seven o'clock. It had seemed the best thing to do, to leave before everyone was up. She couldn't stand the thought of facing Dan's parents over breakfast. When she got home tonight, Glynis and Ronald would be gone and then she and Dan would be able to sit down and talk. She would try to explain to him just how he made her feel at times, how he couldn't go on undermining her in front of Marcus.

With everything now neatly sorted in her mind, she switched on her computer and eagerly embraced the day head on. Suddenly life didn't seem such an uphill struggle. She was back in control.

By nine twenty, the office was buzzing with activity and Sally was drinking her fourth cup of coffee, brought to her by her wonderfully efficient assistant, Chandra. She was flicking through a client's file on the table behind her desk when there was a knock at her partially open door. She heard Tom's voice. 'Morning, Sally. OK if we come in?'

'Sure,' she said. 'You're only interrupting me in my latest bid to make legal history, but I can put that on hold for you.' She looked up to see Tom the other side of her desk. At his side was a man Sally didn't recognise. He was tall, slim and suited-and-booted to kill. His white shirt, complete with cufflinks, showed off a boyishly handsome, tanned face.

'Sally,' Tom said, 'I'd like to introduce Harry Fox. Harry, beware, this is Sally Oliver. She's a human dynamo and takes no hostages when it comes to keeping the rest of us in line.'

Sally got to her feet and stepped round her desk. She'd forgotten all about the New Boy arriving today. 'Hello,' she said, offering her hand, 'good to meet you. And don't believe a word of what Tom says.'

Harry smiled and shook hands with her. 'But just to be safe, I'll take him at his word and do my best to behave myself. I'd hate to get on your wrong side. Especially on my first day.' His dark, glinting eyes dropped momentarily to her legs then back to her face.

Cheeky boy, she thought. We'll have to cure you of that.

'Well, then,' Tom said, rubbing his hands together, 'I'll leave you two to it. Glad to have you on board, Harry. Any problems, you know where to find me. Although I'm pretty sure you're in capable hands here. Sally will be sure to have everything arranged for you.'

Sally did a double take. 'Sorry, Tom?' she said. 'I'm not with you. What will I have arranged?'

'Oh, good lord, Sally,' Tom said. 'There's been an oversight, hasn't there? How embarrassing. My fault entirely. I forgot to tell you that Colin's away on holiday for the next fortnight and while his office is being decorated, I thought Harry could share your office instead.'

It was a while since Sally had shared an office with anyone and she was quick to lay down the ground rules. There would be no bags of sweaty gym clothes brought in. No radios or portable television sets either, no matter how important the cricket, rugby or football match.

'Any rules on the wearing of perfume and aftershave?' Harry asked.

Oh, so he wasn't taking her seriously? 'Depends what it is,' she said.

'Only I have to warn you, the perfume you're wearing is having rather a powerful effect on me.'

Mmm . . . a joker, was he?

'Versace Crystal Noir, isn't it?' he said, when she didn't respond. 'I have a connoisseur's nose for these things. It suits you.'

The impudent boy's self-importance was breathtaking. 'How would you know what suits me?'

He grinned. 'It's a gift. I can size a person up within seconds of meeting them. I'm never wrong.'

She had been out of the office when interviews had been held to find somebody to add to the tax department. If she remembered correctly, Harry Fox had been considered a dynamic 'bright young thing' when it came to Inland Revenue and VAT fraud.

'Exactly how old are you?' she asked.

'How old do you think I am?'

Young enough for a good clip round the ear, sonny! She probably had shoes at the back of the wardrobe that were older than him. 'Twenty-five, twenty-six?' she said.

He stopped what he was doing and sat down, staring at her across the room. 'You think I'm a gauche, wet-behind-the-ears office boy, don't you?'

'I'll leave that for you and your unfailing *gift* to decide.'

Ten minutes later she was on her way to meet a client for a barrister's conference. Darren T. Child was one of her high-profile clients, a premier league footballer who was rarely off the front pages of the newspapers. She was currently handling his divorce.

The conference was over before it had started. Her client hadn't bothered to turn up. None of the numbers she had for him, including his agent, had been answered, and all she could do was leave several messages to call her as soon as possible. She headed back to the office.

'Someone's in luck today,' Chandra said when Sally stopped to check for any messages while she'd been out.

'Any particular reason why?'

'You'll see.'

On Sally's desk was a beautiful bouquet of red roses. Attached to the ribbon that held the stems together was a small envelope. She put down her case. Dan, she thought with a happy smile. The perfect peace offering. She opened the envelope and pulled out the card. *Sorry for getting off on the wrong foot with you. Can we start again, please?*

The sound of tapping on her door had her turning round. Harry Fox was standing in the doorway. Staring earnestly at her, he said, 'Can we pretend that was my cocky brother you met this morning?'

Rosie had been mysterious on the phone earlier that morning, saying she'd met someone recently who she wanted Dan to meet. They'd had an early lunch and then Dan had put Marcus to bed for a nap.

His parents had left shortly after nine thirty with a look on their faces that came nauseatingly close to sympathy. His mother had almost forgotten herself and put a hand on his arm when she'd said, 'You would say if there was anything we could do, wouldn't you?'

'Just get the hell out, that's what you can do!' is what he should have said, instead of the polite non-committal shake of his head that his family was so good at. With Marcus at his side, he'd waved them off, furious that they would be leaving with the case closed on his marriage.

He didn't think he was exaggerating when he thought they would love nothing more than to drive a wedge between Sally and himself. But they were making a big mistake if they thought he'd ever let it happen.

Time to get ready to go to Rosie's. Dan pushed open the door to Marcus's bedroom. He was still asleep and Dan took a moment to absorb his son and to think, as he often did, how similar he was to his mother, not just in appearance with the colour of his eyes or his fine dark hair, but in his temperament. He was as sharp as a tack and Dan didn't doubt he'd grow up to be as ferociously intelligent as his mother. He already had her iron will. Yet Dan wouldn't have him any other way.

Question was, in view of the disastrous weekend they'd just staggered through, would he have Sally any other way? Yes, if he was honest. He did think she had her priorities wrong at times. Yet what if the boot was on the other foot and he was going out to work? Who was to say that he wouldn't be doing the same as Sally? Didn't he used to stay late at the office to get just one more thing sorted?

He sighed. Perhaps he had been unfair to Sally. He'd certainly been unfair forcing her to spend two days with his awful parents. Was it any wonder she'd sought refuge in a few too many glasses of Chablis? Who could blame her? He'd try to make it up to her this evening.

But as he knelt down to wake his son, he had a horrible suspicion that his criticism of Sally might actually be rooted in jealousy. Was there a part of him that felt lost in the long shadow cast by Sally's career as it went from strength to strength? He really hoped it wasn't the case. But he'd be a liar if he didn't admit to occasionally missing the cut and thrust of his old life, but it was nothing like enough to make him regret the sacrifice he'd made. He knew he was doing the right thing, giving Marcus the best possible start in life by being at home with him.

In her efficient way, Rosie Peach had everything organised in the garden to keep Marcus and Charlie occupied while she and Dan sat on the patio waiting for her friend to arrive. They were in the sandpit, digging with sufficient vigour to get them to the earth's centre by teatime.

'Ah, that'll be Tatiana,' Rosie said in response to the sound of a car door shutting. While Rosie went to meet her friend, Dan got to his feet, ready to meet the person who apparently had a proposition for him.

When Rosie reappeared, Dan assumed someone other than her expected guest had turned up. Dressed in jeans and a T-shirt, her hair in two long plaits and carrying a small red canvas rucksack over her shoulder, she looked like a teenaged babysitter from the village. She was slight of build, and he found himself wondering if she'd trained as a ballet dancer as she seemed to glide over to the sandpit. Once there, she knelt beside the two boys and tipping back Charlie's sunhat, she planted a loud raspberry of a kiss on his cheek. He squealed with delight.

'And you must be Marcus,' she said, turning her head. 'I've heard a lot about you. You're Charlie's best friend, aren't you?'

'We're digging,' Marcus said importantly. He pointed to the large hole he and Charlie had created. 'For treasure. We're pirates.'

'Well, avast there, me hearties! Buried treasure! Count me in. Can I do some digging with you handsome pirates? I absolutely love digging.'

Both boys beamed and Marcus promptly offered her his spade.

'Later,' she said. 'I need to talk to your daddy first, Marcus. But make sure you save some buried treasure for me to discover.'

She straightened up in one fluid movement and came over to Dan and Rosie. 'Hello,' she said to Dan, 'I'm Tatiana. What a lovely son you have. He has such a thoughtful and intuitive face.'

Dan felt himself blush with fatherly pride. 'I'm no expert, but from the look on that thoughtful and intuitive face of his, I'd say you've just acquired yourself a fan for life.'

She shrugged off the compliment and sat down at the shaded end of the table. 'Rosie, the garden is looking beautiful. I wish I had your green fingers.' She held out her pale, delicate hands for them to inspect as evidence. 'See, not a hint of green to them. Perfectly useless.' She laughed lightly. 'Ooh, is that a goldfinch at the bird feeder?'

She's like a butterfly, Dan thought, flitting charmingly from one thing to another. He couldn't begin to think what kind of proposition she had in mind for him.

Five minutes later, when Rosie went inside the house to make drinks for everyone, Dan began to think that there might be more to Tatiana Haines than he'd originally thought.

'Has Rosie told you anything at all about me?' she asked, her vibrant green eyes suddenly focusing entirely on him.

'Nothing other than that she met you recently at a fund-raising event,' he said.

'Good. I asked her not to say anything; I wanted to make the pitch myself. Have you heard of a charity called the Kyle Morgan Trust?'

He shook his head. 'Sorry, no, I haven't.'

'It's a charity for terminally sick children and I'm their fundraising manager. We provide respite and specialist nursing care in the home for families who are desperate for a break. And by a break, I'm talking about a couple of hours to go to the shops or time to snatch some much-needed sleep. Or even play with their other children.'

'How did you get involved?'

'Kyle Morgan was my nephew; my sister's son. He was born with a genetic disorder and died before his second birthday. After his death we heard of a charity down in the southwest that provided just the kind of care and support that would have helped my sister and her husband. We decided to try to get something similar started here in Cheshire.'

'How long ago was that?'

'Five years ago. Since then we've supported more than a hundred families, which is great, but we know there are many more in the region that we can't help yet because we don't have the funding. We're aiming to launch a major appeal in December to get a massive leap in donations. We don't receive any government funding; every penny we have is raised through events and rattling collection tins.'

'So where do I come in?'

'From what Rosie's told me about you and your line of work before you took time out to be at home with Marcus, I think you'd be a real asset to the trust. I'm hoping to twist your arm and convince you to join us.'

Sally switched off her computer, tidied her desk and pulled on her suit jacket. As she did so, she glanced at the roses Harry had given her. They were as absurdly showy as the boy himself. Should she take them home with her? No. Dan might wonder why she'd been on the receiving end of such an ostentatious gift. The flowers were fine here in the office.

Out in the corridor, her mind on making peace with Dan, she bumped into Harry. Literally. He'd been walking towards her carrying a tower of box files, his view all but obscured. The files teetered and then the one on the top slid to the floor, banging against her ankle. Gritting her teeth, Sally retrieved the file from the floor and added it to his load.

'Sorry,' he said. 'Is your foot OK?'

'It'll survive,' she said.

'I seem to have done nothing but annoy you today,' he said, putting the files down. 'Aren't you taking my roses home with you?'

'I'm leaving them here to brighten the office. Good night.' She took a step past him.

'Look, could I extend my apology by buying you a drink?' he said.

'I'm sorry,' Sally said. 'I can't.'

'Can't or won't?' he asked. His eyes were bright with mischief.

'My husband's waiting for me at home,' she said curtly. 'And if you carry on with this line of talk, I'll have you bounced out of here faster than you can say sexual harassment. Got it?'

Unabashed, he smiled. 'You have the most amazing eyes. They were what I noticed about you first. Then I spotted your legs.'

Her back straightened with stiffening rage. 'Are you hearing me?'

'Oh, yes. Question is, are you hearing me? I think you're beautiful. Possibly the most beautiful woman I've ever met.'

'Have you got something of a Class A nature in your blood?'

He laughed. 'You know, I think I might have. But it's not what you're thinking. Something this good couldn't be illegal.' He bent down and picked up the files. 'Have a nice evening. I'll see you tomorrow.'

Sally marched off. She would have to talk to Tom. The fool of a boy would have to go. He was intolerable. Not to say unspeakably arrogant. How dare he treat her as some kind of sex object! *Possibly the most beautiful woman I've ever met*. What rubbish! Well, I'll tell you what I noticed first about you, sonny. It was your bloody great ego!

She drove home faster than she should have, seething with anger, and just as she was passing Chloe's house, she noticed her friend's car on the drive. She slammed on the brakes and reversed hard.

'**I** don't believe it!' Chloe laughed. 'He came onto you on his first day? You've got to admire his nerve. Hey, talk about when Harry met Sally.'

'Admire his nerve? He's a menace! A pest!'

'Don't tell me you weren't just an itsy-bit flattered.'

'Certainly not!'

Chloe smiled, which only added to Sally's exasperation. She had come here expecting sympathy and understanding from her friend, but instead she was being made to feel unaccountably worse.

'Is he good looking?'

'Yes,' Sally said, 'but implausibly so. And he damn well knows it. Oh, and he's got one of those sticking-out-a-mile public-school voices.'

'So, let me get this right. You have a young and handsome newbie in the office who thinks you're beautiful. And your problem would be?'

'Oh, Chloe, don't be stupid. You can't have men behaving in such an insulting way in the workplace. It's intrinsically wrong.'

'You genuinely feel insulted?'

'Of course! He treated me like he was picking me up in a bar. He's undermining my position.'

'Mm . . . and that would be senior to him?'

Sally stopped pacing. She considered Chloe's words carefully. Yes, there it was. That was the truth of the matter. Harry Fox hadn't respected her. By treating her as an inconsequential bit of fluff, she had felt disparaged.

Now that she had put her finger on exactly what had enraged her so much, Sally turned slowly round to face her friend. Calm now, she registered that Chloe was dressed for going to the gym.

'I'm sorry,' she said. 'I'm keeping you, aren't I?'

'No worries. I'm glad you stopped by. I wanted to know how things progressed after I left yesterday. You were quite tense, weren't you?'

'Don't remind me. It was one of the worst weekends in a long while.'

'Did you and Dan get a chance to talk?'

Sally shook her head. 'That's what I'm hoping to do tonight.' She picked up her bag. 'I'd better go. Wish me luck.'

Marcus was already in bed, fast asleep, when she got home. She crept into his bedroom and skimmed his forehead with a kiss. How peaceful he looks, she thought enviously. Not a care in the world.

She went to change and, after carefully hanging up her suit, she went back down to the kitchen. Dan greeted her with a glass of white wine.

'Supper will be ready in ten minutes. How was your day?'

She thought of Harry Fox and said, 'I've had better. How about you? Your parents get away all right?'

'I'll tell you about it later. First I want to apologise for the weekend.'

'You can't help your parents,' she said with a tight smile.

'It's not them I'm apologising for; it's . . . it's me. I was out of order when I criticised you for the amount of time you devote to work. Call it an error of judgment on my part. I'm sorry, really I am. Do you forgive me?'

Sally didn't know what to say. This wasn't the conversation she had imagined them having. Everything she'd planned to say now went out of her head. 'You've never asked me that before,' she murmured.

'Let's hope I never have to again,' he said, his expression grave. He put down his glass, then took hers, too. He held her face in his hands and kissed her on the mouth.

'No,' she said. 'It wasn't only you who made a mistake. I did as well. I behaved no better than a sulky teenager. I'm sorry. Am I forgiven?'

He kissed her again. 'Forgiven entirely,' he said as his hands began moving over her body. She kissed him back and pressed herself against him, her desire for him roused in an instant. She suddenly needed to be connected to the strong, hard warmth of Dan, knowing that it would blank out how frustrated and isolated she'd felt these last few days.

'Fancy an addition to the menu tonight?' she whispered in his ear.

He smiled and unzipped her trousers, then lifted her up onto the worktop. Kissing him, she worked at the buttons on his jeans.

She'd just undone the last of the buttons when they heard Marcus calling from upstairs. 'Daddy. Can I have a dink? Daddy.'

'Don't move,' Dan said. 'Stay exactly as you are. I'll be right back.'

But left alone, Sally did move. By the time Dan returned, she had her trousers back on and the timer on the cooker was announcing that supper was ready.

'No chance of hitting the rewind button?' he said with a rueful sigh.

'We'll save it for later.'

He smiled again. 'I'll hold you to that. Now, sit down while I serve. It's fish pie,' he added.

From her chair at the table she watched him take the pie out of the oven. 'Oh, something I forgot to tell you,' she said. 'I'm making a duty visit to Hull to see my mother this coming weekend. Is that OK?'

'But it's Derek Lockley's memorial service this Saturday.'

'Damn,' she muttered. 'I'd forgotten all about that.'

'Can you change your visit to another weekend?'

'I'd rather not.'

'Then you'll have to take Marcus with you,' he said decisively.

'I think I'll ask Chloe to have him for the day,' she said. 'I'm sure she wouldn't mind.'

Chloe had decided she liked Seth a lot. He was warm and kind and made her laugh. He was also intelligent and articulate. And what's more, he didn't appear to be dragging any baggage around with him. There was no ex-wife nor was there a brood of dependent children.

Having showered and changed after their workout, they were now sitting at a table in the bar of Cartwright Hall and tackling a platter of barbecued chicken wings. She was telling him about one of her patients, who had given birth that day to a baby boy and had named him Dyson. 'Can you imagine when the poor boy goes to school? He'll be stuck with some awful nicknames, like Sucker, or Dusty.'

'How about this for a corker of a name for a little girl: Clarity Shine. Brilliant, isn't it? Is having children something you want?' Seth asked.

Taken aback by the question, and not caring if her answer would be committing dating suicide, she said, 'Yes. How about you?'

'Oh, yes, definitely.'

The speed of his reply surprised her again. She mentally added a tick in yet another box for him: he was scoring quite highly.

'I have two brothers and one sister,' he went on, 'all married with six children between them.'

'Which leaves them wondering what on earth's wrong with you?'

'Something like that. I'm going to see my sister tomorrow, over in Whitchurch. It's the last day of the Easter school holidays so I'll get to see my two nieces. Which will be great. Not so great will be that I'll have to submit myself to my sister Rebecca's usual interrogation.'

Remembering that, like her, it was his day off tomorrow, Chloe tried not to feel disappointed. It would have been nice to get together again. While jogging on the treadmill earlier, she had indulged herself in a mild daydream of the two of them going for a walk in the Peak District.

'If I hadn't been anxious about kick-starting World War Three, I might have been tempted to say no to my sister,' he said. 'I was going to ask you if you wanted to spend the day with me. But I lost my nerve and thought you might think I was pushing my luck.'

She smiled, experiencing a genuine rush of pleasure and fondness for him. 'I wouldn't have thought that at all.'

'Really?'

'In fact, I was going to ask you if you wanted to go for a walk in the Peak District. There's a great tea shop in Castleton where they serve the best cream teas in the world.'

'Stop!' He groaned. 'Now you're just torturing me. There I'll be tomorrow, thinking of what might have been.' He turned to face her and put a hand on her forearm. 'Can we go to Castleton another time?'

'I don't see why not,' she said, trying not to read too much into the gesture—a friendly hand on her arm, that's all it was—'but if I remember rightly, you do owe me dinner.'

He feigned a look of shock at the platter of chicken bones in front of them. 'I thought *this* was dinner. You mean you want more?'

'A cheapskate as well as a coward! Now I'm getting to know the real you.'

Outside in the car park, Seth walked her to her car. They'd now reached the tricky stage of bringing the evening to a close.

Would he kiss her? That was the burning issue. As she played for time and pretended to hunt through her bag for her keys, Chloe knew she would feel cheated if he didn't. She looked up to see him smiling.

'Finished?' he asked. He then swooped in for a kiss. A polite little kiss at first and then a long, long kiss.

Mm . . . she thought; that was definitely worth waiting for.

'You have told her, haven't you?'

Seth gave the small screw one last turn then pushed the plug into the socket. He flicked the switch, pushed down the lever and within seconds he could feel heat rising from the toaster. 'As I thought,' he said, 'it was the fuse. You really should learn to change one, you know.'

'That's what husbands and brothers are for,' Rebecca said. 'And I repeat my question: you have told her, haven't you?'

Ignoring her again, Seth went to put the screwdriver back in his brother-in-law's toolbox. Working away in Zambia, Peter was helping local farmers to market their produce more effectively. Seth had been here less than an hour, doing the odd jobs around the house that needed doing in Peter's absence, and already his sister had got more out of him than he'd intended to divulge. He swore her mission in life was to marry him off and have him settled down before his fortieth birthday. With less than a year to go, she appeared to be upping the ante. In the past six months, she'd brought a number of girls to his attention whenever he visited. The last one had been pleasant enough company during dinner, if a touch flaky, but he couldn't have imagined wanting to spend more than an evening with her. Anyway, Chloe had entered his consciousness by then.

The second he'd set eyes on Chloe at the gym, he'd wanted to get to know her better. But he'd deliberately not rushed straight in; he'd kept his distance, watching to see if she ever turned up with a partner. Happily for him she was always alone, and he'd decided to ask her out.

He smiled at the memory of kissing Chloe last night. When their lips had touched, he'd kept it brief, telling himself to go slowly. But there she was, so close, so gorgeous, and so wholly irresistible. So he'd kissed her again. He'd driven home afterwards with a broad smile on his face.

Back in the kitchen, Rebecca was waiting for him.

'No,' he said, 'I haven't told Chloe. I'm waiting for the right moment. I want her to get to know the real me before her view is coloured by prejudice. It's happened too many times in the past, as you well know.'

She wagged a finger at him. 'You're lying to Chloe, aren't you?'

'I can honestly say I haven't once lied to her.'

'Hmmm . . . you mean you've glossed over what makes you the person you are?'

There was no arguing with this uncomfortable truth and Seth was relieved when the kitchen door flew open and a human tornado burst in and wrapped itself around him. 'Uncle Seth, come and play! Come and play! We've built a den!'

'Is it safe to come in?' Harry was peering round Sally's office door. When she gave him the go-ahead, he came in carrying a tray of china—teapot, jug, cups and saucers and a plate of mini chocolate éclairs.

'What's all this?' she asked, as he took the tray over to his desk.

'A peace offering,' he replied. 'I made a prat of myself yesterday and I want to make it up to you.'

She hesitated. She'd come into work this morning all set to do battle with him, only to find a note on her desk saying he wouldn't be in until later and could they talk.

'How do you like your tea? With or without milk?'

'With,' she said, deciding to give him a chance to redeem himself.

He handed her the cup and saucer. 'There,' he said, 'a conversation without me annoying you. You see, it is possible.'

Warily she asked, 'Where have you been all day?'

He smiled. 'I had an on-site meeting with a client that went on. And on. It was stupendously tedious.'

'I guarantee it couldn't have been more tedious than my last client.' She took a sip of her tea. 'Earl Grey,' she said, surprised. 'My favourite.'

'I know,' he said, 'I asked Chandra. I also know you love chocolate éclairs.' He offered her the plate. 'Tell me about your vexatious client.'

'Oh, he's the usual maggot wriggling on the end of a fishing line.'

'And presumably not the reason why you became a lawyer in the first place?'

She looked at him closely, realising that somehow he'd thoroughly disarmed her. 'How old *are* you?' she asked him.

'Ah, we're back to that again, are we? I'm thirty.'

'You look younger.'

'So I'm told. It's a pain in the butt. I occasionally have trouble with people not taking me seriously.'

She suppressed a snort of derision. Surely he couldn't be so guileless? 'I'm not surprised if yesterday was anything to go by.'

He met her gaze. 'I meant what I said. You are beautiful and I really could look at you all day. I just went about saying it entirely the wrong way. From now on I shall do my best to behave myself. More tea?'

The service had already started when Dan slipped into a pew at the back of the church. He didn't recognise anyone around him, but up at the front there were some familiar faces—Jeremy Williams, David Taylor, Hilary Parr, Howard Bailey, Huw Alsop, Diane Fallows, Sue Halloran, oh, and there was Andy Hope.

He'd very nearly opted out of coming, because for the first time ever he'd experienced a loss of confidence. Stupidly, he'd been bothered about how his fellow Durham alumni would react to him being a house-husband, a stay-at-home father. In the end, it was what had propelled him out of the house and into his car. No way would he allow himself to start feeling he was achieving less than anyone else.

During the drive down, he'd made up his mind to find out more about Tatiana Haines's proposition. When he'd stopped for petrol at Taunton, he'd phoned her number and agreed to meet her again at the trust's offices in Crantsford; he'd stressed that he wasn't interested in a full-time job. She'd sounded pleased that he'd got in touch.

Rosie had already offered to have Marcus as often as was necessary, so childcare didn't look like it would pose too much of a problem. While Sally was clearly surprised that he was even considering the job, she had no problem with him pursuing it further.

Sally drew up outside the house. The pocket handkerchief-sized garden was home to knee-high grass, a knocked-over dustbin and a street's worth of litter. A net curtain at an upstairs window was rucked up and resembled a bride's dress caught in her knickers.

She went and rang the front-door bell. Her brother opened the door and, looking over her shoulder, he sneered. 'Latest 5-series BMW, I see. Not stinting yourself, are you?'

'Good to see you, too, Terry,' she muttered, stepping inside and thinking he would never change. With the door shut behind her, the smell of a fifty-a-day habit hit Sally, as did years of accumulated filth and grime. She could barely make it along the hallway for piles of old newspapers and carrier bags of what appeared to be rotting rubbish. The stench made her want to cover her mouth with her hand, run back to her car and drive all the way home to her beautiful, spotless house.

Kath Wilson was sprawled on the sofa in front of the television. The woman looked her usual, miserable, disgustingly corpulent self.

'You've come, then,' Kath said, tearing her eyes briefly away from the television. 'Terry,' she said, 'fetch us a drink, will you? I'm parched.'

'How are you, Mum?' she asked, sitting in the least offensively stained of the two armchairs. 'What has the doctor said about your hip?'

The woman shifted her massive bulk and faced Sally. 'He said it's shot. I need it replacing. And it was a top specialist who told me that.'

'Are you in a lot of pain?'

'Would it please you if I was?'

Yes! Sally wanted to shout back. I hate you for reminding me of the person I once was. 'Of course it wouldn't,' she lied. 'Exactly how long have you been told you'll have to wait before the operation?'

'Too long. That's how bloody long. It's them cutbacks. It's all right for the likes of you going private, the rest of us have to get in line and wait.'

The door opened and in walked Terry with three mugs. Sally silently groaned. Now she'd be expected to drink from a cup she hadn't personally washed. She took the mug from Terry just as he slopped some of it onto the carpet. She had to fight the urge to fetch a cloth.

She also had to fight the rising sense of regret and futility in coming all this way. Why had she done it? Why didn't she just cut the tie and have done with it? She reminded herself why she was here: to discover how badly her mother needed this operation, or if in fact she needed it at all. But how to rule out a possible scam, other than accompanying her mother to the specialist she had allegedly visited. Another few minutes and she'd suggest that.

It had been a teacher at school who'd changed the course of Sally's life. For years, Sally had been getting away with murder—her wildness was legendary and skiving off school came as naturally to her as did stealing, joy-riding, drinking and having sex. She never once got caught; she was too smart for that. Unlike Terry. Running wild kept her enemy—boredom—at bay. That was the one thing she couldn't hack. But gradually boredom began to win out and she derived no pleasure in any of her usual pastimes. She was fifteen years old and could see no point in anything. Others would have turned to drugs in her situation, but the control freak in her wouldn't allow that.

But then Mr Atlee showed up as a new member of staff at school. He was charismatic and dynamic and announced on his first day that he was here to kick arses into touch and anyone who had a problem with that would be first in line for a good kicking. His approach was borderline psychotic but he got results and something in Sally responded to him. 'You've got a brain, Sally Wilson,' he shouted at her one day, when she hadn't bothered to do her homework, 'you're just too scared to use it for fear of losing your credibility and the approval of your peers.'

So she set out to prove to him she could do both: use her brain and keep her credibility. Some weeks later, after a classroom debate about animal testing, he congratulated her on winning the argument for her team—they'd been pro—and he'd said she was dangerously analytical. The description appealed to her like nothing else had in a long time. He'd also said that he didn't see her ever making a career out of losing.

'You're not genetically programmed to come second,' he'd added.

That day was the turning point in her life. From then on, in spite of her mother's disbelief and her brother's taunts, she devoted herself to a future she'd previously never dreamed of. By the time she made it to university, the process of her reinvention was well underway. Chloe became an important part of it and then, with her career rapidly taking off, Dan added the crucial finishing touch of refinement and class, and *voilà*, she was entirely reborn. She was inordinately proud of what she'd achieved. She'd done it all herself. She was beholden to no one.

Chloe was having a brilliant day. Seth had phoned earlier to ask if she was free to take him on that walk in the Peaks that he'd missed out on and when she'd explained about having Marcus with her, she'd invited him to join them for lunch instead. 'What's on the menu?' he'd asked.

'It's Marcus's choice; bangers and mash with baked beans.'

'If there's enough for me, I'll be there in half an hour.'

She'd been surprised to see him arrive in a bright red, two-seater sports car. She'd wondered how comfortable it was for him, being so tall. 'Style above content,' he'd said when she aired the thought. 'A man has to suffer for his style.'

Now, as she cleared away the lunch things, she watched Seth with Marcus. The pair of them created a bitter-sweet tableau of the happy family scenario she so badly wanted for herself: Seth was lying on the sofa with a bandage comically tied round his head and Marcus was listening intently to his heartbeat with a stethoscope. Marcus always liked to play with the stash of toys Chloe kept here for him, including her old stethoscope from her training days, along with a selection of bandages. Willing herself not to think the obvious—that Seth would make the most fantastic father—Chloe could see that Marcus liked him a lot.

He wasn't the only one. Chloe's feelings for Seth were definitely growing, but she was determined not to lose her head.

A knock at the back door had Marcus jumping off the sofa. 'Daddy!'

'Sorry, Marcus,' Chloe said, going to answer the door, 'I doubt very much that will be Daddy for you yet.'

She was right. It was her mother, wicker shopping basket in hand and nosiness radiating off her like steam. 'Hello! Only me! I was just passing.' Craning her neck round the archway to the sitting room, she added in a surprised voice that wasn't fooling Chloe, 'Oh, you've got company. Now I feel awful for barging in.'

Chloe smiled. 'The car on the drive wasn't a big enough clue?'

Jennifer feigned vagueness. 'A car? Is there one on the drive? Silly me.'

'Start displaying too many dotty-old-lady traits and I'll have to take steps with you,' Chloe said. 'But since you're here, come and meet my visitor. Be nice to him,' she warned, 'or else.'

'**N**ow that's what I call a man worth coming home for,' Jennifer said when she was gathering up her basket, having eventually got the hint that it was time she was on her way. 'He'll do very nicely.'

Chloe shot an anxious glance back to the sitting room. 'A little louder, Mum, I don't think he heard you.'

'Nonsense. I'm being the model of discretion. Seriously, though, he's gorgeous. Bring him for dinner some time soon. Now give my love to Dan and Sally, won't you? Is everything all right with those two?'

'Yes, of course. It was just having Dan's parents round. You know how tense that makes them both. Say hi to Dad from me.'

Despite beginning to show signs that he was overtired, Marcus had no intention of missing out on any fun by having an afternoon nap and so Chloe suggested that they have some quiet time together on the sofa.

'I'll read to you,' she said.

'Mind if I join you?' Seth asked. 'I can never resist a good story.'

At which point Marcus took the book from Chloe and insisted that Seth read to him. 'That OK with you?' Seth said.

She nodded happily and lifted Marcus onto her lap. Seth proved an excellent reader and he held Marcus spellbound with the range of amusing voices he adopted for the various characters. Before long, Marcus's eyelids were drooping, and then his body went limp and he fell asleep, his head resting heavily against Chloe's shoulder.

'You've done this before,' she whispered to Seth. She carefully laid Marcus on the sofa. 'Come on, let's leave him to his forty winks.'

They hadn't got as far as the kitchen when Chloe felt a hand round her waist. She turned and found herself neatly wrapped in Seth's arms. He gazed at her for a moment, then lowered his head and kissed her. 'I've wanted to do that ever since I got here.'

'You should have said.'

He kissed her again. When he looked up, his expression was serious. 'Chloe, there's something I want to tell you. You'll say I should have told you before, but I had my reasons, which I hope you'll understand.'

She smiled. 'That sounds ominous.'

He held her hands in his. 'The thing is—'

The sound of the telephone ringing made them both start. Chloe rushed to answer it before it woke Marcus. 'Hi, Dan,' she said, her voice low. 'No, everything's fine. We've had lunch and he's having a nap now. He's been no trouble at all. No, really. How was the service?'

She turned round to mouth that she'd only be a few minutes and was shocked to see Seth pulling on his jacket. He pointed to the back door.

'Hang on a minute, Dan,' she said, confused. She covered the receiver with a hand. 'You're not going, are you, Seth?'

'I better had. I'll give you a ring. Thanks for lunch. It was great. I'll let myself out.' He didn't look like he could get away fast enough.

But why? What had happened? One minute they were kissing and he was about to tell her something important and the next . . . From outside she heard the sound of his car engine starting up.

What on earth had got into him? What had he been about to tell her? She swallowed. Oh, dear God, no. Not that. Oh, please not *that*.

But even as she tried not to think it, she knew that it was the obvious explanation. Seth had been about to admit that he'd been lying to her. He probably had a wife and children. Had his conscience suddenly got the better of him? The lying cheat! Good riddance to him.

A voice from the forgotten receiver in her hand reminded her that Dan was at the other end. 'Yes, Dan,' she said, 'I'm still here.'

Chapter Four

AFTER EMAILING TATIANA a copy of his CV on Saturday evening, Dan was visiting the Kyle Morgan Trust's office to meet the rest of the team, as well as the chief executive. His CV would leave them in no doubt that he was qualified to take on the role of trusts and major donations manager, but if he wanted the job he'd have to convince them he would fit in. As he drove through the village on Monday morning after dropping Marcus off at nursery, he wondered what Tatiana's colleagues would be like. One of his concerns was that the rest of the team might be a bunch of bustling do-gooders in hand-knitted twin-sets. In which case, there wouldn't be a chance in hell of him fitting in.

Point of fact, he wasn't entirely sure where he did fit in nowadays. Derek's memorial service could not have flagged up more clearly how out of step he was with everyone else now. When the service had finished and they'd gathered in the local pub for a drink and a bite to eat, the inevitable round of What Are You Doing Now? ensued.

Jeremy Williams and David Taylor—both married with young children—had said he was a better man than they were as ten minutes in the company of their own kids was enough to drive them mad. *Guffaw! Guffaw! Only joking!* Diane Fallows and Sue Halloran had oohed and aahed over him, saying they'd give anything to swap their workaholic husbands for him. No patronising there, then. And Andy Hope— divorced, no children and based in Hong Kong—had said, 'Lucky old you, a kept man! You always were a jammy sod.'

Not one of them had given the slightest indication that they thought he was doing something as worth while as they were. Was this how mothers who stayed at home to care for their children were made to feel?

The Kyle Morgan Trust was housed in an attractive converted barn on the road to Crantsford. There was a turning circle at the front of the horseshoe-shaped building and a sign with four other businesses listed. An arrow directed him to a car park at the rear.

He'd been waiting in the reception area for no more than two minutes when Tatiana appeared. She was dressed a little more formally than when he'd met her at Rosie's, but she still wore her hair in two long plaits and there was that same effervescent joyful air about her as she shook his hand warmly and led him through a pair of double doors.

'Everyone's so looking forward to meeting you. I think you can safely assume that it's a foregone conclusion that we want you on board with us. All we're worried about is that with your expertise and experience you'll think us very small potatoes. How's Marcus?'

Dan could feel her enthusiasm rubbing off on him. I want this job, he suddenly decided.

Her patient off the examining couch now and sitting next to her mother, Chloe said, 'Exactly how long have you been feeling tired and nauseous, Chelsea?'

'About two weeks,' Chelsea mumbled.

'I'm afraid my next question is going to be rather blunt and personal. Before I ask it, would you prefer your mother stayed or left us alone?'

'What the hell's going on?' Mrs Savage said. 'I'm not going anywhere.

Chelsea's my daughter. What you say to her, you say to me. End of!'

'Chelsea?' Chloe persisted. 'Are you happy with that?'

'Of course she is! Now tell us what's wrong with her. It's probably a bug. Whatever it is, we need it dealt with. We don't want anything to hold up her getting her boob job done. She's booked for next week.'

Ah, yes, the boob job that somehow Mrs Savage had found the money for in the face of the NHS telling her to come back when her daughter was older.

'I have to ask you, are you sexually active?'

'Sexually active?' spluttered Mrs Savage. 'Course she isn't. What do you take her for? One of those cheap girls who fool around?'

'Chelsea, can you answer my question, please?'

'What if I was?' Her reply was hardly more than a whisper.

'You're displaying many of the classic symptoms of early pregnancy. When was your last period?'

'Pregnant! But she can't be! No way. She's going to be a model.'

Chelsea's face collapsed and she started to cry.

'She can't keep it,' Mrs Savage said grimly. 'It'll have to be sorted. And soon.' Her eyes were narrowed and her mouth was set firm.

Ignoring her, Chloe reached for the box of tissues on her desk and came round to where Chelsea was sitting. She plucked a handful of tissues out of the box and gave them to the distraught girl. 'You don't need to make any decision right away,' she said. 'It's important that you make an informed choice. There's more than one option available and I can put you in touch with people who can help you. Meanwhile, I want you to do a urine test for me so that we can confirm the pregnancy.'

Chelsea raised her head. 'You mean . . . you mean I might not be pregnant?' The hope in her voice was pitiful.

'We need to make sure, either way. When that's been done, you can start the process of deciding what to do.'

'The decision's made,' Mrs Savage said. 'Chelsea, come on, you stupid little bitch, we're going home. You and I need a talk.' She pointed a finger at Chloe. 'And you, you keep your mouth shut. If this gets out in the village, I'll know whose big gob spread it about. Got it?'

'I assure you, Mrs Savage, everything discussed in this room is considered private and confidential.'

'Yeah, well, it better had be.'

Snivelling noisily, the girl allowed herself to be led away by her bully of a mother. Chloe closed the door after them and went and sat behind her desk. Thank goodness Chelsea had been her last patient of the day.

And what a day it had been. Ron Tuttle had been admitted to hospital that morning with dehydration as a result of a urinary infection, a hysterical mother had brought her son in with a crayon stuck up his nose and her father had called to say that Margaret Parr had died.

Years ago Margaret had lived in the village and she'd regularly babysat Chloe and Nick when they'd been little. With no children of her own, she had spoiled them at every opportunity. The funeral was to be held on Friday at St Michael's in Crantsford, where Margaret had moved five years ago. There was no question of Chloe not going.

Two days after her visit to Hull, Sally was still trying to get her mother out of her system. She was driving home from work and each time she thought of Saturday she had to ease her foot off the accelerator. Getting done for speeding would be the final straw. Would she never learn to disregard anything that came out of Kath Wilson's poisonous mouth?

She had just suggested that she speak to Mum's doctor when Terry had attacked. 'Why do you want to do that?' he'd demanded. 'Why can't you give us the money? I mean, it's no skin off your nose, is it?'

Patiently, she'd tried to explain that to pay for her mother to have the operation privately would cost a small fortune in one lump sum.

Kath gave Sally one of her famously vicious looks. 'I always did say you had a heart of stone. Now I know I was right.'

'How can you say that when I'm offering to help you?'

'Oh, don't give me one of your, Who-me? faces. You've got no intention of helping me, have you? So why don't you just push off back to that useless wimp of a husband of yours. You're not welcome here.'

Sally had leaped to her feet. 'Dan is not a useless wimp of a husband!'

'Oh, no? Does he stand up to you? Or do you walk all over him?'

'I think you're confusing Dan with the man you were married to.'

'Just goes to show that it must be in the genes, then. I landed myself with a useless loser and you've done the same.'

Sally had grabbed her bag then. 'We've clearly said all we're ever going to say to one another. Please don't bother to get in touch with me again. You'll get no more money from me.'

She was out on the street and opening her car door with a trembling hand when a voice called out, 'Coo-ee. I thought it was you. Not often we get a fancy car like this parked round here. Home for a visit, are you?'

It was her mother's neighbour, Joan. She was clutching a selection of holiday brochures. Battling with the lump of anger in her throat, Sally managed to say, 'Going somewhere nice?'

'I hope so. Your mum and I are planning a little holiday. We're thinking of going to Furta . . . Oh, the name's gone. Must be my age. Your
mum's dead excited about it. Terry and Janice are coming with us.'

'Fuerteventura?'

'Yes! That's it. Clever you.'

Yes, clever me, thought Sally bleakly as once again she realised her
speed had crept up. Clever me for having such a delightful mother. The
kind of mother who'd make out she was in dire need of an operation so
she could con money out of her daughter. Well, those days were gone.
The Bank of Sally Oliver was officially closed.

As furious as she was for her mother's deception, what had angered
and upset Sally most was the way the hideous woman had spoken
about Dan. How dare the bitch compare Dan to her father! A man
who'd buggered off to Spain with some slapper when Sally was ten
years old. A man who never bothered to get in touch with his family
again, other than to send them a postcard saying he wanted to remarry
and was instigating divorce proceedings.

Sally couldn't bring herself to confide in Dan about the way her
mother had described him or the scam she and Terry had tried to pull.
Admitting that Mum and Terry despised her to that extent was just too
humiliating. She loosened her clenched grip on the steering wheel and
reminded herself that the one positive thing to come out of her visit
was that she would never have to make that journey again. She'd been a
fool all these years, paying them off to keep them tidily out of her life.
Pretending they didn't exist would have been a far better option. It was
what she was going to do from now on.

The church of St Michael was almost full and an elderly couple had to
shuffle along the pew to make room for Chloe and her parents. With
sombre organ music playing in the background, people were chatting
quietly among themselves. Her parents had struck up conversation
with the couple on their left. Chloe picked up a Bible and flicked
through it. It reminded her of when she and Nick used to be dragged
along to church by her mother and they would giggle about some of the
lines in the Song of Songs. All that 'browsing among the lilies . . . your
two breasts are like two fawns . . .'

Their father never accompanied them to church and when they were
of a suitably rebellious age, Chloe and her brother claimed that if their
father was allowed to stay at home, tinkering in his workshop, they
should be allowed to do the same. It was getting up early on a Sunday

morning that Nick bucked against; for Chloe it was the total tedium of the exercise that rankled. Anything but sit through a mind-numbingly boring sermon. It was a shame Nick couldn't be here today, but he was stuck in Boston on business.

For a brief moment the organist paused, alerting everyone to stop talking, and then took up with a louder, more strident piece of music. Chloe closed the Bible and placed it on the narrow shelf in front of her. Passing her now were the pallbearers with Margaret's coffin on their shoulders. A great sadness swept over her. Margaret had been such a part of her childhood. She had spent numerous Christmases with the Hennessey family at Laurel House, Chloe's parents refusing to allow her to spend the time alone.

The coffin had been set down now and the pallbearers had found their places in the pews. The vicar stepped forward and announced the first hymn. Chloe reached for her hymn book, but then did a double take. Her senses reeled. *No!* It couldn't be! Surely not? She stared hard, incredulous. If it wasn't him, then he had a twin brother. An identical twin brother. Next to her, her mother whispered, 'Isn't that your handsome young man? You never told me he was a vicar.' She chuckled. 'I hope you haven't been leading a man of the cloth astray.'

As he de-robed in the vestry, Seth could scarcely believe he'd managed to conduct the service without making a comprehensive cock-up of it. He'd had many a distraction to deal with in his time but this had thoroughly tested his mettle.

Avoiding Chloe's eye hadn't been the problem as such—she was looking anywhere but in his direction—it was knowing that there was going to be some hefty fallout to follow.

He hung his robe and stole on the hook on the back of the vestry door and wondered what Chloe's connection had been to Margaret Parr. Possibly a close and long-standing one if Jennifer Hennessey's presence was anything to go by. Presumably that had been Chloe's father in the pew alongside them.

With his jacket on now, completing his black suit, he checked his appearance in the mirror—hair OK, white collar straight, expression calm—he opened the door and went in search of forgiveness.

He found Chloe sitting on a bench in the dappled shade of the chestnut tree. When she heard his footsteps on the gravel and turned towards him, she didn't give the impression of having murder on her mind. She did look annoyed, though.

'May I?' he said.

She moved to one end of the wooden bench to accommodate him. 'Am I supposed to say something like, "That was a nice service, vicar?"'

'You could if you wanted. Except, strictly speaking, I'm not a vicar.'

Her face flickered with scorn. 'What? You're an impostor? You dress up in black frocks and bury people for kicks?'

He smiled. 'I'm an assistant vicar, still in my curacy.'

'Oh. Well, it amounts to the same thing. Why didn't you just tell me what you did for a living? Why the pretence?'

'Would you have gone out with me if I had told you at the outset? And be honest.'

She looked at him with contempt. 'That's rich coming from you.'

He took a deep breath. 'I never lied to you, Chloe.'

'But you weren't entirely straight with me.'

'With good reason. I knew that you'd treat me differently, that you wouldn't regard me as normal. I'd suddenly become this untouchable, unapproachable being. It's what you're doing to me right now. And I know what I'm talking about; it's happened to me before.'

'You mean you've conned girls like me before?'

'Absolutely not. But the minute they know I'm a vicar, they're off faster than you can say *amen*. So hand on heart, now that you know, does it change things?' He watched her face intently.

'Why did you leave so suddenly last Saturday and then not ring me during the week?'

Noting that she hadn't answered his question, he said, 'I was about to tell you the truth that afternoon and then I bottled it. I wanted to get in touch afterwards but I knew that if I did, I'd have to come clean with you and then that would be the last I'd see of you. I was sunk either way I turned. You don't need to tell me that I screwed up in a major way, and with only myself to blame. I'm sorry.'

'I'd decided you were either married or a con artist.'

'Is being a priest as bad, or worse, in your eyes?'

'I don't know. It's weird. I mean . . . well, you know, we kissed and—'

'I'm not a monk, Chloe,' he interrupted her gently. 'And I certainly haven't taken a vow of celibacy.'

'Aha! There you are!'

They both looked up to see Chloe's mother advancing towards them. As one, they rose from the bench.

'Lovely service, Reverend,' Jennifer said, holding out her hand. 'I must say, you'd increase the number of bums on pews at our church no end if you were our vicar. I expect you have more than your fair share of congregational groupies here, don't you? That's the price you pay for being such a dashing clergyman.'

'Mum!'

'Good to see you again, Mrs Hennessey. How are you?'

'Please, call me Jennifer. Are you coming for the bunfight? Chloe, what's that look for?'

Chloe felt like a sulky teenager at a boring grown-ups' party. She only had to watch Seth for a few minutes to realise that her mother had been right about the groupies. Dressed in his black suit and with his dark, curly hair, he looked impossibly glamorous in this setting. And it was clear the good women of St Michael's loved him. They buzzed around him like bees round a honey pot. Chloe pitied the poor girl who ended up marrying him; she would be the most hated girl in Christendom.

An ordained minister. Oh God, she'd kissed a Church of England priest! Well, actually, she'd *snogged* a Church of England priest. Worse still, she'd entertained the occasional fantasy of making love with him. Only now to discover that she hadn't known the first thing about him. And what kind of a clergyman picked up girls in gyms, took them out, kissed them and deliberately led them up the garden path? No wonder the Church of England was in such a mess!

Dan, with Marcus's help, was loading bottles into a wheelbarrow—Tabasco sauce, gin, peri-peri marinade, walnut oil, ketchup, cider, Tango, Grouse, Taylor's Port, Stone's ginger wine, Radox bubble bath, cheap sparkling wine and hair shampoo.

Eastbury was preparing for the May Bank Holiday fete and it was all hands to the pump, as Lardy McFierce kept saying. She'd got herself into a real headless chicken state yesterday when her tombola stall rota fell apart. Dan had taken pity on the woman and had offered to run the stall himself, single-handedly, for the whole afternoon if necessary. It was no big deal, no real sacrifice.

Compare an afternoon's commitment to a village fete to the sacrifices he'd seen in the last month since he'd started working for the Kyle Morgan Trust, and it didn't register. As part of getting an in-depth understanding of the job, he'd now met a number of the families the trust assisted. As harrowing as the lives were that these people were living, their unfailing love and dedication to their children—who were unlikely to live beyond the age of eighteen—was awe-inspiring.

Most of the children had been born with a degenerative disease of some sort and required constant care. This meant the parents were physically and mentally drained, and with other children in the family to look after, it was a wonder to Dan they could face each day. The most important part of the trust's work was letting these parents know that they were no longer alone in caring for a child twenty-four hours a day. One of the things that had struck Dan was that maybe more could be done for the siblings of these families. He had kept his counsel on the matter, not wanting to appear as though he was telling anyone their job. Any worries he'd had about working with a bunch of intense worthies had been dispelled the day he'd gone to meet everyone. He'd been impressed by their enthusiastic drive and sheer hard work.

With Marcus at his side, and pushing the wheelbarrow in the direction of the village green, Dan had to agree that there was some truth in what Andy Hope had said when he'd called him a jammy sod. If it wasn't for Sally's hard work, he would not be able to take on a satisfying, worthwhile but relatively poorly paid job for the trust as well as spend time with Marcus. So far he'd been able to do a fair amount of the work from home and he hoped this would continue. The times he had to be at the office, Rosie had Marcus. It was a perfect arrangement.

And since he'd started work at the trust, his nightmares had stopped; it was as if a great weight had been lifted off his shoulders. It felt as if he'd just emerged from a low point in his life. It had been triggered, he believed, by Marcus being the same age as the boy he'd failed to save. He just wished he and Sally spent more time together. But what married couple didn't say that? Having made the mistake of criticising her for putting work first, he now found himself biting his tongue on a regular basis. He was growing increasingly perturbed by just how little time Sally seemed to want to spend with him and Marcus.

From Chloe's kitchen window, Sally observed her husband setting up the tombola stall on the green opposite. He was wearing a pair of blue knee-length shorts, a cream Polo shirt, his favourite old brown leather deck shoes and a Panama hat. He looked so at home here in the village. More so than Sally did. It had been her dream to live somewhere like this, but now, if she were honest, she wasn't so sure it was right for her.

'Can you chop these mushrooms for me, Sally?'

Chloe's request had Sally turning from the window. 'When are your parents joining us?' she asked, taking a knife from the drawer.

'Any minute, I hope. As usual Dad's made the tomato sauce and pizza bases and without any of that we can't put the pizzas together.'

Running a take-away pizza stall from the kitchen window of Chloe's cottage had gone down so well two years ago, it was now an expected feature of the fete. It was also the biggest money-earner.

'Dan's really enjoying his new job, isn't he?' Chloe said. 'I've never seen him so animated about work before.'

'Yes, I'm really pleased for him.' Sally tried to sound as if she meant it, that she shared her husband's happiness and everyone else's opinion about his new job. In short, they thought he was wonderful, a real hero for giving his time to such a worthy cause when, with his qualifications and experience, he could walk into any high-flying job he wanted.

It wasn't the first time Dan had been awarded this status. When he'd risked his life in the tsunami to save that little girl and her brother, he'd been hailed a hero by everyone there. Back at home, here in the village and in the local newspaper, his efforts had also been applauded. The BBC's *North West Tonight* had wanted to do a feature on him, but Dan had declined. They had both been relieved when the hoo-ha eventually died down and people stopped asking them about their experiences. Sally had hated talking about it, and Dan was the same. Sometimes she felt as if it had never really happened to her, that she had acquired her experience of the disaster vicariously through the lens of a camera. If it wasn't for one particular fear that the ordeal had left her with, she could very nearly convince herself that this was the case.

When the first anniversary of the disaster had begun to loom, people started raking it over again. 'How does it feel a year on?' they kept asking Sally and Dan. Sally had begun to wonder if they would for ever be defined as being tsunami survivors. Or more precisely, in her case, defined as the wife of a tsunami hero.

And here they were once more, she thought, as she heard the sound of Chloe's parents arriving. Dan was being hailed a hero because he was doing something so worth while. Was it wrong of her to feel rankled by this? Wasn't keeping a roof over her family's head and food on the table, which she was working so hard for, also worth while? Did that count for nothing?

For two solid hours, the queue for pizzas at £1.50 a slice didn't let up. Now, though, trade had dwindled and Chloe, her parents and Sally were able to take stock. The kitchen looked as though it had been trashed during the course of a food fight, and they themselves looked as though they'd been thoroughly roughed up.

'It must be about time to reward ourselves with a glass of wine,' Chloe said, as she opened the oven door for the last of the pizzas.

'Already ahead of you,' her mother said, taking a bottle of white wine from the fridge.

Chloe put the pizzas on wooden mats on the table, where Sally was counting the money they'd made so far.

'How have we done, Sally?' Chloe's father asked.

'At this point, we're forty-five pounds up on last year.'

'I think we can safely call that a result,' Chloe said. She took a welcome glass of wine from her mother. 'Well done, team!'

Thirty minutes later, with the kitchen returning to its usual state, Chloe's parents offered to go and mingle with the crowds on the green to sell the remaining slices of pizza. That left Chloe and Sally with nothing to do other than take two chairs outside to soak up the warm afternoon sun. With their glasses refilled, they sank back with a contented sigh. Over the crackling address system, Dave Peach was announcing that following the Best Mongrel in Show competition, they could look forward to the arrival of the newly crowned May Queen, Chelsea Savage's reign having come to an end. Chelsea's plans for becoming a model were currently on hold. Very much against her mother's wishes, she was going ahead with having the baby.

Chloe sipped her wine, and taking her cue from Sally, she too tilted her head back and closed her eyes.

'Still not heard anything from your sexy rev?' Sally asked.

'Nope,' Chloe replied. 'Not a peep.' Since Margaret's funeral nearly five weeks before she had neither seen Seth nor heard from him. To her shame she had stopped going to the gym so that she wouldn't have to face him there. 'And I wish you wouldn't refer to him as my sexy rev,' she said. 'Especially as you never even laid eyes on him.'

Sally laughed. 'I'm going by your mother's description. She said he was a particularly fine specimen of manhood.'

'I'm never going to live it down, am I?' Chloe said crossly.

'What, that you fancied a Church of England priest? I think it's hysterically funny. Just think; you could have ended up a vicar's wife!'

'All right, Sally, no need to make my disastrous love life sound any worse than it already is.'

'But honestly, you, a vicar's wife! Hey, do you remember that list we compiled at university, the list we swore we'd live by?'

'I knew you'd trot that out sooner or later.'

Sally laughed. 'Well, at least one of us has stuck by it.'

Chloe recalled the list with unease. Back then, when they'd been students, it had seemed clever of them to be so discriminatory. The list had been a rule book of men they would never date. Car salesmen were out, as were financial advisers, politicians and journalists, all on the basis that they told lies for a living. But, top of the list, because they pedalled the biggest lies of all, were pompous, sexless, po-faced clergymen.

Opening her eyes, Chloe took a long sip of her wine. Whatever else she thought about Seth, she couldn't accuse him of being sexless or po-faced. As for lying, that was debatable. He'd misled her, that much she did know. But for all that, she occasionally caught herself thinking fondly about him. She missed his cheerfulness and kind demeanour, but most of all, she missed the way he'd made her feel. He'd given her hope—hope that maybe she had found the man of her dreams?

None of this would she admit to Sally. It annoyed Chloe that her friend was deriving so much pleasure from something that had mattered to her. It seemed unnecessarily cruel. Cruel to Chloe and cruel to Seth, who wasn't here to defend himself.

Surprised that she could suddenly feel sorry for him, Chloe thought hard about Seth and the reasons why she had refused to see him again. One, she could never countenance being romantically involved with a man who had such a strong religious bias; a bias she simply couldn't respect. And two, to all intents and purposes, Seth was already married: he was married to the Church. Chloe could only ever be second best.

Sadly, Seth's world could never be her world. But, while it was true that these key points precluded a romantic relationship with him, Chloe wondered now if there was any reason why they couldn't be friends. The thought so instantly cheered her, she resolved to ring Seth.

Having reached what felt like a satisfactory conclusion on the subject, she decided to turn the tables on Sally. 'How's your newbie in the office?' she asked. 'Is he still making a pest of himself?'

She never got to hear Sally's answer, for she heard another voice. A voice she would know anywhere, any time. 'Hello, Chloe.'

Chloe sprang from her seat, spilling wine down her front. 'Paul!'

'I seem to remember wine being spilled the first time we met,' he said. 'How are you, Chloe? You look great. You too, Sally.'

On her feet beside Chloe, Sally stared coolly at him. 'What brings you here?' she asked. Her tone was as ice-cool as her gaze.

He smiled and addressed Chloe, face on. 'I came on the off-chance that we could talk. Did you get any of my messages?'

'I did, but you didn't reply to mine. Why not?'

'I'm sorry, but I didn't know that you had. My car was broken into and I'd left my mobile in it. It was taken, along with my laptop.'

'How did you have Chloe's number in the first place? And her address?' More cross-examining from Sally.

'I'd heard on the grapevine in Nottingham that Chloe had moved back here and all I did was check the phone book. So here I am.'

Here you are, indeed, thought Chloe. How easy and assured he was. Not a flicker of remorse. Dressed in black jeans, he looked every inch the handsome, well-groomed man she remembered of old.

'Since you've come all this way, why don't you sit down?' Chloe said.

'Thank you,' Paul said.

'In that case.' Sally drained her glass and stood. 'I'll leave you to it.'

'Sally's never going to forgive me, is she?' Paul said when they were alone and he was sitting in the chair Sally had vacated. He'd accepted a glass of wine and was looking dangerously at home.

'Do you really expect my best friend, of all people, to forgive you?'

'I'd like to think that one day she might,' Paul said.

'And what about me? Do you expect me to forget what you did?'

He frowned. 'That's my girl, straight to the heart of the matter.'

'Well? Do you?' *That's my girl!* The nerve of him!

'I've changed, Chloe. When I left you, I was a self-centred, arrogant bastard. I thought I had life all figured out. Now I know different.'

'So if you're no longer a self-centred, arrogant bastard,' she said, deliberately echoing his words for the sheer pleasure of saying them out loud, 'what are you? A paragon of goodness and honest virtue?'

'Far from it. I still make plenty of mistakes, but at least now I'm more aware of them.' He turned and faced her. 'I've become a life coach.'

Chloe nearly choked on her wine. 'A life coach? Are you serious?'

'Very serious. And I've never been happier.' He laughed. 'But then who wouldn't be, after escaping the tedium of working in IT?'

'From IT manager to life coach; what brought that on?'

'I lost my way, you could say. I thought that being with Christine would make everything suddenly feel right.'

'And did everything feel right for you with Christine?'

He shook his head. 'We lasted five months together. We were driving each other crazy. In short, we weren't the people we thought we were.'

Five months, seethed Chloe. If he hadn't left her for those five wasted months, who knows what might have been? Paul, the father of the child she'd carried so fleetingly, was here beside her. Suddenly it all seemed more real and more painful than it had in a long while. How would he feel, she wondered, if she told him the truth?

He'd started talking again. 'It wasn't until I met Liz that I began to understand where I'd gone wrong. Liz taught me so much. She opened my eyes to what I really wanted to achieve with my life.'

Liz? Who the hell was Liz?

'Uh-oh,' he said. 'I think your mother's just spotted me.'

Chloe followed his glance and sure enough, striding across the grass was her mother, an empty pizza tray in her hand.

'So it really is you! Well, well, well! Who'd have thought you'd have the cheek to show your dirty, rotten face round here?'

'Hello, Jennifer,' Paul said, rising from his chair, his hand extended.

'Don't give me any of your smarmy patter! You. Snake. In. The. Grass!'

Yes! Chloe silently cheered. Finally, after all this time, her mother had got to say the words to the face of the man she despised.

'You broke my daughter's heart,' Jennifer continued angrily. 'Don't think for one moment I'm going to welcome you back with open arms.' And with that she raised the empty pizza tray in her hands and clouted Paul's head with a satisfying crash.

Other than a blow to Paul's pride, Chloe could detect no signs of any real damage to his head, and she declared him fit to fight another day.

'I've got some bridges to rebuild, haven't I?' he said ruefully as they watched Jennifer marching away.

Chloe said, 'Surely you didn't think it could be otherwise?' She had no intention of apologising for her mother's behaviour.

'I had hoped that sufficient time had passed for everyone's feelings to have calmed down.'

'You thought wrong.'

'Does that mean you're about to hit me, too?'

'I haven't made up my mind yet.'

His expression softened. 'Would a quiet dinner, just the two of us, help you to decide?'

'Dinner?'

'I came here to clear the air between us. I can't think of a nicer way to go about it than to take you out for dinner.'

'And what would Liz have to say about that?'

Without missing a beat, he said, 'She'd say it was exactly the right thing to do.'

Sally was quite used to seeing Dan with other women. It was a standing joke between them that one day he would run off with one of the mums from the nursery. But not once had Sally ever thought that their marriage could come under threat. However, observing this diminutive creature to whom Dan had just introduced her, with her bright, animated face, her tiny waist, her stunning hair and eye-catching dress, Sally experienced a frisson of unease. This perky little thing looked like trouble. She had a way about her that managed to convey inner strength, yet at the same time an air of vulnerability. She was the kind of girl men instinctively want to protect but also want to take to bed.

Not listening to what Dan, Tatiana and Rosie were talking about, Sally backtracked through conversations she and Dan had had about the trust. She couldn't recall him making more than a passing reference to Tatiana—something about her enthusiasm being infectious. The lawyer in her asserted that often it wasn't what people said, so much as what they didn't. And in this instance, Dan had barely opened his mouth about Tatiana, Queen of the Bloody Fairies.

Trying to tune back into the conversation, Sally watched the way her husband interacted with Tatiana. Certainly he was smiling and maintaining eye contact with her, but did that make him guilty of anything more dangerous than being a red-blooded male captivated by a pretty girl? For her part, Tatiana was doing nothing remotely flirtatious, but then she didn't need to. She'd probably still manage to be alluring with her hair unwashed, wearing a shabby old candlewick dressing gown with a Marmite stain down the front.

Thoroughly out of sorts now, Sally stifled a yawn and, thinking of the work she could be doing at home, wondered if anyone would notice if she disappeared. Village fetes were hardly her thing.

Over the public-address system, Rosie's husband was announcing the arrival of the newly crowned May Queen. As if sensing something exciting was about to happen, Charlie came to a sudden stop and Marcus careered straight into the back of him. The collision made both boys fall over and land in a heap; Marcus let go of his balloon and when he saw it drifting skywards he began crying. Sally went to him, but he was inconsolable. He pushed her away, struggled to his feet and wailed loudly, his arms stretched above him.

Then, magically, he was quiet.

Tatiana was kneeling on the grass in front of him. In her hands, and pressed to her lips as she blew into it, was another balloon. As it took shape, puff by puff, a slow smile appeared on Marcus's face. By the time the balloon was its full size and Tatiana had it securely tied—she even produced a ribbon from her bag—Marcus was beaming happily. He could not have looked more adoringly at her.

A shot of hatred mainlined straight to Sally's heart. First her husband, now her son?

'**W**hat the hell happened to you?' Dan asked.

The fete had finished more than an hour ago and after staying behind to clear up and then trundle an exhausted Marcus home in the wheelbarrow, he was dumbfounded to find Sally working at her laptop.

She stared at him. 'I'm surprised you noticed I wasn't there.'

'What's that supposed to mean?'

She shrugged. 'You tell me. At what point did you actually miss me?'

He frowned. 'I don't know what this is about, Sally, but for the record, it would have been nice to have had your support for once. You could have helped me on the tombola stall for a few minutes.'

'Let me get this straight. You want my support? Oh, that's rich. Here I am working all hours to support you and Marcus and somehow that isn't enough.'

'Hey, I'm working too! And Marcus doesn't take care of himself.'

'No, you've got your charming coterie of women to help you on that score, haven't you?'

He laughed at this. 'Since when has Rosie become a one-woman charming coterie?'

'I'm not talking about Rosie, as you well know.'

'Who then? Chloe?'

'Don't be absurd. You know exactly who I'm talking about. Tatiana.'

'Tatiana? You're mad. I barely know her.'

'You work with her; of course you know her.'

'She's a work colleague. Nothing more.'

'So why was she here at the fete?'

'She's a friend of Rosie's.'

'She didn't come to the fete last year. What was the big attraction this time round?'

Exasperated, his voice raised, he said, 'Rosie's only recently met her!' Then, truly stunned at what Sally was accusing him of, Dan took a moment to consider what he said next. 'You're serious about this, aren't you? You really think I'm capable of being unfaithful to you?'

'I see it every day in my work, Dan. No one's beyond reproach.'

'Funny that, because from the outside looking in at our marriage some people might think *you* would be the one most likely to have an affair. Certainly you have more opportunity than me, yet I've never once thought you would. I trust you, Sally. And I believe in our marriage.' He wanted to shore his words up by action, by going over to his wife and embracing her to show that he loved her, but he couldn't. He felt leaden with disbelief. She'd as good as kicked him in the teeth.

What *the hell happened to you?* Dan had asked her and now Sally asked herself the same question. What had she just done? Could she not have found a more subtle way to voice her concern with Dan?

I believe in our marriage, he'd said. But what did that really mean? She couldn't remember the last time they'd made love or exchanged anything more passionate than a hurried kiss on the cheek. Things had definitely got worse since he'd started working for the trust. She thought of Tatiana and how effortlessly she had cured Marcus of his tears. A regular Mary Poppins, Sally had thought nastily.

Shortly after Tatiana had worked her magic with the balloon, Sally had slipped away from the fete; she wasn't needed there.

But the question was, who really needed her at Corner Cottage? Dan and Marcus had such a close relationship there were times when she felt she had to crowbar her way into it.

Chapter Five

TUESDAY MORNING AND SALLY was alone in her office. Harry had moved into an office of his own some weeks before, but today she found herself missing his presence.

Despite their getting off on the wrong foot she had come to appreciate his company. Now that he was behaving himself—he'd stopped all that absurd infatuation nonsense—she had come to respect his keen intellect and his shamelessly ambitious work ethic. He teased her now and then, mimicking the way she said, 'Oh, don't be absurd!' Until he'd pointed this out to her, she'd had no idea that she said it so often. He had a knack for cheering her up, of making her laugh when she least expected to. She could do with a good laugh now. Yesterday had been an unmitigated disaster. After Dan had put Marcus to bed, they had eaten their evening meal in near silence and afterwards watched a programme on the television that she had no recollection of at all.

She had woken up this morning knowing that all it would have taken from her was one word—sorry—and she and Dan would not have slept with their backs to each other. Sorry . . . and she wouldn't have woken feeling everything was slipping away from her.

But was she sorry? Truth was, she wasn't. A woman knows when another woman is a threat and Sally knew in her bones that Tatiana had the capability to cause trouble. Hadn't she already?

She reached for the client file from the top of the pile on her desk and opened it. Twenty minutes later she realised she had lost count how many times she had reread the same page. She couldn't concentrate. Caffeine. That's what she needed. Lots of it.

There was no one in the kitchen and she was glad not to have to make small talk with anyone while she waited for the kettle to boil.

She was on her way back to her office, when the doors of the lift opened and Harry stepped out.

'Aha!' he proclaimed eagerly. 'Just the person I was looking for.' His hand on the lift button, he said, 'Have you got a minute? There's something in my office I want to show you.' And before she knew what he was doing, he'd taken her by the arm and manoeuvred her into the lift.

'No!' she cried, as the doors closed. Spilling her coffee, she jabbed at the panel of buttons. But it was too late; the lift was moving.

OK, she told herself, stay calm. No need to panic. It was two floors up to Harry's office. That was all. It was no big deal.

Harry was staring at her oddly. It slowly registered that he'd asked her something. To her relief the lift juddered to a stop. She'd made it.

She faced the doors, waiting for them to open. But the doors didn't open. She pressed the button. And again. Panic began to rise in her.

'I don't believe it,' Harry said. 'It looks like we're stuck.'

'We can't be,' she said. The knot of panic in her stomach was tightening and she could feel the air being sucked out of her chest. She frantically tried the button once more. The lights began to flicker.

'I don't think that will help,' Harry said. The lights flickered again, then went out. Darkness.

'This is all your fault!' she cried desperately. 'If you hadn't manhandled me the way you did, I wouldn't be stuck here with you.'

'Sally,' he said. Except it didn't sound like Harry. He sounded serious.

Authoritative. In the darkness, she felt the cup of coffee being taken from her hands. 'Listen to me,' he said. He now had her hands in his and was holding them tightly. 'We'll be out of here in no time at all. OK?'

She struggled to speak but couldn't. A low wattage light above their heads came on and in the dim light, she watched Harry press the red emergency button. The lift juddered and she let out a startled cry.

'Please,' she gasped, 'I have to get out of here!' She covered her head with her hands and slid down the mirrored wall of the lift until she was crouched on the floor. She tried to concentrate on her breathing.

It wasn't working. She was going to suffocate. A long way off, almost drowned out by the sound of crashing in her ears, she could hear Harry talking to someone. A hand on her arm made her start. She opened her eyes. It was Harry. He was pulling her into his arms.

'Help's on its way,' he said. 'Hang in there, Sally. Five minutes, ten, tops.'

'I can't . . . I can't breathe,' she rasped. A sob caught in her throat. She was beyond caring. She wanted to curl up and die. Just let it be over.

He turned her face towards him and held it so firmly she had no choice but to look at him. 'Do exactly as I do,' he said. 'Imagine each breath as a step out of here.' He inhaled deeply, then exhaled slowly. 'Come on, Sally, try it. Look into my eyes. Show me you can do it.'

His words began to cut through her panic and the deafening crashing in her ears but, light-headed now, she had no way of connecting with her lungs. She felt clammy all over and was shaking hard.

'Sally, what colour are my eyes?'

His voice was so insistent, she wondered whether it was important. She focused her own eyes on his and said, 'Brown. They're brown.'

'What kind of brown are they? Look closely. Tell me, are they light brown or dark brown? What do you see?'

'Dark . . . brown,' she said falteringly. 'Dark, like . . . like chocolate.'

He smiled. 'Good girl.' He released his hold on her and brushed her hair away from her face. 'Now, take a small breath and think how like chocolate they are and how wonderful it would be to eat some when we get out of here. That's it, breath in slowly. Now out. And again. You're doing brilliantly.' He stroked her cheek. He put an arm round her and she could feel his warm, firm body through his shirt. It felt good. Reassuring. He made her feel safe. She'd stopped shaking now.

'I'm sorry,' she mumbled with a deep, shuddering breath.

'What for?' he asked.

'For this. For you having to see me this way.'

'It's my fault. I had no idea you suffered from claustrophobia. I feel such an idiot for putting you through this. Hang on, I can hear voices.'

He made to stand up, but when the lights flickered, she clung to him, grabbing hold of his hand. 'Please,' she said, 'don't leave me.'

He stayed with her on the floor.

A disembodied voice shouted to them. It declared itself to be part of the emergency services and asked if they were all right.

'We're doing fine,' Harry shouted. 'What seems to be the problem?'

'A power failure. The light you've got on there is hooked up to the emergency generator. How many of you are there?'

'Just the two of us.'

'Any injuries?'

'No.'

'That's good. Now stay nice and calm and I'll be right back with you.'

Sally said, 'You won't tell anyone about this, will you? I couldn't take the shame of everyone knowing what a fool I've been.'

He squeezed her hand. 'Of course I won't.'

'I never used to . . . to suffer from claustrophobia.'

'When did it start?'

'Remember the Boxing Day tsunami?'

'Who could forget it? God, you weren't there, were you?'

She nodded. 'I got trapped and . . . and ever since, I can't stand to be in a confined space.' Tears filled her eyes and her chest tightened. She hated this debilitating weakness that she'd been left with since that dreadful day. It was like a curse. And she despised herself for letting it get the better of her, allowing it to make her so pathetically helpless and vulnerable.

'The scariest situation I've ever been in was the day I met you,' Harry said. 'I took one look at you and knew my life was never going to be the same again. You completely took my breath away. You still do.'

Slowly, she turned to face him. Their eyes met and held. And held. 'Your eyes really are as dark as chocolate,' she murmured. He moved closer to her. Then closer still. Until finally the gap closed, his lips touched hers and they kissed. After all these years, it was a revelation to feel lips other than Dan's against hers.

'That was probably a mistake,' she said, when she pulled away.

'Don't say that.' He kissed her again and she didn't resist him.

It was only when the lights flickered and then came back on with full brightness and a cheer went up the other side of the lift doors that they stopped. By the time the doors had slid open, they were on their feet, perfectly composed and standing a chaste twelve inches apart.

Chloe was nervous about meeting Paul for dinner. She couldn't decide what worried her most. Would all her hurt and anger finally bubble up and cause her to disgrace herself thoroughly in public? Or would something far worse occur? Would she fall for him all over again?

She was fifteen minutes late when she stepped into the restaurant. The old Paul would have glanced pointedly at his watch but the new Paul merely rose from his chair and leaned in to kiss her.

'You look great,' he said. The kiss—as perfunctory as it was on both cheeks—jarred with her. It smacked of assumption. Assumption that she'd forgiven him and they were all set to be lifelong best mates.

'Busy day?' he asked as she settled herself at the table.

'Frantic. It's always the same after a Bank Holiday weekend; there's a stampede to the surgery.'

'A full-on day, then. What would you like to drink?'

His relaxed and ultra-controlled manner further annoyed her. By the time they'd got the business of ordering their drinks and meal out of the way, Chloe was bristling with the need to hold Paul to account.

Her mother had been horrified when Chloe had told her she was meeting him for dinner. Her advice was to slip something deadly into his food when he wasn't looking.

'What's so funny?' Paul asked her when their drinks arrived.

'I was thinking of something my mother said to me earlier.'

'Ah. Did it involve me?'

'Not everything revolves around you, Paul.'

'That was said with feeling,' Paul remarked. 'But I do understand how you feel. I know that deep down you must have harboured a real need to extract some form of revenge on me.'

'You flatter yourself that I gave you that much thought.'

'Didn't you? Don't you?'

His conceit was breathtaking. But he was right. One way or another she did think of him more than was healthy. 'It was quite a stunt you pulled on me,' she said. 'One minute I thought you were planning to propose and the next you were leaving me for someone else. As break-ups go, it was brutal. I was hurt. And very angry.'

'I never once spoke about us getting married. How did you possibly think I was about to propose to you?'

Chloe knew that the honest answer was that it had been a chronic case of wishful thinking on her part. But she couldn't bring herself to admit it.

'It seemed the natural order of things,' she said. 'Seeing as we'd been together so long. But evidently the natural order of things for you was to have two women on the go at the same time.'

'That was an inexcusable mistake on my part. I confused my unhappiness with myself with our relationship. As a consequence, I acted very badly towards you.'

'When did your conscience kick in?' Chloe was intrigued.

'When I met Liz.'

Aha, Liz. 'And is she your latest girlfriend?'

He raised his eyebrows and laughed. 'Definitely not. Liz is my business partner. We run Forward Thinking, a life-coaching business. It's thanks to Liz that I can see things so clearly now.' He smiled. 'I'm a much nicer man to know these days.'

And so modest, she thought when their first course was brought to their table. She asked him if he was still living in Nottingham.

He shook his head. 'I left Nottingham earlier this year. I'm living in Cheshire now, in a village called Lymm. How's your avocado?'

'Rock hard and tasteless, if you want the truth.'

He speared a cube with his fork. It was another overly familiar gesture that jarred with her. What was wrong with saying, 'May I?' She recalled Seth saying these very words to her. Thinking of him made her remember that she hadn't called him.

'You're right,' Paul said. 'It's awful. Much too bitter.' He turned round in his seat and attracted the attention of their waiter. He handed Chloe's plate to the waiter. 'Could you ask the chef if he could rustle up an avocado that's actually fit to eat, please? Thank you so much.'

'You might have asked if I wanted it changing,' Chloe said, nettled.

'But it was inedible,' he said. 'You wouldn't be valuing yourself if you didn't complain about it. Being a life coach has taught me never to put up with anything I don't want to. Self-awareness comes through self-assurance and leads to being truly positive.'

When their waiter reappeared with a tight smile on his face and placed a new starter in front of her, Chloe couldn't help but fear that he and the chef had probably added something unspeakable to it.

'How is it?' Paul asked after she'd taken a mouthful of avocado.

'It's perfect,' she said quickly. Anything less than perfect and he'd be off again, flexing his self-assurance muscles.

'You're sure?' Once again, he helped himself to a piece. 'You're right. Now wasn't it worth complaining about? You mustn't make yourself a doormat, Chloe. Behave like a victim and you'll be taken advantage of.'

She stared at him in disbelief. She put down her knife and fork.

'Paul, the only person who has ever taken advantage of me was you!'

'I can see why you'd think that I took advantage of you, but I didn't. The bottom line is that I took the coward's way out of our relationship because I wasn't thinking straight. I'd begun to worry we were pulling in different directions and that scared me.'

'What kind of different directions?' she asked.

'It was your need to have children.'

'But I never made a big thing of it. I used to tiptoe round the subject, terrified that you'd think I was trying to trap you into parenthood.'

'I know, but I was an idiot back then.'

'And you're not now?'

'I've changed, Chloe. And I'd really like to prove to you that's true. I know it's asking a lot, but do you think you could forgive me so that we can work on making it right between us? I can't stop thinking how great we used to be together.' He shook his head. 'It's one of life's terrible ironies that it's only when we lose something that we realise how precious it was. And you *were* precious to me, Chloe. You really were.'

Chloe swallowed. Here then was the contrition she'd wanted, the apology she had wanted all this time. So why did it feel such an anticlimax? This was nothing but a Pyrrhic victory. The words 'I'm sorry' were never going to bring back what she'd lost.

Almost overcome with the need to share her own confession with him, she felt her eyes pooling with tears. She looked away and blinked hard, hoping he hadn't noticed.

But he had. 'I'm sorry it still hurts after all this time, Chloe,' he said. 'You've no idea how bad that makes me feel.'

His choice of words rankled sufficiently for her to pull herself together. She said, 'Oh, please, don't feel bad on my account.'

He caught her tone and looked hurt by it. 'Tell me about you. What have you been up to? Is there a new man in your life?'

'Yes,' she lied. Her pride would have her say nothing else.

'And is it serious?'

'Is that any of your business?'

'Point taken,' he said. 'But just so that you know, I'm not seeing anyone right now.'

Sally had once watched an episode of *Footballers' Wives* with Chloe. It had been one of their rare, girls' only nights together—a bottle of wine, a take-away curry and something daft to watch on the telly. The glossy lifestyle portrayed in the programme had been about as bizarrely unreal as it could possibly be, and yet here was Sally, chez Darren T. Child, able to testify that what she'd seen on the television had not been a far-fetched aberration of a screenwriter's mind.

Darren T. Child's prowess on the pitch had afforded him a pile of considerable proportions in sought-after Prestbury. The seven-bedroom, five-bathroom house was a monstrosity of vulgarity, equipped with an indoor pool, a snooker room, a gym, a cinema and garaging for five cars.

Sally had been shown through to an enormous sitting room decorated with inexorably bad taste. It was the epitome of teenage-girl chic: pink leather sofas, pink carpets, pink wallpaper. Clearly the decorating had been left to Mrs Child. Either her or Lady Penelope. On the grounds of this room alone, Darren had every right to file for divorce.

The woman who had answered the door to Sally, a housekeeper perhaps, had informed her that Darren was in the swimming pool and wouldn't be long. That had been twenty minutes ago.

Meeting Darren in his own home had been the only way Sally had been sure of nailing her client. He'd refused to come to Manchester to the office, claiming that he'd get mobbed.

The sound of girlish giggling alerted Sally that her wait might nearly be over. Whatever exercise Darren had been up to, it probably hadn't involved the swimming of any lengths. The sound of a slap—a hand on a pert buttock?—followed by, 'Now get lost, like, I got business to do.'

You most certainly have, thought Sally. She stood up.

Dressed in a snow-white towelling robe, Darren slowly swaggered in. All that was absent from his entrance was the 'Eye of the Tiger' soundtrack. 'Hello, Sally, mate. How you doin'?'

'I'm very well, Darren. How are you?'

'I'm good, mate. Bleedin' 'ell! What've you done to that table?' He was staring in horror at the papers she'd spread over a glass coffee table.

'It's important paperwork, which we need to go through,' she said.

'You what? But that's what I pay you to do. I don't do paperwork.'

'We need to go through it together, Darren. Shall we sit down and take a look at what I've brought?'

He took the big pink leather armchair next to the sofa where she'd been sitting. He pressed a button on the arm rest and the chair reclined.

'Now, then,' she said, when he was comfortable. 'Can we get on?'

She drove back to the office thinking about Harry's declaration that he was falling in love with her. 'Oh, don't be absurd,' she'd said. It had come immediately after their getting stuck in the lift together. She had literally run to her office to hide there until the worst of the clamouring guilt shrieking inside her head had subsided. She still couldn't believe that she had kissed Harry. A kiss that could in no way be described as innocent. Oh, no, it had been a kiss loaded with sexual significance.

All she could say in her defence was that it had happened only because the situation had been so wholly unnatural, which in turn had caused her to act out of character. But for all her rationalising, she knew the kiss she had shared with Harry had touched her so profoundly there was a very real risk of it happening again.

When they'd finally been freed from the lift Harry had followed her to her office. He'd sent Chandra off to make some coffee, sat her down in her chair and asked her how she was really feeling.

'You still look very pale,' he'd said.

'It's shock. Shock at what we did.'

'I could apologise, but it won't make it any less true.'

'I know, but we have to go on as if it had never happened.'

'What if I have no intention of doing that? What if I told you there's a very serious chance that I'm falling in love with you?'

'Oh, don't be absurd, Harry.'

He'd smiled, and that was when he'd told her how seductive he found her when she admonished him so primly.

'Please don't tease me,' she'd said. 'Or joke about what we did. I have a husband to think about.'

'Were you thinking of him when I had my arms round you?'

God help her, but she hadn't. 'You won't make things difficult, will you?' she'd said, more of a statement than a question.

'Difficult?' he'd repeated. 'Are you worried that I'm now going to start chasing you round the office or bombarding you with sexually explicit emails?' He stepped towards her. 'I care about you, Sally. Why would I want to do anything to you that would cause you pain?'

'Thank you,' she'd murmured.

'What for?' he'd asked.

'For being so understanding.'

He'd smiled at that. It hadn't been a happy smile.

'I'm sorry,' she'd said, 'that didn't come out the way I wanted it to.'

He'd put a hand on hers.

Don't, she'd thought. Please don't. But she hadn't slid her hand out from under his.

'I don't deserve you,' he'd said, 'but for now it's enough for me to be near you. Don't take that away from me, will you?'

Remembering his words and the expression on his face made Sally's heart lurch. How had she got herself into this mess and allowed Harry to do this to her? How had he got under her skin, to the extent that he made her feel wildly out of control whenever she thought of him?

All in all it was proving to be the kind of week theology college warns you about but in no way prepares you for. The phone had been ringing nonstop since Owen had left for his fortnight's walking holiday in Austria, most of the calls about petty parish squabbles that Seth was expected to resolve.

He'd also had to prepare for three funerals, and it was the home visits he found so difficult. The tears he could cope with, but it was the anger—the need for the griever's shock to be vented—that was more of a challenge. That and the endless cups of tea.

This morning he'd been woken by the phone ringing again. It was bad news: Kenneth Garside, a long-standing member of St Michael's, had been admitted to hospital and wasn't expected to see the day through. He'd hurriedly thrown on his clerical suit, but by the time Seth made it to the hospital, the dying man was beyond recognising who was praying for him. He died ten minutes later.

At home he found his answering machine full of messages. He played through every message, hoping, as he did every day, that there might be something from Chloe. There wasn't. His sister's voice echoed in his ears: call her. Why not? If she refused to speak to him, then so be it.

Sitting at his desk, he leaned forward for the phone and hunted through his address book for Chloe's number. What was the worst she could do? Slam the receiver down?

He tapped in her landline number and almost dropped the phone when he heard her voice after only one ring.

'Chloe, it's me, Seth.'

'Oh,' she said.

'Please don't hang up.'

'I wasn't going to.' He could hear indignation in her voice, as though he'd accused her of lacking courage. 'How are you?'

This was good. She was prepared to talk. 'I'm well,' he said. 'Well, actually, I'm not. I've had a shit week and today's been no better.'

There was a silence and then: 'Are you allowed to swear?'

'Did I swear?'

'You said shit.'

'Now who's swearing?'

She laughed. This was definitely good. 'So how are you?' he asked.

'I've had a weird week. Paul, my ex-boyfriend, showed up unexpectedly.'

Oh, great! Perfect. 'What did he want?' Seth managed to ask.

'Funnily enough, he wanted me to forgive him.'

'And did you?'

'Not really. Although I suppose you would tell me I should or I'll go to hell or something.'

'You know, Chloe, I'm going to have to rid you of these stereotypical images you have of my profession.'

'I've never heard it called a profession before. I thought it was a calling. Or a vocation.'

'You think my job's a holiday?'

'I said *vocation*.'

'I know, I was teasing you.' He paused. Took a breath. 'Would I be pushing my luck if I were to ask if you'd like to meet for a drink?'

'Just a drink?' she asked.

He was sensitive to her testing his suggestion for any strings that might be attached. 'There might be some talking involved,' he added.

'A drink and some talking. Anything else?'

'Don't worry, Chloe, we'll just be two friends meeting for a drink and catching up.' To reassure her, he laid all his cards on the table. 'I promise I won't try to kiss you again. I totally accept where I stand with you. Do you think you can be friends with a curate?'

Dan was in a particularly good mood. His idea to add a new dimension to the work the trust did had gone down surprisingly well.

'You should have more faith in your input,' Tatiana had told him after she'd listened to what he had to say. 'I think what you're proposing is spot on. Only trouble is, funds are limited so we have to prioritise, and sibling care tends to get overlooked. Find us the money, Dan, and we'll do it.'

Dan knew exactly where he was going to start looking for the cash. First he'd approach his old firm in Manchester, then he'd tap his old university mates with their big corporate connections. What was more, and because he so believed in the cause, he would be brazen about it.

He was slicing some leeks when he heard Sally letting herself in at the front door. He glanced at the clock—it was eight forty-five. At once he felt his good mood evaporate. For too long now he and Sally had been chafing at each other. He had no idea how she could have come up with that extraordinary accusation about him and Tatiana, but he'd decided to let it go, putting her behaviour down to problems at work. She had seemed oddly jumpy and on edge this week.

It was also the last thing Marcus needed to be around. Parents were supposed to be the buffer zone in a child's life and Dan was adamant that Marcus's buffer zone would not be breached. To this end, he cranked up his mood and plastered a cheerful smile on his face. 'Hi,' he said brightly when Sally came into the kitchen. 'Good day?'

'Not bad,' she said.

Sally's heart sank. Why did he always have to look so damned happy? She watched Dan return his attention to slicing the leeks. She willed him to put down the knife. Hug me, she thought. Just one hug to make me believe everything's all right between us.

He suddenly turned to face her. 'I'm afraid I'm running late tonight,' he said. 'Supper won't be ready for a while yet. Why don't you treat yourself to a soak in the bath?'

Feeling as if she'd been dismissed, Sally went upstairs. There seemed no room in Dan's life for her; he had his hands full with Marcus, the house and now the trust. He was so deeply entrenched in his own world, he had no idea of the danger they were in.

A practice meeting kept Chloe at the surgery until late and by the time she was on her way home she was starving hungry. As she followed the path round to the back of her house, she tried to remember what she had in the fridge.

The sight of a large bouquet of flowers on the back doorstep stopped her in her tracks. She let herself into the house, dumped her medical bag and jacket on a chair and went back out for the flowers.

She put them on the table in the conservatory and retrieved the card that was attached to a stick poking out from behind a lily. *Dear Chloe, Thank you for giving me a second chance. With love and deepest regret, Paul.*

Chloe stared at the card in her hand. *Deepest regret.* What did he mean by that? It sounded more like the kind of sentiment you'd express to the recently bereaved. And the word *love*, was that just a straightforward salutation, or did he mean something more by it? His last words to her the other night when they'd left the restaurant were that he'd very much like to see her again. She'd said she'd think about it.

But why not see him again? He'd apologised for what he'd done to her; why not forgive him? What if they could not only rekindle what they'd once had, but could develop it into something even better that might lead to marriage and them having children together?

She gasped. What was she thinking? How could she even entertain such an idea? Was she really so desperate to satisfy her intense craving for a child that she would risk getting involved with Paul again?

As shaming as it was, she really was that desperate. Furious with herself, she tossed the card angrily onto the table. How dare he assume she was giving him a second chance? How dare he send her flowers and think that it would make everything right between them?

So worked up was she, she grabbed the bouquet and took it out to the garden. She threw it on the ground and stamped on the flowers hard. She stamped and stamped and then stamped some more. How was that for valuing herself?

It was mid-June and the sun was hot and high in a cloudless blue sky.

Dan was playing superheroes in the garden with Marcus and Charlie when Rosie returned from her visit to the doctors' surgery. He broke off from the game—removing his cape made out of an old beach towel—and offered to make lunch for everyone.

Charlie and Marcus ate their lunch on a blanket under the apple tree and Dan and Rosie sat at a table. Rosie didn't seem to be very hungry. Without wanting to pry, Dan asked Rosie how she'd got on at the surgery.

She smiled. 'Chloe confirmed that I'm pregnant.'

'Hey, that's brilliant! Congratulations! When's it due?'

'January. And before you ask, we're not going to find out what sex the baby is. We didn't with Charlie and we don't see any reason to do things differently this time round. It might sound silly, but we don't want to tempt fate. We've had one perfectly healthy child, and part of me is worried that second time around we might not be so lucky.'

Dan understood exactly what Rosie was saying. He'd thought it himself whenever he'd entertained the idea of he and Sally having another child. Could they really hit the jackpot twice in a row? But having grown up as an only child Dan would prefer Marcus to have a brother or sister as a playmate. He'd been thinking for a while now that it was something he and Sally ought to discuss.

That night, Dan and Sally were in bed early. But they weren't sleeping; they were both working. Sally was making notes for another article for the Law Society's *Gazette* and Dan was putting a report together for the trust. When he was satisfied that the spreadsheet contained all the information he needed, he closed down his laptop, put it on the floor beside the bed and turned to Sally.

'How's it going?' he asked.

She took a moment to reply. 'Slowly,' she said. 'I know what I want to say, but I can't seem to find the right words.' She clicked her Biro, closed her legal pad, and yawned. 'Let's call it a night.'

They turned out the lights. Sally lay on her side. Dan did the same. They had their backs to each other. It was a warm, sultry night and through the open bedroom window, Dan listened to the sound of a car driving by. 'I forgot to tell you,' he said. 'Rosie and Dave are expecting another baby.'

'Really? Was it planned?'

Dan rolled over onto his back. 'Rosie didn't say otherwise, so I assume so. The age gap between Charlie and the baby will be a good one.' In the half-light, he turned his head to look at Sally. 'I know it would complicate things, but would it be so out of the question for us to consider having another child?'

Sally rolled over and stared at him. 'You're not serious, are you?'

Until now, this very moment, Dan hadn't realised just how serious he was. 'I've never wanted Marcus to be an only child,' he said. 'If we're going to have another baby, we should think about it before—'

'Before what?' she interrupted him. 'Before I'm too decrepit? Was that what you were going to say?' She sat up. 'And is that all I am to you now? A baby-making machine? When did I change from being the woman you wanted to make love with, to being a human incubator?'

'Maybe it was when you started being so unapproachable,' Dan said quietly. 'The day you became so touchy about everything.'

'I am not touchy!'

'No? Well then, how come we're having this argument? All I did was suggest we might try for another baby.'

'Oh, that's it; make it sound like I'm the one being unreasonable! You don't touch me in God knows how long and suddenly you want sex to get me pregnant. You're unbelievable!'

'If we haven't had sex recently it's because we've both been so busy. You especially.'

'There you go again, making out that it's my fault.'

'Sally, this isn't about fault. It's about adding to our family.'

'But why? We have Marcus. Isn't that enough for you? Why do you want to risk us having another baby that might . . . that might turn out like the ones your precious trust looks after? Or would that suit you just fine because it would feed into your hero complex? Good old self-less Dan! He saves the life of a child, stays at home to bring up his own, and at the same time devotes himself to the needs of the less fortunate. You'll be walking on water next!'

Dan stared at her, staggered. 'Is that how you see me?'

'Yes. Do you have any idea how hard it is to live with a hero?'

Shocked, Dan got out of bed. He didn't trust himself to say another word. Take this any further and they'd both say things they'd really regret. In silence, he left the room and went downstairs. How had this happened? How had they reached this appalling point when they could say such things to each other?

Chapter Six

'UNCLE SETH, UNCLE SETH, are you going to marry Chloe?'

Seth scooped up the two squealing girls, one in each arm, and dangling them over the edge of the pool, threatened to throw them in. After a good deal of thrashing and hysterical laughter from the pair of them, he set the two girls down. 'Tell us or we'll push you in,' they shrieked.

'Mind your own beeswax,' Seth said, and in one deft moment, he grabbed his nieces by their hands and jumped into the pool with them.

Amused, Chloe watched their antics from her sun lounger. She was glad that she had accepted Seth's invitation to spend the day with him in Shropshire at his sister's house—a converted mill complete with stream, pool and amazing views of the countryside. Rebecca was at a friend's wedding and wasn't expected back until late that night.

Since they'd redefined the nature of their relationship, Chloe really appreciated Seth's presence in her life. He was fun to be around and she always looked forward to spending time with him. Initially, if she was honest, she'd been anxious that he might view their friendship as a way to win her round into pursuing an altogether different relationship. But he'd been as good as his word and never once hinted that he wanted anything more from her. If indeed he did.

Paul had telephoned her, minutes before she had been on her way out to meet Seth for their first let's-be-friends drink. 'Did you receive my flowers?' he'd asked.

She had thought of them lying crushed outside in the garden, and replied, 'I did, thank you.'

'I meant what I said on the card,' he'd gone on. 'I genuinely hope—'

She'd cut him off mid-sentence. 'Paul, I don't know exactly what it is you want from me, but please don't think a bunch of flowers and dinner is going to make me forget what you did. I wish you well, but really, I'd rather not have any more contact with you.'

'I understand,' he'd said. 'It is still too raw and painful for you—'

'Stop! Paul: you really *don't* understand. Now, please, you're making me late. Goodbye.' She'd put the phone down, not with a dramatic bang, but very slowly, very surely. There. That was Paul dealt with.

'Fancy a swim, Dr Hennessey?' Seth was at the side of the pool, his elbows planted in front of him as he raised himself partially out of the water. His curly black hair was slick and wet and swept back from his forehead. He looked like a glamorous male model.

'You know, Reverend Hawthorne, I think I just might.'

He smiled and offered his hand.

'No way,' she said. 'I've seen what you do to poor defenceless girls.' Instead, she dived in just a few feet away from him. When she rose to the surface on the other side of the pool and looked back to where he'd been, he'd disappeared. He then bobbed up behind her.

'I'm sorry about what they said earlier,' he said. 'You know, about me marrying you. It's nothing more than high spirits. They're always like it.'

'You mean they say it to every friend you introduce them to?'

'Oh, yeah, without fail. They're worse than certain members of my parish who are constantly asking me when I'm going to settle down.'

This was the first time Chloe had heard Seth refer directly to his parish and it was a reminder that despite the number of evenings they'd spent together, the one topic that Seth had assiduously avoided was his work.

'Seth,' she said, swimming closer to him, 'can I ask you something?'

'Of course.'

'What made you go into the Church?'

'Ah, a long story. I used to be a policeman.'

'A policeman? You're kidding?'

He shielded his eyes from the sun and looked at her. 'People are always surprised by that. But it's in the family. My dad retired from the Met recently, and his father before him was also in the force.'

'What made you leave?'

'I was working in the vice unit,' he said. 'Day in, day out I was dealing with the kind of stuff that made me despair of the world we live in.

It was the video evidence I had to watch that really did it. Especially when children were involved. I didn't have the stomach for it. Several of my older colleagues had become inured to the horrors of the job and I knew I didn't ever want to reach that point.'

'So you decided you'd try to save these monsters' souls rather than send them to prison?'

He frowned. 'Would that be so very wrong?'

'Sorry, I could have put that better.'

'Whichever way you want to put it, you think I'm misguided and idealistic, don't you?'

'I don't, actually. As a GP I've seen a number of child abuse cases and know as well as you do that there's always a reason why it goes on, that often the abuser was once abused themselves. But back to my original question; why the Church? Why not social work?'

'The simple answer is that I genuinely felt called.'

'How? In what way?'

'It's . . . it's a long story—' he broke off. 'Do you really want to know?'

She nodded.

'Well, I can honestly say, hand on heart, that it was the thought of all that Shlœr that attracted me.'

'Shlœr?'

'Sorry, it's a theology college joke.' He adopted a falsetto tone. 'Can I tempt you into another glass of non-alcoholic grape juice, vicar?'

Chloe smiled.

'That's better,' he said, 'you were looking much too serious.'

'Does that mean I'm not going to get an answer to my question?'

'For now, all I'll say is that I came to the understanding that a life without faith would mean that the hokey-cokey really was what it's all about. Come on, the first one to do four lengths doesn't have to do the washing up.'

It was almost eleven o'clock when Rebecca returned home, and gone midnight by the time Seth was driving Chloe back to Eastbury. Rebecca had invited them to stay the night, but since he had a morning service at eight o'clock the next day, Seth declined.

As he kept his eyes on the road, Seth tried not to feel so pleased that everything about the day had gone so well. The only downside had been that he'd continually had to check himself when he was around Chloe. Countless times he'd instinctively wanted to put his arm round her. He'd promised himself that he'd be able to cope with being just a friend to Chloe, but he'd misjudged how much strength it would take to keep his distance from her, both physically and mentally.

They'd been driving for several miles when Chloe said, 'Seth, does it bother you that I don't go to church or believe in God?'

'Are you asking me that because you're paranoid I'm going to try and convert you?'

'I don't think so.'

'Or is it because my belief makes you feel defensive of your lack of belief, something that until now you've never had to question?'

In the silence that followed, Seth wondered if he'd gone too far.

'No,' she said at last. 'I'm a scientist at heart and so approach things quite differently from you. You appear to have all the answers to something that can't be proved. It naturally makes the scientist in me react with suspicion and distrust.'

'Chloe, if there's one thing I really want you to understand about me, it's that I work consistently within the parameters of my inadequacies; I don't have all the answers. I can't, for instance, explain away the nature of suffering. What I do know is that we're better off with the power of redemptive love than without it.' He paused and glanced sideways at her. 'And that's me sounding one hundred per cent defensive.'

'I'm sorry, I didn't mean to make you feel you had to defend yourself.'

He smiled. 'Don't worry. I'm used to it. As you no doubt gathered, my sister doesn't share my views. That goes for the rest of my family too.'

'Did your family treat you differently when you left the police force to become a vicar?'

'You bet they did! My parents did everything they could to make me change my mind. They thought I was having some kind of breakdown.'

'Are they OK with it now?'

'They're still coming to terms with it. They think I'm some kind of weird Holy Joe and do crazy things when I go to see them, like hide the bottle of wine they've just opened, or apologise if my father swears in front of me. I end up telling them to stop buggering about and to pass the wine before I die of thirst.'

It was August and to celebrate her birthday, Chloe's parents had invited her to lunch, together with Dan and Marcus. Seth had also been invited to join them.

'So, Seth,' Jennifer said when they were all seated and Chloe's father was urging them to tuck into what was on the table—poached salmon, Mediterranean roasted peppers and aubergines, and new potatoes glossy with garlic butter—'What do you think of that bishop who attributes recent natural disasters to God's wrath for same-sex marriages?'

'The man's two shades of stupid,' Seth replied. 'And probably certifiable into the bargain.'

'Mum, I'm sure Seth doesn't want to talk shop.'

'If that's the case, Chloe, I'm sure Seth is perfectly capable of telling me that for himself.'

'He's much too polite to do that.'

Jennifer looked at Seth across the table. 'Good gracious! Is that true? Are you too polite to tell me to shut up?'

Seth smiled. 'Not at all. But with Marcus sitting next to me I'm holding back in the hope of setting him a good example.'

As if several paces behind in the conversation, Marcus dabbed the air with his fork and said, 'What does two shades of stupid mean?'

Lately, with his third birthday coming up next month, Marcus's speech had come on in leaps and bounds.

'It's a way of saying someone is incredibly stupid,' Chloe explained.

'How stupid? As stupid as a baby?'

'What makes you think babies are stupid?'

Marcus looked back at her sagely. 'Charlie says they are. His mummy's going to have one soon. It will cry and cry and then be sick everywhere.' He turned to look at Dan. 'Daddy? Will we have to have a baby like Charlie?'

'It's not a matter of *having* to have one,' Dan said. 'Do you think you would like a baby brother or sister?'

Marcus thought about this. 'I'd prefer a dog,' he said slowly.

Everyone laughed. All except for Dan, Chloe noticed. She had a pretty good idea why. Sally had confided in her that Dan was pressurising her into having another child. Lucky you! Chloe had wanted to say. Just as a good friend should, she'd listened to Sally grumbling but she hadn't been able to summon up any sympathy for her. Didn't Sally know how lucky she was? She had a fantastic husband, a gorgeous son, the career she had always wanted and the chance to make her family complete. What on earth did she have to grumble about?

Chloe wasn't jealous of Sally being married to Dan, but she was jealous that she was married to someone who cared so deeply about her. Thinking that she would give anything to be in Sally's shoes, Chloe suddenly felt the pain of her longing so acutely she was overwhelmed by it. Watching her mother filling Seth's plate, Chloe tried to restore her good mood. It was her birthday, after all.

'I know exactly what will happen when we leave here.'

Her head resting on Harry's shoulder, Sally said, 'You do?'

He stroked her hair. 'You'll feel guilty and regret what we've done. You won't even be home before you'll be planning to tell me it's over.'

She uncurled herself and gazed at him thoughtfully.

'Is that what you want me to do?' she asked. 'To end it now?'

He held her tightly. 'I never want it to end. I love you. I love you in way I've never loved anyone before.' His voice was low and impassioned. 'I don't know what I'd do if you did say it was over.'

'Then stop thinking about it. Let's enjoy the time we have left here.' They both turned and glanced at the clock on the bedside table.

'Six hours and fifteen minutes before we have to go,' Harry murmured. 'Mmm . . . can you think of anything we could do to pass the time?' He was smiling now, dazzling her with what she called his killer smile. She thought, not for the first time, how young he looked.

'Harry?' she said, 'do you ever think of the age difference between us?'

When they'd booked into the hotel last night she had been convinced the receptionist had clocked the age gap and would hurry off to have a good snigger about it with a colleague.

'Never. Why? Do you?'

'Now and then.'

'Eight years is nothing. Besides, you look no more than thirty.'

When Harry had first asked her to spend a night with him, Sally had made it very clear she was never going to have an affair with him. 'But you're having an affair with me already,' he'd argued. 'In your head you've already gone to bed with me.'

'Don't be absurd,' she'd admonished him. Which, of course, had just made him laugh. They'd been in her office at the time—the door firmly closed—and he'd come up behind her, kissed the back of her neck and whispered in her ear how he longed to make love to her.

'It's going to happen, Sally,' he'd said. 'I won't give up.'

For a while, she convinced herself that she could contain her feelings for Harry by allowing herself the occasional daydream about making love with him. Give it a week or two and it would pass, she reasoned. It didn't pass. Instead, the intensity of the attraction grew and grew until it was almost all she could think about.

Then, on Monday of this week, he'd knocked on her office door, stepped inside and told her he'd booked them a room at a hotel for Friday night.

'Where?' was all she said.

'Somewhere miles from here. But don't worry about anyone seeing us,' he'd added, 'your clothes will be confiscated on arrival. I don't have any intention of letting you stray beyond the four walls of our room.'

At home that evening she'd explained to Dan that she had to go to Hull at the weekend to sort out a problem her mother had with an insurance claim over a ruined carpet. She'd explained that she would drive over on Friday evening after work, stay the night in a hotel and deal with the problem the next day.

After they'd checked in at the hotel and had been shown to their room, Harry had opened the bottle of champagne that was waiting for them in an ice bucket. For a few awkward moments they'd behaved like strangers, sipping the champagne and inspecting the room. Just when she didn't think she could keep up the act any longer, he took her glass from her and put it on the dressing table. Standing in front of her, he seemed to be holding his breath. 'I'm going to kiss you now,' he said, finally. 'And then I'm gong to undress you and make love to you.'

He kissed her long and hard, and as he slowly and methodically removed every piece of her clothing, he never once lost eye contact with her. It was like an intensely erotic game that he was playing; she sensed his enjoyment, how he took pleasure in controlling her. She sensed, too, the air of reckless excitement that sparked between them.

Looking at Harry now she thought how alike they were. Or rather, she thought how alike her old self was to Harry. Harry was passionate, impulsive and reckless and being with him allowed her to rediscover the wild Sally of old. Never had she felt so free or euphoric. She didn't kid herself that she loved him, but she did love the way he made her feel: fantastically alive and energised.

In comparison, Dan depressed her and drained the life out of her. He made her feel as though she was always in the wrong. Harry, on the other hand, never found fault with her. He repeatedly said that he needed her. When had Dan last said that to her?

'Can I ask you something about your husband,' Harry said.

She nodded warily.

'Does it suit you, having a husband who stays at home to look after your son, leaving you to be the breadwinner?'

'Suit me?' she repeated. 'In what way?'

'You like to be in control, don't you? And as things stand at home, there's no danger of you being controlled by your husband. You're the decision maker. The one who calls the shots. But now and then, I think you quite like someone else to take the lead for a change. Am I right?'

Sally opened her mouth to respond, but Harry put a finger to her lips. She closed her eyes and the moment she did, she had a sudden replay in her mind of the way Harry made love to her, how he instigated it, how he dictated the pace, and how much that fuelled her desire and intensified her pleasure. How odd, she thought, that she had allowed Harry to take the lead in almost everything they did when it was something she now realised she rarely allowed Dan to do. In or out of the bedroom.

With Chloe's parents booked to go to a local outdoor production of *Midsummer Night's Dream*, the party, at Dan's invitation, had moved seamlessly from Laurel House to Corner Cottage.

It was gone nine o'clock now. Seth had just left to go home and put the finishing touches to his sermon for tomorrow morning and Marcus was upstairs asleep in bed. Alone with Chloe, Dan fetched another bottle of wine from the kitchen and joined her back out in the garden.

Today was the first time Dan had met Seth and while he knew how Chloe felt about him—that it was a platonic friendship—he was pretty sure there was nothing platonic about the way Seth regarded Chloe.

He turned and looked at Chloe. Lost in her own thoughts as she stared up at the darkening night sky, she looked happier than he'd seen her in a long while. Was that down to Seth?

'Chloe?' he said. 'Can I ask you something?'

'No, you can't.' She still had her eyes on the sky

'Why not?'

'Because I know what you're going to ask.'

'You do?'

'You're going to ask me something about Seth, aren't you?'

He smiled, and put his arm round her. 'You know me so well.'

'So, go on, then, get it out of your system. Ask away.'

'OK. And no interrupting and leaping down my throat, but the way I see it, Seth's a great bloke and you could—'

'You're only saying that because he's a fellow *Simpsons* aficionado.'

'I thought I said no interrupting. But, seriously, what would you do if Seth said he wanted more than friendship from you?'

She shook her head. 'That's not going to happen.'

'But if it did?' Dan pressed. 'What if he did hit on you?'

'Don't be silly, Dan, that would be like you hitting on me.'

'You really think Seth and I both feel the same way about you?'

'Yes.'

'But you told me that in the beginning things were quite different between the two of you. You said he kissed you.'

'That was then,' she said, 'this is now. We've recalibrated things.'

Dan snorted. 'Well, I've got news for you. Seth and I view you through very different eyes. Don't get me wrong, you're eminently fanciable, but after all these years, you're like a sister to me. In Seth's eyes, you're no such thing. No, no, hear me out. I'm a man; I know about these things. Trust me, when he looks at you, he sees a real hottie.'

'Dan! You've had too much to drink. Be quiet before I get cross.'

'Get as cross with me as you like, but it won't change a thing. I suspect that if Seth wasn't so concerned about losing you altogether, he'd be making his feelings very clear to you.'

She frowned and hesitated fractionally before saying, 'He's given me absolutely no indication that that's the case.'

'Look, I think I know where you're coming from, but just because Seth doesn't appear to fit the ideal profile, it doesn't mean he's not worth a punt. I really like him, and I'd hate to think that you couldn't give him a chance purely because he's a man of principle and strong belief.'

'This is the last time I'm going to say this, so listen up. I'm inordinately fond of Seth, but a full-on relationship with him is out of the question. Apart from the obvious differences between us, it would be too weird. I mean, well, given his principles and strong beliefs, as you put it, we wouldn't even be able to have sex unless we were married. What kind of a sensible, grown-up relationship would that be?'

Dan sighed. 'It sounds exactly like marriage to Sally!' He immediately regretted his words. 'Forget I said that,' he muttered, swallowing the last of his wine. He could feel Chloe's eyes on him. 'I said forget it.'

She continued to stare at him. Oh, what the hell, he thought. She might know something. Sally might have said something to her.

'I expect it's just a phase,' he said. 'You know, working too hard, crashing out in bed exhausted and falling asleep immediately. It's what happens, isn't it?'

'It can happen, certainly. But who are you talking about? You or Sally? Or the pair of you?'

'Sally. Has she said anything? You know, something in confidence?'

Chloe smiled. 'If it was in confidence I couldn't tell you, could I?'

'Unless it was something serious. You'd tell me then, wouldn't you?'

'What's really worrying you, Dan?'

He blinked. 'I . . . I think Sally's having an affair.'

'You're kidding?'

'Shit, Chloe! Why would I joke about something like that?'

'But why? Why would you think that of her?'

He put his glass down on the wooden table and covered his face with his hands. 'She's been acting so strangely lately. She works ridiculous hours and when she is home she's here in body but not in mind. I can't get close to her. I can't remember the last time we made love. Do you think there could be someone at work she's seeing secretly?'

Chloe put a hand on his arm. 'I think I know what the problem is,' she said. 'And don't be angry that Sally shared this with me, but she told me that you're keen to have another child.'

He nodded. 'That's true.'

'Well, a pound to a penny, that's what's troubling her. She's not sure about taking that step and thinks you only want sex with her to get her pregnant.' She smiled. 'Why not try talking to her about it?'

'About having another child?'

'About everything that's bothering you. Make some time to be alone together and really talk. Go away for a weekend. So long as I'm not on call, I could look after Marcus for you.'

He smiled ruefully. 'I sound paranoid and pathetic, don't I? I'd convinced myself that Sally didn't love me any more. Back in May, when we had the fete in the village, she actually accused me of having something going with Tatiana from the trust. Which, for the record, I wasn't.'

'What made her think you were?'

'I have no idea. But not long after that she asked me if I knew how hard it was to live with a hero.'

'She said that? But why?'

'I don't really know. I'd just told her about Rosie's baby and it all got out of hand and suddenly she was accusing me of having a hero complex ever since we came back from Phuket. Do you think I do?'

'Oh, Dan, not for a single second. What you did back on Phuket was heroic, but it's not as if you ever mention it. I know you don't like to.'

It was dark now, the only light spilling out from the French windows behind them. They stared up at the star-studded sky, deep in thought.

The sound of a car pulling onto the drive at the front of the house broke the silence. 'Sally,' Dan said. 'She's back. She'll probably be in a terrible mood after spending so long with her mother.'

Chloe didn't stick around for much longer. With everything she and Dan had discussed, she felt uncomfortable being with her friends. She would inevitably end up watching their every move and exchange to gauge the situation between them, and she didn't want to do that.

She walked home reflecting on what Dan had said. No way would Sally have an affair. It was crazy. Dan had jumped to an irrational conclusion. But what was all that nonsense about accusing Dan of having a hero complex? What had led her to make such a nasty comment?

She'd reached home and was just putting her key in the lock of the back door when a thought occurred to Chloe. *Do you think there could be somebody at work she's seeing secretly?* Dan had asked Chloe. What if Sally's office admirer had persisted and she had fallen for him?

'Seth, are you gay, or what?'

A cacophony of sniggering broke out in the minibus, along with several ear-splitting whistles. In the passenger seat next to Seth, Patricia O'Connor—mother of fourteen-year-old Abigail, who had predictably opted to travel back from the bowling alley in the other minibus, driven by Owen—glanced at him. The silly woman was pink with embarrassment. But Seth was more than used to the youth group's antics, especially on their monthly night out.

When the noise had finally died down, he looked at Jez Lucas in the rearview mirror and said, 'What's the context of your question, Jez? Are you referring to my sexuality or asking if I'm a sad loser?'

Jez's face coloured. His mate Ricky thwacked him on the head. 'He wants to know if you're a bender, Seth.'

'And why do you want to know that?'

'Cos he's one and want to know if you'll go out with him,' someone shouted from the back row of seats.

Everybody laughed. Patricia whipped round in her seat. 'That's enough, you lot!' she ordered. 'Of course Seth's not gay.' Patricia was known for her hard-line views: homosexuality was an abomination in the eyes of the Lord, the Bible was explicit on the subject. 'Take no notice of them, Seth,' she said. 'No one believes for a moment that you could be a homosexual. The very idea is preposterous.'

'Really?' he said. 'I don't think the idea is that preposterous. In fact, I'd go so far as to say I'd be a perfect candidate. I'm single, I work out, I like to cook.' Despite knowing he was playing with fire, Seth couldn't help himself. He hated prejudice and there was far too much of it within the parish in his opinion.

As he stopped at the traffic lights, he caught Patricia looking at him doubtfully. He immediately regretted what he'd said. Oh hell, how soon before the parish was a bubbling pot of gossip about his sexuality?

Two days later and his prophecy was fulfilled. He was alone at St Michael's, and was enjoying himself by playing 'Intervention' on the organ. He was almost at the end of the song when he noticed Owen making his way up the nave of the church. Seth swung himself off the organ stool and approached the other man.

'Could I talk to you, Seth?' Owen asked.

'Of course.'

'There's no easy way of saying this, Seth,' he said, 'but I feel it's my duty to bring it to your attention before you hear it from another source.'

'Right, I think I know what this is about,' Seth said.

From beneath his straggly eyebrows, Owen looked at him sharply. 'You do? Does that mean there's some substance to the rumour?'

'Substance,' Seth repeated with a hollow smile. 'That's an odd choice of word, isn't it? Are you asking me if there's any truth to my being gay?'

'You mean you are?'

'I didn't say that.'

'Seth, as my curate, your welfare is my responsibility. I also have the parish's welfare to consider.'

'But presumably my private life is not up for consideration. It's no one's concern but my own.'

'I'm afraid that's too simplistic an approach. If your private life is at odds with that of . . . of the parish's best interests, not to mention the Church's teaching, then it's very much my concern.'

'You're saying there's a danger that my sexuality could affect my work here in Crantsford? You have evidence of this?'

'Insomuch as people are talking about you. Yes.'

Seth was working hard at keeping his temper. 'And you didn't think it your *Christian* duty,' he said slowly, 'to discourage the gossipmongers?'

For the first time in the conversation, Owen looked like a man on less sure ground. 'Of course I did,' he blustered.

'Good, so you told them there was categorically, unequivocally, no truth to the rumours. You explained in no uncertain terms that I'm as heterosexual as you are.' Seth didn't mean to, but he suddenly laughed. He snapped forward in the chair and got to his feet. 'Excellent,' he said, 'I'm glad we've got that all sorted out.'

Frowning, Owen didn't give the impression of having got anything sorted out.

Seth felt almost sorry for him. Perhaps he'd been unfair. Instead of trying to prove a point, wouldn't it have been better to have given an outright denial and have done with it? 'Look, if it puts your mind at rest, and the parish's, I'll bring my girlfriend to the barn dance.'

Owen's eyebrows rose. 'You have a girlfriend? Why didn't you say?'

'As I said before, my private life is my own. The last thing I want is people gossiping about me. For whatever reason.'

Leaving a visibly relieved Owen in the vestry, Seth walked back out into the interior of the church. He knelt at the altar rail and prayed. He prayed that God would forgive him for the lie he'd just told Owen.

Girlfriend? What girlfriend? And what on earth had made him say such a thing? Wishful thinking?

Two weeks had passed since their night away and they were taking more and more risks, grabbing each other in their offices, stealing frantic pleasures when and how they could behind closed doors. Sally couldn't help herself. Never had she felt so alive or exhilarated, or so greedy for sex. Harry was her drug of choice and she lived in daily need of him. She loved knowing that when they were apart he fantasised over what he would do to her when they next went away together.

A knock at her office door had her turning round from the window that looked down onto Deansgate. 'Yes,' she said.

It was Marion Brooke, one of the more capable members of her team.

'Have you seen this?' Marion asked. She laid out a tabloid newspaper on Sally's desk. A grinning Darren T. Child had his arms round a blonde girl wearing only the bottom half of a bikini. For the sake of propriety, the girl's Spacehopper breasts were partially hidden by one of Darren's arms. The photograph was of no surprise to Sally—Darren with a blonde on his arm was a regular occurrence—but the headline was a different matter: *Darren and Tasty Tina Back in Sack!*

'Do you want me to call his agent or manager for official confirmation that we're to terminate divorce proceedings?' Marion asked.

'Yes, go ahead.' Sally folded the newspaper. 'When we've received confirmation we'll swing into gear with our bill.'

Left on her own, Sally dismissed Darren from her mind and wondered what Harry was doing. How easy it would be to email or text him to find out. But she wouldn't. Harry was desperate for her to communicate this way in secret, but she'd flatly refused. Emails in the workplace were too dangerous. Who knew who could access them? The same for text messages. Having such a forbidden fruit was all part of the game for Sally: it kept Harry keen. She smiled to herself. Sex and power— was there ever a more powerful combination?

Even wearing an old T-shirt and scruffy knee-length cut-off jeans, Chloe had to admit that Seth still managed to look great.

She'd mentioned last weekend that she was going to spend her day off this week redecorating her bedroom and he'd immediately offered to help her. At eight thirty this morning he'd arrived all raring to go. They'd been painting for three hours now.

'How about an early lunch?' she suggested.

'Excellent idea,' he said, reloading the roller with white paint from the tray on the top rung of the stepladder. 'Just this bit in the corner to do and then I'll be finished.'

She watched him approvingly. It was on the tip of her tongue to say, 'We make a great team, don't we?' but she held back. What if there was the merest hint of truth in what Dan had said to her about Seth? Would a comment like that give him reason to think things had changed between them? But, if she was honest, hadn't things changed?

She couldn't speak for Seth's feelings, but she could think of no one she would rather spend time with. Since her birthday she had caught herself thinking about Seth a lot, wondering where he was, what he was doing. What she couldn't bring herself to dwell on, was how she'd feel if he were to meet someone else who held the same beliefs as him.

Everyone else liked Seth—well, Mum and Dad, Dan and Marcus; Sally had yet to meet him—so really, what was the problem? Why did she continue to hold back, to make a big deal out of something that was nothing of the kind? He was a curate. A clergyman. A priest. A man of the proverbial cloth. Get over it! Did it make him any less of a man?

Not from where she was standing right now—with a fine view of his legs and their perfect muscle tone—that was for sure!

Chloe had always thought of herself as being her own boss, as being intelligent enough to form her own opinions. Never had she knowingly allowed herself to be influenced by another, but with regard to Seth, she was doing exactly that. It went back to when they were students, when having a best friend's approval over a boyfriend was crucial. She wished it wasn't so, but Sally's approval of Seth mattered to her.

Once or twice Chloe had thought of ringing Sally to arrange an evening together so that she could meet Seth properly, but she'd never got further than just thinking about it. She hated the idea that Sally might meet Seth and still think negatively about him.

There was also a more worrying concern: Dan's suspicions that Sally might be having an affair. Since Dan had shared his fear with her, Chloe had shied away from talking to Sally. She knew that if she was left alone with her she would end up asking her if she was seeing anyone. And what if Sally admitted that she *was* having an affair? Would she be able to keep a secret like that from Dan?

Seth was climbing down the stepladder now.

Chloe said, 'You've done a brilliant job. We work well together, don't we?' There, she'd said it. Let him make of it what he wanted.

'Good enough to set up a decorating business?' he replied, smiling.

'I think that would be pushing things. A beer and a bacon sandwich suit you for lunch?'

They ate in the garden, sitting on the lawn on an old bedspread. It was such a beautiful day; a shame to be wasting it stuck inside the house decorating. When Chloe voiced this regret, he said, 'You didn't exactly force me, Chloe. I offered to help you. Besides, I am enjoying myself. I like creating order out of chaos.'

'Watch it, pal. That sounds worryingly like you're saying my bedroom was a chaotic mess before you got your mitts on it.'

He laughed and lay back on the bedspread, his hands clasped behind his head. 'Trust me, I wouldn't be so stupid.'

'Well, any time you need a favour from me, just say the word.'

He looked up at her, his eyes soft and beguiling. 'Do you mean that?'

Seeing him lying stretched out before her, Chloe was startlingly more aware of his physical presence, his inherent masculinity. It really wouldn't take much on her part to kiss him. No effort at all. 'Of course I mean it,' she murmured, remembering the one time they had kissed and how it had made her feel. 'Why wouldn't I?'

'If you really are serious,' he said, raising himself up onto his elbows, 'there is something you could do for me. Are you doing anything this coming Saturday evening?'

Once again, Seth found himself at the top of a stepladder.

The St Michael's Barn Dance was a legendary affair. So Seth kept being told. After ten years of putting on the event, the hard-working committee had the procedure down to a fine art. The band and caller had been booked last year, the marquee had been erected, the hog roast and drinks had been organised, the tickets had been sold, the raffle prizes rounded up, and now there was just the marquee to decorate.

This was where Seth came in. He'd been given specific instructions on where and how to hang the tons of greenery that had been delivered that morning. The instructions had come, and were continuing to come, from Barbara Hicks, a retired head teacher who had an infuriating habit of treating everyone as a five-year-old.

Hovering at the bottom of the stepladder, she was keeping a keen eye on Seth's every movement. Whatever the level of scrutiny he was currently under, Seth knew that this evening the level would be greatly increased. He just hoped Chloe was prepared for the degree of interest her presence would create when they walked in together.

When he'd explained to her what his favour would entail, and the reasons behind it, she'd laughed out loud. 'You're joking?' she'd said. 'How could anyone seriously consider you were anything but heterosexual?' Then the laughter had slipped from her face. 'This is exactly what I can't stand about organised religion,' she'd said hotly. 'Churches are stuffed full of hypocritical, judgmental idiots.'

'I couldn't agree more,' he'd said.

'So how can you be one of them?'

He'd very nearly pointed out to her that she had judged him at Margaret's funeral, but instead said, 'One way or another we're all hypocritical and judgmental. We're all idiots when push comes to shove.'

'But aren't you tempted to ignore Owen and the tongue-waggers? Just let them get on with wondering whether you're gay or not. It's none of their business. Hang on, you're not homophobic, are you?'

'Certainly not. But if people think I am gay and the knock-on effect does affect my work in the parish, then I need to set the record straight.'

'So a twirl around the dance floor with me on your arm will put an end to the gossip? That's essentially what this is about?'

He'd nodded. 'I quite understand if you don't want to do it. Maybe a barn dance is the last way you'd want to spend an evening.'

The smile had slowly reappeared on her face. 'I'll have you know, thanks to Mum and Dad, both my brother and I are champion barn dancers. I could do-si-do for England if it were made an Olympic event.'

'I don't know if that's a good thing or not, seeing as I'm officially a do-si-do virgin. You're going to draw attention to my two left feet.'

'Don't fret; by the end of the evening, there'll be no doubt in anyone's mind about your hetero credentials. We'll Gay Gordon those malicious gossipers to kingdom come!'

Chloe was almost at Seth's house—they'd agreed to meet there and then walk on to where the event was being held—when her mobile went off on the dashboard. Caller ID showed that it was Sally. 'Hi, stranger,' Chloe said. 'Long time no speak.'

'I was thinking that myself,' Sally said, 'hence this call.'

Trying not to think of the last conversation she'd had with Dan, Chloe said, 'What have you been up to?'

'Oh, the usual: work.'

'I've warned you about that before. All work makes Sal a very dull gal. She's never around to go out to play any more.'

'Yeah, yeah, I know. But if it makes you feel any better, I've just left the office and I'm heading for home.'

'You've been at the office today? But it's Saturday.'

'Spare me the lecture. What are you doing at the moment?'

'I'm on my way to spend the evening with Seth.'

'Really? He's not still chasing after you, is he?'

Hackles immediately up, Chloe said, 'He's not chasing me at all.'

'If you say so. Where's he taking you tonight? To a fun-packed pray-in?'

'We're going to a barn dance, actually.'

'A barn dance! How quaint.'

Chloe waited for her friend's laughter to subside. 'Sally?' she said tightly. 'Why do you hate Seth so much?'

'I don't hate him. I just don't think you're cut out to be the girlfriend of a man like him.'

'I'm not his girlfriend. I'm his *friend*. And, anyway, how would you know what kind of a man he is? You haven't even met him. Dan on the other hand has and he likes him. As do my parents.'

'Wow. I've clearly rattled you. You sound cross and defensive.'

'I am. You've done nothing but disparage Seth.'

'That's rich. I seem to recall you falling over yourself to disparage him when you realised he'd been lying to you.'

'He didn't lie. And I regret my behaviour now. I was wrong and acting like the worst kind of idiot.' All at once, Chloe heard Seth's voice in her head saying everyone was an idiot, that everyone was hypocritical and judgmental. She felt her cheeks flush. How easy it would have been for him to point out that she was guilty of the same crime she was prepared to condemn others for. But he hadn't. He'd let it go. 'So what's keeping you so busy at work, then?' she asked Sally, changing the subject.

'Oh, you know how it is. These things just build and build.'

Don't do it, Chloe cautioned herself. But she couldn't stop herself. She wanted to get back at her friend and, petty or not, this was the only way she knew how to do it. 'How's that young admirer of yours?'

'Which young admirer?'

'The one you said was sexually harassing you.'

'Oh, him. I'm pleased to say he's behaving himself impeccably. All he needed was a good dressing down and he soon jumped into line.'

Was it Chloe's imagination or had Sally sounded just a bit too nonchalant in her reply? 'And how's that mother of yours?' Chloe segued. 'I still haven't forgiven you for missing my birthday in favour of visiting her.'

'Yeah, I was sorry about that. But it looks like I'll have to go and see her again soon. She's got herself into debt. I'm trying to sort things out for her. Don't, whatever you do, let on to Dan. You know how he thinks I'm chucking good money after bad with her.'

There was a lot more Chloe could say on this particular subject, but there wasn't time. 'I'm going to have to go now, Sally,' she said. 'I'm at Seth's. Give my love to Dan and Marcus. Bye.'

She put her mobile in her bag, got out of the car and locked the door. It was the first time she'd visited Seth at home and she was curious to see what his house was like inside. Externally it was a classic Victorian mid-terraced house with a bay window, a tiled entrance porch and a stained-glass front door.

She received no response to her first ring, so she tried the bell again. The door opened and there was Seth. Dressed only in a towel wrapped round his waist, his hair wet and dripping down his neck and shoulders, he was clearly running late. 'Sorry,' he said, 'I was in the shower. Come on in. Let me make you a drink and then I'll get dressed. What would you like? There's a bottle of white already open in the fridge. Or there's some red in the rack.' He led her through to the kitchen.

'Why don't I see to my own drink,' she said, 'while you get dressed.'

'I'm really sorry about this,' he said. 'I was all set to jump in the shower an hour ago when the phone rang. It was one half of a couple I've been preparing for their wedding in two weeks' time. She was in tears; the groom's got cold feet. You look lovely, by the way. You've done your hair differently. It suits you. Makes you look— Oh, hell! I'm rambling, aren't I? It must be nerves. Sorry. Really sorry.'

She smiled. 'I don't mind a rambled compliment in the least. You don't look so bad yourself.' She cast her gaze over his sexy, glistening chest. *No! Where had that come from? Sexy, glistening chest?* Embarrassed, she tore her gaze away from him. Inappropriate behaviour, she warned herself. Two strikes and you're out!

'I bet you say that to all the half-naked men you come across, Dr Hennessey,' he said lightly. 'Give me ten minutes and I'll be back down.'

On her own, she poured herself a glass of wine. She stared unseeingly out of the kitchen window, her thoughts wandering and then finally settling on the lasting image of Seth, fresh from the shower. Unsettled at her reaction—an unmistakable rush of undiluted lust— she took a large, steadying gulp of wine, but immediately reprimanded herself: easy girl, no drinking too much. The curate's pretend girlfriend can't let the side down by showing up plastered.

The light was fading when the band took to the stage. There was an accordion player, a guitarist, a girl in dungarees with a fiddle under her chin and a bearded old boy sitting on a bale of hay with a banjo. The caller didn't have any trouble corralling participants for the first dance; a sudden surge of people rushing to form a circle left Seth and Chloe momentarily shipwrecked at their table.

'Nothing else for it,' Chloe said. 'Time to initiate you.'

People smiled when they joined the circle and Chloe could see the looks of endorsement on their faces. As far as she was aware she'd thus far not put a foot wrong in her role as The Curate's Girlfriend and had answered everyone's questions without hesitation or resorting to lying. They'd met in the spring . . . at the gym . . . she lived in nearby Eastbury . . . she was a GP . . . like her father . . . yes, Seth was wonderful . . . yes, he was excellent company . . . yes, very generous, very caring.

The questions she hadn't been asked were anything to do with her church-going habits. Seth had insisted that he didn't want her to feel obliged to lie on his behalf. 'Just tell them the truth,' he'd said.

The caller was walking them through a dance called the Lucky Seven, an easy one to get things started. Seth looked at her anxiously and she squeezed his hand. 'You'll be fine; just follow everyone else.'

'I'll only be fine if I can stick to you like glue.'

'Sorry, after I've danced the first sequence with you I'll have to move on to someone new and dance the next sequence with him.'

'That doesn't sound much fun for me.'

'Don't you believe it,' she whispered in his ear. 'The women here are champing at the bit to get their hands on you. Hey ho, we're off.'

The first sequence completed, Chloe waved Seth goodbye and moved round the circle. Her next partner was Max Wainbridge, a spry, white-haired gentleman sporting a multi-coloured waistcoat. He grasped her firmly. 'If I'm not mistaken, you've done this before?' he said.

'A misspent youth,' she admitted.

'Is there any other kind?' He laughed loudly. 'Seriously, though, my wife Stella and I are delighted that Seth has such a charming companion in his life. Being a vicar can be a tough and lonely job.'

When she moved on to her next partner, Chloe encountered a similar conversation. And the same again with the next partner, the next and the next. The general consensus was that Seth had been a dark horse keeping her slyly under wraps the way he had. When she had very nearly completed the circle, she found herself dancing with Seth's boss, Owen. Seth had introduced her earlier and Chloe hadn't liked him. But there again, she was biased; she despised him for not taking a firmer line with his gossiping flock. She also didn't like the way he was dressed—in formal work clothes, dull grey suit and dog collar.

She looked over to Seth and thought how vibrant and dynamic he looked in comparison. Wearing nothing fancier than a pair of faded jeans and a blue and white shirt, he was easily the most attractive man here. He stood out from the crowd effortlessly. He was also looking her way, she realised. Their eyes met and she thought how proud and happy she was to be here with him tonight. He gave her a dazzling smile and, smiling back at him, she experienced a curious sensation of peace, of letting go. Why had she battled against her feelings for Seth for as long as she had? Why had she been so stupid? She had no answer, but filled with a joyful sense of discovery, she didn't care.

As if floating on air, she felt Owen propelling her away from him to complete the circle and then she was moving slowly but irrevocably towards Seth. He took her in his arms. 'I think I've got the hang of this,' he said with a cheerful smile.

'Me too,' she murmured.

It was gone midnight and they were walking through the quiet streets of Crantsford back to Seth's house. Something extraordinary had happened to Chloe this evening. There had been a seismic shift in her emotions and it scared and thrilled her in equal parts.

He invited her in with the offer of a drink. She was glad he did; she wasn't ready yet to end the night. Nor was he, it seemed.

Laughing and joking, they performed a neat do-si-do round the kitchen as they made coffee. 'You enjoyed tonight more than you expected to, didn't you?' she said when they were in the sitting room. She took the sofa and he took the armchair furthest away from her.

'What can I say?' he said. 'I'm a Strip-the-Willow convert. How about you? Was it very awful for you?'

'Not in the slightest. Do you think we fooled everyone?'

'In what way?'

'Me being your girlfriend.'

Suddenly his expression was grave. Gone was all trace of the carefree laughter of only minutes ago. 'There was no doubt in anyone's mind,' he said flatly. 'You put on a very convincing performance. Thanks.'

Troubled at the transformation in him, she said, 'Seth, what's wrong?'

'Nothing,' he said. His gaze was disturbingly shuttered.

'I don't believe you. Please tell me what's wrong.' She longed to put her arms round him, to remove the expression of misery on his face.

The silence lengthened. 'OK,' he said finally. 'There is something wrong. I thought I could settle for being your friend. *Just* your friend.' He rested his elbows on his knees, covered his face. 'But I can't go on pretending any more. I really can't.'

She put down her mug of coffee and rose silently from the sofa.

'I understand completely,' he said morosely, his head still down. 'You made it very clear to me that we could never be more than friends. You never once gave me reason to hope for more, so I'm not blaming you in any way. It's my fault. I deluded myself. I arrogantly believed that quiet persistence on my part could win you round. I was wrong.'

Chloe knelt down in front of him. She touched one of his hands that was covering his face. He looked up, startled. She kissed him lightly on the mouth, was about to kiss him again when he pushed her away from him. 'Please don't,' he said hoarsely. 'Don't kiss me out of pity. That's more than I can take.'

Her heart ached for him. 'I'm not. Honestly. I—' She saw the raw pain burning in his eyes and her voice broke. She hated knowing that she had done this to him. That all this time he'd been suffering. 'I discovered something very important tonight,' she said. 'I woke up to how I really feel about you. If you'll have me, I'd like to be promoted from your pretend girlfriend to your real girlfriend.'

He stared at her and swallowed. For the longest time, they gazed at each other in silence. Slowly the pain faded from his expression and she saw the depth of his feelings for her in the intense blue of his eyes. He put a hand to her face and when he kissed her, it was with great tenderness and passion. His arms closed round her, and still kissing her, he lifted her onto his lap. Wrapped in his embrace, bending to the shape of him, she felt the perfect fit of their bodies.

Chloe woke with a warm, glowing feeling inside her.

She turned onto her side and looked at the alarm clock: eight forty-five. Dare she risk having a shower? No, she didn't want to miss Seth. He had promised to ring her when he was between services—right now he would be conducting Morning Prayer and at ten thirty he had a family service. She had invited him for lunch, but disappointingly he was going to be busy with the cleaning-up operation after last night.

Last night, when she had reluctantly suggested it was time she drove home, he'd kissed her again. 'Don't go yet,' he'd said.

'But you've got to be up early.'

'Who says I'm going to go to bed?'

'I do,' she'd said firmly. 'I don't want to hear that you dozed off during your early morning service.'

When he eventually agreed to let her leave, they'd then spent an age in the hallway, spinning out their goodbye kiss like a couple of teenagers.

The telephone rang by the side of her bed. Chloe practically jumped on it. 'Hello,' she said in her best M&S this-is-not-just-food voice.

A silence followed by an embarrassed but very recognisable cough at the other end of the line had her sitting up straight. 'Dad!'

'Oh, so it is you, Chloe. I thought perhaps I'd misdialled. Dare I ask who you thought was ringing you?'

'No!'

In the background Chloe could hear her mother saying something to her father and then her father replying, 'She thought I was someone else . . . I don't know who . . . that's what I've just asked her.'

Glancing anxiously at the clock—what if Seth was trying to get through?—Chloe shouted down the phone at her father. 'Dad, stop talking to Mum and get on with why you called me!'

'No need to shout, Chloe,' her father said. 'I'm not deaf. Not yet, anyway. Are you around next weekend?'

'Of course. Where do I ever go?'

'Oh, don't be like that. We're off to Stratford. For four days. Any chance you could water the pots and tomato plants as usual?'

'Consider it done. Sorry, Dad, I can't chat, there's someone at the door.'

'At this time of day? It's not even nine o'clock. People have no manners these days. Bye, love. Speak to you soon.'

There wasn't anyone at the door, but it was the only way Chloe could think to get her father quickly off the phone. She was still feeling guilty about this when five minutes later the phone rang again. Once again she lay back and said breathily, 'Hello, Reverend Hawthorne.'

'Is that you, Chloe?'

'Mum? What are you ringing me for?'

'More to the point, what are you doing sounding as if you're operating one of those kinky sex lines?'

'And what would *you* know about them?'

Ignoring her question, her mother said, 'I take it things have progressed somewhat with the delectable curate? When did this all happen? And don't put the phone down on me, I'll only ring back straight away and hog the line so the poor man can't get through to you.'

Chloe and her brother had often joked of their mother that resistance was futile. 'OK,' she conceded. 'You're right, things have moved on between us. But only since last night. Satisfied?'

'Aha! I knew it! I knew it the moment I clapped eyes on him. Mark my words, Chloe, he's a good 'un.'

The moment she'd got her mother off the line, the phone rang again. 'Hello,' Chloe said, dispensing with any attempt to sound alluring.

'Hello, you. Is your phone always so busy on a Sunday morning?'

She smiled and relaxed back against the pillows. 'It was Mum and Dad making a nuisance of themselves. How are you?'

'Looking forward to seeing you again. I don't suppose that offer of lunch is still on, is it? After last night, your popularity is such that I've been told to sling my hook for the afternoon and spend it with you.'

With a bowl of raspberries between them, Seth lay on his side next to Chloe. Her eyes were closed in the dappled sunlight but her lips were enticingly parted. 'You have a very erotic mouth,' he said.

She opened an eye lazily. 'Are you allowed to say such an outrageous thing on a Sunday?'

He placed a perfectly ripe raspberry between his own lips, bent his head and dropped the raspberry into her mouth with a kiss. 'I can say whatever I like,' he said. When she'd swallowed the raspberry, he moved the dish of fruit out of the way and kissed her again. Her soft, sweet-tasting mouth opened wide against his and he lost himself in kissing her. He'd never felt the way he did when he kissed Chloe.

He pulled her closer to him and slipped a hand under her top. Her skin was silky smooth and he slowly inched his fingers upwards. When his hand settled on her breast, she let out a small but unmistakable breath of pleasure. He slid his hand round to her back and unhooked her bra. He kissed the base of her throat and then, lifting her top, he lowered his mouth to her breast. She moved against him, her hands on his shoulders. But then suddenly she was pushing him away.

'What's wrong?' he said, concerned.

Pulling down her top, she said, 'It . . . it doesn't feel right.'

'You mean I'm not doing it right?'

'Oh God, no! You're doing it right. Much too right, in fact.'

'So what's the problem?'

She looked at him now. 'I'm making you do something you shouldn't do, aren't I? I'm . . . I'm compromising you.'

He'd known this was yet another bridge they had to cross. 'You're worried about my spiritual integrity, is that it?' he asked, trying to keep a straight face. 'You think what we were doing is a violation of my calling?'

'Well, isn't it?' She was struggling to do up her bra.

'I wasn't about to have full-on sex with you, Chloe, if that's what you're worrying about. Here, turn round and I'll do that for you.'

When he had put her back together again, he turned her to face him.

'Now I feel really stupid,' she said. 'Talk about killing the mood.'

He took her hands in his. 'I think we need to be sure of a few ground rules. Basically you want to know where I stand on sex outside marriage?'

She nodded and he could see the embarrassment in her face.

'Sex within the bounds of a loving and committed relationship is what's important to me. Anything else just won't feel as satisfying. It's got to be the real deal. Or nothing.'

'But how do you know for sure if the relationship is the real deal?'

He smiled and stroked her cheek. 'Human nature being what it is, I'd say that's half the fun, wouldn't you?'

'I'm sorry,' she murmured.

'What for?'

'For doubting you. I should have known better than to think this wasn't something you hadn't worked through. I just don't want to wake up one morning feeling that I'm responsible for leading you astray.'

He laughed out loud and pulled her into his arms. He lay her down next to him. 'When I joked the other day that I was a do-si-do virgin, you didn't think that I was implying anything else, did you?'

When she didn't answer him, he said, 'For the record, the old me would have had your knickers off on a second date. I would have chalked your name up with all the others and, what's more, I wouldn't have returned your call the next day.'

She turned in his arms. 'I don't believe you.'

'You think I'd lie to you about something like that?'

She stared into his face. 'How many? How many women have you slept with, Reverend Seth Hawthorne?'

'I'm not saying. I'm too much of a gentleman, as I've told you before.'

'More than twenty?'

'I'm not saying.'

'More than forty?'

'Still not saying.' He mimed the closing of a zip across his mouth.

'My God, Seth, what were you? Some kind of sex addict?'

'Oh, yeah, me and Russell Brand, we were in rehab together. Look, I'm not proud of it, but back then I was a right bastard. How about you? How many partners have you had?'

'Me? I'm practically a chaste nun compared to you.'

'Quality over quantity?'

'Not exactly.'

'Were they all good? Just out of interest.'

'Why, worried you might not come up to standard?'

'No chance.' He brought her face close to his and kissed her.

When he let her go, she said, 'You dodged the bullet once before, but this time I want you to answer my question. What made you leave the police force for the Church?'

'OK,' he said. 'Do you remember the Hill House rail crash?'

She nodded. 'That was the train that derailed in the snow. When more than twenty were killed. You weren't involved, were you?'

'I was one of the lucky ones who walked away with nothing more serious than cuts and bruises. I was knocked out for little more than a minute or so and when I came to there was chaos all around me. In the distance I could hear a girl's cry coming from somewhere. I followed the sound of her cries. When I found her she was in a bad way. She was losing a lot of blood. One of her legs had been ripped off at the knee and her stomach was . . .'

He paused, remembering the shocking scene of utter carnage.

'When she realised I was there,' he continued, 'she asked me if she was dying. There seemed no point in lying to her. She asked me if I would hold her. "Right to the end," she whispered as I held her. "I don't want to die alone." Her last words were to ask me to pray for her. Me, pray? I hadn't done that since I was eight years old and wanted a new bike for Christmas! But I did as she asked. Once I started I didn't feel so powerless or so alone.

'She died in my arms. I later found out that she was only twenty-one. Her family got in touch with me; they wanted to thank me for what I'd done. When I said I hadn't really done anything, they argued that the littlest things in life often created the greatest good. They said they would always remember the kindness I'd shown their daughter. I'd never felt so humbled or so in need of turning my own life around. As conversions go, it took me a while, but two years later I resigned from the police force and took up a place at a theological college.'

'But what convinced you that there was a god in any of that?' she asked quietly. 'Surely it would make you think otherwise. Such needless destruction. All that senseless fear and grief.'

He reached up to run his fingers through her hair. 'It was watching the innate goodness of virtual strangers rushing to the aid of fellow passengers who were dying or badly hurt than convinced me that, whether we realise it or not, there's a force for good working through each and every one of us every minute of the day, and in the least likely situations.'

She lay down beside him, her head resting against his. 'Would it be crass of me to say I'm glad you were one of the lucky ones that day?'

He kissed her lightly on the forehead. 'I'm glad I was lucky too.'

Chapter Seven

IT WAS SEPTEMBER and two days after they'd returned from a week in Cornwall, Dan was in the kitchen blowing up balloons for Marcus's third birthday.

This year's break—a traditional seaside family holiday down in Cornwall—was a throwback to Dan's own childhood when he and his parents used to go to Devon to stay in the same cottage, year in year out. Children liked continuity and Dan could foresee Marcus looking forward to the prospect of returning to St Ives next year. As for Sally, Dan wasn't so sure.

Before their holiday her behaviour had been markedly erratic, up one day, down the next. He'd reached the point of almost dreading their week away. But the holiday had gone better than he'd hoped. Sally had seemed to be enjoying herself, playing with Marcus on the beach, building sandcastles and hunting in rock pools with him for crabs.

They were midway through the holiday when, following the consumption of a bottle and a half of wine over supper one night, he risked touching her in bed. To his surprise, she didn't roll away from him and from then on they made love every night. He knew they were on surer ground when, on their last night, it was Sally who made the first move.

If she was having an affair, would she really do that? It was all the encouragement he needed to believe they were over the worst.

He'd also been encouraged by her decision to leave her mobile and laptop at home. 'I don't want my mother badgering me while we're away or anyone from work being able to get in touch,' she'd said when they were packing up the car. This was a first. She had never cut the tie with work so resolutely before. And if there was a lover on the scene, wouldn't she want the security of being able to stay in touch with him?

With shame, Dan now had to admit that he'd been wrong. He'd been paranoid to imagine Sally was seeing someone behind his back.

Down to the last balloon, Dan gave it a final puff. Although it was Marcus's birthday today, his proper party wouldn't be until the weekend. Today there would be just a small gathering of close friends to mark the occasion. It was both Chloe and Seth's day off, so they would be coming, along with Jennifer and Graham, and Tatiana and Rosie with Charlie. On Saturday it was Charlie's birthday, and he and Marcus were having a combined party in the village hall.

Sally had promised to get back in time, but knowing that she had the inevitable mountain of work to catch up on from last week, Dan wasn't holding his breath in the hope that she would be on time.

'I've got to go,' Sally said.

Standing behind her, one of his hands inside her blouse, Harry said, 'Another five minutes won't hurt.'

'Harry, no,' she said.

He laughed. 'You don't mean that.'

God help her, but he was right. She would willingly stay here in his office for the rest of the day if she thought they could get away with it. He held her closely and she could feel the hardness of him pressing against her. Five minutes was probably all it would take. Certainly if Monday was anything to go by. Within minutes of being back in the office after her week away, Harry had locked her in his office with him and done what he'd threatened to do since they'd started their affair.

'I missed you,' he'd said, as he'd slumped against her afterwards. 'Don't ever go away like that again.'

'But look how the denial has sharpened your appetite for me,' she'd replied, relishing the depth of his need for her.

On her last day at work before going on holiday he'd begged her to let him ring or text her while she was in Cornwall, but she'd stood firm. Being completely deprived of Harry had increased her desire for him and she'd resorted to having sex with Dan just so she could close her eyes and pretend she was in bed with Harry. The first time she had done it she had experienced a vague sense of guilt, but by the following night she reckoned Dan was happy enough, so why worry?

Extricating herself from Harry's grasp, she said, 'I really have to go. I'm going to be late as it is.'

'One more kiss, then I'll let you go.'

Chloe was cross. What was Sally playing at? Sometimes she didn't think her friend deserved Dan and Marcus. Surely she could find the time to be with her son on his birthday? Twice now Dan had had to explain to Marcus that they couldn't light the candles on his cake yet, not until Mummy was here. Frankly, if it were down to Chloe, she'd light the candles, let Marcus blow them out and to hell with his mother sharing the moment. It was high time that girl got her priorities sorted.

Quite apart from Sally letting her son down, Chloe also felt personally slighted. Today was to be the day when Sally finally met Seth. Glancing across the kitchen, she watched with proprietorial pride as Seth chatted with her father. As she continued to observe him, she experienced the by-now familiar stirring in her; a warmth, an inner light. Love? She thought it might be. It both stilled and thrilled her.

'How many times did I tell you when you were a child that it was rude to stare, Chloe?'

Chloe took the glass of wine her mother had fetched for her.

'I can't say I blame you. He's absolutely gorgeous. An unearthly beauty. What helped to change your mind about him?'

'Mind your own business, Mum.'

'You will be careful, won't you?'

Chloe looked at her mother. 'Why do you say that?'

Jennifer took a sip of her wine. 'Be patient with him. He has to play by different rules from the rest of us.'

Sally locked her car, fixed a harassed expression on her face and let herself in. 'Sorry, everyone!' she cried, feigning breathlessness. 'Honestly, those roads just get worse and worse. Forty-five minutes I was stuck on the M—. Hello, Marcus, are you having a lovely time? Any chance of a gin and tonic, Dan?'

Congratulating herself on such a perfect entrance, Sally shrugged out of her suit jacket and began working the room. She spun the usual old baloney to Rosie—pregnancy going well, blah-di-bloody-blah—kissed

Graham Hennessey—Yes, excellent holiday in Cornwall, thanks. Boring. Boring. *Boring!* When would it ever end? How she longed to shock them all out of their smug, small-mindedness. But why was Chloe looking at her that way? And what the hell was Tatiana, Queen of the Bloody Fairies doing here? But check out the angelic, curly-haired, sex god standing next to Chloe! Holy Moses! It wasn't her curate, was it?

A large and welcome gin and tonic in her hand now, Sally strolled over. Oh, oh, time to light the touch paper, stand back and have some fun!

She kissed Chloe's cheek. 'And you must be Chloe's sexy, unobtainable priest, Seth Hawthorne,' she said. 'I've heard so much about you.'

'I've heard a lot about you, too. It's good to meet you at last.'

'I'm disappointed in you, though. You don't seem to have done a very good job on Chloe. If you ask me, she's still as big a sinner as ever. Or is she beyond redemption?'

'Thanks a bunch, Sally!'

'Don't look so grouchy, Chloe, I'm only joking. Seth knows that, don't you, Seth?'

'Sally,' Dan called to her. 'Marcus wants to blow out the candles on his cake now. Do you want to come over?'

Chloe was furious. Could Sally have been any ruder or more patronising? It seemed she could, because now, on her second gin and tonic, she was telling Seth that he didn't look anything like she'd expected.

'How did you think I'd look?' Seth asked her, smiling.

'Well, you know; a bit wet and insipid.'

Chloe stifled an exclamation. But Seth said, 'Based on what? Chloe's previous taste in boyfriends?'

Sally laughed. 'God, no! The one thing you can rely on Chloe for is her impeccable taste in good-looking men.'

On the verge of telling Sally to shut up, Chloe felt Seth slip his hand in hers and squeeze it gently. She took it as a hint not to react. 'I'm intrigued,' he persisted. 'Just why did you think I'd look wet and insipid?'

'Based on just about every religious fanatic I've ever come across.'

Chloe had had enough. 'Sally, I don't know what you're stoked up on, but take it down a notch, will you?'

'It's OK, Chloe,' Seth said. 'Sally's entitled to her opinion.'

'You're damned right I am! Hey, has Chloe told you about the list we used to keep?'

'Not that I can recall,' Seth replied evenly.

Chloe shot her a threatening look. 'Sally, please, just button it. OK?'

'The thing is,' Sally carried on, ignoring Chloe's plea, her eyes glittering with intent, 'a vicar would have been the last man either of us would have considered dating. Back then, you would have been so lame and so low in the food chain as to be worthy of nothing but our derision. Funny how things change, isn't it?'

Chloe let out a strangled cry of incensed disbelief. But his manner quite unruffled, Seth moved his hand to Chloe's shoulder and said with quiet dignity, 'Then I have to consider myself exceedingly fortunate.'

His politeness in the face of such a blatant insult was more than Chloe could bear. She leaned forward to whisper in Sally's ear, then tipped her glass of wine down her front.

If it makes you feel any better, I wasn't offended by what Sally said. I've been on the receiving end of far worse insults and have learned the hard way to ignore them. I was more concerned about her upsetting you. Which she clearly did. What did you whisper in her ear?'

'You don't want to know.'

She and Seth had left the party while Sally was upstairs changing out of her wine-soaked top. Dan had been disappointed to see them leave so early—he'd been expecting them to stay on for supper—but she'd lied and said she had a headache.

'I'm sorry,' Chloe said. 'Sorry that I have such a bitch of a friend. She was horrible to you. I don't think I'll ever forgive her.'

'Don't say that. Nothing's ever that bad.'

'You're not going to go all preachy on me, are you?'

'Do I look that dimwitted? But I'd be interested to know what's really troubling your friend. She gave the impression of spoiling for a fight.'

'Well, she'll get one from me if she doesn't get her act together.'

'Come on,' he said, 'let's go and sit outside. And when I think it's safe and I won't get my head bitten off, I'll risk kissing you to cheer you up.'

Despite her foul mood, Chloe smiled. 'You can kiss me now, if you like.'

He put their drinks down and placed his hands round her waist and bent to kiss her. 'Better?' he said when he pulled away.

'Almost,' she said.

He tutted. 'Almost isn't good enough.' He kissed her again, this time taking her face in his hands. Her heart soared and it wasn't long before her body ached for his touch. It was all she could do to stop herself from ripping his clothes off. Never had she wanted a man as much as she wanted Seth. Abruptly, he stopped kissing her and suddenly hugged her with a fierce shudder. Pressed against him, she could feel his heart hammering in his chest. 'In your professional capacity as a doctor,' he said, 'do you think it's possible to die from abstinence?'

'The way I feel, I think it's highly likely.'

He tilted his head back and gazed down at her. His pupils were fully dilated, the blue of his irises intensely dark. She could see he was suddenly nervous. 'I hadn't wanted to say anything,' he said, his voice low, 'not this soon. But the way I see it, I'm damned if I do and damned if I don't. I love you, Chloe. I love you in a way I've never loved anyone before. I think about you all the time.' He smiled hesitantly. 'And not just about how much I want to make love to you, which I only do on average about twenty-three hours a day.'

'What do you think about in that other hour?' she asked.

The smile broadened. 'OK, I admit it, I lied. It's a full-time, twenty-four-hour job fantasising about you naked in bed with me. Not that I'm complaining. There are worse things I could be obsessed with.'

Chloe rested the palms of her hands on his chest. Through the soft, warm fabric of his shirt, she could feel beating of his heart. 'Can we rewind the conversation a bit, please?' she said.

He frowned. 'To which bit in particular?'

'The part when you said you loved me.'

'That sounds ominous.' The anxious frown instantly clouded his handsome face and eyes. 'I knew I shouldn't have said anything.'

She placed a finger on his lips. 'Ssh . . . It's my turn to speak. When you said you loved me, you didn't give me a chance to respond. I just want you to know that I love you. Nobody's ever made me as happy as you do.' She removed her finger and kissed him. She felt him quiver in her arms and went on kissing him.

Oh, yes, she loved Seth. She loved the littlest thing about him. She loved the soft, sensual way he kissed her. She loved his integrity. She even loved his obsession with Arcade Fire. But best of all, she loved the way he made her feel so cherished. Would it be tempting fate to think that maybe, just maybe, she and Seth had a real future together?

With Marcus finally settled in bed and clasping a newly recruited teddy to his platoon of cuddlies—a present from Chloe and Seth—Dan went to look for Sally. He found her downstairs in the study.

She looked up from her laptop. 'Just finishing,' she said absently.

'That's OK, no hurry. I'll make a start on supper.'

'Actually, I'm not very hungry. Just a sandwich would suit me. Will what you've prepared keep for tomorrow?'

'Probably better if I freeze it. There's rather a lot of it—I was expecting Chloe and Seth to stay for the evening. What did you think of Seth?'

'He's all right, I suppose. Although if I'm completely honest, I found him a bit hard to take seriously.'

Surprised, Dan said, 'In what way?'

'Come off it, Dan, the man believes in virgin births and the dead being raised. How can anyone with half a brain take him seriously?'

'Chloe seems to. I think she's very fond of him. And he of her.'

She shrugged. 'If you say so.' She returned her attention to her laptop.

Leaving her to get on, Dan turned to go. But he hesitated. 'Sally,' he said, 'is everything OK at work?'

She raised her head sharply. 'What do you mean?'

'You would say if things were getting too much for you, wouldn't you? You work so hard.'

She stared back at him wordlessly, her eyes chillingly pale and direct. He feared he might have gone too far and touched a nerve that she would prefer to be left well alone. 'I just want you to know that I appreciate everything you do,' he added.

He closed the door after him and tried to remember when exactly it was that he'd started walking on eggshells around Sally.

As partners' meetings went, it was the same old game of attack and defend. It was as predictable as night followed day and Sally could play the game in her sleep. Which was just as well, because her mind wasn't on what porkadelic Duncan Patterson was bleating on about.

As she doodled absent-mindedly on the notepad in front of her, Sally had something much more important preying on her mind than anything Duncan Patterson had to say. '*How's Harry?*' Chloe had whispered in her ear yesterday. What did she know? And whatever it was she did know—or thought she knew—how had Chloe come by it? No way could she have seen her with Harry. Yet her friend appeared to suspect something and had used it to strike back at her. She had even childishly tipped wine down her front. And because Sally had dared to speak the truth about Seth?

OK, he was a looker—she'd give him that—but could Chloe honestly see herself as a vicar's wife? Really, the whole thing was absurd.

But how had Chloe jumped to such a conclusion about Harry? And if she had, was there a chance that Dan had? Was it something the pair of them had discussed behind her back? But based on what, exactly? She had been so careful. No emails. No texts. No telephone calls when she was at home. That had been the rule. Despite Harry's pleadings.

As soon as she'd arrived at work this morning, Sally had rushed to speak to Harry, but annoyingly he was out of the office for the day.

At last! Pens were being capped, notepads and files slapped shut— the meeting had finally drawn to a welcome close. Up on her feet, Sally hurriedly gathered her things together and headed for the door.

'Could I have a word, Sally?' Tom McKenzie, who had just chaired the meeting, had his hand on her arm.

'Of course,' she said brightly, disguising her irritation at being delayed.

'Let's go to my office,' Tom said, already leading the way.

Stationed outside Tom's office was Fern Elliot, Tom's PA. 'The Iron Lady' was her unofficial office title and she guarded Tom possessively.

Sally gave her a cheery, insincere smile as she followed behind Tom into his office.

Tom offered her a chair, but instead of taking up his seat behind his desk he wandered over to the window. He appeared to be on edge.

'Everything all right, Tom?' she asked.

He turned round. 'That was exactly the question I was going to ask you, Sally. Is everything all right with *you*?'

Taken aback, she said, 'Of course. Why wouldn't it be?'

'Look, quite apart from you being a valued member of the firm, I've always had the utmost respect for you. You know that, don't you?'

She nodded slowly. 'I sense a "but" coming,' she said stiffly.

'I want you to understand that I'm only saying what I'm about to say because I care about you. I'd rather you heard it from me than from anyone else.' Tom paused. 'The thing is.' He cleared his throat again. 'The thing is, certain people in the office seem to think that you . . . that you and Harry are . . . more than just work colleagues.'

Sally kept her gaze level. Then, assuming incredulity, she burst out laughing. 'What is this, Tom, a belated April Fools' Day prank?'

Tom didn't say anything.

Sally stopped laughing. 'My God, this isn't a joke, is it?'

'It would be a strange sort of joke, Sally.'

'But you can't really think Harry and I . . . I mean, come on, he's a boy. He's years younger than me. What the hell would I see in him? Or he in me? Oh, really, Tom, it's too absurd for words. I'm married. And very happily so. Besides which, when would I have time for a sordid office fling with Harry Fox?'

Relief began to show in Tom's face. 'I knew it couldn't possibly be true,' he said. 'But I thought you ought to know what was being said about you. I'll do my best to quash any more rumours, but you know as well as I do that office life plays by its own rules.'

'Thanks. I appreciate that. And not that it really matters, but who brought this outlandish work of fiction to your attention?'

Once more Tom dropped his gaze. Which told Sally all she needed to know. The Iron Lady. It had to be. Tom wouldn't cover for anyone else.

'Whoever it is,' she said coolly, 'I'd be grateful if you dealt with him or her appropriately. Superficially it has its amusement value and I'm prepared to let it go, but if the rumour doesn't go away, then I'll take my own steps to deal with the matter. Now, if there isn't anything else, I need to put my thoughts in order for a conference this afternoon.'

Back in her office, the door firmly shut, Sally leaned against it. That was close. That was bloody close. But what a performance! Adrenaline racing through her, she smiled and punched the air. Oh, yes, it was some performance she'd given. She went over to her desk and sat down. It was all she could do to stop herself laughing out loud.

There was a very different atmosphere at work that morning. Normally there was a mood of cheerful industry about the place, but today everyone was unnaturally quiet and downcast.

The trust had lost one of its most popular children. Jordan Kemp had died from kidney failure last night. Five years old, he had been one of the real stars of the trust, known for his cheeky smile and infectious laughter. His death had hit them all hard. Tatiana had received the news first and Dan knew that she had been especially attached to Jordan.

Leaving his printer to churn out the report he'd been working on, Dan went to make himself some coffee. He pushed open the kitchen door and found Tatiana there. With a start she glanced at him over her shoulder and he saw that she was crying. She looked unutterably sad. He shut the door after him and because it seemed the most natural thing in the world to do, he went to her and put his arms round her. She rested her head against his chest and sobbed helplessly, her tears falling wet and warm on his skin through his shirt.

Finally, she raised her head from his chest. 'I'm sorry,' she stammered, 'I promised myself I wouldn't lose it over Jordan.' She wiped first one eye with the back of her hand, then the other. Her mascara had not survived her tears, yet somehow the smudging emphasised the colour of her eyes, giving them a depth and intensity he'd never noticed before. But then he'd never been this close to her before.

Still standing within the circle of his embrace, she looked up at him and their eyes met. And held. He knew that he should let go of her. But he didn't. Instead, he bent his head and brushed his lips over her mouth. Scarcely making contact with her, it was barely a kiss, but it made him catch his breath. And made him want to kiss her again. He did and she kissed him back in a way that caused something deep inside him to burst free. He pulled away, shocked.

'I'm sorry,' he apologised. 'I shouldn't have done that.' He willed himself to let go of her but he couldn't. 'I'm sorry,' he repeated, even though he realised with dazed disbelief that he wasn't sorry at all.

'Don't be,' she said at length. 'You were being kind. It was just a kiss to comfort me. That was all.'

He shook his head slowly. 'I don't think it was. I think it's something I've wanted to do for some time, only I didn't know it until now.'

'I've wanted you to do it for a long time, too,' she said quietly.

'Really? You never gave me any idea.'

'I was hardly going to advertise how I felt about you, was I? Given your circumstances.' She slipped out of his arms. 'And now that we've both reminded ourselves that you're married, I'm going to get back to work and pretend the last five minutes never happened.'

You might be able to, Dan thought when he was left alone. He put a hand to his chest, where her tears had left a cool, damp patch on his shirt and kept it there, wondering. Just wondering.

That evening, Sally was in a strange, jittery mood. She'd scarcely eaten any of her supper and she kept fidgeting in her chair and laughing exaggeratedly at things on the television. Right now, she was reading the local newspaper, turning the pages noisily and messily.

Or had Dan got it wrong? Was it him who was behaving oddly and being overly sensitive to Sally's manner? Certainly he had more on his mind than usual. Mostly guilt. He couldn't stop thinking of the amazing sense of release he'd experienced when he'd kissed Tatiana. For a split second everything had made perfect sense.

Now, of course, nothing made sense. He'd as good as cheated on his wife and he felt disgusted with himself. What was so disconcerting for him was not the physical betrayal he'd committed, but the knowledge that he'd emotionally betrayed his wife. As fleeting as the moment had been, he'd felt more of a connection with Tatiana when their lips had touched than he had with Sally in a long time.

He'd left work while everyone was having lunch, without speaking again to Tatiana. But he regretted his decision. He should have spoken

to Tatiana before leaving. He should have apologised and assured her—
and himself—that he had no intention of compromising her.

'Oh, I forgot to say,' Sally said, tossing aside the messed up paper. 'I
have to go and see my mother again. I've checked the calendar; this
coming weekend's free, so I'll go then. That OK with you?'

'Are you asking me, or telling me?'

'Don't be silly.' She laughed.

'Not entirely free,' he corrected her, 'it's the Harvest Festival at church
on Sunday and Marcus's class from nursery is taking part.'

'Oh, you don't need me there.'

'But Marcus might like you there,' he pressed.

'I doubt Marcus will even notice my absence,' Sally said. She stood
up abruptly. 'You know what, I think I'll go and see Chloe.'

'But it's almost ten o'clock. She could be in bed. Why don't you ring?'

Sally laughed again. 'Who knows, I might just catch her in bed with
her saintly reverend. Wouldn't that be a blast?'

Dan listened to the front door shutting and shook his head. As
before, he contemplated the imposter who was masquerading as his
wife. The old Sally would never have said what she just had. A blast?
Catching her best friend in bed with a man she was clearly more than
just fond of. Where was the so-called blast in that?

With a bottle of wine in her hand, Sally walked purposefully through
the dark, lamp-lit village. In her head she was rehearsing what she was
going to say to Chloe. She would apologise for her remarks about Seth,
even though she still stood by them. Then, when they'd kissed and
made up, she would wait to see if Chloe raised the subject of Harry.

After Harry had returned from seeing his client in Burnley this afternoon, she'd asked Chandra to buzz his office upstairs to tell him to
come and see her; there was a tax matter she needed to discuss with
him. Once they were alone, she'd told Harry what Tom had said about
them having an affair. She told him about her no-holds-barred denial.
His face had dropped.

'You're going to suggest we end things, aren't you?' he'd said.

'End things?' She'd laughed, grabbing his tie and pulling him to her.
'You've got to be joking! Big kudos to me, I want us to celebrate my
incomparable acting skills by going away together at the weekend!'

He'd laughed, too, and kissed her hard. 'That's what I love about
you; the greater the risk, the greater the thrill. You're incredible!'

There were lights on at Chloe's cottage, but no sign of an extra car on the drive. Which implied that Chloe was alone. Sally rang the doorbell.

'Oh, it's you,' Chloe said when she opened the door to her.

'You don't sound too happy to see me.'

'I can't think why that would be the case. Can you?'

A suitably repentant expression on her face, Sally said, 'That's why I'm here. I want to apologise for what I said. Can I come in?'

'It's a bit late. I was just going to have a shower and get ready for bed.'

Sally offered the bottle of wine. 'An olive branch. I was a total bitch yesterday and I really want to clear the air between us. Please.'

'All right,' Chloe said. 'But your apology had better be good.'

Chloe took the bottle from Sally and led her through to the kitchen. She had no intention of drinking wine at this time of night and she plonked it on the work surface with an inhospitable bang. 'Right,' she said, 'you were outstandingly vile to Seth yesterday. Care to explain why?'

'Call it a moment of madness.'

'I'd call it more than that, frankly. You knew exactly what you were doing. It was a carefully constructed attack on the man I love.'

'The man you love? You can't be serious.'

Chloe bristled, annoyed that she'd shared something so intimate when she was so angry. 'I *am* serious, as a matter of fact,' she asserted. 'What's more, Seth loves me.' Damn! Why did she sound so defensive?

'Bloody hell! This is all a bit quick, isn't it? You'll be telling me next the two of you are planning to marry.'

'Would that be so very awful?'

'Have you been to bed with him?'

Chloe hesitated. 'That's none of your business.'

'Well, if you have, what does that say about the saintly Reverend Hawthorne? And if you haven't, what does it say about you? What's he done to you, Chloe? Turned you into some pathetic, dried up little nun?'

'It's called respect, Sally. Something you wouldn't know anything about, given your behaviour of late.'

'Rubbish! It's my respect for you that makes me want to open your eyes to what's really going on inside your head. The only reason you're so quick to convince yourself that you're in love with Seth is because you're desperate for some man to get you pregnant. Any man will do. Even a man who believes in holy gobbledegook!'

'OK, that's enough. I'm not listening to any more of this. Out. Now.'

'Oh, come on. I'm just hitting the honesty button.'

'Honesty! You want to talk about honesty? Well, try this on for size: how about you telling Dan what a lying, cheating bitch you are?'

'And what's that supposed to mean?'

'It means I know about you and your affair.'

'Affair? What affair?'

'Get real, Sally. I heard your intake of breath when I whispered Harry's name in your ear yesterday afternoon.'

'Oh, so that's what you whispered. I wondered what that was about.'

'You're not fooling me, Sally. Now get your sorry arse out of my house and go home to your husband and child. And when you've got a minute, try looking in the mirror and asking yourself whether you like the person looking back at you. Because right now, I don't much care for the person you've become. I doubt many other people do either.'

After a sleepless night, Dan decided that there was nothing else for it; he had to see Tatiana again. He badly wanted to clear the air. He gave Rosie a call after breakfast and she agreed to look after Marcus for a couple of hours.

He was nervous when he drove to Crantsford. He'd lain in bed for most of last night, unable to stop his brain from replaying that moment when he'd held and kissed Tatiana. Each time he thought of it, his confusion grew. He was a happily married man, right? Happily married men did not kiss their work colleagues. Happily married men did not have the kind of reaction he'd had when he'd kissed Tatiana.

Dan pulled into the car park at the back of the trust's offices, switched off the engine and released his seat belt. He thought about Sally. Could he honestly say that he still felt the same way about her as he used to? And how many times had he made excuses for her behaviour in the past few months? And what of his suspicion that she'd been having an affair? How had he so easily dismissed that from his mind? Because he was a coward, that was why. The consequences of confronting her would be too awful to contemplate.

Staring through the windscreen at the building in front of him, he wondered what he was doing here. Then he remembered: Tatiana. He suddenly doubted whether it had been wise of him to come here to talk to her. In his current frame of mind it would be dangerously easy to do entirely the wrong thing. But she deserves an apology, he reasoned.

It was a persuasive argument and one that had him opening his car door. It was still compellingly persuasive when he reached the reception desk and smiled at Emma. And he was still utterly, one hundred per cent persuaded, right up until he tapped lightly on Tatiana's door and pushed it open. But then it all fell apart. He took one look at her sitting behind her desk and he knew he should have stayed at home.

She put down her pen and smiled uncertainly at him. 'I didn't think you were coming in today.'

'No,' he said.

'And yet here you are.'

He took a step into her office, then another, and then closed the door behind him. Another wrong decision. Keep the door open and he wouldn't do anything he'd regret. 'I wanted to speak to you,' he said.

'I rather thought you might. Do you want to sit down?'

He shook his head and went and stood next to the bank of filing cabinets. Distance was vital. 'How are you feeling?' he asked.

'Slightly shy of you, if you want the truth.'

Realising she'd misunderstood him, he said, 'No, I meant, how are you feeling about Jordan now?'

'Oh. I see. Much better. Thank you for asking. Are you sure you wouldn't like to sit down? How about some coffee?'

'I don't want you to be shy or awkward around me,' he blurted out, ignoring her questions. 'I want you to feel like you've always felt.'

Her cheeks flushed a delicate shade of pink and he saw his gaffe. 'I'm sorry,' he said, 'that was clumsy of me.'

Leaning back in her chair, she sighed. 'I'm sorry, too, Dan. I should never have said how I felt about you. I've ruined everything.'

'No!' he said, moving towards her desk and forgetting all about keeping his distance. 'You mustn't think that. It was me. *I* kissed *you*.'

'I could have stopped you. But I didn't.' She swallowed. 'And to my shame I probably wouldn't stop you if you did it again. See what a bad person I am? I'm a potential marriage wrecker, Dan. In my defence all I can say is that I never intended to fall in love with you.'

He stared at her, profoundly shocked. 'You love me?'

'What's not to love?' She turned huge, sad eyes on him. 'So there it is; the genie is well and truly out of the bottle. I'm sorry.'

'Please don't keep apologising. And don't ever describe yourself as bad. You're the least bad person I know.'

'Your wife might not share your view of me.'

'These days my wife shares very little with me.' The admission was out before he could stop it. He steeled himself to say the right thing. 'Which is why it wasn't a good idea for me to come here. I wanted to apologise to you for yesterday, but deep down I was fooling myself. I wanted to see you again, to see . . . well, let's just say that the way things are at home with Sally, it would be the easiest thing in the world for me to start an affair with you. But I won't do that. I care about you too much to make that mistake. You deserve to be treated better.'

Without knowing how he'd got there, he suddenly found himself on her side of the desk. He knelt down on one knee beside her so that he could look her in the eye. 'I wish things were different. Really I do.'

'I understand.' She touched his face with her hand. 'You're a good man, Dan. I knew that the minute I met you.'

'I'd better go,' he said.

'Yes,' she murmured. 'You better had.'

But he didn't move. Just one kiss like yesterday, he thought. One kiss to lock away in his heart. He tilted his head fractionally closer to hers. If she resists, I'll stop, he told himself.

His lips had just made contact with hers when he jerked his head back. What was he thinking? How could he be so selfish? 'I'm sorry,' he mumbled, full of remorse. 'I want to but I can't. Forgive me, please.'

She nodded sadly.

'Will you be at the Harvest Festival service on Sunday?' he asked, getting to his feet.

'I promised Charlie I'd be there. I don't want to let him down.'

'And nor should you.'

'Will your wife be there?'

He shook his head. 'She's otherwise engaged.'

The sky was bright and glittery and with a sharp nip in the air the weather was hinting that autumn was just round the corner.

St Andrew's had been packed with fidgety children and adults unaccustomed to being in church. Now, everyone stood around in groups outside, children letting off steam by running in and out of tombstones.

The sight of Marcus carefully making his way up the aisle with his cargo of fruit and vegetables had brought a lump to Dan's throat.

With Marcus's help, Dan had spent most of yesterday afternoon decorating a cardboard box with brown paper and straw and filling it with apples, damsons, runner beans and tomatoes, all donated by Chloe's parents from their garden. Chloe had joined him in the pew and Tatiana, along with Rose and Dave, had sat in the pew in front of him.

'OK, everyone? Ready to come back to ours for lunch? You're invited too, Chloe,' Dave said.

Breaking off from her conversation with Tatiana, Chloe said, 'I'd love to, Dave, but I can't. Sorry.'

Dave grinned. 'Got a better invitation from that man of yours?'

'Something like that,' Chloe said with a happy smile.

'No worries. We'll catch you another time.'

Rosie had phoned Dan last night to suggest they all have lunch together after the service. 'It won't be anything special,' she'd explained, 'just a thrown-together affair of whatever's in the fridge. Tatiana's already said she's coming.' His response should have been to apologise and say he and Marcus couldn't make it, but he hadn't.

Having said goodbye to Chloe, he went to round up Marcus and Charlie. When he had them both in hand, he turned to find Tatiana waiting for him. Squealing loudly, both boys let go of Dan and rushed full tilt at her, nearly knocking her off her feet. 'You are all right with this, aren't you?' she asked, when she had them under control.

'As long as you are,' he said.

She nodded.

I'm not doing anything wrong, Dan told himself as they set off with Rosie and Dave. Lunch, that's all this is.

Dan looked through the open doors of the conservatory where they were drinking coffee and out to the garden where Marcus and Charlie were playing on the new wooden climbing frame Charlie had been given for his birthday. It was a stupendous bit of kit; a large, complicated climbing frame that wouldn't be out of place in a public park.

'More wine, anyone?' Dave asked.

Tatiana shook her head. 'I'm driving.'

'Dan?'

'I'd better not,' Dan said, 'I've got some work to do later.' He was just about to start making noises about it very nearly being time he was going when he heard Marcus shouting to him. 'Look at me, Daddy!'

With his hair on end and his arms waving, Marcus was hanging upside down at the highest point of the climbing frame, his legs hooked over a wooden bar. When had he learned to do that? Fighting the urge to rush over, Dan called back, 'You be careful, Marcus.'

'I'm the king of the castle,' Marcus chorused gleefully.

What happened next had Dan's blood freezing in his veins. A wasp came into view and started to dive-bomb Marcus. Since he'd been stung by one very recently, he'd developed a fear of them. He started waving his arms frantically about his head to get rid of the wasp. Dan watched powerlessly as the tension went out of Marcus's body and his legs began to straighten, first one, then the other.

He landed with a sickening thud on the grass below.

Chapter Eight

DAN KNELT BESIDE HIS SON. His son who wasn't moving. His son who wasn't crying. 'Marcus,' he said. He turned him over as gently as he could. Was that the wrong thing to do? Dan didn't know. But he had to do something. He had to hold his son. He had to know he was all right. 'Marcus,' he said again.

With his eyes closed and his face ashen, the only colour to Marcus was the blood round his mouth. There was so much of it, it was difficult to see just exactly where it was coming from.

'Marcus,' Dan tried again, holding him tenderly. The still, limp weight of his precious son reminded Dan of all the times he'd carried him sleeping from the car into the house. But it also reminded him of another time. Of the boy who had been ripped from his arms and swept out to sea. The boy he hadn't been able to save.

Icy fear gripped Dan's heart and he squeezed Marcus tightly. Amazingly his son's eyes then flickered open and his body sprang to life. He coughed and spluttered, spraying blood down the front of Dan's shirt. He started to cry. Never had Dan been more pleased to hear his son cry.

Marcus had very nearly bitten through his lower lip and it was obvious he needed stitches, so Tatiana offered to drive them to the hospital. Sitting next to Marcus in the back of her car—they'd moved Charlie's seat across from Rosie's—Dan phoned Chloe on his mobile. She said she would meet them at A & E.

Next he tried ringing Sally, but there was no answer from her mobile. It was switched off.

Tatiana dropped them off at the entrance to the hospital and went to park the car. It was a quiet afternoon at A & E and by the time Tatiana caught up with them, they were being ushered into a curtained cubicle. A man about the same age as Dan introduced himself as Dr Flannigan and Dan did his best to answer his questions as clearly as he could while trying not to sound like a negligent parent. The doctor was brisk and straightforward and listened impassively.

'Concussion,' the doctor said matter-of-factly. 'We'd better do an X-ray, just to be on the safe side.'

When finally it was over and Dan went to look for Tatiana in the waiting area, he saw that she wasn't alone. Chloe and Seth were with her. It was Marcus who spotted them first. Sporting a collection of stick-on badges and a plaster covering most of his swollen, stitched-up chin, he waved at Chloe, pointing proudly to his badges.

'He's all right, then?' Chloe said, relief in her voice.

'He'll mend,' Dan said. 'There's a danger he might be sick again or feel a bit dizzy, but he's certainly well enough to go home. Sorry to spoil your afternoon.' He said this more to Seth.

'It wasn't a problem. Really.'

'Which doctor did you see?'

'Dr Flannigan.'

'Right, I'll just go and have a chat with him. Then we'll get going.'

Once more, Dan sat in the back of Tatiana's car with Marcus. Once again he tried ringing Sally. 'Still no answer?' Tatiana asked.

Dan shook his head.

'Maybe she's out of range.'

That was one way of describing Sally, Dan thought.

'You OK?'

Dan glanced up and met Tatiana's gaze in the mirror. 'I should have been out in the garden with him. He's three. What was I thinking?'

'Don't beat yourself up. We were all there keeping an eye on Marcus and Charlie. And even if we'd been in the garden with them, Marcus could still have slipped.'

'But he's my son. He's my responsibility. I let him down.'

'You didn't let him down. Don't ever think that. You're a great father to him. The best I know.'

He smiled at her gratefully. 'Thank you,' he said. 'And thanks, too, for offering to drive. I should have said something earlier.'

'You had far more important things on your mind.'

He stared at the back of Tatiana's head. She had a graceful, slender neck. It was beautiful. Even when she was driving she looked poised. He remembered something from the first time he'd met her. 'Did you ever train to be a dancer, Tatiana?' he asked.

She gave him an odd look in the mirror, visibly surprised at his question. 'Yes,' she said, 'I spent five years at ballet school. Why do you ask?'

'I thought so,' he said with a small shrug.

They drove on in silence, following behind Seth's car.

Tatiana parked on the road in front of Corner Cottage and while Dan was lifting Marcus out of Charlie's seat, she said, 'I'll ring you tomorrow to see how he is.'

'Aren't you going to come inside?'

They were on the pavement now. 'I'd better not,' she said, stroking Marcus's cheek. 'Take care, little chap,' she said, kissing his head.

Dan didn't want her to leave. But he knew he had to let her go.

While Seth put the kettle on and made them a drink, Dan watched Chloe lift Marcus up onto the kitchen table and go through much the same procedure with him as Dr Flannigan had earlier. When she had finished, she declared Marcus to be in good shape.

'You'll be amazed how fast the swelling will go down,' she said. 'Thankfully children heal incredibly quickly.' Addressing Marcus, she said, 'Another time, sweetheart, just let the wasp have a sniff around you to satisfy his curiosity and then he'll be on his way.'

'But he wath going to thing me.'

Chloe smiled at the sound of Marcus's newly acquired lisp and lifted him down from the table. 'A sting would have been better than frightening the life out of us all.'

He shook his head doubtfully and looked at Dan. 'Can I have a dink now, Daddy? With a thaw like the doctor thaid.'

'Of course. And then we must get you out of those dirty clothes. Maybe you'd like a bath?'

Marcus looked anxiously at the dried bloodstains on his sweatshirt and jeans. 'Will Mummy be croth?'

'Of course she won't,' Dan said, registering that this was the first reference Marcus had made to his mother. 'Which reminds me, I must try ringing her again.' He took out his mobile and pressed redial. 'Still nothing,' he said seconds later, with irritation.

There was no real urgency to get in touch with Sally now but it rankled with Dan that she had been unobtainable when who knew what the consequences of Marcus's fall might have been. He wasn't proud of it, but he wanted to shame Sally.

Leaving Seth and Chloe to keep an eye on Marcus in the kitchen, he went to the study and opened the desk drawer where Sally kept her address book. If he was going to prove a point with Sally, what better way to do it than via his mother-in-law?

When the telephone was finally answered over in Hull, Dan could hear the blare of a television in the background. 'Mrs Wilson?' he said. He'd never known her well enough to call her by her Christian name.

'Yes. Who's that?'

'It's Dan.'

'Dan who? Terry, turn that telly down? Who did you say you were?'

'Dan Oliver. Sally's husband.'

'Why didn't you say? So what do you want, Dan?'

'I need to speak to Sally. Is she still there with you or has she already left? Only Marcus had an accident this afternoon and—'

'Why the hell do you think she's here? She's not been to see me for months. Chance would be a fine thing.'

The door opened and Dan looked up to see Chloe bringing in a mug of tea for him. It must have been the look on his face, but her expression dropped.

'I'm sorry,' he said into the phone. 'What did you say?'

'I said we've not seen hide nor hair of her in months. She's too lah-di-da these days to bother with her own family.'

'In that case I'm sorry to have bothered you, Mrs Wilson,' Dan said. 'Goodbye.' He rang off.

'What is it, Dan?' Chloe asked. 'What's happened?'

He swallowed back his shock. No. Not shock, exactly. Acceptance. He'd known the truth all along, hadn't he?

'Sally was supposed to be spending the weekend with her mother,' he said quietly. 'Sorting out her debts and loans, she told me. As she's done for several weekends now. Except Kath Wilson claims Sally hasn't been to see her for months. Certainly not this weekend.'

Chloe came and put the mug of tea on the desk.

'Tell me honestly,' he said, 'did you know that she's been having an affair?'

'Not definitely,' Chloe murmured uneasily. 'It was only after you'd put the idea in my head that I began to suspect. It was her behaviour. She just wasn't the same Sally any more. But I didn't know for sure. And let's face it, we still don't.'

'Are you saying that because she's your oldest and closest friend?'

'She might well be my oldest friend, but right now she isn't my *closest* friend. She's behaved appallingly to me recently. Especially over Seth. If she is seeing somebody, I think it's someone from work.'

Dan slumped back in the chair. 'I've had enough, Chloe,' he sighed. 'I've tried everything with her. For Marcus's sake, I really tried. But not any more. She's pushed me as far as she's ever going to.'

'What will you do? Will you confront her this evening?'

'Yes.'

'Do you want me to have Marcus for the night?'

He shook his head. 'After what he's gone through today, I'd rather he slept in his own bed. Don't worry; there won't be a big ugly scene. I wouldn't do that to Marcus. I'll make sure it's all very civilised.'

It was gone nine o'clock when Dan heard Sally's car on the drive. He'd been waiting for her in the kitchen ever since he'd put Marcus to bed.

'How was your mother?' he asked when Sally came into the kitchen.

'Oh God, you *so* don't want to know. I honestly don't know why I'm putting so much effort into helping her. How was your weekend?'

He got to his feet. 'Oh, you know, the usual. I got all choked up with fatherly pride at the sight of Marcus in the Harvest Festival. Afterwards we had lunch at Dave and Rosie's and then the day took on an altogether different shape. Marcus had an accident. He fell from Charlie's new climbing frame. I had to take him to casualty. He needed nine stitches, but don't worry, he's absolutely fine. He's fast asleep upstairs.'

'Why didn't you ring me?'

'I did.' He looked her square in the eye. 'I tried several times. But you didn't have your mobile switched on.'

'Oh, hell!' Sally said with a wave of her hand. 'You're right about my mobile. I only noticed what I'd done when I set off for home.'

'But because I really wanted to let you know what had happened,' he carried on, 'I phoned your mother.'

Sally froze.

'And guess what she told me. She said you weren't there. What's more, she said she hadn't seen you in months. Where were you, Sally? Or more to the point, who were you with?'

Think, Sally! Think! But she couldn't. Playing for time, she said, 'I'll go upstairs and look in on Marcus.' She turned to go.

'Don't,' he said. 'Don't you dare, not until you've told me the truth.'

'OK,' she said, facing him now. 'You want the truth, do you?'

'Yes,' he replied. 'If nothing else, you owe me that.'

'Oh, please,' she said, 'let's not turn this into a cliché fest.'

'I'm not turning this into anything other than what it already is. You're having an affair and you've been caught out. I'd say that just about sums it up. Unless you have something more inventive to offer?'

'An affair? Are you mad? When would I have time for an affair?' Again, playing for time, she walked over to the kettle, filled it at the tap and plugged it in. Until now she hadn't thought of the consequences of being found out. She had been so sure she wouldn't be. Could she get away with saying that she had sworn her mother to secrecy, knowing that Dan wouldn't approve of Sally helping to pay off her debts?

Her brain immediately jumped on this last possibility.

Adopting a contrite expression, she turned to face Dan. 'You're not going to like this, Dan, but yes, I have been lying to you. The thing is, for some time now I've been paying off my mother's debts and the reason she claimed I hadn't been there with her this weekend was because I'd sworn her to secrecy. I told her that you'd hit the roof if you discovered that I was giving her money. So you see, when you phoned her, she obviously took the whole secrecy thing too far.' Sally dropped her shoulders and sighed. 'I'm sorry. I shouldn't have hidden something as important as this from you.' *Oh, my God, she was good! She really was.*

Dan stared at her and she waited for him to apologise. Could she ever forgive him? he'd ask. Yes, she'd say. Because, no matter what, she didn't want anything to change between them. She needed Dan.

Just as she needed Harry.

If Harry was her mind-blowing Class A drug, Dan was her rock. He provided her with a sense of permanence that enabled her to do her job.

Next to her, the kettle started to boil. It clicked off. And then Dan did something that surprised her. He started to clap.

'Bravo,' he said. 'I knew I could rely upon you to be inventive, but that really was some kind of turnaround, Sally.' He stopped clapping. 'I'm almost impressed.'

'I don't understand,' she said. 'I tell you the truth and you throw sarcasm back in my face. Why?'

'OK,' he said, 'if that's the truth, show me your bank statements. Show me these payments you've made to pay off your mother's debts.'

Sally felt the ground moving beneath her. 'What the hell's got into you, Dan? What kind of marriage do we have when you start asking me for proof?'

'You can't, can you?' he said, ignoring her question. 'You don't have any bank statements to show those payments, do you? You're lying.'

Sally wasn't ready to give up yet. 'If you really loved me,' she tried. 'You wouldn't say something as hurtful as that. Don't you trust me?'

'No,' he said simply.

That shook her. She really hadn't seen that coming. 'Don't you love me?'

'Do *you* love *me*? Do you think how much you love me when you're in bed with your lover?'

'Don't be absurd, Dan. I don't have a lover.' Even to her ears her denial lacked conviction.

'You do,' he said. 'I know you do. I've humiliated myself for long enough pretending you weren't seeing someone else, but the game's up, Sally. Your lover might be happy to share you, but I'm not.'

'You ought to try listening to yourself, Dan,' she tossed back at him angrily. The gloves were off now. 'You stand there full of pompous self-righteousness; is it any wonder I looked elsewhere for some excitement? Have you any idea how stultifying our marriage has become?'

'Well, some honesty from you at last. And thank you for your frankness. Presumably he's someone from work? Is it serious?'

She laughed. 'It's anything but serious.'

'What's that supposed to mean?'

'It's about fun, Dan. Excitement. Of feeling alive. Really alive. What's the biggest thrill you get out of life these days? What leaves you feeling exhilarated? What would it take to make you lose control?'

'You're saying I'm boring?'

'Yes. You're safe and predictable. And I'm sorry, but that's not enough for me. I need more.'

'Then I hope you find it with this other man. Because it's over between us. I don't want to stay married to you any more. It's selfish of me, I fully accept, but I'd appreciate it if you moved out. If only for a few days. I'd rather not see or talk to you for a while.'

'How very typical of you to be so rational.'

'Would you have preferred a blazing row? Voices raised? Plates thrown? Sorry, but I wouldn't do that to our son. He deserves better. He certainly deserves a better mother than you.'

Sally glared at him. 'I wondered how long it would take before you would play that card. I just didn't expect you to be so vicious with it.'

'I have no intention of retracting it. Or apologising for it.'

'Good for you, Mr Oh So Bloody Perfect! And what a hero you'll be to everyone now. A fully fledged single father bringing up his son on his own because his wicked wife had a sordid affair.'

'I hope you find the man is worth it. You're throwing away a hell of a lot for him.'

'Oh, he's worth it all right! Don't you worry about that.'

Sally overslept the next morning and woke with a spectacular hangover. She lay very still, piecing together how she'd wound up in a strange bed. Alone.

She hadn't spent the night how she'd expected to. With a hastily packed case in the boot of her car, she'd left Corner Cottage and used the number Harry had given her for his mobile.

Except Harry hadn't answered. All she'd got was his voicemail. She'd left him a message to call her immediately and it was then that it had hit her that she didn't actually know his address. She'd ended up driving into the centre of Manchester and checking in at the Hilton.

She'd launched a massive attack on the mini-bar last night and combined with a bottle of wine from room service, she was now paying the price. Bleary-eyed and smelling none too fragrant, she dragged herself to the shower and blasted herself beneath the powerful jets.

When she was dressed she checked her mobile. Nothing. Zilch. Zippo. Harry hadn't tried ringing her back or texting her.

She checked out and drove the short distance to the office. Just a normal Monday morning, she told herself.

She managed an upbeat 'hi' with Chandra and then collapsed inside her office, the door firmly closed. She snatched up the phone and punched in Harry's extension number. He answered on the third ring. 'Where the hell have you been?' she demanded.

'Sorry, I've got a client with me just now. Could I call you back?'

'How long will you be busy for?'

'Erm . . . an hour should do it. Goodbye.'

She sighed. Things weren't supposed to have taken this direction. So long as she was always careful, she'd really believed she could keep things going with Dan and Harry on parallel tracks.

Maybe she still could. A few days to let Dan stew in his own juices and he'd soon come round. She'd have to play the part of repentant wife, but given the performances she'd given of late, she didn't doubt she could pull it off.

Then again, Dan would insist that she give up Harry. Could she really do that?

No. She couldn't. And wouldn't. She'd carry on seeing him, no matter what lies it took. Even now, just thinking of Harry—the way he touched her—she could feel her heartbeat quickening. It wasn't his fault, but Dan had never had that effect on her.

Feeling marginally more optimistic, she opened her diary and saw to her dismay that Murray Adamson was due in thirty-five minutes. Hell! She'd never be able to get rid of him in half an hour.

To further frustrate her, the wretched man turned up late. 'Sorry about that,' he said. 'I got caught in traffic. You OK? You look a bit green about the gills. Not got something catching, have you?'

'Thank you for your concern, but I'm fine,' she lied. She felt anything but fine. She felt ghastly; sick and clammy. 'Now then,' she said. 'As I told you on the telephone last week, this is what I'm proposing—'

But whatever it was that Sally had been about to say had gone completely out of her head. 'Um . . . I wonder if you would excuse me for a couple of minutes. I've suddenly remembered something.'

She made it to the toilet in the nick of time. Bent over the pan, she heard the outer door open and shut. *Damn!* An audience. Just what she needed. It was impossible to vomit discreetly and after she'd yanked on the handle and flushed away the evidence of last night's excesses a voice called out to her. 'You all right in there?'

Oh great, it was the Iron Lady! No way was Sally going to reply. Her back against the door, she stood there in silence, her eyes closed.

'Sally? It is you in there, isn't it? Anything I can get you?'

'Err . . . no thank you,' Sally was forced to answer.

'Something you ate?'

'More than likely,' Sally muttered weakly. Oh, God, here we go again. She lurched forward in the confined space and bent over the toilet.

Remembering her abandoned client, she thought of a way to get rid of the Iron Lady. 'Fern,' she said, 'could you do me an enormous favour and ask Chandra to make my client a cup of coffee. Oh, and get her to tell him I'll be with him in five minutes.'

'Goodness! I didn't realise you had a client waiting. Why didn't you say? That's not at all professional.'

Oh, silly me, thought Sally when she heard the bathroom door closing. Perhaps you'd have preferred me to throw up all over him!

The coast now clear, Sally emerged from the cubicle. She groaned at the sight of her reflection in the mirror above the basin. She ought to go home. It wasn't fair to inflict this face on anyone.

Home. The word jarred with her. Did she even have a home any more? Of course she did, the lawyer in her snapped. Corner Cottage was as much hers as Dan's. But home. Somewhere she could rest her weary head and be sick in private. A wave of longing for Dan's tender care surged through her. Kind, dependable Dan.

No! No, no, *NO*!

She thumped the ceramic basin with her fist. Kind and dependable wasn't what she needed. She needed Harry. Wild, unpredictable Harry.

'Sorry to keep you waiting so long,' Sally said when she closed the door of her office after her.

'Feeling any better?' Murray Adamson looked at her sympathetically. 'Better?' she repeated.

'The woman who brought my coffee said you were otherwise detained being sick. Not very professional of her. If you ask me, she could have covered for you better.'

Sally smiled grimly. 'You're right, she could have.'

'Would you rather we took a rain check and did this tomorrow?'

'Would that be very inconvenient for you?'

'Not at all.' He grinned. 'I'd much rather see you when you're looking your usual gorgeous self.'

'What time tomorrow?' she said, turning the page of her diary. 'Oh, sorry, I can't do tomorrow. The day's full up. The day after?'

He fished out a small black leather diary from his jacket pocket. 'Yes,' he said. 'That'll be perfect. How about just before lunch? Then when we've finished I can take you for a bite to eat.' He smiled at her. 'You do owe me, after all.'

Five minutes later and she was slowly taking the stairs up to Harry's office. Her head was pounding painfully now.

She knocked on his door and waited for him to answer. She would feel infinitely better once she was wrapped in his arms.

With no response to her knock, she tried again and went in.

But Harry wasn't there. His office was empty.

She went over to his desk and checked his diary. According to the entry, written in his sloping hand, he was out for the rest of the day.

She groaned. No Harry. No bed. Could things get any worse?

Not wanting to let Marcus out of his sight, Dan hadn't taken him to nursery as normal and he was working from home.

Work had so far consisted of watching a whole *Thomas the Tank Engine* DVD with his son and reading a selection of books—*Spot the Dog*, *Paddington Bear* and the endless stories about Topsy and Tim.

He was now making lunch. For Marcus's benefit, soup was on the menu. Dan had no appetite. He may have appeared to Sally to be perfectly in control of himself last night, but inside he'd been close to breaking down. He'd never known such misery. He'd gone to bed and slept only intermittently. He lay there in the darkness trying to come to terms with what he'd done: he'd confronted Sally and the outcome had been to bring about an end to their marriage. Just as he'd feared.

Every time he'd come close to sliding into oblivion, his brain had jerked him awake by picturing Sally with the unknown man who had destroyed their marriage. It had been bearable suspecting the worst of her, but *knowing* it was far more painful. It was a pain that ripped through him. Again and again. There was no let up from it.

He switched off the gas. 'Soup's ready,' he called to Marcus.

The usual rules had been dispensed with and, like Dan, Marcus was still wearing his pyjamas and dressing gown. His hands were full of a fluffy green frog, a colouring book and a small red plastic bucket of chubby crayons. Marcus dumped his hoard onto the table, adding to the debris of breakfast that Dan hadn't bothered to tidy away.

Paying no attention to the mess, Dan helped Marcus into his chair Once again Dan wondered if he'd done the right thing last night. For Marcus's sake, should he have been a better man and told Sally he would forgive her if she promised him she would end the affair?

He poured the soup. Time to face facts, Danny Boy, he told himself. You are not that better man. You are as basic a man as ever walked the planet. If someone hurts you, you want to hurt them back. And if that means banishing the woman you once loved, then so be it.

He swallowed at the thought of how in love with Sally he'd once been. She had been his world. He would have done anything for her. *Anything.* Now he couldn't stand to look at her, never mind forgive her.

But a part of him couldn't shake off the thought that he might be partly to blame. She had described him as boring. Was he? Had being at home with Marcus changed him? And was there another reason why she'd had an affair? Was it because she'd suspected he'd been having one with Tatiana? Had her suspicions made her jealous and insecure, forcing her to seek affirmation elsewhere?

He'd just sat down at the table when there was a knock at the back door. Hardly in the mood for socialising, Dan ignored it. But that was impossible with Marcus sitting next to him.

'Door, Daddy,' he said helpfully. 'Thumone'th knocking.'

Dan reluctantly went to see who it was.

Chloe took one look at Dan—dishevelled and unshaven—and wished she'd come sooner. Without uttering a word, she stepped over the threshold and embraced him. Holding him tightly, she said, 'I'm so sorry, Dan. So very sorry. Tell me what happened. What did she say?'

Sally's day had passed in a nauseous daze. It was now six o'clock and all she'd managed to get down, and keep down, was strong black coffee and paracetamol. Marion, Chandra and Tom had urged her to go home—word had gone round that she was suffering from food poisoning—but she'd battled on.

Chandra had switched off her computer ten minutes ago and left, encouraging Sally to do the same.

On her desk, her mobile went off, making Sally jump. Harry! At last. Swivelling round in her chair, she checked her door was shut. 'Harry!' she cried. 'Where've you been all day?'

'Tied up with a client for hours on end.' He laughed. 'Not literally, of course. There's only one person I'd want to play those games with.'

Sally tried to join in with his good mood but failed. 'Didn't you get my messages?' She'd left three in all. Every one of them asking him to ring her. But not a single one containing the reason why.

'Only now. What's up? You sound glum.'

'I've left Dan,' she said.

'But why? What made you do that?'

This was not the response she had expected. 'We slipped up,' she said. She told him about Marcus having to go to hospital and Dan not being able to get hold of her on her mobile.

'Shit!'

'A fair enough assessment in anyone's book.'

'And your boy . . . he's OK?'

'Apparently so. I didn't get to see him. He was asleep when I got back and when it all hit the fan Dan asked me to leave. When I couldn't get in touch with you, I ended up spending the night at the Hilton here in Manchester. Where were you, Harry? Why didn't you ring me back?'

'You tried ringing my mobile last night? Sorry, I had no idea. I went for a drink with a friend when I got home.'

A drink? With a friend? Sally couldn't believe how blasé he was. 'Well, next time, check your bloody voicemail,' she snapped.

There was a pause. A long pause.

'Listen,' he said. 'I'm going to have to go. My client is insisting on taking me out for dinner tonight.'

'Harry, you can't just leave me like this! I need you. What time will you be home?'

'I'm staying over. With a bit of luck I'll have the preliminaries of the case buttoned up by tomorrow afternoon.'

'But I need you here *now*. Where am I going to spend the night?'

Another pause. 'I'm sorry, Sally, really I am, but surely the best thing all round would be for you to go home to Dan. You have your son to consider. I'll speak to you when I get back.'

The mobile went dead in her ear. Sally stared at the small device in disbelief. Then she threw it hard across her office. It bounced off the wall, dropped to the floor with a crash and split neatly in two.

She checked back into the Hilton. Once again she ordered room service and drank steadily and angrily. For the second morning in a row, she came to with a thumping headache. Groggy and horribly nauseous, she groaned, recalling the red wine and vodka chasers. Not again. Why had she done it? What had she been thinking?

She had been thinking too much; that had been the problem. She'd overreacted. Harry had only said the things he had because he wanted the best for her. He didn't want to be responsible for breaking up her marriage. It was understandable. All she had to do was convince him that her marriage was her responsibility, not his.

It was to his credit, she had concluded by the time she was showered, dressed and applying a mask of make-up, that he hadn't whooped and cheered that she was now a free woman. It was when she was slipping on her watch that she noticed the time. It was gone ten o'clock. She'd never been this late for work before. Furious with herself, she checked out from the hotel. It was ten forty-five by the time she was climbing the stairs to her office.

'I didn't think you'd be coming in today,' Chandra said when she saw her, adding: 'Shouldn't you be at home in bed? You still don't look well.'

'Too much to do,' Sally said offhandedly, breezing past to get to the safety of her office. 'Any calls for me?'

'Nothing. Apart from a message from Tom. He said he wanted to see you urgently if you did make it in today. Shall I tell him you're in? Or would you like some coffee first?'

Sally smiled gratefully. 'Coffee would be wonderful. You're such a star, Chandra.'

She had only managed a few sips of her coffee when there was a knock at her door and Tom came in. His expression was one of solemn concern. 'What is it?' she asked him;

He pulled out a chair and sat down. She noticed what appeared to be a piece of folded A4 paper in his hands. 'Tom?' she repeated.

'I'm afraid it's not good, Sally,' he said.

'I can see that. What's the problem?'

He swallowed. 'It's Harry Fox. He's formally accusing you of sexual harassment.' Tom waved the piece of paper in front of him. 'It's all here in an email he sent me this morning. He's also sent a copy to the rest of the partners. He claims you actively pursued him from the day he started work with us. He says you abused your position by saying you would blight his chances of promotion if he didn't do as you wanted.'

Sally's head began to spin. 'But he . . . he can't have said all that. It's simply not true. Please tell me you don't believe a word of it, Tom.'

Tom shook his head grimly. 'I don't know what to believe, Sally. He's been most explicit, giving dates when you insisted the two of you spend weekends together. He says it finally got too much for him this weekend, when you announced that you'd left your husband to be with him. He claims you've deluded yourself all along, imagining him to have feelings for you. He hasn't stated in his email who he's instructed to act for him, but he's hinted it's a firm here in Manchester.'

Sally gasped. Then she rushed from her office to be sick.

By mid-afternoon the only topic of conversation of any interest to anyone was Sally. Emails were circulating at the speed of light, most of them titled *When Sally Met Harry*. Sally only knew this because Chandra had offered to keep her informed. Her loyalty touched Sally.

'I know you couldn't possibly have done those things you've been accused of,' the young girl said. 'You're not that kind of a woman.'

Sally could have wept. What did Chandra know of her? What did any of them know of the real Sally Oliver?

Tom had suggested that she should go home and stay there until he and the rest of the partners had decided what to do next. Apparently Harry was lying low. He'd taken a fortnight's holiday as of today.

But home was the last place Sally wanted to go. She sat in her office in a state of shock. In one fell swoop, her reputation would be shot. Not just here at McKenzie Stuart, but in the whole of Manchester's legal system. She would be a joke. A laughing stock.

How could she fight back? How could she retain any semblance of respect? And how could Harry have done this to her? More to the point, why? Why had he turned on her this way?

On the brink of wasting vital energy on crying, she pulled herself together. Self-pity wouldn't get her anywhere. She needed a plan. She also needed some clean clothes; she'd worn the same suit for two days running. Nothing else for it, she would have to go home.

She would tough it out with Dan, she told herself after she'd informed Chandra she was going home after all. What's more, there was no reason on earth why she shouldn't move back in properly. It was her house as much as Dan's. Hell, she was the one paying the mortgage!

By the time she was driving into the village, she wasn't feeling quite so sure of herself. Moving back in was an admission that Harry didn't want her. First Dan had rejected her, now Harry.

Dan's car was in its usual place on the drive and she parked behind it. She put her key in the lock of the front door and let herself in. She closed the door and stood very still on the mat, listening for signs of Dan and Marcus. Nothing. The house was as still as the grave. She hadn't anticipated that. She went through to the kitchen. It looked like a bomb had hit it. There were plates, bowls, mugs, plastic cups, pans and toys strewn everywhere.

She went upstairs, following a trail of toys and discarded clothes. Marcus's bedroom carpet had disappeared beneath a sea of Duplo, cars, trains, track, jigsaws and cuddly toys. His bed was unmade and the small wooden table and chair he liked to sit at were tipped over.

She had never seen the house look like this before. She bent down to pick up Marcus's pyjamas from the floor. She could smell her son on the patterned fabric. His warm, tucked-up-in-bed little boy smell.

She crossed the landing to her and Dan's bedroom. Here again the bed was unmade and while the room was nowhere near as untidy as Marcus's, it was a far cry from its customary neat order. She went and sat on the bed, suddenly feeling overwhelmingly tired. How tempting it was to lie back and pull the duvet up over her. But what would that solve?

What might solve everything was apologising to Dan. *I'm sorry, Dan.* Would that be so very difficult? She hadn't fully comprehended until the other night, when Dan had found her out, just how much she had subconsciously relied upon his calm, dependable nature to contain that dangerously wild streak within her. Yet perhaps it had been inevitable that one day the Sally Wilson of old would break free.

But what if she begged Dan to forgive her? Would he? And if her marriage looked to be rock solid, would Tom and the rest of the partners somehow make Harry's accusations go away?

Even if he did, her reputation would always be tarnished. The worst-case scenario that Sally dreaded was that she might be asked to leave the firm. One of them would have to leave; that much she knew. It was her or Harry. Why was he doing this to her? How could he be so cruel? Had he meant any of what he'd said and done?

A tear slid slowly down her cheek. She dashed it away with her hand, determined not to give in to self-pity. Hearing the sound of car doors slamming, she got up from the bed and looked out of the window. Dan and Marcus were on the road standing next to a Honda Civic. They weren't alone. Tatiana, Queen of the Bloody Fairies, was with them. Marcus was reaching up to kiss her and Dan was . . .

Watching what happened next—Dan putting his arms round Tatiana and holding her close—sent a roar of fury crashing through Sally's ears. The other night Dan had been so full of self-righteousness, playing the part of a wronged husband, when all along he'd not been so innocent after all. She'd suspected that there was more than just a work relationship between them; now she knew her instinct had been right.

Furious that he'd played her for a fool, she watched Tatiana get back in her car and drive off, then flung open the wardrobe doors and began chucking clothes onto the bed.

Downstairs she could hear voices. 'Mummy must be home,' she heard Dan say, followed by, 'She's not down here. Let's try upstairs.'

'Hello, Marcus,' she said brightly when they came in. 'Come and let me see your chin. I hear you've had quite a time of it while I was away. Fancy falling off Charlie's climbing frame like that! How many stitches did you have put in?'

'Nine.'

'Goodness! And were you very brave when it happened?'

Marcus glanced over towards the door where Dan seemed to be rooted to the spot. 'I wath a bit brave, Daddy, wathn't I?'

'You were extraordinarily brave, Marcus. Much braver than I would have been.' Dan switched his gaze to Sally. 'We've just been down to the surgery for the nurse to check him out. She says he's healing well.'

'And let me guess,' Sally said, 'you just happened to meet your chum from work at the surgery?'

Dan stiffened. 'Don't, Sally. Just don't.'

'You seem to be saying that to me a lot these days. I wonder why. A guilty conscience?'

'My conscience is clear. Can you say the same? Marcus, do you want to do downstairs and choose a DVD for us to watch later?'

'Thomath, Thomath, Thomath,' Marcus chanted as he scooted off happily.

'What have you told him?' Sally asked.

'The usual, that his mother is busy with work. How have you been?'

'I've been OK,' she'd said.

'If you don't mind me saying, you don't look it.'

'Thanks! But then nor do you.' It was true; Dan did look a mess. He didn't look like he'd slept much in the last forty-eight hours.

She was about to make a bigger effort to ease the hostility between them when Dan said, 'So how's it going with the new man in your life? It must be some cosy love nest you've got going; the two of you spending the day working together and then spending all night together.'

'You disappoint me, Dan. I thought you'd be more adult about this. Resorting to cheap shots really isn't helpful.'

He stepped towards her. 'I'll tell you what isn't helpful,' he said. 'It's you carrying on as if none of this matters. Divorce might be part and parcel of your everyday life, but for me it's near enough the end of the world. So if it's all the same to you, an occasional cheap shot from me is my way of dealing with the unthinkable.'

'Divorce? Who said anything about us getting divorced?'

'Isn't that the inevitable consequence of you falling out of love with me and falling in love with someone else?'

Sally blinked. 'I never said I'd stopped loving you.'

'You didn't need to. Your actions said it for you. And if I'm brutally honest, I don't love you any more. At least, not the woman you've become. I'd have expected that to make the situation more bearable. But it doesn't.' He looked at the clothes she'd thrown on the bed. 'I'll leave you to your packing. Do you have an address you can give me?'

Shocked at the cold finality of his manner and his words, Sally said, 'Work. You can contact me at work. And of course my mobile . . .' She stopped herself short, remembering her smashed phone. 'My mobile's broken,' she said. 'I'll let you know when I've replaced it.'

'**M**ummy's got to go away again,' Sally said.

His eyes glued to the television screen, Marcus nodded vaguely.

Sally moved so that she was directly in front of his line of vision. When she was sure she had his full attention, she said, 'I want you to know that while I'm away, I'll try and ring every evening to speak to you before you go to bed. OK?'

He nodded and strained his neck so he could see the television. 'Look,' he said, pointing, 'Perthy'th thtuck in the thunnel.'

Dan helped Sally put her luggage in her car. It was as if he couldn't wait to get rid of her. She switched on the ignition and when she looked up after putting on her seat belt, there was no sign of Dan. He was back inside the house, the door closed.

She'd driven no further than the village green when she stopped the car and burst into tears. What was she doing? Why hadn't she told Dan the truth, that Harry didn't want her and that she had nowhere to go?

Go back and tell him, she told herself. Go back and tell him it has all been a terrible mistake. Beg his forgiveness. But her pride wouldn't let her. She just couldn't admit that she'd made such a mess of things.

She lowered her head to the steering wheel and cried harder still, loudly and messily. A gentle tapping sound on the side window had her nearly jumping out of her skin. To add to her humiliation, there was Chloe's boyfriend looking at her.

Chapter Nine

SETH WAS SURPRISED at the way Chloe was treating her friend. He didn't know all the details, but he was aware that their last meeting had been acrimonious and that, since then, Sally had confessed to having an affair and Chloe was upset about the effect this was having on Dan.

When he'd arrived outside Chloe's cottage to spend the evening with her, he'd recognised Sally in her car across the road. Slumped over the steering wheel, there was obviously something wrong. Concerned, he'd gone over to see if there was anything he could do to help. She had been sobbing so violently, he'd insisted he take her inside to Chloe's. But now here was Chloe, treating her with brutal contempt.

'You should have thought more about the consequences of what you were doing,' Chloe said hotly. 'Have you any idea what you've done to Dan? You've destroyed him. I'll never forgive you for that.'

Sally blew her nose loudly. 'He didn't look too destroyed just now when I saw him,' she mumbled.

'He's putting on a brave front for Marcus's sake, of course. Didn't you once think about Marcus when you were cheating on Dan?'

Sally started to cry again.

'Oh, go on, when all else fails, turn on the waterworks.'

'Chloe,' Seth said quietly, 'I don't think this is helping.'

Chloe shot him a fierce look. 'And what would? Telling her she's done nothing wrong?' Chloe turned back to Sally. 'I've had enough of your crocodile tears. Why don't you go and seek solace in the arms of the man who clearly means so much to you?'

Sally started to wail. 'I . . . I can't,' she stuttered. 'It's over. He's . . . he's not interested in me any more. I don't think he ever was . . . And now I have nowhere to go.' She buried her face in another tissue.

'Whoever said bad people don't get what they deserve, got it wrong. Wow, Seth, I could almost believe in that God of yours based on this turn of events. Is this what you call biblical justice?'

If Seth had been surprised earlier, now he was shocked. And dismayed. He couldn't believe Chloe's behaviour.

'Could I have a word with you?' he asked, tipping his head towards the sitting room. Alone with her, he said, 'Chloe, you've made your point with Sally, why not show a little compassion now?'

Chloe looked at Seth with astonishment. 'Compassion?' she repeated. 'You didn't see Dan. You didn't see what she's done to him. Oh, no, if you don't mind, I'll save my compassion for people who deserve it.'

He put a hand on her arm. 'Chloe, she's totally messed up. What's more, she knows it. Don't make it any harder for her.'

'You'll be telling me next to offer her a bed for the night.'

'Would that be so out of the question?'

'You're serious, aren't you? Forget it; I couldn't be that disloyal to Dan.'

'Doesn't loyalty to an old friend mean anything?'

'She's not my friend any more. She's crossed too many lines for me to value what we once had.'

He frowned. 'Surely not?'

'If you'd heard the things she said about me and you, you'd think the same. The last time I saw her she was doing her best to split us up.'

'But you said yourself, she hasn't been herself for some time.'

'That doesn't give her the right to criticise and make fun of you. Or accuse me of only being interested in you because I'm desperate to have a baby. Now, if you'll let go of me, I'm going to tell her to leave.'

'Please don't,' he said, removing his hand. 'She has nowhere to go.'

'Not my problem,' Chloe said emphatically.

Disappointed, Seth followed Chloe back to the kitchen.

'Time to bring the curtain down on your performance,' Chloe said brusquely. 'I want you to go now.'

Sally stood up, her shoulders hunched. She was at the door when she turned and said, 'I'm sorry, Chloe. Really I am.'

'Me too,' Chloe said off-handedly.

When Sally had closed the door after her, it took Seth all of two seconds to make a decision he hoped he wouldn't regret.

Chloe couldn't believe it. How could Seth have taken Sally's side over hers? 'I can't stand by and not do anything to help,' he'd said when Chloe had tried to stop him. He'd grabbed his keys and then hurried after Sally. 'I'll ring you later,' he'd called over his shoulder.

'Don't bother!' she'd shouted. 'I wouldn't want you to take time out from letting that manipulative piece of work cry on your shoulder!'

She didn't know who she was more cross with: Seth for interfering, or Sally for duping him. How could he have been so easily taken in?

But there was another source of her anger. It was the comment she'd let slip about her being desperate for a baby. Of all the things she wouldn't want him to know about, it was that. Nothing would more effectively make a man lose interest in a girl than thinking he was being fast-tracked into fatherhood. But that all seemed hypothetical now. Did she really want to be involved with a man who could so easily dismiss her opinion and favour Sally's feelings over hers?

Calm now, and more in control of herself, Sally looked around her. From the looks of things, the bedroom that Seth had shown her up to doubled up as his office. Crammed into the small space was a single bed and a cheap pine desk with a computer and printer on it, along with an anglepoise lamp, two black plastic 'in' and 'out' trays stacked on top of each other, and a framed photograph. The photograph was of Chloe.

Sally picked it up and stared at it. The one and only true friend she'd ever had now hated her. Her eyes filled with tears. Yet more tears. Not since she'd had postnatal depression had she cried so much.

She put the photograph back in its place, sat on the bed and thought of Seth's wholly unexpected offer for her to stay with him until she got herself sorted. Her accommodation might not be up to much, but it had to be better than another soulless, drunken night at the Hilton.

Her unexpected host was currently downstairs making them some supper. She could smell onions frying and hear music playing. There was something faintly comforting about the combination.

But why? Why was he doing this for her? She was practically a stranger to him. Christian duty, she supposed. This was too good an opportunity for him to pass up, playing the part of Good Samaritan.

She cringed at the thought. Who'd have thought she would sink so low as to be a charity case? He better not think she was a captive audience for him to hit her with some moralising, preachy number. One hint of that and she'd hightail it back to the Hilton.

After a good night's sleep and zero alcohol intake, Sally was sitting at her office desk feeling a little more like herself. What that actually meant, she wasn't sure. When was the last time she had felt entirely herself? And who was she anyway? Was she Sally Oliver, wife and mother and respected top divorce lawyer? Or was she Sally Wilson, reckless headcase bent on self-destruction? She had the sensation of having gone through a prolonged period of madness. She felt exhausted and weirdly disengaged. It was almost impossible to know what was real and what wasn't. What did feel real was the certainty that there was no way back.

When she'd arrived for work it had been evident that no one had expected her to show her face. With a demonstration of bravado she'd fended off the raised eyebrows and whispered comments. Mostly, though, everyone was leaving her alone. Thank God work had always been her refuge. Without it, she'd be lost.

She'd woken early that morning and, eager not to be late again for work, she'd dressed hurriedly and headed downstairs. Seth had beaten her to it. The smell of bacon and freshly brewed coffee welcomed her. 'Nothing like a bacon sandwich to set you up for the day,' he said, poking about under the grill with a fork. They'd eaten in the kitchen, where they'd had supper the night before.

She'd told him outright that she didn't want to discuss her marriage and to her relief he'd respected her wishes. He'd offered no moralising advice, only reiterated his invitation for her to stay with him as long as she needed. She really didn't know what to make of his generosity.

'Did you manage to speak to Chloe?' she'd asked him, knowing that he'd tried several times during the course of the previous evening.

'No,' he'd said. 'She's not answering her phone or her mobile. I think . . . I think she's cross with me.'

As Sally waited for Murray Adamson to arrive for his appointment, She recalled that hesitation in Seth's reply and felt a trickle of guilt. She hoped that she hadn't caused a rift between the two of them. Surely Chloe couldn't be that angry? But even as she wondered this, she knew that she'd never seen Chloe so furious. Never.

Murray Adamson arrived his customary ten minutes late. 'Let's talk business over lunch,' he said. 'I've booked us a table at Heathcote's.'

Sally didn't argue. She was glad to get out of the office.

The restaurant wasn't busy and they had the pick of the tables. Once they were settled and their order taken—Murray having insisted on asking for two glasses of champagne—Sally reached for her briefcase.

'Put that away,' he said.

'But you said business over lunch.'

He flashed her one of his I-always-get-what-I-want smiles. 'I say a lot of things, not all of which I mean. Relax and enjoy the meal. Or at least try to. I've never seen you look so strung out. What's troubling you?'

A waitress brought them their champagne. 'Well?' Murray said. 'You haven't answered my question. What's wrong?'

'Nothing's wrong,' she replied, annoyed. 'Other than resenting the fact that you've tricked me into having lunch with you.'

'For which I make no apology.' He raised his glass and waited for her to do likewise. 'Cheers,' he said when she'd obliged. 'Here's to the future and a successful outcome to my divorce.' He put his glass against his mouth, took a long sip, then said, 'I sincerely hope you won't disappear from my life entirely when my divorce is final.'

'That remains to be seen,' she said. 'If you marry again and find someone other than your wife irresistible, who knows, you might require my services a third time.'

He laughed. 'Trust me, that won't happen. I intend to find exactly the right woman to be wife number three. I've had it with arm candy and nothing more substantial than candyfloss between the ears. I want a woman with a brain. A woman who's complex and who fascinates me. A woman who doesn't bore me. Someone like you, for instance.'

Sally put down her glass. 'Stop it, Murray. I'm really not in the mood to listen to any of this nonsense. If you can't be sensible I suggest we return to the office and go through the points we need to cover.'

He put a hand out to her, touching her wrist lightly. 'I'm sorry,' he said. 'Forgive me, please. It's just—' His words fell away.

She stared at his fingers, then looked up at his face. 'It's just what?'

'I like you. I like you a lot. Surely you must have realised that? But I respect the fact that you're happily married. That's why I've never pushed it. You *are* happily married, aren't you, Sally? Sally? Oh my God, I've made you cry. I'm so sorry.'

Two choices, Sally told herself when she accepted that she couldn't hide in the ladies' room any longer. She could either lie to Murray and say she wasn't feeling well, or she could brazen it out, insist they keep their personal lives to themselves, and discuss business only. She would have to do it tactfully, of course. She couldn't afford to offend a client like Murray Adamson. But that was the least of her concerns. If Harry took her to court for sexual harassment, she'd be lucky to have a job.

Thinking about Harry was a mistake. The pain of his betrayal ripped through her. What wouldn't she do to ring him and tell him exactly what she thought of him . . . But no. She mustn't do that. She must have no contact with him whatsoever.

She wrenched open the door, marched back to the table where Murray was waiting for her and decided upon the latter option. But his anxious expression as he rose to pull out her chair caused her throat to bunch and she slumped into her seat.

He sat down, slid his chair nearer to hers and placed his hand on her shoulder. 'Sally, can I say something?'

She nodded.

'As someone who cares about you,' Murray said, his voice low, 'I want you to know that you can talk to me as a friend. Nothing you tell me will go any further. I mean that.'

'There's nothing to tell,' she managed to say.

'Is it your husband? Is he having an affair? Is that it?'

She closed her eyes at the absurdity of what Murray was saying.

'The man's a fool,' he went on. 'He doesn't realise how lucky he is to have you. If I was married to you I wouldn't—'

'It's not him,' Sally said, 'it's me. I'm the one who's been having an affair. It's over now.' She looked directly at Murray. 'And I don't know why I've just told you all that. Not when I hardly know you.'

'In my experience, it's usually easier to confide in someone outside the immediate circle of one's friends. What happened? Was your husband neglecting you?'

'You sound as if you're trying to lay all the blame at my husband's feet. I can face up to the fact that I, and I alone, am responsible for my actions, you know.'

'I don't doubt that for a minute. But what did your lover give you that your husband didn't? That's the question. Excitement? Great sex? Or, as I suspect, did you get a kick out of playing by different rules?'

In spite of everything, Sally smiled. 'I would never have had you down as so perceptive. Or such a relationship expert.'

'What can I say? I've cocked up enough to have learned something along the way.'

It was Seth's and Chloe's day off. He'd left countless messages for her to ring him, but he hadn't received a single reply. Whichever way he viewed her silence, it didn't look good.

He parked on the road outside her cottage and with the engine still running and the wipers working at the rain on the windscreen, he rehearsed one more time what he was going to say. He got out, pressed his finger to the doorbell and waited. Then he went round to the back of the house. He found her in the garden where, despite the rain, she was digging with considerable energy in one of the flowerbeds.

'Need a hand?' he called out.

She spun round. 'Oh, it's you. What do you want?' She drove the spade into the damp earth, pushing down on it hard with her foot.

'I want to talk to you. Why haven't you answered my messages?'

'I would have thought that was blindingly obvious.'

He drew closer to her. 'Any chance we can go inside and talk?'

'No. I want to get this laurel out.'

'Why don't you give me the spade and I'll do it for you?'

'No.'

He held his hand out for the spade. 'Don't be churlish.'

'Go to hell! You've got a cheek coming here and telling me what to do.'

The rain was coming down harder now. It was drenching them both.

'If this is about Sally,' Seth said, 'you have to understand that I'm neither condoning what she's done nor condemning her for it. I'm merely trying to help her find a way through the mess she's created.'

'Bully for you!'

'Chloe, please. Don't let a little thing like this come between us.'

'It might be little to you, but it's not to me. You made a choice and it's a choice I can't live with.'

'So that's it? Because I'm trying to help Sally, it's over between us?'

'Looks that way.' She sighed. 'Let's face it, Seth, it was never going to work between us. We're too different. And if you're really honest with yourself, you'd accept that I was never going to be able to live up to the high standards you'd expect of me.'

'You don't really believe that?'

'I do, as a matter of fact. I've come to understand that I could never be good enough in your eyes.' Her face looked as if had turned to marble.

'I don't believe you.'

'You're calling me a liar now?' Again the same cold, stony expression.

Suddenly it was more than Seth could take. Anger blazed inside him. He grabbed the spade out of her hands and hurled it with all his strength. It shot through the air and landed with an explosive clatter against the fence at the end of the garden. 'I'm not leaving here until I've made you change your mind,' he shouted.

She took a small step back from him. 'That's never going to happen,' she said. 'For the simple reason that we're chalk and cheese. One of us would have to compromise and I'm sorry, but I'm not prepared to do that. You have your principles you live by and I have mine.'

'You couldn't be more wrong, Chloe.'

'See! That's the problem between us. You're always judging me. I can't do anything without you telling me I'm wrong.'

'I've never judged you!' he shouted again. 'Not once. Don't you dare ever accuse me of that.'

'You do it all the time. Only you don't realise it.'

'For fuck's sake, Chloe, this is crazy. As far as I can see, the only person judging you is you. Perhaps you ought to ask yourself why.'

As the rain continued to hammer down mercilessly, she slowly turned away from him. In furious disbelief he watched her calmly go and retrieve the spade.

Would it make any difference if he threw his arms round her and told her how much he loved her? Rooted to the spot, he opened his mouth to call out to her, but the words wouldn't come. He blinked as the rain continued to drench him, and then he walked away fast.

Chloe turned and watched him go. Through the rain and her tears, she swallowed the urge to cry out to him, 'Come back! Don't leave me!'

'You've broken up with Seth? But why?'

Much against her will, Chloe was at Corner Cottage. Ten minutes ago she had phoned Dan to see how he was and when he'd asked if she was feeling all right, she had stupidly, oh, so stupidly, burst into tears. Dan had then insisted she come round to talk properly. And so here she was, unburdening herself to a dear friend who had more than enough troubles of his own to contend with.

Trying hard to hold it together, she said, 'Dan, you have more important things to think about than my silly problems.'

'But Seth was the best thing to have happened to you in ages. You were so right together. I hadn't seen you so happy in a long while. I can't believe you've ended things with him because of Sally.'

She shook her head vehemently. 'It isn't just because of Sally. It's because we weren't right together. Not really. It was that job of his. Let's face it; the Church is no place for someone like me. I could never have shared Seth's world.'

'Would you have had to?'

'I think he would have wanted me to, eventually.'

'I'm not so sure. I think he cared about you too much to do anything that would put him at risk of losing you.'

Chloe turned away from Dan. She should never have agreed to come here. Ringing him had been a mistake. She didn't need to hear him singing Seth's praises. It only made her feel worse. If that was possible.

As far as I can see, the only person judging you, is you. Perhaps you ought to ask yourself why? The truth of Seth's words had hit home in a way nothing else could have done. Those few words had shocked her more than even his anger. But it added to her conviction that she had been right to end it. Better that she did it before he turned on her.

It was easy for him to profess now that he didn't judge her, but if he ever found out what she was capable of, he would definitely look at her anew. And he had judged her over Sally, hadn't he? He'd accused her of not being compassionate. And if he could judge and condemn her for siding with Dan, what else could he judge and condemn her for?

Exhausted, Dan went straight to bed after Chloe left. The endless, grinding effort to retain an air of outer confidence was getting to him, leaving him drained with a cold, inner emptiness.

He lay on his back in the dark, his eyes closed, waiting for sleep to come, but knowing it would be some time yet. And because the nightmares he'd thought he'd put behind him had resumed, sleep, when it did come, meant that he was plunged into the familiar circle of hell, caught up in the relentless nightmare of failure. Of failing to save that little boy's life. Of failing to save his marriage.

He forced himself to think of practical things. Work. If he was to provide for Marcus, he'd have to work full time. And not for the trust. They wouldn't be able to afford the level of salary he now needed. He'd ring Tatiana in the morning.

He'd been leaving the surgery yesterday afternoon with Marcus when he'd spotted her car driving through the village. She'd stopped to offer him and Marcus a lift home. She'd been unable to hide the look of shock in her eyes at his appearance, and, as quietly as he could so that Marcus wouldn't overhear, he'd explained why he looked like hell. When they'd got home he'd hugged her. Big mistake. It had felt good. It had also been witnessed by Sally, something he regretted.

He hustled his thoughts on. Top of his list was to find himself some legal representation. He opened his eyes. Did he really want a divorce? What if he and Sally could turn things round? It was possible. For Marcus's sake he could almost imagine trying to do that. It would save his son from so much heartache and confusion. But would it be enough for Dan? Would he be happy? Or would he drive himself mad wondering if Sally was being unfaithful to him again?

Dan glanced at the alarm clock on the bedside table. He could just about make out from the luminous hands that it was twenty minutes past one. It was going to be a long night.

Thursday morning and Sally was sitting in her office in a state of numb incredulity. She had just been told she had been suspended for the foreseeable future. She must gather her things and leave straight away. What's more, Tom hadn't even had the courage to tell her himself. Bill had informed her of the firm's decision. 'We don't have any choice,' he had said. 'We've suspended Harry as well, but he's resigned.'

She shouldn't have been surprised by the decision. After all, it was standard procedure in these cases. It still came as a shock, though. Somehow she had convinced herself it wouldn't come to this.

A knock at her door had her snapping, 'Yes!'

It was Chandra. 'I've been instructed not to put any more calls through to you,' she said nervously, 'but Murray Adamson is insisting he talks to you. What shall I do?'

'Put him through,' Sally said with a sigh. 'And don't worry, I'll deal with the consequences if anyone finds out.'

'What the hell's going on?' Murray demanded. 'I was told you were unavailable and would be so for some time.'

'I've been suspended.'

'What on earth for?'

'You don't need to know.'

'Sally, I meant what I said yesterday. Whatever you tell me is strictly between the two of us. What's happened?'

She hesitated. Then thought, Oh, what the hell! 'What I didn't tell you yesterday is that the man I was seeing was a colleague and now he's accusing me of sexual harassment.'

'The bastard! Has he been suspended as well?'

'Yes. But apparently he's taken the moral high ground by resigning.'

'And what have you told Tom and Bill?'

'I've admitted nothing.'

'Does anyone in the office know for sure that you'd been having an affair with this man?'

'Absolutely not. I may have behaved recklessly, but I didn't lose all reason. I was still careful.'

Murray was silent. 'In that case,' he said at length, 'seeing as you've got some time on your hands, are you free to meet for a coffee?'

'I should say no to you. I'm in enough trouble as it is.'

'No point in doing anything by half. Meet me at Harvey Nicks in the brasserie. And then you can tell me the whole story and we'll see if we can't find a way out of it. How does that sound?'

Murray was waiting for her at a table where he was reading a copy of the *Financial Times*. He stood up and kissed her on each cheek. 'Right,' he said when they were seated and two cups of coffee had been brought to them. 'Tell me the whole story. Leave nothing out. I think I might have come up with something to help you.'

She frowned. 'What on earth do you mean?'

'I'll explain in a moment. But first I want to know all the details and *exactly* what you've told Tom and anyone else in the office.'

The sincerity on Murray's face compelled Sally to do as he asked. It felt good to tell someone the truth.

Resting his elbows on the table he said, 'So, this is how it currently stands. At no stage did you ever admit there was a shred of truth to the allegations. You've denied everything. Have I got that right?'

She nodded. 'Which, I know, makes me a liar.'

Murray laughed. 'Give me a break; all lawyers are liars. Now, listen carefully; this is what we're going to do. And I think you'll agree that as ideas go, it's the sweetest. Together we're going to tuck that Harry Fox up good and proper.'

Since the next two days would be taken up with an ecumenical confer-ence in York, Seth was working at home, trying to squeeze an extra ten hours into his day. He was also praying for inspiration. This coming Sunday it was his turn to take the family service, and the theme of his sermon—as he'd planned earlier in the week—was forgiveness. His opening line was: '*The unforgiveable sin is that of refusing to forgive another.*' As well as being his opening line, it was, so far, his only line. He was stuck.

For the last hour and a half he'd been staring at the screen of his laptop, trying to think of something insightful and inspiring to say. But his brain had shut down, owing to his inability to forgive Chloe's cold-ness towards him. And, yes, anyone tempted to point out the irony of this would get short shrift.

It was beyond his comprehension to understand how she could have treated him the way she had. Not only that, there was the manner in which she had turned her back on her old friend so heartlessly. Fair enough, Sally may have made a colossal error of judgment in having an affair, but hadn't Chloe ever made a mistake? He certainly had.

He would never have thought Chloe would be one of those people who would condemn another out of hand, yet this was exactly what she'd done. What bothered him most were her remarks about her not living up to the high standards he would expect of her, and that she would never be good enough in his eyes.

He stood up and went to the window. It was raining again. He sighed and wondered how much longer Sally would remain here. As yet there had been no mutterings in the parish about him having a lone female guest staying, but it wouldn't be long before word went round.

Perhaps he had been misguided to invite Sally to stay, but if a similar situation arose again, he'd do exactly the same thing. Let people leap to their conclusions. What did he care? He'd lost the woman he loved.

'What do you think?'

'I think you're mad. Stark raving bonkers. It would never work.'

Murray laughed. 'But you like the idea, don't you? Admit it.'

Sally didn't know what to make of the man sitting opposite her. What he was suggesting was breathtaking in its audacity.

'You're not really serious, are you?' she said.

'You bet I am.'

'But why? Why would you go to such lengths on my behalf?'

With what she suspected was practised ease, he slid his hand across the table and touched hers. 'I think you know why.'

With equal ease, Sally slid her hand out from under his. 'You're not expecting something in return, are you? Because I'll warn you now: that isn't going to happen.'

He smiled. 'All I want is for the best lawyer in town to take care of my divorce. I don't trust anyone else. Are we on? Can I talk to Tom? Persuade him Harry has no case and that you should be reinstated?'

Sally chewed on her lip. 'OK, tell me again how it's going to work.'

'It's quite simple. I tell them you and I have been having an affair since April. Along comes Harry, who makes a play for you. You tell him to back off, but he won't. He starts hassling you, discovers our secret relationship, tries to force you into having an affair with him, says if you don't he'll tell the senior partners about us. When you still refuse to play ball with him, he turns nasty and sends that email to

Tom and the rest of the partners, accusing you of sexual harassment.'

'And the reason I never told Tom what Harry was up to?'

'You were between a rock and a hard place. You were worried how the firm would react to you shagging one of its most valued clients.'

'How about the messages I left on his mobile when I broke my golden rule and tried to get in touch with him?'

'You'd decided you'd had enough and wanted to talk to him about his behaviour or you'd go to Tom and the rest of the partners.'

'And the dates he'll say he and I went away together?'

'We say he's deluded because those were the weekends you spent with me.'

'But what if Harry persists and takes this to court? I can't commit perjury. Do that and my career really will be over.'

'Trust me, it won't go to court. Harry Fox will climb down. I know his sort. He's so low he could look up a snake's arse.'

'Do you really think they'll buy our version of events?'

'Completely. I'm one of the firm's most valued clients; they won't argue with me for fear of losing my business. And, as I said earlier, it will be me who goes to them with the story. You won't have to be there. That way, it's me lying and not you. Now then, when do you want me to hit Tom with our revelations?'

The next day Sally had no reason to get up early and so she lay in bed listening to Seth moving about the house.

She decided that one of the things she had to do today was find somewhere to live. Should she look for a small flat closer to the office, or something near to Eastbury so she could see Marcus without too much difficulty? She pictured Corner Cottage and experienced a flash of anger. It was as much her home as it was Dan's. Why shouldn't she return there? But then she remembered why she hadn't wanted to go back; she couldn't admit to Dan that she had been rejected by her lover.

Thinking of Dan made her realise that she had hardly thought of him in the last twenty-four hours. All her thoughts had revolved around her job—perhaps a stark reflection of what was important to her. But why shouldn't it be? She'd worked hard to get where she was. What she'd achieved at McKenzie Stuart was as crucial to her identity as any part of her DNA. It was who she was. Should she have to apologise for that?

But mothers weren't supposed to think or behave the way she did. Mothers were supposed to feel guilty if they didn't put in the regulation amount of time with their children.

She flung the duvet away from her and sat up. None of this meant that Marcus wasn't important to Sally. He was. He just wasn't the centre of her world, as he was for Dan. Secretly she harboured the hope that one day, when Marcus was older, they would have more in common and that he would understand the person she was and maybe respect her.

A knock at the door had her getting out of bed, slipping on her dressing gown and opening the door.

'Sorry to disturb you so early,' Seth said, 'I just wanted to let you know I'm going now.' He'd explained to her over supper the night before about the conference he was attending in York. He told her to treat his house as her own during his absence. He handed her a piece of paper. 'My mobile number, in case you need me.'

'Thank you. Is there anything I can do while you're away?' she asked. 'Any shopping you need? Or perhaps . . . look, I know it's none of my business, but I was just wondering, and I know it's a long shot, but if Chloe will agree to see me, would you like me to talk to her?'

'That's very kind of you, but you might just as well know, I very much doubt I'll be seeing Chloe again.'

'But why, what's happened?'

'Chloe's decided it was never going to work out for us and has pulled the plug on me.'

'Is it because of me?'

She could see he was choosing his words with care. 'It might look that way,' he said slowly, 'but, essentially, it's me Chloe's got a problem with and I don't think you can fix that.'

Seth had attended enough ecumenical conferences to know they all had one thing in common; they were a sizzling hotbed of diocesan gossip. It was usually what made attending them worth while.

However, by lunchtime, following two plenary sessions on Inner City Outreach, he was regretting being there. The ecumenical tom-toms must have recently been given a sound thrashing because he was repeatedly being asked about his new girlfriend. 'Old news,' he kept saying with as much indifference as he could muster.

He joined the lunch queue with Father Jim O'Brien, a rascally septu-agenarian from Waterford. He was one of the speakers for the conference and someone Seth had always admired for his plain speaking.

'So what went wrong, then, Seth? The way I heard it, the parish was anticipating wedding invitations.'

Seth pushed his tray along the counter ledge until it was nudging another tray in front of him. 'It's complicated,' he said evasively.

'These things always are. Was it the job? Did she not share your commitment? That can be the devil for buggering up a relationship.'

'Partly.'

'Not much you can do about that. Hang in there, lad. Have you got anyone you can talk to? I can't imagine Owen would be much of a listener in his current state. The word is,' Jim lowered his voice, 'Owen wants out asap. And you know what that means. Especially as you're due to be fully priested in December.'

A week ago and Jim's words, would have had him inwardly cheering. To take over the running of St Michael's would have been exactly what he'd have wanted. But now it wasn't. He needed to move on. He wasn't strong enough to stay in Crantsford and risk bumping into Chloe. He needed distance between them.

'You look like I've just flicked you with a wet towel, Seth. I thought you'd be pleased.'

Forcing a smile to his face, Seth said, 'To satisfy my curiosity, from whom did you hear it?'

Jim laughed. 'As an ex-copper you should know better than to ask who my informant is. Now, would it help to mend your broken heart if I indulged in some matchmaking? I know of a pretty curate in Matlock who might be just the thing to lift your spirits. Her name's Eleanor.'

On tenterhooks for the last hour, Sally grabbed her new mobile as soon as it went off. Just as she hoped it would be, it was Murray. 'How did it go?' she asked him.

'Is there any chance you can come into town?' he replied gravely.

Everyone at the trust responded with sadness and disappointment to Dan's news that he would be leaving.

'You've made quite an impact here,' Tatiana said when he accepted her offer of a cup of coffee. 'We're all desperately sorry to be losing you.'

They were in her office, the atmosphere taut and awkward.

'Thanks,' he said. 'I'm sorry for letting you all down.'

'Don't apologise, Dan. Your priorities have changed; we understand that. How's Marcus?'

'He's fine. His mouth's healing well. He'll have an impressive scar to show off to the girls when he's older.' Dan knew Tatiana wasn't referring solely to his son's accident, but he didn't want to tell her that Marcus hardly seemed to notice his mother's absence.

'And you?'

He shrugged. 'Not bad. I'd suspected for a while that things weren't right and initially I felt a sense of relief when I learned the truth. But now I'm angry and can't stop thinking how badly this will affect Marcus.'

'Don't let it get to you, Dan. My parents divorced when I was very young. I was five at the time. But I like to think I've turned out OK.'

'You seem more than OK to me. You're one of the most cheerful and optimistic people I know.'

She smiled. 'There you go, then. Marcus will be fine. How could he be otherwise with a great dad like you?'

'I haven't been so great lately.'

She looked at him with sad eyes. 'Why are you so hard on yourself?'

Beneath her scrutinising stare, he shifted uneasily in his chair. 'Perhaps it's because I blame myself. If I'd been a better husband, Sally wouldn't have needed to look elsewhere for excitement. She described me as boring and our marriage as stultifying. I had no idea she felt that way. So where does that leave me?'

'It leaves you free to make a new life for yourself, Dan,' she said quietly.

They stared at each other in silence. Dan was remembering their last conversation in this very room. *I wish things were different*, he'd said. He may have got his wish, but he knew it would be a mistake to take things further with Tatiana. Maybe it would never be right between them because they'd both always worry that any relationship they embarked upon would be based on the worst reason of all: him seeking a quick and immediate fix of consolation from her. But she was right. He did have to make a new life for himself.

Chapter Ten

ON A FREEZING-COLD, pale-skied morning in December, Chloe drove to Crantsford. She parked her car at the back of the library and checked her watch. She had an hour to do her shopping before she would have to keep her lunch appointment. She nearly hadn't agreed to come but then she had decided that surely it was time to let bygones be bygones.

Her first stop in her bid to make a start on her Christmas shopping was to call in at the new Waterstone's store. Thirty minutes later and she was back out onto the street and making for the toy shop where she hoped to find Marcus's present. Wrapping her scarf round her neck and turning the corner, she collided with a couple coming towards her. She murmured an apology and carried quickly on. But the sound of her name being called had her looking back. 'It is Chloe, isn't it?'

She stared at the man in his smart woollen overcoat, felt hat and leather gloves. There was something vaguely familiar about him.

'Max and Stella Wainbridge,' the man said helpfully. 'How are you?'

'Oh,' she said awkwardly. 'I'm well, thank you. And you?'

'We're not doing so badly,' Max replied. 'We both went down with some bug last week but we've bounced back.'

His wife leaned forward. 'We were sorry to hear that things didn't work out between you and Seth. You seemed so happy together, we—'

Max shushed her embarrassedly. 'Come on, darling, that's none of our business. These things happen.'

'But you said it yourself only the other day. You said what a shame it was that Seth was working so hard and that the new girl wasn't—'

A young mother with a pushchair was having trouble getting round them. They stepped aside and when the girl had passed, Max terminated their stumbling conversation. 'It's good to see you again,' he said, giving his wife a little tug. 'Have a lovely Christmas.'

Seth hadn't wasted any time in replacing her, Chloe thought as she pressed on towards the toy shop. Be glad for him, she told herself.

With Marcus's Christmas present added to her bags of shopping, she checked her watch. It was one o'clock.

She hurried off down the street. As she pushed open the door of Café Gigi—his choice—and felt the warm air hit her in the face, her stomach churned with nerves. Bygones, she reminded herself again. Be nice to him. No bitterness. No grudges. It's all in the past.

She spotted him at a table on the far side of the restaurant. She went over and he helped her out of her coat. 'It's so good to see you,' he said.

'Thanks,' she said. 'And how about that: you've grown a beard.'

'Do you like it?'

'Yes,' she lied politely. It was one of those fiddly beards, the sort that she imagined required masses of careful grooming. 'So what have you been up to since I last saw you?' she asked.

He smiled. 'It's been an extraordinary few months,' he said. 'But let's order and then I'll tell you everything. It really is good to see you again.'

His cheerfulness irritated her. Why couldn't he be miserable like her?

The waiter took their order and when he'd returned with a bottle of water and two glasses of red wine, Chloe said, 'Go on, then, tell me what's causing you to be so pleased with yourself.'

The boyish eagerness was back. 'I'm getting married.'

'Married!' she blurted out.

'I know what you're thinking. That it's all a bit sudden. I can hardly believe it myself. Don't laugh, but it was love at first sight. I took one look at Anna and just knew.'

'Congratulations,' Chloe managed to say.

'Do you mean that? I'd hoped that you could be happy for me. But I wasn't sure.' He frowned. 'You and I didn't part too well and I . . . well, let's just say I'd like nothing more than to know that we could be friends.'

With a leaden hand, she raised her glass to him. 'Congratulations Paul,' she repeated. 'I think it's great you've found the woman with whom you want to spend the rest of your life. Good luck to you both.'

'Thank you. You don't know how much that means to me.'

'Where does Anna live?' she asked.

'Skyros. She's a local girl I met when Liz and I were running the summer school. Her family own a nearby taverna. As soon as I've got things wrapped up here, I'm going back to start my own life-coaching business there. Anna's going to help me run it. We're planning to marry in February. But I haven't told you the best bit. Anna's pregnant! I'm going to be a father. Who'd have thought my life would take this particular turn?'

Chloe tensed. She slowly lowered her knife and fork. Bygones, she warned herself. No grudges. 'A baby,' she murmured. 'How wonderful.' But inside she was screaming: *It's not fair! It's not fair!* On and on she could hear Paul twittering away, completely unaware of the pain he was causing her. She couldn't bear to hear another word.

'Chloe? Are you all right?'

'We were going to have a baby,' she said flatly.

He blinked. 'What did you say?'

'You heard. And if you hadn't left me when you did, our child would be nearly three and a half years old now.'

He stared. And stared. 'What are you saying, Chloe?'

'I was pregnant.'

'Why didn't you tell me?'

'Would that have made you stay?'

The bitterness in her voice made him frown. 'Are you saying what I think you're saying? Did you have an abortion?'

'And if I did? Would you have cared? You couldn't get shot of me fast enough when we came back from Phuket. So what if I didn't want your child and got rid of it in the same offhand way you got rid of me?'

'You killed our child? I can't believe it. I can't believe you didn't tell me.' He was struggling to keep his voice low, to stay in control.

'Like I said, would it have made any difference?'

'I don't know. I don't know what to feel. I'm in shock.'

'Well, don't bother trying to figure it out. It's not worth it. I've had to live with it all this time and I still haven't come close to figuring it out.'

'You regret it?'

'I . . . I regret everything.' To her horror she started to cry. She snatched up her napkin from her lap and buried her face in it. When she raised her head, Paul was looking at her in a way she'd never seen before; he looked truly concerned. 'I'm sorry,' she said. 'I never meant to tell you. In fact, I never meant to tell anyone. I'm so ashamed of what I did. And now it looks like I'm destined never to have a child of my own.'

Paul reached across the table and took one of her hands. He was calmer now. 'Tell me about it,' he said. 'Tell me everything.'

She sniffed loudly and took a deep breath. 'Do you mean that?'

'Yes.'

When she'd finished, he said, 'And you've never told anyone this before now? Not even Dan and Sally?'

'I couldn't. Not when Sally was pregnant and Dan was so looking forward to being a father. What would they have thought of me? Then, when Marcus was born, I couldn't ever bring myself to admit what I'd done. He was such a beautiful baby. So perfect.' Tears filled her eyes again. 'There,' she said. 'Now you know everything.'

He looked at her sadly. 'I'm so sorry, Chloe. No wonder you hated me.'

'I hated myself more. I still do.'

Sally hadn't been entirely sure it would be a good idea to come here to Antigua, but now she was glad she had. It was wonderful to exchange the freezing temperatures of winter and pre-Christmas madness for the sun and a steady twenty-six degrees. Better still, and for the first time ever, it was a relief to have left work behind her.

Just as Murray had predicted, when confronted with what he had to say, Tom and the rest of the partners had reinstated her. They'd still taken her to task over having an affair with a client, but had said they would let it go in the circumstances. 'That's big of them,' Murray had said to Sally in private. 'The circumstances being that I'd have switched horses in an instant if they hadn't done as I'd asked.'

What happened next had taken them all by surprise. With Harry's claims now officially dismissed, Tom had done some digging and had unearthed some surprising results. Harry Fox was not the man they'd imagined him to be. His CV proved to contain some highly creative touches. He did have a law degree, but it certainly wasn't a first as he'd made out. A housemaster at his old school admitted that he'd been suspended twice, once for stealing and another time for trying to pass off a dud cheque in the nearby post office. His skill, so it seemed, was for talking himself up in such an impressive way it never crossed anyone's mind to check his CV. And the one thing nobody could take away from him—even Tom admitted this—was that he'd been extremely good at his job. The irony of a low-level fraudster working on important tax fraud cases was not lost on the firm.

Nobody had heard from Harry since his past had been revealed and Sally could almost admire him for his bravado. He'd been so convincing. But her admiration soon withered whenever she thought how he had tried to ruin her career and her reputation. She often thought about the dynamics of their relationship. In particular the sexual dynamics. As he'd pointed out, now and then she had enjoyed the novelty of relinquishing control to him. She had yet to fully understand why she had done that with Harry, but never with Dan.

Her marriage was unquestionably over. 'You're better off without me,' she'd told Dan during one of their meetings to discuss the future.

'I might be,' he'd said, hardly able to look at her, 'but I'm not so sure Marcus will be. Children are better off with both parents.'

'I'm sorry,' she'd said, meaning it. 'But I'm just not like other women. Or other mothers. And I can't pretend I'm something I'm not.'

She was making the effort to see Marcus as often as she could, but with her workload it wasn't easy. He'd spent last weekend with her in her rented apartment in Didsbury and things had gone far better than she'd expected. It was after they'd watched a couple of the DVDs she'd stocked up on that they had an interesting discussion based on the theory Marcus had that shadows were frightened of the sun. She had no idea where this theory of his had come from, but his ability to push home his point with such persuasive argument had impressed her and even left her with a feeling of pride.

She'd been exhausted when she'd dropped him off at Corner Cottage on Sunday afternoon. She had wondered, with renewed respect how Dan had managed it full time.

Dan was now working in Manchester—for his old firm again—and she had to give him credit; he wasn't going out of his way to be difficult or unreasonable over the divorce.

Chloe, on the other hand, was being extremely difficult and unreasonable. She had utterly refused to have anything to do with Sally. Losing the only friendship that had ever been important to her upset Sally. But what could she do about it if Chloe wouldn't talk to her? Sally knew from Dan that Chloe and Seth had never got back together again. And that bothered her. It bothered her a lot.

She put down the book she was trying to read and watched the man who was swimming backwards and forwards across the small bay until he eventually emerged from the unfeasibly blue water. For a man of his age he was in pretty good shape. Not quite Daniel Craig in those famously skimpy blue swimming trunks, but not bad at all. Squinting in the bright sunshine, he walked up the beach to where Sally was lying. When he was directly in front of her, she said, 'Good swim?'

'Excellent,' he said. He bent down and wrapped his cold, wet hands around her ankles. 'Have I told you, you have the sexiest legs I've ever had the good fortune to set eyes upon.'

She smiled and tried to kick him off. 'I do seem to recall you mentioning them at some point or other.'

'Good, because I'd hate to think you didn't know just how much I appreciate every little bit of your delectable body.'

He lay down on the sun lounger next to her and reached for her hand, slipping his fingers through hers. 'I know we only arrived last night, but do you have any regrets about coming here with me?'

'Funnily enough, none at all.'

'I'm so pleased you agreed to come. I'd have hated to celebrate my decree absolute alone.'

'I doubt you'd have been alone for long.'

He let go of her hand, raised himself up onto his elbow and turned to look at her. 'I told you before; I'm not interested in anything trivial. I want the real thing. I want to be with someone I can respect and admire. We make a good team, you and me.' He leaned over and kissed her.

They had booked separate accommodation for Sally, but that night she didn't sleep in her own bed. She spent the night with Murray in his private villa attached to the hotel. They both knew that she would. The speed with which she'd moved from one relationship to another gave her a few misgivings, but Murray was quite untroubled by it. 'Don't give it another thought, Sally,' he'd said. 'I certainly won't.'

In the morning, breakfast arrived on a large wooden tray and was placed on the verandah overlooking the sea. 'Fresh fruit and a glass of champagne: how else would we start the day?' Murray said.

'It certainly has the edge on driving into wet, dreary Manchester,' Sally replied. The air was arm and fragrant and the only sound to be heard was that of birdsong and the ocean. 'Work feels a million miles away,' she added.

'Since you've raised the subject, there's something I want to discuss with you. How would you feel about coming to work for me?'

Taken aback, she said, 'I'd have thought you of all people wouldn't want to mix business with pleasure.'

'As I said yesterday, we make a great team. I've been thinking of finding an in-house legal expert, an expert I can trust implicitly. You'd be a great asset to my business concerns.'

'But my speciality is family law.'

His eyes danced with amusement. 'Are you saying you couldn't meet the challenge of extending your skills?'

'Don't ever do that to me, Murray. Don't ever suggest or even imply I'm not up to the job.'

He raised his glass of champagne to her. 'I'll take that as a yes, then.'

'Inasmuch as I'll think about your offer. No more. No less.'

'Can't say fairer than that.'

They were halfway through the holiday when Sally did reach a decision. She had spent many hours in the intervening days cross-examining Murray and his motives, as well as her own. She was torn. Half of her saw it as a great move—certainly the salary was tempting enough—but what if things went wrong with Murray? She had no intention of becoming his third wife and had told him so.

'You say that now,' he'd said, 'but I sense I'm growing on you.' Really the man was incorrigible.

An abandoned two-day-old tabloid newspaper on the sun lounger next to her caught her eye. Splattered across the inner pages was a series of lurid photographs of a bleary-eyed Darren T. Child leaving a nightclub at three in the morning. Hanging off his arm was a young blonde girl falling out of a chiffon dress that only just managed to skim her bottom. The main headline was: *Darren Does it Again!* The article then went on to speculate about the state of his marriage.

Here we go again, thought Sally. Was that what she wanted to do for the rest of her life? Represent idiots like Darren? A nasty jolt of reality shot through her, forcing her to accept the unpalatable truth that she, too, had now joined the ranks of those very people she was so quick to despise. What would a tabloid newspaper make of her recent behaviour?

She sat up. Down at the water's edge, Murray was talking into his mobile. Working for him would be a huge risk. But a life without taking a chance would be a life simply not worth living. Wasn't it existing in the risk-free zone of her marriage that had driven her to have an affair with Harry in the first place?

She stood up decisively and went down to the water's edge to join Murray. She had no idea how things would work out between them, but they were two of a kind. Getting to know him properly, she had come to appreciate that he was uniquely understanding of what made her the person she was. She had surprised herself one day when they'd been strolling along the beach by confiding in him about the person she'd been when she was growing up and how she'd worked to reinvent herself. She had already shared things with him that she'd never dared tell Dan.

So, yes, Murray was right; he had grown on her.

When she was level with him at the water's edge, he turned and smiled. Still talking into his mobile, he put his arm round her. She put her mouth to his free ear and whispered into it.

He immediately told whoever it was he was speaking to that he'd call them back later.

'I won't be able to start for some months,' she said.

'I don't care how long I have to wait,' he said.

She had the feeling it wasn't only work that he was referring to. He took her hand and they stared at the sea and the hazy line of the distant horizon. The water, sparkling in the dazzling sunshine, was calm and benign. It was extraordinarily beautiful.

How could it be so different from the menacing sea that had claimed all those lives almost four years ago, when its savage force had convinced Sally she was going to die alone and terrified in that hotel room?

Four years. Was it possible that so much time had passed? Or that her life had changed so dramatically? She thought of Dan. When this holiday was over, she would go and see him. She would try to explain to him just how sorry she really was. It suddenly seemed important that he understood that none of what had happened was his fault.

There was no mistaking the glint of jittery panic in Lardy McFierce's eye. She looked every inch a woman on the verge of meltdown. Whatever chaos was about to come her way, Dan reckoned she deserved it.

Of course, his opinion had nothing to do with Lardy McFierce sending Marcus home the other day with strict instructions that he was to wear a clean tea towel on his head today. Dan had toed the line and supplied Marcus with the appropriate headwear.

'I know how difficult it must be for you now, Daniel,' Lardy had said when he and Marcus had turned up with Rosie, Dave and Charlie, 'but we can't let standards slip because there are personal problems at home. It won't help Marcus in the long run.' Patronising bitch!

Her condescension echoed that of Dan's mother. 'I can't say that I'm surprised,' she had said stiffly when he told her the news. 'She never struck me as being the kind of girl who'd make a loyal and devoted wife. You're well out of it, Daniel. Mark my words, you'll soon find someone a lot more suitable. Why don't you come down with Marcus for a weekend and I'll organise a bit of a get-together for you. The Irving-Millers' daughter still hasn't married, you know.'

'I'm not surprised,' he'd snapped back. 'She's as appealing as last week's fish. God knows what you think we'd have in common.'

'There's no need to take that tone of voice. I'm only trying to help.'

'You think marrying me off before I'm even divorced is helpful?'

'Life goes on, Daniel. You being alone and miserable won't help Marcus one iota. Will she fight you to have custody of him?'

'I doubt it.'

'Have you thought about boarding school?'

'Don't you think I'm a little old for that?'

'Not for you! For Marcus. Boarding school in a couple of years' time would be ideal for him. It would be a marvellous environment to give him some much-needed stability, not to say the best possible start in life. It would also free you up to meet the right woman.'

'It would also kill me. Give my best wishes to Dad.' Dan had hung up then, breathless with anger.

Taking his seat in the pew with Rose and Dave and Chloe's parents, he was just about to switch off his mobile when it went off. He hurried outside to take the call. He hoped it wasn't work.

Sliding back into the world he'd left behind to take care of Marcus had not been without its problems. The job itself was fine. He didn't have any trouble accepting that he couldn't walk straight back into the role he'd once held, that he would have to take what he was offered.

What did trouble him was guilt. He felt guilty that he was not only spending so little time with his son, but also depending on Rosie so much. It didn't matter how often she promised him that having Marcus around made her life easier with Charlie, he still didn't want to impose on her. She'd reluctantly agreed that he could pay her the going child-minding rate and the arrangement was working like clockwork.

It wasn't work calling him; it was Simon Frinley from Frinley and Baker, the estate agents in Crantsford. 'Good news, Dan,' he said heartily. 'I've just received an offer from Mr and Mrs Hughes, the couple you showed round at the weekend. It's as close to the asking price as we're likely to get. What do you want me to tell them?'

'Tell Mr and Mrs Hughes that I accept,' he said.

'Right you are. I'll get the paperwork started this end and will be in touch again tomorrow.'

Dan turned to go back inside the church, but was distracted by the sight of a flash of red crossing the road and coming towards the lych gate. It was Tatiana, strikingly dressed in an ankle-length, red Cossack-style coat. Perched jauntily on her head was a black beret. She looked like she'd just stepped out of a Smirnov advert. As Dan waited for her on the gravelled pathway, he couldn't ignore how happy he was to see her again. It was five weeks now since he'd stopped working for the trust. Five weeks since he'd last seen Tatiana. He'd missed her.

She smiled tentatively at him. 'Hello, Dan. How are you?'

'I'm OK. You look great. Nice coat.'

'Oxfam's finest,' she said with a light laugh. 'It's my Christmas coat. You look very smart too.'

He glanced down at his dark woollen overcoat and Hugo Boss suit. 'Work clothes,' he said. 'I came straight from the office.'

'How's the new job working out?'

'In some ways it's as if I've never been away.'

'That's good.'

'I suppose it is. How's everyone at the trust?'

'It's our busy time, organising parties for the families.'

For an awkward moment they seemed to have run out of things to say. Until Tatiana, her face flushed with either the cold or embarrass-ment, said, 'We'd better go inside, or we'll miss Charlie and Marcus's big performance and that would never do.'

Loud, enthusiastic applause rang out.

The play had gone off without too many hitches. The relief on Lardy McFierce's face was plain to see. Only two pieces of scenery wobbled and collapsed, only one of the angels cried, and only one of the three wise men tripped, dropping his wooden chest of gold. Marcus and

Charlie spent most of the time nudging one another and grinning inanely at the audience.

Following frequent discussions on the subject, Marcus seemed to have grasped the concept of them moving house and all that appeared to worry him was that they wouldn't live too far from Charlie. Which meant finding a house in the village, and last week fate had shone benevolently on him in the form of a three-bedroomed cottage that had just come on the market. It was a fraction of the size of Corner Cottage and needed a fair amount of updating, but it had a good feel to it and a decent-sized garden for Marcus and Charlie to play in. It was also within easy walking distance of Rosie. Dave had already looked over the house for Dan and pronounced it as sound as a bell.

There had been no urgency to put Corner Cottage on the market, but he'd wanted to get the wrench of moving over and done with. Not for financial reasons, but because he was through with putting things off. He'd done that time and time again with Sally, repeatedly talking himself out of confronting her. He wouldn't ever behave that way again. He'd act quickly and decisively from now on.

He reminded himself of this when he was buying two plastic cups of mulled wine at the Christmas Fair in the crowded village hall. He'd left Marcus and Charlie with Tatiana and she was encouraging them to dig deep into the lucky dip barrel.

He gave her one of the cups. 'Happy Christmas,' he said.

'Happy Christmas,' she replied.

He moved in closer to hear her. 'Are you around on Christmas Day?'

'No definite plans as yet. It's always a bit last minute with me.'

'In that case, would you like to join Marcus and me? Chloe and her parents are coming. What do you think? Could you bear it?'

'Are you sure that's what you really want?'

He knew what she was asking him. 'I've missed seeing you, Tatiana,' he said. 'If you're prepared to take things slowly, I'd like to see a lot more of you. So will you come?'

She gave him a soft, gentle smile. 'Yes. I'd love to.'

Christmas and the run up to it was the busiest time of the year for Seth. But being rushed off his feet was a blessing. It meant he had little time to torture himself with thoughts of Chloe. He'd tried to push her out of his mind, but in a short time she had become a fundamental part of his life and nothing seemed to be filling the void she'd left behind.

He missed their long phone calls, especially the late-at-night ones.

He missed being able to share the stresses and strains of his work. He missed her humour and encouragement. He missed kissing her. And the sheer bloody sexiness of her.

He kept waiting for his feelings for her to change, but they wouldn't. Every day he prayed for some kind of let-up, but God was distant and silent on the subject.

So what could he do, other than throw himself into his work? Or try replacing her with someone new. He'd taken up Father Jim O'Brien on his offer to introduce him to the 'pretty curate' from Matlock. Eleanor had been pleasant company, but he'd known from the outset that it wasn't going to work between them. She was too serious and intense for him. He'd cited the distance from Crantsford to Matlock and their hectic work commitments as an excuse to end things with Eleanor. She hadn't been able to disguise her disappointment, but then she'd shrugged and wished him well.

He wished he could say the same of Chloe. She plainly had no intention of ever forgiving him for helping Sally. He couldn't decide whether to send her a Christmas card or not. Obviously, the right thing to do would be to send her a card. But he was scared of doing that. What if she didn't return the gesture? There was only so much rejection he could handle.

Chloe was coming to the end of her afternoon round of home visits. Her next one was with Chelsea Savage. Her baby had arrived three days ago and she was now home from hospital.

Chloe parked on the road outside the Savages' house. The daylight was beginning to fade, and the front of the house was lit up with a surfeit of gaudy coloured Christmas lights. She could see flowers and cards on the windowsill of the front room as she walked up the short path.

Mrs Savage opened the door. From behind her came the sound of a party in full swing. 'Come in, come in!' the woman bellowed. 'Come and join the fun. It's been nonstop ever since Chelsea got home last night. Friends and neighbours keep calling in to get a look at the baby. And what a looker! She's a stunner all right. Come and see for yourself.'

It was quite a different atmosphere from the one Chloe had expected. Knowing how disapproving Mrs Savage had been about her daughter's pregnancy, this was quite a turnaround.

Chloe caught her first glimpse of Chelsea's three-day-old daughter and felt her own heart melt. She was astonishingly beautiful. Swamped in a pale pink Babygro, sleeping peacefully in Chelsea's arms, she could not have been more perfect. It was all Chloe could do not to snatch the baby out of Chelsea's arms and run away with her.

Whatever feelings Chelsea and her mother had experienced throughout the last nine months, Melody-Joy, as Chelsea proudly said her baby was called, was now very much the centre of their world.

After examining mother and child, Chloe drove home. She hadn't held Melody-Joy for more than a few minutes, yet she could still feel the comforting weight of her in her arms.

Many times since her lunch with Paul, Chloe had wanted to do what he'd advised. 'You need to talk about this with someone you trust,' he'd said. 'You were always so close to Dan; why not open up to him?'

But whenever she thought of telling Dan, she felt sick with fear. She didn't want him to view her differently, as she knew he would. As a father, he would find it incomprehensible. Hadn't Paul looked at her in horror when she'd told him? He hadn't said it, but the word 'murderer' must have been there on the tip of his tongue. Did she want Dan to think that of her? She'd lost Sally; could she bear to lose Dan as well?

The only person judging you, is you. How right Seth had been. But that was only because no one else knew about the abortion. It had been easy for Seth to forgive Sally's adultery, but forgiving Chloe would be beyond him; she'd taken a life.

As a doctor, Chloe would be the first to point out the obvious: that ethically she had done nothing wrong. Moreover, she would say that she hadn't been thinking straight when she'd booked herself anonymously into the clinic to terminate her pregnancy; that she'd been under a lot of stress, what with coming so close to dying in the tsunami and then Paul leaving her. It didn't help, though. In fact it made it worse. She should never have taken such an important decision when she was least equipped to do it. All that had been in her mind at the time was the terrible need to be free of Paul's child.

Oh, yes, she'd wanted a child, but she hadn't wanted the child of a man who could treat her so brutally. She hadn't wanted to live with such a cruel and lasting reminder of him.

And yet she had. All this time, whenever she thought of the child she desperately wanted, she was reminded of Paul.

What would Seth say to that? We reap what we sow?

Oh, Seth, she thought with an ache of longing. How different things could have been for us. If only I hadn't . . . If only you weren't . . .

But what was the point in even thinking about it? Her anger for Seth had long since evaporated. She had now accepted that he couldn't help being the man he was. Seth had criticised her for lacking compassion for Sally. Even now that hurt. Because it had shown up her true colours. She wasn't a very nice person when it came right down to it.

Understanding how and why it had gone wrong with Seth in no way lessened the pain of their break-up. If anything, it made it worse because she now realised exactly what she'd lost. She had thrown away the love of a truly good man.

Nothing changes, thought Dan when he heard Sally's car on the drive. Christmas Eve, and she still manages to be late. 'Mummy's here,' he said to Marcus, who was sitting at the kitchen table eating his tea.

Marcus looked up, his brows drawn together in an anxious frown. He shook his head. 'I don't want to stay with Mummy tonight. Father Christmas won't find me at her house. She doesn't have a chinney.'

'Don't worry, Marcus, you're not going anywhere tonight. Mummy wants to see you here.'

He went out to the hall to let Sally in. She still had her own keys to the house, but had tactfully not used them in a long time.

'Good holiday?' he asked, when she was slipping her coat off. Her face was attractively tanned; she looked well.

'Yes,' she said without expanding. 'Where do you want me to put Marcus's presents?' she whispered.

'For now I'll hide them in the understairs cupboard,' he replied. When he'd taken the Hamleys bags from her, he said, 'Come through. Marcus is just finishing his tea. Can I get you something to eat?'

'No, thanks. A drink would be nice, though. But before that, could I . . . could we have a talk on our own? There's something I want to say.'

'Can it wait until Marcus has gone to bed? Only he probably won't be too accommodating in giving us any time alone before then.'

She glanced at her watch. Dan experienced a spark of irritation. Why did Marcus always have to come second in her world?

'That's if you have time,' he added pointedly, not caring what reaction he provoked.

'Of course I have time,' she said quickly.

Dan didn't believe her. How could he ever believe anything she said these days?

While Sally was upstairs putting Marcus to bed, Dan tidied the kitchen. The chances of Marcus going to sleep in the next hour or two were slim. It was the first Christmas he had really been old enough to look forward to, and, according to Rosie, he and Charlie had been as high as kites for most of the day.

With the last of the dirty plates put away in the dishwasher, he poured out two glasses of Chablis and waited for Sally. Just like old times, he thought wryly.

They sat at the kitchen table and, seeing the grim expression on Sally's face, he braced himself for bad news.

'I want to apologise,' she said. 'I've come to the conclusion I couldn't have treated you much worse. You really didn't deserve any of it. I said some terrible things to you and I wish I hadn't. Words can never be unsaid, but I want you to know that I'm sorry, Dan. Truly I am.'

'I don't know what to say,' he murmured, shocked. A repentant Sally was the last thing he'd expected.

'Then don't say anything. There's something else I need to tell you. You might not believe me, but I do love Marcus. Just not the same way you do. I can't help that. I wish I could be more like you, more loving and caring, but it simply doesn't come naturally to me. I did try. And I'll continue to try. But what I found so impossible to live with was the knowledge that I was failing on a daily basis. No matter how hard I tried to be a better mother, the more I understood it was never going to happen. The sad truth is, Dan, I can't compete with you.'

He struggled to take in what she was saying. 'Parenthood isn't a competition, Sally. It couldn't be more straightforward. It's about love and wanting to do everything in your power to make your child happy.'

'It might be straightforward to you, but surely you realise that for me, life is one big competitive event. It's not enough for me to take part; I have to win. That's what Chloe and I always had in common with each other: our competitive edge. It was why we became friends. But with Marcus, you beat me fairly and squarely. You did it effortlessly, and I'm ashamed to admit it, but I think I came close to hating you for that.'

'You make it sound as if I did it deliberately.'

'Didn't you, just occasionally? Can you put your hand on your heart and say you didn't feel closer to Marcus, knowing that he always behaved perfectly for you but badly for me?'

To his regret, Dan knew there was an element of truth in what she was saying. 'I'm sorry,' he said.

'Don't beat yourself up over it, Dan. I may have given birth to Marcus, but he's always been your son. You're a better person than me. Stronger, too, for putting up with me for as long as you did. I'll always respect you for that.' She smiled. 'You know, you really are a superhero.'

He flinched. 'Don't say that. Please.'

'Too late, I already did.' She took a sip of her wine.

'I'm no hero,' he said, staring down at the table. 'Nothing could be further from the truth. I'm one of life's big, unsung cowards. I still get nightmares about the tsunami. They come and go, but essentially the dream never changes. I'm back there trying to save that boy all over again and then he changes into Marcus and I can't save him either.'

Sally lowered her glass. 'Why did you never tell me?'

He looked up at her. 'How could I, when you'd proved how easy it was to put it behind you? I wanted to be as strong as you, but I wasn't. I thought you'd despise me for my weakness.'

'I would never have done that.'

'But you did. As good as. You accused me of being safe and pre-dictable. You might say now that you think I'm stronger than you, but then you saw me as being weak, didn't you?'

'I told you before, I'm sorry for what I said. I wasn't in my right mind. Do you think you could ever forgive me?'

'Oh, I imagine so. Not right now, though. Don't expect that of me.'

'Thank you,' she said quietly.

A heavy silence fell on the kitchen. From upstairs came the sound of Marcus singing 'Jingle Bells'.

Dan smiled. He looked at Sally, who was also smiling. 'You know,' he said, 'for two intelligent people, we made a colossal job of cocking it up, didn't we?'

Sally nodded.

Sally drove out of the village satisfied that she had said everything she had planned to say to Dan. While she knew it was early days, she was hopeful that it would eventually help to reconcile them.

Of course, she hadn't told Dan everything. He knew about Harry's allegations—rumour and gossip had reached him at his office when he'd gone back to work—and he knew that Harry had disappeared off the face of the earth. He also knew—or thought he knew—just as everyone else did, that it was Murray Adamson with whom she'd been having the affair all along. Not Harry.

During their flight home from Antigua, in one of his unexpectedly perceptive moments, Murray had said that in his experience things invariably went wrong in a relationship when people didn't confront the small irritations.

'The next thing you know,' he'd said, 'those petty little irritations escalate until they are seemingly insurmountable. You must tell me when I start irritating you,' he'd added.

'What do you mean, when you *start* irritating me?' she'd replied with a smile.

She had stopped to fill up with petrol when her mobile went off on her dashboard. Not recognising the number, she answered cautiously.

'Is that you, Sally?'

Harry!

'I'll take that stunned silence as a yes,' he said. 'How are you?'

'You've got a bloody nerve ringing me.'

'I like to call it spirit. Or chutzpah. Something you're not short of yourself. That's why we were so good together.'

'We were never good together, you little shit!'

'Oh, don't be like that. You're not going to say I meant nothing to you, are you? Don't say that, not after all the fun we had. And it *was* fun, wasn't it? How I enjoyed playing you. One little hint of denial and you were practically on your knees begging for it.'

Suddenly fearing that Harry might be recording their conversation, Sally put her guard up. Better still, why not cut him off? Not, she couldn't do that. There was something she had to know. 'Why did you do it?' she asked. 'Why did you try to destroy my career.'

'Oh, that,' he said airily. 'Well, I did it to teach you a lesson.'

'But why? What did I ever do to you?'

'The fact that you even have to ask the question disappoints me. Cast your mind back to my first day at McKenzie Stuart. You treated me like dirt. You thought you could put me in my place, didn't you?'

Sally thought back to that fateful day. She hadn't treated him like dirt, but, yes, she had tried to put him in his place. But he'd deserved it. He really had. 'I don't understand,' she murmured. And choosing her words carefully, just in case he was recording their conversation, she said, 'I thought we'd put that misunderstanding behind us.'

'You might have done. I didn't. From the moment you didn't take me seriously, I knew how I'd teach you a lesson you wouldn't forget.'

'You mean, based on my not wanting to be eyed up as a bit of office fluff, you set out to destroy me? How pathetic you are, Harry.'

He laughed. 'Don't you realise, Sally, it's always the littlest things that cause the most trouble in life. By the way, nice move bringing in Murray Adamson. Presumably you traded with him; sex for a few lies. Nice touch. You're a real pro, Sally.'

'Goodbye, Harry. I hope I never have the misfortune to meet you again.'

'You probably won't. I'm giving law a break and moving to France.'

'One more question,' she said. 'Why did you ring me?'

''Tis the season for goodwill to all men, and since I knew you'd be tearing yourself apart wanting to know why I did what I did, I thought I'd put you out of your misery. Call it a Christmas present. Au revoir!'

The line went dead.

Sally thought about what he'd said. You didn't call to put me out of my misery, Harry, you called because you needed to brag about what you did. You wanted to show off how clever you think you are.

She made a mental note to change her mobile number and drove on to Prestbury, where Murray would be waiting for her.

Chapter Eleven

'WHY IS IT THAT Christmas Eve always makes me feel ten years old?'

Chloe laughed and flicked a handful of soap suds at her brother. She was so glad he had decided to come home for Christmas, bringing with him Madeleine, his latest girlfriend.

'Could it have anything to do with the fact that we're both sleeping in our old bedrooms and have been banished to the kitchen to do the washing up just as we always used to be?' she said.

Madeleine, as a guest, had been let off washing-up duty and was upstairs wrapping some last-minute presents. 'Not that you need my approval,' Chloe said, 'but I really like Madeleine. Is she likely to stick around long in your life?' Nick had a history of cutting and running if things started to get too serious. He liked his freedom and his own space.

'She might do,' Nick said casually. Then he smiled. 'I hope so.'

Chloe smiled, too. 'Then just you make sure you treat her nicely.'

'I fully intend to. And since we're having a cosy share-and-tell moment, why did things go wrong between you and the guy you were seeing in the summer? Was it the whole churchy thing that you couldn't cope with?'

She rummaged around in the washing-up bowl for the last of the silver cutlery that couldn't go in the dishwasher. It would be so easy to say yes to her brother and leave it at that. But she desperately wanted to tell someone how much she still loved Seth. She had even promised herself that if he sent her a Christmas card, she would get in touch with him to try to explain her behaviour. Not because she thought he would want her back, but because she owed him an apology. And maybe apologising would start the healing process for her. But there had been no card from him, so she had kept her apology to herself, deciding that he really had moved on. After all, he had a new girlfriend.

'Houston, we have a problem. The lights are on but nobody's home.'

'Sorry, Nick,' she said. 'It must be my age; drifting off without answering a question.'

He looked quizzical. 'Either that or I prodded where you don't want to be prodded.'

Chloe had always been close to her brother, so could she risk telling him everything?

'If I tell you something I did, something I regret, will you promise not to think badly of me?' she asked.

'I could never think badly of you, Chloe.'

'Just say you promise. Please.'

Frowning, he said, 'OK, I promise.'

She moved away from the sink, dried her hands and took a deep breath. She told him everything.

When Chloe had finished, Nick said, 'You couldn't have been harder on yourself, could you? Don't you think we'd have all supported you in whatever decision you wanted to make?'

She reached for a tissue and blew her nose. 'I thought Mum was so keen to be a grandmother that she might persuade me to keep the baby.'

'I very much doubt she would have done that. Do you miss Seth. Do you still think about him?'

'I'm trying to cut down how often I think of him. I've got it down to a mere every other minute now.'

'You don't think it's worth telling him what you've just told me? I'm sure he'd understand.' Nick hesitated. 'He's not a red-hot pro-lifer, is he?'

'That's what I'm afraid of. I do know he was keen to have children. It was something we discussed very early on in our relationship.'

Nick went quiet. 'I still think you have to risk talking to him,' he said finally. 'If he practises what he preaches, then he should be able to forgive you. And when it comes down to it, what have you got to lose?'

'Even if he could forgive me, I think it's too late for there to be anything between us again. I heard that he's started seeing someone else.'

'Classic rebound behaviour,' Nick said. 'It won't mean anything.'

'I wouldn't count on that.'

'Who's for a glass of devil juice before we go for the midnight carol service?' It was their father. Standing in the doorway, he was dangerously armed with a bottle of sloe gin. Last Christmas morning they'd all woken late and with hangovers due to polishing off a bottle of their father's homemade liqueur.

'I think I'll pass, Dad, if you don't mind,' Chloe said.

It was as well she did, because when they were putting on their coats, gloves and scarves to go to St Andrew's, Chloe made a split-second decision. 'I'm not going with you,' she said.

'But what will you do instead?' her mother asked.

'I'm sure I'll find something to do. Now go! Or you'll be late.'

Thirty minutes later, Chloe hurried up the path towards the church. Lights blazed at all the windows and the loud, robust sound of 'Hark the Herald Angels' met her ears.

She was nervous. Petrified would be a more apt description. But she had to do it. Nick had been right. She had to take the risk.

It was always possible, though, that he wasn't here.

She pulled open the heavy door and stepped into the small porch. She helped herself to a hymn book and a carol service sheet, and pulled open a second door. Greeted by a brightly lit interior and a packed church, she spotted an empty seat right at the back. She squeezed in next to an elderly couple. Just as she got herself settled, the singing came to an end and the congregation sat down. She was so nervous her hands were shaking as she searched the front of the church for Seth.

Oh, God, there he was! Her heart crashed against her ribs. She slumped as low as she could in the pew without attracting unwanted attention or losing sight of Seth. Fully robed up—fancy, embroidered stole over a white surplice—he looked well. What was she saying? He looked amazing, just as he always had.

So lost in scrutinising him, she hadn't realised that the service had come to an end and that everyone was on their feet. A procession of choir boys and girls was making its way along the nave of the church. At the rear came the choir's older members and then . . . and then Seth was following behind. He was smiling and shaking hands with members of the congregation, wishing them a Happy Christmas.

He was five pews away from her. Chloe's knees began to shake. Oh, God, she was in real danger of cardiac arrest.

Was there a chance he wouldn't recognise her, bundled up in her hat and scarf? Was there a chance he would pass by and not notice her?

He turned, his hand already outstretched, the warmth of his smile aimed directly at her. He stopped dead. The smile vanished. There was shock in his face. Was she imagining it, or was there regret too?

His hand finally made contact with hers. 'Happy Christmas,' he murmured. She held his gaze, her cheeks burning.

And then he was gone. Swept away on a tide of well-wishers.

She stayed in her pew, alone and trembling. A team of men and women were tidying up the pews, putting away hymn books and Bibles.

'Are you all right, dear?' asked a woman with a small, festive pine cone pinned to her coat lapel. 'Only we'll be locking up in a minute.'

'I won't be long,' Chloe said, as if she'd come here for some late-night shopping. The woman smiled and went about her business.

Chloe got up. To steady her nerves, she walked the length of a side aisle and went to look at the nativity scene. Surrounding the model of the lowly cattle shed and figures were pots of poinsettias and home-made Christmas cards. She picked one up. A child's wobbly hand had written the words: *Congratulations Reverend Seth, love from Tabitha (aged six) and William (aged three)*.

She put the card back and wondered what Seth was being congratulated for. Then it hit her. He'd got engaged! He was due to be married!

No wonder he'd just looked at her the way he had. Perhaps his girlfriend—his fiancée—was here with him.

Oh, what had she been thinking in coming here? But how to escape without causing him any embarrassment?

From behind her, she could hear what sounded like the last of the goodbyes being said. Then she heard the sound of a heavy door closing. Then the main lights were being turned off. Filled with panic, she wanted to run and hide behind the nearest pillar. Which, unbelievably, was exactly what she did.

'Chloe?' The sound of Seth's voice caused her heart to leap. 'Chloe?' he repeated, his footsteps advancing towards her. 'Where are you?'

He was closing in on her. Not wanting to appear any more foolish than she did already, she stepped out from her hiding place.

'There you are. I was beginning to think I'd imagined seeing you.'

'Would you be happier if you had?'

He frowned and looked at her as if he hadn't understood. 'Shall we sit down?' he said. 'Or do you feel uncomfortable being here? Would you rather we went somewhere—'

'Please,' she interrupted him, 'don't be so considerate. I don't think I could cope with that.'

They sat down, side by side, each staring straight ahead. 'I'm sorry I missed most of the service,' she said. 'It was a last-minute decision to come. Owen not here?'

'He's gone. He retired a couple of weeks ago. St Michael's is officially my parish. We had a party here last week to celebrate my new position.'

Did that explain the cards? 'Congratulations,' she said.

'What made you come?' he asked.

She turned at his question, found herself looking straight into his intensely blue eyes. Her pulse quickened. 'Selfishness, pure and simple,' she said. 'I wanted to see you, to tell you something. It won't undo what I said or did, but I'm hoping it might help you understand why I behaved the way I did. Do you remember that day when you came to see me, the last time we spoke? You said the only person who was judging me was me? Do you remember saying that?'

He nodded.

'You were right.'

'I'm sorry. Nobody likes a smart arse.'

'Actually, it's the truth we don't like, and I was doing my best to keep that from you. It was my reaction to your comment that I should show some compassion towards Sally that did the damage. Your words were like a judgment of me and I knew then that I couldn't live up to your high expectations. I also felt that if you could judge me over something like that, what else would you judge me for?'

'So what is it that you're so frightened I'll judge you for?'

'When Paul left me, I discovered I was pregnant. I hated him so much for leaving me the way he did that I didn't want to keep his child and so I secretly had an abortion. It wasn't long before I hated myself more than I hated Paul. It seemed a cruel twist of fate that I'd got rid of the one thing I then longed for most: a child.'

'Who did you turn to for help and support?'

'No one. Not my parents, Dan or Sally. Certainly not Paul. I hadn't told them that I'd been pregnant. Not until recently. I finally confessed to Paul what I'd done. And then tonight I told my brother about it.'

'Either one of them judge you?'

She shook her head.

'But you thought I would? Because of this?' He indicated his robes. 'You think I'm so perfect it gives me the right to attack others for their flaws? You didn't know me at all, did you?'

'I was frightened of losing you. I was jumping the gun a bit, I know, but you were everything I wanted in a partner. I could see us having a real future together. Except deep down I knew it couldn't be possible because of what I was keeping from you.'

'So instead of sharing any of this with me, you destroyed that future?'

'I didn't want your condemnation. Not when I cared about you the way I did.'

'Better to condemn me then?' His voice was edged with sadness.

A long and heavy silence passed between them. Chloe broke it by getting to her feet. 'I've done what I came here to do. I wanted you to know that it wasn't anything you did or said; it was entirely me who messed up our relationship. I wish you the best of luck with your new girlfriend.'

He stared at her, his head tilted, his eyes dark. She thought he'd never looked more handsome. Her heart skittered.

'What new girlfriend?' he asked. He was standing up now.

'The one Max and Stella told me about when I bumped into them a couple of weeks ago. As I said, I wish you all the best.' She started to walk away. Fast. She'd got as far as the middle of the nave when she felt a hand on her arm.

'Chloe,' he said. 'Please don't rush off. At least not until I've had a chance to say something.'

'It's late,' she croaked, her words trapped in her throat. 'You need to go home.'

'Don't tell me what I need, Chloe. Not when I know my own mind so well.' With a swiftness that took her by surprise, he took her in his arms and kissed her. He kissed with such passion that when he released her she swayed in the firm circle of his embrace.

'I must be hallucinating,' she murmured, dazed and breathless. 'I can't really be standing in a church being kissed by a vicar.'

'It's real enough,' he answered. 'And there is no new girlfriend. I saw someone a couple of times, but it was never going to work. For the simple reason I couldn't get you out of my head. I still love you, Chloe.'

'How can you, after all the things I said?'

'God only knows!' He let out a short laugh. 'But the fact that I do only goes to show how strong my feelings are for you.'

'I don't know what to say. I never dreamed you'd still feel the way you do.'

'Then say you'll give me two minutes to change and lock up and then come and have a drink with me.'

'But everywhere will be closed. It's well past midnight. And haven't you got to be up early in the morning?'

'I doubt I'll sleep much tonight. Come home with me, Chloe.'

Christmas morning and Seth woke late, a little after nine o'clock.

After checking that last night hadn't been a dream, he allowed himself a small smile. A smile that soon developed into a hopeless, mile-wide grin of euphoria. He felt he'd been given the best Christmas present of his life. It was a gift he had no intention of ever letting slip through his fingers again. There would be no more secrets between them. No more destructive, misplaced guilt.

He should have known there was more to their break-up than just that business with Sally. But an abortion. And one that she regretted so deeply. He would never have guessed. It saddened him to think that she had carried such a dreadful weight on her shoulders for as long as she had and that she'd suffered so much for it. He hoped he'd convinced her that he would never judge her for what she'd done. What right-thinking person would?

How glad he was that Chloe had come looking for him last night! What courage that must have taken. He was glad, too, that his request to be moved to a parish as far away from Crantsford as possible had been turned down. He'd approached the bishop at a seminar in Chester last month and had been informed that there were already plans in place for him. Owen did indeed want to retire, which meant Seth was the ideal person to take over from him.

But it was what else the bishop had in mind for Seth that had clinched matters. A new scheme backed by the Church was being set up in the New Year to help young offenders, and given Seth's background, it had been suggested he was the perfect candidate to take an active role in the initiative. He was to be attached to the police station in Crantsford as of the middle of January.

He lay as still as he could for a further ten minutes, staring up at the ceiling, then gave in to temptation. What man wouldn't?

He turned over, gently lifted Chloe's hair away from her cheek and kissed her. When her eyelids fluttered open and she smiled sleepily at him, he kissed her again. 'Happy Christmas,' he said.

'Happy Christmas to you.' She sighed and stretched languidly, then put a hand against his chest. 'You OK this morning? Any regrets?'

He raised her hand to his lips. 'None at all. You?'

'Only that I wish I had a present to give you,' she said.

'You've given me more than I ever expected. Although there is one other thing you could give me.'

'Name it and it's yours.'

'Give me your trust,' he said, still holding her hand. 'Trust and believe in me when I say that for as long as I live, I'll never want you to be other than the person you are, that your happiness is more important to me than my own. Can you do that?'

'Already done,' she said.

'Good.' He stroked her cheek. 'But as much as I wish I could lie here all day making love to you, I'm afraid I must tear myself away and have a shower. Family service is in less than an hour.'

'Would you like me to join you?'

He smiled. 'Only if you want to.'

'I want to.'

'In that case, we'd both better get a move on.'

Before setting off to walk the short distance to church, Chloe telephoned her parents to tell them she'd be home later than planned that morning. She'd called them late last night, just to put their minds at rest that she hadn't been abducted and her mother had been ridiculously overjoyed at the latest development. 'Bring him back with you tomorrow,' she'd said, making Seth sound like a new toy Chloe had just been given for Christmas. 'I'm sure Dan won't mind an extra one for dinner. We can always rustle up some extra food to help out.'

She sat in the second row of seats from the front with Max and Stella. She watched Seth conduct the service with pride and happiness. It was obvious that he loved what he did and that he was good at it. Equally obvious was that his congregation loved him and held him in high regard. Would their opinion of him change if they knew that he hadn't slept alone last night?

He hadn't needed to, but Seth had explained they would have to be discreet. He'd said he didn't mind people drawing their own conclusions as to what they may or may not be up to—after all, most of his congregation was aware of his views on sex; that what was important was that it took place within the context of a committed relationship— but to flaunt the fact blatantly that they were sleeping together was a different matter. Apart from anything else, the bishop might feel compelled to say something if it were brought to his attention.

Not so long ago Chloe would have been compelled to say something about it, too. Such as wasn't this a classic example of Church of

England hypocrisy? But for Seth's sake she would keep quiet.

She watched and listened to him as he gave his sermon, which he'd assured everyone would be quick and painless. He moved about at the front of the church, his body language relaxed and expressive, his face animated. It was difficult for Chloe to concentrate on what he was saying, though. Her thoughts had drifted elsewhere, to making love with the Reverend Seth Hawthorne, the vicar of St Michael's.

He'd asked her to trust him and she did. She really did. Her love for him was deep and aching and she knew that at last her heart was connected to him in a way she'd never allowed to happen before. He'd shown nothing but kindness and understanding after her confession about the abortion she'd had. There had been no condemnation. No criticism. Not a single word of censure. Only love and acceptance.

St Michael's wasn't as packed as it had been last night, but there was still a good-sized crowd. Everyone was smartly dressed, including the children. Each and every one of them was guarding a wrapped present on their laps. The significance of this became clear when Seth called the children up to the front of the church and explained that they were going to distribute the presents randomly to everybody in the congregation, along with the ones he had in the sack he was holding.

The distribution started in a quiet, orderly fashion, but rapidly gained its own momentum as presents were opened and members of the congregation began expressing surprise and delight. Laughter broke out when Max stood up to show off a pair of comical spectacles complete with furry eyebrows and mini windscreen wipers. Stella got a book of jokes, and the couple in the pew behind them were given a box of chocolates and a coffee mug.

A small, dark-haired girl handed Chloe an envelope with her name on it. Touched that she had been included, she opened the envelope and pulled out a card; a printed watercolour of St Michael's on a snowy day.

'What have you got?' Stella asked, leaning over to get a better look.

Chloe opened the card, then snapped it shut. But not before Stella saw what was written inside and let out a small gasp.

Her heart racing, Chloe glanced up and saw Seth at the front of the church. Surrounded by happy, laughing children, he was staring directly at her. He looked unbearably anxious. How could he think she would say no? She smiled at him and nodded, very slowly, but very surely. His face was instantly transformed and he smiled back at her.

The rest of the service passed in a blur.

Afterwards, when they were alone in the vestry and Seth was changing out of his robes, he admitted that it had been the same for him.

'I can't remember a single word of what I said in the remaining minutes of the service,' he said. He came over to put his arms round her. 'Did I tell them at the end to go in peace and serve the Lord? Or did I blurt out that I couldn't hang around as I had a pressing engagement in bed with the girl who'd just agreed to marry me?'

'It was definitely the latter. That's why they were all smiling so much.'

Boxing Day. Dan had it all planned. Or he hoped he did. It had taken very little effort or persuasion on his part, which only added to his conviction that he was doing the right thing.

The idea had come to him yesterday afternoon. It was opening the door to Chloe and her family and seeing Seth standing at the back of the group that had started him thinking. If one reconciliation was possible, why not another?

The best part of the day had been when Chloe, pink-faced and grinning, had tapped her knife against her glass and announced she had something to tell them. 'This morning Seth asked me to marry him,' she said, her face growing pinker, her grin widening, 'and I said yes.' They all went a bit crazy after that: lots of whooping, kissing and hugging. Another bottle of champagne was opened and Marcus sat on Tatiana's lap, asking her to explain why everyone was making so much noise.

It had been one of the best Christmas Days Dan could remember. Which was why he was determined to make today as much of a day to remember. It was senseless not to try. They had too much history not to put the last few months behind them. If they'd learned anything from their experience, surely it was that life was too short and too precious to do otherwise?

Sally was perplexed. When Dan had phoned first thing this morning and invited her for a drink at Corner Cottage, she had agreed because it would have been churlish not to.

It had seemed odd not to spend Christmas Day with Dan and Marcus, but spending it quietly with Murray had been a very pleasant experience. They had shared the cooking of lunch—something she and Dan hadn't done in years—and she had surprised herself by how much she had enjoyed the day.

At the back of her mind was the worrying thought that Dan might have an ulterior motive for inviting her to Corner Cottage. He'd sounded oddly upbeat on the phone and she really hoped she wasn't going to have to disappoint him. Relations between them had been good recently and she didn't want anything to jeopardise that.

Dan and Marcus opened the front door to her. With his usual high level of enthusiasm, Marcus grabbed her hand and said, 'Mummy, Mummy, we've got a surprise for you. Come and see! Come and see!'

She looked at Dan. Was it her imagination or did he look worried? Dear God, surely he wasn't going to ask her to come back in front of Marcus? He wouldn't do that to her, would he?

She allowed herself to be dragged to the sitting room. Standing at the shut door Marcus suddenly turned and said very solemnly, 'Close your eyes, Mummy. Then the surprise will be even better.'

She did as he said and let him lead her into the room.

'*Ta daar*!' Marcus sang after she'd heard him turn the door handle.

She opened her eyes, and . . . and there was Chloe.

'Happy Christmas, Sally,' she said. 'Dan decided it was high time we settled our differences. I think he's right, don't you?' She smiled. 'After all, he knows us better than anyone and knew we'd never put our stubbornness behind us without help.'

Stunned, Sally glanced back to where Dan was hovering in the doorway. He still looked anxious. But she now understood the cause of his apprehension. That he could have thought to do this for her and Chloe touched her deeply. Overcome with emotion, her voice tight, she said, 'I don't know who to hug first.'

'But Daddy, why are they crying?' Marcus said, his little brow puckered. 'Didn't they like our surprise?'

Out in the kitchen, Dan got down on one knee in front of his son. 'They loved it. That's why they're crying. When something really nice happens, grown-ups sometimes cry.'

Marcus didn't look convinced. 'That sounds silly.'

Dan wrapped his arms around Marcus and held him tightly. 'One day you'll understand,' he said. 'One day you'll realise just how silly we really are. And the really silly part is that sometimes we get so much wrong we forget just what we get right.' He tilted his head back so he could look into his son's face. Straightening Marcus's reindeer antlers, he said, 'And the best thing I ever got right was you.'

Marcus frowned. 'Now *you're* crying, Daddy.'

'Because I'm happy.'

'Really?'

'Yes. Really.'

Erica James

Like the characters in *It's the Little Things*, you were caught up in the Boxing Day tsunami. Did it cause you to reassess your life?

As I said in the introduction to the novel, I knew that one day I would write about the tsunami but it's taken me until now to do so. On that fateful day I was on holiday in Phuket with my sons, Edward and Samuel, and having breakfast alone on the hotel terrace when the first wave came in, then the second. Once I was reassured that the boys were all right, the scale of the disaster began to hit. It was like a scene from a disaster movie. I still find it very hard to talk about. We were very lucky and it certainly brought home to me just how fragile and precious life is. But, that said, I don't think it caused me to reassess my life specifically, maybe because I was already very happy with where I was and what I was doing.

How long did the novel take you to write and how did it develop?

My novels usually take about ten months and this is my fourteenth. Dan and Sally were the first characters to take shape in my head, with Sally proving to be the more complex. I saw her very clearly as a woman whose career means the world to her, having fought so hard for it in the first place. Motherhood comes as an incredible shock to her, as it does for so many women. She is strong, capable, ambitious, and she and Dan are trying to make sense of the losses in the tsunami by creating another life.

Have you ever thought of being anything other than a writer?
No. It would be like giving up food. It's the best job in the world.

Do you have any tips for a would-be author?
Don't tell anyone your idea. And trust your instincts.

What's your greatest indulgence?
My flat on Lake Como that I bought last year. It's on the third floor and overlooks the lake. It's just wonderful. I try to go there at least once a month and it's the perfect place to write.

How is your Italian?
I've been learning Italian now for a couple of years and am quite proficient. I've just had a new kitchen put in the Como flat and all my dealings with the workmen were in Italian—and sign language! I also like to read in Italian and at the moment I'm enjoying the Italian edition of *Can You Keep a Secret?* by Sophie Kinsella. I've only marked a few difficult words that I need to look up later!

Do you love Italian clothes?
Yes, I admit that I buy most of my clothes in Italy these days.

Who do you most admire and why?
The people I admire most are my sons, Edward and Samuel. And why? For putting up with me!

A selection of 'little things' that make Erica happy . . .

- I have a large framed photograph of me with my eldest son—we're striking a particularly silly pose and I can't look at it without smiling.
- The sight of my garden in Cheshire, early on a summer's morning, never fails to fill me with a calming sense of happy well-being.
- I have a weakness for whimsical things and arranged on the shelves in my study is the complete set of Vauxhall Nova C'mon puppets from the TV advert. They always make me smile, especially when I squeeze them and they tell me to 'C'mon!'
- There are two pieces of music from my childhood that are guaranteed to make me laugh—Morecambe and Wise's 'Bring Me Sunshine' and Benny Hill's, 'Ernie (The Fastest Milkman in the West)'.
- The purchase of a long-awaited book from one of my favourite authors is an unbeatable pleasure.
- The heavenly scent of my favourite rose. One sniff of a Gertrude Jekyll rose and the world suddenly seems a much better place.
- And there's nothing like a new relationship to lift your spirits. I'm currently in love with my new car—an Audi A5. It's beautiful, all sleek, curvy lines and, unlike a man, it never puts up a fight when I put my foot down!

What a wonderful job I have! It's an absolute joy spending time with my lovely characters, interacting with them, steering them through the story and hoping that all the ends will tie up neatly when the last chapters are reached. As I only have the very roughest of outlines when I start a new book, there are always plenty of surprises along the way—for me, and hopefully for you too. Rumour Has It took quite a few unexpected twists and turns but I'm very happy with the way it's turned out. I do hope you'll feel the same way when you turn the final page!

Jill Mansell

Chapter 1

HOW WEIRD that you could push open your front door and know in an instant that something was wrong. Tilly stopped in the doorway, her hand fumbling for the light switch. Back from work at six o'clock on a cold Thursday evening in February, there was no reason to believe that anything should be different. But it was, she could feel it.

Flick went the light switch, on came the light. So much for spooky sixth sense; the reason opening the door had felt different was because the hall carpet had gone. Mystified, Tilly headed for the living room.

What was going on? She gazed round the room, taking everything— or rather the lack of everything—in. OK, they'd either been targeted by extremely picky burglars or . . .

He'd left the letter propped up on the mantelpiece. Gavin was nothing if not predictable. He had probably consulted some etiquette guru: Dear Miss Prim, I'm planning on leaving my girlfriend without a word of warning—how should I go about explaining to her what I've done?

To which Miss Prim would have replied: Dear Gavin, Oh dear, poor you! In a situation such as this, the correct method is to convey the necessary information in a handwritten letter—not in an email and *please* not in a text message—and leave it in the centre of the mantelpiece where it can't be missed.

Because, in all honesty, what other reason could there be? Tilly conducted a rapid inventory. Why else would the DVD recorder— hers—still be there, but the TV—his—be missing? Why else would three-quarters of the DVDs be gone (war films, sci-fi and the like), leaving only the slushy make-you-cry films and romantic comedies?

'Tilly? Coo-eee! Only me!'

Damn. Babs from across the landing.

'Hello, Babs.' Tilly turned; maybe Babs had a message for her from Gavin. Or maybe he'd asked her to pop round and check that she was all right.

'I just wanted to see how you're doing. Oh, you poor thing, and there was me thinking the two of you were so happy together. I wish you could've told me, you know I'm always happy to listen.'

Happy to listen? Babs *lived* to listen to other people's woes.

'I would have told you,' said Tilly. 'If I'd known.'

'Oh my GOOD LORD. You mean . . .?'

'Gavin's done a runner. Well,' Tilly reached for the letter on the mantelpiece, 'either that or he's been kidnapped.'

'Except when I saw him loading his belongings into the rental van this afternoon he didn't have any kidnappers with him.' Her expression sympathetic, Babs said, 'Only his mam and dad.'

The commuter-packed train from Paddington pulled into Roxborough Station the following evening. And there was Erin, waiting on the platform, waving madly as she spotted Tilly.

Just the sight of her made Tilly feel better. She couldn't imagine not having Erin as her best friend. Ten years ago, when she had been deciding whether to do her degree course at Liverpool or Exeter, she could have chosen Liverpool and it would never have happened. But she'd gone for Exeter instead—something about the seasidey feel to it—and there had been Erin, in the room next to hers in the halls of residence. The two of them had hit it off from day one. It was weird to think that if she'd gone to Liverpool instead she would have a completely different best friend, a tall skinny triathlete, say, called Helena. God, imagine *that*.

'Oof.' Erin gasped as Tilly's hug knocked the air from her lungs. 'What's this in aid of?'

'I'm glad you aren't a triathlete called Helena.'

'Blimey, you and me both.' Erin tucked her arm through Tilly's. 'Come on, you. Let's get home. I've made sticky toffee pudding.'

'You see?' Tilly beamed. 'Helena would never say that. She'd say, "Why don't we go out for a nice ten-mile run, that'll cheer us up!"'

Erin's flat, as quirky and higgledy-piggledy as the properties that lined Roxborough's High Street, was a one-bedroomed affair situated on the first floor above the shop she'd been running as a dress exchange for the past seven years. Working in a shop hadn't been her dream career when she'd graduated from Exeter with a first-class degree in French, but Erin's plans to work in Paris as a translator had been dashed the month after her twenty-first birthday when her mother had suffered a stroke. Devastated, Erin had given up the ideal job in Paris and moved back to Roxborough to nurse her mother.

Three years after the first stroke, a second one took her mother's life. Having always intended to move back to Paris once the unthinkable had happened, Erin realised she no longer wanted to. Roxborough, an ancient market town in the centre of the Cotswolds, was a wonderful place to live. The people were caring and supportive, there was real community spirit and the business was doing well. This was where she was happy and loved, so why move away?

And now, almost four years on, Erin had even more reason to be happy with her decision to stay. But she wouldn't tell Tilly yet, not while her friend was still reeling from Gavin's disappearing act. That would definitely be insensitive.

Although it had to be said, Tilly didn't seem to be reeling too badly.

'I phoned him this afternoon,' Tilly said between spoonfuls of sticky toffee pudding. 'He couldn't face telling me in person in case I cried. He's moved back in with his parents, which leaves me stuck with a flat there's no way I can afford on one salary.'

'Would you have cried? If he'd told you face to face?'

'What? God, I don't know. Maybe.'

'*Maybe?* If you're madly in love with someone and they dump you, you're supposed to cry buckets.'

Tilly looked defensive. 'Not necessarily.'

'Buckets,' repeated Erin. 'Which makes me think secretly, deep down, you *wanted* him to finish with you because you couldn't bring yourself to be the one to do the deed.'

Tilly flushed and said nothing.

'Ha! See? I'm right, aren't I?' Erin let out a crow of delight. 'It's Mickey Nolan all over again. You really liked him to begin with, then it all got a bit boring and you didn't know how to chuck him without hurting his feelings. So you did that whole distancing yourself thing until he realised the relationship had run out of steam. And Darren Shaw,' she suddenly remembered. 'You did the same with him. You feel guilty about finishing with boyfriends so you force them to finish with you.'

It was a light-bulb moment. 'You could be right,' Tilly admitted. 'Did I ever tell you about Jamie Dalston?'

'No. Why, did you do it to him too?'

'No, we went out for a couple of weeks when I was fifteen. Then I realised he was a bit weird so I dumped him.' Tilly paused. 'That was when it started getting awkward, because Jamie didn't want to be dumped. He used to phone the house all the time, and walk up and down our road. If I went out, he'd follow me. Then, when it was my birthday he sent me some quite expensive jewellery. My mum took it round to his mum's and the police got involved. He'd stolen the money to buy the jewellery. Anyway, his family moved away and I never saw him again, but it frightened the living daylights out of me. I'd rather let the other person do the dumping. That way, they're less likely to stalk you afterwards.'

'So you are actually quite glad Gavin's gone,' said Erin.

'Well, I did feel kind of trapped,' Tilly confessed.

'Come on.' Erin's tone was consoling as she put the empty pudding bowls on the coffee table and stood up. 'Let's go to the pub.'

The joy of living at one end of Roxborough High Street was that the Lazy Fox was situated at the other end of it, far enough away for you not to need ear plugs at home if they were having one of their karaoke evenings but close enough to stagger back after a good night. Tilly enjoyed the atmosphere in the pub. She loved the way Declan, the landlord, upon hearing her just-been-chucked story from Erin, said easily, 'Fellow must be mad. Come and live in Roxborough. Fresh country air and plenty of cider—that'll put hairs on your chest.'

Tilly grinned. 'Thanks, but I'm a townee.'

'Damn cheek. This is a town!'

'She means London,' said Erin.

'That's a terrible place to live.' Declan shook his head.

'Our newspapers have proper news,' Tilly riposted, poking at the copy of the *Roxborough Gazette* he'd been reading between customers. 'What's that on your front page? Cow falls through cattle grid?'

'Ah, but isn't it great that we aren't awash with terrorists and murderers?' Declan winked at her. 'That's why I like it here.'

'What happened to the cow anyway?' Tilly leaned across but he whisked the newspaper away.

'Oh no, anyone who laughs at our headlines doesn't get to find out how the stories turn out. Was the cow left dangling there to die a horrible death? Now that's what I call a *moo*-ving tale . . .'

Declan relented as they were leaving two hours later, slipping the

Gazette into Tilly's bag. 'There you go, you can read the rest yourself. It may not be the *Evening Standard* but our paper has its own charm, you know. In fact, in some ways it's *udder*ly compelling.'

The awful thing was, after three pints of cider Tilly secretly found this funny. Somehow she managed to keep a straight face.

Once outside on the street, closing-time hunger pangs struck and they were forced to head up the road to the fish-and-chip shop.

Back out on the pavement, Tilly greedily unwrapped the steaming hot parcel and tore off her first hunk of batter. 'Mm, *mmm*.'

'I'm going to save mine until we get home,' said Erin.

'You can't! That's what old people do!'

'I'm twenty-eight,' Erin said happily. 'I'm knocking on. And so are you.'

'Cheek!' Outraged, Tilly threw a chip at her. 'I'm a spring chicken.'

A couple of teenage boys, crossing the street, snorted and nudged each other. Tilly heard one of them murmur, 'In her dreams.'

'For heaven's sake!' Indignantly Tilly spread her arms. 'Why is everyone having a go at me tonight? Twenty-eight isn't geriatric.'

The other boy grinned. 'In two years' time you'll be thirty. *That's* geriatric.'

'I can do anything you can do,' Tilly said heatedly. 'Pipsqueak.'

'Go on then, try peeing up against that wall.'

Damn, she hated smart kids.

'Or do *this*,' called out the first boy, effortlessly leapfrogging the fixed, dome-topped litter bin just down from the chip shop.

Oh yes, this was more like it. Leapfrog was practically her specialist subject. Dumping her parcel of fish and chips in Erin's arms, Tilly took a run-up and launched herself at the bin.

Vaulting it went without a hitch; she sailed balletically over the top. It was when she landed that it all went horribly wrong. Honestly, what were the chances of your left foot landing on the very chip you'd earlier thrown at your best friend after she'd called you old?

'EEEEYYYYAAA!' Tilly let out a shriek as her leg scooted off at an angle and her arms went windmilling through the air. She heard Erin call out in horror, 'Mind the—' a millisecond before she cannoned into the side of the parked car. *Ouch*, it might have broken her fall but it still hurt. Splattered against it like a cartoon character, Tilly belatedly noticed that it was an incredibly clean and glossy car.

'Hey!' yelled an unamused male voice from some way up the street.

Well, it had been incredibly clean and glossy up until five seconds ago. Peeling herself away from the car, Tilly saw the marks her fish-and-chip greasy fingers had left on the passenger door, the front wing and the side window. With the sleeve of her jacket she attempted to clean off the worst of the smears. The male voice behind her, sounding more annoyed than ever, shouted out, 'Have you scratched my paintwork?'

'No I haven't, and you shouldn't have been parked there anyway. It's double yellows.' Glancing over her shoulder and checking he was too far away to catch her, Tilly retrieved her fish and chips from Erin, then did what any self-respecting twenty-eight-year-old would do and legged it down the road.

'It's OK,' panted Erin, 'he's not chasing us.'

They slowed down and Tilly carried on eating her chips. As they made their way along the wet pavement she said, 'Lucky there was no one around to take a photo. In a place like this, getting greasy fingers on a clean car could've made the front page of next week's *Gazette*.'

'You know, Declan's right. You'd like it here.' Erin, who was still saving her own chips, pinched one of Tilly's.

They'd reached the bottom of the High Street. All they had to do now was cross the road and they'd be home. Tilly waited next to Erin for a bus to trundle past, followed by a gleaming black car—

'You sod!' Tilly shrieked as the car splashed through a puddle at the kerbside, sending a great wave of icy water over her skirt and legs. Leaping back—*too late*—she glimpsed a flash of white teeth as the figure in the driver's seat grinned and raised a hand in mock apology before accelerating away. 'It was him, wasn't it? The one who yelled at me.'

'It's the same car,' Erin confirmed. 'Some kind of Jag.'

'Bastard, he did that on purpose.' But she was inwardly impressed. 'Quite clever though.' Tilly pointed at Erin's unsullied cream coat. 'The way he managed to avoid you and get only me.'

Tilly woke at ten o'clock the next morning. Erin had tiptoed past her an hour ago in order to open the shop. Later Tilly would join her, but for now she would enjoy being lazy and spend a bit of time wondering what to do with the rest of her life.

Tilly made herself a mug of tea and a plate of toast before hauling the duvet back onto the sofa and crawling under it. Plumping up the pillows, she pulled the *Roxborough Gazette* out of her bag and leafed through it. There was a piece about a tractor auction—be still, my beating heart—and a whole page devoted to a charity bazaar at Roxborough Comprehensive. Actually, it was quite sweet. Sipping her tea, she came across the jobs section. Garage mechanic required, bar staff wanted for the Castle Hotel . . . Her attention was caught by a small box ad at the bottom of the page: *Girl Friday, fun job, country house, £200 pw.*

That was it, brief and to the point. Tilly wondered what 'fun job' meant; after all, some people might call Chancellor of the Exchequer a fun job. She took a bite of toast, turned over the page and began reading the articles for sale—a size eighteen Pronuptia wedding dress, never worn . . . fifty-nine-piece dinner service (one plate missing—thrown at lying, double-crossing ex-husband) . . .

She reached the end, then found herself turning back to the page with *that* advert on it. Almost as if it were calling her name.

Which was ridiculous, because it didn't even say what the job involved and the money was rubbish, but a quick phone call to find out wouldn't do any harm, would it? Scooping up her mobile, Tilly pressed out the number and listened to it ringing at the other end.

'Hello,' intoned an automated voice, 'please leave your message after the . . .'

'Tone,' Tilly prompted helpfully, but the voice didn't oblige. All she got was silence. The answering machine was full.

Oh well, that was that. Whoever had placed the ad had been inundated with calls. It was probably a vacancy for a topless waitress anyway. Better get up instead.

Erin drove Tilly to the station on Sunday afternoon.

'So, any idea what you're going to do?'

Tilly pulled a face, shook her head. 'Not yet. Find somewhere cheaper to live, that's all. What else can I do?' She gave Erin a kiss and said, 'Thanks for the weekend. I'll keep you up to date.'

Erin hugged her. 'Sure you don't want me to wait with you?'

'Don't worry, I'm fine. The train'll be here in ten minutes.'

Famous last words. Within two minutes the announcement came over the Tannoy that the train bound for London Paddington would be delayed by forty minutes. Clutching at straws, Tilly looked at the elderly woman next to her. 'Fourteen or forty?'

The woman clicked her tongue in disgust and said, 'Forty. This is going to be fun.'

Fun. *Fun job, country house.* Tilly wished she'd tried calling the number again. Then with a jolt she realised all she had to do was press LAST NUMBER REDIAL.

'Hello?' The voice was young, female and breathless.

'Oh, hi, I was calling about the ad in the paper,' began Tilly.

'Hang on, I'll get Dad. DAAAD?' bellowed the voice.

'Ouch.' Tilly winced as the noise bounced off her left eardrum.

'Dad, it's another one about the job.'

'Oh, bloody hell, haven't we got enough to choose from?' The voice was flat, fed up and Liverpudlian. 'Just tell her she's too late, we've given it to someone else.'

Tilly's competitive spirit rose to the surface; until two minutes ago she hadn't even wanted the job. But now, if he was going to try and fob her off . . . 'Actually, you can tell him I heard that. Could he at least have the decency to speak to me?'

The girl said cheerfully, 'Hang on,' and, 'Ooh, Dad, she's cross.'

Tilly heard the phone being passed over, coupled with fierce whispering. 'Right, sorry.' It was the father's voice, marginally more friendly than before. 'If you want the truth, this whole thing's been a prize cockup. We've just got back from holiday to find the answering machine jammed with messages. The ad was meant to go into next week's paper, not last week's. All I want right now is a mug of tea and a bacon sandwich and I'm not getting either of them because the damn phone keeps ringing. Give me your name and number and I'll call you back, fix up a time for the interview.'

'Hang on,' said Tilly, 'I don't even know if I want an interview yet. What does a Girl Friday *do*, exactly?'

'Everything.'

'And you said it was a fun job. What does *that* mean?'

'It means there's a chance you might enjoy it for about two per cent of the time. The other ninety-eight per cent will be sheer drudgery.'

'OK, now you're just trying to put me off,' Tilly said suspiciously. 'This so-called job. Is it anything to do with porn?'

'No. Sorry.' He sounded amused. 'Why, was that what you were hoping for?'

'No, it was not.' Tilly did her best to sound ladylike but not off-puttingly prissy. 'And why are you only paying two hundred a week?'

This time he actually laughed. 'It's a live-in position. Everything else is paid for, including a car.'

OK, this was definitely a good-enough reason. Tilly said promptly, 'You know what? I'd be great at this job. Are you in Roxborough?'

'No, we're in Mumbai, that's why I advertised in the *Roxborough Gazette*.' There it was again, that laconic deadpan Liverpudlian wit.

'Well, I live in London. But right now I'm on the platform at

Roxborough Station, waiting to go back there.' Going for broke, Tilly took a deep breath and said, 'So what would be really fantastic would be if I could come over and see you now.'

Silence.

Finally she heard a sigh. 'Did I tell you how bloody knackered I am?'

'While you're interviewing me,' Tilly said innocently, 'I could always make you a fantastic bacon sandwich.'

He gave a snort of amusement. 'You're sharp, aren't you?'

'Just think. If I'm perfect, you won't have to interview anyone else.'

Another pause. Then he said, 'Go on then, get yourself over here. We're at Beech House on the Brockley Road, just over the bridge and on the right as you're heading out of town. Do you know it?'

'No, but I'll find you, don't worry.' That sounded nice and efficient, didn't it? 'I'll be there in ten minutes.'

Well, she would have been if there'd been a taxi outside the station. But that was wishful thinking, because this was Roxborough Station on a wintry February Sunday. Tilly couldn't bring herself to phone Erin. How far away could Beech House be, anyway? Surely not more than a mile. She could be there in fifteen minutes on foot . . .

It rained. It was more than a mile. It rained harder and the sky darkened along with Tilly's grey sweatshirt and jeans, because of course she didn't have anything so sensible as an umbrella. Her case-on-wheels jiggled and bounced along the pavement as she dragged it behind her.

After twenty-five minutes she saw a house up ahead on the right and quickened her pace. There, thank God, was the sign saying Beech House. She turned into the stone-pillared entrance and headed up the gravelled driveway. The Regency-style property was imposing.

Panting and drenched, Tilly rang the bell. What was she even doing here? The man would probably turn out to be a right weirdo.

'Bloody hell, kid. Look at the state of you.' Having flung open the door, the right weirdo hauled her inside. 'I thought you'd stood us up. Don't tell me you've walked all the way from the station.'

Tilly nodded, the blissful heat causing her teeth to start chattering wildly. 'There weren't any t-taxis.'

He looked askance at her drenched sweatshirt. 'If you'd called me again I'd have come and picked you up. If you catch pneumonia and drop dead I'm going to have it on my conscience now, aren't I?'

'I'll sign a disclaimer.' Tilly stuck out her hand and shook his. 'I'm Tilly Cole. Nice to meet you.'

'Nice to meet you too, Tilly Cole. Max Dineen.' He was tall and grey-hound thin, aged around forty, with close-cropped wavy blond hair and friendly grey eyes behind steel-rimmed spectacles. 'Come along in and we'll get you dried off. That's what I usually say to Betty,' he added as he led the way into the kitchen.

'Your daughter?'

Max indicated the brown and white terrier curled up on a cushion in one of the window seats. 'Our dog, but it's an easy mistake to make. I get them mixed up myself. Betty's the one with the cold nose,' he went on as a clatter of footsteps heralded his daughter's arrival in the kitchen, 'and the noisy one in the stripy tights is Lou.'

'Hi!' Lou was in her early teens, with mad red hair corkscrewing around her head and an infectious grin. 'It's Louisa actually.'

'Lou, this is Tilly. Run upstairs and fetch her the dressing gown from the spare room.' Max turned to Tilly. 'We'll chuck your clothes in the tumble drier. How about that then?' He winked. 'How many job interviews have you done in a dressing gown, eh?'

The thing was, he wasn't being sleazy or suggestive. He was simply making the suggestion because it made sense. Nevertheless, it would be surreal . . .

'It's OK, I've got something I can change into.' Tilly pointed to her case. Max said, 'Spoilsport.'

The house was amazing, decorated with an eye for colour and real flair. Whether Max Dineen was married or divorced, Tilly guessed this was the work of a woman. In the bottle-green and white marble-tiled downstairs cloakroom she stripped off her wet things and changed.

Back in the kitchen, Max took her jeans and sweatshirt through to the utility room and put them in the tumble drier. Then he handed her a cup of coffee and pulled out one of the kitchen chairs.

'Right, let's make a start, shall we? The situation is this. Lou's mum and I split up three years ago. Her mum lives and works in California. For the first couple of years Lou stayed out there with her, but she missed all this . . .' he gestured ironically at the rain-splattered window, 'so last year she decided to move back for good. I tried changing my name and going into hiding but she managed to track me down.'

'Dad.' Lou rolled her eyes at him. 'Nobody's going to want to work for you if you say stuff like this. OK, here's the thing,' she took over, 'I'm thirteen. Dad cut back on work when I first came home, but now he's stepping it up again.'

'It's a question of having to,' said Max. 'You cost a fortune.'

'Anyway,' Louisa ignored him, 'we decided we needed a Girl Friday to help us out, someone to pick me up from school and stuff, do a spot of cooking sometimes, help Dad out with the business—just anything that needs doing, really. We kept it vague, because—'

'We kept it vague,' Max interjected, 'because if we advertised for someone to look after a bad-tempered old git and a whiny teenager, everyone would run a mile.'

'Just keep on ignoring him.' Louisa's eyes sparkled. 'So. Does that sound like the kind of thing you might like to do?'

Tilly shrugged. 'That rather depends on your dad's business. If he's the town rat-catcher I'm not going to be so keen on helping him out.'

'How about gravedigging?' said Max.

'Dad, will you leave this to me? He's not a gravedigger,' said Louisa, 'he has an interior design company. It's good fun. He's very in demand.' She nodded proudly. 'Now it's your turn to tell us about you.'

Tilly hid a smile, because Louisa was so earnest and sparky and bossy and young, and she, Tilly, was being interviewed by a thirteen-year-old freckly redhead wearing huge hooped earrings, a lime-green sweater dress and multicoloured stripy tights. She'd also been wrong about the ex-wife being responsible for the way the house looked.

Plus no rats, which had to be a bonus.

'OK, the truth? I live in London, my job's pretty boring and my boyfriend's just done a bunk. Which doesn't upset me, but it means I can't afford to stay on in the flat we shared, which *does*. Then I came down here for the weekend to stay with my friend Erin, and—'

'Erin? Who runs Erin's Beautiful Clothes?' Perkily Louisa said, 'I know her. I used to go in the shop with Mum. She's cool!'

'I know she's cool. And she'll be thrilled to hear you think so too,' said Tilly. 'We've been best friends since university. Erin says this is a really nice place to live. She'd love it if I moved down here. So here I am.'

'Can you cook?' said Max.

'Ish. I'm not Nigella.'

'Don't look so worried, we're not after Nigella. Criminal record?'

Shocked, Tilly yelped, 'No!'

'Like yellow?'

'Excuse me?'

'Do you like yellow? That's the colour of the room you'd be sleeping in if you came to live here.'

They went upstairs and Max showed Tilly the room, which was

fabulously decorated in shades of pale gold with accents of silver and white. The curtains were sumptuous. And as for the bed . . .

'Well?' said Max.

Tilly's mouth was dry. Was it wrong to take a job just because you'd fallen in love with a bed?

Except this was so much more than just a bed. It was an actual four-poster, draped in ivory and silver damask, pure Hollywood, the bed of her dreams, and she wanted to roll around on it like a puppy.

Louisa surveyed Tilly beadily. 'So? What's the verdict?'

'I want this job,' said Tilly. 'Although I should talk to Erin first, check out your credentials. You might be the ASBO family from hell.'

'Oh, we're definitely that.' Max nodded. 'And maybe we should give Erin a call too, find out all about you.'

'She'll say nice things, tell you I'm lovely. If she doesn't,' said Tilly, 'she knows I'll give her a Chinese burn.'

Over bacon sandwiches and mugs of tea they carried on getting to know each other. 'Are you bright and cheerful when you get up in the morning?' asked Max.

'I can be.'

'Christ, no, I can't bear people being cheerful in the mornings.'

'He's a grumpy old man,' Louisa said comfortably, 'aren't you, Dad?'

Tilly pointed a teasing finger at her. 'If I came to work here, it'd be like *The Sound of Music*.'

'Minus the singing nuns,' said Max.

'And with a lot fewer children to look after,' Louisa pointed out.

'And you won't end up marrying Captain von Trapp,' said Max.

Oh. Right. Not that she wanted to marry him, but still. Tilly guessed it was his way of letting her know right away that she wasn't his type. God, did he think she'd been flirting with him? Because she genuinely hadn't. Talk about blunt, though.

Across the table she intercepted a look passing between Louisa and Max. 'Oh, Dad, don't tell her,' Louisa wailed. 'Can't we just leave it for now? Wait until she moves in.'

'Tell me what?' Tilly sat up, her stomach tightening with apprehension. Just when everything had been going so well, too.

'I have to,' Max said evenly. 'It's not fair otherwise.'

For heaven's sake, were they *vampires*?

'Please, Dad, don't,' begged Louisa.

The phone started ringing out in the hall. Max looked at Louisa. 'Go and get that, will you, Lou?'

For a second she stared at him, her jaw rigid. Then she scraped back her chair and ran out of the kitchen, red curls bouncing.

'Is this to do with your wife?' Tilly had done *Jane Eyre* at school; had Louisa's mum gone loopy? Was she actually tied up in the attic?

'In a way.' Max nodded. 'The reason Kaye and I got divorced is because I'm gay.'

Crikey, she hadn't been expecting *that*. Tilly put down her sandwich. Was he serious or was this another joke? 'Really?'

'Really.' Max surveyed her steadily. 'OK, let me just tell you before Lou comes back. When I was in my twenties it was easier to be hetero-sexual. I met Kaye and she was great. Then she got pregnant. Not exactly planned, but that was fine too.' His smile was crooked. 'So we got married and Lou was born, and I told myself I had to stay straight for their sakes. Well, I lasted nearly ten years. And I never once cheated on Kaye. But in the end I couldn't do it any more. We split up. Poor old Kaye, it wasn't her fault. And Lou's coped brilliantly. She's a star.'

'I can see that,' said Tilly.

'But it's obviously been a lot for her to cope with. I don't have a part-ner right now, which makes things easier.' Max paused, then said, 'The thing is, you have to remember this isn't London, it's Roxborough. I spoke to a woman who runs an employment agency and she said I shouldn't mention the gay thing at all. Apparently a lot of poten-tial employees would be put off, especially if half the reason for taking the job was because they fancied their chances with a wealthy single father.' He half smiled before adding archly, 'And then you came out with your *Sound of Music* comment.'

'I didn't mean it like that,' Tilly protested.

'Well, that's good news. But according to this woman, some people just might not want to live in a house with a gay man.' Max shrugged. 'Apparently some people might find it a bit . . . yucky.'

A noise behind them prompted Tilly to swivel round. Louisa was back, standing in the doorway. 'Well?' Louisa looked anxious.

Tilly was incredulous. 'This woman who runs an employment agency. Is she by any chance two hundred and seventy years old?'

Louisa's narrow shoulders sagged with relief. 'Does that mean it isn't a problem? You still want to come and live here?'

Unable to keep a straight face, Tilly said, '*That's* not a problem. But if we're talking yucky, I'm going to need to know exactly what your dad's like when it comes to digging butter knives in the marmalade, dump-ing tea bags in the sink and leaving the top off the toothpaste.'

Chapter 2

WAS THIS HOW shoplifters felt as they made their way round a store stealthily pocketing small items, nerve-janglingly aware that at any moment the tiniest slip-up could lead to them being caught out? Erin did her best to stay relaxed, to keep her breathing steady, but any minute now she could make that slip, give herself away. And to add insult to injury she was in her own shop.

Not trusting herself with the portable steamer in case her hands trembled too much, Erin busied herself with the computer and pretended to be engrossed in a spreadsheet. Three feet away from her, riffling through a rail of tops, Stella Welch carried on chatting to her friend Amy through the door of the changing cubicle.

'I saw Fergus again last night, by the way. Bumped into him in the Fox.'

That's because you've been stalking him, thought Erin.

'How's he looking?' Amy's voice floated out of the cubicle.

'The truth? Pale.'

It's February.

'In fact, I told him he could do with a few sessions on the sunbed.' Stella flicked back her tawny hair and held a pomegranate-pink silk shirt up against herself. 'Does this colour suit me? It does, doesn't it?'

'It looks great.' Erin nodded, because the colour was perfect against Stella's permatanned skin.

'I also told him he was a bastard.' Stella seamlessly continued her conversation with Amy. 'I can't believe it's been six months since he left. I mean, why would anyone want to leave *me*? It's not even as if Fergus is amazing looking! Eleven years of marriage and then he ups and goes. He was lucky to get me in the first place, for God's sake.'

'Did you tell him that?' said Amy.

'Only about a million times. Oh, he just makes me so mad. I asked him last night if he was seeing someone else but he still says he isn't. He'd better not be, that's all I can say. Oh yes, that's perfect on you.'

The changing-room door had opened. Amy did a twirl in the

midnight-blue Nicole Farhi dress. 'Not too over the top for a first date?'

'Go for it,' Stella pronounced. She turned to Erin and said, 'Amy's being taken out to dinner tonight. By Jack Lucas.'

'Gosh. Lovely.'

Amy's eyes sparkled. 'I can't believe it's actually happening!'

Erin couldn't think why she couldn't believe it; when you'd been out with as many girls as Jack Lucas had, it was hard to find someone who *hadn't* been one of his conquests. In fact she, Erin, was practically the only female she knew who hadn't been there, done that. It was far more entertaining to stand back and let all the other girls do their moths-round-a-flame thing, and to watch them crash and burn.

'I'll take it,' said Amy, dancing back into the cubicle to change.

'See, if Fergus looked like Jack Lucas I could understand him doing what he's done.' Stella shook her head in disbelief. 'But how does he have the nerve to do it when he looks like Fergus?'

'Maybe he'll change his mind and come crawling back,' Amy offered.

'That's what I've been waiting for! But it's been six months now and he still hasn't. You go to the Fox sometimes, don't you?'

Her skin prickling, Erin realised this question was being directed at her. Unwillingly, she looked up from the computer. 'Sometimes.'

'Have you heard any rumours about my husband? Any gossip, any signs that he's seeing another woman?'

Erin's mouth was dry. 'No. No signs, nothing.'

Stella gave a nod of satisfaction. 'He'd better not be. He's trying to ruin my life. Talk about selfish. I mean, how old are you, Erin? Thirty-three?' she hazarded. 'Thirty-five?'

Ouch. 'Actually I'm twenty-eight,' said Erin.

'Oh. I thought you were older than that. And I know I look young for my age but I'm thirty-seven. Thirty-seven! We were supposed to be starting a family this year, and my husband's had some kind of bizarre mental breakdown and buggered off instead. Meanwhile my fertility is declining. Ooh, it just makes me so *mad*.'

'Quick, I didn't realise it was nearly two o'clock.' Bursting out of the cubicle, Amy frantically waved the Nicole Farhi dress at Erin and scrabbled for her credit card. 'I've got an appointment at the hairdresser's in five minutes. Can't meet Jack Lucas tonight without having my roots touched up!'

Two minutes later they were gone. Erin could breathe again. Fergus was the best thing that had happened to her in years; he was the light of her life. But nothing was ever simple, was it? Because Fergus had spent the past eleven years being married to Stella and although he was now desperate to put those years behind him and divorce her, Stella was digging her heels in.

The irony was that although she had known them both for years, in all that time Erin had never secretly lusted after Fergus. With his messy, unstyled dark hair, merry eyes, large feet and eternal struggle to dress smartly, Fergus Welch was simply a lovely person to know. He and Stella had always been generally regarded as something of a mismatched couple, but even the news of their separation hadn't caused Erin's heart to give a secret leap of hope.

Which had only made it all the more surprising when, just six weeks ago, they had bumped into each other and *whoosh*, out of nowhere the spark had ignited. And just think, if it hadn't been raining that day, it would never have happened.

Although to call it raining was an understatement. It had been a full-on thunderstorm, with rain hammering down like bullets. It was also undoubtedly what had inspired the bored teenagers to run round the car park flipping up the windscreen wipers of an entire row of cars.

Erin's Fiat, sadly, had been the oldest in the row and her windscreen wipers had been the most fragile. When she emerged from the supermarket on the outskirts of Cirencester and got soaked to the skin unloading her bags of shopping, she didn't immediately realise what had happened. When she leaped into the driver's seat and switched on the ignition and wipers, she couldn't work out why they weren't working. It wasn't until she climbed back out of the car that she found the wipers on the ground. A posh middle-aged woman in a nearby 4x4 unwound her window a couple of inches and bellowed, 'I saw 'em doing it, little sods. Gave 'em an earful and they ran orf. Bloody hoody types. Set the hounds on 'em.'

Which was all well and good but it didn't exactly solve the problem to hand. Erin, her hair plastered to her head and her clothes clinging like papier-mâché to her body, gazed in dismay at the snapped-off windscreen wipers. Driving the car would be impossible in this downpour. She was stuck here ten miles from home until the rain stopped, and in the meantime her three tubs of honeycomb ice cream were going to melt all over the—

'Erin! Stand there for much longer and you might get wet!'

Turning, Erin squinted and saw Fergus Welch hurrying towards her across the car park, holding a half-broken golfing umbrella over his head and waving his key at a dark green Lexus. As he slowed, Erin held up the amputated wipers.

'Oh no.' His forehead creased with concern. 'Vandals?'

'Well, I didn't do it myself.' Rain dripped off Erin's eyelashes and nose. 'And from the look of the sky, I'm going to be stuck here for hours. It's Monday, my precious day off—what could be nicer?'

'Hey, no problem, I can give you a lift home.'

And that was how it had started. She'd waited in the car while Fergus had shown a client round a house in Tetbury, then he'd driven her back to Roxborough and helped to carry her bags into the flat. Erin had made coffee and they'd shared an entire tub of honeycomb ice cream—semi-melted by now, but still delicious.

They didn't leap on each other in an unstoppable frenzy of lust. But each of them silently acknowledged that . . . well, they'd quite like to.

Stella was a major stumbling block.

'She's spent the past eleven years telling me I don't deserve her, that she's better than me,' said Fergus as Erin made another pot of coffee. 'I thought she'd be thrilled when I moved out. But she's taking it so badly. I wasn't expecting this to happen at all.'

'Do you think you'll get back together?' Erin did her best to sound impartial.

'No, never. It's over.' Fergus shook his head. 'Stella doesn't love me, she's just outraged that I had the nerve to leave.'

'Maybe she'll meet someone else,' Erin said hopefully.

Fergus nodded in agreement. 'That's what I'm hoping.'

Fergus had had to head back to the office after that. He worked as a senior negotiator at Thornton and Best, the estate agents at the top of the High Street. Later that evening he'd given Erin a lift back to her car and the evening had ended with her planting a careful thankyou kiss on his cheek. Perfectly chaste and innocent on the surface but seething with longing and less-than-innocent possibilities underneath.

Erin was jolted back to the present by the phone shrilling on the desk in front of her. Since that night she and Fergus had carried on secretly meeting up and the chastity aspect wasn't set to last for much longer; she was besotted with Fergus and, blissfully, he appeared to be just as—

OK, enough, no more daydreaming about Fergus. Answer the phone.

Ooh, it might even *be* Fergus!

'Hello? Erin's Beautiful Clothes.'

'Hey, you!' It was Tilly's voice. 'Are you busy or can you talk?'

Erin's heart sank as the bell jangled above the door, heralding the arrival of another customer just when she'd been about to settle down for a good chat. Then her head jerked up and her mouth fell open because there, standing in the doorway, was . . . 'Tilly! What's going on?'

Tilly flung her arms wide. 'Surprise!' Her eyes dancing, she explained, 'You said I'd like it here. Well, you'd better be right, because I've done it, I live here now. As of today.'

'What? Where? Where are you living?'

'Beech House. I'm working as a Girl Friday for Max Dineen.'

Erin sat bolt upright. 'Dineen! Max Dineen who was married to Kaye? Daughter with red hair called . . .'

'Lou. That's right.' Tilly pulled a face. 'Please don't tell me he's a raving psychopath.'

'Don't worry, everyone likes Max. And Lou's a cutie. I can't believe it.' Erin shook her head, still in a daze.

'I know, isn't it great? New job, new home, whole new life!'

'Here she is,' Max announced as Tilly, back from her visit to Erin, padded into the kitchen in her socks. 'Here's the girl I was telling you about.'

Tilly turned to greet the visitor and stopped in her tracks. Because there, leaning against the Aga with his arms casually folded in front of him and a devastating grin spreading across his face, was one of the most disconcertingly good-looking men she'd ever seen in real life. Thickly fringed green eyes surveyed her with amusement and glossy dark hair flopped over his forehead. His face was tanned, emphasising the whiteness of his teeth, but the teeth themselves were just imperfect enough not to have been the work of a dentist. Phew. And he was wearing faded paint-splashed jeans, Timberlands and a pale brown polo shirt beneath a well-worn dusty grey gilet. Pretty spectacular body too.

Max performed the introductions. 'Tilly, this is my . . . *friend*, Jack Lucas. Jack, meet Tilly Cole.'

'OK, let's just make something clear, shall we? From the word go? I'm not Max's . . . *friend*,' said Jack. 'I'm just his friend. No hesitation, no significant emphasis. Max likes to make people wonder what he's insinuating. He thinks it's hilarious. Just ignore him.' He reached forward and shook hands. 'Hi, Tilly. Good to meet you.'

'You too.' Tilly did her best to behave as if being introduced to knee-tremblingly attractive men was a daily occurrence.

'You know, something about you reminds me . . .' Letting go of her hand, Jack circled an index finger as the connection eluded him.

'Oh God, here he goes.' Max shook his head in disgust. 'You don't waste any time, do you? And talk about unoriginal. Watch out, girl,' he told Tilly. 'Next he'll be saying he's sure he's met you before, and you'll believe him and start wondering where.'

'Max, shut up. This isn't a chat-up line, it's the truth.' But Jack Lucas was laughing as he said it, making it impossible for Tilly to know whether he was telling the truth or not.

'I'm from London. We haven't met before.' If she had, Tilly knew she would definitely have remembered.

'Well, you're here now. And Max and I sometimes work together, so I'm sure we'll be seeing more of each other.' The playful glint in his eye told her he was perfectly well aware of the double entendre. But something altogether more impressive was happening, Tilly discovered, at the same time. When he spoke to her it was as if all he cared about was what she might say in return. Neat trick. It was also, of course, the sign of a champion seducer.

At that moment the front door opened and slammed shut, and Louisa erupted into the kitchen in her navy school uniform.

'You're here!' Her eyes lit up. Then she rushed over and flung her arms round Tilly. 'I'm so glad!'

'Hey, how about me?' Jack was indignant. Louisa hugged him in turn. 'You smell of paint.'

'So sorry.' He gave one of her coppery plaits a fond tweak. 'Rush job on today and we were two men down. Anyway, you can talk,' he added, pulling a face. 'You smell of . . . ugh . . . blackcurrant.'

'Nesh's mum drove us home. She gave us some sweets. It's what kind parents do. Hi, Dad.' Louisa gave Max a kiss.

'And then you aren't hungry and you don't want your tea,' said Max.

'Dad, that's so not true. I'm hungry now! What are we having? Jack, are you staying for something to eat?'

Eek, Tilly hoped not. If cooking dinner was her job, she didn't need Jack Lucas distracting her on her first day.

'Not today. I'm out for dinner this evening.' Jack gave Tilly that thrilling look again. 'What am I missing?'

Tilly didn't have the foggiest. 'Something fabulous.'

Jack grinned. 'I'm sure. Never mind, some other time.' Raising a hand and moving to the door, he said, 'Right, I'm off. See you soon.'

When he'd left, Tilly said, 'Well, *he* thinks he's irresistible, doesn't he?'

Max looked amused. 'Jack's all right. He's a good mate. To be fair, most of the women round here think he's pretty irresistible too. He'll make a play for you, don't worry. It's up to you, but if you go for it, don't go getting your hopes up,' he said. 'Strictly no-strings, that's Jack. Bedpost? There's been that many notches there's no bedpost left.'

As if she would be attracted to Jack Lucas for one moment. Tilly said bluntly, 'Don't worry, I'm not planning on being anyone's notch—'

The kitchen door swung open and Jack stuck his head round.

'Bloody hell, you're supposed to have gone,' said Max. 'How are we meant to talk about you behind your back if you're going to creep back and eavesdrop?'

'Sorry.' From the way Jack was grinning it was obvious he'd overheard every word. 'I *was* leaving, then I spotted something interesting out in the hall.' He raised an eyebrow at Tilly. 'Two interesting things, actually.'

Tilly blinked as he reappeared in the kitchen holding the boots she'd kicked off and left by the front door five minutes ago. Were emerald-green leather cowboy boots with customised glittery heels not allowed in Roxborough? Might their glitteriness cause herds of cows to take fright and stampede through country lanes?

'I love Tilly's boots.' Louisa leapt loyally to her defence.

'I didn't say I didn't like them,' said Jack. 'I think they're very . . . individual. The kind of boots you might wear when you're leapfrogging over litter bins, in fact.' He paused.

Tilly let out a squeak of dismay. 'That was your car?'

'My brand-new car,' Jack emphasised. 'Only two days out of the showroom. You left grease marks all over the window.'

'It was an accident. Unlike you,' Tilly added pointedly, 'splashing me when you drove through that puddle.'

'It was only meant to be a little splash. But look on the bright side, at least now you know I wasn't spinning you a line.' His eyes glittered good-humouredly. 'I knew I remembered you from somewhere.'

'Come in, come in. Sorry my room's a mess.' Lou was sitting up in her double bed wearing purple pyjamas and reading *A History of the Industrial Revolution*.

'Doing your homework?' said Tilly.

Lou beamed and waggled the school textbook at her. 'Revision. It's really boring . . . oh no, Dad *told* you!'

'Sorry. He's the boss.' Having lifted the pillow next to the one propped up behind Lou, Tilly located the copy of *Heat* and whisked it out of reach. 'He said if I looked under here I might find one of these.'

Lou pulled a caught-out face. 'I was only going to glance at it.' She sat back. 'So, do you think you're going to like it here?'

'I hope so.' Tilly sat on the edge of the bed, checking out the framed photos on top of the bookcase. 'I like that one of you and your mum.'

'That was taken on the beach in Hawaii. Everyone else was tanned and glamorous.' Lou grimaced. 'And there was me with my stupid red hair and my spindly white legs. I don't know how my mum stands it out there in LA. I'm more of a cold-weather person. I like living here.'

Carefully Tilly said, 'You must miss her a lot.'

Lou shrugged. 'Yes, but when I was over there living with Mum, I missed Dad loads too. And I talk to her all the time. She's happy, and work's going really well. She loves her job.'

Who wouldn't? Tilly had discovered over dinner this evening that Kaye Dineen, mother of Lou, ex-wife of Max and unsuccessful British stage actress, was in fact well known in America and throughout large parts of the rest of the developed world as Kaye McKenna, one of the stars of the Emmy-garlanded TV drama series *Over the Rainbow*.

'Here's a good one.' Lou reached for another photo, of a group of cavorting teenagers round an LA pool. 'That's me and some friends after a wedding party. You know the actress Macy Ventura? She's the main star of Mum's show. Anyway, she was getting married for the fifth time to some ancient film producer and she'd never met me but she asked my mum if I'd like to be one of her bridesmaids. So we went along to meet Macy and Macy's people and the wedding coordinator.'

'And?' Tilly was frowning, wondering what the giant pink mushrooms were doing in the swimming pool.

'Oh, it was hysterical. Macy and the wedding guy took one look at me and were horrified! I was too ginger, too pale, too freckly, too tall . . . The bridesmaids were wearing sugar-plum pink. Well, you can guess how I'd look in sugar-plum pink. They ended up offering me five hundred dollars to not be a bridesmaid.'

Tilly shook her head in disbelief. 'Did you take the money?'

Lou snorted with laughter. 'Too right I did! I never even wanted to be her bridesmaid. I got chatting to the other bridesmaids at the party afterwards and they were so great. As soon as I told them what Macy had done, they all took off their dresses and chucked them into the pool. I thought that was really nice of them.' Adopting an earnest Californian accent, she said, 'Like, you know, totally supportive?'

'So those are the dresses.' Tilly pointed to the floating mushrooms.

'They were proper designer ones, too. Vera Wang. They cost thousands of dollars.' Lou giggled. 'Macy was furious.'

'Bloody hell, you're the one who should have been furious.' Tilly was outraged on her behalf. 'I can't believe you even went to the wedding after she did that to you.'

'Oh, I don't care. It's all panto. All I did was fail the audition.' Lou seemed genuinely unperturbed. 'Anyway, it was a Hollywood wedding, not the proper kind. They were only married for six months.'

'Well, if I ever get married,' said Tilly, 'you can definitely be my bridesmaid. I've never been one. Never even been asked.'

'I was nearly one once. When I was nine.' Lou yawned, tiredness catching up with her. 'That was for Jack and Rose's wedding.'

Jack? 'You mean Jack who was here this afternoon?' Ready for gossip, Tilly perked up. 'What happened? Did they cancel it at the last minute?'

'Well, they had to.'

Ooh, lovely. Eagerly Tilly said, 'Why, who finished with who?'

'Nobody. It wasn't anything like that. They would have got married,' Lou explained, 'except they couldn't. Because Rose died.'

Downstairs in the living room Max was uncorking a bottle of red wine.

'Here's to the end of your first day.' He clinked his glass against Tilly's.

'I've hardly done anything. I feel like a fraud.'

'Hey, that's because I haven't started cracking my whip yet. Now, I've written a list of things I need you to do tomorrow. I'm off up to Oxford first thing, but any problems and you can give me a ring.' Max showed her the sheet of paper, which said: *8 a.m. Take Lou to school. Then drop wallpaper books back to Derwyn's in Cirencester. Buy food, cook dinner, take Betty for a walk, collect six framed prints from Welch & Co. in Roxborough. Pick up Lou and Nesh from school at 4.10 p.m.*

'That looks fine. Um, what would you like me to cook?'

'Oh, we're not fussy. I'll be home by six,' said Max. 'And the day after you can give me a hand with measuring up the next job.'

'Fantastic.' Tilly wondered how soon she could swing the conversation round to Jack. She was longing to ask questions.

'Nothing too fancy, just one of Jack's.'

Bingo! 'Actually, Lou and I were—'

'Here, I can show you the details, he left me the brochure earlier.' Max reached for a folder on the table. 'Jack's in buy-to-let, did you know that? He picks up properties at auction and renovates them, then I make them look great before he rents them out. This one is a second-floor flat in a Victorian house in Cheltenham—'

'Lou told me about his girlfriend dying,' Tilly blurted out. 'The week before their wedding. Lou said she drowned.'

Max paused, smiled slightly, drank some wine. Finally he turned to look at her. 'That's right. Oh dear, and now you've joined the club. I can see it in your eyes.'

'What? I don't know what you mean.'

'The romance of it all. The tragic widower—except he isn't a widower because they didn't quite manage to get married.' Max shook his head, his tone wry. 'Jack's one of my best friends and what happened *was* terrible, but it just amuses me to see the effect it has on the opposite sex. As if he isn't bloody good-looking enough to start with, and smart and successful with it. The moment women hear his history, that's it, they lose all control. And now it's happened to you.'

'It hasn't,' Tilly protested, turning red.

'Don't give me that.' Looking resigned, Max said, 'D'you know what? If Jack seduces you and dumps you and breaks your heart, and you bugger off leaving me and Lou high and dry, I swear to God, best friend or no best friend, I'm going to break the tragic widower's neck.'

Tilly was still longing to hear all the details. 'I already told you, I'm nobody's notch.'

'Ah, but that was before you knew the whole story.'

Frustration welled up. 'I still don't know the whole story!'

'OK. Ready for a top-up?' Max refilled her glass. 'Get those tissues ready, girl. Jack and Rose were together for three years. She was gorgeous. Everyone loved her. They got engaged on Christmas Eve five years ago. The wedding was booked for the following December in the village church in Pembrokeshire where Rose had grown up. Then they found out Rose was pregnant, which was the icing on the cake. They couldn't wait to become parents. Anyhow, the week before the wedding, Rose went on ahead to Wales to stay with her parents and do all that last-minute faffing about and Jack stayed behind here, tying up loose ends to do with the business. On the Sunday morning, Rose took her parents' dog for a walk along the seafront. It was a stormy day, the sea was rough. Basically, the dog was chasing a seagull into the surf and it got into difficulties. The next moment Rose had jumped off the rocks into the sea.'

Tilly's mouth was bone dry.

'And you know what?' said Max. 'She *did* rescue the dog. But she couldn't save herself. The currents swept her away. By the time the lifeboat reached her, it was too late. She was dead.'

'I don't know what to say.' Tilly shook her head, trying and failing to imagine the horror of it. 'Her poor family.'

'It was tough,' Max agreed, taking another glug of wine. 'The parents were devastated. And of course Jack blamed himself. He was convinced that if only he'd gone to Pembrokeshire instead of staying here, it would never have happened.' He paused, exhaled heavily. 'Anyway, that was it. No more wedding; we had a funeral instead. Jack went through the whole thing on autopilot. Afterwards he threw himself into his work. Then, about six months later, he started . . . socialising again.'

Drily Max said, 'And he's been socialising ever since, in pretty epic fashion. We're thinking of contacting the *Guinness Book of Records*. Except they'd send some poor innocent girl down here to check him out and we all know what would happen next. Imagine the next year, opening the book and reading: "The world record for seducing women is held by Jack Lucas, aged thirty-three, of Roxborough in the Cotswolds, who *said* he'd phone me, but oh no, he's just a rotten lying bastard who thinks he can get away with treating us women like rubbish."'

There was a not-so-subtle message in there somewhere.

'Everyone wants to make him better,' Max went on. 'They all think they'll be the one to make Jack fall in love again. But it's been four years now. Take it from me, he'd rather steer clear of commitment and stay single. That way he can't be hurt again. And that,' Max concluded, 'is what makes Jack irresistible. That's the challenge.' He stopped and looked sideways at Tilly, to gauge her reaction.

'What happened to the dog?' said Tilly.

'It died a year later. Old age. Went to sleep and never woke up. Pretty good way to go.' Max held up his glass and said deadpan, 'Although given the choice, I'd prefer a night with Johnny Depp.'

So far, so good. Tilly was delighted with the way her first proper day was going. She'd dropped Lou off at school, driven over to Cirencester and taken the wallpaper books back to Derwyn's and called into the butcher's for a three-pack of beef en croute. The potatoes were ready to be roasted, the carrots were chopped, and Betty had enjoyed her walk through Roxborough woods. It was two o'clock and all she had to do now was pick up the framed prints. Then she'd have time to call in on Erin before collecting Lou and her friend Nesh from school.

Ha, there was even a parking space practically outside Welch & Co., which was the kind of shop you go to when you want to buy something nice for your house and you're feeling flush. Everywhere you looked, you saw something that made you say, 'Ooh, *that's* nice,' then go a bit light-headed when you saw the price.

The woman chatting on the phone at the back of the shop looked expensive too, with long tawny hair that might just be extensions, a pink shirt, a white pencil skirt and a lot of make-up.

'. . . OK, but don't get your hopes up. He always says he'll give you a ring, and he never does.'

Designery-looking shoes, Tilly noticed.

'Well, I'm glad you had a nice time. Yes, I know, he is, isn't he?'

Sheeny, superfine tights. No wedding ring. Musky, heavy perfume.

'Hang on a sec, Amy. Customer.' The woman looked at Tilly and said charmingly, 'Can I help you, or are you happy to browse?'

'Actually I'm here to pick up some prints. For Max Dineen?'

The woman said into the phone, 'Amy, I have to go, someone interesting's just come into the shop.' Pause. 'No, not *him*. God, you're obsessed.'

'Crikey,' said Tilly. 'I didn't know I was going to be interesting. I hope you aren't expecting me to do a tap dance.'

'Not if you don't want to.' The woman was now giving her an unashamed once-over, her confident gaze taking note of Tilly's wind-blown hair, lack of make-up, battered jeans and pink spotted wellies. Evidently having decided that her visitor didn't present any threat— Tilly felt like announcing that she did scrub up well—she said, 'You must be Max's new girl. He told me you were starting this week.'

'Tilly Cole.'

'I'm Stella Welch. Pleased to meet you. So what d'you think of him?' Stella leaned forward conspiratorially. 'Pretty dishy, wouldn't you say?'

Flummoxed, Tilly said, 'Um . . .'

'And so *funny*. I bet you secretly fancy him, don't you?'

OK, getting weird now. 'But he's . . . gay,' said Tilly.

'Oh that.' Stella dismissed the protestation with a shrug. 'Not completely, though. He was married to Kaye for long enough. There's definite room for manoeuvre.'

'Um, I hadn't realised.' Hastily Tilly said, 'But I still don't fancy him.'

'Why not? Are you gay?'

Blimey. 'No, he's not my type. And I just split up from my boyfriend so I'm taking a bit of a break from all that stuff.'

'Hmm, but it's all right for you. You're younger than me. How old are you?' Stella was alarmingly forthright.

'Twenty-eight.'

'I'm thirty-seven. I know I don't look it, but I am.' Stella was alarmingly modest too. 'And my husband and I broke up six months ago. He just left me high and dry. At thirty-seven! So it's not as if I have time to take a break. I want babies before it's too late.'

'Crikey, poor you. Is he . . .' Tilly wavered; how could she put this tactfully? '. . . seeing someone else now?'

'No, no. Definitely not.' Vigorously Stella shook her head. 'I'm on the prowl for another man just in case, but I can't help thinking that sooner or later he's going to beg me to take him back.'

'And would you really want that?'

'Of course I would. I want babies. He'll be a great dad.' With a determined nod, Stella changed the subject. 'Let's get you what you came for.'

'**W**ho? Stella? Oh God,' said Erin.

'Why? What's up with her?' said Tilly. 'She seemed quite nice. Blunt though. I heard all about her husband running off.'

'Oh *God*.' Carefully, Erin put down the red beaded evening dress she'd been checking over. 'I've been seeing Fergus.'

'Who?' Honestly, this was like twenty questions.

'Stella's husband.' Erin licked her lips. 'I was going to tell you.'

Tilly winced. 'Oh my God. Is that why he left her?'

'No! Nothing like that. They broke up six months ago. We only started seeing each other a few weeks ago. But obviously no one else knows. Especially not Stella. I don't think she'd take it very well.'

'I only just met her and I already know that's the understatement of the year. Scary,' said Tilly. 'Is he worth it?'

A dreamy look spread over Erin's face. 'He's the nicest, *nicest* man.'

'Does he know she's waiting for him to go back to her?'

'Of course he knows. She's told everyone!' Defiantly Erin said, 'But it's not going to happen. Sooner or later she'll have to accept that.'

'Crikey,' Tilly marvelled. 'You're really serious about him.'

'I've waited a long time for something like this to happen. And now it has.' She was all aglow. 'Fergus is worth being serious about.'

While they were on the subject . . . 'Guess who I met yesterday? The owner of the car I skidded into when I leapfrogged over that bin!'

'Oh bloody hell, you mean he recognised you? Was he cross?'

'He was pretty good about it, all things considered. It was a brand-new car.' Tilly couldn't suppress a squiggle of excitement at the thought of seeing him again tomorrow. 'He seemed quite nice too. His name's Jack.'

Had she secretly been wanting Erin to shriek, 'My God, you two would be *perfect* for each other!'? Secretly, maybe she had.

Instead Erin did a comical double take. 'Jack? You mean Jack Lucas?' She looked horror-struck. 'Oh no, don't even *think* of going there, that's one man you definitely wouldn't want to get serious about.'

'See how shiny my car is? That's because I put it through the car wash last night,' said Jack. 'So try not to throw yourself over the bonnet.'

'I'll do my best to control myself.' Tilly emerged from Max's BMW, parked behind the Jag. Jack was waiting for them on the frosty pavement outside his newly acquired flat on Marlow Road.

'Hey, you. Stop flirting with my assistant. And you,' Max addressed Tilly, 'stop encouraging him.'

Tilly spread her arms. 'What did I do?'

'You don't have to do anything, that's the trouble.'

'It's OK, I'll behave myself.' Jack led the way to the front door. 'Come on, let's show you the flat.'

Tilly swallowed as she followed him up the stairs; they'd arrived only a minute ago and here she was, palpitating already. Long legs, broad shoulders, piece of thread stuck to the back of his jeans . . . Tilly dug her fingers into her palms, resisting the tantalising urge to pick it off.

'Are you looking at my backside?'

'Give it a rest, will you?' Max exclaimed. 'Leave the poor girl alone.'

Tilly looked suitably grateful.

'She was, though,' said Jack.

The second-floor flat smelled of fresh plaster. 'The plasterers finished last night,' Jack explained to Tilly as Max strode from room to room, scribbling notes. 'Now it's time for Max to come in and do his thing.'

'I thought property developers just painted everything magnolia.'

'Most do. But first impressions count, and Max knows his stuff. Make the place look a bit special and you'll attract a better class of tenant.'

'Paying a better class of rent,' said Max. 'He doesn't hire me out of the goodness of his heart. It's all about making a profit. OK, hold this tape measure. Keep it steady,' Max ordered. 'Let's get to work.'

His mobile rang twenty minutes later. Max, with his hands full, nodded at the phone on the windowsill. 'Can you get that?'

The name flashing up was Kaye. 'Hooray,' said a cheery female voice when Tilly answered. 'You must be Tilly—I tried calling the house, but no reply. So, what's it like working for the old slave-driver?'

'Fine so far. We're just measuring a place up at the moment, a flat in Cheltenham. For Jack Lucas.'

'Oh-ho! And have you been introduced to Jack yet?'

Aware of Jack's gaze on her, Tilly said, 'Um, actually he's right here.'

'Oh-ho-*ho!*' Kaye chuckled knowingly. 'Say no more. I get the picture. And how are the two of you getting along?'

Turning away from Jack—who was evidently telepathic and was

grinning broadly—Tilly murmured, 'He seems OK.'

'He is OK. Keep reminding yourself though, he's not to be taken seriously. Buckets of charm but you must never believe a word he says.'

'I know.'

'Excuse me,' Jack drawled. 'Am I being discussed here?'

'Tell Jack I'm just issuing the standard Government Health Warning. I rang because I wanted to say hello to Max's new Girl Friday. Lou emailed me last night to tell me how lovely you are.'

Touched, Tilly said, 'Lou's lovely too. She's a real credit to you.'

'I miss her so much.' Kaye exhaled and audibly gathered herself. 'I'll be back for a holiday at Easter. Only a few more weeks to go. Now listen, any time you want to call me, don't even hesitate.'

'Absolutely.'

Max announced, 'Kaye just asked Tilly if I'm the best boss she ever had.'

'No no no.' Jack shook his head. 'She asked her if I was the most fanciable man in Roxborough.'

'Tell them I can hear them. One other thing, has Lou said anything about a boyfriend? She's mentioned a boy at school a few times recently, that's all. In a God-I-can't-*stand*-that-idiot kind of way. So of course I'm wondering if she has a bit of a crush on him.'

'I'll keep an ear out.' Tilly felt for Kaye; it must be agonising being so far away while your thirteen-year-old daughter was making her initial foray into the confusing world of boys.

'Thanks . . . oops, I'm going to have to go now,' said Kaye. 'Give my love to everyone.' Cheerfully she added, 'Even Jack.'

Chapter 3

THE DOORBELL RANG at eight on the dot. As she let him into the flat, Erin's heart was hammering against her ribs. 'You didn't stand me up.'

'I'd never stand you up.' Fergus enveloped her in a hug.

And that was the brilliant thing; she knew he wouldn't.

'Come on in.' Erin led him inside, still super-aware of her heart hammering away. Did Fergus know that tonight was *the* night? Had the fact that she'd invited him round for the evening and was cooking him a proper dinner told him that the rest would follow?

'Fantastic smell.'

'It's roast chicken.'

He shook his head. 'Nope. It's you.' Fergus flashed his lopsided boyish smile. 'You're the one who smells fantastic.'

She was wearing her favourite perfume. Jo Malone's Pomegranate Noir. Erin felt all warm inside; wait until she got him into bed and he discovered she'd sprayed it on the sheets.

'That was brilliant.' Finishing his dinner, Fergus pushed his plate to one side and gave her hand a squeeze. 'Clever girl. Thank you.' He grinned, then pulled a face as his phone burst into life.

'You'd better answer it,' said Erin. 'Might be work.'

'I'm not being dragged out this evening.' When he saw who was calling, he grimaced, but he didn't answer it and the next moment the ringing stopped. 'No one important.'

'Pudding?' Relieved, Erin collected the plates.

Fergus relaxed. 'Now that's what I call important.' *Bee-eep* went the phone in his hand, indicating that a message had been left. He put it down on the table.

'Aren't you going to listen to your message?'

'Nope.' He broke into a smile. 'I told you, it's my evening off.'

As they were eating their pudding, the phone rang again. This time Fergus switched it off before calmly helping himself to more cream.

'One of your other girlfriends?' Erin meant it jokily but regretted it the moment the words were out of her mouth; she was implying that *she* was his girlfriend. Presumptuous or what? 'Sorry. Just ignore me.'

'Hey, don't worry. As if I could ignore you anyway.' Fergus shook his head. 'I've loved these past few weeks. You have no idea how much.' He paused, mentally replayed what he'd just said, then blurted out, 'Oh God, now it's my turn. That sounds as if I'm telling you it's all over. I'm not, I promise. In fact, quite the opposite. I think you're fantastic . . . Shit, look at me, getting all flustered and tongue-tied. This never happens at work. Ask me to sell a house and I can do it, no problem. But here with you, trying to tell you how I feel . . . well, I suppose I'm out of practice.'

Erin couldn't eat any more. 'It doesn't matter.'

'It *does*. I really like you.' Fergus hesitated, the tips of his ears going pink. 'A lot.'

For a mad moment Erin wanted to burst into tears of happiness. But that would definitely be enough to scare him off. Gazing into his eyes—bluish grey and fringed with blond-tipped lashes—she said breathlessly, 'Have you finished?'

He looked startled. 'You want me to say more?'

'Actually, I meant the pudding.'

'Oh right, sorry, yes, yes . . .' Fergus shook his head. 'God, sorry.'

'OK, here's an idea.' Feeling brave by comparison, Erin said, 'How about we both stop saying sorry to each other? And how about we make some coffee and go and sit on the sofa?'

Fergus nodded, relieved. 'Coffee. Sofa. Sounds great.'

But when he followed her out to the kitchen seconds later, he stood behind Erin and slid his arms round her. He kissed her on the shoulder. And carried on dropping a tantalising trail of kisses along her collarbone until she was squirming with desire. Finally swivelling round in the circle of his arms, Erin said breathlessly, 'Or we could give the whole coffee-and-sofa thing a miss.'

Fergus stroked her face. 'You know what? That's an even better idea.'

And it was.

'What are you thinking?' Fergus murmured in her ear.

Erin lay in his arms, smiling uncontrollably into the darkness. 'I'm thinking it went . . . very well, considering how nervous we both were beforehand. It was lovely.' She hesitated, wondering if it was too personal a question. 'Am I . . .?'

'Lovely too? Oh yes.' He hugged her more tightly.

'I didn't mean that.'

'Right, so you were wanting to know if you're the first since Stella?' He'd known what she was trying to ask. 'That would be another yes.'

Erin's heart expanded; she was glad he wasn't the kind of man who just slept with any woman who happened to cross his path.

'And seeing as we're being honest, it was Stella trying to call me earlier.'

Oh. That put a bit of a dampener on proceedings.

'Sorry. I just thought you should know.'

'Shouldn't you call her back, then? There's nothing worse than sitting at home waiting for the phone to ring.' Magnanimous in victory, Erin ran her hand over his furry teddy-bear chest. 'Give her a quick ring, get it out of the way.'

He leaned over and kissed her. 'You're a nice person.'

When he came back into the bedroom he was no longer smiling.

'What's wrong?'

'Seven messages.' Fergus stood in the doorway frowning and pressing buttons on his phone. 'In one hour. Bing's been sick and all the lights have fused in the house.'

Who? *What?* 'Who's Bing?'

'The cat.' Listening to the next message, Fergus said, 'Stella's in a panic. The fuse box must have blown.'

Erin said, 'Can't she call out an electrician?'

'You don't know what Stella's like. She's terrified of the dark. And Bing's the love of her life. You have no idea.'

Erin wished she hadn't been quite so nice now. This was what happened; it came back to bite you on the bum. The happy, relaxed atmosphere had gone and Fergus was now visibly on edge. As he listened to the third message, they were both able to hear Stella's desperate voice spiralling upwards.

'Call her.'

Fergus nodded and switched off the message. The next second, the phone burst into life in his hand.

'Hi . . . yes, no, I was just about to . . . OK, calm down. I turned it off because I was busy. With *work*, Stella.' As he said this, Fergus turned away slightly, too guilty to meet Erin's gaze. 'Have you checked the fuse box?'

The high-pitched shriek at the other end of the phone reached new heights. Erin flinched.

'All right, all right.' Fergus heaved a sigh. 'I'll come over.'

Oh *fantastic*.

'Sorry, I couldn't say no. She's in a terrible state.' Off the phone now, Fergus was dressing hurriedly.

Bravely Erin said, 'Never mind. But if you're keen to see me again,' she smiled, secure enough to say it, 'I'm free tomorrow night.'

'OK, just in case you were thinking I have a cushy job, here's the kind of crap I have to put up with.' Max's voice crackled down the phone from Oxford, where he was meeting a new client. 'Robbie and Clive are supposed to be making a start on the Marlow Road flat but they aren't going to be able to let themselves in because, get this, Robbie left the key in the pocket of his denim jacket. And guess what?'

Dutifully Tilly said, 'What?'

'Brain of Britain Robbie managed to leave his jacket in some girl's house. So could you be an angel, get yourself over to Jack's place and pick up the spare key, then take it over to Cheltenham? No rush, they won't get to Marlow Road before midday.'

'OK.' Eek, Jack's place. 'I don't know where Jack lives though.'

'It's the house at the top of Miller's Hill, the one with the black iron gates and the best view over the valley.'

Of course. What else? Tilly wondered if the gates were to keep out the hordes of women who chased after him, or to lock them in.

The gates were open and the view was as spectacular as Max had said. There was Jack's beloved Jag on the driveway. Parked next to it was a girlie lime-green Golf. So who did that belong to, then?

Tilly approached the L-shaped, ivy-strewn Cotswold stone house. The front door swung open as she reached it.

'Saw you coming.' Jack was grinning at her, his hair wet from the shower and his white T-shirt clinging damply to his torso. His feet were tanned and bare and he was wearing grey jogging bottoms. 'Come in.'

She followed him through the parquet-floored hall and into a long sunny kitchen. It was all very tidy, very clean.

'Got time for a coffee?' Jack was already filling the cafetière.

'Why not?' She perched on a high stool. 'This is nice.'

He half smiled. 'I know. If it weren't nice I wouldn't be living here.'

Tilly fell silent. This was the house he and Rose had bought together at auction five and a half years ago; Max had told her. They had spent eighteen months restoring it from a shell. OK, don't think about the rest of that now. Sad stories had a way of bringing tears to her eyes.

'Jack?' A female voice, huskily seductive, called down from the top of the stairs. 'Are you finished in the bathroom now? OK if I go in?'

Tilly examined her fingernails and did her best to look as if it made no odds to her who he had stashed away upstairs. Not bothering to disguise his amusement, Jack raised his voice and drawled, 'Feel free, darling.'

He made the coffee and they talked about Max's plans for the flat in Marlow Road. From upstairs they heard the sound of the shower running and Tilly wondered if his compulsion to sleep with more women than Robbie Williams actually brought him happiness. After ten minutes, as the shower was turned off upstairs, she drained her cup.

'Another one?'

'No, thanks.' She didn't particularly want to meet his latest conquest. 'I'm going to pick up some food then head over to Cheltenham.'

'I'll get you the key. Sorry to have put you out. I could have driven over there with it myself but my business manager's due in twenty minutes and we're going to be tied up all morning. Give me two minutes and I'll be right back.'

Jack disappeared upstairs. Left alone, Tilly instantly slid off the stool and sidled out to the hall. One of the other doors, slightly ajar, looked as if it led into the sitting room, which might be more interesting.

Oh all right then, it was photos she was looking for. But that was only natural, wasn't it? Tilly pushed open the oak door.

It was a light sun-filled room with huge squashy sofas. Tilly's attention was instantly drawn to the photographs in silver frames on the table next to the fireplace. Stealthily she approached the table, focusing on each of the photos in turn: a small boy—Jack?—racing across a field; university-age friends in evening dress . . .

Whoops, footsteps on the stairs. Caught off guard, Tilly abruptly shot into reverse and half turned, desperate not to be caught snooping in—

'Ow.' The heel of her boot caught in the fringed border of the rug behind her, catapulting her to the ground. Pain shot through the hand that had semi-broken her fall. Mortified, she heard a voice behind her.

'Oh, my *word*. Are you all right?' A sexy female voice, needless to say. 'Hang on, mind how you go, let me help you up.' A powerful pair of arms hauled her to her feet. Her rescuer was a well-built woman in her mid-fifties with a generous helping of turquoise eye shadow and an emerald-green nylon housecoat. Behind her, plonked on the coffee table, was a wicker basket bristling with cleaning products.

'So, looks like the two of you have met.' From the doorway, Jack said drily, 'Monica, this is Tilly. Tilly, this is my fantastic cleaner, Monica.'

'Hi. Thanks.' Tilly clutched her painful left hand. 'Sorry.'

'Here, let me have a look,' Jack said. 'I can't imagine how you managed to fall over. Were you leapfrogging the TV?'

Could she lie? Would he believe her? 'I was looking for the loo.'

He carried on testing each of her fingers. 'We decided against installing a lavatory in the sitting room. It didn't go with the furniture.'

OK, so he didn't believe her. 'I looked in here to see if it was a bathroom,' Tilly amended. 'Then, when I saw it wasn't, I spotted the photos. And I was . . . interested.' She retrieved her hand, decided to come clean. 'When Max was telling me about Rose he said she was gorgeous. I was curious.'

'I don't keep a photo of Rose on that table.' Jack paused. 'But at least you're honest.'

'Sorry.'

'Right,' Monica announced. 'I'm due a break.'

As Monica bustled out of the room, Jack said, 'Here's the key, by the way.'

'Thanks.' Tilly stuffed it into the front pocket of her combats.

'Is Max still calling me the tragic widower?'

She pulled a face. 'Um . . . yes.'

Jack looked amused. 'Did he also warn you off me?'

'Oh yes.'

'I suppose he would. So how does that make you feel?'

Tilly hesitated. Truthfully, it made her feel like a fifteen-year-old whose mother has told her that hitching up her school skirt isn't a flattering look. Just because you hear it, doesn't mean you're going to take a blind bit of notice.

'I'm sure it's good advice. OK, I'm off. One thing,' said Tilly. 'Was that deliberate? Letting me think you had a woman upstairs?'

Jack grinned as he showed her out. 'I did have a woman upstairs.'

Tilly gave him a look. Ha, she knew she'd been right.

Erin watched the woman squeeze into the size eighteen Jaeger wool coat with the big faux-fur collar. 'I love the shape. What do you think?'

Oh dear, sometimes she really wished she had less of a conscience. The coat had been here for over a fortnight and this was the first time anyone had shown any interest in it. Furthermore, she knew that Barbara, who had brought the coat into the shop, was desperate to raise some cash.

Then the door swung open and her heart leaped into her throat as— *oh God*—Stella came into the shop. 'Don't mind me. Just looking.'

'Well?' said the woman in the Jaeger coat.

It was no good, she couldn't do it. 'The shape's really flattering,' said Erin, 'but I'm wondering if it might be a bit tight across the shoulders.'

The woman turned hopefully to Stella. 'Do you think it's too tight?'

'Honestly? Put it this way, if you lost three stone it'd fit you a treat.'

That was the thing about Stella, she wasn't the type to stab you in the back. She stabbed you right there in the front so you could watch all the blood gushing out.

'Tuh.' Stella sniffed as the door swung shut behind the woman. 'If she didn't want my opinion, she shouldn't have asked for it.'

'Mm.' Erin started busily rearranging the handbags.

'Then again, you were the one who said the coat was a bit tight. She'd probably have bought it if you hadn't told her that.' She tilted her head enquiringly. 'You must be a pretty honest person.'

Oh God, where was this leading? Did she have a gun hidden under that white jacket? With a casual shrug, Erin said, 'I just like people to buy clothes that suit them.'

'And that coat definitely didn't suit her.' Stella's tone was dismissive. 'Can you pass me that cream leather bag? I might treat myself.' Pause. 'I deserve a treat after last night.'

'Oh?' *Just sound natural.* 'What happened last night?'

'Oh God, a fuse blew in the house and all the lights went out.'

'Did you manage to get them back on?'

'In the end. Fergus came over.' Exhaling noisily, Stella said, 'You know, I really think he might be seeing someone behind my back.'

'Do you?' *Oh help, just breathe . . . and breathe again . . .*

Stella handed the handbag back. 'He'd better not be, that's all I can say. I won't bother with this. The buckle on the front looks a bit cheap.'

It was hilarious, watching everyone come streaming out of school. Tilly, leaning against the car waiting for Lou to emerge, saw gaggles of girls freeing their hair of scrunchies. Groups of boys with deliberately untucked shirts sauntered along. There was plenty of texting going on. Girls eyed up boys and boys chucked things at girls. And there, bless her heart, was Lou coming down the stone steps. With her wild red-gold curls, she stood out from the rest, maybe not the prettiest girl in the school but surely the one with the sparkiest personality.

Then Tilly straightened up and focused more intently as Lou turned and said something to the boy behind her, clearly replying to some remark he'd just made. The boy, tall and lanky, was carrying a tennis racket. As Lou swung round, a trainer fell out of her backpack and with lightning reflexes he reached down with his racket, scooped it up and batted it high into the air. Even from this distance, Tilly could see the look Lou shot him as her trainer landed in a hedge. Shaking her head in disgust, she stalked past him and retrieved it. Laughing, the boy said something else and Lou tossed back her hair as she retaliated.

Tilly smiled. It looked like Kaye had been right. Watching Lou's reaction to the boy's attention brought back memories of her own first tentative foray into the scary but thrilling world of boys. Her particular nemesis had been a fourteen-year-old called Lee Jarvis and he'd teased her nonstop, driving her demented. And then somehow she had mysteriously found herself agreeing to dance with him at the school disco. And somehow Lee had ended up mumbling, 'You know, I've fancied you for ages,' and to her own amazement she'd found herself realising that she fancied him too. And right there and then, in the middle of the dance floor in front of *everyone* while George Michael sang 'Careless Whisper', they'd ended up kissing, *with tongues . . .*

Lost in a nostalgic glow, Tilly jumped a mile when Lou appeared in front of her. 'Boo! You were miles away.'

'Sorry, I was just thinking back to my schooldays.'

As they climbed into the car, Tilly glanced over her shoulder and saw the boy with the tennis racket.

'Who's he, then?'

'A complete idiot.'

'He looks quite nice.' The boy had floppy dark hair, no spots and killer cheekbones. You could imagine girls falling for him.

'Well, he's not. I hate him. What's for tea?'

Tilly kept a straight face. Oh yes, that was familiar. How many times, when her friends had said Lee fancied her, had Tilly announced she hated him? Then abruptly changed the subject.

'What's his name?'

'Eddie Marshall-Hicks. What are we having for tea?'

'Fish pie and blackberry crumble.' Tilly mentally squirrelled the name away. Next time she spoke to Kaye on the phone she'd find out if this was the same boy.

'It was weird.' Erin didn't mean to go on about it but her lunch-time visit from Stella had put the wind up her. 'She seemed . . . different.'

'So don't try. Let's just relax and have fun.' Fergus twirled Erin through from the kitchen and pulled her down with him onto the sofa. 'If Stella knew about us, trust me, *we'd* know about it. She'd come right out and say it. But she hasn't, so that means she doesn't. And I'm not going to let the thought of my ex-wife spoil our evening.'

Ddddrrrringgg went the doorbell, causing Erin to catapult upright in fear. 'Oh God, it's her!'

'Don't be daft, of course it isn't. It could be anyone.'

'I suppose it might be Tilly.' Erin began to relax. Leaving the living room, she ventured halfway down the stairs; the fact that her front door led out into a narrow side alleyway was a bonus when it came to enabling Fergus to enter the flat unobserved, but the downside was that it meant she had no way of peering out to see who was on the doorstep.

'Hello?' Please, *please* let her visitor be Tilly.

'Erin? Can you open the door, please? It's Stella Welch.'

Oh God, oh God. Erin collapsed back on the stairs in fright. 'Um . . . I can't come down at the moment . . . I'm not dressed . . .'

'Please, just open the door. I need to see you.'

Erin's heart was banging like a cannon. 'What about?'

'Well, for a start, the fact that you're refusing to open the door. What's wrong, Erin? What are you afraid of?'

You, you, *you*. 'Nothing.'

'So why won't you let me in? Could it possibly be because you have my husband up there with you in your flat?'

How could she possibly know? Erin said, 'I don't, OK? He's not here. Look, I'm not answering the door, so please just . . . go away.'

Unbelievably, Fergus hadn't heard any of this. As she stumbled back into the living room, he patted the sofa and said, 'Who was it?'

'Stella.' The word felt like ice in her mouth.

His expression abruptly changed. 'You're joking. It can't be.'

They both jumped as a shower of gravel rattled against the window.

'Come on, Fergus, I know you're in there.' Stella was outside on the pavement now, in full view of anyone who happened to be passing. 'Fergus, you cheating BASTARD!' she bellowed.

'Oh God.' Erin covered her mouth as Fergus rose to his feet.

'Right, that's it.' He crossed the room and flung open the window.

'Ha! I knew it!' Stella yelled.

'Fine, good for you. But this is exactly why I didn't tell you before.' Fergus shook his head in despair. 'I knew you'd make a fuss.'

'Why wouldn't I make a fuss? You're my husband!'

'Stella, we're not *together* any more. We broke up six months ago.'

'Thanks to *her*,' Stella screeched like a parrot.

Oh no, no, *no*. Leaping up, Erin raced over to the open window. 'Hang on, that's not true, you can't—'

'*You*,' Stella jabbed an accusing finger up at her, 'are a lying, marriage-wrecking bitch!'

'I'm not, I'm really not, I promise. This only just happened.'

'Oh yes, and of course I'm going to believe that,' Stella said bitterly.

'I swear to God, I'm telling the truth!'

'Really? Just like you did when I came into the shop and asked you if you thought Fergus was seeing anyone? And you said no?'

God, this was a nightmare. People heading along the High Street were turning to stare, stopping to listen.

'Right, that's enough.' It was Fergus's turn. 'You're being unfair—'

'*I'm* being unfair? My God, you hypocrite! My life is in tatters thanks to you, and you expect me to just stand here and take it?'

'Everyone's looking at you.' Exasperated, Fergus said, 'Go home, Stella.'

'Hang on.' Erin knew she wouldn't be able to rest until she'd asked the question. 'Look, I *swear* I've only been seeing Fergus for a few weeks, but how did you know he'd be here tonight?'

'When Fergus came to the house last night, he smelled different. I thought I recognised the perfume but I couldn't be sure. That's why I came into the shop at lunch time. And there it was again, on you.' Stella paused. 'Very distinctive. No one else in Roxborough wears that scent.'

Possibly because there was no Jo Malone shop within fifty miles. Tilly had sent her a bottle of the fabulously exotic perfume for Christmas.

And the moral of the story was, if you don't want people to know you have a secret lover, you're probably better off *not* spraying Pomegranate Noir all over your brand-new Egyptian-cotton sheets.

The phone rang as Tilly was doing her impression of a chef in the kitchen. Feeling super-efficient, she tucked the cordless phone between ear and shoulder, stirred the frying mushrooms with one hand and whisked the cheese sauce with the other.

'Hi there.' It was Kaye's voice. 'How's everything going?'

'Oh, fine. I'm multi-tasking! Just making—*oops*.' Tilly jumped back as the cheese sauce spat, causing her to lose control of the phone, which slid down her chest and landed in the frying pan. In a panic she hurriedly scooped it out with the spatula, sending the phone clattering across the stove and mushrooms flying through the air like confetti.

Having given the phone a hasty wipe with kitchen towel, Tilly said, 'Hello, are you still there?'

'Just about.' Kaye sounded amused. 'What happened to me?'

'I just dropped you. I'm only a trainee multi-tasker. Sorry about that.'

'No problem. Is Lou around?'

'She's upstairs doing her homework, I'll just take the phone up. By the way, I saw her bickering with a boy yesterday. I asked her what he was like and she said he was a complete idiot. Then she changed the subject.'

'Ooh!' Avidly Kaye said, 'Was his name Eddie?'

Bingo. 'That's the one. Eddie Marshall-Hicks . . . Sshh, Betty.' Betty had bounded up onto the window seat and was barking at the rooks.

'Oh, Betty! Let me speak to her,' Kaye begged.

OK, slightly weird but never mind. Tilly knelt on the window seat and held the receiver to Betty's ear.

'Betsy-Boo! Hello, Betsy-Boo! It's *meee*,' crooned Kaye. Betty tilted her head to one side, then returned to gazing intently out of the window. 'Betsy-Boo? Betsy-Boo-Boo-Boo! Can she hear me?'

'Bark,' Tilly whispered in Betty's other ear. 'Woof, woof, go on, do it.'

'She's not barking.' Kaye's voice rose to a wail. 'She's forgotten me!'

'She hasn't, she's just distracted.'

Now Tilly really felt sorry for Kaye. She crouched down next to Betty, did a doggy-type snuffle into the phone.

'Is that her? Betsy-Boo?'

Tilly closed her eyes and did an experimental high-pitched *yip*. Actually that wasn't bad at all. Who'd have thought she'd be so good at this? Even Betty had turned to look at her in surprise. Encouraged, Tilly moved closer to the phone. 'Yip, yip-yip, yip . . .'

'Hang on.' Evidently she wasn't the world-class dog mimic she'd imagined. Kaye said slowly, 'That wasn't Betty. That was you.'

Tilly's heart sank. Oh well, she'd done her best. 'Yes. Sorry.'

'Never mind. Thanks for trying. I'll speak to Lou now.' Wryly Kaye said, 'That's if she wants to talk to me.'

Swivelling round, Tilly saw she wasn't the only person in the room. Just inside the doorway were Max and Jack. Honestly. Keen to retain some dignity, she slid off the window seat and crossed the kitchen. As she passed between them, she waggled the phone and said, 'Call for Lou. I'll just take it up to her.'

Thankfully, Lou seized the phone with delight. 'Hey, Mum, I got fifty-eight per cent in French today. Euw,' she added, wrinkling her nose. 'This phone smells of mushrooms.'

Back downstairs, Tilly resumed cooking without looking at either Max or Jack. For several seconds there was silence in the kitchen.

Then, behind her, she heard, 'Woof. Woof-woof.'

'All right.' Tilly turned to face them. 'It was Kaye on the phone. I was just trying to make her feel better.'

'Does it for me, every time,' said Jack. Being barked at. Or there's growling. Maybe a growl beats a bark. I can't decide.'

Max beckoned with both hands. 'Come on, Tilly, give us a growl. We'll see which one we like best.'

'You know how much you hate mustard?' Tilly levelled the spatula at him. 'I could always put mustard in every meal I cook.'

'Can't mess with this girl.' Grinning, Max searched among a pile of papers on the dresser before pulling out a folder. He passed it over to Jack. 'Here's the plan for the Avening conversion. See what you think.'

'Great.' Jack moved towards the door, jangling his keys. 'Coming down to the Fox later?'

Max grimaced. 'What, and spend the evening having to stand there like a spare part while every woman in the place chats you up?'

'It's Declan's fiftieth. He asked if you'd be there. Bring Tilly.'

'I can't go,' said Tilly. 'Who'd be here to look after Lou?'

Lou bounded into the kitchen. 'Look after me when?' She looked puzzled.

'This evening.'

'Excuse me! I'm thirteen, not *three*. I don't need a baby sitter.'

'Fancy it?' Max turned to Tilly. 'Declan's the landlord of the Lazy Fox on the High Street.'

Proudly Tilly said, 'I've been there. With Erin. Declan was really nice.'

'Must've been having an off day.' Jack headed for the door. 'Right, maybe see you later.'

'Maybe.' Tilly returned her attention to the mushrooms.

The Fox was busy, crammed with friends and customers helping their favourite grumpy landlord celebrate his birthday.

'It's you!' Recognising Tilly, Declan said, 'The one who made fun of our headlines.'

'You said I'd like it here,' said Tilly.

'And now she's taken you up on it,' said Max.

'Ha, so you're the one Max has got working for him.'

'All thanks to you. I wouldn't have seen the ad if you hadn't given me that newspaper.'

Declan patted her on the back. 'You'll be fine. We're not so bad. Let's get you two a drink.' He ushered them over to the bar.

At that moment the crowd shifted and they glimpsed Jack, surrounded by a gaggle of girls in their twenties. Max called out, 'Hey, Lucas, never mind them. I'm here now.'

Jack came over. He grinned at Tilly. 'You made it, then.'

'And by the look of things we got here just in time.' Max nodded at the group of girls, who were still watching him. 'Once that lot get their claws into you, there's no escape.'

'Scouse poof to the rescue.' Drily Jack said, 'You have your uses.'

Then the door to the pub swung open and Tilly saw Jack register the arrival of someone whose presence didn't fill him with joy. A split second later he raised a hand in greeting, flashed a friendly-but-distant smile and mouthed, 'Hi.'

Turning, Tilly saw a thin blonde who ignored the 'but-distant' part of the message and determinedly battled her way through the crowd towards them. With a start Tilly realised she was dragging a friend along in her wake, and that the friend was Erin's chap's ex-wife.

'Amy.' Jack greeted the blonde with a nod. 'Stella.'

'Hi, Jack, how are you? I had such a fantastic time the other night.' Amy gazed up at him, adoration in her eyes. 'Wasn't it great?'

What might have become an awkward pause was averted by Stella clutching Max's arm and blurting out, 'Never mind that. Oh, Max, wait till you hear what's happened. You will not *believe* this.'

Uh-oh.

'*You.*' Recognising Tilly, Stella said, 'Remember I told you about my husband? Well, I found out why he left me.' Addressing everyone now, she declared, 'Because he was having an affair! And get this, it's not even with someone amazing. Compared with me, she's eugh, not even close. And she stole my husband!'

Amy trilled, 'And you'll never guess who it is!'

'Edwina Currie?' said Max. 'Peg-leg Aggie from the corner shop?'

Hang on. 'Actually, that's not fair,' Tilly blurted out. 'It wasn't a question of stealing him. Nothing happened until *well* after he left you.'

Every head instantly swivelled in her direction. Jack's expression was unreadable. Max exclaimed, 'Fuck me! *You're* having an affair with Fergus? Is that why you were so desperate to move down here?'

'Not me.' Vigorously Tilly shook her head. 'I've never even met Fergus. Oh, thanks,' she added gratefully as Declan handed her a glass of wine.

'Come on then,' said Max. 'Who's he seeing?'

Stella announced, 'You know the dress exchange at the bottom of this street? Erin's Beautiful Clothes? Well, it's her! I've been going into her shop and she's been pretending to sympathise with me, and all this time that witch is the reason I was distraught in the first place!'

Tilly swallowed. Aware that Max had made the connection, she said, 'Look, Erin's my friend. I didn't know about all this when I met you the other day, but she's told me since. And she told me herself, she only started seeing Fergus a few weeks ago.'

Stella half laughed. 'Well, she's always going to *say* that, isn't she?'

'Let's change the subject,' said Max.

'Absolutely.' Declan presented his cheek. 'Happy birthday to me.'

'Sorry, Declan. Happy birthday.' Stella gave him a kiss.

Then Amy said gaily, 'Ooh, now I just want to kiss *everyone*,' and gave Max a kiss. Realising why, Tilly kept a straight face as Jack neatly turned to greet a friend, just as Amy had been about to launch herself at him. For a moment disappointment flared in her lavishly mascaraed eyes, then the smile was plastered firmly back in place. 'So you're Max's new assistant,' she said brightly. 'Stella told me about you. No boyfriend at the moment.' Clearly sensing danger, she gave Jack's arm a possessive squeeze. 'Jack and I went out to dinner the other night. We had such a great time, didn't we?'

'Of course we did.' Jack's reply was warm; it would be easy to humiliate someone so gushy but Tilly sensed he would never do that.

Amy glowed. 'Maybe next time we could try out that new restaurant in Tetbury. I can't remember, did I give you my mobile number?'

'Yes, yes . . . oh, could you excuse me for a minute?' Across the pub a tall brunette was calling his name, beckoning him over. With a genial smile, Jack removed himself, easing his way through the crowd.

'Marianne Tilson.' Amy shot the brunette a look of disdain. 'Honestly, talk about desperate. She's so *obvious*. Jack doesn't even like her.' She turned back to Tilly. 'Do you fancy Jack?'

There was more than a hint of accusation in her tone. It seemed only sensible to say no. Shaking her head, Tilly said, 'Um . . . no. I don't go for men with his kind of track record.'

Amy looked suspicious. 'So if he asked you out, you'd turn him down? You wouldn't even be tempted?'

'No,' said Tilly, 'I definitely wouldn't be tempted.'

'Tempted to do what?' Jack's voice behind her made her jump.

'Run the London Marathon.' She turned and looked at him. 'Amy was just saying, she's very keen to do it next year.'

If ever a girl was surgically attached to her spindly four-inch stilettos, it was Amy. Her face was a picture.

'You should give it a go too,' Max told Stella. 'Take your mind off other things. It'd do you the world of good.'

'No, thanks. God, aren't I already miserable enough?' Stella smartly sidestepped that trap. 'Anyway, if anyone should be running marathons it's my husband's new girlfriend.'

'Stella.' Max shook his head at her.

'What? She's fat! Why can't I say that?'

'Because Tilly's here and Erin's her friend.'

'And Erin stole my *husband*. I'll call her whatever I like.'

Tilly briefly imagined the reaction if she were to chuck her drink in Stella's face. But no, this was Declan's birthday—and he'd supplied the drink, come to that, so she wouldn't waste it. Instead, she would rise above it, meet rudeness with grace and serenity.

'Jack! Jack! Oooh, you naughty creature, come here and give me a big kiss!' Tilly, knocked to one side by a slinky-hipped brunette, spilled her drink over Max's sleeve. So much for not wasting it.

'Bloody hell,' said Max, shaking his arm. 'See what I mean about coming out with him? We should get danger money.'

'Lisa.' Jack allowed her to kiss each cheek. 'How nice to see you again.'

'If it's nice to see me again, why haven't you been in touch? You promised you would.' Lisa pouted and clung to him.

Tilly escaped to the Ladies and phoned Erin. 'It's me. I'm at the Fox. Stella's here. She *knows*.'

Erin wailed, 'I know she knows! Is she still furious?'

'And outraged. I told her you didn't break up the marriage.'

'So did I. Did she believe you?'

'Not for a second.'

Erin heaved a sigh. 'Oh well, who else is there?'

'Loads of people. Me and Max. Stella and her friend Amy.' Tilly paused. 'Jack's here. Women keep coming up and grabbing him.'

'Always fun to watch. So long as you're not tempted to join in.'

'Don't worry, I'm not. The more I see him in action, the easier it becomes to steer clear.' Tilly meant it. Watching the other girls clamouring over Jack made her determined not to join in.

Making her way back from the Ladies, Tilly met Jack in the corridor. He smiled. 'Enjoying yourself?'

'Yes, thanks. I hardly recognised you without all those women clinging to you like barnacles.'

'Sorry about that. I don't ask them to do it. Pretty embarrassing really.' When he did that self-deprecating shruggy thing he looked irresistible. 'Actually, you could do me a big favour.' He gazed at her intently. 'I'm being put under a bit of pressure by, um, a couple of people in there.' His head tilted in the direction of the bar.

'A couple? Or maybe three?'

'OK, three. I've been invited to a charity dinner in Cheltenham and I have to take a guest along with me. The thing is, all three of them are angling to be the one I ask. So I'm thinking the best way round it would be to take you instead.'

Was he serious? Tilly said, 'Are you trying to get me publicly stoned and run out of Roxborough?'

'But you're new. I can tell them you're already involved with the charity, and that the organisers asked me to bring you along. That way, nobody feels snubbed. And we'll have a great evening, I promise.'

'I can't.' Tilly shook her head. 'Amy was quizzing me earlier. She wanted to know if I'd go out with you if you asked me. I said no.'

'God, like a bullet through my heart.' Clutching his chest, Jack said, 'But Amy meant would you go out with me if I asked you out on a date.

And this wouldn't be a date, would it?' He shrugged. 'It wouldn't be romantic. If I had a sister I'd take her along with me. But I don't, so the next best thing is if I take you instead. Purely platonic.'

Perversely, it rankled to be thought of as the next best thing to a sister. But if she said no, would he think that was what was bothering her? Oh God, now this was starting to get complicated.

'Unless you don't want it to be,' said Jack.

Which didn't help *at all*. Now her stomach was going like a washing machine on spin. He was a nightmare.

Having waited, Jack raised his hand. 'I'll take that as a no.'

Nooo! Tilly got that eBay feeling when you see the lot you've been bidding for slip from your grasp. 'When is it? I'd have to ask Max, see if he'd give me the night off.'

As they rejoined the others in the bar, Tilly was aware of Amy's eyes on her. Then she saw she was the focus of Lisa and Marianne's scrutiny too. This was the kind of attention Jack had to deal with all the time.

Then again, only because he'd slept with them.

'I was looking at some of the websites this afternoon.' Stella, deep in conversation with Max, said, 'It's brilliant. I had no idea! If you want George Clooney you can have him!'

'Well, that would be the answer to all our prayers,' said Max. 'But you can't *really* have him, can you? Because George isn't *really* advertising himself on the Internet, is he?'

Stella rolled her eyes. 'You haven't been paying a bit of attention, have you? Honestly, Max. I'm not talking about dating websites here!'

'Oh. Sorry, I drifted a bit,' said Max. 'Websites to do with . . .?'

'Donor sperm!'

Spraying wine, Max clapped a hand over his mouth. 'Is this a joke?'

'I want a child.' Stella's back was very straight. 'My husband's buggered off and the thought of having sex with another man makes me feel physically sick. So this seems like the answer.'

Amy was perplexed. 'You can't really buy George Clooney's sperm.' She frowned. 'Can you?'

'Of course you can't buy George Clooney's *actual* sperm.' Stella shot Amy a despairing look. 'I meant if you wanted a sperm donor with his qualities and physical characteristics.'

'Just don't get him confused with Mickey Rooney,' said Max.

'And how much would it cost?' Amy was clearly concerned.

Stella sipped her drink. 'It's a baby, not a new sofa. You can't put a price on a child.'

'But think how many beautiful new shoes you could buy! Jimmy Choos,' Amy said dreamily. 'I'd rather have new shoes than a baby any day.'

'Shoes are better,' Max agreed. 'Shoes don't throw up on your shoulder.'

'Now you're just making fun of me.' Stella mock-punched him on the arm. 'And it's no laughing matter. Men don't understand how it feels to have that clock ticking away inside you. I just hate feeling this help-less.' She shook her head. 'All my life I've made plans. I like to be in control. And now, thanks to Fergus, I'm not. It's just *killing* me.'

'Speaking of making plans . . .' Amy nodded at Stella meaningfully.

'What? Oh right. Yes.' Prompted by Amy, Stella turned to Jack. 'While you were gone just now, Marianne came over and said something about going with you to the charity ball in Cheltenham. She's so pushy. And I said I wasn't sure but I thought you might be inviting *someone else*.' As she spoke, she subtly tilted her head in Amy's direction.

'As a matter of fact, I'm not taking Marianne,' Jack said easily. 'And I am inviting someone else.'

A tiny smile of anticipation tweaked at the corners of Amy's mouth.

No, no. Tilly winced inwardly. Not here, not now, not like this.

'I've asked Tilly to come along with me and she's said yes.'

Oh bugger, he'd said it.

Amy stiffened. Her gaze accusing, she blurted out, '*What?*'

Stella said bluntly, 'You said you wouldn't.'

'It's not a date,' Tilly put in hastily, 'and I haven't said yes either. I said I'd ask Max.'

'Next Friday.' Jack looked over at Max. 'Can you spare her?'

'Fine by me. No hanky-panky, mind,' Max said, wagging a finger.

'What's going on?' Eavesdropping on her way to the bar, Marianne's head snapped round. 'What's happening?'

'Jack's taking *her*.' Amy indicated Tilly.

'*What?*'

Oh please, she didn't need this. Tilly said, 'This is crazy. Forget it.'

'Don't be daft. I'm inviting Tilly for a reason.' Jack eyed each of the indignant girls in turn. 'She's been raising money for the charity for years. This is her chance to get to know the fundraisers down here.'

Marianne's face fell. Amy looked resigned. Stella said suspiciously, 'Which charity is it?'

Honestly, why did people have to be so *nosy*? The really frustrating thing was, Stella was asking *her* and Jack was waiting for her to give them the answer because he'd told her the name of the charity moments before they'd come back through to the bar.

Except it had gone, slithered away like mercury. And everyone was standing there waiting, gazing expectantly . . . Ooh! 'Help for Alzheimer's!' Tilly gave a nod of triumph. Phew, just in the nick of time. 'And it's not a date,' she reminded them, because there were still looks of hate winging her way. She checked her watch. Was it time to go home yet?

Chapter 4

AFTER THREE YEARS IN LA you'd think she'd be used to its funny little Californian ways but the parties still made Kaye smile. This one, thrown by the director of *Over the Rainbow*, was glitzy and lavish in so many aspects, yet it still ended at five o'clock on the dot. Even more bizarrely, guests were leaving in chauffeur-driven limos because they were too rich, rather than too paralytic, to drive themselves home. Denzil and Charlene Weintraub's house in the Hollywood Hills had been spectacular but it wasn't the kind of party you'd remember for the rest of your life. Over here you were expected to network rather than enjoy yourself. Fun was frowned upon and actually eating in this world of size zeros was categorised as a dangerous sport.

Anyway, sod hiring a chauffeur-driven limo for no reason other than to show off. Kaye slid behind the wheel of her convertible and wondered whether Charlene's manner towards her had been a bit odd. Out by the pool earlier she'd drawled, 'So, found yourself another man yet, Kaye? One of your own, I mean, rather than somebody else's?'

Which had been a weird thing to say, hadn't it? Then again, the wife of your director wasn't the kind of person you took issue with. Charlene was pampered, prickly and famously indulged by Denzil. Kaye had heard on the grapevine—well, Macy Ventura, who knew pretty much everything about everyone—that Charlene was secretly battling an addiction to painkillers, so it was best to stay on the right side of her. She could be volatile when crossed.

Putting the car into gear, Kaye reversed out of her parking space and headed down the drive. She pressed PLAY on the CD player and cranked up the volume as Jennifer Hudson launched into 'And I Am Telling You I'm Not Going'. Oh yes, this was her favourite song of all time. Kaye sucked air into her lungs and bellowed along with Jennifer, 'And I am *telling* you . . . I'm not *goooooooinggg*—'

Shit, what was *that*?

In a split second the tiny brown creature had appeared out of nowhere and disappeared under the front wheels before she even had a chance to react. She stamped on the brakes and let out a shriek of fright as the car slewed to a stop on the drive. Oh God, please don't say she'd hit it, even if it was only a rat.

Having stumbled out of the car and dropped to her knees, she saw the sight she'd been most dreading. The little body lay unmoving in the shadows under the car. She'd killed the rat.

'Nooooooo!' shrieked a high-pitched voice in the distance as a door slammed and footsteps came racing down the drive.

'No,' Kaye croaked as she saw that it wasn't a rat after all. Oh no, oh no, oh no. She went hot, then ice-cold all over, appalled by the sight of the tiny creature, Charlene's pet Chihuahua, on the ground.

'You killed Babylamb! You killed my baby!' Charlene had reached them, panting and distraught. Scooping the little body into her arms, she began rocking to and fro. 'Oh, my Babylamb, wake up, wake up . . .'

'I'm so sorry. It was an accident. He just came out of nowhere, ran straight under the car. There was nothing I could do, I'm so sorry.'

'You bitch, you did it on purpose!' screeched Charlene.

Kaye stumbled backwards, stunned by the ferocity of the attack. 'That's not true, I wouldn't do that, it's not *true*!'

'You hate me. You're jealous,' Charlene spat vehemently. 'You want Denzil and you can't bear it that I have him. You're nothing but a skinny ginger husband-stealing tart and you ran over my Babylamb on purpose.'

'I didn't, I didn't.'

'Oh, don't lie. Look at you, you're drunk.' Charlene jabbed a bony finger at her. 'And I know you did it on purpose. I was up there on the balcony and I saw you deliberately swerve to run over him.'

This was a nightmare. Kaye couldn't believe it was happening. Guests, security guards and household staff hurried over.

'She's drunk,' Charlene yelled over and over again.

'I had one glass of wine. *One glass*,' Kaye protested, but it was no use.

'She's a murdering bitch and she is *finished* in this town!' screeched Charlene. 'C-call the cops. That bitch is going to pay for this.'

There were two customers in the shop when Stella made her entrance. Erin's heart sank like an anchor.

'What d'you reckon, Sandra? How about this for our Angie's wedding?' A middle-aged woman reverently stroked a pale green matching dress and jacket. 'Lovely material. Eighty pounds, but it's Frank Usher.'

Stella said to the woman, 'It's a pity you didn't try the Oxfam shop yesterday morning. You could have bought it in there for six pounds fifty.'

The middle-aged woman and her friend instinctively took a step back from the outfit and turned to look at Erin in shocked disbelief.

'That's not true.' Erin shook her head at the two women. 'Just ignore her. It's not true.'

'By the way,' Stella said sweetly, 'did you ever hear back from that woman who complained about the cardigan she'd bought from you, the one with maggots in the pocket?'

The two women backed out of the shop, one surreptitiously wiping her palms on the side of her coat.

'She's lying,' Erin called out before the door clanged shut.

'Worked, though.' Stella looked pleased with herself. 'Didn't it?'

'You can't do this. It's not fair.'

'I think it's fair,' said Stella. 'I think you deserve it.'

'I didn't steal Fergus from you. And marching in here like this and causing trouble isn't going to make Fergus want to come back to you.'

'I know that. I'm not *stupid*.' Her chin raised and her shoulders stiff, Stella said, 'Thanks to you, I'm not going to have the life or the family I'd planned to have. Which, funnily enough, I find really upsetting.'

Trembling, Erin said, 'I don't want you coming into this shop again.'

'I won't. But just remember.' Stella paused with her hand gripping the door. 'You've hurt me. And now it's my turn to hurt you.'

'There's a photographer up a tree across the street.' Clutching the phone, Kaye ducked away from the window before he could get a shot of her. 'And a load more milling around on the sidewalk.'

'But it'll blow over, won't it?' Max said. 'Give them a day or two and people will lose interest, move on to the next bit of gossip.'

'I hope so.' Except she wasn't so sure, and now an outside broadcast truck was pulling up. She hadn't been arrested—the police had released her without charge—but she already knew Charlene wasn't going to let it go. Journalists contacted by Charlene had been ringing for her response. This was Hollywood. The right story could be whipped into overdrive. And let's face it, who wouldn't love the idea that one of the stars of *Over the Rainbow*—the cute British one, no less, who seemed so ladylike—was really a man-hungry, puppy-murdering psychopath?

'Hey, you'll be fine,' Max said helpfully. 'Just tell everyone to fuck off.'

'Oh yes, that'll work.' A reporter was standing outside the house wielding a microphone and addressing a camera.

'OK then, come home. We'll look after you.'

Kaye's eyes abruptly filled with tears, because what he was suggesting was so tempting and so impossible.

'Except I have this little thing called a job,' she reminded Max. 'And a contract for next season about to be renewed. And something tells me the studio wouldn't be too thrilled if I did a bunk.'

Above a faint tapping sound, Max said, 'Well, we're here if you need us. Don't let the buggers get you down—bloody hell.'

Oh God, what now? Her mouth dry, Kaye said, 'What is it?'

'I've got the laptop here. I've just been googling you. There's a piece calling you the bunny boiler of Beverly Hills.'

'**P**oor Mum.' Three days had passed and Kaye was now officially the most reviled woman in America. Clicking onto the next link, Lou was confronted with a photograph of Charlene tearfully hugging a portrait of Babylamb.

Tilly said, 'Stop reading them now.'

'I can't. That's my mum they're talking about. Look, here's a photo of her being carted off to the police station. They're saying she's got a drink problem. If she didn't have before, she'll end up with one at this rate.'

Tilly peered over Lou's shoulder at the photograph of Kaye. 'Perfect English Rose or Deranged Drunk?' screamed the headline. 'Kaye McKenna's career is in tatters, thanks to an unrequited crush on her boss and a moment of murderous madness.'

'My mum isn't like that! She doesn't chase after ugly old men just because they're rich!'

'We know that. Turn off the computer now, sweetheart.'

'I can't. I've got to look up some stuff about Shakespeare. *Boring.*'

'My daughter the philistine,' Max announced, coming into the kitchen. 'If it isn't *Heat* magazine, she's not interested.'

'Thanks for that, Dad. I just don't happen to like Shakespeare.'

'That's because you haven't seen it being performed. Right, let's do something about it.' Max expertly nudged Lou out of her seat and took her place in front of the laptop. 'Royal Shakespeare Company, Stratford. Here we go. *Richard the Third* . . . maybe not. *Coriolanus,* hmm. *Twelfth*

Night, you'll like that. Right, fetch my wallet, we'll book the tickets now. Tilly, you up for this?'

Startled, Tilly said, 'Are you serious? You really like Shakespeare?'

'Ha, she thinks I'm too common to appreciate the Bard. But I'm not.' Max wagged a finger at her. 'He's bloody brilliant. Bugger, I can't do the Wednesday or Thursday, I'm up in London with a client. It'll have to be Friday the 20th.'

Phew, reprieve. 'I can't make that. It's the night of the charity ball. What a shame,' said Tilly.

The atmosphere on the set hadn't improved. Everywhere she went, Kaye encountered groups of people whispering together. She was also aware that the team of writers were currently working away on last-minute alterations to the script for the final episode of the series. Hmm, wonder what that could possibly be about? *And* she was still waiting for her contract to be renewed. Funny that.

In the make-up trailer, the only sound came from the TV. '. . . And now the Kaye McKenna affair,' announced the presenter.

Ellis, the make-up girl, said, 'Want me to change channels?'

'No, leave it. I don't care any more,' Kaye said.

'And this morning we have here in the studio three guests who all have something in common with Charlene Weintraub.' The presenter paused significantly. 'Paula here says she was walking along the street one day last year when a car driven by Kaye McKenna came careering at top speed towards her. If she hadn't leapt out of the way she's convinced she would have been killed, just like Babylamb.'

'Oh my God . . .' breathed Ellis. 'You did *that*?'

'No, of course I didn't do that! I've never seen the woman before!'

'Next we have Jason, who tells us that Kaye McKenna deliberately tried to run over his pet dog, Brutus. And finally we have Maria who says she was verbally abused in the street by a deranged red-headed woman whom she now believes to have been Kaye McKenna.'

'I should sue them all! How *dare* they?' bellowed Kaye.

There was a tap at the door, then Denzil entered the trailer. 'Can we get this new scene shot?'

'OK. Sorry.' He'd come empty-handed. 'Do I get to see the script?'

'No need.' Denzil shook his head. 'You don't have any dialogue.'

Kaye looked steadily at him. 'Let me guess. Am I going to be floating face down in a swimming pool?'

His tone abrupt, Denzil said, 'Something like that.'

'Just water for me.' Tilly was going to hang on to her faculties tonight.

Jack said, 'Hey, the whole point of getting a taxi here was so we didn't have to worry about driving home. One glass of wine wouldn't hurt, would it?' Grinning at the waiter with the wine bottle, Jack confided, 'She's scared I'll seduce her.'

The waiter in turn pulled a Graham Norton-type face and stage-whispered in Tilly's ear, 'Go for it, darling. Lucky old you.'

Which was a great help.

'I'm not going to,' said Jack. 'I gave my word I wouldn't.'

'Don't worry.' The waiter winked at Tilly. 'I'm sure you can persuade him to change his mind.'

Just the thought of it made her go hot. Glad of the reprieve as the young waiter minced off and Jack was collared by a couple of florid businessmen, she stood back and surveyed the scene.

The ball was being held at a huge wedding cake of a hotel in Cheltenham; the ballroom was glamorous, vast and high-ceilinged and thronged with people chatting and dancing along to the band. An older woman resplendent in purple silk came swishing up. 'I've been meaning to come over and say hello! Dorothy Summerskill, from the committee,' she introduced herself. 'And you're Jack's girlfriend.'

'Friend,' said Tilly. 'We're just friends.'

'Oh, right! Probably safer that way!' Dorothy had a jolly laugh. 'We all love him to bits, you know. He's done so much for our charity. One of our greatest supporters here in Cheltenham.'

'Is that because a member of his family had Alzheimer's?'

'Actually, it was through Rose, his fiancée. Darling Rose, her grand-mother was affected, which is how she got involved with fundraising. After she died Jack stayed on board. Wonderful for us.'

After dinner the dancing began in earnest. Tilly spent the next couple of hours being twirled round the dance floor. Barely even aware that she still wasn't drinking, she was having a whale of a time.

Then Jack had to come along and spoil it all.

Exhausted after a couple of energetic tangos, she was perching on the edge of a table resting her feet when she saw Jack heading towards her. 'What?' said Tilly, because he was checking his watch. 'Is it time to go?'

'No. Actually, I was thinking it was time we had a dance.' He paused, watching her reaction. 'Sorry. It's just that people might think it a bit odd if we don't. Don't worry, I'll behave myself.' Grinning, he drew her to him as the music restarted.

Right, just relax, she told herself, move in time with the music and keep on moving until it ends. Then that's it, job done. How long would it take anyway? Three or four minutes, she could manage that. Even if she had to count the seconds. OK, one . . . two . . . three . . .

'Are you *counting?*'

'What? Oh, sorry.' Tilly ducked her head, tinglingly aware of the fact that most of the front of her body was touching most of the front of his; if she completely lost control of herself and reached up on tiptoe she could lick his neck . . . OK, stop that, start counting again.

'Having fun?' said Jack.

She nodded; he had absolutely no idea how dancing with him was making her feel. 'Everyone's really friendly. Dorothy was saying nice things about you.'

'Could be because I'm a nice person. Every now and again,' Jack amended with a brief smile. 'When I want to be.'

That smile. At such close quarters it was even more devastating. Tilly closed her eyes for a second and thought about Amy and Marianne and . . . Lisa, that was it. Because that was the thing about Jack, he bestowed his smiles indiscriminately and left a trail of havoc in his wake. He wasn't remotely interested in any kind of meaningful relationship either. All he cared about was sex. *Remember that.*

'OK, you can stop now,' murmured Jack.

She realised the music had ended and she was still swaying.

'We've done our duty, haven't we?' Jack released his hold on her, disappointing all her nerve endings at once.

Jack had promised to treat her like a lady and behave like a perfect gentleman but Tilly hadn't actually expected him to do it. All the way home to Roxborough in the back of the taxi she'd been mentally bracing herself, waiting for him to make a move. But he hadn't.

'Bye.' Jack nodded.

'Bye.'

Did he find her *ugly?*

They'd got the dates muddled; when Max had been booking the tickets for the RSC Tilly had thought the ball in Cheltenham was being held on the Friday evening. Happily, by the time she'd realised the mistake—the ball was on Thursday—it had been too late for him to book another seat. Max still thought she'd done it on purpose.

After school on Friday afternoon Lou grumbled, 'I don't know why Dad thinks seeing people prancing around on a stage is going to make me like Shakespeare. You want to go in my place?'

'You are so *sweet*, but one of us has to stay at home and look after Betty.'

'Bloody hell,' complained Max, just home from a meeting with a client in Bristol. 'You'd think I was threatening you with a night in a torture chamber. Right, I'm off for a shower.' Shrugging off his jacket, he added, 'By the way, Jack rang me earlier. You left your pashmina on the floor of the taxi last night, Tilly. He's got it.'

'Oh brilliant.' Tilly exhaled with relief. 'I thought I'd lost it.'

'He said he can drop it back, or you can call in and pick it up.'

'So what are you doing this evening while we're gone?' said Lou.

'Nice long bath. Chinese takeaway. And a Marks & Spencer cappuccino walnut whip.'

'Lucky thing,' Lou sighed.

They left just after six to drive up to Stratford. Tilly took Betty for a long run through the woods. When they got home Betty collapsed into her basket and Tilly ran herself a bath. By eight o'clock she was dressed again in her post-bath grey velours track suit.

On her way to the only Chinese takeaway in Roxborough it occurred to Tilly that she could pick up her pashmina en route, seeing as she would practically be passing Jack's house.

'Hey, you. Quick, come in.' Jack opened the door wider.

Tilly hesitated. 'I just came to collect—'

'I know, I know, but my sauce will stick if I don't get back to it.'

Tilly followed him through to the kitchen. There was no earthly reason to be impressed just because a man was cooking an actual proper meal rather than poking holes in Cellophane, but somehow she couldn't help herself. And it did smell fantastic.

Jack was busy stirring the contents of a Le Creuset pan. A teaspoon of caster sugar and a splash of lemon juice later, he tasted and gave a nod of satisfaction.

'Do you have company?' Tilly asked.

'Oh no, all on my own.'

'I didn't know you were into all this.' Tilly mentally compared him with Jean-Christophe Novelli; God, imagine if he were to adopt a sexy French accent, think of the chaos *that* could cause.

'I do a pretty good bolognese sauce. It's my signature dish.' He paused. 'Actually, it's more or less my only dish.' He turned to look at her. 'How much of a hurry are you in?'

'For what?'

'The pashmina. Thing is, there were a couple of marks on it from where it had been on the floor, so I put it in the wash.' He indicated the utility room, where Tilly could see a washing machine merrily churning away.

'Oh no. My pashmina is one hundred per cent cashmere! It cost two hundred pounds from Harvey Nichols and it's dry-clean only!'

Jack had stopped stirring the sauce. 'Shit. Really?'

Yee-ha, got him. 'No. Polyester, loves washing machines, six pounds fifty, Camden Market.'

The relief was visible on his face. 'Managed to get myself into major trouble once with a white lacy top thing and a load of filthy rugby kit.'

'I wouldn't have had you down as the white lacy top type.'

He took a bottle of red wine and glugged a good couple of glassfuls into the pan. 'I thought Rose was going to explode when she saw what I'd done. It was the first time she'd worn it.' Then he said, 'And the last.'

She watched him put the finishing touches to the sauce he still hadn't asked her to taste. 'How long before the washing machine finishes?'

'Thirty, thirty-five minutes.'

'OK,' said Tilly. 'Well, why don't I go and order my takeaway? Then when I've got it, I'll pop back here and pick up the pashmina.'

'Is that your plan for the evening?' Jack shrugged. 'You could stay here with me and try my signature dish instead.'

Was this why he hadn't offered her a taste? Because the fact that he hadn't meant she now *really* wanted to know what his sauce was like.

'I was going to have Chinese.'

'But hasn't Max taken Lou to Stratford? You'd be all on your own.'

Amy and Lisa and Marianne would have said yes by now.

'I wouldn't be on my own. I'd have Betty. I don't want to leave her on her own for too long.'

'A couple of hours wouldn't hurt.' Jack's eyes glittered with amusement. 'You could give her a ring if you like, *yip-yip*.'

'Don't make fun of me.'

He broke into a smile. 'I actually thought that was a really sweet thing to do. And if you go home to Betty, I'll be the one left here on my own.' Jack gave her a soulful look. 'Just me and a big vat of bolognese.'

Which smelled *fantastic*.

Anyone else would have said yes by now, wouldn't they?

Wake up, love. Is this the place?'

Kaye, who hadn't been asleep, opened her eyes. Home.

Well, not *home* home. But it had been until three years ago. And she knew she was welcome here, which meant a lot just now . . .

OK, don't cry, just pay the taxi driver and get your cases out of the trunk. Boot. You're back in England now.

Within ten seconds of ringing the doorbell she began to regret sending the driver away. How stupid not to have checked first that someone was at home. Bending down, she pushed open the letterbox and yelled, 'Max? Lou? Anybody there?'

Her hopes soared as a door creaked inside the house, followed by the sound of someone approaching at a fast pace—

'Woof!' Betty let out a volley of barks, bouncing up at the letterbox on the other side of the front door. 'Woof! Woof!'

'Oh, Betty, it's so lovely to see you again. I've missed you so much.' Stuffing her fingers through the letterbox, Kaye felt them being licked by the little dog's dear familiar tongue and almost burst into noisy sobs. Then she accidentally let go of the spring-loaded letterbox with her other hand and gave a yelp of pain instead.

OK, what to do next? Phone Max, obviously. She unearthed her mobile and called his number. Switched off. *Where was he?*

Next she tried Lou's phone. Oh yes, and this time it was ringing, thank God. Shit, she could hear it chirruping away from the other end too. Opening the letterbox again, Kaye's heart sank as she recognised the jaunty ringtone. Lou might not be at home but her phone was.

Right, think. Stay here and hope someone comes home before she dies of hypothermia? Or leave her cases and walk into Roxborough?

Oh well, there was bound to be someone she knew in the pub.

It was nine thirty, they'd eaten the meal Jack had cooked and now here Tilly was, sitting on the sofa gazing at a photo of Rose Symonds.

And she hadn't had to creep around the house to get her hands on it. Jack had said, 'Still curious to know what Rose looked like?'

Just like that. And when she'd nodded, he'd left the living room, returning a couple of minutes later with the photograph.

Now he resumed his seat on the sofa. 'I have to say, I don't usually do this. I just keep thinking that if you two had ever met, you'd have liked each other. You would've got on together really well.'

Tilly carried on taking in every last detail. Rose had had conker-brown eyes and long, fantastically glossy dark hair. In the photo she was standing in the middle of what looked like a building site, laughing into the camera. Love radiated from her eyes. Tilly knew without having to ask that the person taking the photo had been Jack.

'I think we'd have got on well together too. She looks . . . fun.'

'She was.' Jack nodded, his expression controlled.

'And you took her to all the best places.' Tilly indicated the building site.

'That was here. In the back garden.'

All those months of work to put together the house of their dreams. Then the dream had been shattered. Tilly wondered how you ever got over something like that. Perhaps by sleeping with hundreds of women and making a point of not getting emotionally involved with any of them. But did it work? Was that getting over it or getting through it?

'Thanks.' She handed the photo back. 'She was beautiful.'

'I know.' Jack glanced at it again, smiled briefly. 'She's laughing there because her grandmother's just come out carrying a tray of mugs. We'd asked for coffee, no sugar. We got tea, six sugars.' He paused. 'Does that sound cruel? We weren't laughing *at* her, just making the best of a situation that had its funny side. Rose loved her to bits. We both did.'

'Was she still alive when . . . the accident happened?'

'Oh yes.' Jack exhaled slowly. 'At the funeral she kept asking who'd died. And every time someone told her, it was as if she was hearing it for the first time. Which was pretty hard to bear.' He stopped, shook his head. 'I can't believe I'm telling you all this. I don't usually.'

There was a lump in Tilly's throat the size of a tennis ball.

'Actually, that's not true,' Jack amended. 'I think I do know why.' Another pause. 'Shall we change the subject?'

Tilly nodded, not trusting herself to speak. All of a sudden, like some kind of weird chemical reaction, her whole body was reacting to his. Every nerve ending in her body was jangling and buzzing. She wanted to hold him, lessen the terrible pain and make him feel better . . . Oh God, this must be the infamous tragic-widower effect.

'Go on then.' He looked at her. 'You choose. Change the subject to something happier.'

Happier. She swallowed with difficulty. 'How about handbags?'

'That's cheating. Let's talk about cricket.'

'I hate cricket.' Was it her imagination or was he moving closer?

'We could discuss Italy.' OK, his mouth definitely wasn't as far away as it had been twenty seconds ago. 'Ever been to Italy?'

'No.'

'Oh dear. We're running out of things to talk about.' He waited. 'If I told you that I like you, would you think I was spinning you a line?'

Tilly managed a nod.

'Well, I'm not. It's the truth. I really do like you. A lot,' said Jack. 'In fact, it almost scares me. I'm not sure I want it to be happening.'

Was this how he did it? Was this the well-spun line? It probably was. But what if it *wasn't*? What if this was the one time he actually meant it?

'And in case you were wondering,' Jack's voice was low, 'it almost killed me, keeping my promise last night.'

Had it? Really? He looked as if he was telling the truth. Breathlessly Tilly said, 'I thought you weren't bothered.'

He half smiled with his incredible mouth. 'Oh, I was bothered.'

Tilly's stomach was by this time awash with butterflies. 'I wish you didn't have such a reputation.'

'I know. Me too. I'm not proud of some of the things I've done.'

'Like that girl Amy, from the Fox. She was so thrilled and besotted, because she didn't realise she was just a meaningless one-night stand, and that's so *sad*. You're just making her look stupid.'

Jack surveyed her for a long moment, his expression unreadable. Then he said evenly, 'I don't want to talk about Amy. I never discuss my relationships. Everyone knows that.'

'Is that part of the attraction? That they can trust you to be discreet?'

A glimmer of amusement. 'I'm sure it helps.'

He was right, of course. Tilly had never forgotten the desperate humiliation of going back to school after breaking up with Ben Thomas, only to discover he had broadcast intimate details of their relationship to everyone they knew. But instead of telling them what a great kisser she was, he'd spread the news that she'd once laughed so hard at a video of *Mr Bean* that she'd accidentally wet herself.

The jokes she'd had to endure had kept everyone else in Year 12 entertained for months. So, yes, the prospect of a relationship with someone who knew the meaning of discretion definitely had its upside.

'What are you thinking?' The little finger of Jack's left hand brushed against her wrist as he spoke, reminding her that he was still there.

What am I thinking? That I could sleep with you and no one would ever know. We could go upstairs and have sex right now and it would stay our secret. All I have to do is be home before midnight—

Dddddrrrrinnnngggg. Doorbell. *Bugger*. Back to earth with a bump.

'Shouldn't you find out who that is?'

Jack wasn't moving. 'They might go away.'

Dddddrrrinnggggg, the bell went again, followed by the sound of the letterbox being pushed open. 'Jaaa-aaack! Are you there?'

A female voice, surprise surprise. Tilly looked at Jack, who was frowning. 'Who's that?'

'Jack, it's meee! Please open the door, I'm *desperate*.'

Jack was on his feet, his face clearing. 'My God, I don't believe it . . .' He hurried out to the hall. The next moment Tilly heard the front door open and exclamations of delight, followed by hurrying footsteps.

Jack returned to the living room, shaking his head and smiling. 'She was desperate for the loo. She'll be through in a minute.'

'Thank goodness you were in,' the female voice called out. 'I was going to use the loo in the Fox but it's Declan's night off. I didn't know a soul in there and a group of teenagers recognised me and started making smart remarks so I got out fast—oh, hello!'

The mystery visitor materialised at last in the living room. Tilly's mouth dropped open as she realised who it was.

'Oops, am I interrupting something?' Kaye pulled a face.

Yes, yes, *yes*.

'Not at all. Kaye, meet Tilly Cole.' Easily, Jack effected the introductions. 'Tilly, this is Lou's mum, Kaye.'

'Tilly!' Kaye's eyes lit up. 'How lovely to meet you.' She crossed the room, greeted her with a hug and a kiss. 'Although it would have been lovelier if you'd been at home when the taxi dropped me off! No one there but Betty. I've had to walk all the way from Beech House.'

'Max and Lou have gone to Stratford,' said Tilly. So much for no one ever knowing she'd spent the evening here with Jack.

'The RSC!' Kaye smacked the side of her head. 'Lou told me. My memory's gone completely to pot since I became public enemy number one in the States. Oh God, here I go again.' Abruptly her sapphire-blue eyes filled with tears. 'Sorry, sorry, it's been a hell of a week.'

'Hey, sshh, don't cry.' Jack was there in a flash, folding Kaye into his arms and rubbing her back comfortingly. Over her head, he said, 'There's a box of Kleenex in the kitchen.'

Tilly obediently found them then paused in the doorway on the way back, pierced with envy as she watched Kaye and Jack standing together in the middle of the living room. Which was ridiculous and shameful, because Kaye had been through a horrible time.

'Tissues,' she said lamely, and Kaye turned, grateful and pink-eyed.

'Thanks so much. I'm not usually such a crybaby.' Noisily blowing her nose she said, 'What time are you going home? Can I hitch a lift? Oh . . . unless you weren't planning on going home.' Kaye glanced from Tilly to Jack, the thought belatedly crossing her mind.

'No, no.' Tilly hastily shook her head. 'Of course I'm going home! I just called in to pick up my pashmina. We can leave now if you want.'

They drove back to Beech House and Kaye had an emotional reunion with Betty, prompting yet more tears, but happy ones this time.

Then she opened a bottle of Max's wine. 'Just as well I turned up on Jack's doorstep.' She clinked glasses with Tilly across the kitchen table. 'I think I probably did you a big favour tonight.'

'There's nothing going on between us.'

'Jack can be very persuasive. Not that he usually needs to do much persuading. Most of the women round here just fling themselves at him.'

Tilly flushed slightly; had she done that?

'It's like the deli counter at the supermarket,' Kaye went on. 'They all queue up, take their tickets and wait their turn to be served.' She gave a snort of laughter. 'Or serviced.'

Which made Tilly feel *so* much better.

'Never mind.' Kaye patted her arm. 'You may just have had a lucky escape.' She waved the wine bottle, ready to top up their glasses.

Mischievously Tilly said, 'He must be pretty good, though.'

'Oh, he is.'

Excuse me? *What?* Tilly opened her mouth to ask if that meant what she thought it meant, but the beam of headlights swung across the kitchen. Max and Lou were back.

Opening the front door, Tilly said, 'Well? How did it go?'

'Fantastic.' Max was on a high. 'Bloody brilliant.'

Lou rolled her eyes. 'It was better than having to sit down and read Shakespeare from a book. But only just.'

'Never mind.' Tilly gave her a consoling hug. 'Come on into the kitchen. I've got a surprise for you.'

Eleven o'clock on Saturday morning and Jack was on the doorstep. For a mad moment Tilly fantasised that he'd come to grab her and bundle her back to his house. But no, that would be too much to hope for. Plus, Lou might have something to say about it.

'Yay, you're early!' Lou cannoned into Tilly before Jack had a chance to open his mouth. 'Mum's nearly ready. And I'm coming with you. I'll go up and tell her you're here.'

Curiously, Tilly said, 'So what's happening?'

He followed her into the kitchen, pinched the still-warm croissant from Lou's plate and added extra butter. 'Kaye rang me an hour ago. She wants a place of her own while she's over here and I've got a couple of properties free at the moment. Easier for her.' Jack shrugged. 'She can use one until she decides what she wants to do next.'

'Nice of you.'

He half smiled. 'I told you, I can be nice when I want to be.'

Tilly wrestled with staying super-casual but the question was crashing round inside her head. 'Can I ask you something?'

He raised an eyebrow. 'Fire away.'

Oh help. It was too personal. She braced herself. 'Are you . . .'

'Am I what?' Jack looked mystified. 'A vegetarian? Fond of flower arranging? Am I still a virgin? Is that it?' Still guessing away, he said cheerfully, 'What did I tell you yesterday? I never discuss my sex life.'

He had indeed said that. Which pretty much meant there was no point in asking the question. Then Lou erupted back into the kitchen and let out a squeak of protest at the sight of her empty plate. 'Who's had my croissant?'

'That was Tilly,' said Jack.

Out of the two vacant properties, Kaye had gone for the small but charmingly furnished cottage in Roxborough.

'I like it,' said Tilly when they went over to see the place on Monday.

'Small but perfectly formed. Handy for the shops, and close to home. Well,' Kaye amended, 'close to *your* home.'

'You could have stayed with us,' Tilly pointed out.

'It's OK, best not to. Stay separate, stay friends, always the best way.' Kaye seized the suitcase. 'Want to give me a hand with this?'

Upstairs in the only bedroom, they took out the bed linen borrowed from the airing cupboard at Beech House and made up the double bed.

'Not that I need a double.' Kaye pulled a face. 'I've been living like a nun for the past two years.'

Tilly's mouth went dry. Anyone with manners and an iota of decorum wouldn't dream of asking the question she was about to blurt out, but not knowing the answer was killing her.

'Can I ask you something really personal? About something you said the other night.' Tilly felt her heart thudding very fast. 'When I made a jokey remark about how, um, Jack must be great in bed.'

Kaye's hair swung to one side as she tilted her head. 'And?'

Oh God, was she offended? Was she going to be as infuriatingly discreet as Jack? 'Well, and you said he was.'

'Uh-huh.' An enigmatic nod.

Oh well, she'd come this far. 'So does that mean you and Jack . . .?'

Kaye's eyes sparkled. 'Did it? Slept together? That kind of thing?'

Oh, the shame. Tilly shrugged and said, 'Pretty much. Sorry.'

'No problem. Yes, we did. And he was great. In every way.'

'Gosh.' Now Tilly really didn't know what to say. 'I didn't realise.'

'It's OK, I'd be curious too. It wasn't a relationship. More like therapy. Max and I were no longer a couple. Logically I knew it wasn't my fault that my husband was gay but I lost all my self-confidence. I'd never felt so physically unattractive, so completely undesirable. And poor Max, he felt terrible about it too. It was killing him, seeing me so upset. Then one night I ended up yelling at him that I was going to go out and pick up a complete stranger and have sex. I followed that up by bursting into tears and saying nobody would want to have sex with me anyway because I was such a hideous turnoff.' Kaye paused, shrugged. 'A week later, I ended up in bed with Jack.'

Tilly digested this. 'You mean you went out and picked him up, instead of a stranger. You *chose* him.'

'No, we just met up for a drink and a chat and it went on from there. It was really nice and really natural, the way it happened. But you know something? I've never worked out if it was Max's idea.'

'You think Max could have asked Jack to do it?'

'I think it's a possibility. Who knows? Anyway, it happened.' Kaye was unrepentant. 'And it did the trick. Jack was wonderful and he made me feel normal again. He gave me back my self-esteem. I owe him so much for that. Talk about a night you'll never forget.'

Phew. 'But . . . didn't you wish it could have been more?'

'No, I didn't. Because Jack and I had been such good friends for so long, it would just never happen. We both knew that. The spark wasn't there, it simply didn't exist. We had fabulous sex, but that was all. And afterwards we were able to go back to being just friends again.'

Tilly quelled a stab of envy. Kaye's might not have been the standard reaction of a woman whose husband announces he's gay, but who was to say it hadn't been the right thing to do? If it works, don't knock it. And don't knock it till you've tried it. Except she hadn't had the chance to try it, had she? Oh well, it was probably for the best.

Kaye's mobile began to ring as they arrived at Harleston Hall at four o'clock to pick up Lou. The name of the caller flashed up onscreen.

'It's my agent,' said Kaye. 'Maybe Charlene's admitted she lied. Maggie, hi! Has America stopped sending me to Coventry yet?'

'Is that meant to be some kind of joke?'

'Sorry. Any news?'

'Charlene's still flogging her story. She's seeing a grief therapist now.

And she's hired some pet sculptor to produce a six-foot marble statue of the damn dog.'

'Any happier news? Like maybe someone wants to give me a job?'

Maggie didn't find this amusing either. 'Nobody wants to employ you, Kaye. Just keep your head down. Maybe do a little charity work. Or get yourself snapped coming out of an AA meeting, that might be an idea. But don't go giving any interviews. Keep a low profile.'

'That won't be a problem.' Her level of celebrity over here was far lower than in the States, thank God. 'So . . . um, why did you call?'

'Just to tell you that a delivery arrived here for you. Some guy sent you flowers. Pretty decent ones, too. About six hundred dollars' worth, at a guess. And a box of chocolates. Godiva, or some such.'

'Godiva chocolates? I love Godiva chocolates! Who sent them?'

'Some nobody guy.' Maggie's tone was dismissive. 'He sent the stuff to cheer you up. So there you go—you still got one fan out there. Obviously I took the flowers home, save them from going to waste.'

Obviously. Kaye said, 'That's fine. But you'll post me the chocolates?'

'What? You kidding me? I threw them straight in the trash.'

Kaye's voice rose. 'But they were Godiva!'

'Honey, they were *carbs*.'

'OK.' Kaye sighed. 'Anyway, it's nice that someone's still on my side. I'll have to write and thank him.'

'Don't bother. It only encourages these stalker types.'

The first pupils had begun to spill out of the school. Kaye said, 'You threw away his address, didn't you?'

'Oh, *hi* there!' Her whole manner transformed, Maggie exclaimed, 'Take a seat, you look *fabulous* . . . Kaye, sorry, have to go, bye now . . .'

Dial tone. Hollywood's way of letting you know you weren't important. Kaye closed her phone.

Next to her, Tilly said consolingly, 'We'll stop on the way home and buy you a Snickers bar. Who wants Godiva chocolates anyway? Look, there's Lou coming out now . . . ooh, is that Eddie with her?'

Tilly leaned sideways to get a better look. 'Yep, that's him.'

Eddie was brandishing a sheet of paper and Lou was making a grab for it. The next moment he was racing across the gravelled driveway, laughing and waving the piece of paper above his head.

'Isn't it sweet?' Tilly grinned as Lou launched herself after him.

Together they watched fondly as Lou caught up with him. In one swift movement she snatched the sheet of paper from his grasp, then gave him a hefty shove and stalked off, reducing the paper to shreds.

'That's my girl.' Kaye experienced a burst of satisfaction. 'Don't be a pushover.'

'Then again, if you really fancy a boy, probably best not to push *him* over either. Crikey, who's *that*?' Tilly pointed.

'Oh, I *say*.' Together they gazed at the broad-shouldered, tightly muscled vision of sportiness wheeling a racing bike down the drive.

As Kaye marvelled at the outline of his thighs, Lou reached the car and flung herself into the back.

'Hi, sweetheart. Who's the chap on the bike?'

Lou rolled her eyes. 'Yes, thanks, I've had a good day at school, got a commendation in maths and we had chicken Kiev for lunch.'

'You know what?' Flapping away the great gusts of garlic fumes, Kaye said, 'I could tell. Is he one of your teachers?'

'It's Mr Lewis. He teaches French and PE. Please don't tell me you fancy him, that would be *so* embarrassing.'

Mr Lewis was heading towards them on his bike.

'Hmm, when's the next parents' evening?'

'Mum! Oh God, he's coming over! Please don't say anything . . .'

Having spotted Lou, Mr Lewis drew to a halt beside them. He indicated to Lou to buzz down her window. 'Louisa, you left your hockey stick outside the changing rooms. I've put it in the staffroom for safekeeping.'

'Sorry, sir, I forgot. I'll pick it up tomorrow.'

Mr Lewis glanced at Kaye and Tilly, acknowledging them with a brief nod. Then, addressing Lou again, he said, 'You played a good game today. Couple of nice tackles there. Well done.'

'Thanks, sir.'

Thanks, sir, your tackle's not bad either. The renegade thought zipped through Kaye's brain. Lou would faint if she could mind-read. Battling to keep a straight face, she caught Tilly's eye and saw that she'd been thinking along those lines too. Mr Lewis rode off, Lou buzzed the window shut and Kaye and Tilly burst out laughing.

'Honestly,' Lou heaved a sigh, 'you two are *so* immature. Just because he said tackle, you've gone all giggly and stupid. You're too old for him anyway. He's got a girlfriend called Claudine and she's stunning. Promise me you won't make a show of yourself, Mum.'

'Looks aren't everything,' Kaye teased. 'If he starts racing across the grass waving a sheet of paper, would that count as a sign that he secretly likes me? What was it, a love letter?'

'Oh please. Now you're being even more childish. Eddie Marshall-Hicks is a prize prat and I hate him, so don't even go there.'

Chapter 5

WHEN YOU WERE twenty-eight years old and a responsible adult there was no reason whatsoever to feel awkward and embarrassed about visiting your GP and asking to go on the Pill. No reason *at all*. The trouble was, Roxborough was a small enough town for people to know who you were and what you'd been getting up to lately.

'Erin Morrison,' the receptionist called out. 'Doctor will see you now.'

Was that a note of disapproval in her voice? Erin stood up, aware that not only the receptionist but everyone else in the waiting room was looking at her. God, did they all know too?

Fifteen minutes later the appointment was over. Dr Harrison, bless him, hadn't lectured her at all. Clutching her prescription, Erin left his office feeling a hundred times better. Until she reached the waiting room and saw who was now seated on the chair she'd been occupying earlier. Stella looked up, her lip curling with hatred, and there was an intake of breath from the rest of the room. From the avid expression on the receptionist's face it was clear that she was up to speed with the situation and had probably given them adjacent appointments on purpose.

'Marriage wrecker,' said Stella.

Next to her, an ancient woman put down her knitting and said, 'Eh?'

Oh great.

Stella said extra-loudly and extra-clearly, 'That one there, just leaving. She stole my husband, you know.'

'Really?' The ancient woman did a double take. 'What, *her?*'

Erin's face burned as she hurried past them across the waiting room. Just get out, get out, *now*.

Two hours later she was wrapping a turquoise and silver Karen Millen skirt in tissue paper when she heard a commotion outside.

'What's that?' The girl buying the skirt frowned.

Oh God, please no. No no no . . .

'Don't shop in there! The woman's a trollop!'

Outside on the pavement, acting a lot braver than she felt, Erin confronted her nemesis. 'You can't do this, Stella.'

'Why can't I? You banned me from your shop, but this isn't your shop, is it? I'm out here on the pavement.'

'This is my business and I'm not going to let you ruin it.'

Stella stared at her, her manicured hands clenched at her sides. 'But you've wrecked my life! Why do I have to sit back and take it? Why can't I hurt you like you've hurt me?' she wailed. 'I'm better than you! And I'd *never* steal a married man from his wife!'

There was no getting through to her. Sadly, however, she was getting through to a lot of passers-by who were stopping to watch the drama with interest. Erin was at her wits' end. Could she call the police? Should she try a solicitor first? Or how about a hit man to bump Stella off?

'Hey up, what's going on here?' It was Max Dineen. Had Tilly told him about the hassle they'd been getting from Stella?

Stella took one look at Max and promptly burst into tears.

'Bloody hell,' Max exclaimed. 'I'm not that ugly, am I?'

From his laconic tone and the glance he directed at her, Erin guessed he knew the score.

'Oh, Max!' Stella let out a wail of despair. 'I'm so miserable I just want to *die*.'

She stumbled into Max's arms.

Max's heart sank. Fuck, this was the moment you really wished you hadn't got involved. Having Stella burst into noisy sobs on his shoulder was the last thing he'd expected, but she was definitely doing it now. He could feel her tears on his neck, and her hair was plastering itself against his face, an unnerving experience when you considered that it wasn't actually Stella's hair and had probably originally belonged to some Russian peasant.

'It's OK, it's OK.' Max patted her on the back and pulled a clean handkerchief from his pocket. 'Here, use this.'

Erin turned away. 'I have to get back. I've left a customer in the shop.'

'Off you go.' He smiled briefly. 'I'll take care of this one.'

'Where are we g-going?' hiccuped Stella as he steered her up the road.

'Your place. You're in no condition to open the shop this afternoon.' Reaching his car, Max pulled open the passenger door. 'In you get.'

'Oh, Max. Thank you. And will you stay with me for a bit?'

Great, because he only had about a million other things to do today. Oh well, too late to worry about that now. Stella wasn't exactly a close friend, but they'd known each other through their complementary businesses for several years and he was fond of her.

'I'll come in,' said Max. 'For a bit.'

Back at her modern, super-clean, super-tidy house, Stella opened a bottle of white wine and knocked back the first glass in one go. 'I'm just in knots, Max. *Knots*. I wake up in the morning and everything *hurts*. That woman stole my husband.'

She wasn't looking so great, actually. Her face was drawn and the super-polished exterior was missing. This was what jealousy did to you, it ate away at your appearance like a maggot invading an apple.

Max said flatly, 'She didn't, you know. You just need to get on with your life. Living well is the best revenge. Being happy!'

'But the only thing that could make me happy is a baby!'

'So do it.'

Stella was looking at him oddly. 'Would you do it?'

'What? If I were in your shoes?'

'No. I meant would you give me a baby?'

Oh shit. 'You don't mean that.'

'I do! Max, don't you see? It makes perfect sense. I like you. I always have. You like me. And you're a great dad to Louisa.'

'Plus I'm gay,' said Max.

'If you were really gay, you'd have a boyfriend by now. OK,' Stella blurted out as Max rose to his feet, 'we can just do the sperm thing. Artificial insemination, how about that? If I go to a sperm bank, how do I really know what I'm getting? I'd much rather know for sure who the father is. And I'd love it to be you. You're funny and kind and better looking than bloody Fergus. Picture it, we'd have a beautiful baby . . .'

Max backed away. 'Stella, you aren't thinking straight. You're a great girl and you'll find someone who's right for you, once you get over Fergus. But you have to promise me you'll stop hassling Erin.'

'It makes me feel better,' said Stella.

'Sweetheart, it's not dignified.' At that moment the cat flap rattled and Bing slunk in. Max glanced at his watch and grimaced. 'Look, I'm really sorry but I have to get off now. I'm meeting a new client this afternoon. Promise me you won't top yourself, OK?'

Stella, who doted on her cat, scooped Bing into her arms. 'Don't worry, I wouldn't give them the satisfaction. Especially when I've just had my extensions redone. They cost me three hundred quid.'

Jamie Michaels and his fiancée had just moved into a six-bedroomed, eight-bathroomed mock-Tudor mansion in a gated community on the outskirts of Birmingham. 'Me mate recommended you. Cal Cavanagh, yeah? He said you was the business.'

'What's good enough for the Cavanaghs is good enough for us,' giggled Tandy. 'And we've got loads of ideas. I can't wait to get started. Can I offer you a drink before we get going? We've got Cristal champagne on ice, if you want. Eighty quid a bottle!'

Tilly kept a straight face, because Max had warned her that any sniggering would get her sacked. He'd also explained that just because young Premiership footballers had more money than sense, there was no cause to turn your nose up at their ideas. 'They pay good money for our services and it's our job to give them whatever they want. People are entitled to live with an end product they bloody well like.'

Which was fair enough. Tilly completely agreed with that. And it was just as well, too. Because as they followed Jamie and Tandy around the house, they certainly had some eye-popping ideas.

'I'm thinking of, like, tartan walls in silver and pink metallic hand-painted wallpaper for the dining room. Because when I was little I had a Barbie with a pink and silver tartan dress.' Tandy was tiny, blonde and doll-like herself; the ring on her engagement finger was the size of a walnut. 'And you know the chandelier you put in Cal's kitchen? Well, we want one bigger than that. And could you do one of those disco floors that light up, like in *Saturday Night Fever*?'

It was Tilly's job to write down each of their ideas while Max made suggestions as to how they might be adapted, explaining that if the chandelier was any bigger, Jamie would crack his head every time he walked under it, and a disco floor was a fantastic idea but how about having it in the karaoke room rather than the kitchen, because that was where more dancing might take place.

Turquoise and pewter leopard print en-suite bathroom?

Perfect, said Max, he knew just the suppliers.

After two hours the preliminary meeting was over. Tandy threw her arms round Max and cried, 'I love your plans! This is so cool!'

'Hang on,' said Max. 'You haven't had your estimate yet. You might go off me when you find out how much it's going to cost.'

Jamie frowned and rubbed his hand through his spiky bleached hair. 'More than two hundred grand?'

'No.' Max shook his head. 'There's nothing structural. I'll get home and work on the figures, but I'm thinking around one eighty.'

'That's all? Cool. No problem.' His face cleared. 'We're doing a shoot for *Hi!* magazine once it's done, for two hundred. So, quids in!'

'It's going to be a huge party to officially celebrate our engagement.' Having done the maths, Tandy said brightly, 'We'll have twenty grand left over! How about if we get a dear little church built in the garden, for when we get married?'

'Or,' said Max, 'why not get married somewhere really spectacular and have a massive hot tub installed instead.'

'You're brilliant!' Tandy clapped her hands, then hugged Tilly. 'And so are you. You'll both have to come along to the party.'

Then the doorbell went and Tandy disappeared upstairs for her weekly session with her nail technician. Jamie showed Max and Tilly out.

'She's nineteen,' Tilly marvelled. 'This is where I've been going wrong.'

'Bag yourself a footballer. Become a WAG,' said Max.

Except Tilly knew she didn't have it in her to become high-maintenance; the endless fake tans and having to get her nails done would drive her nuts. 'I think I'm more of a SAG. Slobby and geriatric.'

'Or how about a DROOP?' Max grinned as he unlocked the car and said, 'Dumpy, ropy, 'orrible, ordinary and past it? *Youch.*'

'So sorry,' said Tilly. 'My foot slipped.'

The more you didn't want to bump into someone, Sod's Law dictated that the more often you would. When Erin paid a visit to the chemist after work, a few days after her last run-in with Mad Stella, she was blissfully unaware that Stella was in the shop.

Only when she was queuing up to pay did she find out. The woman behind the counter asked, 'Can I help you, love?' and a voice behind her rang out, 'Well, she's having an affair with my husband so she's probably here to stock up on condoms.'

That drawling, sneering, all-too-familiar voice. Erin experienced the swoop of fear that went with it and the sense of mortification that invariably—actually, no, damn it, why should *she* stand here and take it? Adrenaline surged up from goodness knows where and Erin slowly turned to lock stares with Stella. Enough with the pussyfooting. In a voice every bit as loud and clear as Stella's, Erin said sweetly, 'Condoms? Too right! It's amazing how many we get through.'

'I can't believe I said it.' When Fergus arrived at the flat an hour later, Erin was still shaking.

'So what happened next?'

She shuddered. 'Stella shouted, "I don't know how you can live with yourself." Then she stormed out.'

Fergus folded her into his arms. 'Oh, baby, shh. You haven't done anything wrong. I'm sorry. I love you.'

'I love you too.' Despite all the horrors, happiness still flooded through her. Fergus was everything she'd ever dreamed of, from his gentle personality to his easy warmth and innate goodness. Better still, he was attractive without being physically perfect, which was wonderfully reassuring when you were less than svelte yourself. Not having to suck in your stomach and pretend you were a size twelve was a heart-warming bonus.

'Look, the next fortnight's chaotic at work but I'm pretty sure I can swing a week after that. How about I book us a holiday? Somewhere hot, my treat. We deserve a break. Could you get someone to run the shop?'

Maybe . . . maybe not . . . but what the hell, some offers were just too good to turn down. 'If I can't find anyone, I'll close it for the week.' Oh God, a holiday was *so* what she needed right now.

'Right. You tell me where, and I'll book everything.'

'I've always wanted to go to Gdansk.'

'Really?'

It was just another reason to love him. Erin grinned and kissed him. 'No. But I've definitely always wanted to go to Venice.'

It was Friday evening and Max was taking Kaye to dinner with old friends in Bristol. 'Right, are we setting off now? Where's Lou?'

'Noooo! Don't go before you've seen me!' Lou, clattering downstairs, landed with a thud in the hallway. 'Right, what about this?'

It was her third outfit change in thirty minutes, in honour of tonight's school disco. Having swapped jeans and a purple T-shirt for slightly different jeans and a blue cropped top, she was now wearing a grey-and-white-striped T-shirt, grey jeans and Converse trainers.

'You look just right.' Kaye gave her daughter a hug and a noisy kiss. 'Have a fabulous time tonight. Be good.'

Lou rolled her eyes. 'I'm always good.'

'No getting bladdered,' said Max.

'Dad, this is the Year 9 disco. It's a choice of Pepsi or water.'

'And no snogging.'

'Dad,' Lou wailed. 'Shut *up*.'

'Hear hear!' Kaye threw the car keys over to Max. 'And we're going to be late if we don't set off now. Come on, let's go.'

The timing was a minefield. Lou's disco ran from seven thirty to ten o'clock. But only tragic losers—obviously—were uncool enough to turn up at seven thirty. Following much frantic texting, the consensus among Lou's friends was that ten past eight was the optimum time.

Which gave Lou long enough to discard her third outfit and instead change into the *first* pair of jeans, an olive-green boat-neck T-shirt, silver flip-flops and a plaited green and silver leather belt.

'Perfect.' Solemnly Tilly nodded; bless her, Lou was desperate to impress someone.

Lou checked her watch. 'Is it a quarter to eight?'

'Yep. Ready to go?'

The key turned in the ignition and nothing happened.

Tilly tried again. The car still didn't start.

'I'm missing the disco.' Lou began to hyperventilate.

'OK, go and get the Yellow Pages. Find the number of Bert's company and we'll call him. I'll keep trying here.'

Lou raced into the house and Tilly tried polishing the ignition key with her T-shirt, just in case it made that all-important bit of difference.

When Lou reappeared she was clutching the Yellow Pages in one hand and the cordless phone in the other. 'Hello? Hi, Bert, this is Lou Dineen. Can you come and pick me up from home in, like, thirty seconds?'

Tilly's heart went out to her when Lou's face fell. 'No, that's no good. OK, thanks, bye.' Ending the call she said, 'He's picking up a fare in Malmesbury. Oh God, why does this have to happen to *me*?'

Eight o'clock came and went. The line to the next taxi firm was engaged nonstop. Lou's friend Nesh had gone away with her parents for the weekend. In desperation Tilly tried calling Erin but there was no reply and her mobile was switched off.

'This is *so* unfair.' In a panic now, Lou began riffling through the Yellow Pages again. 'Does this count as an emergency? Would the police be cross with me if I dialled 999?'

She was joking, but only just. The phone rang in Tilly's lap.

'Hi, it's me.' In the midst of all the panic, it was odd to hear Jack sounding so relaxed. 'I know I've missed Max, but can you pass on the message that the electrician's finishing off at Etloe Road tomorrow.'

'Who's that?' Lou had found another cab number to try and was marking it with her finger.

'And if you've got a pen handy, I've found a number for a new marble supplier he might be interested in.'

'Get them off the phone.' Lou gave Tilly a nudge.

'Er . . . I don't have a pen . . .'

It wasn't easy to concentrate, what with Jack murmuring in one ear and Lou buzzing like an agitated wasp in the other. 'Sorry, Jack, it's just—'

'JACK?' Lou let out a screech and grabbed the phone, nearly taking Tilly's ear with it. 'Why didn't you SAY? Jack, where are you? The car won't start and we're stuck here and I'm missing my disco . . .'

His Jaguar shot up the drive seven minutes later. Lou catapulted herself into the passenger seat and declared, 'You are my most favourite person in the whole *world*.'

'**M**y hero,' said Tilly, when Jack returned thirty-five minutes later. Checking her watch, she added, 'That was quick.'

'I did have Lou sitting next to me, bellowing, "Faster!" Stick the kettle on. We've got until ten to ten. Lou wants to be picked up at ten past.'

'Tea or coffee?' said Tilly.

'Coffee, black, one sugar.' He smiled slightly. 'You forget how exciting discos are when you're thirteen. I remember having a crush on a girl called Hayley and wondering how the hell I was going to get her away from her friends so I could kiss her.'

Tilly passed him his coffee. 'Did you manage it?'

'Oh yes, I was very suave. I told her the headmaster wanted to see her outside, and that I had to take her.'

'Suave and devious. So, what did she do when you kissed her?'

'Carried on chewing her chewing gum and asked me to buy her and her three friends a Coke. Each.'

Tilly started to laugh. 'And did you?'

'No! I told her I didn't have enough money and she said oh well, in that case I couldn't afford her. And then she went back inside.'

'So you haven't always been irresistible to women.' She loved the way he could tell a story against himself.

'God, no. The first few years were disastrous. I went out with a girl when I was fifteen and she told all her friends when I tripped up and fell flat on my face outside the cinema.'

Telling stories against yourself was all very well but Tilly couldn't quite bring herself to share the one about wetting herself while watching *Mr Bean*. There was such a thing as too much information.

'One boyfriend took me home to meet his mum and I had to pretend to like this gristle casserole she'd made for dinner. It was awful. And after that, she made it every time we went to his house.'

'Maybe she didn't think you were good enough for her precious son and that was her way of getting rid of you.'

'Oh my God, I never thought of that!' Caught in a light-bulb moment, Tilly excitedly flapped her hands. 'And I've actually done it too! Years ago I was seeing this guy and I was cooking more and more horrible meals for him and it wasn't until he complained about them that I realised I'd been doing it on purpose!'

Jack raised an eyebrow. 'You mean . . .?'

'I didn't want to be with him any more, but I didn't want to hurt his feelings either. I don't like being the one to do the finishing.'

'What happens if they don't want to finish with you, though?'

'I just make myself horribler and horribler until they do.'

'And is that what happened with the last one? Max told me you came home from work one day and he'd moved out of your flat.'

Hmm, so did that mean he'd been asking Max about her? Tilly said, 'That's right, he did.'

'Because you'd been horrible to him?'

'I wouldn't call it horrible. I just . . . distanced myself.'

'So that's why you weren't devastated when it happened.'

'I suppose.' She took a sip of her coffee. 'He just wasn't . . . The One. God, it's a funny business, isn't it? You can line up ten thousand men and know immediately that nine thousand nine hundred and ninety of them aren't your type. So then you're left with ten who are possibles and you have to narrow it down by a process of elimination. And it can all be going really well, then someone says or does one tiny thing that makes you realise you could never have a relationship with them.'

Jack's smile broadened. 'So you'd reject ten thousand men before you found someone you liked. That's kind of picky, isn't it?'

'I don't mean finding someone just to go out on a date with. I'm talking about the one person you'll end up sharing the rest of your life with. And as you get older, you naturally get pickier.' Struggling to explain, Tilly went on, 'When I was at school, all the girls used to imagine being married to the three or four best-looking boys in the class. There were things you could do to work out how happy you'd be together. You'd write out both your names, one above the other, then cross out all the letters you had in common, then add up the ones that were left and divide the boy's final number into the girl's, and if it made a whole number, you were a perfect match.'

His face was a picture. 'You're kidding. You seriously did *that*?'

'Many, many times.' It was all coming back to her now. 'And if you didn't get the answer you were hoping for, you had to find out what their middle name was and start all over again.'

Jack looked dumbstruck. 'Hang on. Girls at school used to ask me my middle name!'

'Now you know why. That's what they were doing.'

Amused, Jack said, 'And do girls still do this?'

'I don't know. We'll have to ask Lou.' Tilly grinned. 'I know whose name she'd be doing it with. Eddie Marshall-Hicks.'

'Lou's got a boyfriend?' He sounded shocked.

'Not yet. Ask Lou and she'll tell you she hates him. But we've seen them together at school,' said Tilly. 'It's so sweet, they obviously fancy each other like mad but can't bring themselves to admit it.'

Jack nodded wisely. 'Ever done that?'

Hang on, was this a trick question? Did he mean here? With him?

'God, yes.' Tilly nodded vehemently. 'When I was fifteen I had a huge crush on this boy who used to catch the same bus as me in the morning. He used to look over at me. I used to look at him. Each day I'd start an imaginary conversation with him. But in real life I was sitting there, waiting for *him* to make the first move, because what if I said something first and he snubbed me?'

'So what happened?'

'Nothing. For months and months he caught the same bus every morning. Then one day he just stopped and I never saw him again. But I can't tell you how upset it left me. I learned my lesson. Grasp the nettle. Don't waste opportunities. Never let a chance slip by.'

'Which is how you came to be working for Max, living here in this house. And you're glad you did, aren't you?' He sat back in his chair, his eyes glittering. 'So it works.'

Distracted by the look he was giving her, Tilly said, 'How about you then, when you were at school? Ever have that thing where you really liked a girl and didn't know how to tell her?'

He tilted his head. 'Because she might have rejected me? Oh, yes.'

'Really? Did you finally pluck up the courage to ask her out?'

He nodded solemnly. 'I did. But she explained it probably wouldn't be a good idea, what with her being my maths teacher.'

Tilly just managed to avoid spraying coffee. 'How old was she?'

'Twenty-five. And I was seventeen. So that was that, she turned me down.' Jack paused. 'But three years later she called me up out of the blue and asked if I'd like to meet up for a drink. So I got to go out with her in the end.'

It was nine forty-five and, leaving Betty asleep in her basket, they set out to pick up Lou.

'I hope she's had a good time.' As they sped along narrow country lanes, Tilly pictured the scene in the school hall. 'What if Eddie asked her to dance? Or what if he asked some other girl instead? Oh God, poor Lou, and she was just left on her own, propping up the wall . . .'

'OK, that definitely happened to you.'

'Maybe just the once. Or twice. Shut *up*,' Tilly said as he broke into a grin. 'It's a horrible feeling . . . What are you doing?'

They were still several miles from Harleston Hall and Jack was slowing down. He stopped the car and switched off the headlights. Had all those cups of coffee proved too much for him? He unfastened his seat belt, then turned to look at her. Why wasn't he speaking? Probably embarrassed; a weak bladder wasn't exactly macho. It wasn't something you'd want to shout about.

To help him out, Tilly said discreetly, 'It's OK, I won't look.'

Pause. 'Excuse me?'

'Don't be shy,' said Tilly. 'If you need to go, go.'

Jack laughed and shook his head. 'Is that what you think? Oh dear, talk about cross-purposes.' Next moment, he'd resumed the journey to Harleston Hall, before Tilly had even dared to guess at why else he might have stopped.

They gathered speed, hedgerows on either side whipping past. It was five past ten now; they'd be there in less than—

'Sod it.' Jack slammed his foot on the brake, screeched to a halt and switched off the engine. '*This* is why I stopped before.'

He pulled her into his arms and Tilly was dizzily aware of his mouth on hers, his fingers stroking the back of her neck, his hair falling forward onto her left cheek . . . God, he was a fantastic kisser.

Doing her best not to hyperventilate or appear overimpressed, Tilly said, 'What was that for?'

'Just curious.' He sounded as if he were smiling. 'Don't tell me you weren't too.'

How was she meant to speak normally when she was still zinging from the feel of his mouth on hers? She exhaled slowly. The clock on the dashboard indicated that it was nearly ten past. 'We have to collect Lou.'

In the darkness, Jack nodded. 'You're absolutely right.'

The disco had finished. Groups of teenagers hung around outside the school waiting for their lifts. The first person Tilly recognised was Tom Lewis, keeping an eye on the gaggles of overexcited pupils and an arm round a strikingly pretty twenty-something brunette.

'There's Lou's PE teacher, over there on the steps. That must be his girlfriend with him. Lou told us about her. Ooh, and there's Eddie!'

'Which one?'

'Tight black jeans, Jackie Chan T-shirt.' As they watched, Eddie loped across to a group of girls. 'There's Lou, behind the girl in the pink skirt. He's going over to her . . .'

Eddie said something to Lou. Lou tossed her head and looked away, determinedly unconcerned. Oh dear. Tilly's heart went out to her; she hoped they hadn't had a tiff.

Finally they reached the head of the queue. Jack briefly tooted his horn and Lou, spotting them, came over and threw herself onto the back seat. 'Hiya!'

She seemed chirpy enough. Tilly swivelled round. 'Good time?'

'Brilliant. I've had three Pepsis and two packets of crisps.'

Bless. 'So, did you dance?'

'Loads!' Animatedly Lou said, 'You should have seen Gemma—she was moonwalking across the dance floor! Then the DJ started playing the music from *Grease* and we were all doing the moves.'

'The boys were dancing too?' Crikey, things had changed since Tilly's day. Had Eddie been Lou's Danny Zuko?

'The boys? Dancing to *Grease*? You must be joking!' Lou's tone was disparaging. 'They were superglued to the walls.'

'Oh. But how about when the slow dances came on? They must have joined in then.'

Lou gave her a thirteen-year-old's look that signalled Tilly was hopelessly deranged. 'Of course they didn't! A few of the old people danced, that's all. The DJ asked if we wanted another slow song and everyone yelled no, so he played Girls Aloud instead!'

'So, no snogging then.' As he said it, Jack caught Tilly's eye.

'Eeurgh, no *way*. Who'd want to snog any of the boys at our school?'

Tilly couldn't resist saying it. 'Even Eddie?'

'Oh, don't start that again. I hate him,' Lou said bluntly. 'He's vile.'

Twenty minutes later they arrived back at Beech House.

'Thanks, Jack.' Lou gave him an exuberant hug. They watched her race into the house to greet Betty.

Tilly climbed out of the car and said, 'Yes, thanks for helping out.'

He half smiled. 'Don't mention it. My pleasure.'

OK, awkward moment. Feeling incredibly self-conscious, Tilly said, 'You're welcome to come in for another coffee if you'd like to.'

'Thanks, but I'd better get back. Paperwork to do.'

She nodded. Paperwork, of course that's what it was. Could he still feel the sensation of their mouths meeting for the first time, or was it just her? Oh God, unless the kiss had been a *disappointment* . . .

Jack turned to look directly at Tilly. 'You asked earlier if I'd ever had that thing where I didn't know how to tell a girl I liked her.'

Tilly's stomach did a somersault. 'And you told me about your teacher.'

'Well, there's you too. Sounds like a line, doesn't it?' He looked rueful. 'Like the kind of thing you wouldn't take seriously because I can't possibly mean it, because you don't trust me, because I have a bad reputation and I've probably said it a hundred times before.'

True to form, Tilly heard herself say flippantly, 'Only a hundred?'

He shrugged, restarted the car. 'See? But what if I haven't said it before? What if I'm serious?'

Did he seriously expect her to believe he was serious? Was he honestly expecting her to answer that question?

'Well?' said Jack.

Blimey, he did. 'I'd say you had some persuading to do.'

'OK.' A glimmer of a smile. 'Let's see if I can manage persuasive.'

Chapter 6

ERIN HADN'T SEEN KAYE since her last visit home at Christmas. Delighted to see her again when Tilly brought her into the shop, she updated Kaye with the story of Scary Stella while Tilly, in the changing room, attempted to battle her way into a lace-up-the-back summer dress that was infinitely covetable but two sizes too small for her.

'Fergus is lovely.' Erin sighed. 'We're so happy together. It's just impossible really to relax and enjoy ourselves when we're forever wondering what Stella might do next.'

'We think she might kidnap Max and force him to have sex with her,' said Kaye with a wicked grin.

'Oh God, don't,' Erin groaned. 'I'm so sorry he got dragged into it.'

'Don't worry about Max, he can look after himself. Ooh, is that a von Etzdorf?' She flung the yellow devoré velvet scarf round her neck.

'That colour really suits you.' Erin wasn't angling for a sale; it was the truth.

'Ha. Stella once said to me, "Poor you, being so pale. I bet you wish you had skin that tanned like mine." Right, I'm going to have this. You know, the brilliant thing about buying secondhand clothes is you never have to feel guilty, because everything's such a bargain.'

'And it's a form of recycling.' Tilly's disembodied voice drifted out.

'Are you winning in there?' said Erin.

'No. This isn't a dress for a human being, it's Barbie-sized.'

'Here, I've got something you might like. It just came in this morning.' Nipping into the back room, Erin returned with a spaghetti-strapped lilac silk dress. 'Give this a go.'

Tilly emerged two minutes later. The dress fitted like a dream. Erin clapped her hands. 'I love my job. You look . . . fab.'

Flushing with pleasure, Tilly said, 'I had a panic yesterday. Tandy asked me what I'd be wearing to their party. Then she took a phone call from one of the other WAGs and I overheard her saying her biggest nightmare would be if anyone turned up wearing High Street.'

'Cheek!' Kaye was indignant. 'That would make me *want* to.' She sighed. 'I've got so many gorgeous dresses over in the States. I may as well sell them all, seeing as it's going to be at least fifty years before anyone invites me to another party.'

Erin felt for her. 'We're in the same boat, aren't we? Both of us blamed for something we didn't do.'

'At least you've got Fergus. Look at me,' said Kaye. 'The only male attention I've had since Christmas is from the old bloke with the squint who collects the trolleys at the supermarket.'

'There's that fan who sent you chocolates,' Tilly protested.

'Which I didn't get to eat. And he lives six thousand miles away. Plus, we've never actually met. So he doesn't count.'

'Now you're going to make me feel guilty about telling you my happy news.' Erin brought out a holiday brochure. She rolled it up and clonked Tilly on the head to stop her admiring herself in the full-length mirror. 'Hey, are you listening? I'm going away on holiday!'

That caught Tilly's attention. 'What? But you always said you couldn't afford to close the shop.'

'I did, but this time I'm going to do it anyway. We need the break. And guess where we're going? Venice!'

'Now that,' said Kaye, 'is seriously romantic.'

'I know,' Erin said joyfully. 'I'm so excited! We're going for a week at the end of the month. I can't *wait*.'

'And you're closing the shop?' said Kaye.

Erin nodded. She'd asked Barbara, who had helped her out on occasions in the past, but Barbara was unable to do it this time.

'Because I could always look after it for you. If you want,' Kaye added when she saw the stunned look on Erin's face.

'Are you serious?'

'Absolutely. I like clothes. And it drives me nuts, doing nothing.'

Tilly's phone began to ring. She answered it.

'Hello, this is Mrs Heron calling from Harleston Hall.'

'Oh! Hi!' Astrid Heron, tall and terrifying, was Lou's headmistress. Tilly unconsciously stood to attention. 'Is everything all right?'

'Louisa isn't unwell. But I'm afraid there has been an . . . incident.' Mrs Heron was choosing her words with care. 'I've been trying to contact Louisa's mother but she isn't answering her phone.'

'Oh, but she's here!' Tilly thrust the mobile into Kaye's hands.

'Hello? This is Lou's mum. What's happened?'

Tilly and Erin watched Kaye's face as she listened intently. Finally she said, 'We're on our way now,' and hung up.

'What kind of an incident?' Tilly's heart was in her mouth.

'She said she'd explain everything when I got there. But it's something to do with Eddie Marshall-Hicks. There's been a fracas.'

'We'd better call Max.' Tilly reached for the mobile.

'No, don't. Mrs Heron said not to. Lou doesn't want him to know.'

The school secretary was waiting for them in reception. She ushered them through to the head's office.

'Oh my God . . . sweetheart, what did he *do* to you?' Lou's face was pinched and white. Her shirt was torn and there were holes in her black tights. Kaye flew across the room and scooped her out of her chair. 'We're calling the police, that boy's going to suffer for this—'

'Mrs Dineen . . . er, Ms McKenna, would you please let me speak?' Astrid Heron indicated that Kaye should take the seat next to Lou. 'I think you need to calm down and listen carefully to—'

'Calm down? CALM DOWN? How can you *say* that?' bellowed Kaye. 'My daughter's been attacked and we're getting the police.'

'Mum, I haven't,' said Lou.

Kaye gazed from Lou to Mrs Heron. 'You said there'd been a fracas.'

Mrs Heron said grimly, 'That is correct. And I'm afraid your daughter was the instigator. She launched a serious physical assault on another pupil and I'm afraid there will be consequences—'

'Lou!' Shaking her head in disbelief, Kaye said, 'Is this true? You were actually *fighting* with another girl? Over Eddie Marshall-Hicks?'

'Oh, Mum, no.' Vehemently Lou shook her own head.

'Edward Marshall-Hicks is the person she attacked,' said Mrs Heron.

'I blacked his eye.' Lou was unrepentant. 'And I *almost* broke his nose.'

Bloody hell. Tilly heard the pride in Lou's voice.

Kaye's hand had flown to her mouth. 'Why? I thought you liked him.'

'Mum, I told you I hated him. He's a bastard.'

'*Louisa*,' thundered Mrs Heron. 'Aren't you in enough trouble already? I will *not* tolerate that kind of language in my school.'

'Oh well, I'm probably expelled anyway.' Lou shrugged and folded her arms. 'In fact, why don't I just clear my locker and leave now?'

'Stop it!' Kaye was beside herself. 'Tell me why you did it.'

'OK, you really want to know? Because I have put up and *up* with that brain-dead idiot making pathetic comments and saying horrible stuff and today I decided not to take it any more.'

'Oh, sweetheart. Has he been making fun of your hair?'

Lou bit her lip and said nothing.

'Louisa.' Mrs Heron employed her headmistressy don't-mess-with-me voice. 'We need to know.'

'OK, it's not about my hair. If you *must* know,' Lou said evenly, 'it's to do with having a dad who's gay.'

Kaye asked to see Eddie Marshall-Hicks, who was being kept in a separate room. As the door opened, she braced herself.

Eddie was standing gazing out of the window. Mr Lewis, the PE teacher, was sitting on the desk.

'Hello, I'm Lou's mum. I've come to see how you are.'

Turning, Eddie said, 'I don't know, how do you *think* I am?'

Maybe sarcasm was allowable, given the circumstances. His left eye was almost completely closed, his nose was swollen and there were splashes of blood on the front of his untucked white shirt.

Kaye experienced a secret surge of pride that her skinny thirteen-year-old daughter had managed to wreak such havoc. Calmly she said, 'I'm sorry this happened. But I gather Lou was provoked.'

'She just went mental. It was like being attacked by a wild animal,' Eddie said furiously. 'Look what she did to my face!'

'He's been thoroughly checked out by matron,' Tom Lewis put in. 'His nose isn't broken. There's no permanent damage to the eye.'

'Well, that's good. But I'm sure you can understand why Lou was upset,' said Kaye. 'You've been making comments about her father.'

Eddie's face reddened. 'It was just a bit of fun.'

'To you, maybe. It hurt her. A lot.'

'Oh yeah?' He pointed at his face. '*Snap*.' The phone began to ring in his pocket at that moment. Eddie answered it. 'Dad? Uh . . . yeah, I know you're busy. Sorry. The school said I had to call and tell you I was in a fight today.' He paused, listened, then said, 'No, nothing serious. I'm fine. Mrs Heron just said I had to ask if you wanted to come over and talk about it.' Another pause. 'No, that's OK, you go to your meeting. I'll see you tonight. Bye.' Eddie switched off his phone. 'He's got stuff on at work. Anyway, he's cool about it.'

Tom Lewis looked relieved; evidently they'd been worried Eddie's father might roar up flanked by lawyers at the first mention of assault.

'**S**he didn't want you to know,' Kaye told Max when he arrived home that evening, 'but I said we had to tell you. She's in a terrible state.'

Max briefly closed his eyes.

Shit. *Shit*. How could he ever have imagined his daughter wouldn't be made to suffer as a result of his own selfishness? His chest tightening, Max left Kaye and Tilly in the living room and made his way upstairs.

'Oh, Daddy, I'm sorry.' As soon as Lou saw him, she burst into tears.

Clasping her tightly, he said, 'Don't apologise. It's my fault.'

'It is not. It's *his* fault. Boys are just so immature. And ignorant. I hate hate *hate* Eddie Marshall-Hicks.'

There was a lump in Max's throat. He stroked her bony shoulders. 'You should have said something before.'

'I couldn't tell you. And Mum was over in LA when it started. The hilarious thing is, Mum and Tilly both thought I fancied Eddie because they kept seeing us together.' Her lip curled with a mixture of derision and amusement. 'Once they saw me chasing him and ripping up a piece of paper, and they thought it was a love letter. *As if*.'

'What was it?'

'A horrible note he'd stuck on my back. Don't ask me what it said.'

'Oh, sweetheart.' Max exhaled slowly. 'What have I put you through?'

'I'm not ashamed of you,' she said fiercely. 'I'm *proud*.'

Oh shit, now she'd stopped crying and he was in danger of breaking down completely.

'Do you want to switch schools?'

'No.' Shaking her head and hugging him, Lou said, 'Who's to say any other school would be different?' She pulled a face. 'I might *have* to leave. I could be out on my ear by next week.'

'I'll make sure that doesn't happen. After what that little bastard's been putting you through? No way. I'm going to meet up with Mrs Heron tomorrow.' Max gazed at Lou intently. 'We'll sort this out.'

The thing about fancying someone rotten was it made you want to make more of an effort with your appearance so when you bumped into them you could at least relax in the knowledge that you were looking great. Tilly was wearing nicer clothes, taking more care with her hair and make-up, and had upped her leg-shaving rate from once-a-fortnight-if-you're-lucky to twice a week. Which just made the fact that she hadn't clapped eyes on him for the past fortnight all the more infuriating.

'Yeek!' Lou dodged out of the way as Tilly, not concentrating on the task in hand, accidentally sprayed her with the hose.

'Sorry, sorry.' But it was a hot day, the warmest of the year so far, so Tilly wasn't too apologetic. Playfully she sprayed her again. Lou, spluttering and squealing, darted out of sight behind the garage.

Amused, Tilly carried on washing and rinsing the car. Any minute now, Lou would race back and attempt to turn the hose on her, but she'd be ready and waiting—

'WAAAHHH!' Tilly let out a shriek as a torrent of ice-cold water almost knocked her off her feet. Staggering backwards, she turned and realised, too late, that Lou had flung only half the contents of the bucket at her back. *Whoosh*, the rest of the water hit its target.

'Right, that's it. You're in big trouble now.' Blinking water out of her eyes and shaking herself like a dog, Tilly turned the nozzle on the hose from medium-fine spray to superjet.

'Help! Child abuse!' Shrieking with laughter as an icy jet hit her in the leg, Lou yelped, 'Someone ring ChildLine!' She pointed exaggeratedly behind Tilly, urging her to turn round. 'It's Esther Rantzen, she's come to arrest you.'

'Yeah yeah.' What did Lou think she was, five years old? 'Of course I'm going to look behind me so you can grab the hose.'

Lou cried piteously, 'Help, help!'

Having shaken the water out of her ears, Tilly belatedly heard the sound of wheels on gravel and realised Lou hadn't been bluffing. Although, hopefully, it wasn't Esther Rantzen. Keeping Lou covered, Tilly slowly turned her head. Oh buggering *poo*.

'Jack, help me, Tilly's being *cruuuuel* . . .'

Tilly blasted one last jet of water at Lou before releasing the trigger. Jack, emerging from his car, came towards them holding his arms aloft.

Thirteen whole days of mascara, lipstick, coordinated clothes, leg-razoring and scent squishing. And *now* he had to turn up.

'OK, I've stopped being cruel.' Had he been abroad? He must have been away, to get so tanned. Had he taken anyone with him? Had they had fantastic sex? Oh God, she was turning into Stella. *Stop it.*

'Glad to hear it. My chain saw's buggered so I've come over to borrow Max's. Do you know if it's in the garage?'

'Yeugh, my trousers feel gross.' Pulling a face and emptying her trainers, Lou said, 'I'm going to get changed.'

When she'd squelched off into the house, Tilly led the way over to the garage. 'What's the chain saw for? Chopping up troublesome tenants?'

'Can't say I'm not tempted sometimes,' said Jack. 'I've got a couple of trees to take down and some branches to trim back.'

It was no good, she had to ask. 'Been away? You're tanned.'

'I've been working outside for the past few days, clearing the gardens of people too bone idle to do it themselves. So you were wondering why I hadn't been around? That's encouraging.'

Honestly, did he have to say things like that? Having lifted the garage door, Tilly surveyed the boxes piled against the walls.

'In fact, it's what I was hoping,' Jack went on.

What?

'In *fact*,' he amended, 'I stayed away on purpose.'

Her pulse racing, Tilly said, 'Why?'

'To see if it made a difference.'

Her mouth was dry. 'And?'

There was that look again. 'I think we can both guess, can't we? At least, I know how *I* feel,' said Jack. 'It might be different for you.'

But since he wasn't stupid, he couldn't really think that. There was a crackling electricity in the air that only a turnip could miss.

Or a thirteen-year-old girl with powerful quick-change skills.

'Honestly, haven't you found it yet?' Lou pointed to the box containing the chain saw. Tut-tutting, she said, 'It's there.'

For a split second Jack and Tilly's eyes met, then Jack crossed the garage and lifted out the chain saw. He turned to Lou and held it up. 'Want me to cut your hair while I'm here?'

'No way. We're going up to Auntie Sarah's wedding this weekend.' Lou darted out of the way. 'I don't want to look like a scarecrow.'

'Sarah's wedding? In Scotland?'

Tilly nodded; Sarah was Max's cousin and on Saturday she was getting married in Glasgow. Max, Lou and Kaye were flying up there on

Friday afternoon for a weekend of epic celebrations, Glaswegian style.

Was Jack thinking what she hoped he was thinking?

Happily, yes. When he'd finished putting the chain saw in the boot of the Jag, he waited until Lou was out of earshot then beckoned Tilly over. She kept a neutral I-have-*no*-idea-what-you're-about-to-say expression on her face. Well, tried to. Inwardly she felt gorgeous and desirable, like a goddess.

'So, are they leaving you here on your own?'

'Mm.' Goddess-like, Tilly nodded.

'Well, if you don't have any other plans, how about I pick you up on Friday? Around eight?'

This was it. She gave him a tiny, goddessy smile. 'OK.'

'Deal.' Jack smiled too.

He waved to Lou as he drove off. Lou waved back then turned to look at Tilly.

'Sorry about your face. I didn't mean it to happen,' she said. 'I just found the bucket of water under the garden tap. I didn't realise the bottom of it was full of gunk and mud.'

Oh bum. Peering into the car's wing mirror at her reflection, Tilly no longer felt like a goddess.

If Jack hadn't minded her looking like the creature from the black lagoon, the chances were that he wouldn't be too bothered whether she wore her silver-grey top or the navy one. But it mattered to Tilly. A lot. She wanted to look her best. After so many weeks of prevarication and wondering if she would be making a horrendous mistake, she knew that this evening things were finally going to . . . well, happen. Tonight, everything would change. Now, at last, she truly trusted him. This wasn't yet another of his meaningless flings.

OK, too much thinking about it was getting her all jittery with anticipation, and jitters could only result in badly applied mascara. Deliberately clearing her mind, Tilly said, 'What d'you reckon, Betty? Grey top or blue? Or my white shirt . . .' Honestly, what a kerfuffle. Was Jack having this much trouble getting himself ready for tonight?

The TV was on, the newsreader was reaching the end of the news, and for the life of him Jack couldn't have named one item on the programme. Because all he could think about was tonight. And Tilly. Shit, this was serious.

What's more, she had no idea. How could she know how he felt, how life-changing this evening would be? When Rose had died, his world had changed for ever. It had been like a giant prison door clanging shut. That was what happened when you allowed yourself to fall in love with someone; when they were ripped away from you, the pain and grief were unimaginable.

So he had vowed never to let it happen again. It had been so much easier to act the part of the flirtatious philanderer and avoid any emotional involvement. But now everything was about to change. Because Tilly had unlocked that door. And it might be terrifying, but it was also a fantastic feeling, like being sprung from prison after four years.

Jack wondered what Tilly was doing now. She wasn't the type to flap around, spending ages trying to decide what to wear. That was one of the great things about her, she wasn't high-maintenance or vain.

Jack crossed to the window to close the curtains. He froze as a car turned into his road. Then he gripped the window ledge for support, a great wave of shock and hope and nausea rolling through him. He wasn't hallucinating. It was Rose's car.

This was crazy. Jack shook his head, ordered himself to get a grip. Rose was dead. It might be Rose's car but Rose wasn't the one driving it. *Because she was dead.* He knew that. It was just the shock of seeing it so unexpectedly. Following Rose's death he hadn't known what to do with her beloved red Audi. When her parents' rusting old Fiesta had failed its MOT, he'd been only too glad to hand it over to them. Jesus, though. They'd given him a heart attack. And for them to turn up tonight of all nights. It was almost as if Rose had sent them here on purpose.

On the driveway below, the Audi's doors opened. Bryn emerged first, followed by Dilys. They looked older, slower, tireder, worn out with grief. Jack felt his stomach plummet at the sight of them now. He was meant to be picking up Tilly in an hour.

Jack opened the door, dreading what lay ahead and awash with guilt at dreading it.

'Oh, Jack.' Dilys dissolved into tears, as she'd taken to doing every time they'd seen each other since the day her daughter had died. He knew why, of course. Because he reminded her of the happy life Rose was supposed to have had. And who could blame her for that? If the accident hadn't happened, Bryn and Dilys would have been proud grandparents, turning up at the house today to visit their daughter and son-in-law, and to shower gifts and affection on their adored three-year-old grandchild . . . OK, don't think about it, just blank it out and *don't* start trying to imagine what the child might have looked like.

He hugged Dilys, shook hands with Bryn and invited them in.

'Oh, thank you, love.' Dilys dabbed at her eyes with an ironed hand-kerchief as Jack put a cup of tea down in front of her. 'Sorry to land ourselves on you like this. I hope we're not being a nuisance.'

What could he say? 'Of course not. It's great to see you again.'

Another lie, another wave of shame.

'Well, it's been quite a while.' Bryn quietly stirred sugar into his tea.

'I've been pretty busy here.' Jack felt worse and worse.

'It's all right, love. We know. We understand,' said Dilys.

'And how have things been for you?' He hated even asking the ques-tion, already knowing the way the conversation would go.

'Oh well. Not good.' Dilys was off again, breaking down completely this time.

Bryn, doing his best to comfort her, said to Jack, 'It feels like everyone's forgetting about Rose. They used to ask us how we were, and talk about her. But now it's as if they think we should be putting all that behind us. We can't put it behind us, though, and we don't want to forget.'

'That's why we had to come and see you today.' Dilys wiped her red-rimmed eyes. 'Because you're the only other person who loves Rose as much as we do. I mean, I know they can't help it, but it's like she's f-fading away, being rubbed out, getting fainter and fainter. And every-one else is just moving on as if she'd never existed.'

Jack escaped from the kitchen and went upstairs. It was eight thirty already and he could no longer even remember whether he'd been meant to pick Tilly up at eight o'clock or nine. Bryn and Dilys Symonds's grief had had that much of an effect on him. He took out his phone. What other choice did he have?

What was going on? Jack had said he'd be here at eight. From not having had the slightest twinge of anxiety that he might not turn up, Tilly was now in knots. This was like being sixteen again, beginning to realise that the boy you'd fancied for months had stood you up.

Disbelief mingled with misery as, slowly and sickeningly, the hands of the clock slid round to eight thirty. *Bbbbrrrrinnngg.* The phone rang at last and Tilly launched herself at it like a rugby player. Of course he'd rung, of course he had a genuine excuse. He was probably calling to say he was on his way and would be here in two minutes . . .

'Hi, it's me. Look, sorry, but I'm not going to be able to make it tonight. Something's come up.'

It was Jack's voice, but it didn't sound like it. He was distracted, distant.

'Are you OK?' Tilly's palms were slippery. 'Are you ill?' As she said it, she heard a door opening in the background, a female voice saying apologetically, 'Oh . . . sorry . . .'

'No. I'm fine. Um, I can't talk about it now. Sorry about tonight. I'll call you tomorrow. Bye.'

'Wait—' But it was too late, the phone had already gone dead. She stared at it, trying to imagine what could have happened to cause him to do this. Except she knew the answer to that, didn't she? It had to be something to do with another woman. Or women, plural. Because let's face it, women were the focus of Jack Lucas's life. He surrounded himself with them, amused himself with them and broke their hearts.

And she'd nearly, *so very nearly*, got herself sucked into the madness.

Oh God, and she'd wanted it to happen *so much*. This hurt.

Tilly closed her eyes. And if she was miserable now, well, then she'd really had a narrow escape.

Every time the doorbell rang, Erin's stomach contracted with fear that it could be Scary Stella. When it happened at ten o'clock that evening, Fergus went downstairs. He was soon back. 'It's someone less scary.'

'Tilly!' Relief turned to concern. 'God, what's happened? You look awful!'

'You're too kind. I brought wine.' Flopping down onto the sofa, Tilly passed the bottle to Fergus. 'Big glass for me, please.'

Within seconds they heard the cork being popped out of the bottle. Fergus returned from the kitchen with two brimming glasses.

Tilly took hers. 'Thanks. You're allowed to have some too, you know.'

'I was about to go and pick up the food. We've ordered Indian. Want me to get some for you too, or will you share ours?'

'I'm too churned up to eat.' Tilly took a glug of wine. 'Well, maybe some poppadoms. Seeing as I've been stood up.'

Erin said, 'Who by?'

'I've been stupid.'

'Who by?'

'Gullible.'

'WHO BY?'

'It's my own fault. Should've known better.'

'I'll take your wine away if you don't tell me.'

'*Don't.*' Tilly whisked the glass out of reach. 'OK, OK. Jack. And you aren't allowed to say I told you so. I already know that.'

'You didn't even tell me!' Erin was stunned.

'That's because there hasn't been anything to tell. Nothing's . . . happened. It was supposed to happen tonight,' said Tilly. 'But he phoned and cancelled. And to think I thought I was different from all the rest.'

The look on Erin's face told her all she needed to know. Every single one of Jack's conquests believed they were different from the rest.

'What did he say when he called you tonight?'

'Nothing. That he couldn't make it, that's all. That something had come up. *Tuh*. And I heard some girl's voice in the background. So now you're stuck with me while I bleat on about myself like a big girl's blouse.' She waggled a finger at them both. 'And you can't tell anyone, either. I don't want the whole of Roxborough knowing what a prat I've made of myself.' At that moment her stomach gave a huge rumble of protest. Disgusted with her ability to be simultaneously heartbroken and ravenously hungry, Tilly said, 'OK, better get me some samosas.'

The headlights lit up the road ahead as Jack drove. Bryn and Dilys had left at eleven thirty. By the time he'd shown them out of the house, the pain and grief was as fresh as if Rose had just died all over again. Guilt about having failed Rose fought inside him with guilt about the way he'd treated Tilly tonight. He owed her an explanation at least. He'd tried calling her but the phone hadn't been answered, and she deserved more than a phone call anyway. Braking sharply, he swung the car up the drive to Beech House.

Shit. After all that Tilly wasn't even here. Jack saw that the top of the drive was empty. Her car was missing. She could be anywhere, and could he blame her? He swung the Jag round in a circle.

Time to go back home.

'There he is! That's *him*. That's his car!' Tilly let out a shriek. 'Stop!'

They were just driving over the bridge on the Brockley Road. Fergus braked, as did Jack.

'Oh great.' Fergus sounded resigned. 'Now he'll probably throw me into the river.'

But Tilly, emboldened by drink, was already scrambling out of the car. The driver's door of the Jag swung open and Jack stepped out, illuminated by the silvery light of the almost full moon behind him. The fact that he looked so perfect made it easier for Tilly. How could she ever have imagined they might have a future together?

'Thanks for tonight.' Her voice carried clearly.

Jack shook his head. 'I'm sorry. I said I was sorry. I've just been over to see you.'

'Don't apologise. I'm not being sarcastic. I really mean it,' said Tilly. 'Thanks for standing me up tonight, I'm glad you did. And I'm sure you had a lovely time too, with whoever it was who turned up.'

Evenly Jack said, 'It was Rose's parents.'

Oh. Tilly hated it when you were all geared up for a shouting match and the other person said something that stopped you in your tracks.

'You could have told me that earlier, when you rang me.'

'Maybe.' Jack nodded slightly. 'But I was distracted. Dilys was upset.'

'Um . . . sorry to interrupt,' Fergus called from the car, 'but this is a narrow road and we're blocking it.'

'OK. I'm coming now.' Tilly turned and headed back towards him.

'Tilly. I'm sorry. I'll speak to you tomorrow.'

'No need.'

'There is. We have to talk. I didn't *want* this to happen tonight.'

Tilly climbed back into Fergus's car. 'I know. But it did. I'm not trying to punish you, Jack. I'm doing it to protect myself.'

By eleven o'clock the next morning the Nurofens had kicked in, Tilly's hangover was gone and her mind was made up. When the doorbell rang, she braced herself and went to answer it. Except it wasn't Jack.

Dave, the postman, was standing on the doorstep clutching a large flat rectangular parcel. 'All right, love? Hello, Betty!'

'Hi, Dave. Present for me?'

'Sorry, love. It's for Kaye. They've addressed it care of Max. Sent it all the way from America too.'

'Thanks. They're all away for the weekend. I'll give it to Kaye when she gets back.' Over Dave's shoulder she saw the Jag heading up the drive. At the sound of wheels on gravel, Dave twisted round too.

When he turned back, he gave Tilly a doubtful look. 'And Max and Kaye are away? Is there something going on between you two?'

'No.' Honestly, was nosiness part of the job description?

'Oh, right. Just as well.' Lowering his voice, Dave leaned closer. 'Gets sent a lot of Valentine cards, that one does.'

Dave made his way back to the post van, nodding and saying hello to Jack as they passed each other. Then he glanced at Betty, who was now racing across the gravel and launching herself at the new arrival like an overexcited It girl. The look Dave shot at Tilly spoke volumes; dogs or girls, it didn't matter. They all superglued themselves to Jack.

'But I said I was sorry.' In the kitchen, Jack frowned. 'I know I let you down last night, but it was for a reason. You can understand how I was feeling, surely? Everything came flooding back and I thought I was betraying Rose. But I've had time to sleep on it now, and it doesn't have to be like that. This doesn't have to be the end for us.'

Tilly stood her ground. 'You can't end something that hasn't had a beginning.' This was one of the hardest things she'd ever had to do. But she also knew it was for the best. Self-preservation.

'You can't do this. Bryn and Dilys turned up out of the blue. What was I supposed to do? Chuck them out of the house?'

'They're not the ones who changed my mind. They just gave me time to think. And I think we should forget . . . you know, *that* side of things. Let's just be friends, OK? That's what I want.'

'Why?'

Why? Now that was the killer question. Because a night or a week or a month with Jack would never be enough and what she really wanted would never happen. Sooner or later he would back off as he always did, leaving her bitter and eaten up with jealousy like Stella.

Tilly gave a tiny shrug. 'Just because.'

'Are you open to persuasion?' said Jack.

'No, no.' She shook her head, simultaneously relieved and utterly desolate. 'I've made up my mind. That's it.'

Chapter 7

TILLY SAID, 'How was the wedding?'

'Noisy, boozy, lots of dancing with hairy-legged men in kilts. Lou peered interestedly at the parcel on the kitchen table. 'What's this? Has someone sent me a present?'

'No, it's for your mum.'

'Me? Ooh, I love presents.' Kaye tore into the outer wrapping and unwound a ream of Bubble Wrap, finally pulling out a painting in a simple black frame. 'Oh my God, it's a Dinny Jay!' Kaye let out a squeak of disbelief. 'Who sent me this? I *love* Dinny Jay.'

Lou said, 'There's an envelope taped to the back.'

Detaching the envelope, Kaye opened it and began to read the letter aloud.

Dear Miss McKenna,

In a magazine interview you mentioned your fondness for the work of Dinny Jay. I saw this in a gallery last week and thought you might enjoy it, so I do hope you will accept this small gift from me. Having read in the paper about your move back to the UK, I am sending it via your ex-husband, whose address I found on his website. Don't worry, I'm not a stalker, just someone who wishes you well. Stay happy.

Best wishes,

P. Price

PS Hope you liked the chocolates and the flowers.

'So he's a stalker.' Tilly grimaced. 'Anyone who has to tell you they aren't a stalker, definitely is one.'

Kaye was gazing adoringly at the painting. 'He might just be a really nice man.'

'Shouldn't you send it back?'

'Oh God, should I? I'd hurt his feelings if I did. I think the best thing to do is graciously accept and write him a really nice letter. At least I've got an address this time. And he lives in New York, so that's OK, that's safe enough.'

Max came in with their cases. 'Until he turns up on your doorstep with an axe.'

'That's all right. I won't be giving him my address, will I?' Kaye hugged the painting to her chest. 'I'll keep using yours.'

In forty-six and a half hours they would be boarding their flight and setting off from Bristol Airport, bound for Venice, tra-la. Willing today to be over, Erin checked her watch. Three more hours before she could close the shop, head upstairs and get on with her packing. The cases were lying open on the living-room floor and she'd spent ages between customers working on her list. She loved lists, and holiday lists were extra-special.

The door to the shop flew open and Erin dropped her pen in fright. There, standing in the doorway with a grim, almost robotic look on her face, was Stella. 'I need to speak to Fergus.'

'He's not here.'

'I know he's not here. And his phone's switched off. Where is he?'

Erin didn't dare bend down and pick up the dropped pen. What if

Stella took the opportunity to attack her? 'I don't know.'

'I need Fergus to look after Bing. I'm going away, so he needs to pick him up from my house after work today. I'll leave all the food out, and Bing's basket, and—'

'Hang on, Fergus can't look after him. He won't be here.' Erin felt her stomach clench. 'We're going away too.' Ha. *So there.*

Stella stood there looking as if she'd been punched. 'Away? But I *need* someone to look after Bing.'

This was crazy. 'So get one of your friends to do it. Amy,' said Erin.

'Amy's too busy with her new man.' Stella's jaw tensed. 'There isn't anyone else I can ask. And I *won't* put Bing into a cattery—he couldn't handle it. Where are you going, anyway?'

Erin said, 'Venice. Look, I'm sorry. If we weren't going away, we would have looked after Bing for you.' Crikey, who'd have thought five minutes ago that she'd be saying this and meaning it? But Stella was clearly desperate and in a complete state.

'Right. OK. Well, tell Fergus I've . . . no, don't bother.' For a second, tears brimmed in Stella's eyes before she abruptly left the shop.

Erin watched her jump into the car she'd left recklessly parked on double yellows across the road. Next moment it shot back at an angle, mounted the pavement and went smack into a lamppost behind it.

By the time Erin reached her, Stella was hyperventilating and rocking to and fro in the driver's seat, moaning, 'I don't know what to *doooo.*'

'Stella, what's going on? Tell me.'

Stella shook her head wildly. '*Noooo.*'

'You can't drive in this state. You just hit a lamppost.'

'Who's going to look after Bing?'

Erin raised her voice. 'Where are you supposed to be going?'

Covering her face, Stella mumbled something.

Oh, for God's sake. '*What?*'

Stella said dully, 'Hospital. I have to go into hospital this afternoon.'

'Why?' Erin stared at her.

'Oh, nothing much. I have cancer, that's all. Could you close the door?'

'*What?* You've got cancer? Really?'

'Really. Cross my heart and hope to—' Stella stopped abruptly, shook her head. 'Anyway, I have to go now.'

'You can't drive like this. You've already dented your bumper. Wait here.' To be on the safe side, Erin leaned inside the car, reached across and grabbed the keys. 'I'll take you. Just give me two minutes to lock up the shop.'

As they made their way through Roxborough it crossed Erin's mind that maybe Stella had been lying. What if this was a trap, and she was being lured to Stella's house . . . Except it wasn't, she knew that. Stella had been telling the truth. *Cancer.*

'I feel like I'm falling off a cliff in slow motion,' said Stella. 'All the pain and cramps I've been having, I just ignored them for ages. Took more painkillers, drank more wine. I thought the reason I was feeling so awful was because my marriage was over. I only went along to the surgery to see if Dr Harrison would prescribe me some happy pills. But because I'd lost weight he started poking and prodding me. Turn left down here, it's the house by the second lamppost.'

Erin pulled up at the kerb and they climbed out of the car.

'Then he said how about a scan to be on the safe side, so I had one done on Monday just to shut him up, then this afternoon I went back to Dr Harrison, and that's when he told me. I've got cancer.' Her hands were shaking so badly she couldn't fit her front-door key in the lock.

'Here, let me do it.'

Taking over, Erin opened the door then stepped aside to allow Stella in first. Stella uttered a loud gulping sob as Bing sauntered over to her, his blue-grey furry body as sinuous as a snake. Scooping him up into her arms, she broke down completely.

An hour later, with Stella's overnight case packed, they set off for the hospital. As Erin drove, Stella said, 'I'm scared. I want my mum.'

'Where is she? Do you want to phone her?'

'She's dead.' Stella wiped her face. 'But I still want her.'

A lump formed in Erin's own throat.

'I don't want to have cancer. I want a *baby.*'

Feeling helpless, Erin said, 'But thousands of people have cancer and they beat it. You can still have a baby afterwards.'

They'd reached the hospital. Stella checked her face in the rearview mirror. Then she blurted out, 'Will you come with me?'

Erin sat by Stella's bed while a young blonde nurse filled out the information page of Stella's notes in careful loopy handwriting. Verrrry slooooowly indeeeed.

'Now, religion?'

'None,' said Stella.

'OK. Shall we just put C of E then?' It took her thirty seconds to write it. 'That's great. And who's your next of kin? Mum? Dad?' the nurse prompted helpfully. 'Brother or sister?'

'I don't have any relatives.' Stella looked as if she was struggling to hold back tears. She glanced over at Erin and said brusquely, 'Put Erin's name down.'

Outside the hospital, Erin tried Fergus's mobile again. This time he answered. 'Fergus, something's happened. It's Stella.'

'Oh God, what's she done now? Where are you?'

'I'm at the hospital.'

'*What?* Jesus, are you hurt? Did she attack you?'

'She's ill, Fergus. She didn't attack me. She's been admitted for tests.'

Back on the ward, the orange and blue curtains had been drawn round Stella's bed. Then they were pulled back with a flourish and a tall, rather good-looking man emerged, white coat flying. Spotting Erin hovering, he pointed and said, 'Stella's friend? Let's have a quick chat while Stella's having her bloods taken. I'm Mr Wilson.'

He led her into a small windowless office. 'Well, I won't beat about the bush. Your friend Stella is going to need all your support. I'm very sorry, but the cancer appears to be significantly advanced.'

Now didn't seem an appropriate time to tell him that, actually, she wasn't Stella's friend at all, and what's more she really needed to finish her holiday packing. 'But you can treat it?'

'We'll check out every option, of course. But I have to warn you that it's not looking good. The scan shows evidence of spread to the bowel, the lungs and the liver. It's a very aggressive form.'

Well, someone like Stella was hardly likely to have a shy retiring cancer, were they? Oh God. Bowel. Lungs. Liver. *Aggressive.* She felt sick.

'Cancel?' Fergus looked at Erin as if she were mad. 'Stella's ill, so you seriously want to cancel *our holiday?*'

They were outside the hospital. Erin clutched his hands. 'We have to. She's got no one else. I was with her this afternoon when she phoned a couple of her girlfriends. Deedee and Kirsten?'

Fergus's lip curled. 'Right, I know them.'

'Yes, well. They're too busy to come and visit her. Deedee's put on a couple of pounds so she daren't miss her session at the gym. Kirsten's really busy at work. And Amy's found herself a new man.'

'Look, I'm shocked too. But we'll only be away for a week. She could be back home by then!'

'The consultant spoke to me. The cancer's bad, Fergus. It's *everywhere.*'

Talk about being thrown in at the deep end. With Erin staying at the hospital with Stella, Kaye had found herself thrust into the job a day early and—as it turned out—woefully unprepared. God, but it was so hard not to offend people when they were trying on outfits that didn't suit them, or were blind to the faults of their own castoffs. By lunch time she had upset five customers. When Tilly came through the door at one thirty she greeted her with relief. 'Hi! You look fantastic!'

Tilly gave her an odd look. 'I've been using a floor-sander. I'm covered in dust.'

'Oh, but I love your T-shirt! And your jeans fit you so *well*, although with a figure like that, you'd look great in anything!'

'You're starting to scare me,' said Tilly. 'Is this one of those hidden-camera shows?'

Kaye pulled a face. 'I'm practising being nice. Paying compliments. Customers don't like it if they try something on and you tell them it makes them look like a hippo.'

'You have to say it in a nice way. Erin's great at that. She's honest but tactful.' Tilly exhaled. 'I can't believe she's not going to Venice.'

Kaye nodded in sympathy and handed her the key to Stella's house. 'I can't believe we're all taking it in turns to look after Scary Stella's cat.' Since Bing was so pampered, it had been decided that he should stay in his own home. Four or five times a day, one of them would drop in to check on him, keep him fed and watered and make sure his litter tray was scrupulously clean. Erin had organised it.

'Right,' said Tilly now, 'I'll get over there and check on Bing.'

An hour later, a tall woman in her sixties came into the shop. She eyed Kaye with surprise. 'You're not the usual lady.'

'I'm the reserve team.'

'But you still know about fashion? I certainly hope so anyway! I need a new evening dress, size fourteen. But I also want to ask your advice.' As she rattled on, the woman plonked a handbag on the counter. 'I feel dreadfully guilty doing this, but we're a bit desperate. You see, my son's mother-in-law gave me this for Christmas. It's Hermès, and one of the big prizes in our charity auction has just fallen through, so I've decided to offer this instead.' She looked hopefully at Kaye. 'And I wondered if you'd tell me roughly how much it's worth.'

Kaye examined the shoulder strap and tugged at a loose thread. 'Look, I'm sorry, but this isn't a Hermès bag. It's a copy.'

'Oh no! Really? So how much is it worth?'

Kaye shook her head. 'Nothing. It's a cheap market knock-off.'

'Right. Bugger.' The woman heaved a sigh. 'I dare say we'll sort something out. We can at least find me a dress for the night. Stopping and frowning, the woman looked more intently at Kaye. 'I keep thinking we've met before. But we haven't, have we?'

'I don't think so.'

'You're very familiar, though. Have you worked in any other shops?'

'Um, no. I've been living over in the States for the past few years.'

'We spent a month in Texas last year! Were you there too?'

'No, LA. I'm an actress,' said Kaye.

'Good heavens! *Over the Rainbow*!' The woman gave an excited yelp of recognition. 'We used to watch you on that show!'

'That's right.' Kaye smiled.

The woman clapped her hands in delight. 'This has to be fate!'

Fate. Really? 'Why?'

'Because you're a famous Hollywood actress! And if you wanted to do me a huge favour, you could.'

Kaye eyed her with caution. She owned only one really good designer bag and she loved it with a passion. 'What kind of favour?'

'Well, the whole reason I'm in such a flap is because this girl's just pulled out of our event. Antonella Beckwith? The singer? Have you heard of her?'

This was a bit like saying the Rolling Stones? They're a band? Ever heard of them? Kaye nodded, anxiety unfurling in her stomach.

'Well, the event's two weeks away and the wretched girl's cancelled on us. We've been racking our brains to come up with another celebrity, but everyone we've approached has other commitments.'

'OK, two things. One,' said Kaye, 'I'm not really a celebrity. Not over here anyway. Nobody would know who I am.'

'*I* know who you are! We'd tell everyone you're a Hollywood star!'

OK, so far, so toe-curlingly embarrassing. 'The other thing is, I'm not working on *Over the Rainbow* any more. They dropped me. That's why I'm living back here now.'

'Perfect!' As she spoke, the woman dug out a business card. 'If people don't know you, they won't know about that either, will they?'

The woman was a whirlwind, an unstoppable force. Examining the card, Kaye saw that her name was Dorothy Summerskill.

'It's a week on Saturday at the Mallen Grange Hotel,' said Dorothy. 'It's for a very good cause. The charity's called Help for Alzheimer's.'

'Oh! I've got a friend who supports them! Jack Lucas.'

'You know Jack? But how marvellous! He's going to be there.'

'OK, I'll do it.' Not that she'd ever had a choice, Kaye realised. Hadn't her agent said she should get involved in charity work? 'What will I be doing, just opening the evening?'

'Oh, yes,' Dorothy nodded, 'that too. But of course the main draw will be the auction. You'd be taking Antonella's place as the star lot!'

What?

'The highlight of the evening,' Dorothy continued. 'People will be bidding for a dinner date with you. It'll be fabulous!'

Stella had slipped from shock into flat-out denial. Erin knew the doctor had spoken to her but Stella insisted on talking about future holidays, while sitting up in bed applying copious amounts of make-up. In less than a week, the changes in her physical appearance were pronounced. Watching it happen day by day was horrifying and having to pretend you hadn't noticed harder still. Stella's skin had turned greenish-yellow, her eyes had become sunken and she was losing weight practically by the hour. Her movements were slowed too, curtailed by pain.

The doctor had spoken to Erin again. 'I'm sorry. We can control the pain but I'm afraid the cancer isn't treatable. I did broach the subject, but Stella didn't want to hear it. Her husband does need to be aware of this, though. We're talking a matter of days now.'

Not even weeks. *Days.* Erin had had no idea cancer could be this quick.

You missed a bit.' Stella's tone was querulous.

On her deathbed and dissatisfied with the way her nails were being painted. Erin, redoing the edge of the nail, said, 'Sorry.'

'I want to look my best for Max. Why isn't he here yet?'

The doors to the ward crashed open. 'You're late,' said Stella.

Max arrived at the bedside; if he was shocked by the change in Stella's appearance since his last visit, he covered it well. 'Bloody hell, woman, can't you give me a break? Some of us have work to do, WAGs to fight with.' He gave her a hug. 'Anyway, how are you feeling?'

'Like shit. I hate this place. And Erin's completely mucking up my nails.' Raising her face for a kiss, Stella said, 'Do I look all right?'

'You look fab. Here, I brought you some mags.'

'Thanks. I've already seen that one. And that one.'

Max shook his head. 'Did nobody ever tell you it's polite, when someone gives you something, to at least pretend to be pleased?'

Stella managed a smile. 'Sorry. I haven't read the rest of them.' Fumbling for one of the glossies, she studied the cover. 'Did you choose this one on purpose?' She pointed a still-wet fingernail at the words 'Biological Clock Clanging? Phone a Gay Friend!' then added, 'Changed your mind?'

'No.'

'Not now, obviously. When I'm better. I want a baby, Max. *Please.*'

Erin stared at him. Max shook his head. 'I know you do, but it's not going to be with me. Sorry, you'll have to get some other sucker to do it.'

'Fine then. I will.' Summoning up another brief smile, Stella said, 'Wouldn't want any child of mine inheriting a nose like *that*, anyway.'

Max stayed for another forty minutes, swapping insults, regaling them with gossip and eating the contents of Stella's fruit bowl.

When he left, Stella sighed. 'He's great, isn't he?'

'Hmm.' Erin shrugged and semi-nodded, privately outraged by Max's earlier behaviour. Would it have killed him to *pretend* that—

'He's made me feel so much better. I feel silly even saying this, but at least I know now that I'm definitely not dying.'

'*What?*'

'Oh well, you know.' Sheepishly Stella said, 'When you feel this rough and people keep being nice to you, it crosses your mind. And that's pretty terrifying, right? But if I was dying, Max would have gone along with anything I said, wouldn't he? So that means I'm all right.'

'Well, good.' Erin didn't know what else to say.

'So, when are you and Fergus planning on getting married?'

Erin was having trouble keeping up with this conversation. 'We haven't even talked about it. You aren't divorced yet.'

'That won't take long. We can get it sorted. I don't care about Fergus any more, you can have him. I just want you to promise me one thing.'

Oh help, what now? 'Promise you what?'

'That you'll invite me to the wedding. So I can turn up looking absolutely fantastic. I'll be thin and classy and gorgeous,' said Stella, 'and everyone will wonder why Fergus ever divorced me.'

'You know something?' said Erin. 'I have the strangest feeling your invitation's going to get lost in the post.'

'Don't worry, I'll gate-crash.'

'**G**uess what I've been doing all day?' Tilly burst into the shop and flung her arms above her head. 'You'll never guess!'

Kaye, who had been carefully de-bobbling a cashmere sweater, eyed Tilly with her arms in the air and said, 'Pretending to be an orang-utan?'

'I've been gluing Swarovski crystals to a thousand square feet of midnight-blue ceiling. All the feeling's gone from my fingers.' Wincing as she lowered her arms, Tilly said, 'And I had the completely brilliant idea of rollering glue over the whole ceiling then just flinging handfuls of crystals at it, but Max wouldn't let me.'

'He's an evil slave-driver.'

'Tell me about it. Oh, and you have to see the Alzheimer charity's website.' Tilly reached past her and waggled the mouse to bring the computer's screen to life. 'Jack called Max and told him to take a look.'

'Oh my *God*,' Kaye wailed when she reached the charity's home page. Beneath the headline NEWSFLASH! came the announcement, 'Due to unforeseen circumstances, Antonella Beckwith has had to pull out of our charity auction. However, we are thrilled and *delighted* to inform everyone that her place will now be taken by the much-loved award-winning Hollywood superstar, KAYE McKENNA!!!'

Kaye let out a groan and covered her face. 'Oh, that is *soooo* embarrassing. Who's going to bid to spend a couple of hours with *me*? They could come and sit in here for free. I bet Max thinks it's hilarious.'

'Just a bit.'

The door opened and a couple of well-groomed women came into the shop. Tilly had seen them somewhere before. In the Lazy Fox, probably. Ignoring her and Kaye, they began flicking through the rails. Kaye shrugged slightly and turned back to the computer. Tilly checked her watch; she should be heading over to Harleston to pick Lou up from school.

'. . . I mean, can you believe it? I know she's always been a tart, but not knowing who the father of your kid is, God, that's just *tacky*.'

Tilly exchanged a glance with Kaye; honestly, they might as well be wearing an invisibility cloak. Still, it had its own entertainment value.

'Well, if it's Andrew's,' said the taller, blonder woman, 'it's going to be born with weird little stumpy legs.'

'And if it's Rupert's,' the brunette grimaced, 'God help it! It'll have a bald head and hairs sprouting out of its pointy ears.'

They both snorted with laughter at this.

'Ha, no wonder she's worried. At least she knows it won't look like a gargoyle if it's Jack's. Now, what about the buttons on this shirt?'

Tilly's insides dropped. Kaye looked equally stunned.

'Those shoulders look a bit square. And I'm not sure about the collar. If it's Rupert's,' giggled the brunette, 'it might come out doing that laugh of his, like a hyena on helium.'

Who were they talking about? *Who?* Please let it be some other Jack.

'She must be desperate for it to be Jack's. At least he has a decent surname. Imagine if she married Rupert!'

'God, how *awful*,' squealed the other woman. 'She'd be Amy Pratt!'

Amy, oh no. Tilly remembered being interrogated by skinny, stiletto-heeled Amy in the pub on the night of Declan's birthday. She'd been besotted with Jack then. How could Jack have been so reckless?

'So what does Amy's new bloke make of it all?' The blonde was carefully examining a Ghost dress.

'Haven't you heard? He's legged it. Dropped her like a stone.'

'So she's going to be chasing after all three of them.'

'Um, excuse me.' Frowning, Kaye said, 'Is this Jack Lucas you're talking about?'

The two women turned to look at her, eyebrows raised as far as Botox would allow. The blonde said, 'That's right. Do you know him?'

Kaye was visibly dismayed. 'Yes, I do. *Very* well.'

'Ohhhh.' The brunette gave a slow, knowing nod. 'You're another one. Well, I know it's his own fault, but you can't help feeling sorry for him.'

Fergus shifted uncomfortably on the hospital chair. Years ago, he had loved Stella enough to marry her. But her towering ego and endless capacity for criticising others had worn that love away. Now, seeing her growing visibly weaker by the day was really churning him up; he felt ashamed of himself and resentful and . . . guilty because if she hadn't put her physical symptoms down to the fact that her husband had just left her, she might have gone to the doctor months earlier . . .

'Come on, come on, you're supposed to be making polite conversation.' Even now, Stella was able to mock him.

It was true. He was being a lousy hospital visitor. He didn't know how Erin did it. Day in and day out, for hours at a time, she stayed here and kept Stella company, talking easily about anything and everything.

'You look like someone waiting to see their bank manager,' said Stella.

Fergus made an effort to cheer up. But that was exactly how he felt. Checking the clock on the wall, he saw that it was almost three.

'Erin'll be here soon.'

'Thank God. She's a damn sight better company than you are.'

'Sorry.'

'I like Erin, you know. She's nice. I'm coming to your wedding, did she tell you?' Stella smiled. 'When it gets to that bit where the vicar asks if anyone knows of any reason why you shouldn't marry, I'm going to stand up and say yes, because you wear women's underwear in bed.'

It was Fergus's turn to smile. It wasn't true, but he could imagine Stella doing it. Except she wouldn't get the chance, would she? Because by then she'd be—oh God, no, no, don't let him cry. But it overtook him without warning, a great tidal wave of emotion. Fergus buried his face in both hands and sobbed and sobbed, unable to control himself.

Finally he got himself back on an even keel. He wiped his face, noisily blew his nose and looked up to see Stella impassively watching him.

'Sorry.' Fergus shook his head, embarrassed by the outburst. 'I don't know where that came from.' Did Stella know she was dying? Or, if she hadn't before, had he just given the game away?

She slid her skinny arm across the bed and clasped his hand in hers. 'It's all right, I know why you're crying.' With a ghost of a smile Stella said, 'You've just realised you're stuck with Erin now. And you wish you were still with me.' And, being Stella, it was impossible to know whether this was a joke or if she meant it.

Fergus, who had no intention of finding out, checked the clock again and said, 'She'll be here in a minute. Let's get you into a chair.'

Between them, he and a cheerful nurse managed to transfer Stella from the bed into a wheelchair. This, one of Erin's ideas, was the highlight of Stella's day. Fergus wheeled her out of the building. Seated on a bench opposite, beneath a chestnut tree, Erin was waiting for them.

Fergus parked Stella in front of the bench and Erin opened the front of the carrying case next to her. Bing snaked out, yowling impatiently, and stepped across onto Stella's bony, blanket-covered lap.

'Oh, Bing. My baby.' Stella lovingly stroked her cat.

Erin watched her cradling him and murmuring endearments into his ear. Bringing Bing along had really lifted Stella's spirits. She sat back and turned to look at the comings and goings at the hospital entrance.

Hang on. Who was that, heading up the road? Wasn't that . . .? It *was*.

'Stella.' Erin gave the side of the wheelchair a gentle nudge. 'Looks like someone's come to see you.' *At last*, but better late than never. Pleased for Stella, Erin pointed the visitor out to her: Amy.

Stella smiled, visibly relieved to see her friend at long last.

Amy grew closer. Recognising first Erin, then Fergus, she nodded briefly in acknowledgment. Then carried on. Boggling, they stared after her as she click-clacked past in high-heeled sandals.

'Amy,' Fergus called out, stopping her in her tracks.

Mystified, Amy looked at him, then at Erin. Finally her gaze went to Stella in the wheelchair and her expression became horrified as recognition dawned. Belatedly Erin realised that Amy hadn't come to visit Stella.

'Stella? How *are* you?' Staying where she was, Amy waved across the distance between them. 'How nice to see you! You're looking . . . um . . .'

'Stunning,' Stella murmured sarcastically. 'I know.'

'Gosh, I'd love to stop and chat, but I'm late for my appointment. Having my first scan. Wish me luck,' trilled Amy. 'See you around!'

They watched in silence as Amy teetered in through the glass doors.

Stella carried on stroking Bing. Finally she spoke. 'That poor baby. Fancy not even knowing who the father is. D'you think the scan will be able to see if it's got Rupert's ears?'

Chapter 8

THE SCHOOL CAR PARK was alive with activity. Max pulled into a space and hauled Lou's case off the back seat of the car. She threw her arms round him; her curls tickled his nose. 'Love you. Bye, Dad.'

'Hang on a sec.' Releasing her, Max strode round to the back of the car, clicked open the boot and pulled out a second case.

'What's going on? Who's that for?'

The coach was already filling up with pupils and teachers; in ten minutes it would be setting off on its journey to Paris.

'Me,' said Max. 'I'm coming.'

'Oh, Dad, no!' Lou looked panicky and upset, and Max knew why.

'Hey, it's OK. It'll be fine.'

'It won't be fine! Eddie Marshall-Hicks is going on the trip, and his friend Baz . . . They're vile. This is going to be awful.'

Which just went to prove that the snide remarks *hadn't* stopped.

'Sweetheart, do you think I can't handle a couple of spoilt brats? Coming along on the trip was my idea, after Mrs Heron and I had our chat. She was all for it. Oh, don't look at me like that.' Max prayed he hadn't made a terrible mistake. 'I'm not doing this to punish you.'

Lou's eyes narrowed, but there was nothing she was able to do about it; he'd presented her with a fait accompli. Over the next fifteen minutes, forty children were installed on the coach. Astrid Heron turned up to see everyone off. She stood at the front of the coach and gave a brief headmistressy speech. 'Now, you already know Miss Endell and Mr Lewis, so just let me introduce our two volunteer parent helpers. Mrs Trent, mother of Sophie.'

Next to Max, a beaming Fenella Trent leaped to her sensibly shod feet, waved enthusiastically and trilled, 'Hello, everyone!'

'And Louisa's father, Mr Dineen.'

OK, he definitely wasn't going to beam or wave. Max rose to his feet, gazed at the sea of faces and said, 'Hi there, you can call me Max.'

Everyone on the bus heard the sniggers at the back and the loudly whispered, 'Or we could call you Poof.'

Outraged, Mrs Heron barked, 'Who said that?'

'It's OK.' Max stopped her with a brief smile. Addressing Eddie and his sidekick at the back of the bus he said pleasantly, 'You *could* call me that, but you might not like what I'd call you in return.'

Astrid Heron was now looking as if she might be regretting her decision. 'Well, have a wonderful trip, all of you. And behave yourselves!'

The coach trundled down the driveway. Max sat back and wondered if *behave yourselves* applied to him too. If the ferry crossing was rough, would it be so very wrong to tip Eddie over the rail?

God, keeping an eye on forty overexcited thirteen- and fourteen-year-olds was knackering. Following an afternoon of sightseeing, they'd all eaten dinner at tables outside a vast pizza restaurant. (*Pizza? Mais naturellement!*) Now they were chatting and eyeing up other groups of teenagers in the vicinity. Some of the boys were kicking screwed-up balls of foil around, showing off their skills.

Max drank his black coffee and watched the history teacher, Josie Endell's, body language as she chatted animatedly to Tom Lewis. She was leaning forward, using her hands a lot to illustrate whatever she was saying and flicking her hair. Oh yes, the classic mating ritual. No doubt about it, Miss Endell was not-so-secretly smitten with Mr Lewis. And she wasn't the only one. Adolescent girls flitted round Tom Lewis like moths, practising their fledgling flirting skills in the most harmless way, on someone who was attractive but safe.

'Sir? Could you look after my Zen for me?'

The other interesting thing was watching the interaction—

'Sir?'

'Oh, sorry.' Belatedly Max turned. 'Didn't know you meant me. No one's ever called me sir before. Yes, I'll take care of it.' He slipped the Zen into his jacket pocket. 'It might be easier if you called me Max.'

'OK, sir—Max.' The girl giggled.

'Now that sounds good. Sir Max. I like it.' He nodded. 'How are you getting on, anyway? Having fun?'

'Oh, yes. Paris is dead cool. I liked seeing the *Mona Lisa*. I saw a programme about Leonardo da Vinci once. He did so many brilliant things.'

One of the balls of foil had just been kicked under Max's chair. Eddie Marshall-Hicks, deftly hooking it out with his foot, gave a snort and said with derision, 'Leonardo da Vinci was *gay*.'

The girl rolled her eyes. 'Eddie, you are such a div.'

'That's right. He was a genius,' said Max.

As Eddie dribbled the makeshift ball back to the game on the pavement, he said under his breath, 'And a shirt-lifter.'

The girl shook her head in disgust. 'Sorry about him, sir . . . Max. We're not all like Eddie. I think you're OK.'

Max grinned. 'And guess what? You're absolutely right.'

When the girl had rejoined her friends, Tom Lewis said to Max, 'Are you all right? Want me to have a word with him?'

'No, thanks, I'm fine.' Max shook his head briefly and signalled to the pretty waitress for another coffee. Bringing it, her gaze slid with sultry appreciation over the PE teacher's solid, super-trained body. Josie Endell, possibly without even realising it, gave the waitress a possessive hands-off-he's-mine smile.

Max stirred sugar into his coffee. Was Superman the one with the X-ray vision? Because this was how he felt right now, being the only one who knew without a shadow of a doubt that Josie was wasting her time.

No two ways about it. Gaydar was a wonderful thing.

Climbing onto the coach the next morning, Max could almost sympathise with the children. When you were thirteen or fourteen and there was a Disneyland in the vicinity, it wasn't easy to get excited about the fact that you were having to visit the Palace of Versailles instead. Oh well, whoever said school trips were supposed to be fun? And this one was about to get worse for Eddie Marshall-Hicks.

'Right, I'm sitting back here today. You,' Max indicated Baz, 'can move up to the front. I'm going to sit right here, next to Poison Eddie.'

Eddie bristled. 'What? Why? I don't want you sitting next to me!'

'Sorry, I'm the parent helper so you have to do as I say.'

The girl from last night crowed, 'Yay, Sir Max! Way to go!'

Out of the corner of his eye, Max glimpsed Lou's anxious face. He ignored her and sat down. If he'd had a plan to win Eddie round with his generally irresistible personality, well, he now knew that wasn't going to work. Which meant he was going to have to go with Plan B.

'So, looking forward to Versailles? It's pretty spectacular, you know.'

'If chandeliers and mirrors and fancy curtains are your thing.' Turning to stare pointedly out of the window, Eddie said, 'They're not mine.'

'Well, that's my job. Did Lou tell you I'm an interior designer?'

Eddie snorted. 'What a surprise.'

'Yes, well. It's not a bad career. You meet some interesting people.'

'What, like Laurence Llewelyn-Bowen?'

Max shrugged and unfolded yesterday's newspaper. Twenty silent minutes later, he took out his mobile and rang home. 'Tilly? Hi, sweetheart. Listen, did the lads finish tiling that bathroom floor last night?'

'They finished at ten o'clock,' said Tilly. 'How's everything with you?'

'Oh, fine.' Max grinned. 'Everyone loves me to bits.'

Next to him, Eddie heaved a sigh of you're-so-funny irritation.

'Now I know you're lying,' Tilly said cheerfully.

'Thanks. Anyway, about the bathroom. Jamie's happy with it, is he?' Lowering his voice slightly, Max went on, 'And Tandy?'

Eddie abruptly stopped picking at the loose threads on his jeans.

'They're over the moon. When Tandy saw it, she cried.'

'Tandy cried? God, that girl's soft in the head. When she sees the bill for the finished job, that's when she'll want to start crying.'

'Except they've covered their costs, remember?'

Max chuckled. 'God bless *Hi!* magazine. Anyway, we'll be at Versailles in a minute, so I'll leave you to it. Speak to you later. Bye.'

He put away his phone. Eddie carried on gazing out of the window. Max returned his attention to the crossword.

'So, what was that about then?'

Yee-ha! Bait taken!

'Hmm?' Max glanced up from the paper. 'Oh, just making sure the clients are happy.'

'Right.' You could almost feel the curiosity burning through his Led Zeppelin T-shirt. 'So . . . who are they, then?'

Because that was the great thing about Jamie and Tandy. Their names, together, were recognisable—the new Wayne and Coleen.

'I'm not meant to talk about my clients.' Max hesitated then said reluctantly, 'It's just a footballer and his girlfriend.'

Eddie was staring at him now. 'Jamie Michaels and his girlfriend?'

'Sshh. Don't tell everyone.'

'Bloody hell. And you've actually met them? Like, properly?'

'Of course I've met them.'

'But, Jamie Michaels isn't . . . you know, *gay*.'

'No.' Max marvelled at the workings of a fourteen-year-old's mind. 'I did his friend's house last year, and his friend recommended me. Colin, was it?' Frowning as if trying to remember, he said, 'No, Cal, that's the one. Cal Cavanagh.'

Eddie sat bolt upright and shouted, 'You are joking! Cal *Cavanagh*! But . . . but he's, like, the most genius footballer on the planet.'

'Is he? I don't know a lot about football. Lucky old Cal.'

Eddie leaned his head against the seat back. 'That is so amazing. You have, like, no idea. Cal Cavanagh and Jamie Michaels play for the best team in the world and you actually *know* them. Any minute now, your phone could ring and it could be them on the other end. I can't believe it. So . . . Cal Cavanagh. Does he live in, like, a huge mansion?'

Max nodded. 'Pretty huge. Electric gates. Eight bedrooms, nine bathrooms, a snooker room and an indoor pool with the names Cal and Nicole spelled out in gold tiles on the bottom of the pool.'

'Cal and *Nicole?* But they broke up six months ago.'

Max nodded briefly. 'I told him those gold tiles were a mistake.'

On Saturday evening they ate outside in the courtyard of the hotel. As the children let off steam, playing pétanque against teams of French teenagers, Max and Fenella Trent sat at a long trestle table with Tom Lewis and Josie Endell. Max had finally managed to swing the conversation round to favourite films.

Tom Lewis leaned back on his chair and counted off on his fingers. 'OK, top three. *Terminator. Gladiator. Rambo.*'

Josie Endell gave him a playful thump on the arm. 'You and your testosterone. Honestly, you are such a *boy*.'

For a split second Max caught Tom's eye and something unspoken passed between them. Tom knew that he knew. The silent acknowledgment was there. Then the moment passed and Tom shrugged. 'What's wrong with that? They're the kind of films I like to watch.'

'Audrey Hepburn!' Fenella clapped her hands. '*Breakfast at Tiffany's*!'

Josie said comfortably, 'My favourites are *Love Actually* and *When Harry Met Sally*. Can't beat a good old romantic comedy.' Dimpling, she addressed Tom. 'And I bet Claudine's the same, isn't she?'

Claudine, that was it, Mr Lewis's seriously attractive girlfriend. The question was, did Claudine know her boyfriend was gay?

'Oh, yes, all that girlie stuff. There's only one film we both like. *The*

Great Escape.' He looked at Max and said cheerfully, 'How about you?'

'Black and white with subtitles for me. Fassbinder,' said Max. 'Wenders, Almodóvar, Truffaut.' He paused, nodding in a thoughtful, intellectual way. 'But I suppose if I'm forced to narrow it down, I'd have to say my top three would be *Borat*, *Mr Bean* and *ET*.'

Tom grinned. Josie clutched at Tom's wrist and shrieked with laughter. Eddie and Baz, who had been hovering a short distance away, moved closer. Fenella gave Max a sympathetic look. 'And they're all outsiders seeking acceptance, aren't they? Is that why they're your favourite films, because you identify with the lead characters?'

'No, they're my favourite films because they make me laugh,' said Max. 'Same as you liking *Breakfast at Tiffany's* doesn't mean you secretly want to become a prostitute.'

Sniggering under their breath, Eddie and Baz casually pulled up a couple of chairs and joined them at the table. '*Mr Bean's* funny,' Eddie ventured. 'He's hilarious. Have you seen the one where he's a spy?'

'I like that one too.' Max nodded. 'How about Bruce Lee?'

'Yeah! Bruce Lee, brilliant!' Eddie began to yowl like a cat

Max nodded. '*Enter the Dragon* may have to go into my top three.'

'Three's not going to be enough.' Tom shook his head. 'We haven't even started on James Bond yet.'

'James Bond's all right.' Max intercepted Eddie's grimace. 'But I prefer *Shrek*.'

'*Shrek* is cool.' Vigorously nodding, Eddie said, 'Uh, sir? You know you know footballers? Well, do you know any, like, famous film stars as well?'

Max shrugged. 'I suppose maybe one or two.'

'**O**ooh, I need a wee, I'm *scared*.' Kaye was bleating with fear as they pulled up in the taxi outside the hotel.

Tilly didn't blame her, but she said consolingly, 'It'll be great, everyone'll be bidding for you. Dorothy won't let them *not* bid. And it's all in a good cause, isn't it? Even if you only raise fifty quid for the charity, that's still fifty quid more than they'd have had without you.'

Kaye let out a wail of anguish. 'Fifty quid!'

Inside the hotel, the buzzy atmosphere embraced them. Vaguely familiar faces from the ball were dotted around. Tilly spotted Dorothy and carted Kaye over to her. Having greeted her effusively, Dorothy then dragged Kaye off—looking like a baby seal about to be clubbed to death—to meet and greet potential bidders.

'She'll be all right,' said a voice behind her.

Tilly's heart did a dolphin leap in her chest. She'd known Jack would be here tonight, and he'd still managed to catch her off guard.

Jack was damaged, scarred by grief and incapable of giving himself fully to anyone. Irresistible he might be, but she was going to resist him.

And now he was waiting for her to say something. Damn, what was it they'd been talking about? Oh yes, Kaye. 'She's terrified,' said Tilly.

'Watch her.' Moving to her side, Jack nodded over. 'She'll click into actress mode any second now. Ha, there, see it?'

And he was right. Kaye had pressed the switch and metaphorically lit up. She was confident, dazzling, completely at ease as she chatted and effortlessly won over a group of complete strangers.

'Neat trick,' Tilly marvelled. She summoned a breezy smile. 'Don't tell me you're here on your own tonight?'

Jack shook his head. 'My partner's been held up. She'll be along later. See the big guy with the white hair?' He indicated the men clustered round Kaye. 'That's Mitchell Masters. He owns half the nightclubs this side of London. Seriously loaded.'

Maybe, but he still had a Santa-sized stomach. Without thinking, Tilly said jokily, 'He looks a bit pregnant.' *Oops.*

'Don't worry.' Jack sounded amused. 'I'm sure he isn't.'

Oh help, now she'd started she couldn't stop. Tilly blurted out, 'So, what's happening with Amy, then?'

Jack surveyed her steadily. 'Now I hear she *is* pregnant.'

'And have you talked to her?'

He shrugged. 'No.'

'But you could be the father! She's twelve weeks pregnant! That's when you slept with her. What if she's having your baby?'

A passing couple turned to look at them. Jack murmured, 'Sure you don't want a megaphone?'

Oh God, she was turning into a shrew. With an effort Tilly controlled herself. 'But she could be. Doesn't that even bother you?'

Jack certainly didn't look bothered. 'I hear she slept with a couple of other guys too. I doubt the baby's mine.'

How could he *be* like this? 'What'll you do if it does turn out to be yours? Will you marry Amy?'

Jack tilted an eyebrow. 'I think we can safely say no to that question.'

In desperation, Tilly said, 'Will you even *see* the baby?'

Jack raised his hands. 'Do you seriously think I'm that much of a bastard? OK, I'll make you a promise. If I'm the father, I will absolutely see the baby and support it financially. Scout's honour.'

The main business of the evening got started after dinner. It was a jolly, unstuffy affair, accompanied by much cajoling, blackmail and laughter. The first, smaller items up for auction were an eclectic bunch—dinner for six at an Indian restaurant, a signed football shirt, a hand-knitted sweater featuring the cartoon character of your choice.

'Come on, Mitchell, show us what you're made of!' Dorothy Summerskill, up on the stage with the auctioneer, was in full flow.

Mitchell Masters obediently sat back and stuck his hand in the air. When he discovered he'd just acquired a month's membership of a health and fitness club, he let out a shout of dismay and had to knock back a double brandy to get over the terrible shock. But minutes later he was off again, bidding generously for salsa lessons.

'Oh God,' Kaye whispered to Tilly when he won them. 'Can't he stop spending his money now? He won't have any left for me.'

The next few lots were auctioned. Kaye grew more and more jittery. Jack appeared at their table and gave her shoulder a squeeze. 'Max just called from France. He's told me to bid for you if no one else does.'

Kaye said gloomily, 'Better than nothing, I suppose.'

'Hey, you'll be fine. I'd have done it anyway.'

Tilly turned to him. 'Did your guest turn up?'

'Yes, she's here. Why? Did you think I might have been stood up?'

Kicking herself for having asked, Tilly looked away. Even more annoyingly, when Jack returned to his own table at the very back of the room, she discovered it was impossible to see who this evening's companion was. Unless she clambered onto a chair and peered over everyone's heads, and he'd be bound to spot her doing that.

The next lot was sold, then it was Kaye's turn. Dorothy gave her the most tremendous build-up then invited her onto the stage and led the applause. A couple of tables away from Tilly, Mitchell Masters gave an earsplitting wolf whistle. This was promising.

Behind Tilly, a woman grumbled, 'Kaye who? I've never heard of her.' Which made Tilly itch to throw a coffee spoon at her head.

Again Kaye hid her nervousness as the auctioneer launched into his spiel. Thankfully Mitchell Masters kicked off proceedings, a couple of other people joined in, then at £300, Tilly heard Jack make his bid from the back of the room.

'Four hundred!' cried Mitchell.

Tilly relaxed. There, Kaye could stop worrying now. Four hundred pounds was a perfectly respectable amount.

'Five? Do we have five hundred? *Yes*,' cried the auctioneer, pointing to the back of the room. Blimey, Jack was really giving it some.

'Six,' bellowed Mitchell.

'Seven at the back,' confirmed the auctioneer as people began to whoop with delight.

Mitchell yelled, 'Dammit! Make it a thousand!'

Tilly exhaled. You had to admire Jack's nerve. Now he could relax—

'Fifteen hundred,' announced the auctioneer, pointing at Jack.

Gordon Bennett, what was Jack playing at? Unable to contain herself, Tilly jumped up and peered over the heads of the applauding diners. She located Jack just as Mitchell said loudly, 'Two grand!'

Jack spotted her looking at him. From the stage, the auctioneer was saying, 'Gentleman at the back? Do I have two thousand two hundred?'

Tilly gazed in disbelief at Jack. Jack shrugged in return, signalling bafflement. Then she saw an elderly man standing behind him raise a gnarled hand at the auctioneer. The man was in his eighties, wearing a baggy grey cardigan and a pair of slippers. Who the hell was he?

'Two thousand two hundred!'

'Two five,' bellowed Mitchell, who clearly hated to be outdone.

'Three thousand pounds!'

'Four!'

'Five thousand!' roared the auctioneer. 'We have five thousand pounds at the back of the room!'

'Oh, sod it.' Mitchell shook his head. 'I give up. I'm out.'

And that was it. Ancient cardigan man had won. Everyone in the room cheered and applauded wildly, and Tilly expected the victor to make his way onto the stage to be introduced to Kaye.

Instead, he slid out through the double doors and disappeared. The organiser came to the front and spoke to Kaye and Dorothy. Moments later, Kaye rejoined Tilly at their table.

'Oh my God!' Tilly topped up both their glasses. 'Who was he?'

'OK, the woman who owns this hotel? He's her dad. He was just bidding on behalf of someone else.'

'Seriously? Who?'

Kaye was still trembling and hyperventilating from the ordeal. 'Someone who couldn't be here tonight because he lives in New York. His name's Price,' she said. 'Parker Price.'

Hang on. That name rang a distant bell. Price . . . Price . . .

'Oh my God!' Tilly jerked upright. 'The stalker!'

'Numbly, Kaye nodded. 'I know.'

'Who is he?' Jack had reappeared with his guest in tow. It was

Monica, Jack's cleaner, her sparkly turquoise eye shadow exactly matching her Mae West-style Spandex dress.

'The chap who's been sending her stuff.' Tilly shook her head. 'Well, he can't expect you to fly to New York to have dinner with him.'

'He doesn't. He'll come over here. We just have to fix a date.'

'But . . . he could be deranged! You can't meet him.'

'I have to. He's paid all that money. I still can't believe he found out about this thing here tonight . . . it's just so bizarre.'

'It was advertised on the Internet, wasn't it?' Ever-practical Monica in her throaty, sexy voice said, 'He'll have had your name on Google Alert, love. They can track your every move. Don't take this the wrong way, but you want to be careful. He's paying five grand to go out with you. If you ask me, that means he's got to be some kind of maniac.'

It was now eleven fifteen and Lou couldn't sleep. Everyone had been sent up to their rooms at ten thirty but the adults had stayed downstairs in the bar. Making up her mind, she pulled on a T-shirt and jeans.

Tonight was Saturday, their last night in Paris. The bar was still busy but she couldn't see Max anywhere. Or Mr Lewis. Only Miss Endell and Mrs Trent were still there, sitting at a small table being chatted up by a couple of middle-aged Frenchmen. Which was totally gross for a start.

Spotting Lou, Mrs Trent said, 'You should be upstairs asleep.'

'Sorry, I wanted to talk to my dad. I thought he'd be in here.'

'He went upstairs . . . ooh, about twenty minutes ago. With Mr Lewis,' said Mrs Trent. 'They were both tired. I expect your father's fast asleep by now. As should you be, my girl.'

As should you be. Seriously, only Mrs Trent could come out with a sentence like that. 'OK, I'll go up.'

'Straight to bed now.' Miss Endell was enunciating with care—she'd clearly sunk a fair few glasses of wine. 'See you in the morning.'

'Yes, miss.' Except I won't have a stonking hangover, Lou thought gleefully, and you will.

Anyway, of course her dad wouldn't be asleep. It was only half past eleven and he never went to bed before midnight. Heading back upstairs, Lou knocked on her dad's door. She had to see him.

No reply. Surely he hadn't fallen asleep so early? 'Dad? It's me.'

Finally the door opened. 'Hi, sweetie, everything all right?'

'Fine, thanks.' Lou followed him into the bedroom. Her dad finished brushing his teeth in the bathroom then came back through. He'd been reading. She picked up the paperback and said, 'This any good?'

'A damn sight better than sitting downstairs in the bar with Fenella and Josie.' He shuddered. 'I had to get out of there.'

'I know, I just saw them. Miss Endell's getting trolleyed and chatting up Frenchmen. But that's not why I'm here.' Lou bounced onto the bed. 'Eddie caught up with me on the stairs as we were coming up to bed.'

Max eyed her carefully. 'And?'

'He gave me a little shove in the back. Just like old times.'

'That little shit,' seethed Max.

'Hang on, and then he said, "I just wanted to tell you that I've been talking to your old man. You know what? Your dad's pretty cool."'

Max adjusted his spectacles. 'He said that?'

'He really did.' Breaking into a grin, Lou lunged forward and gave him a hug. 'The funny thing is, he seems to think you're best friends with all sorts of famous people.'

'Cal Cavanagh. Jamie and Tandy.' Her father shrugged modestly.

Lou raised an eyebrow. 'Not to mention Johnny Depp.'

'Probably best not to mention Johnny Depp then.'

'Dad! You *lied*. That's naughty!'

'Hey, so what?' Flashing his unrepentant smile, Max said, 'How's he ever going to find out? If the kid's shallow enough to be impressed by something like that, I'm shallow enough to say it.'

Chapter 9

THE MOMENT TILLY clapped eyes on Max on Wednesday morning, she knew what it was. 'I hate to say I told you so,' she lied.

He sat down with a groan. 'But you're going to.'

'It's your own fault! Oh, you look awful. Is it really bad?'

Max nodded, his skin green-tinged and pallid. 'I'm going to sue that bloody takeaway.'

'Well, you can't do that. It's not their fault you left it out all night and finished it up the next morning.'

'It tasted all right.' He clutched his stomach. 'God, my muscles hurt. Do you know how many times I've thrown up?'

'I don't *want* to know, thanks. I'm just wondering how we're going to manage today. I can't do Jamie and Tandy's on my own.'

'I know, I know. You take Lou to school and I'll sort something out.'

By the time Tilly returned from dropping Lou at school, Max had made the necessary arrangements. 'The schedule's too tight to cancel. So I gave Jack a call. He's on his way over.'

Just what she needed. Now Max wasn't the only one feeling sick.

Jack arrived ten minutes later. Max opened his design portfolio and ran through the list of jobs needing to be completed.

'No problem. We'll take care of that.' Having checked through the detailed plans, Jack tucked the portfolio under one arm.

'Thanks,' Max croaked.

As they were loading everything they needed into the back of Jack's van, his phone rang. Tilly was forced to stand by and listen as some female did her best to persuade him to go out with her tomorrow night. Gently but firmly, Jack turned her down.

'See? I can say no when I want to.'

'Actually, can we not do this?' Stepping back, Tilly held up her hands. 'Could we please stick to talking about work, because I really, really don't want to hear about your social life.'

'But—'

'No, I mean it. Sorry. You have to promise, or I'm not getting in the van.' She meant business. Being in his company was hard enough without having to worry about him getting personal.

Jack gazed at her for several seconds. She didn't flinch. Finally he shrugged and said, 'Fine.'

The first sign that something was up was the level of activity outside the front gates. 'Are there usually this many paparazzi?' said Jack.

'No.' Recognising Tilly and the van, the security guard opened the gates and let them through.

'Hi there! What's going on today then?' Tilly asked chattily when Tandy opened the door. Then she saw Tandy's swollen, pink-rimmed eyelids and clapped a hand to her mouth. 'Oh God, what's *happened?*'

'The engagement's off. Jamie's been shagging some hideous slapper. Come on in.' Tandy gazed dully past her at Jack, busy unloading the platinum-plated wall sculptures from the back of the van. 'Who's that?'

'Jack Lucas. Max has food poisoning. Is Jamie here?'

Miserably, Tandy shook her head. Fresh tears sprang out. 'He left last night. I said I never wanted to see him again.'

'Oh, look at you.' Desperately sorry for her, Tilly enveloped her in a hug. 'What a bastard. You don't deserve this.'

'I know. And she's, like, some desperate little tart who works as a pole-dancer. It's just . . . oh God, it's so *humiliating*. How could he *dooo* this to *meee?*' Tandy wailed. 'I just want to *screeeeam!*'

Ouch. Bit close to the eardrum, that.

'Of course you do.' Tilly inched away, aware of Jack waiting. Turning, she said, 'The wall sculptures are for the master bedroom. Turn left at the top of the stairs and it's the fourth door on the right.'

'Hi. Sorry to hear about Jamie.' Addressing Tandy, Jack said, 'Does this mean the party on Friday is cancelled?'

God, talk about insensitive. Tilly glared at him in disbelief.

'Of course it's cancelled.' Tandy eyed him stonily. 'It was going to be an engagement party.' She held up her left hand, bereft of rings.

Definitely no party then. Tilly felt sorry for Tandy but also a teeny bit sorry for herself. So much for buying that new dress.

Jack, meanwhile, was shaking his head. 'So . . . excuse me, but Max did mention that a magazine was buying the rights to the party, and that the payment for that was covering his bill.'

'Riiiight.' Tandy nodded slowly.

'So no party means no money from the magazine. Now I really don't mean to be rude,' said Jack, 'but could that cause a problem?'

'The party's cancelled.' Tandy lifted her tiny pointed chin. 'But I'm still doing sixteen pages for the magazine, so don't worry about Max getting paid. In fact, my agent's negotiated an increase in my fee.'

Tilly was taken aback. 'What, just for photos of the house?'

The look Tandy gave her was filled with pity. 'It'll be an exclusive. My heartbreak at Jamie's betrayal after I'd worked so hard to create our dream home. They'll take loads of photos of me around the house. So it all still has to be perfect.'

'In that case, we'd better get on with what we came here to do.' Jack hefted some of the wall sculptures into his arms and headed up the stairs.

When he was out of earshot, Tilly said consolingly, 'You'll get over this, I promise. You'll meet someone else and be happy again.'

'I won't.' Tandy shook her head. 'I don't *want* to meet anyone else.'

'Oh, you think that now, but just give yourself time,' said Tilly.

Tandy gave her an odd little look. 'No, you don't get it. I mean I won't need to meet anyone else because me and Jamie'll be back together next week.'

'Excuse me?'

'He played away. He got caught. I could kill him for what he's done.' Tandy took a deep breath then exhaled noisily. 'But he doesn't want us to break up. It's not like he's in love with this other girl.'

Tilly shook her head. 'You're going to forgive him?'

'Without Jamie I'll be just another ex-WAG.' Tandy's eyes glittered with tears. 'I'd have to go back and live with my mum. And everyone would be sniggering at me behind my back, and what if I couldn't get myself another footballer? What if I had to settle for some boring bloke who works in Comet?'

Tilly was stunned. 'But if you stay with Jamie, he'd know he could do anything, sleep with anyone he wants, and you'd put up with it.'

'I suppose so.' Tandy shrugged. 'It's what all the girls do.'

Tilly's voice rose. 'I wouldn't!'

'I don't mean girls like you,' Tandy retaliated. 'I mean girls like *me*, who go out with Premiership footballers. It's just the way it goes. We kick up a fuss when they do it, but then we forgive them.'

'And you honestly think it's worth it?' said Tilly.

Tandy shook her head at her as if she were five. 'Look at this house. Look at my shoe collection. I'm living the dream, aren't I?'

Having opened her mouth to protest, Tilly promptly closed it again. Jack had come back downstairs and was shooting her a warning look from the doorway. 'Yes.' She gave up. 'Anyway, I'd better get to work.'

Jack carried the rest of the sculptures upstairs and they started organising them on the walls. After ten minutes he said, 'I heard a saying once: if you marry for money, you end up earning every penny.'

'Hmm.' Tilly was still inwardly seething at Jamie's inability to keep it in his pants and Tandy's reasoning in letting him get away with it.

'Are you cross with her?'

'I wouldn't call it cross.' She reached up and held one of the large intricate sculptures firmly in place while Jack, behind her, drilled one of the fastening screws into the wall. 'I'd call it furious.'

He laughed and she felt his warm breath on her neck. 'Thought so.'

'Jamie's going to break her heart.' Super-aware of his proximity, Tilly supported the second section of the sculpture.

'For what it's worth, I agree with you.' Jack's hand brushed against her arm as he prepared to drill in the next screw. 'I'm on your side.'

'Tuh.'

'I was always faithful to Rose.'

'Well, you would say that,' said Tilly, possibly unfairly.

Zzzzzzzrrrrrggghhh went the electric drill.

'Because it's true.' Jack's mouth was now perilously close to her ear.

'Fine. I believe you.' Taking extreme care to avoid any physical contact, Tilly slid away from her position between Jack's body and the wall. 'There, can we get on with the rest of the jobs now? There's loads to do.'

The end was near. The curtains were now kept permanently drawn round the bed and Stella was drifting in and out of sleep. For the past forty-eight hours she'd been like a clock whose batteries were wearing out. For Erin, sitting by the bed stroking her hand, the periods of silence were lasting longer and longer.

When Stella stirred and mumbled something unintelligible, Erin leaned closer and said, 'Sorry?'

Stella opened her eyes. 'I'm not scared.'

'Good.' A lump expanded in Erin's throat. Yesterday, for the first time, Stella had admitted, 'I know this is it. I just don't want to say it.'

Now Stella murmured, 'Shame I'll have to miss the funeral.' She managed a smile. 'Hearing people say nice things about me. Even if they don't mean it.'

Erin just carried on stroking her hand.

'No black,' said Stella after a while. 'Bright colours only.'

'OK.' Erin nodded. 'Bright cheerful colours.'

'Ha, my so-called friends won't be cheerful. The only reason they go to funerals is to look thin and beautiful in black. Serve those bitches right.'

Hiss-clunk went the electronic pump dispensing morphine.

'And make sure Bing's all right.' Stella's eyes began to close. 'Promise.'

'Absolutely promise.'

'. . . Good . . . home.'

Good home? What did that mean? Was Stella saying she wanted her, Erin, to give Bing a good home? Or that Bing should go to a good home with someone else?

'What was that?'

No reply. Stella's breathing was slow and even. Erin wasn't going to get an answer out of her just now. She'd have to wait till she woke up.

After an hour Stella opened her eyes, gazed blankly at the ceiling then closed them again before Erin could ask the all-important question. One of the nurses rested a hand on Erin's shoulder and said discreetly, 'You might want to give Fergus a call. It won't be long now.'

Erin's heart gave a leap of panic. 'What? But there's something I need to ask Stella!'

'Don't worry about that. Now, do you want to phone him or shall I?'

Fergus arrived forty minutes later.

Stella's breathing was very slow now. Erin found herself counting the seconds between each delayed rasping breath . . . *nine* . . . *ten* . . .

'Is it going to happen?' whispered Fergus.

Erin nodded sadly.

'Oh God.' He sat down. 'She's not in any pain, is she?'

Erin shook her head. *Eleven* . . . *twelve* . . . *thirteen* . . .

'Oh God . . .' Fergus was staring at Stella's motionless chest. *Fourteen* . . . *fifteen* . . . *sixteen* . . .

Erin carried on stroking Stella's hand. She stopped counting at thirty and tidied a strand of hair away from Stella's marble-smooth forehead. It had happened. It was done. Stella was no longer here with them.

Hiss-clunk went the electronic pump, dispatching its hit of morphine into a body that no longer needed it.

Answering the phone, Tilly said cheerfully, 'Hello, how's it going?'

Erin picked at the flakes of peeling paint on the wall. 'Stella's gone.'

'*Oh.*' Tilly's voice dropped at once. 'Oh, Erin. I'm sorry.'

Erin felt the aching lump in her throat. Swallowing it, she said, 'It was peaceful at the end. She wasn't in any pain.'

'Oh, sweetheart. She was lucky to have you with her. I'll tell Max, shall I? And let other people know.'

'Thanks. That'd be good.' Tears began to slide down Erin's face as she leaned against the wall. 'Is it strange to say I'm going to miss her?'

'Sshh. Of course not. It's not strange at all.'

'**R**emember before the auction last week when I thought I was scared? This is fifty times worse.' Kaye's eyes darted round the hotel. 'I feel like I'm about to do the world's highest bungee jump.'

'Look, it's going to be fine. We're all here, aren't we? You're safe.'

'I feel sick. And I need a wee.'

Tilly gave Max a meaningful look; it was all thanks to his Anthony-Perkins-in-*Psycho* impressions that Kaye was such a gibbering wreck.

'Off to the loo? Check he isn't hiding behind the door.'

'Dad, shut up,' said Lou. 'You're not helping.'

It was ten to eight and the four of them were in the bar of the White Angel, a busy restaurant in Tetbury. Max had arranged everything with Parker Price, who was due to arrive at eight o'clock. While he and Kaye were eating dinner, the rest of them would be seated at a nearby table keeping a discreet eye on them.

At that moment, Max's mobile rang. He checked caller ID and said, 'It's him.' They all listened to Max's side of the ensuing conversation, which comprised a series of Rights, OKs and Fines.

'He's not coming.'

'*What?*' Tilly sat up. 'Why not?'

'Just doesn't feel it's right.' Max shrugged. 'Fine by me.'

'Are you serious?' Kaye's voice rose. 'It's not fine at all! I've been . . . oh my God, I've just been stood up by a stalker! Here, give me that phone.' Snatching it from him, she jabbed at the buttons. 'Hello? Hello? Is that you? Yes, of course it's me! Oh, well spotted, Einstein, I *am* upset, I've never been so insulted in my life! Where are you now?' Pause. 'Well, get yourself over here this minute. You paid to have this dinner with me and that's what you're damn well going to do.'

They all thought she was off her rocker but Kaye didn't care. After hyping herself up to meet him and enduring all that anxiety, not going through with it would have been a complete *waste*.

Parker Price didn't look like a fanatic. He looked perfectly normal. His hair was dark with a few silvery threads. He was in his early forties, lightly tanned, with warm grey eyes and nice hands.

The moment she'd clapped eyes on him, Kaye's nerves had melted away. Calmness descended. Across the room, Max and Tilly and Lou were watching like hawks but here at her table she was in control.

'So tell me why you tried to cancel. I can't believe you came all this way over from the States and decided to pull out at the last minute.'

'OK, I'm going to level with you. I was getting ready to come here and *really* looking forward to meeting you. Then all of a sudden it hit me.' Parker shook his head. 'I wondered how you'd be feeling about it, and realised you'd probably be scared witless.' He paused. 'Was I right?'

'Well, maybe. Maybe not scared *witless*,' said Kaye. 'Call it . . . wary.'

'Now you're just being polite. Let's face it, I could have been a complete psychopath. I still might be, for all you know.'

'You're not.' Kaye's confidence was absolute.

'*I* know I'm not.' He smiled. 'But you don't. Anyhow, that's why I suddenly decided I couldn't see you. I couldn't bear the thought of you sitting opposite me, wishing you could be anywhere else.'

'I'm not frightened any more,' said Kaye. 'I promise.'

'Glad to hear it.' He relaxed visibly. 'It's really good to meet you.'

'Very nice to meet you, too.' Kaye couldn't begin to describe the way she was feeling about this gentle, sensitive man; all she knew was that he was someone she would trust with her life.

'We're being watched,' said Parker.

'I know. Sorry about that.'

'Your security team. We could invite them to join us if you want.'

'No, thanks, they're fine where they are.' Kaye didn't want Max and Lou constantly interrupting. 'I can't tell you how much I love that painting you sent. It's hanging up in my living room. So kind of you.'

'My pleasure. You'd been through a rotten time. Trial by tabloid. I just wanted to cheer you up,' said Parker.

'You shouldn't have spent that much.'

He shrugged. 'Money isn't too much of an issue.'

He had the nicest eyes, warm and sparkly and crinkling at the corners each time he smiled. Kaye, who didn't make a habit of asking impertinent questions, said, 'How'd you get so rich?' Well, she wanted to know.

'I'm an architect. Not very exciting, but we have a successful practice. P. K. Price, over on Hudson Street.'

He seemed so normal, yet what he'd done definitely came under the heading of unusual. Kaye said bluntly, 'How much would you have bid up to, at the auction?'

'Twenty thousand. Dollars,' he added hastily as her eyes widened.

Kaye shook her head. 'I can't believe you thought I was worth so much.' She looked at him, completely unafraid now, and said, 'Why am I? Why did you come all this way?'

Parker said steadily, 'I can't tell you why. It'd sound . . .' He stopped, shook his head. 'No, sorry, I can't tell you why.'

Kaye liked it that he couldn't tell her. He wasn't exactly blushing but he looked as if he might be on the verge of it. Spotting the waitress hovering at a discreet distance, she said, 'We're holding up the kitchen. Let's decide what we're going to eat.'

'Look at them.' It was ten thirty and Max was getting fed up. 'They haven't stopped yakking all night. Bloody hell, he's getting his money's worth, isn't he?'

'Dad, calm down. He paid a *lot*.'

'But it's late and you have to go to school in the morning.'

'I know,' said Lou, 'but it's only double geography first thing. Everyone sleeps through that.'

'Here comes the cavalry,' said Parker. 'Looks like my time's up.'

'Hi. Good evening. We have to go now,' Max said without preamble.

'That's fine. You go,' Kaye said. 'We're having a lovely evening and

I don't want to leave yet. I'll catch a taxi home when I'm ready.'

'No you *won't*,' said Max, 'because leaving you with a stranger who could be a complete *freak*—no offence—would be a crazy thing to do.'

'Parker isn't a freak, so you don't have to worry any more.'

Parker raised a hand. 'Hey, it's OK. He's right. We've had a great evening but now we should call it a night.'

Kaye felt like a teenager being picked up early from the disco by her dad. She heaved a sigh and said to Max, 'Just give us two minutes.'

As soon as he was out of earshot Kaye said, 'Sorry about my ex-husband. Tact was never his strong point.'

'He's looking out for you. That's a good thing.'

She gazed at Parker, whose features were becoming more wonder-fully familiar by the minute. They'd talked about everything, darting from one subject to the next because there was so much to say. And still so much to learn. Was this how it felt when you met your soul mate?

Without even stopping to think about it, Kaye blurted out, 'So anyway, are we seeing each other again?'

Parker's whole face lit up. 'I'd love that.'

'Tomorrow night?'

'**A**t bloody last,' said Max when Parker left the restaurant and Kaye joined them at the bar. 'Job done. Let's go.'

'What was he like?' Tilly was curious.

Kaye could feel herself glowing. 'Really, really nice. In fact, he still is nice. I'm seeing him again tomorrow night.'

'Over my dead body,' snorted Max.

'OK.' Pointing two fingers at him, she fired. 'Bang, you're dead.'

'That's what you'll be when he does it to you. Don't you get it?' Max was incredulous. 'You have no idea who this man is!'

Kaye shrugged. 'I'm still meeting up with him tomorrow night. You don't have to tag along.'

'Of course I do! Somebody has to! Bloody hell, I don't believe this is *happening!*' bellowed Max.

There were some things you really didn't expect to see on your way to work at seven forty-five on a Thursday morning, and Jack Lucas hold-ing a wailing half-naked baby at arm's length was one of them.

Tilly, having pulled into the filling station for petrol, queued behind a white van and observed the goings-on with a mixture of emotions. Jack's car was parked at one of the pumps and a red Fiat stood with its doors flung open in the valeting bay. A toddler was screaming in his car seat while his harassed mother peeled a sodden white Babygro carefully down over the baby's frantically kicking legs so as not to splash baby sick over Jack's polo shirt. The nappy-clad baby, still being held under the arms by Jack, promptly threw up again, missing Jack's jeans by a whisker. Handing it over to the mother, he went over to his car and re-emerged with a pack of tissues, which the woman gratefully took from him.

The white van drove off. Tilly moved up and began filling her car with petrol. Farther along the row of pumps, Jack was now doing the same. Having mopped clean her bawling infant and stuffed it back into its baby seat, the mother effusively thanked Jack before driving off.

Tilly was torn. Half of her acknowledged that he'd done a good thing. The other half simmered with frustration because it was genuinely beyond her how he could be so thoughtful one minute and so selfish the next. Nodding across at her, Jack called out, 'Morning!'

'Morning.' Conflicting emotions continued to tussle inside Tilly's chest. In his sand-coloured polo shirt, faded Levi's and desert boots he was looking . . . pretty damn fit. Physically he was perfect. Which only made the other side of him that much more of a letdown.

'See my narrow escape back there with the incredible puking baby?'

'Yes, I did. What a complete hero you are. Then again, who's to say it wasn't one of yours anyway?'

'I'd never seen the woman before in my life.' He sounded amused.

'Have you even been in touch with Amy yet?'

Jack's smile faded. 'No.'

'So you'll go out of your way to be nice to the baby of a complete stranger, but you couldn't care less about one that could be your own flesh and blood.' Tilly's tank was full of petrol now and she clunked the nozzle noisily back into its holster. 'Don't you see how cruel that is?'

Jack shook his head; now she'd really annoyed him. Good.

'OK, let me just tell you something. The reason I haven't spoken to Amy is because I'm not the father of that baby of hers. And I know that for a fact because I haven't slept with her.'

Tilly stopped dead. What? *What?* Was he serious?

She looked at Jack. 'You mean . . . you haven't *had sex* with her?'

The older woman at the next pump was listening avidly.

'That's another way of putting it,' said Jack.

'But she said you had! Why would she say that if it wasn't true?'

'Who knows?' bawled the man in the Volvo behind her. 'Bloody women, they drive us all bloody nuts. And you're another one.' He jabbed an irate finger at Tilly. 'Standing there, yakking away while the rest of us sit here waiting for you to SHIFT YOUR BLOODY CAR!'

Eek. Blushing, Tilly hopped into the car and moved it over to a parking space. Back at the pumps, Jack was hanging up his nozzle. Tilly headed on into the station shop to pay, expecting him to follow her so she could continue the interrogation. Ten seconds later, through the window, she saw his Jag disappearing up the road. Tilly let out a squeak of surprise, prompting the cashier to raise an eyebrow and look up.

'Someone just drove off without paying,' Tilly bleated.

The cashier looked bored. 'That's because they were in the Express lane, love. You put your credit card in before you start.'

Oh. Right.

What had happened between him and Amy anyway? Why had they both lied about it? Tilly couldn't imagine, but she had to find out.

When she'd come down from London to work for Max, how could she ever have imagined that part of her job description would be chaperone-cum-gooseberry?

'I've got an appointment in Bath tonight,' Max had said earlier. 'You'll have to keep an eye on Kaye.'

Which was how Tilly came to be sitting, like a right Nelly No-mates, all on her own at a table in the garden of the Horseshoe Inn on the outskirts of Roxborough. Well, not completely on her own. She had Betty with her. At the other end of the garden, Kaye and her stalker were laughing together and generally having a brilliant time.

Ten minutes later, Jack emerged from the pub and stood surveying the scene. Betty raced over to her hero, greeting him like an ecstatic groupie. See? Even Betty was under his spell. But Tilly was glad he'd turned up. Max must have told him to come over to keep her company.

'Hi.' Tilly beamed. 'Let me guess, Max rang you.'

Jack nodded. 'He did.'

'Betty, leave Jack alone. Let him sit down.'

'I can't stop.' Shaking his head, he said, 'I've got new tenants moving into the Farrow Road flat this evening. Said I'd meet them there.'

What? 'So why did you come?'

'Because Max asked me to. It's OK, I'm pretty good on first impressions. Five minutes'll be enough to check him out, see what I think.'

So, not here for her benefit then. Tilly watched Jack head over to where Kaye and the stalker were sitting. He greeted Kaye with a kiss, shook Parker by the hand and joined their table.

'I'm off.' Four minutes had passed and Jack was back.

'One thing before you go.' Tilly blurted the question out; it had been driving her nuts all day. 'Because there's something I *really* don't understand. Why would Amy say she'd slept with you if she hadn't? And if it's true that you didn't sleep with her, why didn't you tell me *that* before, instead of letting me carry on thinking you had?'

'Listen to me.' Jack regarded her steadily. 'What did I tell you months ago? I said I never discussed my sex life. Never have, never will.' His eyes glittered. 'If you and I were to . . . have any kind of relationship, would you be happy to know that I was off telling everyone all about it?'

Tilly flushed and shook her head. 'No.'

'No, you wouldn't. And neither would any girl. So I respect that and say nothing.' Pause. 'I shouldn't have told you about Amy this morning, but this baby business was getting out of hand. So that's your answer.'

Well, that told her. Feeling thoroughly chastened—and frustratingly none the wiser—Tilly murmured, 'Yes.'

'Good.' With a wink he added, 'Who knew I had morals? Tell me you aren't secretly impressed.'

After chastising her like that? Not a chance. Ignoring this, Tilly said, 'What's the verdict on Kaye's stalker?'

'Seems OK. Not obviously howling at the moon. Kaye's keen. I'm off.'

To say that Kaye was keen on Parker Price was an understatement. She was besotted. When they'd said their goodbyes and Parker's taxi had taken him back to his hotel, Tilly and Kaye walked with Betty the short distance into the centre of Roxborough. Well, Tilly and Betty walked. Kaye was probably floating along a couple of inches above the pavement.

'He's just lovely, isn't he? You do like him, don't you? Honestly, I can't remember the last time I felt this comfortable with a man.'

'You still have to be sensible.' Tilly felt duty-bound to say it. She was a chaperone, after all.

'I know, I know. I am!' Kaye gleefully grinned and shook back her hair.

'Can I ask you something?'

'About Parker? Anything!'

'No, about Jack. Listen, remember you told me you'd slept with Jack. Well, did you really?'

'Sorry?' Kaye sounded puzzled. 'Did I really what?'

'Sleep with Jack.'

'Of course.' Incredulously Kaye said, 'Why would I say I had if I hadn't?'

Well, exactly. *Exactly.*

Max was already back from his meeting in Bath, frying eggs and bacon. 'Lou's gone up to bed. How did it go with the stalker?'

'Fine. She's seeing him again tomorrow. But she doesn't want a chaperone this time. She says she's a big girl now, you're not her dad and you have to let her and Parker go out together on their own.'

'OK.'

'Really?' Tilly was astounded.

Max shrugged. 'They can go out together. Not stay in.'

'Well, that's a start. Kaye'll be pleased.'

As Max flipped the rashers, his phone began to ring on the kitchen table. 'See who that is, will you?'

Tilly peered over at the screen. 'It's Kaye. Shall I answer?'

Was he struggling to keep a straight face? 'Be my guest.'

'Is Max there with you? Oh my God, you won't believe what he's done,' Kaye shouted over the phone. 'Tell him he's a complete bastard!'

'You're a complete bastard,' Tilly reported. 'Why, what's he done?'

'Only gone and phoned up Parker's offices and interrogated everyone who works there! I'm so *embarrassed*,' shrieked Kaye.

'OK.' Seizing the phone, Max said laconically, 'I can hear you squealing away, but I happen to think it was the sensible thing to do. They told me he was a nice normal guy, everyone likes him, no history whatsoever of chopping women up into small chunks.' Pause, tinny squawk. 'Look, I just want you to be safe. And Jack says he seems OK, too. So now that we know all this, I'm happy to let you go out with him tomorrow night on your own.' Pause, brief tinny squawk. 'Well, charming.'

'What did she say?' Tilly busily piled rashers of crispy bacon onto the lined-up slices of bread.

'She just called me something *very* rude.'

Tilly studied the order of service in her hands and felt guiltily void of emotion. It felt faintly fraudulent, attending the funeral of someone you'd barely known and hadn't even liked. But, petrified that the turnout would be pitiful, Erin had been badgering practically everyone Stella had ever met in her determination to ensure that the church would be reasonably full.

And over a hundred people had turned up. The so-called friends who hadn't visited Stella in the hospital were all here today. Either their consciences had been pricked by Erin or the opportunity to look glamorous in black was simply too good to pass up. The request to wear bright colours had been ignored by most of the women, including a visibly pregnant Amy in an elegant black velvet wraparound dress. Tilly still hadn't been able to get her head round the Amy conundrum. Had Jack hypnotised her into somehow believing she'd had wild sex with him?

Tilly gulped. Oh dear, now she was imagining wild sex with Jack, which had to be inappropriate at a funeral . . . *Stop it this instant.* And speak of the devil, here was Jack coming into the church now. Tilly did her best to look as if she wasn't looking.

Then again, was there really any need when everyone else was?

Just the sight of him was enough to set off the usual reaction in Tilly. She wondered if it would ever stop. It couldn't be good for you, feeling like this about another human being and not allowing yourself to do anything about it. OK, breathe. Of course it hurt, but wasn't keeping your distance safer in the long run? It indisputably was. And breathe again.

Anyway, never mind that now. The vicar was readying himself to begin the service. It was time to say goodbye to Stella Welch.

There was a good turnout at the Fox afterwards. Nobody felt the need to rush back to work; far easier to soften the blow of mortality with a few drinks instead. And it was a jolt, to think that someone you knew had died before reaching forty. Suddenly you realised it was no longer safe to assume that one day you'd be a pensioner. The prospect induced an atmosphere of almost wartime recklessness and everyone was drinking that bit more rapidly than usual. Well, why not?

As one of the barmaids approached with an open bottle of Moët, Tilly stuck out her glass for a refill. Kaye had volunteered to pick Lou up from school today, so it was allowed. She smiled at Fergus. 'Stella would be pleased with all this.'

'She would.' Fergus nodded in agreement. 'Most of it's thanks to Erin, getting everyone here today. She's been amazing.'

'Of course she's amazing. She's my best friend.'

'She feels guilty. We both do. No expensive messy divorce. We can just get married now, whenever we want. And I *do* want, but Erin says we can't because it would look bad . . . Oh hello . . .'

Fergus had been buttonholed by the man who ran the antiques market a couple of doors up from Stella's shop. Slipping tactfully away, Tilly made her way over to Erin.

'Well, if Fergus isn't going to be moving back into the house, I do hope it'll go to a nice family. We don't want any rowdy teenagers.' The hectoring tone belonged to one of Stella's neighbours.

Erin was nodding, looking anxious. 'I'll tell Fergus.'

'And what about Bing? The reason I asked is if you don't have a home lined up, I wouldn't mind taking him.'

Since Erin was hesitating, Tilly said quickly, 'That would be brilliant. Wouldn't it, Erin? The perfect answer. Stella wanted him to go to a good home. It was her last wish.'

When the woman had moved on, Tilly murmured triumphantly, 'There you go. Sorted.'

Erin was worried. 'But what if that wasn't what Stella wanted? What if she was trying to say she wanted *me* to give Bing a good home?'

'No. Listen to me. You've done enough for Stella, more than she deserved, and now you can stop. Let someone else take care of Bing.'

Slowly, Erin's shoulders sagged with relief. 'OK. I will. Thanks.'

'You don't have to feel guilty.'

Erin managed a wry smile, took a sip of wine. 'I just can't help it. Because I'm still here and I'm going to be living the life she wanted.'

Marrying someone you love, having babies, watching them grow up, staying married till death do you part . . . well, that was the fairy tale, but how often did it actually happen? Look at Max and Kaye, Jamie Michaels and Tandy, and what about Jack and Rose?

Tilly's gaze was drawn across the room. An exotic-looking girl with waist-length black hair was busily flirting away with Jack. 'Who's that talking to Jack?'

'Oh, Stella used to belong to a fitness club in Cheltenham. I think she teaches ashtanga yoga there. Looks like Jack's got his evening entertainment sorted out.'

She was undoubtedly right. Then Tilly's attention was caught by the conversation to the right of them, between a curvaceous blonde in an emerald-green summer dress and a reed-thin brunette in black.

'. . . I mean, I know it's not the done thing to speak ill of the dead, but she could be pretty intimidating sometimes,' the blonde confided.

Her friend said, 'You're not kidding.'

Erin gave Tilly a tiny nudge, letting her know she was listening too.

'Stella told me I should sue the surgeon who left me with a nose like this.' The brunette shook her head. 'I said I hadn't had a nose job. So *she* said wasn't it about time I got one?'

'But if you tried to tell her she was being mean, she'd be really surprised. As far as she was concerned, she was just being honest.'

'I'll tell you something else,' the brunette confided. 'My auntie Jean always does my hair for me. But when Stella asked me where I'd had it done, I knew she'd laugh if I told her that. So I said Toni and Guy.'

'Well, guess what I did,' countered the blonde. 'She wanted me to go with her to that new health spa in Cirencester last year. I mean, you can just picture it. Stella looking amazing in a bikini, me and my cellulite wibbling around in my swimsuit. Yeurgh, no thanks! So I said I couldn't go because I had to visit my granny in hospital in Dundee. But then Stella didn't go to the spa, which meant I had to hide in the house all weekend.'

'Nightmare,' agreed the brunette.

'Then afterwards Stella asked me how my gran was and I couldn't remember whether I'd said she'd had a stroke or a heart attack, so I had to pretend she'd had both. God, the lies I was telling! And talk about tempting fate. How would I have felt if my gran *had* had a stroke?'

'Awful.' The brunette shook her head in sympathy. 'Still, I suppose it was nice of Stella to ask after her.' Then she perked up. 'Ooh look, Declan's bringing out more of those smoked-salmon thingies.'

They rushed off. And then it came to Tilly. Not a definite answer to her question, but a possible explanation so bizarre yet so feasible that it might . . . *might* . . . just be true. My God. Could it be?

Erin was staring at her. 'Tilly? What is it?'

'OK, I need you to do me a favour.' She checked out the gathering of mourners—yes, there was Deedee, there was Kirsten, there was thingummy with the red hair who was another one. 'When I tell you, don't ask any questions, just go along with everything I say.'

They didn't have long to wait. After twenty minutes Deedee and her red-headed friend went off together to the loo.

'Here we go,' Tilly murmured, nudging Erin in the same direction.

The cubicles were both engaged by the time Tilly and Erin got there. Taking out her make-up, Tilly said, 'The thing is, I've got a confession to make. I don't know why I lied to you, I just felt so embarrassed.'

The great thing about Erin was she knew her so well; throw her a ball and she'd catch it. 'So now you're going to tell me the truth? Go ahead.'

Tilly uncapped a lipstick. 'You know I went out with Jack last week.' As she said it, she shook her head.

Grinning at her in the mirror, Erin played along and said, 'Ye-es.'

'And you know I said the sex was fantastic. Well, I was lying.'

Erin pulled an ohmygod face. '*What?* You mean it was awful?'

'No, no, I mean there was no sex. We didn't sleep together. I'm sorry.' Miming disbelief, Tilly mouthed, *Why?*

'I don't get it!' Erin rose effortlessly to the occasion. 'Why would you *lie* about something like that?'

'Why do you think? Jack's been out with hundreds of girls and he *always* sleeps with them. We had a really nice evening, I thought it was going to happen,' Tilly wailed, 'and it just didn't! He dropped me home and said good night! I was so humiliated! Total rejection!' Pause. 'So I'm sorry, but I was ashamed. That's why I lied.'

There was silence then. Poor Erin searched Tilly's face for clues as to how she was meant to react but Tilly pressed a finger to her lips.

Wait. Wait. Oh God, had she just made a hideous mistake?

Then they heard flushing and the first cubicle door swung open to reveal the redhead. Moments later, Deedee emerged. They glanced sheepishly first at each other, then at Tilly.

'You're not the only one it didn't happen to,' Deedee blurted out.

The redhead clapped a hand to her mouth and let out a shriek of disbelief. 'WHAT? Are you serious? *I* was just going to say that!'

Yesssss. Bingo. Exhaling slowly, Tilly sent up a prayer of thanks for the tongue-loosening properties of Moët.

Deedee and the redhead stared at each other. 'You too?'

'Me too! I thought I was the only one! I felt like a complete *troll* . . .' Starting to laugh incredulously, the redhead exclaimed, 'But I couldn't admit it, could I? So I just pretended it had happened . . .'

'And everyone else has always said he's spectacular in bed, so I said it too.' Deedee shook her head.

'Hang on a second.' Bemused, Erin surveyed them. 'Are you sure you're all talking about the same person here?'

'Of course we are. Jack Lucas.' Deedee's eyes were like saucers. 'Oh my God, this is unbelievable. There's three of us!'

'There's four,' Tilly added. 'Amy. She didn't sleep with him either.'

The door opened and someone else came into the loos. 'Kirsten!' squealed the redhead. 'Listen to this! You know we've all had sex with Jack? Well, we were lying! None of us has!'

From the look in Kirsten's blue eyes they knew at once. 'Thank God. I thought there was something horribly wrong with me.'

Then they were all gabbling away at once. Erin looked at Tilly and whispered, 'How did you know?'

'I didn't, not for sure. But I knew Amy hadn't slept with him. Then we heard those girls talking about how intimidated they'd been by Stella, and how they'd lied to her, and I suddenly thought *what if* . . .?'

'And you were right.' Erin thought it over. 'Does this mean he's . . . gay?'

Kirsten swung round and squealed, 'That's it! Of course. Jack's gay!'

Deedee was triumphant. 'No wonder he gets on so well with Max.'

Eek, this was getting out of hand. Tilly said hastily, 'He's not gay. He definitely slept with a friend of mine.' Better not say the friend was Kaye, whose track record when it came to telling hetero from homo wasn't exactly stellar. But the problem had been solved at last.

'I'm back.' Kaye approached Max at the bar. 'I've dropped Lou at the house and fed her. I said you'd be home in an hour or two.'

'Fine. And where are you off to?' Max raised an eyebrow, noting the change of clothes, the perfume, the redone make-up.

'Parker's on his way over in a taxi. He's picking me up and we're going to have dinner at the Hinton Grange.'

He considered this. 'OK, but stay on your guard. If you're worried about anything, call me. And don't let him book a room.'

Kaye nodded obediently. 'Don't worry, I won't.'

In the taxi, Parker leaned forward and addressed the driver. 'Right, we're going to the Hinton Grange, it's—'

'Straight down to the end of this street,' Kaye interrupted, 'then turn left.' The taxi driver obeyed. 'Just pull up here by the postbox.'

Parker looked at her. 'This is your cottage, isn't it? Have you forgotten something?'

God, he was lovely. So lovely that she wasn't even nervous, and that was a first. 'No. I'm not hungry. I don't want to go to the Hinton Grange.'

The taxi drove off and Kaye led Parker by the hand into her tiny cottage. First she pointed out the painting he'd bought her, hanging on the wall in the living room. Then she took him upstairs.

Afterwards she lay back against the pillows gazing up at the ceiling. A tear slid out of her eye down to her ear.

'Oh, Kaye. You're crying.'

'Because you're only here for a few more days. Then you have to go back to the States.' Looking at him, Kaye felt bereft already.

'You know something?' He was holding her. 'I love you.'

She clung to him and burst into tears. 'I love you too.'

'OK, now I'm going to tell you something else. I couldn't before,' said Parker. 'Forty-five years ago, in New York, my father was shopping in Bloomingdale's when he happened to see a girl in a red coat. She was chatting with the staff in the hat department. And there and then, my father knew this was the girl he wanted to marry. It was love at first sight.'

'Oh my God, did he just march up to her and—'

'Sshh, no, he was still wondering how to make his approach when the girl turned and left. So of course he followed her, but it was really busy out on the streets and he lost her. My father couldn't believe it. His future wife and he'd found and lost her again in the space of five minutes.'

Kaye couldn't bear it. She'd thought it was going to be a story with a happy ending and instead it was turning into one of lost opportunities.

'My father did the only thing he could do and went back to the millinery department. He asked the women who worked there and found out that she worked at Bloomingdale's, upstairs in ladies' fashions.'

'Oh!' Kaye clutched her chest with relief.

'That day was her afternoon off. Well, he went back the next morning and trawled through the fashion department until he found her. He told her why he was there. Leaving out the love-at-first-sight bit, of course. But he asked her to meet him for a coffee after work, and she liked the look of him so she accepted. Her name was Nancy.'

'Nancy's your mother.'

'She is. They're still together. But my father always told me that one day I'd see a girl and that would be it. Love at first sight.' He took a deep breath. 'And guess what? He was right. I saw this beautiful woman on TV and knew she was everything I'd ever wanted.'

Was this one of the very best moments of her life? Absolutely. She wriggled closer and kissed him on the nose. 'But I still don't know what's going to happen to us. Bloody Atlantic Ocean.'

Chapter 10

'I'M SORRY, I FEEL LOUSY.' Erin shook her head apologetically. 'Should we just call it a night?'

Tilly felt sorry for both Erin and herself. Erin had a virus and would clearly prefer to be at home in bed, which was disappointing when you'd been looking forward to a girlie evening out together on your Friday night off. Lou was spending the weekend at Nesh's house. Max was at home working. When she'd left the house she'd told him to expect her back around midnight. Well, it was going to be more like nine.

There were bats flitting and darting round Beech House at warp speed. Never able to convince herself that they were harmless, Tilly made a dash across the gravel, unlocked the front door and—*oof*.

The bicycle that had been propped against the wall clattered to the floor, nearly taking her with it. Letting out a shriek of surprise, Tilly thought three things in quick succession. First, what a stupid place to leave a bike. Second, who would have cycled here at nine on a Friday night? Third . . . *crikey, bloody hell, surely not*?

Then a door opened upstairs and Max appeared at the top of the staircase in his dressing gown.

'God, I'm sorry.' Tilly wished she could evaporate on the spot.

'Well, at least it's only you.' Max looked relieved. 'You said midnight.'

'Erin was ill. I'm really sorry . . . I'll go out again . . .'

Max shook his head. 'It's OK. He was just leaving anyway.'

Mortified, she waited in the kitchen. Max came downstairs less than three minutes later, followed by a clearly embarrassed Tom Lewis.

Max came straight to the point. 'Look, this is the first time. I thought we'd be undisturbed. Tom's moving up to a school in Dundee next term. For his sake I hope we can trust you to keep this to yourself.'

Tilly flushed. As if she would broadcast it. 'Of course I will.'

'Thanks,' said Tom. 'Right, I'll be off.' With a brief smile he was gone.

'Oh, I'm so sorry,' Tilly groaned again. 'I can't believe he's gay. Lou *told* me he'd broken up with Claudine. Is that why? Did she find out?'

Max shook his head. 'Claudine never was his girlfriend. Just his flat-mate. She helped out when Tom had to produce a partner.'

'Oh, Max. And now he's moving to Scotland. Do you really like him?'

He shrugged. 'What's not to like? But we both knew nothing could ever develop. Poor Lou, it was traumatic enough when she thought her mother might make a play for him.'

'Poor Kaye too. Everyone she's attracted to turns out to bat for the other side. Oh God!' Tilly exclaimed. 'Don't say Parker's gay too.'

Max grinned. 'Don't worry, some of us have better gaydar than my ex-wife. Parker's definitely straight.'

Saturday night, and it was Tilly's turn to be alone in the house. Max had caught the train up to London and would be back tomorrow lunch time. Lou was continuing her weekend sleepover at Nesh's and Kaye had whisked Parker off to Oxford. Still, there were worse ways to spend an evening than at home on a comfortable sofa with a cute dog on your lap. Outside, rain was bucketing down, whereas inside it was warm and one of her favourite films was about to start on TV.

With impeccable timing Betty jumped off her lap and trotted over to the door. She turned and gave Tilly a meaningful look.

'Fine, but you have to be quick.' The trouble with dogs was they didn't appreciate how much you hated to miss the first few minutes of a film. As she opened the kitchen door a smattering of rain hit Tilly in the face. 'Yeuch, I'll wait here. No hanging about out there, OK?'

The little dog slipped past her into the darkness of the back garden. The next second, a volley of high-pitched barks rang out, there were sounds of a furious scuffle and Betty shot across the grass, closely followed by a fox. Letting out a shout of alarm, Tilly glimpsed the fox's long bushy tail as it chased after Betty, down the lawn and into the depths of the bushes at the end of the garden.

Oh God, *Betty* . . .

Tilly raced barefoot after them but they were gone, vanishing into the woods beyond. Foxes were nasty creatures who killed for the fun of it, and Betty was only small. Tilly raced back into the house, dragged on a pair of wellies and found a torch . . . oh please, please don't let the fox have ripped her to pieces . . .

Twenty minutes later Tilly was back again, soaked to the skin and hoarse from shouting Betty's name. This was serious. Sick with worry, she reached for the phone. She needed help, but who to call? Max, who was a hundred miles away? Kaye in Oxford? Or how about Erin, except she was still laid low with her virus . . .

OK, she knew what she had to do. There was someone Betty was so besotted with that she'd crawl over broken glass to reach him. Not unlike most of the single females in Roxborough.

'Jack?' Tilly's voice cracked with emotion as he answered the phone. 'I'm really sorry, but Betty's missing. Can you help me?'

Jack arrived less than eight minutes after her phone call, listened grimly to Tilly's description of the fox chasing Betty out of the garden, and from his car fetched a far more powerful torch than her weedy one. 'Right, we'll start in the woods. Got your mobile on you?'

Tilly nodded and patted her jacket pocket.

'OK.' Putting up the collar of his Barbour, Jack said, 'Let's go.'

By midnight Tilly's hopes were fading fast. The rain was still hammering down and the wind was howling like a wolf through the trees. There was still no sign of Betty. They would surely have found her by now if she were alive. It didn't bear thinking about . . .

Phone ringing in her pocket. 'Yes?'

'I've got her. She's safe.'

The words reverberated through her brain. For a moment she wasn't sure she'd heard him right. Tilly said, 'Is she alive?'

'Alive and kicking and very muddy. Meet you back at the house.'

Tilly ran all the way. Jack and Betty arrived two minutes later.

'Oh, Betty.' Bursting into tears of relief, she held out her arms but Betty, predictably, preferred to stay in Jack's. 'Where have you *been?*'

'She was trapped in a rabbit hole. I called her name and heard this tiny bark,' said Jack. 'The grass was muffling the sound. Then I had to haul her out. It was like helping a cow to give birth to a calf.'

'Oh, sweetie, how horrid for you.' Tilly lovingly stroked the little dog. She was covered in slimy mud. 'We need to get you into the bath.'

Jack's mouth twitched. 'Thanks.'

'Not you.' Tilly paused. 'But thank goodness you came over.'

Upstairs in the bathroom they scrubbed and shampooed Betty. Jack wrapped her in a bath towel and gently patted her dry. Downstairs, he lowered a gently snoring animal into her basket.

'Well, thanks again.' Now the drama was behind them Tilly thrust Jack's Barbour at him, anxious to see him gone.

He took the jacket from her. 'So I'm leaving now, am I? Tilly.' He shook his head slightly. 'Why are you still giving me such a hard time?'

'I'm not, I'm just tired.' *Please leave, please leave.*

Jack followed her to the door, then turned and kissed her.

It felt like coming home. The feel of his mouth on hers, warm and dry, was simultaneously the most perfect experience of her life and the most agonising. Her body wanted him but her brain was yelling that she couldn't—*absolutely couldn't*—let it happen. Her whole life she'd held back a part of herself for this reason. Fear of hurt meant she needed to be in control of any relationship, particularly when it involved someone who could have anyone they wanted, because why would they choose you? Even now, while her whole body was fizzing, she knew the subsequent untold misery would far outweigh the fleeting moments of joy.

Jack murmured, 'See? I'm not so bad, am I?'

Tilly closed her eyes. Come on, weigh it up. A night, even a week with Jack. Versus years of gut-churning misery and regret. 'I want you to go.'

Jack surveyed her steadily. 'OK, I don't get this. You hated it when you thought I'd slept with a million girls. And now you know I haven't. I thought you'd have been happy about that.'

She swallowed; it hadn't taken long for *that* irresistible snippet of gossip to become common knowledge. 'But it's not just that, is it?

There's trust and commitment. I know I could never trust you, and *you* know you have a problem with commitment. I don't blame you. But at the same time, I don't want to get involved with someone when I know it's never going to work out.'

'Who says it won't? It might.' He smiled persuasively. 'The way I feel about you . . . well, it's different. I really think there's something special going on here. And I think you know it too.'

'I think you want me to believe you mean that. And it's still not going to happen. I'm not interested in becoming another name on your list of conquests. Whether you've slept with them or not,' Tilly added, because the sex was irrelevant. Either way they were still conquests.

'You wouldn't be.'

'You say that now. But look at your track record.'

'So I can't win.' His eyes glittering, Jack said evenly, 'You're the one I want, but you don't trust me because you're convinced I'm incapable of maintaining a normal, happy, committed relationship. So the only way I could possibly change your mind about me would be by having a normal, happy, committed relationship with someone else.'

In a weird way, it was true. Don't give in, *don't give in*. Jack looked at her. Then he turned and let himself out.

Unable to get to sleep, Kaye lay in Parker's arms and watched him sleeping peacefully beside her, breathing easily and—

'Shit, what's *that*?' Jerking awake and sitting bolt upright, Parker clutched his chest as an unearthly wailing noise filled the bedroom.

'It's OK, sorry, that's my phone.' Snatching it from the bedside table, Kaye marvelled at her own stupidity in having allowed Lou to choose a new ringtone, some thrash-metal rocker screaming AAAANNSWER MEEEEEE! at the top of his lungs.

'Kaye, honey, it's Macy!'

Macy Ventura, one of her costars on *Over the Rainbow*. Kaye let out a groan. 'Macy, it's one o'clock in the morning. Everyone's asleep here.'

Macy shouted, 'Never mind about that! Baby, brace yourself. I am holding something that's gonna rock your world. In my hand I have a little tape containing CCTV footage of you running over Babylamb. Or rather *accidentally* running over him.'

'*What?*'

'It's all there on the tape, clear as day. You're heading slowly down the drive, the dog shoots out from nowhere, you brake as hard as you can but it's too late, there's no way you could avoid him.'

Kaye sat up, her heart racing. 'How did you get a tape of it? There *was* no CCTV footage. That camera wasn't switched on when it happened.'

'That's where you're wrong.' Triumphantly Macy said, 'The camera was working just fine. Charlene saw the accident happen. First thing she did was tell the security guy to destroy the tape.'

Kaye closed her eyes. 'Why would he do that?'

'Charlene was schtupping him, wasn't she! Plus, she threatened to sack him if he didn't. So he took the tape and told her it was sorted.'

'Charlene was sleeping with this security guy? But she was furious with me because she thought I was flirting with Denzil!'

'Yeah, well, she was feeling neglected because Denzil had stopped sleeping with her. She was also convinced this meant he was getting it somewhere else. Which it turns out he was,' Macy continued. 'And now he's divorcing Charlene so he can marry his one and only true love. So Charlene's moved out, the security guy no longer has to worry about losing his job, and what with him being a good Catholic and all, he confesses everything to the new love of Denzil's life and she knows she has to get right on the phone to Kaye McKenna and let her know she's about to be completely exonerated. In fact, she's doing it right now.'

'You *what?*'

'Isn't it fabulous news? The new love of Denzil's life is me!'

Tilly gulped down a cup of coffee with one hand and ironed Lou's PE kit with the other. It was eight o'clock in the morning, and Kaye and Parker had turned up on the doorstep half an hour ago.

'. . . Denzil's already got his publicist onto it. They're releasing the CCTV tape to the news stations. Everyone's going to know I'm innocent.'

'Tell them what else Denzil said,' Parker prompted.

'He wants me back on the show.' Kaye beamed. 'The writers are already working on it. And he's quadrupling my salary. Can you believe it? They're desperate to have me back!'

Tilly switched off the iron, glancing at Parker. He was doing his best to look pleased but she could sense his concern that he might be on the verge of losing Kaye back to her old Hollywood life.

'Well, I think they've got a damn cheek.' Unlike Parker, Max didn't bother to hide his feelings. 'They turned on you like a pack of wolves. If you go back, it's like you're forgiving them. I'd tell them to fuck off.'

'Dad. Language.'

'Lou.' Max tapped his watch. 'School.'

'OK, two things,' said Kaye. 'First, I'm an actress. Hollywood is where I work and telling Hollywood to fuck off would be cutting off my nose to spite my face.'

'Mum! Honestly, we're going to have to set up a swear box.'

'And second.' As she spoke, Kaye reached for Parker's hand. 'If the rest of America hadn't hated me, this man wouldn't have sent me flowers and chocolates to cheer me up. Parker and I would never have met. So how can I be angry? This is the happiest I've been in years.'

'That's really sweet.' Lou hugged her, then hugged Parker too. 'I never thought you were a mad stalker, I promise.'

Visibly touched, Parker said, 'Well, thanks.'

'I did.' Max refilled Parker's coffee cup. 'But I admit I was wrong.'

'What'll happen with you and Parker if you go back to Hollywood?' Lou's eyes were bright. 'Will he move over there too?'

Out of the mouths of thirteen-year-olds. From the look of things, Lou was voicing the question neither Kaye nor Parker had yet dared to ask.

'School,' Tilly announced, expertly tipping Lou off her chair.

The next couple of days were completely crazy. The high-quality CCTV clip aired on American TV, America fell in love with Kaye McKenna all over again and Charlene Weintraub slunk off into rehab. Kaye barely had a moment to breathe. Reporters descended on Roxborough and the phone didn't stop ringing. It was lovely to have been exonerated but all she really wanted was to be with Parker, whose time over here was running out fast.

On the evening of the second day, Kaye switched off her phone and they holed up together in his hotel room. 'Denzil's desperate for me to sign that new contract. And he's upped the offer again.'

Parker stroked her hair. 'Well, that's good, isn't it?'

'I know.' Finally plucking up the courage to ask the question, she took a deep breath. 'Would you move to LA?' There, done. She'd said it.

'Listen to me. I love you. But I can't just abandon my company. It wouldn't be fair on my staff, or to my clients. I can't let them down. And I couldn't move in with you and not work. I'd look like a parasite.'

He was absolutely right, and no one knew better than Kaye did how vituperative the Hollywood gossip machine could be.

'I'm sorry.' Parker hugged her. 'We can still see each other, can't we? New York to LA is only a six-hour flight.'

It sounded reasonable when he said it like that, but when you factored in Parker's working hours and her own gruelling filming schedule, how much time would they end up spending together really?

There were seven of them gathered in the drawing room at Beech House, and having Jack in the vicinity was making Tilly nervous. The nerves, in turn, were making her ravenous. She snapped yet another breadstick into quarters and trawled through the bowl of guacamole on the table beside her. She'd been taking the different dips in turns. Chilli cheese next, then salsa, then mayonnaise . . .

'Phew, you *reek* of garlic.' Lou flapped her hands in protest.

OK, garlic mayonnaise.

'These are great. You should try some.'

'Yeurgh, no thanks, I've got to go to school tomorrow.'

'Well, here comes Erin. She's not scared of a bit of garlic.'

Erin wrinkled her nose. 'Actually, you are a bit strong.'

'OK, I'm going to say a few words.' Clapping her hands, Kaye captured everyone's attention. 'As you know, Parker and I are leaving tomorrow.' Kaye gestured for Parker to come and stand beside her. 'And I'm going to miss you all terribly. The thing is, I've come to a decision. I'm not going to renew my contract with *Over the Rainbow*. I've decided I'd far rather go to New York.' Turning to watch the look of disbelief spreading across Parker's face—he'd clearly had no idea she'd been about to say this—she added, 'If this man here is sure he doesn't mind.'

Parker was gripping Kaye's hands. 'Are you sure? Really?'

'Oh, please, what's more important? Working on some stupid soap or being with someone who means the world to you?' Tears glittered in Kaye's eyes. 'Hopefully I'll be offered something in New York, but who knows? Either way, I've been lucky enough to find a wonderful man. I'm not going to be stupid enough to risk losing him.'

To her horror Tilly realised she was on the verge of crying too. Hastily she stuffed another breadstick into her mouth, because it was physically impossible to eat and cry simultaneously. She ended up coughing and spluttering and being vigorously whacked on the back by Erin. Oh God, and now Jack and Max were coming over. She croaked, 'Crumbs . . . windpipe . . .' and dodged past them on her way out of the room.

Upstairs in the bathroom she cleared her throat. Not wanting to head back down just yet, she picked up the magazines Lou had left on the floor after her bath this morning. Emblazoned across the cover of *Hi!* magazine were the words 'STOP PRESS!! He Broke My Heart But I Forgive Him!' above a shot of Tandy and Jamie. Overwhelmed with sadness, Tilly placed the handful of magazines on the window ledge.

She opened the bathroom door and came face to face with Jack.

'I came to see if you were all right.' He studied her.

Damn, why hadn't she thought to brush her teeth? Tilly nodded.

'So . . . have you changed your mind about me yet?'

Tilly's teeth were tightly clenched to stop any stray deadly fumes from leaking out. She shook her head. Only when she was halfway down the staircase did she open her mouth enough to say, 'Please don't, Jack.' Because this was hurting, actually *physically hurting*, more than she could ever have imagined. And she couldn't cope.

'**W**here's Jack?' said Erin twenty minutes later.

'Had to see a tenant or something.' Max shrugged as a phone beeped somewhere in the room. 'Mind you, he's been a miserable bugger today. No idea what's wrong with him. Woman trouble, maybe.'

'Oh noooo!' Beside her, Lou was gazing in dismay at her mobile. 'I don't *believe* it. Mr Lewis is leaving at the end of this term!'

Erin said, 'Who's Mr Lewis?'

'He teaches French and PE.' Lou, who had been allowed the afternoon off for Kaye's leaving party, frantically scrolled through the rest of the message from Nesh. 'He's got a job in Scotland. Mum? You'll never guess what! Mr Lewis is leaving! And you fancied him, remember?' She pulled a comical face. 'Although I'm not sure you'd have been his type.'

'**R**ight, back to work.' Max collected his files. 'I'm heading on over to Bristol. I need you to get hold of those bloody electricians and tell them we want polished chrome sockets in the Rowell Street flat, not brushed. And the curtains have to be picked up.' He tilted his head to one side. 'Can I tell you something? You look like crap. And you still smell of garlic. In fact, just breathe on the electricians. That'll do the trick.'

'You know how to make a girl feel good about herself.'

'Sorry, pet. You just look as if you haven't slept well.'

'I didn't.' She'd spent half the night miserably tossing and turning, and the other half watching the sun come up on the most beautiful June morning. The air was zingily clear and the sky was a cloudless cerulean blue. Somewhere overhead, Kaye and Parker were on their way to New York and a whole new life together. Whereas she, Tilly, was stuck here with her increasingly hard-to-handle old one.

'OK, I'm off. Oh, hang on, nearly forgot.' Rummaging in a kitchen drawer, Max picked out a key. 'I was supposed to give this to Jack yesterday; it's the master for Devonshire Road. Can you drop it off at his place before you do anything else? He's not at home, I tried ringing him earlier. So all you have to do is shove it through the letterbox.'

At least she wouldn't have to face him. 'OK, I'll drop it off.'

Max left. Tilly headed out to the car. Swing past Jack's house first, then over to Rowell Street in Cheltenham to give the electricians hell.

The driveway was empty. Thankful that Jack was still out, Tilly let the key fall through the letterbox. Right, done. Electricians next. *Oh God.*

Sod's Law dictated that of course it was Jack's car pulling up.

'Here to see me?' He was wearing yesterday's clothes. There was stubble on his chin too. He hadn't shaved. What did that tell you?

'I just dropped off the master key for Devonshire Road. Max forgot to give it to you yesterday.' Edging sideways in a wide arc round him, Tilly said, 'Actually, I need to get over to Cheltenham.'

'I don't bite,' said Jack.

'I know that! I'm just in a hurry, that's all!' He was twelve feet away but how far were the hideous garlic fumes capable of wafting?

Jack rubbed the flat of his hand over his stubbly jaw and looked down at the ground. Then he raised his gaze, fixed it on Tilly and said, 'I've only just got home. Aren't you going to ask me where I've been?'

Tilly did her best to sound as if she couldn't care less. 'I don't know. Where were you?' *Please don't let him start rattling on about a girl.*

'I was with Rose's mother.' He kept his tone level. 'And her father.'

Completely wrong-footed, Tilly said, 'Oh.'

Jack's gaze was unwavering. 'Yesterday, when you couldn't even bring yourself to speak to me, I realised I had to prove to you that I was serious. So I went to see Bryn and Dilys. We visited Rose's grave together. And after dinner I told them that I'd met this girl . . . I didn't know how they'd react.' Jack shook his head. 'But they were amazing. Dilys said she was so happy for me, and they'd been waiting for this to happen, that Rose would have wanted me to meet someone else.'

Tilly felt as if the ground were tilting underfoot.

'So I had to explain to them that things weren't exactly going full steam ahead,' said Jack. 'Bryn told me if I needed one, he'd write me a reference. And I've just driven back from there this morning. With Bryn and Dilys's blessing. Not to mention half a baked gammon wrapped in foil. So, is that enough to convince you I'm serious?'

Tilly closed her eyes for a moment. She wanted to believe him, of course she did. But who was to say Jack wouldn't change his mind?

When she opened her eyes again, Jack was approaching. Oh God . . .

'Still not convinced, then.' Shaking his head, Jack said, 'Dilys did wonder if that'd be enough. Fine, we'll move on to Plan B.'

'No!' Tilly darted sideways and covered her mouth. 'Please no . . .'

'Oh come on, I'm not that bloody scary.' He frowned in disbelief.

'It's not that.' Tilly hung her head and muttered, 'I have garlic breath.'

'You don't.' He was in the vicinity now. Less than eighteen inches from her face. Definitely inside the danger zone. 'I can't smell anything.'

'I do. Max told me this morning. It's really bad.'

Jack began to smile. 'Lucky I had lamb studded with garlic last night.' He took another step closer and said, 'Do I smell of it as well?'

Despite everything, Tilly smiled too. 'No idea. Can't tell.' So that was it. Fumes-wise, they were immune to each other. Neat trick.

For several seconds they stood there, gazing into each other's eyes. Finally Tilly said, 'Is this Plan B?'

'No. Plan B was going to be me asking you to marry me.'

OK, now the ground had definitely disappeared beneath her feet. Shakily Tilly said, 'This is crazy.'

'No? Not good enough? Ah, you *still* don't trust me, because I could say it today, then next week call it all off. Fair point.' Jack's eyes began to crinkle at the corners. 'That moves us along to Plan C.'

'What's Plan C?' gulped Tilly as he clasped her left hand firmly in his right one. Expecting him to lead her into the house, she was taken by surprise when he headed out through the gates instead. As he hauled her down the street, Tilly said breathlessly, 'Where are we going?'

'Wait and see.' Jack waved at the middle-aged man pruning his roses next door. 'Morning, Ted, this is the girl I've just asked to marry me.'

What?

Ted looked equally astounded. 'Really? Well, um, excellent.'

'Oh God,' squeaked Tilly as they made their way down the street.

'Morning, Mrs Ellis, how are you?' Cheerily greeting an elderly lady walking her Pekingese, Jack said, 'This is Tilly, my future wife.'

'Jack!' Mrs Ellis stopped dead in her tracks, almost garrotting her dog. 'Good heavens, how marvellous. I had no idea!'

'There's Declan! Hey, Declan!' Jack yelled. 'Meet my future wife!'

Declan did a double take, then waggled an imaginary glass at Tilly, cringing behind Jack. 'How many's he had, love?'

'No, I haven't been drinking. I've just come to my senses. Come on.'

Erin's shop next. He barged in, startling Erin and a curvaceous brunette who was in the process of trying on a ballgown. 'Jack! Long time no *see*,' cried the brunette. 'How've you *been*?'

'Never better. Just asked Tilly to marry me.'

'Sorry?' Erin's mouth dropped open in disbelief.

The brunette's gasp was audible. 'You're getting married?'

'Well, she hasn't said yes yet.' Jack flashed a grin. 'Wish me luck.'

'I'm meant to be working,' Tilly said breathlessly.

'Leave Max to me.' Jack stopped as they reached Montgomery's the jeweller's, and rang the bell to be let in. Jack said, 'This is Plan C. I want you and everyone else to know I'm serious. And I'm warning you . . . There is no Plan D.'

Inside the shop, expertly angled pools of light illuminated the polished cabinets of both antique and modern fine jewellery. Twenty minutes later, and without once even letting her glimpse how much any of them cost, Martin Montgomery had succeeded in narrowing the choice of rings to two solitaire diamonds, both so beautiful Tilly could barely breathe. One was square and princess cut, the other oval and cushion cut. The square one was her favourite but the diamond was bigger, so she had to choose the smaller one because just the thought of how many thousands of pounds each must cost was enough to bring on a panic attack.

Tilly looked at Martin Montgomery. 'If he changes his mind next week and brings the ring back, will you give him a full refund?'

Startled, Martin Montgomery said, 'Er . . .'

'I'm not going to change my mind.' Jack held up the two rings. 'Come on, which one do you prefer?'

The big square one, obviously. The shape suited her hand. It was the most beautiful ring she'd ever seen. 'I like the oval one best.'

Jack raised an eyebrow. 'Are you sure?'

'Absolutely.' Oh God, disappointment welled up. Which was completely ridiculous, because the oval one was the second most beautiful ring she'd ever seen in her life.

'Not just saying that because you think it's cheaper? Because it isn't.'

It wasn't? Adrenaline shot through her entire body. 'Is that true?'

The jeweller smiled slightly and nodded.

'OK!' Tilly grabbed the square-cut diamond and said joyfully, 'I'll have this one then!'

'Not just saying that because it is cheaper?' Jack's mouth was twitching.

'No! I love it!'

'Good. Me too. That's it then, Martin. This is the one we'll have.'

As Jack took the ring from her and slid it slowly and deliberately onto the third finger of her left hand, Tilly felt her eyes fill with tears. Because she now knew he was serious. He really, really meant it.

In her ear, he murmured, 'So has Plan C done the trick?'

'You know what? It really has.'

He broke into a wicked smile. 'I'm going to take you home now.'

Tilly quivered in anticipation. 'You haven't paid for the ring yet.'

She waited a discreet distance away while Jack took a card from his wallet. Then her mobile began to trill.

'Oops. It's Max.'

'Here, let me. Hi, Max.' He pressed speakerphone.

'What's going on? Why are you answering Tilly's phone?'

'She's here with me now. I've just asked her to marry me.' Jack's amused gaze went to Tilly's hand. 'And she's more or less said yes.'

Silence. Tilly's mouth was bone dry. She waited for Max to roar with laughter. Instead he said, 'Is she the one?'

Jack gave Tilly's hand a reassuring squeeze. 'Yes, she is.'

'Thought as much,' said Max. 'Put her on.'

Still trembling, Tilly took the phone. 'Hi, Max.'

'So it's serious between you and Jack? Are you still working for me?'

'Yes! Though obviously not at this minute.'

'Where are you?' demanded Max.

'Um, in Montgomery's the jeweller's.'

'So you haven't been in touch with the electricians?'

Tilly winced. Oops. 'Sorry, Max.'

'Max?' Jack stepped in. 'I love Tilly. I'm hoping she loves me, although she hasn't actually said as much yet. This is a pretty special day for us. Basically, bugger the electricians.'

'OK, tell Tilly I'll deal with them myself.' After a pause, Max said, 'It's finally happened, then?'

Jack squeezed Tilly's hand and gave her a look that melted her insides. He nodded and smiled. 'It's finally happened.'

'Well, it's about time too. And trust me, it really must be love if you've just asked her to marry you.' Max sounded both impressed and amused. 'Because that girl absolutely reeks of garlic.'

Jill Mansell

Do you think that there is a happy ending out there for everyone?

Of course! It's just a question of being lucky enough to find it. There's a saying that I love: Every pot has a lid. Being with the right partner is such a joy—and the thing is, they don't have to be perfect, just perfect for you.

Where does your inspiration for each book come from?

I'm a complete magpie. I'll pick up from plot-lines in soaps, features in newspapers, eavesdropping on trains and in restaurants . . . no one's safe!

If you could change tack completely, what would you do?

I'd love to be a restaurant critic and eat fabulous meals every day. Although I suppose you'd get bored eventually. OK, forget that. I'd like to be Pierce Brosnan's personal masseuse instead—wouldn't get bored with that!

Erin's shop in *Rumour Has It* is a dress exchange. Have you ever used one?

Definitely! I love a bargain, and picking up fantastic outfits for a fraction of their original cost is always a thrill. I'm one of those people, too, who tells everyone I'm wearing secondhand clothes. Except these days we call them vintage!

What would you say your fashion style was?

Long skirts, lots of silk and velvet, loose floaty tops, scarves, jewelled flip-flops in summer, pointy boots in winter. I don't actually own any shoes at all . . .

Do you have a special place to write?

On the sofa in the living room, or in bed with a view of the sports field behind our house. I have the TV on, and write by hand with a Harley Davidson fountain pen.

Do you have foods/chocolates/treats that you can't resist close by you when you write your books?

I'm always eating, mainly crisps and liquorice and fruit gums. My new discovery is dried pineapple slices, which are delicious and actually healthy. I have to stock up at my local delicatessen every week. I think I'm their best customer!

How do you switch off?

Very easily. Too easily sometimes—can switch off while I'm still supposed to be working! I love TV, reading, shopping, bouncing on the trampoline in our garden, exploring the internet, eating gorgeous meals . . . oh dear, doesn't sound too healthy, does it? I'd love to say I'm training for a triathlon. But that would be a filthy lie . . .

Rumour Has It That . . .

You can't resist sparkly rings . . .

So true! Sparkly anything, in fact. If it glitters, I'll wear it.

You have a secret fantasy about George Clooney . . .

Also true, but just in case nothing comes of it, I'm adding Pierce Brosnan to the list. Since *Mamma Mia!*, he's become my crush *du jour*. And I love that he can't hold a tune in a bucket—me neither!

You have to start a new book before you've finished the one you are writing . . .

Not true! I can't bear to think of an idea for the next book before finishing the current one. If I did, I'd want to start writing it straight away.

You're a member of an online authors group . . .

A couple of writers groups, yes. It's brilliant to be in daily touch with other authors—no one else can understand how weird it is to sit at home making up stories for a living!

Your favourite food is Cambozola cheese . . .

Oh yes. And fillet steak . . . perfect chips . . . liquorice Catherine wheels . . . Hmm, sounds like a recipe Heston Blumental might dream up!

Your dream is to have one of your books made into a film . . .

Absolutely. I can just imagine what I'd wear to the premiere.

The one thing you'd never tell your partner is how much you spend on things . . .

Well, who does? Hope he never finds out how much my new coat cost!

BAKING CAKES IN KIGALI

GAILE PARKIN

The two years that I spent in Kigali were extremely busy and particularly intense. I had no time to analyse experiences as they were happening, no time to step back and gain perspective——and after I left, I found that very few of my friends were interested in hearing any details. I was treated as some kind of curiosity——a woman mad enough to have volunteered to go and live in Rwanda. But there was so much I wanted to say about Rwanda and Rwandans! I was going to have to write a book . . .

1. An Anniversary

IN THE SAME way that a bucket of water reduces a cooking fire to
ashes—a few splutters of shocked disbelief, a hiss of anger and then a
chill all the more penetrating for having so abruptly supplanted intense
heat—in just that way, the photograph that she now surveyed extin-
guished all her excitement.

'Exactly like this?' she asked her guest, trying to keep any hint of
regret or condemnation out of her voice.

'Exactly like that,' came the reply, and the damp chill of disappointment seeped into her heart.

Angel had dressed smartly for the occasion, in a state of great anticipation of the benefits that it might bring. Completing her ensemble by
pushing a pair of small, gold hoops through her earlobes, she had
stepped out of her bedroom and into the lounge, scanning the room to
check that it was ready for her special guest. The children's clutter had
all been put away in their bedroom, and the tiled floor had been
scrubbed to a shine. The wooden frames of the three-seater sofa and its
two matching chairs had been polished, and each of their cushions had
been plumped to the full extent capable of a square of foam rubber. On
the coffee table she had placed a gleaming white plate of chocolate cupcakes, each iced in one of four colours: blue, green, black and yellow.

Then the shout had come through the open doorway that led off the
lounge on to the small balcony: the signal that she had been waiting for
from her neighbour Amina, who had been standing on the balcony
immediately above her own, on the lookout for the expensive vehicle
making its way up the hill towards their compound.

With a renewed surge of excitement, she had slipped back into the bedroom and watched as the black Range Rover with its tinted windows had pulled up outside the building. A smartly uniformed chauffeur had stepped out from behind the wheel, and holding the passenger door open, had called to the two security guards lounging beneath a shady mimosa tree. The taller of the two had shouted a reply and had stood up, dusting the red earth from his trousers.

Mrs Margaret Wanyika had emerged from the vehicle looking every inch the wife of an ambassador: elegant and well groomed, her tall, thin body sporting a Western-style navy-blue suit with a silky white blouse, her straightened hair caressing the back of her head in a perfect chignon. As she had stood beside the vehicle talking into her mobile phone, her eyes had swept over the building in front of her.

Angel had ducked away from the window and moved back into the lounge, imagining, as she did so, the view that her visitor was taking in. The block of apartments, on the corner of a tarred road and a dirt road in one of the city's more affluent areas, was something of a landmark, its four storeys dominating the neighbourhood of large houses and high-walled gardens, where drivers hooted outside fortified gates for servants to open up and admit their expensive vehicles. People knew that it was a brand-new building only because it had not been there at all a year before: it had been constructed in the fashionable style that suggests—without any need of time or wear—the verge of decay and collapse.

With mounting excitement, Angel had awaited the security guard's knock at the door of her apartment, and when it had come, she had opened the door, beaming with delight and effusively declaring it an honour indeed to welcome such an important guest into her home.

But now, sitting in her lounge and staring at the photograph that she held in her hand, all of her excitement fizzled suddenly, and died.

'As you know, Angel,' the ambassador's wife was saying, 'it's traditional to celebrate a silver wedding anniversary with a cake just like the original wedding cake. Amos and I feel it's so important to follow our traditions, especially when we're away from home.'

'That is true, Mrs Ambassador,' agreed Angel, who was herself away from home. But as she examined the photograph, she was doubtful of the couple's claim to the traditions that they had embraced when choosing this cake twenty-five years ago. It was not like any traditional wedding cake she had seen in her home town of Bukoba in the west of Tanzania or in Dar es Salaam in the east. No, this cake was traditional to *Wazungu*, white people. It was completely white: white with white patterns decorating the white. Small white flowers with white leaves encircled the outer edges of the upper surface, and three white pillars on top of the cake held aloft another white cake that was a smaller replica of the one below. It was, quite simply, the most unattractive cake that she had ever seen. Of course, Mr and Mrs Wanyika had married at a time when the style of *Wazungu* was still thought to be fashionable—prestigious, even. But by now, in the year 2000, surely everybody had come to recognise that *Wazungu* were not the authorities on style and taste that they were once thought to be? Perhaps if she showed Mrs Wanyika the pictures of the wedding cakes that she had made for other people, she would be able to convince her of the beauty that colours could bring to a cake.

Setting down the photograph, she removed her spectacles and, delving into the neckline of her smart blouse to retrieve one of the tissues that she kept tucked into her brassiere, began to give the lenses a good polish. It was something that she found herself doing whenever she felt that someone could benefit from looking at things a little more clearly.

'Mrs Ambassador, no words can describe the beauty of this cake . . .'

'Yes, indeed!' declared the ambassador's wife, leaving no space for what Angel was going to say next. 'And at the party, right next to our anniversary cake, we're going to have a big photo of me and Amos cutting our wedding cake twenty-five years ago. So it's very important for the two cakes to be *exactly* identical.'

Angel put her glasses back on. There was clearly nothing to be gained from helping Mrs Wanyika to see that her wedding cake had been ugly and plain.

'Don't worry, Mrs Ambassador, I'll make your anniversary cake exactly the same,' she said, smiling widely to disguise the sigh of regret that she could not entirely prevent from escaping. 'It will be just as beautiful as your wedding cake.'

Mrs Wanyika clapped her meticulously manicured hands together in glee. 'I knew I could depend on a fellow Tanzanian, Angel! People in Kigali speak very highly of your baking.'

'Thank you, Mrs Ambassador. Now, could I ask you to start filling in an order form while I put milk on the stove for another cup of tea?'

She handed her guest a sheet headed 'Cake Order Form' that her friend Sophie had designed on her computer, and Angel's husband, Pius, had photocopied at the university. It asked for details of how to contact the client, the date and time that the cake would be needed, and whether Angel was to deliver it or the client would collect it. There was a large space to write in everything that had been agreed about the design of the cake, and a box for the total price and the deposit. At the bottom of the form was a dotted line where the client was to sign to agree that the balance of the price was to be paid on delivery or collection, and that the deposit was not going to be refunded if the order was cancelled. Angel was very proud that her Cake Order Form spoke four languages—Swahili, English, French and Kinyarwanda—though less proud that, of these, she herself spoke only the first two with any degree of competence.

Their business concluded, the two women sat back to enjoy their tea, made the Tanzanian way with boiled milk and plenty of sugar and cardamom.

'So how is life for you here compared to at home?' asked Mrs Wanyika, sipping delicately from one of Angel's best cups, and continuing to speak English—their country's *second* official language—in defiance of Angel's initial attempts to steer the conversation in Swahili.

'Oh, it's not too different, Mrs Ambassador, but of course it's not home. As you know, some of the customs here in Central Africa are a little different from our East African customs, even though Rwanda and Tanzania are neighbours. And of course French is difficult, but at least many people here also know Swahili. And we're lucky that here in this compound most people know English. *Eh*, but you're too thin, Mrs Ambassador; please have another cake.'

Angel pushed the plate of cupcakes towards her guest, who had failed to comment on the colours—which were the colours of the Tanzanian flag—and had so far eaten only one.

'No, thank you, Angel. They're delicious, really, but I'm trying to reduce. Youssou has made a dress for me for the anniversary party and it's a little bit tight.'

'*Eh*, that Youssou!' commiserated Angel, shaking her head. She had had a couple of unfortunate experiences of her own with the acclaimed Senegalese tailor of La Couture Universelle d'Afrique in Nyamirambo, the Muslim quarter. 'He can copy any dress from any picture in a magazine and his embroidery is very fine, but *eh!* it doesn't matter how many times Youssou measures your body, the dress that he makes will always be for a thinner somebody.'

This was a rather sore point for Angel, who used to be a thinner somebody herself. In the last couple of years she had begun to expand steadily—particularly in the region of her buttocks and thighs—so that more and more of her clothes felt like they had been fashioned by the miscalculating Youssou. Dr Rejoice had told her that gaining weight was only to be expected in a woman who was experiencing the Change, but this had not made her feel any better about it. Still, running her business in her own home meant that she was able to spend most of her time wearing a loose T-shirt over a skirt fashioned from a *kanga* tied round her waist—an ensemble that could accommodate any size comfortably.

'And how is life in this compound?' asked the ambassador's wife.

'We're secure here,' said Angel. 'And even though all of us in the compound are from outside Rwanda, we're a good community. *Eh!* We're from all over the world! Somalia, England, America, Egypt, Japan—'

'Are they all working at KIST?' Mrs Wanyika interrupted Angel before she could complete the entire atlas of expatriates. The Kigali Institute of Science and Technology—a new university that had recently been established in the capital—was attracting a great number of expatriate academics.

'No, it's only my husband who is there. KIST doesn't accommodate the ordinary staff, but Pius is a special consultant, so his contract says they must give him accommodation. The others here are mostly from aid agencies and non-governmental organisations. You know how it is when a war is over, Mrs Ambassador: dollars begin to fall like rain from the sky and everybody from outside rushes in to collect them.' Angel paused for a moment before adding, 'And to help with reconstruction, of course.'

'Of course,' agreed the ambassador's wife, shifting rather uncomfortably on the orange and brown cushions of the wooden sofa.

Angel knew that Ambassador Wanyika's salary would have been boosted dramatically by an additional bonus to compensate him for the dangers and hardships of being stationed in a country so recently torn apart by conflict. She observed Mrs Wanyika casting about for a change of subject, and saw discomfort giving way to relief when her guest's eyes found the four framed photographs hanging high up on the wall next to the sofa.

'Who are these, Angel?' She stood up to get a better look.

Angel put down her cup and stood to join her. 'This is Grace,' she said, indicating the first photograph. 'She's the eldest, from our son Joseph. She has eleven years now. Then these two here are Benedict and Moses, also from Joseph. Moses is the youngest, with just six years.' She moved on to the third photograph while Mrs Wanyika produced well-rehearsed exclamations of admiration. 'These are Faith and Daniel. They're both from our daughter Vinas.' Then Angel touched the fourth and final photograph. 'These are Joseph and Vinas,' she said. 'Joseph has been late for nearly three years now, and we lost Vinas last year.' She sat down again rather heavily, the wood beneath the cushions of her chair creaking perilously, and knotted her hands in her lap.

'*Eh*, Angel!' said Mrs Wanyika softly, sitting down and reaching across the coffee table to put a comforting, well-moisturised hand on Angel's knee. 'It's a terrible thing to bury your own children.'

Angel's sigh was deep. 'Terrible, Mrs Ambassador. And such a shock to lose both. Joseph was shot by robbers at his home in Mwanza . . .'

'Uh-uh-uh!' Mrs Wanyika shook her head, giving Angel's knee a squeeze. 'And Vinas . . .?'

Angel put her hand on top of her guest's where it rested on her knee. 'Vinas worked herself too hard after her husband left her. It stressed her to the extent that her blood pressure took her.'

'Ooh, that can happen, Angel. *Eh!* Stress? Uh-uh.'

'Uh-uh,' agreed Angel. 'But Pius and I are not alone in such a situation, Mrs Ambassador. It's how it is for so many grandparents these days. Our children are taken and we're made parents all over again to our grandchildren.' Angel gave a small shrug. 'It can be a bullet. It can be blood pressure. But in most cases it's the virus.'

Mrs Wanyika moved her hand from beneath Angel's and reached for her tea. 'But of course, as Tanzanians,' she said, her tone suddenly official, drained of compassion, 'that is a problem that we don't have.'

Angel's eyebrows rushed to consult with each other across the bridge of her nose. 'I'm sorry, Mrs Ambassador, but you're confusing me. It sounds to me like you're saying that we don't have the virus at home in Tanzania. But everybody knows—'

'Angel!' Mrs Wanyika's voice, now a stern whisper, interrupted. 'Let us not let people believe that we have that problem in our country!'

Angel stared hard at her guest. Then she removed her glasses and began to polish the lenses with her tissue. 'Mrs Ambassador,' she began, 'do you think that the virus is in Uganda?'

'In Uganda? Well, yes, of course. Even the government of Uganda has said that it's there.'

'And in Kenya?' continued Angel. 'Do you think that it's in Kenya?'

'Well, yes, I've heard that it's there.'

'And in Zambia? Malawi? Mozambique?'

'Yes,' admitted Mrs Wanyika, 'it's in those countries, too.'

'And what about the Democratic Republic of Congo?'

'Oh, it's very well known that it's in DRC.'

'And surely you've heard that it's in Burundi, and here in Rwanda?'

'Well, yes . . .'

'Then, Mrs Ambassador, if you know that the virus is in every country that is our neighbour, then there are others who know that, too. And if people know that all of Tanzania's neighbours have it, why will they think that Tanzania *doesn't* have it? Will they think that there's something special about our borders, that our borders don't let it in?' Angel stopped, anxious that she had gone too far and that she might have offended her important guest. She put her glasses back on and looked at her. To her relief, Mrs Wanyika appeared more contrite than angry.

'No, you're right, Angel. It's only that Amos is always very careful not to admit that we have that disease in Tanzania. It's his job.'

'That's easy to understand,' assured Angel, 'and, as the ambassador's wife, you must do the same, especially when you're talking to people from outside our country. But we're both from there, and we both know that it can come to any family there and take away somebody close.'

'Yes, of course. Although . . . not *every* family,' Mrs Wanyika countered. 'Not ours. And not yours, Angel, I'm sure.'

But the ambassador's wife was wrong. Had the robbers' bullet not found Joseph's head when he returned home that night from visiting his wife as she lay dying in Bugando Hospital, Angel would be telling a very different story about his death. But Angel recognised that it was best not to say this to her guest, who would not be comfortable with the idea and might even feel moved to tear up her Cake Order Form. She decided to move away from the subject.

'You know, Pius and I were careful to have just two children so that we could afford to educate them well. Back in those days, family planning was still very modern. We were pioneers. Our lives should be growing more peaceful now. Pius should be relaxing more as he works the last few years to his retirement, but instead he has to work even harder. Our children should be preparing themselves to take care of us now, but instead we find ourselves taking care of their five children. *Five!* Grace and Faith are good girls, they're serious. But the boys? Uh-uh.' Angel shook her head.

'Ooh! Boys? Uh-uh,' agreed Mrs Wanyika, who—Angel knew—had herself raised three sons, and she also shook her head.

Both women were silent for a while as they contemplated the problems of boys.

Then Mrs Wanyika said, 'God has indeed given you a cross to bear, Angel. But has He not also given you a blessing? Is a child's laughter not the roof of a house?'

'Oh, yes!' Angel agreed quickly. 'It's only that we won't be able to provide for these children as well as we did for our first children. But we must try by all means to give them a good life. That's why we decided to leave Tanzania and come here to Rwanda. There's aid money for the university and they're paying Pius so much more as a special consultant than he was getting at the university in Dar. OK, Rwanda has suffered a terrible thing. Terrible, Mrs Ambassador; bad, bad, bad. Many of the hearts here are filled with pain. Many of the eyes here have seen terrible things. Terrible! But many of those same hearts are now brave enough to hope, and many of those same eyes have begun to look towards the future instead of the past. Life is going on, every day. And for us the pluses of coming here are many more than the minuses. And my cake business is doing well because there are almost no shops here that sell cakes. A cake business doesn't do well in a place where people have nothing to celebrate.'

'Oh, everybody talks about your cakes! You can go to any function and the cake is from Angel. Or if the cake is not from Angel, somebody there will be talking about another function where the cake *was* from Angel.'

Angel smiled, patting her hair in a modestly proud gesture. 'Well, being so busy with my cake business keeps me young, Mrs Ambassador. And I must keep young for the children. You know, many people here don't even know that I'm already a grandmother. Everybody just calls me Mama-Grace, as if Grace is my first-born, not my grandchild.'

'But you are Grace's mother now, Angel. Who is Mama-Grace if it is not you? Who is Baba-Grace if it is not your husband?'

Angel was about to agree when the front door opened and a short, plump young woman with the humble demeanour of a servant walked quietly into the room. 'Ah, Titi,' said Angel, speaking to her in Swahili. 'Are the girls not with you?'

'No, Auntie,' Titi replied. 'We met Auntie Sophie at the entrance to the compound. She invited us up to her apartment so the girls could play with Safiya. She's given me money to go and buy Fantas from Leocadie, but she said first I must come and tell Auntie that the girls are with her.'

'*Sawa*. OK,' said Angel. 'Titi, greet the wife of our ambassador from Tanzania, Mrs Wanyika.'

Titi approached Mrs Wanyika and, with a small curtsy, shook her hand, respectfully not looking her in the eye. '*Shikamoo.*'

'*Marahaba*, Titi,' said Mrs Wanyika, graciously acknowledging Titi's respectful greeting, and submitting to the pressure to reply in her country's *first* official language. '*Habari?* How are you?'

'*Nzuri, Bibi*. I'm fine,' replied Titi, still not looking at Mrs Wanyika.

'*Sawa*, Titi, go and buy the Fantas now for Auntie Sophie,' instructed Angel. 'Greet Leocadie for me. Tell her I'll come to buy eggs tomorrow.'

'*Sawa*, Auntie,' said Titi, making for the door.

'And leave the door open, Titi. Let us get some air in here.' Angel was suddenly feeling very hot. She fanned her face with the Cake Order Form that Mrs Wanyika had completed. 'We brought Titi with us from home,' she explained, switching back to English in deference to her guest's choice. 'It was our son, Joseph, who first employed her; then when . . . when the children came to us, Titi came with them. She's not an educated somebody, but she cleans and cooks well, and she's very good with the children.'

'I'm glad you have someone to help you, Angel,' said Mrs Wanyika, 'but do you all manage to fit into this apartment?'

'We fit, Mrs Ambassador! The children and Titi have the main bedroom. It's big. A carpentry professor at KIST made three double bunks for them, and still there's room in there for a cupboard. Pius and I are fine in the smaller bedroom. And the children aren't always inside; the compound has a yard for them to play in when they're not at school.'

'And how is the school here?' asked Mrs Wanyika.

'It's a good school, but quite expensive for five children! *Eh*, but what can we do? The children don't know French, so they have to go to an English school. But the school sends a minibus to fetch all the children from this neighbourhood, so we don't have to worry about transport. The boys are visiting some friends from school who live down the road, otherwise you could meet them. Titi took the girls to the post office to post letters to their friends back in Dar, but now they've gone to visit Sophie. It's a pity. I wish you could meet them, Mrs Ambassador.'

'I'll meet them one day, Angel,' said Mrs Wanyika. 'Who is this Sophie that they're visiting?'

'A neighbour upstairs in the compound. She's a good friend to our family. She shares her apartment with another lady called Catherine. Both of them are volunteers.'

'Volunteers?' queried Mrs Wanyika, raising a pencilled eyebrow.

'Yes. There are some few people here who have come to help Rwanda without demanding many dollars.' Angel gave a slightly embarrassed smile, knowing that neither her husband nor her guest's husband fell into that category.

Again Mrs Wanyika shifted uncomfortably on the sofa. 'And what do these volunteers do?'

'They're both teachers. Catherine's a trainer for the Ministry for Gender and Women, and Sophie teaches English at that secondary school that's for girls only.'

'I see,' said Mrs Wanyika. 'So these two volunteers are helping women and girls. That is very good.'

'Yes,' agreed Angel. 'Actually, they told me that they're both feminists.'

'Feminists?' queried Mrs Wanyika, and her other eyebrow shot up to join the one that had still not quite recovered from the idea of volunteers. '*Feminists?*' she repeated.

Angel was confused by her guest's reaction. 'Mrs Ambassador, is there something wrong with a feminist?'

'Angel, are you not afraid that they'll convert your daughters?'

'*Convert?* Mrs Ambassador, you're speaking of feminists as if they're some kind of . . . of *missionaries*.'

'Angel, do you not know what feminists *are*? They don't like men. They . . . er . . .' Here Mrs Wanyika dropped her voice to a conspiratorial whisper and leaned closer to Angel. 'They do sex with other ladies!'

Angel removed her glasses and began to polish the lenses with her tissue. She took a deep breath before speaking. 'Oh, Mrs Ambassador, I can see that somebody has confused you on this matter, and, indeed, it is a very confusing matter. I believe that a lady who does sex with other ladies is not called a feminist. I believe she is called a lesbian.'

'Oh,' said Mrs Wanyika, registering both relief and embarrassment at the same time. 'Right. Yes, I've heard of a lesbian.'

'It's very easy for us to get confused because these ideas are so modern for us in Africa,' said Angel, mindful of her guest's embarrassment and anxious to smooth over her mistake.

'Indeed,' agreed Mrs Wanyika.

'I only know about these ideas myself because I spent some time in Germany with my husband when he was there for his studies,' confided Angel. 'The women in Europe have many modern ideas.'

'I believe so. And is it not true that too many ideas drive wisdom away? I'm relieved that no harm will be done to your girls! I was confused to think that your neighbours are lesbians. They're simply volunteers.'

It was clear to Angel that Mrs Wanyika found the idea of volunteers—disconcerting to her as that was—less alarming than the idea of feminists. She looked for a fresh direction for their conversation, and, glancing at the coffee table between them, cried, '*Eh!* Mrs Ambassador! Your cup is empty and cold! Let me make some more tea!'

'Unfortunately I can't stay for more tea, Angel,' said Mrs Wanyika.

'Amos and I have been invited for cocktails at the Swedish embassy this evening, and I must go and get myself ready. I'll send my driver for the cake next Friday afternoon. I've enjoyed my tea with you so much. Thank you.'

'It's a pleasure, Mrs Ambassador. Please come to see me anytime. In my house it's teatime all the time.'

'Thank you, Angel. And once or twice a year we have parties for Tanzanians and friends of Tanzania at the embassy. I'll make sure that you get an invitation.'

'Thank you, Mrs Ambassador. I'll look forward to that.'

Alone in the apartment, Angel discarded her tight, smart outfit in favour of a comfortable T-shirt and *kanga* before gathering up her good china from the coffee table and taking it through to the kitchen. She filled the sink with warm soapy water, thinking as she did so about the deeply disappointing cake that she would have to bake for the ambassador's wife. It was not going to be a cake that would inspire people to come and order their own cakes from her—unless, of course, there were some *Wazungu* at Mrs Wanyika's party who did not know any better. No, it was going to be a cake that would try to hide its face in shame. The best that she could hope for was that nobody would ask who had made it. Or, if they did feel inspired to ask, perhaps they would see from the Wanyikas' wedding photo—the one of the couple cutting their wedding cake—that Angel had been obliged simply to copy the original cake, no matter how unsightly that had been.

Having washed the cups and saucers, she set about scrubbing the milk saucepan, finding it rather satisfying to take her disappointment out on it. Mrs Wanyika might not be a big person in the way that Ambassador Wanyika was, but she was a woman who entertained; and, as a woman who entertained, she had the power to tuck a great deal of money into Angel's brassiere. The afternoon could have gone quite differently: Mrs Wanyika could have ordered a beautiful cake with an intricate design or an original shape and lots of colours; it would have taken centre stage at the ambassador's party, and nobody there—surely almost all of them big people—would have left without knowing that Angel Tungaraza was the only person in Kigali to go to for a cake for a special occasion.

She set the pot on the draining board and looked at her watch. Pius would be home from work before too long, and it would soon be time to start preparing the family's evening meal. In a short while she would go upstairs to fetch the girls from Sophie's apartment, and she would send Titi to fetch the boys from their friends' house down the road. But before all of that, she had some time alone to enjoy one of her greatest pleasures, something that would surely go a long way to undoing the terrible disappointment that the afternoon had brought.

Drying her hands on a tea towel, she went into her bedroom and took from a shelf in the wardrobe a white plastic bag, inside which lay a bundle tightly encased in bubble-wrap. Back in the kitchen, she placed the bundle on the counter, and her fingers began to search for, and unpeel, the strips of sticky tape that bound it. She did this slowly, prolonging the pleasure, building the anticipation.

The parcel had come to her all the way from Washington DC, via a neighbour in the compound who returned there regularly to see his wife and children. Ken Akimoto was happy to act as a courier for Angel, and his wife never seemed to object to being sent to the shops on Angel's behalf. In fact, she regularly enclosed a card for Angel, usually to thank her for being a friend to Ken or for baking such beautiful cakes for him. And here was one of those cards now.

Snatching it quickly from inside the bundle, she spun round and leaned back against the counter to read it. She had managed to take it without yet seeing what was in the bundle: her pleasure would be all the greater for the delay. This time, June was writing to express her admiration for the cake that Angel had made for Ken's fiftieth birthday party. What a great idea it had been—June wrote, having seen Ken's photos— to make, for a man who so loved karaoke, a cake in the shape of a microphone, in black and grey with a small box positioned on it to make it look like it belonged to a particular TV station. The box on this microphone—red on one side, green on the other, blue on top—carried on all three sides the name KEN in white above a large number 50, also in white. Ken had reported afterwards that everybody at the party had praised it; and now here was praise from Washington, too.

After reading June's card twice, Angel knew that the moment had come for her to turn round and savour—slowly—the contents of the bundle. Ken had delivered it to her earlier that afternoon, on his way home from the airport, and she had resisted opening it immediately, because Mrs Wanyika would be arriving soon. As she had put it away in her cupboard, she had thought that perhaps she would delay opening it until the following day, because—surely—the commission of a beautiful cake from the wife of her country's ambassador to Rwanda was going to provide more than enough pleasure for one day. But now she was very grateful that she had the bundle to lift her mood this afternoon.

She turned round. Gently, carefully, lest any of the contents should fall from the counter and spill over the kitchen floor, she peeled back the folds of bubble-wrap. What treasures lay inside! Yes, here were the colours that she had asked for: red, pink, yellow, blue, green, black, some big blocks of marzipan, and, as always, June had included some new things for Angel to try. This time there were three tubes that looked rather like thick pens. She picked one up and examined it: written along its length were the words *Gateau Graffito*, and underneath, written in upper-case letters, was the word *red*. Reaching for the other two pens—one marked *green* and the other, *black*—she saw a small printed sheet lying at the bottom of the bubble-wrap nest. It explained that these pens were filled with food colour, and offered a picture showing how they could be used to write fine lines or thick lines, depending on how you held them. *Eh*, now her cakes were going to be more beautiful than ever!

This conviction made her feel emotional, and tears began to well in her eyes. Pulling at the neck of her T-shirt with her left hand, she reached with her right hand for the tissue that was tucked inside her brassiere—next to the deposit for Mrs Wanyika's cake—and dabbed at her eyes. Then she became aware that her face was beginning to feel extremely hot, and she extended the dabbing to her forehead and cheeks before picking up the card from June and using it as a fan.

Really, this Change business was not dignified at all.

2. A Christening

THE BUILDING in which the Tungaraza family lived clung to the side of the hill over whose crest the city centre sprawled, so that the apartments that were on the ground floor at the front of the building—as was the Tungarazas'—were one storey up at the back as the hill sloped steeply away at the rear. Angel's work table stood in the corner of her lounge, which was at the back of the apartment, in front of a large window that afforded a good view out over the wall encircling the compound. From there she could watch, as she worked, the busy comings

and goings of people and vehicles up and down the hill, while simultaneously keeping an eye on the children as they played down in the
compound's yard.

Today the boys were kicking their football around noisily, while
Faith was patiently braiding Grace's hair into neat cornrows. Titi had
gone down to the yard to bring their washing in off the line, and was
chatting there with Eugenia, who cleaned for the Egyptian upstairs.

The cake on Angel's work table today was for Ken Akimoto's dinner
party, which would take place that night. Ken was by far her best customer, ordering cakes from her two or three times a month. He loved to
entertain, and it was well known that he was very good at preparing
dishes from his native Japan, even though he had lived most of his life
in the United States.

Angel enjoyed baking cakes for him because he allowed her the freedom to decorate them exactly as she pleased. Today, she had baked a
simple round vanilla sponge cake in two layers with crimson icing
between the layers. Then she had coated the cake with a vibrant
turquoise-blue icing. Across the top she had created a loose, open,
basket-weave design in bright yellow bordered with piped yellow stars
alternating with crimson stars, and she was now finishing off by piping
scrolls of crimson round the base of the sides. It would be a handsome
cake: beautiful, but at the same time masculine. As she refilled her plastic icing syringe with the last of the crimson, she heard a knock at the
front door and a man's voice calling, 'Hodi!'

'Karibu!' she answered, looking up from the table as the door opened
and Bosco, the gangly young man who worked as Ken Akimoto's driver,
came into the lounge. She wiped her hands on a cloth and greeted him
with a handshake, in the traditional Rwandan way.

'You are welcome, Bosco,' she said, speaking in Swahili. 'But I hope
you haven't come to collect Mr Akimoto's cake. As you can see, it isn't
quite finished yet.'

'Ooh, Auntie!' exclaimed Bosco, his lean, youthful face breaking into
a wide smile. 'That is a very, very fine cake! The colours are very, very
good. Mr Akimoto will be very, very happy. Eh! But, Auntie, what is
that?' Bosco's eyes had slid away from Ken's cake and his expression was
registering distaste.

Angel saw that he had noticed the cake that sat at the back corner
of her work table, waiting to be collected that afternoon by Mrs
Wanyika's driver.

'That's an anniversary cake for some big people,' said Angel, adding quickly in her defence, 'That's exactly how they want it to look.'

'*Wazungu?*' asked Bosco.

'*Wazungu* taste. *Wazungu* thinking.' She did not want to say more; it was not professional to gossip about her customers, and as a business-woman she was obliged to remain professional at all times. 'But I'm happy that you like Mr Akimoto's cake, Bosco.'

'He'll come for it later himself, Auntie. I'm not here for Mr Akimoto; I've come to you about a personal matter. Well . . . two personal matters, Auntie.'

'*Sawa*, Bosco,' said Angel. 'Why don't you go into the kitchen and make tea for us while I finish decorating Mr Akimoto's cake? Then we'll sit and drink tea while you tell me your personal matters.'

Bosco glanced with admiration at the finished cake as he and Angel settled into their chairs with their cups of sweet, milky tea.

'Auntie, it is about a cake that I've come to see you,' he began.

'You've come to see the right person, Bosco. Are you perhaps bringing me news of your marriage?'

Since returning from Uganda, where his family had fled many years ago, Bosco had been pursuing—at first rather vaguely and now with greater single-mindedness—the idea of settling down and raising a family of his own. But despite his having identified a small succession of women to propose to, he had not yet had any success in securing a wife.

'No, Auntie,' said Bosco, giving an embarrassed laugh. 'Not yet. No, Auntie, it's my sister Florence. She has delivered her first-born.'

'Congratulations! A boy or a girl?'

'She's a girl, Auntie. She'll go for her baptism next weekend, and Florence would like a cake for the christening party. I told her that you are the one to make the best cake.'

'Thank you, Bosco. I'll be very happy to make the cake for your sister. I'll give her a good price.'

'Oh, no, Auntie,' said Bosco quickly, 'you can charge *Mzungu* price. Mr Akimoto will pay for the cake. He says it will be his gift.'

'*Eh!* Your boss is a very generous somebody!' declared Angel.

This was true. Ken frequently made his driver and Pajero available to friends—although, strictly speaking, both the vehicle and the driver belonged not to Ken himself, but to his employer, the United Nations. Angel herself had benefited from this generosity a number of times when she had needed to deliver cakes to customers who lived on roads where no ordinary *taxi-voiture* was able to travel. And, of course, Ken also helped her by buying supplies for her business whenever he went home to America, where his job gave him a week's leave every two months. Her supplies came into the country in his unsearched luggage along with his own big bottles of soy sauce, tubes of wasabi paste and sheets of processed seaweed—and he would never accept any payment for them from Angel. But despite his constant generosity towards her, she felt no guilt in charging him an exorbitant rate for every cake. When Sophie had found out exactly how high Ken's salary was, she had come to Angel in a state of high emotion, ricocheting between rage and exasperation. Angel had made tea for her and had tried to calm her down, suggesting that perhaps these big organisations needed to pay big salaries if they wanted to attract the right kind of people; but Sophie had said that they were the wrong kind of people if they would not do the work for less. Ultimately they had concluded that the desire to make the world a better place was not something that belonged in a person's pocket. No, it belonged in a person's heart.

Angel rose to fetch her photo album from her work table, and brought it over to her guest. 'Let me show you other christening cakes that I've made, Bosco. Perhaps they'll help you to decide exactly how you want your cake to look.'

Bosco looked carefully at each photograph. '*Eh*, Auntie, these are all very, very fine! How will I be able to choose one?'

Angel laughed. 'You don't have to choose one; you can design a different one. I'm only showing you these for ideas. But always for a christening, the name of the baby must be written across the top of the cake.'

Angel thought of her new Gateau Graffito pens. It would surely be easier to write a name on a cake with one of those than with her bulky icing syringe—although, of course, the colours of the three pens that she had were not suitable for a baby's cake.

'Goodenough,' said Bosco.

'Good enough?' queried Angel. 'What is good enough?'

'The baby's name, Auntie. She's called Goodenough.'

'Goodenough? *Goodenough?* What kind of name is Goodenough?'

'It's because they wanted a boy very, very much, but the baby is a girl. She's not what they wanted, but she's good enough.'

Angel removed her glasses and began to polish the lenses with her *kanga*. 'Do you think that is a good name for a girl to have, Bosco?'

'It is not a bad name, Auntie.'

Angel was silent for a while as she polished her glasses vigorously. Then she said, 'Do you know what, Bosco? I think perhaps it is not you who should choose the cake for Goodenough. You are only the uncle. Really, it's the baby's mother who should choose the cake for the baby's christening. Do you think it will be possible for you to take me with my photo album to meet Mama-Goodenough?'

Bosco's face lit up. 'Oh, Auntie, that is a very, very good idea! I wouldn't like to choose the wrong cake. I'll ask Mr Akimoto if I can drive you there on Monday. We can't go now; I have to fetch him soon from the office and bring him home to prepare for his party tonight. You know he likes me to help him by carrying the TV from the bedroom to the lounge and connecting up all the wires for the speakers and the microphone for the singing machine.'

'*Eh*, we will have another night of noise, then!' said Angel, putting her glasses back on. The whole compound knew when Ken Akimoto's parties included karaoke. As the night wore on and alcohol increasingly loosened inhibitions, even those guests who should never be allowed to sing into a microphone would be persuaded to do just that. But nobody ever complained. Neighbours were often guests themselves, and those who were not invited had usually received some favour or another from Ken.

Angel picked up her diary and a pen from the coffee table. 'On Monday we'll decide about the cake with Florence. But now I must write the day and time of the christening party in my diary so that it cannot be forgotten.'

She made the entry in her diary as Bosco gave her the details. She was careful to record all her orders in her diary so that she could keep track of them. That was the professional thing to do—and besides, Dr Rejoice had warned her that sometimes the Change could make a woman forget things. Angel knew that forgetting to make somebody's cake would be a shame from which she would never recover.

'Now, Bosco,' she said, replacing the diary and the pen on the coffee table, 'your sister's cake is one personal matter. You said that you were coming to me with two.'

'Yes, Auntie,' said Bosco. Then he said a loud *eh!* and looked away disconsolately.

'What is in your heart, Bosco?'

He sighed deeply. 'It's Linda, Auntie.'

'Ah, Linda,' said Angel, immediately picturing the young British human rights monitor who lived in the compound. Men tended to regard her as very beautiful, but Angel wondered how they had formed that opinion. As far as she understood it, the beauty of a woman rested in her face, but Angel had never seen a man look at Linda's face; there were always other parts of her body asking more urgently to be observed. Really, that was not a polite way to dress in a country where women were modest. Even Jeanne d'Arc—the sex worker who occasionally came to see customers in the compound—did not advertise her body like that.

Bosco looked embarrassed and remained silent. Angel did her best to move the conversation on. 'Bosco, last time we spoke you told me that you had stopped liking Linda.'

'Yes, Auntie,' said Bosco. Then he was silent again.

'You told me that you could see that there was a problem with Linda and drink.'

'Yes, Auntie.'

Silence.

'So I hope you're not going to tell me that you've decided to like her again?'

Bosco remained silent.

Taking off her glasses and beginning to give them another good clean, Angel continued, 'Have you forgotten the stories that you told me about her? I haven't forgotten the story of the time you saw her outside Cadillac nightclub and you greeted her, but all the drink in her made you a stranger and she said something to you that was not polite. I haven't forgotten the story of the morning when you went to Mr Akimoto's house to help him clean up after a party and you found Linda asleep on the carpet and she had vomited there, and she simply got up and left you to clean up her vomit. Bosco, please tell me that you have not forgotten those stories yourself.'

Bosco rose from his chair and moved towards the window, from where he could see the children in the yard below. Then he turned to Angel and spoke at last.

'Auntie, I haven't forgotten those stories.' He began to pace. 'But now I have another story to tell Auntie. It is a story that gives me pain in my heart, even though it is many weeks since I decided not to like Linda.'

'Eh! Bosco! It's making my head feel confused to watch you walking up and down, up and down. But I can see that you don't want to sit. Come into the kitchen and we'll make more tea together.'

Putting her glasses back on, she led Bosco into the kitchen. It was a small room, made smaller by the presence of two ovens: the electric one that belonged to the apartment, and the gas one that the Tungarazas had brought with them from Tanzania. Kigali's unstable electricity supply meant that Angel would have lost a lot of business had it not been for her gas oven.

Bosco washed the mugs from which they had drunk their tea, and measured two mugs of water into a small saucepan. Angel spooned in some Nido milk powder and a great deal of sugar and added a few cardamom seeds.

'Now, Bosco, I am going to watch this milk and before it has boiled you are going to tell me about this new pain in your heart before it eats you up like a worm inside a mango.'

'*Eh*, Auntie!' said Bosco, and his story came tumbling out. 'I've just seen Linda. Mr Akimoto sent me to Umubano Hotel to pay his tennis fees. After I paid, I saw Linda in the car park, but she didn't see me. She was with a man, and they were kissing. Kissing like in a film, Auntie. They were leaning against her vehicle, and he was touching her body. *Eh!* I got into Mr Akimoto's Pajero and I watched them. At first I didn't recognise the man because I only saw his back, but after they finished kissing he put Linda in her vehicle and then he went to his own vehicle and I saw who it was. *Eh!*'

Angel stopped looking at the milk and looked at Bosco. 'Who was it?'

'Auntie, it was the CIA.'

'*Eh?* The CIA? From here in this compound?'

Bosco nodded.

'Ooh, that is bad.'

'It is very, very bad, Auntie. The CIA!'

'He's married and he's living right next door to Linda with his wife!' said Angel. Rob and Jenna lived on the same floor as Linda. Officially Rob worked for an American aid organisation, but it was well known that he really worked for the CIA.

'She could be with me,' said Bosco, looking wretched. 'I'm a young man and I have a very, very good job. It's four years now that I've been a driver for people at the UN. But instead she's with a man who is old like her father.'

'A man who is married, Bosco,' said Angel. 'Surely what matters is not that he's older than her, but that he's married.'

'Auntie, many men come here without their wives, and they get girlfriends. There's one who works with Mr Akimoto. That one has even built a house for his girlfriend and they live together and they have a child, and for holidays he goes home to his wife in Europe. Mr Akimoto says that man's wife doesn't know about his girlfriend and his child. She'll never visit him here because he's told her that Rwanda is too dangerous.'

'I've heard of that man,' said Angel. 'And there's the Egyptian upstairs. He came here on his own, without his wife, and he had many girlfriends. But when his wife came to visit, somebody told her, and now she's divorcing him.'

'You cannot have a secret in Kigali, Auntie. Eyes have no curtains here. Somebody will tell the CIA's wife, and then the CIA's wife will take the CIA's gun and shoot Linda.'

Angel was shocked. 'The CIA has a gun?'

'Auntie, can you be a CIA and not have a gun? The milk!' Bosco lunged towards the oven and rescued the milk as it was about to boil over.

They were busy filling their mugs when Titi came in with the basket of dry washing from the lines in the yard and wanted to make a start on the ironing. Angel and Bosco moved into the lounge and switched to speaking English, which Titi could not understand well. They both wanted to talk more about this story, but it was a story that could become dangerous if it was overheard.

They could not talk much more about it, however, because very soon Mrs Wanyika's driver brought a thick envelope of Rwandan francs to Angel and took away the ugly white cake, and very soon after that Bosco looked at his watch, said *eh!* several times and rushed off to bring Mr Akimoto home to prepare for his dinner party.

3. A Scholarship

WEDGED UNDERNEATH THE BACK of the Tungarazas' apartment, where the hill sloped away beneath the building, was the office of Prosper, whose job it was to manage such matters as supervising the compound's security guards, collecting rents and overseeing the general upkeep of the building—roles that he filled, it had to be said, with only token commitment. It therefore came as no surprise to Angel when, having descended the stairs into the compound's yard and knocked on the door to Prosper's office, she received no reply.

She went back up the stairs to the ground floor of the building and left through the front entrance. On the street corner outside, she found Modeste and Gaspard, the day security guards. They had just bought a pineapple from a woman who was now hoisting her basket of pineapples, bananas and avocados back onto her head and moving on down the hill.

Angel greeted the guards and then, ignoring Gaspard—who spoke only French and Kinyarwanda—addressed Modeste in Swahili.

'Modeste, will you find Prosper for me?'

'Yes, madame.'

'Thank you, Modeste. Tell him I'm waiting at his office.'

Modeste set off up the hill, his tall, skinny frame breaking into a slow trot. Angel knew where he was going. On most days Prosper could be found two streets up, at a small roadside bar.

Angel went back down the stairs and waited in the yard outside Prosper's office. It was not a beautiful yard. The last of the builder's rubble still lay in one corner, in a pile partially concealed behind the trailer that had carried Angel's gas oven behind the family's red Microbus on its journey from Dar es Salaam to Kigali.

Wedged under the ground floor of the building, alongside Prosper's office, were four more rooms. One of these accommodated the Electrogaz cash-power meters for each apartment, nestled in an alarmingly haphazard tangle of wires and cables. Another room housed the water meters that had been installed just one month earlier, and that now made it possible for the compound's owner to present a bill for water to each of the apartments. The next room was nothing more than an empty space that would apparently house the diesel-powered generator that had been promised but had not yet materialised. Finally, tucked underneath Ken Akimoto's flat at the far end of the building was a room housing toilet facilities for Prosper and the guards.

Angel heard her name being called from above where she stood. Looking up, she saw Amina leaning over the small balcony of the apartment just above her own.

'Angel! What are you doing there?'

'I'm waiting for Prosper. Modeste's gone to fetch him.'

'Safiya's waiting for the girls to come and do homework.'

'They'll be there soon, Amina. While I'm here they are at home with Benedict. He's still sick with malaria. Titi has taken Moses and Daniel to play with their friends down the road, so the girls must stay with Benedict until I've finished with Prosper. *Eh*, here he is now.'

Prosper was making his way unsteadily down the stairs into the yard.

'Madame Tungaraza!' he declared, extending his hand and shaking Angel's. 'I'm sorry to have delayed you. Come in, come in.'

'Thank you, Prosper,' said Angel, following him into the gloomy little room that accommodated a table and one wooden chair. 'No, no, Prosper, that chair is yours. I'm happy to stand. I must be quick because I have a sick child at home.'

Prosper seated himself behind the table and attempted to convey an air of efficiency by rearranging the file, the notebook, the ballpoint pen and the Bible that lay upon it.

'Now, Prosper,' said Angel, taking two pieces of paper from where her *kanga* was tied at her waist, unfolding them and placing them on the table for Prosper to look at. 'I've come about these.'

Prosper glanced at the pages. 'Yes, madame, these are bills for water.'

'Mm-hmm. But what I want to ask is how are you calculating these water bills.'

'There are meters, madame. The meters tell us how much water an apartment has used. They are new.'

'Yes, I know about these new meters, Prosper. But please look at these two bills and help me to understand.' Angel moved around the desk. The smell of Primus beer threatened to overwhelm her. 'First, this is the bill for my family. See here, Prosper, it says fifteen thousand francs.'

'Yes, I see that. I myself wrote that number there,' said Prosper.

'And now this one. This is the bill for Sophie and Catherine. It says here thirty thousand francs.'

'Yes,' said Prosper. 'What is it that you need me to explain, madame?'

'I am confused, Prosper,' said Angel. 'In my apartment we are eight. *Eight!* We all wash, we all use the toilet, we cook. But in that other apartment they are two. *Two!* How can it be right that two people use twice as much water as eight people? How can it be right that two people must pay twice as much as eight people?'

Prosper shifted in his chair. 'Madame, of course they must pay more. They are *Wazungu*.'

'*Eh!*' cried Angel, looking at Prosper as if he had shocked her to the core. 'Those girls are not *Wazungu*, Prosper!'

It was Prosper's turn to register shock. 'They are not *Wazungu*, madame?'

'No, Prosper. They are *volunteers!*'

'*Volunteers?*'

'Yes, volunteers. A volunteer is not a *Mzungu*. A volunteer does not earn a *Mzungu's* salary. Those girls look like *Wazungu*, but they are not.'

Prosper thought for a while, and then he asked, 'How much does madame think volunteers can pay?'

'I think they can pay five thousand francs,' suggested Angel, having agreed the sum with Sophie and Catherine the previous evening.

'OK,' said Prosper, and he took his pen and altered the amount on the bill. 'I did not know, madame. I thought they were *Wazungu*.'

'Thank you, Prosper.' Her business with Prosper concluded, Angel went back up the stairs and out through the building's entrance to the street. Modeste and Gaspard had now finished eating their pineapple, and were sitting on the ground on the other side of the road with their backs up against the trunk of a mimosa tree. They acknowledged her wave as she turned down the dirt road and headed towards Leocadie's shop, which was housed in a container at the side of the road about a hundred metres from the compound.

On the way to the shop, she passed another kind of container, longer and lower, dark green in colour with a flatter shape and four hinged lids across its top. This was the skip to which the neighbourhood brought its household rubbish in the expectation—sometimes unmet for extended periods of time—that a truck would eventually come and take it away and bring it back empty.

Angel found Leocadie sitting in the dim interior of her shop, breast-feeding her baby. Short and solid, with small eyes set deep in a rather hard face, she was not an attractive girl until she smiled—at which point she would light up as if her cash-power meter had just been replenished, and she was suddenly quite beautiful. She looked up now as Angel's frame blocked the natural light from the doorway, and beamed when she saw who it was.

'Mama-Grace! *Karibu!* How are you?'

'I am well, thank you, Leocadie. How is little Beckham?' The baby had been named long before his birth for his incessant kicking at his mother's belly.

'He's fine, Mama-Grace. But he's always hungry!'

'*Eh!* There are babies who are like that. And how is Modeste?' Modeste was Beckham's father. Angel knew very well how Modeste was, because she had just seen him. But that was not what she was asking.

'*Eh!*' said Leocadie, as she transferred Beckham from her left breast to her right. 'That other woman's baby will come in one month. Modeste says if it is a girl he will choose me. He says a man must be with his son. But if it is a boy then we don't know. He'll try to decide.'

Angel shook her head. 'I hope that he'll take the matter to his family. A family can always help a person to make the right decision.'

'*Eh*, Mama-Grace, there is no family to help him to decide. Everybody died. It is only Modeste now. He must decide alone.'

'That is very difficult,' said Angel. She meant that it was very difficult to lose your whole family, and that it was very difficult to make alone a decision that a family should make, and that it was very difficult to wait for a man to decide between you and another woman. 'Let us hope and pray, Leocadie.'

'That is all we can do, Mama-Grace.'

'But I cannot stay and chat. Benedict has malaria and I must go home and be with him. I have only come to buy sugar.'

Stepping into the container, Angel helped herself to a small bag of sugar from the sparsely stacked shelves lining its walls. It was more expensive to buy from Leocadie than from the market or one of the small supermarkets in town, but the shop was very convenient for things that had been forgotten on the family's weekly shopping trip, or for things that had run out sooner than expected. The shop stocked essentials only: goods such as sugar, powdered milk, tea, eggs, tins of tomato paste, salt, soap, washing powder, toilet paper. A wire wound surreptitiously up the trunk of the jacaranda tree next to the container to join an overhead electrical cable; this powered the small fridge inside the container that kept bottles of Primus and soda cool.

As Leocadie was trying to count out Angel's change without disturbing Beckham, Faith appeared breathlessly in the shop's doorway to report that a lady had come about a cake, and that Angel must come home at once.

Angel found the lady seated in her lounge, encouraging Grace as the child struggled with her few words of school French. The visitor rose to shake Angel's hand.

'*Bonjour,* madame. *Comment ça va?*'

'*Bien, merci,*' replied Angel.

'*Vous êtes* Madame Angel?'

'*Oui, je suis Angel.* But, madame, we have now used up all the French that I know! *Unasema Kiswahili?* Do you speak Swahili?'

'*Ndiyo.* Yes.'

'Good. Then let us speak Swahili and we will understand each other. Please sit down, madame. Girls, Safiya is waiting for you upstairs. Take your homework.'

The girls had their homework books ready. They bid *au revoir* to their guest and hurried out of the apartment as Angel perched on the edge of the sofa and smiled at the woman, who smiled back at her from across the coffee table. She was of medium build with long, delicate braids falling loosely around her pretty face, which was adorned with a pair of gold-rimmed glasses. Angel guessed that she could not be more than thirty years old.

The woman introduced herself. 'Madame Angel, my name is Odile. I am a friend of Dr Rejoice. She is the one who sent me here to you.'

'I'm happy to meet you, Odile. If you're a friend of Dr Rejoice you're my friend too, so let's not be formal with each other. Please call me just Angel; let's forget about madame.'

'OK, Angel,' said Odile, smiling widely.

Angel stood up from the sofa. 'Odile, you are very welcome in my home. But could I ask you to excuse me for just one minute? I have a child here with malaria, and I need to check on him.'

'Eh!' Odile rose to her feet, her face registering concern. 'It's lucky that I came to you when you have a sick child, Angel, because I'm a nurse.'

'Eh! A nurse? Come with me, then, Odile, we'll check on him together. But really, I think the fever is almost over now.'

Angel led Odile into the children's bedroom, where Benedict lay asleep in one of the lower bunks. Quietly they took turns to place a hand on his damp forehead and, feeling that the fever had at last broken, they smiled at each other with relief.

'He's going to be fine,' whispered Odile.

'Yes,' agreed Angel, as they made their way out of the room.

They took up the same seats as they had before, on opposite sides of the coffee table.

'Obviously you've been keeping his fluids up?'

'Yes, and fortunately he's been thirsty, so I haven't had to force him.' Angel clapped her hands together. 'Eh! I feel blessed that a nurse has come to me today to help me to check on him!'

Odile smiled. 'Actually, I didn't come to you as a nurse, Angel. I came to you as a person who is wanting to order a cake.'

'Then I'm blessed twice today! But before we begin to talk business, let me make some tea for us to drink. While I'm doing that, you can look through my photo album and see some cakes that I've already made, and there is also one on the table over there that's waiting to be collected.'

When Angel emerged from the kitchen with two steaming mugs of milky tea, apologising for not having a slice of cake to offer her guest, Odile was at the work table looking admiringly at the cake that waited there. Angel put the mugs down on the coffee table and went to join her.

'That cake is for a christening,' she explained. 'The baby is the daughter of the sister of a neighbour's driver.'

'It is truly perfect!' declared Odile. The oblong, one-layer cake was coated in powder-pink frosting. Around the sides of the cake the pink was decorated with white frills resembling lace. Both the top left corner and the bottom right corner of the upper surface were adorned with lilac roses and white rosebuds tipped with strawberry pink. And across the centre of the cake, starting at the bottom corner on the left and sloping up towards the top corner on the right was the baby's name in lilac cursive script: *Perfect*.

'That is a wonderful name for a girl,' said Odile.

'Indeed,' beamed Angel. 'I helped the mother to choose it. But come and sit, Odile. You know, I thought of becoming a nurse myself, but then I became a mother instead. But the world is different now. Now a woman can become a nurse *and* a mother.'

The two women sat and took a sip of their tea.

'Are you perhaps a nurse *and* a mother, Odile?'

'Oh, no, no.' Odile shook her head, putting her mug down on the table. 'No, Angel, I'm just a nurse.' Her voice had become quieter, and a little sad. Angel watched as Odile's eyes stared through and beyond her mug of tea, and saw a vertical furrow beginning to deepen just above where the young woman's glasses met across her nose. It was clear that thinking about not being a nurse *and* a mother was making her guest feel uncomfortable.

'And tell me, Odile,' she said, her voice as cheerful as she could make it, 'where is it that you are a nurse?'

To Angel's relief, Odile's smile returned. 'I work at the Centre Médico-Social in Biryogo. Do you know it?'

'No, I don't know that place. But my husband and I have driven through Biryogo. *Eh!* The people in that part of town are too poor!' The tiny makeshift dwellings of wood, corrugated iron, cardboard and plastic sheeting that the people of Biryogo called home were not a new sight to Angel. Such places clung to the outskirts of most cities on the continent, providing shelter for those with nothing who had come to the city in the hope of something, only to find themselves contending instead with a different kind of nothing.

'It's not a beautiful place to work,' agreed Odile. 'But it's where God needs me. The centre is for people who are infected. We do testing and counselling, and we educate people, especially women. For example, we're training sex workers to do sewing; then they can earn money from sewing instead of from sex.'

'*Eh!* That is good work,' said Angel, and her thoughts went to Jeanne d'Arc, the sex worker who did occasional business in the compound. She was a nice enough girl, but really, that was not a good job to have.

'This disease is a very bad thing,' said Odile.

'*Eh!* Uh-uh,' agreed Angel, shaking her head.

'Uh-uh,' echoed Odile, and she shook her head, too.

'One of the girls you met here today, Odile, the one you were talking with in French. Grace. She has two brothers who are also with me here. The disease you are talking about took their mother, and it would have taken their father, too. It's only that robbers shot him instead.'

'*Eh! Grace* mentioned her *frères*; she showed me the family photos,' Odile indicated the four framed pictures mounted on the wall, 'but I thought they were all your children. I didn't know that you had adopted orphans.'

'In fact they're my grandchildren. It's my son who got shot.'

'Oh, I'm very sorry, Angel, I didn't know.'

'Thank you, Odile. In fact there are five grandchildren who are now my children. *Five!* Because my daughter is late, too.'

'Oh, that is very sad.' Odile shook her head. 'May I ask . . . forgive me, Angel, as a nurse I'm curious about the late. May I ask about what took your daughter?'

'Of course you can ask, Odile, and to tell the truth I don't mind at all to talk about such a thing with somebody who is a nurse. It was stress that took her.'

'Stress?'

'Blood pressure. She drove herself too hard after her husband left her. Worked herself to death. Everybody knows that such a thing is possible.'

Odile hesitated for a moment before saying, 'It's certainly not impossible, Angel. Was it her heart?'

'No, no. Her head.' Angel pressed her right hand to her temple.

'Her head?' Odile mirrored the gesture. 'Something like a stroke?'

'A very bad headache. That's how her friend explained it to us. And really, Odile, that was not unexpected, because even as a child Vinas would get headaches sometimes, especially at the time of school exams and so on. Her friend said she'd been having a lot of headaches from working too hard, and also from her blood pressure.'

'I see . . .' said Odile.

'And of course everybody knows that stress and blood pressure go together with headaches.'

'Yes. What exactly did the doctor say, Angel?'

'Well, no, we didn't speak to a doctor,' said Angel. 'By the time Pius and I got to Mount Meru Hospital, Vinas was already late.'

'Mount Meru? In Arusha?'

'Yes. Vinas fell in love with Winston in Dar es Salaam while she was studying to be a teacher; then when she qualified she went to live in Arusha with him because his family was there. *Eh!* She loved him so much, Odile! When he left her, we begged her to come back to us in Dar, but by then she was deputy to the *Mwalimu Mkuu* at her school, next in line to be head herself, and she preferred to stay there. But she pushed herself too hard. *Eh!*' Angel closed her eyes and shook her head. 'I wasn't by her side, Odile. I didn't see what she was doing to herself.'

'That is very sad.'

'I failed to recognise the signs of stress. The last few times I saw her I noticed that she was reducing nicely,' Angel patted the sides of her ample thighs, 'but I didn't know it was dangerous to be so stressed.'

Odile mirrored Angel's sad smile, and they sipped their tea in silence for a while before Odile spoke again. 'Angel, may I ask you another question? As a nurse?'

'Yes, of course.'

'I'm wondering . . . bearing in mind . . . are your grandchildren well?'

Angel knew at once what she meant and nodded her head. 'When my son and his wife found out that they were positive, their doctor in Mwanza said the children should be tested, just to be sure. We were worried about Benedict,' she gestured towards the door of the children's room where the boy lay, 'because he sometimes doesn't seem as strong as other boys, but all three are negative.'

'That's good. I'm sure that five grandchildren make a heavy enough load, even when they're well.'

Angel forced a smile. '*Eh*, they keep me busy enough! The two girls that you met are the oldest, and I must confess to you as a nurse that recently I've started to become afraid for them. They'll start to become young women soon and boys will start to notice them. I think my heart will stop beating if the virus gets to one of them.'

'Angel, that's not going to happen,' assured Odile. 'Obviously you've spoken to them about it?'

'*Eh!* It's difficult for somebody who is my age, Odile. We are the ones who did not talk to our own children about sex. That is how our own parents raised us. Now, how can we talk to our grandchildren about sex?'

Odile was quiet for a while as she drank the last of her tea. Then she said, 'Perhaps I can help you, Angel. At the centre we have a small restaurant. It provides jobs for women who are positive. They're not sick, but they cannot find other jobs because some employers discriminate when they know that a person is positive. So they cook and serve in our restaurant, and that teaches the community that the food cooked by a positive somebody is safe to eat. It also brings in a little bit of money for the centre. Now, I'm thinking this: perhaps the girls can come and have lunch with me at our restaurant one day. I can tell them about the work of the centre and even show them the things that we do there. We can talk about the disease and about sex, and I can answer their questions. Do you think that is perhaps a good idea?'

Angel's eyes began to fill with tears, and she reached into her brassiere for a tissue. Odile's idea was a very good one indeed. 'Would it be OK with your boss?'

'Yes, of course. It would be during my lunch break, so it wouldn't take me from my duties. You can just tell me what day you'll bring them. I've been on leave this week, but I'll be back there from Monday.'

'I'm very grateful, Odile! You're lifting a big burden from my shoulders. But how can I repay you?'

Odile smiled. 'You can give me a good price for my cake.'

'Eh! Nobody will get a better price than you! But forgive me, Odile, you came to order a cake, meanwhile I've bothered you as a nurse. That is not a professional way for me to behave towards a customer!'

'Oh, no, Angel, there's nothing to forgive. In any case, I'm not simply your customer, am I? You've already said that you and I are friends because we're both friends of Dr Rejoice.'

'That is true.' Angel slipped her tissue back into her brassiere, smiling at Odile. 'So tell me about this cake that I'm going to make for my friend.'

'Actually, the cake is for a celebration party for my brother. The Belgian embassy has awarded him a scholarship for further studies in Belgium.' Odile was radiant with pride.

'Eh! Congratulations! What will he study there?'

'Thank you, Angel. He'll study for a Master's in public health. He qualified as a doctor at the National University in Butare.'

'Eh! He is a very clever somebody!'

'Yes, but he will deny that. He says it's only hard work and the help of God that have taken him so far.'

'And you, Odile,' Angel said with a smile, 'are you not also a clever somebody to be a nurse?'

'Oh, no, Angel! For me also it was hard work and the help of God.' Then Odile was quiet for a moment before she said, 'Actually, my brother and I are both survivors.'

Angel knew what that meant: unlike the many Rwandans who had grown up outside the country and had come back home after the recent genocide was over, Odile and her brother had lived through it. They might have lost loved ones, they might have witnessed terrible things, they might have experienced terrible things. But they had survived.

'I'm sorry, Odile,' said Angel, knowing that this was not enough to say but also not knowing the words that could say enough. She shifted uncomfortably on the sofa, unsure what to say next. Perhaps the best— the most professional—thing for her to do was to bring the conversation back to the much easier topic of the cake.

But before Angel could say anything, Odile spoke again.

'I feel I can tell you about it, Angel, because you've already told me something of your own pain and loss, and because we're already friends through Dr Rejoice.' Angel gave her a small nod of confirmation. 'Actually, we were lucky. They killed me, Angel, but I did not die. My brother saved me, even though he wasn't yet fully qualified. And when they saw that he could be useful to them as a doctor they spared him and he protected me.' Odile was quiet for a few seconds before she continued, 'Afterwards, I got a job with Médecins Sans Frontières, translating for them between Kinyarwanda and French. They saw that I worked well with patients. They encouraged me to train as a nurse, and they even found sponsorship for me.'

Angel shook her head and clicked her tongue against the back of her teeth. 'You are strong, Odile. And your brother is strong, too.'

'It's God who made us strong, Angel.' Odile gave a big smile. 'And my brother will be even stronger when he gets his Master's degree. Really, I'm too, too proud of him! But as for his cake, I should tell you that I need it on Sunday. Is it possible for you to make it by then?'

'No problem. We can even deliver it to your house on Sunday morning on our way to church.'

'That will be very fine. Thank you.'

'Is there already a picture of this cake in your mind?'

'Actually, I've seen it in your photo album,' said Odile, picking up the album and turning a few pages. 'Perhaps something simple, like this. We'll not be many: maybe five or six friends, and of course my brother and his wife and their two small children. Can you write "*Félicitations, Emmanuel*" on it?'

'No problem,' said Angel, making notes on a Cake Order Form. 'Will Emmanuel's wife and children go with him to Belgium?'

'Unfortunately, the scholarship isn't enough for that, so they'll stay here. Actually, I live at their house, so while Emmanuel is away his wife isn't going to be alone with the children.'

'You are not married yourself?'

'Not yet.' Odile gave a small, shy smile. 'But perhaps one day soon, God will give me a husband.'

'Has He given you a fiancé at least?'

'Actually, not even a boyfriend!'

The front door flew open suddenly, and Daniel and Moses, the two youngest boys, clattered noisily into the apartment, followed by Titi. Angel made introductions, during which Benedict appeared in the doorway of the children's room with the thin and drawn look of a child who has at last stopped sweating and shivering in turn and will very soon—and very suddenly—demand a great deal of food.

Angel and Odile finished their business quickly and walked out into the street together to wait for a passing *pikipiki* to take Odile home. The motorbike-taxis were a relatively cheap form of public transport; bicycle-taxis were cheaper, of course, but this particular slope of the hill was too steep for the riders to climb and too nerve-racking for them to descend with their unreliable brakes.

As they waited, Ken Akimoto's Pajero turned off the tarred road onto the dirt road and pulled up outside the compound: Bosco had come to fetch his sister's christening cake. Angel introduced him to Odile, and amid much shaking of hands, he insisted on driving her home himself.

4. An Independence

DESCENDING THE STEPS that led down to the Chinese shop on Rue Karisimbi in central Kigali, Dr Rejoice Lilimani successfully deflected both a woman intent on selling her some baskets handwoven from banana-fibre, and a man who was urging her to buy one of his small stone carvings of mountain gorillas. She was on the point of entering the shop's busy and shadowy interior, crammed with shelves of kitchen and household goods, when somebody called her name.

She turned and looked back up towards the road from which the steps descended. Crowds of Saturday-morning shoppers weaved their way past the cars that were parked on the unsurfaced verge, while behind them packed minibus-taxis raced along the road on their way to the central minibus station on Rue Mont Kabuye.

She heard her name again: 'Dr Rejoice!'

'Who is calling Dr Rejoice?' she asked, a look of puzzlement furrowing her brow.

'It's me,' said a voice. 'Here I am.'

The doctor became aware of a movement to her left, where scores of brightly coloured plastic goods—enormous bowls, basins, dustbins and wash-baskets—lined the landing at the bottom of the steps outside the doorway into the shop. Above a purple dustbin a hand waved a piece of white tissue. Dr Rejoice took a step forward and peered around the dustbin into the patch of shade in which Angel sat on a tiny wooden stool.

'My dear! Hello! What are you doing sitting there?'

'Hello, Dr Rejoice.' Angel smiled as she dabbed at her face with the tissue that had attracted the doctor's attention. 'You didn't see me!'

'How was I to guess that you were sitting behind a purple plastic dustbin?' laughed Dr Rejoice. 'Are you OK, my dear?'

'Oh, I'm fine, really, thank you. I was inside the shop when I began to feel hot like someone had thrown a blanket over my head, so I had to come outside. They brought me a stool to sit here in the shade till I feel better.'

'Then let me ask them to bring a stool for me, too. I'll sit with you a few minutes.' Dr Rejoice went into the shop, returning moments later with a man carrying a plastic chair. He put it down next to Angel.

'*Murakoze cyane!*' Dr Rejoice thanked him in Kinyarwanda as she sat down. Then she addressed Angel. 'Now tell me, my dear, are you simply flashing, or are you ill?'

'Oh, I'm fine, really, Dr Rejoice. I'm just flashing. But I'm happy to see you, because I want to thank you. You sent me a new customer.'

'Oh, yes, and you made a delicious cake for her! I was at the party for her brother, Emmanuel.'

'Odile is such a nice girl,' said Angel. 'I'm very happy that I met her because she's going to teach my girls about the virus.'

'She'll do an excellent job,' Dr Rejoice assured her.

'She's encouraged me to learn about it, too,' said Angel. 'I'll go and spend some time at that place where she works, and I'll speak to the people who go there. My son would have been like them, Dr Rejoice.

He was positive, but then he got shot. I never warned him about it when he was a child; I didn't even know about it then. None of us did. It was only later, as others around us began to get sick and die, that we learned what it was and what to call it. So when Joseph brought his children to us in Dar from their home in Mwanza, and he told us that AIDS had come to his house, then I felt somehow that I had failed him as a mother because I hadn't warned him.'

'*Eh*, my dear!'

'Now my heart will stop beating if I fail my grandchildren, too. As a grandmother, it's my job to be wise. But how can I be wise if I don't educate myself about this disease?'

'You are very wise to think that way, my dear. Next time you're at the clinic I'll give you some information to take home to read.'

'Thank you, Dr Rejoice. You know, I'm not even going to wait for next time when one of the children is sick. I'll come to the clinic to fetch that information on Monday.'

'I'll leave it with the nurse at reception in case I'm busy when you come. You know how crazy it is there! Now, what did you come here to buy, my dear? I've come for an extra blanket because some members of my family are coming to visit from Nairobi. I don't want you to go inside and feel again like someone has thrown a blanket over your head. Would you like me to shop for you?'

Angel laughed. 'Thank you, Dr Rejoice, but I'm fine now, really. I'll come in with you. I need to buy another mixing bowl for my cakes, because my orders are increasing.' Angel looked at her watch and started to get up from the tiny stool, using the arm of Dr Rejoice's plastic chair for leverage. 'My husband has gone to the market for our weekly groceries. He always manages to get a better price than I do. He says I'm unable to concentrate only on the price of the sweet potatoes that I want because I look at the seller and I think about the work that she has done to clear the land and to plant the seeds and to harvest the sweet potatoes, and I know that she has children to feed. My husband says that as soon as you look at the seller, the seller is going to get more from you. He says that you must ignore the seller and see only what she is selling.'

'He sounds like an economist,' said Dr Rejoice with a smile. 'Are you sure he doesn't work for the World Bank?'

Angel laughed. '*Eh!* If he worked there he wouldn't need to negotiate a fair price: he'd have money to waste. But let's go in now. I must be waiting for him outside the German butchery when he's finished at the market.'

In the afternoon, Angel looked forward to some peace and solitude. Titi had already taken the boys to play with their friends who lived down the road, and the girls were busy dressing up for the birthday party of their friend Zahara, who came from Uganda. Pius had gone to his office to send some emails, but he would be back shortly to take the girls—and Zahara's aeroplane cake that Angel had made—to the party. From there he would go straight to a colleague's house to watch football on TV.

Angel had borrowed a Nigerian video from the wife of one of Pius's colleagues. Such videos were generally unsuitable for children, and she had been warned that this one was particularly full of witchcraft, adultery, betrayal and vengeance. An afternoon alone in the apartment with a good film was exactly what she needed.

'Are you ready, girls?' she called. 'Baba will be here very soon and you know he doesn't like to wait.'

The girls came out of the bedroom looking so pretty in their party dresses that tears began to prick the back of Angel's eyes. Grace was tall, with long, thin arms and legs that seemed to have little more than bone in them. Her skinny neck seemed barely able to support her head, yet she was fit and strong. Neat cornrows controlled her long hair, ending today in pale blue ribbons that matched her blue and white dress.

Though just a year younger, Faith was a good deal shorter and much rounder. She liked to keep her hair short, and this could make her cheeks appear rather chubby. While Grace looked like a girl on the verge of blossoming into a beautiful young woman, Faith still looked very much like a child. Her lilac and pink party dress stretched tight across her belly.

Physically, the two girls could never be mistaken for sisters. But even though they had barely known each other until they had suddenly found themselves part of the same household a year ago, they had become closer friends than many sisters that Angel knew. In fact, all the children got on well with one another—which was rather a relief, as it would have been very awkward if there had been problems between the two sets of siblings. Benedict was a bit of a worry, though: he was still struggling to find his niche in his new family. He was closer in age to the girls than he was to the younger two boys, and while he found much of his brothers' play somewhat childish, he did not share his sisters' interests either. This made him a rather lonely child, and Angel suspected that his frequent bouts of illness were at least in part a way of calling attention to himself. Not that he pretended to be ill, but perhaps he was more susceptible to germs because he did not feel emotionally strong.

Pius arrived back from his office, bringing Zahara's father with him. Dr Binaisa had escaped from home to the campus, as the busyness and excitement of party preparations had made it difficult for him to concentrate on his students' essays. Pius had found him there a few hours later, and it made sense to bring him to the apartment to collect the cake and then to deliver him to his own home along with the girls.

When he saw the cake waiting on Angel's work table, Dr Binaisa let out a low whistle. Appearing to float above the deep blue sky with white clouds that decorated the cake-board was a magnificent grey aeroplane with wings and tail fins. A pale blue window across the front indicated the cockpit, while both sides of the fuselage were lined with oval passenger-windows in the same pale blue. Across the centre of each wing ran a diagonal band bearing narrow stripes of black, yellow and red—the colours of the Ugandan flag—and on either side of the vertical tail fin, written with the red Gateau Graffito pen, were the words *Air Zahara*. Two rows of candles, five in each row, fanned out from behind the tail within a stream of white icing vapour trail.

'When you light the candles it will look like the plane's engines are firing,' explained Angel.

For a moment Dr Binaisa was lost for words.

'This is a very fine cake, Mama-Grace,' he managed. 'A very fine cake indeed. You know, after I placed the order for this cake I began to feel uncomfortable about the price. I told myself it was a lot of money to pay for a cake for a child who is only ten. A girl. I didn't discuss the price with my wife, of course, because financial matters are not a woman's concern. And I didn't want to ask anyone else what they thought about the price, because I didn't want to appear foolish for having agreed to such a high price. But now that I'm looking at the cake, I'm thinking that Mama-Grace has surely charged me too little for all this work.'

'If just one person comes to me to order a cake because they like this one that Dr Binaisa ordered for his child, then I will not think that I charged too little,' replied Angel.

'I'll make sure that many people come to you, Mama-Grace,' assured Dr Binaisa.

'I'm glad you're happy, Baba-Zahara. I think this is a cake that will be talked about for many weeks.'

'No, Mama-Grace, you are wrong. It is a cake that will be talked about for many *months*. But I'm worried that Zahara will love it too much. She won't want to cut it and eat it.'

Angel laughed. 'Baba-Zahara must tell her that it's a chocolate cake. Eating it will be the best part.'

A few minutes later, after she had seen the cake safely into the red Microbus and waved goodbye to everyone, Angel put the Nigerian video into the video machine and settled into a chair with her feet up on the coffee table. She was about to press play on the VCR's remote control when somebody knocked on the door.

'*Karibu!*' she called, taking her feet off the table.

But nobody came in. Instead, they knocked again.

'*Karibu!*' she repeated, more loudly this time. But the person on the other side of the door was either deaf or unable to understand plain Swahili. Angel pushed herself up out of the chair and went to open the door. She was hoping it would be just a passing beggar or someone intent on trying to sell her something—although it would be unusual for such a person to get past Modeste and Gaspard.

She opened the door to find a woman standing there, someone with whom she had exchanged greetings often, but who had never before knocked on her door.

'Hello, Angel,' said Jenna, the CIA's wife. 'I hope I'm not disturbing you. I saw you saying goodbye to your family outside, so I thought you'd be alone and it might be a good time to call.'

'You're not disturbing me,' lied Angel. 'You're welcome, Jenna.' She led her guest to the sofa and indicated that she should sit down.

'Thank you,' said Jenna, perching on the edge of the sofa and clasping her hands together in her lap.

Angel looked at her guest. She was an attractive young woman with short dark hair and green eyes. Her smart, cream-coloured trousers and long-sleeved white blouse indicated that this woman knew how to dress respectfully in a country where women were modest. Her only piece of jewellery was a gold cross that hung from a chain round her neck.

'These apartments all look the same,' she said to Angel, her eyes darting around the room. 'We all have the same furniture and curtains.'

'Yes,' agreed Angel. 'Sometimes when I'm with Amina, after a while I find myself thinking that it's time for her to leave so that I can go into the kitchen and start baking. But then I realise that it's me who must leave because we're in Amina's apartment, not mine.'

Jenna laughed. 'I've made that same mistake myself. Sitting on the couch at Ken's or Linda's I could just as well be sitting on the couch in my own apartment.'

Angel experienced a sudden feeling of discomfort at the mention of

Linda, whom Bosco had seen kissing Jenna's husband. She must change the subject at once.

'I'm happy that you feel at home in my apartment!' she declared, smiling warmly. 'Let me make some tea for us to drink.'

'Oh, no, Angel, I don't want to disturb you for very long. I only came to order a cake.'

'But ordering a cake is something that takes time and care,' countered Angel. 'And when you're bringing me business, then you're not disturbing me at all. Here, let me give you my photo album to look at while I make tea. You can see pictures here of other cakes that I've made.'

'Thank you. But do you have coffee instead? We're not big on tea in the States.'

'No problem. My husband prefers coffee sometimes. I'll make you some coffee that comes from my home town of Bukoba, on the western shores of Lake Victoria. It's very good.'

When Angel returned to the lounge with a mug of coffee, another of sweet and spicy tea, and a plate of cupcakes, Jenna pointed to a few of the photos in the album. 'I've seen these cakes,' she said. 'I've eaten them, too. At Ken's place.'

'Ken is one of my best customers,' said Angel. 'I've almost lost count of the number of cakes I've made for his dinner parties. Do you want to order a cake for a dinner party of your own?'

'Oh, no, I'm not a good cook. I couldn't possibly give a dinner party. If Rob wants to invite people, then we take them out for dinner. No, I'm actually here to order a cake on behalf of the American community.'

'*Eh*, that's an important job,' exclaimed Angel, 'to speak on behalf of the American community.'

'Yes, I suppose it is important. I hadn't thought of it like that!'

'And why does the American community want a cake?'

'It's for our Independence Day celebrations. We want a big cake decorated to look like the American flag.'

'*Eh*, that's a good flag!' declared Angel. 'It has red and blue and white, and there are stripes and stars. It's not boring like the Japanese flag. Did you see that photo? I made that cake for Ken.'

Jenna found the right page in Angel's photo album. 'This one here is nice, though.'

Angel looked at the photo that Jenna was indicating. 'That's the flag of South Africa. It's a very fine flag; it has six colours. *Six!* That cake was for someone who works at King Faycal. There used to be many South Africans working at that hospital, but most of them have left now. You know, one thing I enjoy about Kigali is that you can meet people from all over the world here.'

'I guess so,' agreed Jenna. Then she hesitated for a few moments before adding, 'But it's not like that for everyone.'

Angel was confused. 'What do you mean?'

'Well, I'm sure people from everywhere come and order cakes from you, and your husband probably has colleagues from everywhere, and I guess anyone who has a job here is able to meet people from everywhere. But I don't have a job.'

'What kind of job are you looking for?'

Jenna gave a small, strained laugh. 'Oh, I can't take a job. Rob doesn't like me to leave the compound without him. It's not safe.'

Angel had been about to swallow a large sip of tea. She fought the shocked urge to spray the tea out of her mouth and, swallowing it badly, she began to cough. Jenna tutted with concern. Eventually Angel managed to calm the coughing with a few small sips of tea, but by then her face had grown very hot and her glasses needed a polish.

'Are you OK, Angel? Shall I bring you some water?'

'I'm fine.' Angel dabbed at her face with a tissue before rubbing her glasses with the edge of her *kanga*. 'It's only that I was surprised when you said it's not safe here. Personally, I've found it very safe.'

'Well, Rob has told me not to go out without him,' shrugged Jenna.

'And when you go out *with* your husband, how is it that you're not meeting people from everywhere in the places that you go?'

'Oh, we go to the American Club every Friday night. That's when all the people from the States get together. Others are welcome, of course, but usually there are just a handful of people from other places— England or Canada, mostly. And often we go for dinner or parties at the homes of other Americans, or we take them out for a meal. And of course there are Ken's parties here in the compound.'

'And what is it that keeps you busy when you're not out with your husband?' asked Angel.

'Oh, I read a lot,' said Jenna. 'My family sends me books and magazines from home. And I have a laptop, so I spend hours emailing friends and family back home. And I'm on the committee of wives who organise social events for the American community. We meet in my apartment over coffee once a fortnight.'

'You know, Jenna, I've always found that tea and cake make a meeting run more smoothly, and I'm sure that for Americans coffee and cake can work just as well. You can order a plate of cupcakes like these from me anytime. I can even make the cupcakes taste of coffee, or I can make the icing taste of coffee.'

Jenna laughed. 'I'll remember that, Angel.'

Angel continued to rub gently at her glasses with the edge of her *kanga*. 'Tell me, Jenna, do you like to stay in your apartment so much? Do you never wish that you could just go out by yourself?'

Jenna breathed in deeply and gave a long sigh. 'Sometimes. Sometimes I feel like I'm going to go mad with boredom. Sometimes I wonder what on earth I'm doing here. But I knew when I married Rob that his work would take him all over the world. We talked about it, and he made it clear that he wanted me to travel with him; he didn't want a wife who was going to insist on staying at home in the States. He was married twice before, you see; he's quite a bit older than me, so he knows about life and about the world. But I'm just a small-town girl. I lived at home with my mom and dad the whole time I went to college, and then I married Rob, and this is the first time I've ever been out of the States. He did warn me it wouldn't be easy. I can't complain. And he would never let me do anything that would put me in any danger, because he really loves me. So if he says it's not safe for me to go out, then I have to respect that. He . . . he knows a lot of stuff.'

Angel thought that it was only to be expected that the CIA knew a lot of stuff, because knowing a lot of stuff was the CIA's job. But she also thought that he might be making up a lot of stuff to make his wife believe that it was not safe to leave the compound. That way he could be certain that she was never going to be in the car park of the Umubano Hotel when he was there kissing Linda.

'OK,' said Angel, 'let's imagine just for a moment that your husband didn't bring you here to Kigali. Instead, you went with him to another place, any other place, and he said that place was safe and you could get a job there. What job would you look for?'

'Oh, I don't know.' Jenna thought for a while. 'At college I did a degree in modern languages: French and Spanish. But I married Rob as soon as I graduated, so I've never worked—except for teaching kids at Sunday school.'

'So maybe you'd like to teach languages at a school?' suggested Angel.

'Oh, no, I don't think so. I know this'll sound crazy, but to be honest, I don't like kids so much. But I think I could be a good teacher to adults. I thought of offering to teach French to some of the American wives here, but Rob said it wasn't a good idea. He said if I became their teacher, it would make things difficult for me socially.'

Still not sure that her glasses were properly clean, Angel continued to worry at them with the corner of her *kanga*. 'And what is it that *you* say, Jenna?' she asked. 'You've told me many things that your husband has said, but he's not the one who's sitting here with me this afternoon. You told me that you're here on behalf of the American community, but you didn't tell me that you're here on behalf of your husband.'

'I'm sorry?'

'Well, imagine that I was sitting here telling you that my husband says what-what-what, my husband thinks what-what-what, my husband knows what-what-what. Then you're sitting there telling me *your* husband's what-what-what. Then our husbands may as well be sitting here talking together instead of us. Really, we would just be mouths to speak our husbands' words.'

Jenna looked surprised and did not speak for a while. Then she said, 'I guess I do spend a lot of time repeating what Rob says. I never noticed that before.'

Angel put her glasses back on. 'That's why I'm asking you about Jenna, because it's Jenna who is visiting me now, not her husband. What is it that *Jenna* says? What is it that is in Jenna's heart?'

Jenna opened her mouth to speak but no words came out. Her eyes began to well with tears. Angel was alarmed: making a customer cry could surely not be a good thing; she must try to fix her mistake at once.

'*Eh*, Jenna, I didn't mean to upset you, I'm very sorry. Let me make you another cup of coffee and we can talk about the Independence party that the American community will have.'

Jenna dabbed at her eyes with a tissue that she had retrieved from the pocket of her smart cream trousers. 'I'm sorry, Angel. It's not your fault that I'm crying, really it's not. It's . . . well, it's Rob. You asked me what's in my heart, and . . . and I know I talk about him all the time, but . . . but . . .' She blew her nose. Then she took a deep breath. 'Angel, I suspect . . . I suspect that my husband . . .'

Jenna did not finish her sentence, but Angel could have finished it for her: *I suspect that my husband is having an affair*. This was a suspicion that needed some very sweet tea. 'Jenna, I am going to let you sit here and calm down while I make tea for both of us. I know that you prefer coffee, but really, when someone is upset it is only tea that can help. When someone is unhappy, tea is like a mother's embrace.'

Angel went into the kitchen and set about boiling some milk, leaving Jenna on the sofa to blow her nose and to take deep breaths. She was visibly calmer when Angel returned with their mugs of tea.

Jenna took a sip. 'Hey, this is good. Spicy.'

'It's how we make our tea back home.'

A short silence followed, during which Jenna savoured the tea and prepared herself to speak, and Angel nibbled at a cupcake and prepared herself to register surprise at what Jenna was about to reveal.

'Can I speak to you in confidence, Angel?'

'Jenna, you are my customer and I am a professional somebody. I do not spread my customers' stories. Tell me what is in your heart.'

'Thanks, Angel. It's a real relief to have someone to talk to about this. I don't even know if what I suspect is true or if I'm just imagining it, and I know that if I voiced my suspicion to anyone in the American community, the news would spread like wildfire. God knows what would happen . . .'

Angel thought of the gun that Bosco was sure Rob had. 'It's always wise to confide in the right person,' she said.

'Yes.'

'So what is it that you suspect, Jenna?' Angel put down her mug of tea so that she would not spill any when she pretended to be surprised.

Jenna sighed heavily. 'I suspect that my husband has been lying to me about where he's been and what he's been doing. And you know, he always told me that he left both his previous wives because he caught them having affairs, but now I'm sure *they* were the ones who left *him*. I bet they both found out for sure what I suspect now.'

Angel wanted the surprise to come, and to be over. It was making her head hurt and she wanted her tea. 'And what is it that you suspect?'

'Angel, I suspect . . . I suspect that my husband is working for the CIA.'

Angel did not need to pretend. Surprise shot through her body like a bolt of lightning, causing her to jump in her chair and knock the coffee table with her knees so that tea slopped out of both mugs and the cupcakes shook violently on their plate. '*Eh!*' she cried, getting up and rushing into the kitchen for a cloth, and '*Eh!*' again as she mopped up the spilt tea. Then she sat down and took a big swallow of tea before she could look Jenna squarely in the face. 'The CIA?'

'Yeah. I know it sounds crazy, and I keep trying to convince myself that I must be wrong, but I've overheard bits of phone calls and I've seen Rob locking documents in his briefcase, and I've often felt one hundred per cent sure that he's lying to me when I've asked him where he's been. His colleagues have let slip at socials that he's been one place when he's told me that he's been another place. And he's so secretive.'

Was it really possible that Jenna only suspected what everybody else knew? Was she really so naive that she did not think that all these signs could be telling her that her husband was having an affair? Angel took her glasses off and looked at them. Did they really need cleaning? She put them back on again. This was a very awkward situation indeed.

'*Eh*, Jenna, I don't know what to say.'

'Yeah, it's a shock, isn't it?'

'*Eh*, I am truly shocked.' Angel thought carefully before she spoke. 'You know, when I was at school in Bukoba, I had a teacher who told us that when you see smoke you can be sure that it is coming from a fire.'

'You mean there's no smoke without fire?'

'That's what our teacher told us. But it wasn't the truth. When I grew up, I found that there is something called dry ice. Do you know it?'

'Sure. It keeps ice cream cold out of the fridge.'

'Do you know that when you put water on dry ice it makes smoke?' Jenna nodded. 'So it's possible to see smoke and to think that there is a fire, but really the smoke is from dry ice that has got wet.'

Jenna thought for a moment. 'Are you saying that I might have jumped to the wrong conclusion about Rob?'

Was Angel saying that? No. Rob *did* work for the CIA; everybody knew it. That was not a wrong conclusion. But at the same time, Jenna had not reached the right conclusion, the conclusion that her husband was having an affair.

'What I'm saying is simply that you must think very carefully about what you've seen and heard, and what it might mean.'

'I've done nothing *but* think about it for weeks. It's not like I have much else to do with my time.'

'It must be very difficult. But I see from your cross that you're a Christian. Perhaps if you pray for guidance at church tomorrow . . .'

'Oh, I don't go to church here. Rob isn't a churchgoer and he says it's not safe for me to go without him. And if it's true that he's with the CIA, he must surely know how unsafe Kigali really is. That's why he doesn't let me do what other husbands let their wives do.'

Really, this was becoming too complicated. It was time to head back towards the safer business of ordering the cake.

'You know, Jenna, I cannot give you God's guidance, but I can give you my own—and I think that's why you've spoken to me about this. Number one, you need to find out the truth about your husband. Number two, you need to decide what to do with the truth that you find. Those are both things that are between you and your husband. But there is also a number three, and I think I can help you with number three. Number three, you must find a way to keep yourself busy at home to stop this thing eating at your mind like a plague of locusts. You have said that you want to teach adults, and your husband has said that you cannot go out of the compound and you cannot teach the American wives. To me, the answer is clear: you must teach Rwandan women, and you must teach them in your apartment.'

Jenna looked at Angel with big eyes. In the silence that followed, Angel finished her tea and swallowed the last bite of her cupcake. When she had finished, Jenna was still looking at her.

'What on earth would I teach them?'

'How to read.'

'I don't know how to teach that.'

'But you know how to read yourself. It's a skill, just like making a cake. I can teach somebody how to make a cake, even though nobody has taught me how to teach somebody how to make a cake.'

'But where would I get my students from?'

'I'll find them for you,' said Angel. 'Leocadie at the shop can read very little, mostly numbers for prices. And Eugenia who works for the Egyptian struggles to read. That's two students already. I won't have to go far to find a small class for you, maybe just four or five. They'll all be women that I know, not strangers. You'll tell me when you're ready to start teaching, and I'll bring the students to you.'

'I . . . I don't think Rob would like it . . .'

'You can teach for maybe an hour or so each day when he's at work. He won't even know.'

'But if I don't tell him what I'm doing, that would be dishonest . . .'

'Jenna, do you believe that honesty is important to your husband?'

Angel watched Jenna as she looked distressed and reached for her tea. She took a sip and swallowed it. Then she looked at Angel, and a smile began to play on her lips, stretching wider and wider until she was laughing out loud. Angel laughed with her. Even she had to admit that she had had a very good idea indeed.

'Angel, you're a genius!'

'*Eh*, thank you, Jenna. I'm not a genius, but I *am* very, very good at making cakes. So let's discuss the Independence cake that brought you to me this afternoon.'

After Jenna had gone and Angel had cleared the tea things off the coffee table, she removed the Nigerian video from the VCR and hid it away on top of the wardrobe in her bedroom where the children could not find it;

there would be no time for her to watch it now before her family started arriving home. And before they all came in with their clatter and their noise and their stories of the afternoon, she must climb the stairs to the top floor of the building and get a tablet from Sophie to take away the pain that had moved into her head with its boxes and was beginning to hammer nails into the walls for its pictures.

But Sophie and Catherine were both out and nobody answered her knock. Ken had helped her out with Tylenol before, but on a Saturday afternoon he was sure to be playing tennis at the Umubano Hotel. One flight down from Sophie and Catherine's apartment was Linda's, but Angel was not going to knock on Linda's door because who knew what might be going on behind it.

Across the landing from Linda's flat was Jenna's. Well, it was Jenna who had invited the pain into her head, so perhaps Jenna owed her a painkiller. She knocked on the door.

The CIA opened it.

Angel opened her mouth but no sound came out.

'Oh, hi, Angel. You OK?'

She cleared her throat and told herself to behave normally. 'Hello, Rob, I'm sorry to disturb you, I was just wondering if you could give me something for my headache. Sophie usually helps me, but she's out.'

'Sure, come on in. Jenna's just been telling me about visiting you this afternoon. I hope she didn't give you the headache!'

'No, no,' assured Angel, walking into the apartment past Rob and seeing a slightly anxious-looking Jenna. 'I think it was your flag that gave me the headache. We had to count all the stripes and all the stars in the picture in the children's atlas to be sure that I don't make a mistake with the cake. Do you know how difficult it is to count stripes? Your eyes tell you one number; meanwhile your head tells you a different number.'

Rob laughed. 'Well, I think we owe you a painkiller. Honey, go and see what we've got in the bathroom. Angel, sit down, take a load off.'

'No, thank you, Rob, I can't stay. The children will be home soon.'

'Hey, you know your cakes are really great. We've had them at Ken's.'

'Thank you, I'm glad you like them. Ken is one of my best customers.'

Angel noticed that Rob's hair was damp and he smelled of soap. Kigali was not a hot place like Dar es Salaam, where you sweated a lot and had to shower in the afternoon; the altitude here was too high for that. Of course, Angel sweated a lot herself occasionally—but Rob was definitely not having to deal with the same problem. She did not want to think about why he might have needed to shower at the end of a

Saturday afternoon that he had not spent with his wife.

Jenna came back from the bathroom rattling a small plastic container of tablets. 'There are only a few left in here, so you may as well take the lot with you. We've got plenty more.'

'Oh, no, Jenna, thank you, but Pius and I don't keep tablets at home. It's too dangerous . . . for the children. You know how children can think a tablet is a sweet. Just give me one to take now.'

'You're very wise,' said Jenna. 'Tell you what, I'll keep them here for you and you can come and get one anytime you need to.'

'Thank you very much. I'll remember that. Thank you, Rob. I'm sorry I disturbed you.'

'*Hakuna matata*, as you people say. No problem.' Rob put his arm around Angel's shoulder as he led her to the door. The intimate gesture surprised and shocked her. She barely knew this man; how could he insult his wife by embracing another woman while his wife was standing there watching? OK, he was an American, but surely in his CIA training he had learned what was acceptable behaviour in other countries and cultures? He was so close to Angel that she could smell the dampness in his hair. The intimacy made her feel as though a fat snake was slithering slowly over her bare feet and she had to remain absolutely still even though her instinct was to scream and run. She had to fight this man, even if only in a small way.

Breaking away from his encircling arm, she said, 'Oh, I almost forgot. Rob, I know that you're not a churchgoer yourself, but my family would very much like to invite Jenna to worship with us. Just up the road here at St Michael, near the American embassy. It's a very safe area, and a beautiful service, in English. I was wondering, would it be OK for her to join us one Sunday morning?'

Rob looked reluctant. Angel persevered.

'Of course, I'm probably asking too much of you. I'm sure that you work very hard during the week, and at weekends you simply want to spend time with your wife. I'm sure you wouldn't like to be without her for some two hours on a Sunday morning, left alone and looking for some way to fill that time.'

Rob's face lit up as if he had just had a very good idea. 'I'm sure I could manage, Angel. Of course Jenna can join you anytime she wants. You'd like that, wouldn't you, honey?'

'I'd love it,' said Jenna. 'Thank you, Angel. Thank you.'

As she went down the stairs, Angel carried with her the uncomfortable knowledge that she both deserved and did not deserve Jenna's thanks.

5. A Homecoming

EVERYONE AT *La Coiffure Formidable!*, just a short walk from the compound where the Tungarazas lived, was deeply impressed by the invitation card. It had been passed around from hairdressers to clients and back again, and was now in the hands of Noëlla, who took care of Angel's hair for a discount in gratitude for the good price that Angel had given her on her wedding cake. Noëlla ran the tips of her long, delicate fingers over the Tanzanian coat of arms on the card, exploring its ridges and dents.

'In English that's called embossed,' said Angel, rather more loudly than was necessary over the hum of the hairdryer under which she sat with her hair in green plastic rollers. 'That picture is the emblem of my country. Do you see there, in the middle of the shield, there's a small picture of our flag? And do you see that the shield is standing on top of our famous mountain, Mount Kilimanjaro? There's a man and a woman holding that shield there on top of the mountain. That's because in my country women are supposed to be equal with men. And do you see there it is written *Uhuru na Umoja*, freedom and unity? That's my country's motto. It means that we're all one people, united and free and equal.'

'*Eh!*' declared Noëlla. 'You have a very fine country.' Giving the invitation back to Angel, she switched off the dryer and lifted it away from her client's head.

'We're trying to be like that here,' said the young woman seated next to Angel who was having long braids woven into her hair by Agathe. 'We're striving to be united and equal. We are all Rwandans now.'

'Exactly,' agreed Noëlla, unwinding the rollers from Angel's hair. 'It doesn't matter if in the past some of us thought we were this and some of us thought we were that. There is no more this or that now. Now we are all *Banyarwanda*. Rwandans.'

'That is a very fine thing to be,' said Angel, who was always heartened by such talk of unity. But she had noticed that this was usually the talk of groups; it was possible for the talk of an individual away from a group to be quite different. She was grateful when the woman seated on the other side of her changed the subject.

'So tell us, madame, what is it that you will wear to this important party at your embassy this evening?'

'Yes, and who has made it for you?' added Noëlla.

Angel laughed. 'I'm sure you're expecting me to complain that Youssou has made a dress that's too tight for me!'

'Eh!' said the woman. 'I've heard about this Youssou, although I've never been to him. But don't think that he's the only tailor in Kigali who makes clothes that are too tight; they all do it. It's because they want to accuse you of gaining weight between when they measure you and when your dress is ready. Then they can charge you extra for the alterations. You know, my neighbour has taught me a very good trick which you must try. You must take a friend with you when you go to your tailor and when the time comes for the measuring, your friend must slip two of her fingers between the back of your body and the tape measure wherever he measures. So the tailor will write down a number which is bigger, and then when he makes a dress that is smaller than that number, it is the right size for your body.'

A collective eh! echoed around the small salon as the women looked from one to another with wonder on their faces.

'That is a very fine trick,' said Angel. 'I wish I had known about it before. But let me tell you another trick that I have discovered. I have found a group of women at a centre in Biryogo who are learning how to sew. You can go to them and they'll measure you correctly and they'll sew your dress carefully, and all the time their work is being supervised by their teacher, so it's good. OK, they're not yet experts like the tailors; they cannot yet make a dress from a picture. But if you take them a dress that you already have, they can copy it and make it in a different colour or a different fabric, and they can even make some small additions like adding frills or making the sleeves wider than they are on the original dress.'

'How are their prices?' asked Noëlla, who was now styling Angel's hair delicately with a wide-toothed comb so as not to destroy the curls.

'Eh, they're much cheaper than a tailor,' assured Angel. 'They've made my dress for tonight's reception and it fits perfectly. I'm going to look very beautiful among all those smart ladies.'

Of course, when Mrs Margaret Wanyika complimented Angel's dress that evening—as a hostess must—Angel was not going to tell her that it had been made by women who not only prostituted themselves, but may or may not be infected. If she were to do so, she was sure that Mrs Wanyika's hair would turn white immediately, and an emergency appointment would have to be made at the expensive salon in the Mille Collines Hotel. She did not share this thought with the women in this salon, though; Mrs Wanyika was, after all, her customer.

When Noëlla walked Angel out of the salon and stood with her in the morning sun for a brief chat before her next client arrived, Angel took the opportunity to ask her a question about Agathe.

'Do you think she'd like to learn to read?' asked Angel.

'Of course she would! She's often said that it's embarrassing for her when her children come home from school and they want to show her what they've written that day. But she cannot go to school at her age, and she needs to be at work: she has to feed and educate her children.'

'Do you give her time off for a break every day? To eat her lunch?'

'Of course I do.'

'Now what if I told you that she could go to school to learn to read during that time every day?'

'What?' Noëlla looked sceptical. 'Where? How would she pay for it?'

'The school is free and the teacher knows French. Agathe would learn to read in French. It would be nearby, in my compound. She would just have to walk two streets along and then two streets down and she would be there.'

'Agathe!' called Noëlla loudly, her voice filled with excitement.

A few moments later, Angel was on her way back two streets along and two streets down. She was just passing a half-built house that had never been completed because the people who had planned to live there had not survived, when Ken Akimoto's vehicle slowed beside her.

'Hello, Auntie!' called Bosco. '*Eh!* What are you doing walking in the street with such a beautiful hairstyle? A lady with such a hairstyle must travel in a car with a driver.'

Angel laughed. 'Hello, Bosco! Are you offering me a lift?'

'Yes, Auntie. I'm on my way to your compound but I can take you anywhere.'

'Thank you, Bosco, I'm on my way home.' Angel opened the door and struggled to climb up into the Pajero without splitting the long skirt that was already straining over her expanding hips. Really, these big vehicles with their high seats were not designed with ladies in mind; it was almost impossible for a lady to remain elegant as she got in. Fortunately the children always thought it a great honour to be the one chosen to sit up in the front of the red Microbus, and Angel was happy to sit on one of the seats in the back part that could be entered via a more manageable step.

'I've been shopping at the market for Mr Akimoto,' said Bosco, noticing Angel glancing at the big cardboard box of vegetables in the back as they set off towards the compound. 'He's having guests for dinner again this weekend.'

'I know. I'll be making a cake for him again. But tell me, Bosco, how is Perfect?'

'*Eh*, Auntie, she's a very, very nice baby! She's quiet and still, not like Leocadie's baby. *Eh*, that Beckham can cry! I used to think I wanted lots of babies; then I met Beckham and I thought, Uh-uh, babies are not a good idea. But then Perfect came, and she's very, very good, and I can see how much Florence loves to be her mother, so I thought again that babies were a very, very good idea.'

Angel laughed. 'You haven't even met the lady yet who will help you to get all these babies.'

Bosco pulled the Pajero to a stop outside the compound and turned to look at Angel with a big, happy smile on his face.

'*Eh*, Bosco! *Have* you met the girl who is going to become your wife?'

'I have met a very, very nice girl, Auntie.'

'Then you must come and drink tea with me and tell me all about her!'

'I can't come now, Auntie. I still have to unpack Mr Akimoto's vegetables in his apartment and take his crate of empties to Leocadie for sodas for his party, and then I must fetch him from his meeting.'

'Then tell me quickly now, Bosco. Who is this girl that you've met?'

'Do you remember that when I came to fetch the cake for Perfect's christening, I gave a lift to Odile?'

'*Eh!* Odile! You're in love with Odile! I was just telling the ladies in the salon about the place where she works.'

Bosco laughed. 'No, Auntie, it's not Odile. When I took her to her house I met her brother, Emmanuel, and his very, very beautiful wife.'

Angel felt her heart sinking. 'Bosco, please tell me that you have not fallen in love with Emmanuel's wife.'

'No, Auntie! Emmanuel's very, very beautiful wife has a young sister who is also very, very beautiful. That sister has a friend called Alice. Alice is the one that I love.'

Angel shook Bosco's hand. '*Eh*, Bosco. I am too happy! You must bring Alice to meet me soon.'

'Yes, Auntie. But I think Modeste is waiting for you. He is with a man. Perhaps he is a customer.'

The young man with Modeste was indeed a customer. Arriving at the compound, he had asked Modeste in which apartment he might find the madame of the cakes, and Modeste had reported that Angel was out but would probably be back soon. She had not waited for a *pikipiki* at this corner, and she had not gone along the unsurfaced road to where she could catch a minibus-taxi; she had gone up the hill on foot, so she had not gone far. The man had decided to wait.

Now he sat opposite Angel in her apartment, dressed in a suit and tie and looking extremely handsome and smart. There was something familiar about him, but Angel could not place him.

'Madame, allow me to present myself to you,' he said in English. 'I am Kayibanda Dieudonné.'

The local formality of stating a name backwards, with the first name last, had initially confused Angel, but she was accustomed to it now. She still found it too uncomfortable, though, to introduce herself to anyone as Tungaraza Angel.

'And I am Angel Tungaraza, but you must please call me Angel. May I call you Dieudonné?'

'Of course, madame.'

'Not madame. Angel.'

'Forgive me.' The young man flashed a smile that made him look even more handsome. 'Angel.'

'Do I know you, Dieudonné? There is something about your face that makes me think that we have spoken before.'

'We have never spoken, mad . . . Angel. But I have spoken to Dr Tungaraza when you have been with him. I'm a teller at BCDR.'

'*Eh!* Of course!' declared Angel, suddenly able to place her guest. Her husband's salary was supposed to be paid into his account at the Banque Commerciale du Rwanda at each month-end, but for one or other reason payment of expatriate salaries—in US dollars—was invariably delayed. It was only Dieudonné who could explain the situation clearly in English to Pius's colleagues from India. Many of the Indians would not deal with any other teller.

'Your English is very good, Dieudonné. I know that your president wants everyone to speak French and English equally now, but that is new; most Rwandans are still learning English, but you've already progressed very far in the language. That tells me that you've spent much time outside your country.'

'You are right, Angel.'

'Then I'll make tea for us and you can tell me your story while we drink it. Here is my photo album of cakes for you to look at.'

Angel made two mugs of sweet, spicy tea and brought them into the lounge on a tray along with two small plates, each holding a slice of pale green cake with chocolate icing. She handed tea and cake to her guest and then settled down opposite him. Dieudonné cut a mouthful from his slice of cake with the side of his teaspoon and tasted it with obvious enjoyment.

'Mm, delicious!' he declared. 'But this is not my first time to taste your delicious cake. In fact, I've found a picture of the very cake that I've tasted before.' He indicated a photograph on the page at which Angel's album lay open on the coffee table.

'Oh, that one I made for Françoise, for one of the parties that was held at her restaurant.'

'I was at that very party, and in fact I was the one who arranged it. My house is in the same street as Françoise, so I know her place. When I asked if some few of us from the bank could celebrate a colleague's promotion there, she told me that she could get a cake for us. Never before had I heard of eating cake after chicken and tilapia, but Françoise told me it is modern. She said that a cake can say anything that a person wants. This is the very cake that I asked for.'

As Dieudonné spoke he made large gestures with his hands and arms. This was not the usual Rwandan manner, which was calmer and more controlled; perhaps there was no space for big gestures in a very tiny country that had to accommodate eight million people. No, Dieudonné moved his body more like Vincenzo, Amina's husband, who was half Italian. Angel watched him as he took a sip of his tea.

'*Eh!*' he declared, and took another sip. 'I haven't drunk tea like this since I was in Tanzania!'

'You were in my country?'

'I looked for my family there for almost four years.'

'They were lost?' asked Angel. 'Did you find them?'

'They were not there.' Dieudonné took another mouthful of cake.

'You know, Dieudonné, I think you should tell me your story right from where it begins. I don't want to become confused by starting to hear the story in the middle. Start at the beginning, please.'

'Then I must start in Butare, because that is where I was born. My father was a professor there at the National University of Rwanda. I was still a small boy when Tutsis were chased from the university.' He paused, interrupting his story. 'Forgive me, Angel, we do not talk of Tutsis and Hutus any more; we are all *Banyarwanda* now. But I must use those words to talk about the past because in the past we were not yet *Banyarwanda.*'

'I understand,' assured Angel. 'You can speak freely with me, Dieudonné, because you are my customer and I am a professional somebody. We are confidential here.'

'Thank you, Angel.' Dieudonné cleared his throat and swallowed some more tea. 'My father was killed and we fled with our mother into Burundi, but only for a short time because then we fled again, this time to Congo, more specifically the town of Uvira. *Eh!* There were many refugees there, and there was a lot of confusion. I became separated from my family and I found myself being transported south to Lubumbashi with other small boys. We were schooled there by nuns. I was a good student, so the sisters arranged for me to go for secondary schooling with some fathers at a mission school across the border, in the north of Zambia. One of the Fathers there became like a father to me.'

'Let me guess, Dieudonné. Was that father from Italy?'

Dieudonné looked startled. '*Eh!* How did you know that?'

Angel laughed. 'The way you make gestures with your arms reminds me of someone I know who has Italian blood from his father.'

Dieudonné thought for a while as he chewed and swallowed another mouthful of cake. 'There are ways to father a child even when that child does not have your blood. Father Benedict was helping me by making enquiries to try to find my family, although it was difficult. By then many years had already passed since I'd been with them in Uvira. And at the time we became separated I was still small and I didn't know my mother's name. You know we Rwandans don't have a family name; there can be mother, father and six children, and no two of those eight will share a common name. In fact, by the time Father Benedict began to help me, I could no longer remember the name my parents had given me because the nuns in Lubumbashi had given me a new name: Dieudonné. It means God-given.'

He paused in his story to sip more tea and finish the last of his cake.

'So anyway, Father Benedict got news that two girls who might be my sisters were living in Nairobi. By then he had learned that my father had been called Professor Kayibanda at the university, and that my name had been Tharcisse. So he managed to get papers for me with the name Kayibanda Tharcisse Dieudonné, and through the Church I got a scholarship to study accounting in Nairobi. I found those two girls, and they were not in fact my sisters. *Eh*, that was a very sad day for me! Anyway, I stayed in Nairobi for three years until I qualified. In that time I got to know other Rwandans living there, and one of them was convinced that he had met one of my brothers and my mother in Dar es Salaam.'

'So of course you had to go to Dar yourself.'

'Exactly. I went to the place where the man who was supposed to be my brother was supposed to be working, but they told me there that he had left some months before, nobody knew exactly where. I went to the place where he was supposed to have lived with my mother, but the people there didn't know where they had gone.'

'*Eh!* That was a very difficult time for you.'

'Very.' Dieudonné shook his head. 'Anyway, I took a job in Dar doing the accounts for an Indian gentleman's businesses, and at weekends and in holidays I travelled to almost every town in Tanzania. Babati. Tarime. Mbeya. Tunduru. Iringa. Everywhere! I did that for nearly four years, but my family was not there.'

Angel tutted sympathetically.

'Anyway, by that time it was 1995. The genocide here was over, and many Rwandans in exile were coming home. I hoped that maybe my family would be among them, so I came home, too. I went to the UN High Commission for Refugees and gave them all the information I knew. I never heard anything from them until Monday morning this week . . .' Tears welled up in Dieudonné's eyes and he reached for a wad of toilet paper from his inside jacket pocket and dabbed at his eyes. 'Forgive me,' he said.

'There is nothing to forgive you for,' assured Angel. 'There's no shame in a man shedding tears. But I'm going to leave you here to cry the tears that you need to cry while I make some more tea for us.'

When Angel came back from the kitchen she saw that her guest had composed himself. She had cut him another thick slice of the cake, which she carried in from the kitchen, together with their fresh tea.

'Now,' said Angel, settling herself back in her chair and trying to get comfortable despite the restraints of her tight skirt, 'tell me about what happened on Monday morning.'

'A lady from the UNHCR telephoned me at the bank. She told me that they had found my mother and one of my sisters.'

'*Eh!*'

'In fact, they had crossed back into Rwanda from DRC at Cyangugu and they were looking for me. The lady told me that they were on their way to Kigali that very day, and would be reporting to the UNHCR offices by that evening. Immediately I went to my boss at the bank and requested compassionate leave because my family was alive.'

Again tears welled, and again Dieudonné dabbed. Angel found herself reaching into her brassiere for a tissue and dabbing at her own eyes. Dieudonné calmed himself with a sip of tea before continuing.

'I went home immediately and prepared my house for their homecoming. I went to Françoise and told her my news, and she agreed to cook tilapia for my family's dinner and to send someone with it to my house that night. Then I went to the UNHCR offices and waited for my family to come.'

'That must have been a very difficult wait,' said Angel.

Dieudonné blew his nose. 'Yes, it was not easy. They gave me a chair to sit on but I couldn't sit for more than a few seconds. But when I stood, my legs didn't want to hold me and I had to sit. But I couldn't sit still and I had to stand up. *Eh!* I was up and down like the panty of a prostitute.'

Angel laughed, and Dieudonné laughed with her. 'You must have been very happy and excited.'

'In fact, no,' said Dieudonné. 'What I felt most was fear. I was afraid that they had made a mistake and that the people would not be my mother and my sister. And I was also afraid that I wouldn't recognise my mother. I had been such a small boy when I had last seen her. But in fact, as soon as my mother stepped into the UNHCR compound I knew it was her, and she told me that she had seen my father's face in mine the very minute that she saw me. I was so relieved! Of course my sister and I didn't know each other, but we couldn't stop smiling at each other and crying.'

'*Eh*, Dieudonné, you have told me a very happy story!'

'Yes. And it's only this week that it became a happy story. Last week my story would still have been a sad one.'

They drank tea and ate cake in silence for a few moments, both of them thinking about how suddenly sadness and happiness can change places. It was Angel who broke the silence.

'And what about your other siblings?'

'My one brother is late and the other is still lost; we will continue to look for him. My other sister was violated by some soldiers and she gave birth, but the baby was ill and then my sister became ill and they're both late now.'

Angel heard the word that he was not saying.

He finished his slice of cake. 'So, Angel, I've come to order a cake because on Sunday afternoon my friends will come to my house to meet my family and help me to welcome them home.'

'For sure it will be a very happy party. I can make the cake on

Saturday and deliver it on Sunday morning on the way to church. If you're in the same road as Françoise, I'll find your house easily.'

'You're very kind, Angel.'

Angel laughed. 'You may think that I'm kind; meanwhile, I'm curious! I want to shake the hand of the mother and the sister that you've told me about in your story, so it's not a matter of kindness that I'll bring the cake to your house.'

'Then I must thank you for your curiosity.' Dieudonné reached into a pocket of his jacket and brought out a piece of paper. 'I've drawn a picture of the cake that I'd like you to make. Down the left side here it's red, and down the right side here it's green, and in the middle it's yellow.'

'Like the flag of Rwanda.'

'Yes, but our flag has a black R for Rwanda in the middle of the yellow. On the cake that R is still there, but it's part of the word *KARIBUNI*, which is written going downwards on the yellow.'

'*Eh*, you are a clever somebody, Dieudonné! This will be the perfect cake to say "Welcome home" to your family!'

Just then Titi arrived back from one of her frequent trips to the Lebanese supermarket to buy flour, eggs, sugar and margarine for Angel. She seemed a little agitated and Angel suspected that Titi wanted to speak to her alone, so she declared that Dieudonné had already been away from his family for quite long enough, and that they should complete the formalities of the Cake Order Form as quickly as possible.

As soon as Dieudonné had left the apartment, Angel went into her bedroom to release herself from her tight skirt. When she emerged dressed in a comfortable *kanga* and T-shirt, Titi broke the news that she had just been told by Leocadie: Modeste's other girlfriend had gone into labour. Modeste would go after work at the end of the day to see if she had delivered yet. Very soon the sex of the baby would be known, and that could determine which of the mothers Modeste would choose.

Angel longed to rush upstairs to share the news with Amina at once, but the children would be home from school very soon, and lunch must be prepared for them. Titi put some water to boil in a big pot on the stove and then began to slice some onions. Angel set a smaller pot of water to boil and started chopping some cassava leaves into very small pieces.

'You know, Titi, I'm worried for Leocadie. I'm worried that Modeste will simply not choose. Because why should he? If he can have two girlfriends and two babies, why should he choose to have one?'

'Ooh, Auntie.'

'That's how it is here, Titi. There are more women than men. Many men are late; many men are in prison. There are not enough men for every woman to have a husband. Some women agree to share a husband, because they've told themselves that a woman who is without a man is nothing. There are even men who've told themselves that, under these circumstances, taking more than one woman is like a service to the community.'

'Ooh, Auntie.'

'But let us not be sad today, Titi. Today I met somebody who told me a very happy story. Come, it's time for you to go and wait outside for the children's transport from school. I'll finish the cooking; then while we're eating our lunch I'll tell everybody the happy story that I've heard today.'

Later that afternoon, it was Amina's turn to hear Dieudonné's story from Angel. Amina had come to Angel's apartment to help her to dress for the function at the Tanzanian embassy.

The fabric of Angel's new dress was royal blue patterned with small butterflies embroidered in gold. The sleeves puffed up and out from the bodice, tapering to a small cuff at the elbow, and a broad row of frills spread out at her middle above a long, straight skirt to create the illusion of a waist. A simple gold chain adorned her neck; small gold hoops hung from her ears; her smart black sandals had kitten heels. She twirled for Amina, who looked at her friend critically before giving her judgment.

'When your husband comes home from work and sees you looking like this, his eyes will jump out of his head and run around the room like they've just scored a goal at football.'

Angel laughed. 'Thank you, Amina. *Eh*, it's nice to wear something smart that isn't tight. When do you think we'll hear news of Modeste's other girlfriend?'

'I don't know. It depends how long the girl is in labour.'

'I'll send Titi to the shop when Leocadie opens tomorrow. She'll come and tell us the news.'

'We must all support Leocadie tomorrow, because if the girl has not yet delivered it will be a difficult day for her. And of course it will be a difficult day for her if the girl has already delivered a boy.'

'Yes,' agreed Angel. 'I'll speak to Eugenia and some of the others, and we'll form a group and take turns to go and sit with her in the shop. Leocadie has no mother and no sister to support her; we will be those things for her tomorrow.'

6. An Inspiration

ON SATURDAY MORNING Angel baked two cakes: a round one in two layers for Ken Akimoto's dinner party that night, and a large oblong one for Dieudonné's homecoming celebration the following day, both in plain vanilla; the remaining batter made up a batch of cupcakes. In the afternoon, when the cakes had cooled, she settled down in the peace of the empty apartment to decorate them. Pius had gone off in his smart suit to attend the funeral of a colleague—TB, everybody said, although everybody knew that TB was not what they meant—and the children were all upstairs with Safiya, putting together a large jigsaw puzzle her uncle had sent her. Titi was keeping Leocadie company at the shop.

Modeste's other girlfriend had been in labour for more than two days now, and she had still not delivered. While some were convinced that the long labour heralded a baby boy—because boys were difficult even before they came into the world—others speculated that the mother was deliberately delaying the delivery because she feared that the baby was a girl whose birth would mark the end of her hold on Modeste.

'I don't want to be alone again, Mama-Grace,' Leocadie had said in the small, quiet voice of a child when Angel had been in the shop earlier that morning. 'After . . . afterwards . . . I was alone. Everyone was gone. Then I got Modeste and Beckham. I got a family.'

As the neighbourhood held its breath for the news, people found reason after reason to visit Leocadie's shop for some or other forgotten purchase. For Leocadie—at times tearful, at times brave—business had never been so good.

Angel once again had free rein in decorating Ken's cake, and she decided that she would use the same colours that she would be mixing up for Dieudonné's cake: red, yellow and green. Of course, it was possible for so few colours to be boring, but she was going to create a design that she knew would be meaningful to Ken. When she had delivered a cake to his apartment once before, her eye had been caught by a round design on a big black-and-white poster on the wall of his lounge. She had asked him about it.

'That is yin-yang,' he had explained. 'It's a Chinese symbol meaning balance.'

'It looks like two tadpoles,' Angel had observed. 'A black tadpole and a *Mzungu* tadpole.'

Ken had laughed. 'Yes, I can see that. A black tadpole with a big white eye and a white tadpole with a big black eye. But it's supposed to remind us that nothing is purely black or purely white; nothing is completely right or completely wrong, totally positive or totally negative. We need to find a balanced way of looking at every situation.'

'But why do you have a Chinese something on your wall?' Angel had asked. 'Are you not a Japanese?'

'Actually I'm Japanese-American. But that symbol has become universal. I like to sit here and look at it; it can help me to think more clearly.'

So Angel set about re-creating that same symbol now on the top of Ken's round cake. Not in black and white, but in red and green: a green tadpole shape with a big red eye curving round a red tadpole shape with a big green eye.

Having completed the design on the top of the cake, Angel smoothed yellow icing all the way round the sides and then, round the bottom of the cake where it sat on Ken's large round plate, she piped alternating red and green scrolls in a similar curved tadpole shape. Standing up, she inspected the cake from the three sides of her work table that were not up against the window. Yes, it was a very fine cake indeed: a universal cake; a cake that spoke about balance.

Sitting down again, she moved Ken's finished cake to the back of her work table and pulled Dieudonné's cake towards her on its board. As she smoothed red icing onto one end of the cake, the quiet of the neighbourhood began to be interrupted by a shout, distant at first, then taken up and brought closer by other voices.

'*Umukobwa!*'

'*Umukobwa!*'

It was a Kinyarwanda word that Angel knew well because she had once had a conversation with Sophie and Catherine about what it meant. The word described someone's function within the family: it said that the purpose of this person's life was to bring in a bride-price to increase the family's wealth. It was the word for a girl.

The door of the apartment flew open and Titi stood in the doorway, breathless and excited.

'Auntie! The baby is a girl!'

'*Eh!* That is good news for Leocadie! Now she and Modeste can marry.'

It had been a happy day, thought Angel that night, sitting propped up with pillows, hot and unable to sleep, as Pius snored quietly beside her under a blanket. She fanned her face with the copy of Oprah's new *O* magazine that she had borrowed from Jenna, listening to snatches of song from Ken Akimoto's party at the other end of the building.

Ken had been very excited by the cake and had declared it Angel's most beautiful yet. That had been very gratifying indeed. Now she thought about the meaning of the symbol on the cake and worked at applying it to the major event of the day. She would think of the good parts of the situation as belonging in the green half of the symbol, and the bad parts as belonging in the red half.

Modeste was going to marry Leocadie, and they were going to be a family with their baby, Beckham. That was green. But there was a circle of red inside the green, and that was that Leocadie already knew that Modeste was the kind of man who would have other girlfriends, and that he must give some of his small salary to help with his other baby. The other girlfriend's situation was red: she had lost her boyfriend to another woman and would be raising her baby daughter alone. What could be in that girlfriend's green circle? Perhaps that her situation was now clear—which it would not yet be if she had delivered a boy—and that Modeste had promised to help her financially with the child. There were not many men who could be relied on for that. Paternity tests had not yet come to Rwanda; here a man could decide not to pay without even knowing about such a test.

Then Angel tried to think about the marriage of Modeste and Leocadie, which would happen soon. That was definitely on the green part of the cake. Modeste was alone because everybody else in his family had been killed. Leocadie was also alone. Her father had been late for a number of years; her mother was in prison, and her two brothers had fled into DRC with others who were also thought to be *génocidaires*. Perhaps it was even possible that members of Leocadie's family had personally killed members of Modeste's family; there was still so much confusion, and there were still so many accused whose cases had not yet even been scheduled for trial, that it was not yet possible to piece together the story of every individual death. So for two such people to find love together was definitely green: they were true *Banyarwanda*. But was the red circle inside that green the history of their families, or was that so big that it was the entire red half of the cake? *Eh!* She must not think about it too much because it might give her a headache and she could not go to anyone so late at night to ask for a tablet. Perhaps Ken Akimoto's symbol was only useful for thinking about things that were small and simple. Perhaps there were some things that were just too big and too complicated. Politics, for example. And history. Perhaps those were things that were not about balance.

She put down the magazine and eased herself down to a horizontal position, careful not to wake Pius.

Eventually she heard the sounds of Ken's party spilling out into the street and dissolving into shouted goodbyes and slamming of car doors.

Finally she slipped into sleep.

But not for long.

In the early hours of Sunday morning, she was dragged from her sleep by sounds of screaming and shouting in the street outside the compound. She sat up and reached for her glasses from their usual night-time spot, on the floor under the bed where she would not tread on them by mistake. Pius was already at the window, looking out from between the curtains.

The screaming outside began to be echoed from inside as the children in the next bedroom awoke in fear. Angel rushed into their room, switching on the overhead light and speaking as calmly as she could.

'It's all right, children. That noise is outside; there's nothing bad in here.'

Daniel and Moses were crying; Benedict was torn between being a child and joining in, and being brave as the oldest boy. Faith was still too sleepy to react, and Grace was peeping between the curtains to see what was happening in the street. Titi sat bolt upright in her bed and stared at Angel with very big eyes.

'Auntie, has the war come again?'

'No, Titi, everything's fine.'

When Angel was sure that all of them were OK, she went back into her bedroom and joined Pius at the window.

'What's going on?'

'It's all Kinyarwanda and French, so I can't follow exactly,' said Pius. 'It seems there's a problem between Jeanne d'Arc and that *Mzungu*.'

Angel peered into the darkness. While there were some streetlights on the tarred road that went past the side of their compound, the dirt road on to which the building fronted was not lit. Angel saw that Patrice and Kalisa, the night security guards, were trying to interpose themselves between Jeanne d'Arc and a young man whose shirtless torso glowed palely in the darkness as he gesticulated wildly. Angel recognised him.

'That's the Canadian from the top floor.'

'Who is he? Have I met him?'

'No, he's new. I don't know his name. He's come for just a short time, as a consultant.'

'His words sound very angry.'

'Jeanne d'Arc is very upset. I'm sure it's about money. Perhaps the Canadian is refusing to pay her and she's demanding the amount that was agreed. But how will anybody hear anything if she cries like that?'

'Should I phone the police?'

'The police? But they'll arrest Jeanne d'Arc because she's a prostitute!'

'No, they'll arrest the Canadian because he's a *Mzungu*! They won't believe a foreigner over a Rwandan.'

'But they'll have to take both of them to the police station because everybody is looking now. That *Mzungu* can easily pay them dollars to go free, but Jeanne d'Arc will have to pay them in another way. That will be very unfair. It's best if Kalisa and Patrice can sort out the problem without the police.'

'You're right.'

'I'm going to make hot milk for the children. Shall I make some for you, too?'

'Yes, thank you. Call me when it's ready; I'll keep an eye on things until then.'

By the time the water had boiled and the sweet milk had been made, Pius had joined the children in their bedroom.

'It's all over now,' he said, 'and the police didn't need to be called. Everyone's gone home. Let's drink our milk and go back to sleep.'

But the broken night of sleep left everyone drowsy, and later that morning—much to her embarrassment—Angel found herself sitting in a pew at St Kizito's suddenly aware that she had slept through most of the sermon. In the afternoon, Pius, Titi and the children all took a nap, and Angel settled herself on the sofa, with her feet up on the coffee table, to read Jenna's *O* magazine. She had not got very far when Sophie came to visit. Angel made tea for them and they took it down to a shady corner of the compound's yard, where they sat on *kangas* spread out on the ground.

'Did you hear all the noise in the night?' asked Angel.

'No,' said Sophie. 'Catherine and I slept in Byumba last night; the volunteers there were having a party. We just got back a while ago. But Linda told us about it. We met her on the stairs.'

'What did Linda say? Does she know what it was about?'

'Mm, she spoke to Dave this morning, so she got the inside story.'

'Dave is the Canadian?'

'Mm. Apparently he agreed a price with Jeanne d'Arc, and afterwards he took the money out of a box in his cupboard and paid her.'

'Oh, I was thinking that maybe he didn't pay her.'

'No, he did pay her. But wait, that's not the end of the story. Then Dave goes to the loo, and when he comes out again his cupboard is open, the box is open and all his money's gone—and so is Jeanne d'Arc.'

'*Eh?* She took his money?'

'All of it—nearly two thousand dollars. So he runs to the window and sees Jeanne d'Arc coming out of the building and he shouts for Kalisa and Patrice to stop her. Then he pulls on his trousers and runs down to the street to get his money back.'

'*Eh!*'

'Apparently Jeanne d'Arc denied taking his money. She told the guards that the only money she had was the money he'd given her for sex. Dave threatened to call the police, but of course he would never have done that; he wouldn't exactly have been seen in a good light himself. But anyway, she believed the threat and it frightened her, so eventually he managed to get all of his money back.'

'All of it? Including the money for the sex?'

'And some other money that was hers! And apparently he's feeling very full of himself today, bragging about getting free sex and how a sex worker tried to . . . Well, excuse my language, Angel, but he's bragging that she tried to screw him and he screwed her instead. Apparently he thinks that's hilarious.'

'*Eh*, this Canadian is not a nice man. How can he cheat Jeanne d'Arc like that?'

'He was stupid. He opened that box of money in front of her and she saw him putting it back in the cupboard. That was throwing temptation in her face.'

'Exactly. OK, he doesn't know Jeanne d'Arc, but surely he knows that somebody who is doing that job is not a rich somebody. Stealing is wrong, but if he was showing her a box of dollars it's like he was asking her to take it. Now he hasn't even paid her for her work.'

'And it's not like she can take him to court to get her money.'

Angel shook her head and said, 'Uh-uh.'

'And he thinks it's a big laugh,' said Sophie.

'But, *eh*! What is he doing with two thousand dollars in his apartment? Who is he consulting for?'

'The IMF—the International Monetary Fund.'

'The IMF? He's working for the IMF and he doesn't want to give a poor somebody the money that he promised to give? Even after that poor somebody did what was agreed? Uh-uh-uh. He can afford to pay Jeanne d'Arc a hundred times that money and instead he's made her an even poorer somebody while he puts all the money in his own pocket and laughs at her with his friends.'

At that point the sound of a door opening on to a balcony made them both look up at the building. The Egyptian appeared in the small space next to the enormous satellite dish that occupied most of his balcony, yawned and stretched.

Sophie spun round on the *kanga* so that her back was to the building and whispered, 'Oh, please, please don't let him see me!'

Taken by surprise, Angel cast her eyes downwards to avoid any interaction with the man. 'What's wrong?' she whispered to Sophie.

'Is he still there? Can you see?'

Angel made a show of glancing towards the side entrance to the yard, swinging her eyes in a casual upward arc along the way. In the split second that her eyes took in the Egyptian's balcony, she saw that only the satellite dish remained there.

'He's gone back in,' she whispered, 'but the door's still open. What's going on?'

Keeping her voice low, Sophie said, 'I'm just too embarrassed to greet him. God knows how I'll behave if I meet him on the stairs or end up at a dinner party with him.'

Angel was very confused. 'Why? What has he done to you?'

'Oh, it's an embarrassing story, Angel. Actually, I don't know whether to laugh or be angry.'

'Then you must tell me the story,' insisted Angel. 'Maybe I can help you to decide.'

Sophie smiled. 'Well, yesterday morning, around noon, I was getting ready for our trip up to Byumba, and waiting for Catherine to come back from the ministry, when his maid came knocking on my door.'

'Eugenia.'

'Eugenia? Oh, I didn't know her name, but I recognised her as Omar's maid.'

'Omar? That's his name?'

'Mm. Anyway, she said that her boss had sent her to me . . . to ask for some condoms!'

'*Eh?* Condoms?'

'I mean, I hardly know Omar! We've just greeted each other on the stairs and that's all. If we were friends then maybe he could ask me that, or even if maybe we'd had a discussion once and I'd told him I was teaching the girls at school about HIV and AIDS and using condoms. *Maybe.*'

'*Eh!* For a man to ask a girl for condoms is not a polite thing. Uh-uh. More especially when you're not even his friend.'

'Mm! So I was really shocked and all sorts of things went through my head. I thought maybe he fancied me and was trying to see if I was available. Because you know, there are men who think that if a woman has condoms it means she's available for sex with anyone.'

'Yes, I've heard that. So what did you do?'

'Well, then I thought that maybe Omar wanted to have sex with this woman, with Eugenia, because we've seen him coming and going with one girlfriend after the other. So I thought he was maybe insisting on sex and she was insisting on a condom and she came to me as another woman to ask for one. So if that was the case, then I couldn't refuse.'

'You're right, Sophie. Under those circumstances you cannot refuse.'

'Mm, and all of this happened in my head within about a second, and as soon as I'd decided that I couldn't refuse, then I was stuck with another decision. She said Omar had sent her to ask for *some* condoms. Not *a* condom: *some* condoms. So how many was I expected to give?'

'*Eh!*'

'Everybody knows that when a neighbour comes and asks you for some sugar, you give a *cup* of sugar. That's the etiquette. But what's the etiquette for condoms? How many do you give?'

'So what did you decide?'

'Well, eventually I decided to give him one of those packs of Prudence that Catherine gives out at her workshops. There's a strip of three or four in there.'

'I'm sure that was a good decision,' assured Angel, casually glancing up at the Egyptian's balcony again to satisfy herself that he was not standing there listening to their conversation. 'But I can understand why you don't want to greet him now.'

'Mm, what's he going to say to me: *Hello, Sophie. Thanks for the condoms. I really enjoyed them*?'

Angel started laughing and Sophie joined her, and soon their laughter was echoing around the compound's yard.

'I'm sorry, Sophie, I know I shouldn't laugh, because this could be a serious something, but I can't help it.'

'It's OK, Angel, you've made me laugh about it, too.'

'Then you've found the answer to your question!'

'What question?'

'The question about whether you should laugh or be angry about this story.'

Sophie smiled. 'What would I do without you to talk to?'

'*Eh*, you have many friends to talk to,' said Angel, 'and I'm happy to be one of them. But I'm sorry to be giving you tea without cake today. I made many cupcakes yesterday but there were many visitors.'

'That's OK, Angel. Actually, that's what I came to talk to you about. You've fed me so much of your delicious cake this year, and now at last I'd like to place an order.'

'*Eh*, Sophie, is your birthday coming?'

'No, no. Actually, the cake I'd like to order is only part of what I'd like to ask of you. Perhaps I should tell you everything before I presume to place my order. You might not agree, and then I won't need the cake.'

Angel looked confused. 'Sophie?'

'OK, let me explain. All this year I've been trying to encourage the girls at my school to think about their futures. They don't know how lucky they are to be attending secondary school—most girls in Rwanda never go beyond primary level.'

'Yes, and not just in Rwanda. Ask anyone you meet from any African country and they'll tell you it can be like that at home, too.'

'Mm, a girl's only a temporary member of the family; she's going to grow up and marry into somebody else's family, so educating her is seen as a waste of money. So these girls are very lucky to be getting a secondary education. But there are very few jobs available in Rwanda, especially for the girls who aren't academic enough to go on to university, so I want them to think about *creating* jobs for themselves.'

'You mean they must become entrepreneurs?'

'Mm! Anyway, some of the girls have at last understood what I'm on about, and they've formed their own club, and to flatter me as their English teacher they've given it an English name. It's called Girls Who Mean Business.'

Angel clapped her hands together. '*Eh*, that's a very good name for that club! And that club is a very good idea.'

'Mm, and once a fortnight they're going to invite someone to come and talk to them after school. They want to ask women who run their own businesses to come and tell them their own stories.'

'To give them some steps that they can follow themselves?'

'Mm, and to inspire them generally.'

'That's a very good idea.'

'So, Angel, will you agree to come and inspire them?'

Angel looked at Sophie. 'Me?' Then she clapped her right hand over her chest and asked again, '*Me?*'

'Of course you, Angel! You're a woman! You run your own successful business! You're ideal!'

'But what would I say to them?'

'Just tell them how you started your business; tell them about any mistakes you made or any important lessons you learned along the way.'

'*Eh!* I remember at first I didn't know how to calculate how much I must charge for a cake. I only thought about what the customer would think was a good price to pay. I didn't know about counting the number of eggs in a cake and calculating how much I had paid for each egg and what-what-what. It was a while before I learned how to make a profit!'

'You see? That's *exactly* what the girls need to hear! And you can tell them about your successes as well, and show them your photo album of all the beautiful cakes that you've made.'

Angel was warming to the idea. 'And I can speak to them about what it means to be a professional somebody.'

'That will be wonderful, Angel.'

Then suddenly Angel stopped smiling and looked at Sophie with a disappointed expression. 'But, Sophie, how will I be able to tell them anything? I don't know Kinyarwanda! I don't know French!'

'No problem,' assured Sophie. 'Their English is OK; not great, but OK. I speak enough French to help out if there's anything they can't follow, and I'm sure some of them will understand if you want to use a few words of Swahili. We'll all translate for one another and everyone will understand.'

'Are you sure it'll work?'

'Listen, if people want to understand something, they find a way to understand it. I know those girls. I'm sure they'll all be very interested in what you have to say.'

'OK. And I can show them my Cake Order Form, the one you typed for me. That speaks many languages.'

'Good idea. Practical stuff is what they need, not just theory. And that's why I want to order a cake from you; I want them to experience your product!'

'That's a very good idea! Of course they must taste my cake! And of course I'll give you a very good price because you're a volunteer.'

'Thank you, Angel. And thank you for agreeing to come and inspire the girls.'

'I'm happy that you invited me, Sophie. And I'll be happy to meet your

Girls Who Mean Business. Now, what is their cake going to look like?'

'Oh, I'll leave that to you, Angel; I'm sure you'll have much better ideas than me. When you've made a decision and calculated a price, just let me know and we can fill in a Cake Order Form and I'll give you the deposit.' Movement on the stairs into the yard caught Sophie's attention. 'Grace! Faith! Hello!'

'Hello, Auntie Sophie,' said the girls as they took turns to bend down and give her a hug.

'Would you girls like to come and play on my laptop for a while?'

'Ooh, Auntie, yes, please!'

'Are you sure, Sophie? They won't be in your way?'

'Of course not. You know I love them; they remind me of my nieces back home. And Catherine's out with her boyfriend, so they won't be disturbing her.'

'OK, let's all go upstairs, then.'

The girls shot off up the stairs as Angel and Sophie gathered their empty mugs, shook the red soil from the *kangas* they had been sitting on, and headed back up towards their apartments.

'You were very brave, Benedict. Nobody likes to go to the dentist, but you were strong like a big boy, a teenager. Mama was proud of you.'

Benedict attempted a smile.

'Now, I know that when we get home you won't be able to eat because your mouth is still hurting, but you can drink. Would you like Mama to make you some tea, or shall we stop at Leocadie's shop and buy you a soda?'

'Fanta, please, Mama!' Benedict declared emphatically.

Of course, the dentist had just lectured Angel on the advisability of cutting down on the amount of sugar in her children's diet. He had even specifically mentioned sodas and cakes as being very bad for a child's teeth. But until somebody could persuade her that his advice was indeed good, it was better simply to ignore it. She would try to remember to ask Dr Rejoice about it.

As Angel and Benedict neared Leocadie's shop, its owner stepped out, and saw them approaching.

'Mama-Grace!' she called, giving a wave and a big smile. Really, she was so much happier now that the business with Modeste's other girl-friend had been settled. Apparently the girl had decided to go with her baby and stay with her aunt near Gisenyi, in the north of the country.

'Benedict, why are you not at school today?' Leocadie asked, when

Angel and the boy reached her shop. 'Are you sick?'

'I went to the dentist,' said Benedict, opening his mouth wide to show Leocadie the hole where a tooth had been extracted.

'*Eh!*' said Leocadie. 'You're a brave boy. Was he brave, Mama-Grace?'

'Very,' assured Angel. 'He'd like a Fanta *citron* now to help him to feel better, but all our empties are in the apartment.'

'No problem, Mama-Grace. You can take a Fanta now and I'll remember that you owe me one empty.'

'Thank you, Leocadie. Now tell me, have you and Modeste started to make plans for your wedding?'

'Not yet,' said Leocadie, stepping into the shop and reaching into the fridge for a Fanta. As she opened its door, the fridge cast just enough light into the dim interior of the container for Angel to make out the still form of Beckham, lying asleep on the lowest shelf between the bags of sugar and the rolls of pink toilet paper. 'But what plans will we make, Mama-Grace? We have no family, so there'll be no negotiations about bride-price. And we can't have a wedding party because we don't have money.'

Angel suddenly felt very sad for this girl, whose only happiness was that her fiancé had chosen her above another girl who had had his baby too. And, Angel noticed, Leocadie had now reached the stage of dis-owning her relatives—incarcerated and in exile—as family. Then Angel thought about her own daughter, and about the silence, the distance, that had grown between them over the years.

Suppressing the startling urge to sob, Angel heard herself speaking before she even knew what it was that she was going to say.

'Leocadie, it is not true that you have no family, because I'm going to be your mother for this wedding.'

'Mama-Grace?'

'I'll help you to plan everything, and of course I'll make your wed-ding cake for the reception.'

'*Eh*, Mama-Grace!' Leocadie's eyes began to fill with tears. 'But we cannot afford . . .'

'Nonsense! God will help us to find a way. You leave everything to me. Now, take my hundred francs for Benedict's Fanta so that I can take him home and put him to bed. He needs to rest after all his fright and pain.'

Leocadie reached for the note that Angel handed her. 'Thank you, Mama-Grace. You're a very good mother.' Then she began to weep. 'I'm very happy that you'll be my mother for my wedding.'

'Don't cry, Leocadie: you'll wake up Beckham, and then *he'll* cry.' Angel did not add that she might join them.

After saying their goodbyes, Angel and Benedict walked the last few metres along the road, past the big green skip that had at last been emptied of the neighbourhood's rubbish, towards the corner where their compound lay.

Once Benedict had finally drifted off to sleep tucked up in his bed, and after Angel had changed out of her smart, tight clothes, she settled down to review what she was going to say that afternoon to the Girls Who Mean Business.

On the table sat an oblong cake decorated in a way that made it immediately recognisable—though its design had been simplified and modified—as an enormous version of the Rwandan 5,000-franc note. Against a pale pink background, the words *Banque Nationale du Rwanda* ran across the top edge of the cake in capital letters that were dark green at the top and red at the bottom; to the right of these words was the large figure *5,000*, also green at the top and red at the bottom. Running across the bottom edge of the surface of the cake was a red stripe with a green stripe immediately above it, and outlined in pale pink above the two stripes, with the colours showing through, were the words *cinq mille francs*, and again the number *5,000*. Those letters and numbers had been very difficult for Angel to write with her icing syringe; next time Ken Akimoto went home to Washington, she would send a note to June requesting a white Gateau Graffito pen.

For her talk to the Girls Who Mean Business, Angel wore the same dress that she had worn to the function at the Tanzanian embassy; it made her look smart and professional, and it had the added advantage of being sufficiently loose to ease her ascent to, and descent from, the front seat of Ken Akimoto's Pajero, which had been reserved in advance for the trip to Sophie's school.

'Eh, Bosco! Please go more slowly on these corners, otherwise my cake will be spoiled.'

'Sorry, Auntie, it's only that I want you to arrive at the school on time. I promise that I won't let your cake be spoiled. It's very, very beautiful and says that those girls will make a lot of money from their businesses.'

'Thank you, Bosco.'

At the school gates, two girls in smart school uniform were waiting to welcome Angel and to lead her to the classroom where the club was meeting and where Sophie was waiting for her.

Before following the girls, Angel tried to insist that Bosco should go home because without the cake to carry it would be fine for her to travel home in a minibus-taxi, but Bosco was vehement about waiting there for her.

The talk went very well indeed: the girls were excited and interested, and there was not a single problem with language that could not be overcome. Some were grateful to discover that Angel had a business *and* a family, as they had imagined that they were going to have to choose one over the other. The cake, of course, was a tremendous success.

At the end of the talk, the president of the club stood up and gave a short speech, thanking Angel in particular for her practical tips, and Angel was presented with a gift: a small picture frame woven from strips of banana-fibre. The applause warmed Angel's heart.

Leaving Sophie to gather up her books and lock the classroom, Angel walked to the Pajero carrying the now empty cake-board at her side, with her photo album tucked under her arm, and holding in her other hand the slice of cake that she had saved for Bosco. He was not in the vehicle. She looked around and saw him sitting in the shade of a tree, talking to a girl in school uniform. Leaving the cake-board leaning against the Pajero and the photo album on the vehicle's roof, she made her way towards the tree.

Seeing her heading towards him, Bosco scrambled to his feet, brushing down his trousers to rid them of any leaves or dirt that they may have picked up.

'Hello, Auntie. Did it go well?'

'Very! *Eh*, I've enjoyed myself this afternoon!'

Bosco indicated the girl, who had picked herself up and dusted herself down much more delicately than he had. 'Auntie, please meet my friend Alice.'

'*Eh!* Alice!' said Angel, shaking the girl by the hand. 'I'm happy to meet you.'

'I'm happy to meet you, too, Auntie.' The girl spoke to her in English. 'I'm sorry that my Swahili is not good, but I have a good English teacher.'

'Miss Sophie is your teacher?'

'Yes, Auntie. We are very lucky to have an English teacher who has come to us from far away in England.'

'Very lucky,' agreed Angel. 'So, Alice, I believe you are the friend of Odile's brother's wife's sister?'

'Yes, Auntie. My friend is here at this school with me, and it is her older sister who is married to Odile's brother, Emmanuel.' The girl's pretty smile transformed her rather plain face.

'And are you not a Girl Who Means Business?'

Alice laughed. 'No, Auntie, I am a girl who will study at university.'

'That is very good. *Eh*, Bosco, I saved a piece of cake for you, but now I see that I should have saved two pieces.'

'No problem, Auntie,' said Bosco, taking the piece of cake that was wrapped in a paper serviette and giving it to Alice. 'I've tasted Auntie's cakes before, but now it is Alice's turn.'

'Oh, thank you, Bosco. Thank you, Auntie. I will not share this with my friend because she has already had a piece; she is a Girl Who Means Business. I will hear from her everything that you said, Auntie.'

'That is good.' From the corner of her eye, Angel saw Sophie walking towards the Pajero to get a lift back to the compound with her and Bosco. She shook Alice by the hand again and told Bosco to take his time saying goodbye as she wanted to hear Sophie's opinion of her talk.

7. A Farewell

THE SEASON OF SMALL RAINS had come to Kigali, settling the dust and bringing short and sudden showers that the dry red soil drank thirstily. But the rain had done little to improve the water shortage in the city, and for the past hour or so the taps in Angel's apartment had failed to yield as much as a drop. Fortunately, in the kitchen the Tungarazas kept a yellow plastic jerry can that was always full of water so that tea could still be made under such circumstances.

Angel and Thérèse now sat sipping their tea in the shade of the compound's yard as they waited for the results of the baking lesson to cool. Thérèse examined the notes she had been making.

'So, if a four-egg cake needs two cups of flour and a cup each of sugar and Blue Band, can we say that for each and every egg there must be half a cup of flour and a quarter of a cup each of sugar and Blue Band?'

'Exactly, Thérèse. And half a teaspoon of baking powder. You mustn't forget the baking powder, because without it the cake will not rise. When I came to your house to test your oven, that mixture that I brought with me had only two eggs and one cup of flour. That was a very small cake, but it's wasteful to make a big cake in an oven that might not work.'

'I was so happy that it worked!' declared Thérèse.

Angel had met Thérèse during one of her visits to the centre in Biryogo where Odile worked. Thérèse had sought her out as she sat chatting to a woman who lay on a mat on the floor of the small hospice area at the back of the centre.

'Madame,' Thérèse had said, 'I believe you are the lady of the cakes.'

'Yes, I am. My name is Angel.'

'I am Thérèse.' They shook hands. 'Nurse Odile told me that you were here.'

Angel glanced at the woman lying on the mat; she was now drifting towards sleep. 'Please sit with us, Thérèse. I don't want to leave this lady alone.'

Thérèse lowered herself to the ground, sitting opposite Angel with her legs stretched out in front of her. Unwittingly, she blocked from Angel's view the mother and baby who had unsettled her like a hundred startled frogs leaping into a still pond. For a moment—just a brief moment—the mother and her desperately ill little one had looked like Vinas and her third baby, the one who was late after only a few months.

Angel smiled with relief at the woman who now offered those hundred frogs the opportunity to climb back onto dry land and to settle there, allowing the water in the pond to be still again. 'Tell me about yourself, Thérèse, and tell me why you have come to talk to the lady of the cakes.'

Thérèse smiled back. Something about her reminded Angel of Grace: she was tall and slight, but with an air of strength.

'I am sick, Angel, but I am well. I'm lucky that the centre has chosen me to receive the medication. I have two young daughters and I must remain well to look after them until they grow big. My husband is late and also my youngest child, a boy, but my girls are well; they are not sick. It's my responsibility to earn money to feed us all and to send my girls to school. If they can complete their schooling, then one day they'll be able to live in a better part of Kigali than Biryogo.'

'That is a good dream for your girls. How are you earning money, Thérèse?'

'That has been a problem because I don't have a job. But, Angel, I have an oven! It belonged to my husband's mother and it came to me after she was late and I never used it because it needed a tank of gas and that is too expensive. We were using the oven as a cupboard, but then I heard about you and I got the idea that maybe I can use it to bake cakes and sell them.'

'That is a very good idea!'

'Yes. I've been buying boxes of tomatoes at the market and then selling them in small bags on the street, and from that I've managed to save money. Now I have enough to buy a tank of gas, and I've cleaned the oven and it's ready to use for baking cakes.'

'*Eh*, you've worked hard.'

'Yes. But I don't know how to bake cakes.'

'*Eh?*'

'No. So I'm asking you, Angel, will you teach me how?'

Angel had explained to Thérèse that it was not every oven that could bake a cake: some were too slow, some became too hot, and some became hotter on one side than the other. First they would have to test Thérèse's oven, and if it was a good oven for cakes, then Angel would be very happy to teach her. The following week Angel had visited Thérèse, taking with her a small baking tin—already greased and floured—and a plastic container that had once held Blue Band margarine, in which the mixed ingredients for a two-egg cake were sealed.

The gas oven had stood gleaming in the corner of the cramped one-roomed home, with the tank of gas standing next to it. Angel could see at once that the oven was tilting slightly backwards on the uneven surface of the bare soil on which it stood. She had sent Thérèse's daughters to ask around among the neighbours for the loan of a bottle of Fanta, and when the girls had returned she had laid the bottle on its side on the top of the oven. Together with Thérèse, she had pushed bits of cardboard under the two back feet of the oven until the girls, standing on a crate to see, had declared that the bubble of air was now in the middle of the bright orange liquid in the bottle. The oven was now level.

Anxiously, they had waited for the oven to heat up to number three on the dial, and then they had put the cake inside and waited anxiously again while it baked. Neighbours had joined them in their vigil. When Angel had at last declared the cake done and withdrawn it from the oven to reveal an evenly browned, level surface, the neighbours had erupted in applause and Thérèse had shed a few tears. Somehow, that two-egg cake had stretched far enough to allow every onlooker a taste.

Now the time had arrived for Thérèse to learn how to bake her own cakes, and her first efforts were cooling in Angel's apartment as the two women sat in the yard drinking their tea.

Angel was about to speak when Prosper came down the stairs into the yard, stamping his feet down hard on each step and muttering to himself angrily. Ignoring Angel's greeting, he marched to the door of his office, unlocked it and went inside, slamming it shut behind him.

'*Eh!* Why is that man angry?' asked Thérèse.

'I don't know,' replied Angel. 'Maybe he went to drink Primus at the bar nearby and he found it closed.'

Both women shook their heads and tutted for a while, then Angel said, 'When we've finished our tea, I'll teach you how to make two kinds of icing, one with Blue Band and one with water.' She shifted slightly on her *kanga* to move her bare feet out of the encroaching sunlight. 'It's enough to know how to make those two kinds. There are other kinds, but they're expensive because they need chocolate or eggs.'

'No, I don't want to know about expensive icing. I'm not going to be a person who makes expensive cakes, and I don't think that I'll take orders for beautiful colours and shapes like in your photo album. I think I'll mostly make cupcakes, because those will be easy to sell on the street, and then I can make a big cake when there's a big event like football or basketball, and I can sell slices there.'

'That's a good plan.'

'I think I'll make more money from cakes than from tomatoes.'

'That is true,' agreed Angel. 'There are many tomatoes in Kigali, and anybody can sell a tomato. A tomato is not a special thing. But a cake is a very special thing.'

'Very special,' agreed Thérèse. 'It is only a person who has an oven who can bake a cake.'

Smiling, they drank their tea quietly for a few moments as Angel prepared herself to raise a subject that, when she allowed herself to focus on it, troubled her deeply.

'Tell me, Thérèse, may I ask you a personal question?'

'Of course, Angel.'

'Is your mother still alive?'

'My mother? No, unfortunately she's late.'

'And did you . . . Did you ever tell her that you were sick?'

Thérèse took a sip of her tea before answering. 'Yes, I did. It was only when my baby boy died that they advised me to have the test. I was shocked when they told me I was positive—'

Angel interrupted. 'Odile told me that that is the way, the time, that many mothers discover that they're positive. When a baby is late.'

'It's true, Angel.'

'And, Thérèse, how was it when you told your mother?'

'*Eh*, it's a very hard thing to tell a mother! And I regret so much that I told mine. It upset her too much. Truly, Angel, I think it was my news that made her late so soon.'

'*Eh?*'

'It shocked her too much, and I think she preferred to die before she had to watch me die. We didn't know then about the medication. If I could go back in time and untell her, she could be alive today and not worrying about me being sick—because I'm well.'

'That is not an easy thought for you to have, Thérèse. I'm sorry.' Angel swallowed a sip of tea. 'Now . . . say you met a girl who was sick. Would you advise her not to tell her mother?'

'*Eh!* That is a very difficult question to answer. Each and every case is different, and only the girl herself will know what to do.' She drained her mug. 'Although, in my case I thought I knew what to do but I did the wrong thing. I wish I hadn't told the truth, Angel. A lie would have been so much kinder to my mother. Sometimes a lie can hold more love in its heart than the truth.'

Angel was contemplating this when a shout began in the street, distant at first and then brought nearer by voices closer to the compound: '*Amazi!* Water.'

'*Eh*, the water has come back,' said Angel, scrambling to her feet. 'Let us wash the mixing bowls so that we can make the icing.'

Later, as they had arranged, Angel and Thérèse knocked on the door of Jenna's apartment. It was exactly eleven thirty.

'Perfect timing, Angel,' said Jenna, opening the door. 'We've just finished today's lesson.'

'That's good,' said Angel. 'Jenna, this is Thérèse, my student.'

'Delighted to meet you, Thérèse,' said Jenna in French, shaking Thérèse's hand. 'Let me introduce you to *my* students. That's Leocadie, and next to her is Agathe, and on the other side of the table there's Eugenia and Inès.'

Thérèse worked her way around the table, greeting the women in Kinyarwanda and shaking each of them by the hand.

'Good morning, ladies,' said Angel in English. 'I'm sorry that I don't know French, and if I speak Swahili, then Jenna and Agathe will not understand me, and if I speak the small bit of Kinyarwanda that I know, Jenna won't understand me. So I'm going to speak in English and Jenna will repeat after me in French.'

As Jenna translated, Angel put down the plate that she had been holding.

'Ladies, you are honoured to be the first people in Kigali to taste cakes baked by our sister, Thérèse.' As Jenna translated, everyone looked at Thérèse, who beamed and dipped her head. 'It's a new business for her, a new way of supporting her two girls. Our job today is to taste these cakes and to help Thérèse with our opinions and advice.'

Nestled together on the plate were a number of cupcakes: half of them decorated with pale yellow butter icing—made with margarine—and half with white glacé icing. Not wanting to spoil her first cakes in any way, Thérèse had been too nervous to add colour to her own icing, but she had observed and taken notes as Angel had coloured the icing for her own batch of cupcakes. She had been amazed by the number of colours it was possible to make from just three: red, blue and yellow.

Jenna and her students applied themselves earnestly to their task. The cakes were unanimously declared to be extremely delicious, and there was discussion about which type of icing would be more popular. Finally, agreement was reached that, while some adults might prefer the glacé icing, children would probably prefer the butter icing—and that Thérèse could probably charge more for a cake with butter icing on it because it made the cake look a bit bigger.

'Eh, that is very good advice,' said Thérèse. 'Thank you. Now I'm going to ask my teacher to try one of my cakes, and then I'm going to eat one myself.'

Silently, six pairs of eyes watched Angel as she peeled away the paper case and took a bite. She chewed slowly, savouring her mouthful, then swallowed.

'Thérèse,' she said, with a serious and solemn expression befitting a teacher, 'this is a very fine cake indeed.'

Five pairs of eyes swung towards Jenna, who mimicked Angel's expression as she translated. The women erupted into laughter and applause, and finally Thérèse felt that she could relax and eat a cake herself. As she took her first mouthful, a broad grin spread across her face.

'OK, ladies,' said Jenna, clapping her hands together with an air of authority, 'time to go. You all need to get back to your jobs, and I need to make this place look like you were never here before my husband even thinks about coming home for lunch.'

'Eh, Inès,' said Angel as the women walked down the stairs, 'I think you should fetch Prosper from his office before you go and open up the bar. I think he wanted to have a beer there earlier when you were closed for your lesson.'

'*Eh*, that Prosper!' said Inès, shaking her head. 'I've told him many times that the bar is shut from half past ten to half past eleven on week-days now.'

'I'm sure that he doesn't want to accept that,' said Eugenia. 'When there's something that a man wants, it is *now* that he wants that something. Waiting is something that is very difficult for a man to do.'

Angel thought of Eugenia being sent to get condoms for the Egyptian.

'*Eh*, men?' said Leocadie, shaking her head. 'Uh-uh.'

'Men? Uh-uh-uh,' agreed Inès.

'And my shop was shut, too,' said Leocadie. 'Prosper couldn't buy beer there, either.'

'Exactly,' said Angel. 'Now he's sitting inside his office with the door shut, and you know there's no window there, and no light. He's sitting in the dark.'

The women laughed. They had reached ground level now.

'OK,' said Inès with a sigh. 'I'll go and get him.' She headed towards the stairs leading down into the yard.

'*Eh*, and make sure he takes his Bible with him,' Angel called after her, still laughing. 'Ask him to show you the verses that talk about the virtue of patience.'

Angel looked at her watch. It was almost half past two; she had half an hour to supervise the children's homework before Mrs Mukherjee would arrive with her sons Rajesh and Kamal, and their nanny, Miremba. At 2.55, she sent Grace and Faith up to Safiya's apartment to continue with their homework,

At exactly three o'clock the Mukherjees arrived, and Angel suggested that Titi and Miremba should take all the boys down to the yard with their football so that she and Mama-Rajesh could talk business.

'Yard is safe, no?' asked Mrs Mukherjee, a thin, nervous woman who was constantly wringing her bony hands together.

'Completely safe,' assured Angel. 'The children play there every day.'

'Not too much of germs?'

This was difficult. Angel knew from Dr Rejoice that there were germs everywhere, so of course there must be germs in the yard. But Dr Rejoice had also told her that it was wrong to protect children from all germs. That was the fashion in Europe now, and many *Wazungu* were becoming sick because they had never learned how to fight germs when they were small. But Angel did not think it would be useful to try to explain that to Mrs Mukherjee.

'No germs,' she assured her.

The boys and their carers were dispatched to the yard and Mrs Mukherjee stationed herself at the window to watch them while Angel made tea. She was barely able to coax her guest away from the window when she brought the tea and cupcakes to the coffee table, and it was with great reluctance that the woman sat down opposite her. Angel tried to distract her from the imminent deaths of her boys in the yard.

'These cakes look beautiful with your outfit,' she said. She had deliberately picked out the cakes from the morning's colour-mixing lesson that would compliment the deep purple of her guest's *salwar kameez*. She eyed the design of the outfit now: surely the long dress over the trousers—with slits where it passed over both thighs—would enable a woman to get into and out of a big vehicle elegantly. It looked very fashionable on Mrs Mukherjee's thin body: would it work over her own expanding hips?

Mrs Mukherjee gave the plate of cakes a cursory glance. 'Mrs Tungaraza, did you read *New Vision*?'

'Call me Angel, please, Mrs Mukherjee. I do read it sometimes.' Once a week Pius would bring a copy of the Ugandan newspaper home.

'Ebola!' declared Mrs Mukherjee, leaning forward across the coffee table with an air of conspiracy. Then she sat back in her chair and said again, this time almost defiantly, 'Ebola!'

Angel was not quite sure what to make of this. 'Has Ebola come to Kigali?'

'No!' Mrs Mukherjee's bony hands flew to the sides of her head for a moment. 'No! If Ebola is coming to Kigali then we are booking tickets to Delhi. Immediately!' Her right hand added emphasis to this final word by executing a chopping motion into the palm of her left. She shook her head vehemently.

'Where exactly is this Ebola, Mrs Mukherjee?'

'Uganda!' Mrs Mukherjee raised both her arms in an exaggerated gesture. 'Right next door to Rwanda! Ebola is killing in two weeks. *Two weeks*, Mrs Tungaraza!'

'Angel, please. Let us not be formal.'

'Two weeks. Blood is coming from the eyes, the ears, the nose. *Finished!*' The chopping motion came again.

'But I think we're safe here in Kigali.' Angel removed her glasses and began to clean them with the corner of her *kanga*.

Mrs Mukherjee shook her head. 'Ugandans are here! In Kigali! Working with our husbands! Dr Binaisa. Mr Luwandi . . .'

'But Ebola is not a disease specifically of Ugandans, Mrs Mukherjee.' Angel's rubbing of her lenses became more insistent.

'Ugandan children are at school with our children. My boys will stay home until the Ebola is finished. I told my husband. He agrees to my decision.'

Angel had met Mr Mukherjee, who lectured in information technology. He was the exact opposite of his wife: big and broad with a quick sense of humour and sensible ideas. He would definitely have disagreed with his wife on this issue, but he probably understood that there was nothing to be gained from saying so. Angel saw the wisdom in this.

'You are very wise, Mrs Mukherjee,' she conceded. 'I'll discuss it with my husband tonight, and perhaps we'll keep our children at home, too.'

The lie was rewarding: for the first time since her arrival, Angel suddenly had her guest's full attention. The two women smiled at each other as Angel replaced her glasses.

'Do try your tea, Mrs Mukherjee. I've heard that it's similar to a tea that is made in India.'

Mrs Mukherjee took a sip. 'Oh, yes, cardamom. In India we are putting cardamom and lemon in green tea.'

'I've always wanted to visit your country,' Angel lied.

'It is a very beautiful country,' beamed Mrs Mukherjee.

'And your country has delicious food, very spicy. In my country, especially along the coast, the cooking is still influenced by the people who came from India to build the railway many years ago.'

Mrs Mukherjee slapped both her hands on her thighs and declared, 'I cook for you one day.'

'That will be wonderful. Thank you. But I've cooked for you today. Please have a cake.'

Mrs Mukherjee chose a cupcake with lilac icing, peeled away its paper cup and took a bite. Angel savoured the secret that—that very morning—a woman with HIV had stirred that cake mixture to get a feel for the correct consistency. To reveal that secret to Mrs Mukherjee would surely be to send her into a frenzy of panic and ticket-booking.

'Very tasty.'

'How long have you been here, Mrs Mukherjee?'

'Almost three years. *Three years!* I told my husband if he is renewing contract I am taking the boys home to Delhi. Too much of germs are here.' Mrs Mukherjee finished her cupcake.

'Are there no germs in Delhi?'

'The Ebola is not there.' Mrs Mukherjee shook her head vehemently. 'And no AIDS.'

Angel resisted the urge to polish her glasses again. Without saying a word, she picked up the plate of cupcakes and held them out to her guest, who took one iced in crimson and peeled away its paper case before continuing.

'And the servants in Delhi are better.'

'Are you not happy with Miremba?'

'She isn't knowing good English. Now the boys are speaking bad English. But what to do?' Mrs Mukherjee raised both her arms into the air again. 'Rwandans are not speaking much of English.'

Mrs Mukherjee was clearly unaware that the reason why Miremba spoke English at all was that she had been raised in Uganda, the country where Ebola was even now killing people in two weeks. Angel must remember to warn Miremba never to reveal this fact to her employers. It was time to move the conversation on.

'So, Mrs Mukherjee, tell me about the cake that you want to order for your husband's cousin. Will you be having a party to say farewell to him?'

'Yes. Most of the Indian community here will come.'

'And what was your husband's cousin doing here at the National University, Mrs Mukherjee?'

'Computers, just like my husband. All men in my husband's family are doing computers.'

'I have an idea, Mrs Mukherjee. Perhaps the cake should look like a computer keyboard?'

Mrs Mukherjee thought about this idea while Angel looked for a page in her photo album.

'I have never made a keyboard cake before so it will be unique for your husband's cousin. But here are some cakes that I've made to look like things. This one here is a tipper truck, and this one's a mobile phone, and here's a microphone, and an aeroplane. I've also made one that looks like a pile of 5,000-franc notes, but that photo is not yet printed.'

Mrs Mukherjee examined the photos carefully. 'Computer keyboard,' she said. Then she looked at Angel and said, 'Good idea, Mrs Tungaraza. The cake will be a computer keyboard.'

'Good!' declared Angel, and for the next few minutes they busied themselves with the Cake Order Form. Angel began by quoting an exorbitant price, knowing that Mrs Mukherjee would insist on negotiating it down. The final price was only slightly lower than what she had hoped to get away with, and since it was substantially lower than the price she had originally quoted to Mrs Mukherjee, both women were happy with the deal. They sat back to finish their tea.

'Tell me, Mrs Mukherjee,' began Angel. 'I'm busy organising bride-price for Leocadie who works in the shop in our street. By the way, I'll be coming to each and every family in the street about that soon. But for now I'm very interested to ask about bride-price in your country. I've heard that in India it's the girl's parents who must pay bride-price to the boy's parents.'

'Yes. Dowry. My parents were giving to my husband's parents the fridge, the freezer, the motor car. All new; nothing secondhand. Also jewels; many, many jewels. My husband is an educated man, so there were many gifts.'

'Eh! Here it is different. The boy's parents must give bride-price to the girl's parents. Pius's parents gave my parents eight cows. Eight! But they would have taken six. Pius was already close to getting his degree when we married, and he was going to become a teacher. In those days there were not many boys from Bukoba who were getting degrees at Makerere University in Uganda.' Angel stopped speaking suddenly and looked anxiously at her guest. 'Of course, there was no Ebola in Uganda then, Mrs Mukherjee. My parents knew that it was a good marriage for me.'

'Good marriage,' agreed Mrs Mukherjee. 'The girl in the shop is not yet married?'

'Leocadie? No. But she'll marry soon.'

'What about the baby?'

'It's the father of the baby that she'll marry.'

Mrs Mukherjee shook her head and raised both her arms in the air. 'Baby before marriage is bringing shame to the family!' she declared. 'In India, there is no marriage for girls with babies. Those girls are no good.'

'But sometimes a man wants to be sure that a girl is fertile and can deliver a healthy baby. He doesn't want to find out after he's already paid bride-price and married a girl that she cannot deliver. And if a girl has already delivered a healthy baby to a man, then her family can negotiate for more cows.'

Mrs Mukherjee shook her head. 'No. No good.'

Angel recognised that it was going to be difficult to persuade Mrs Mukherjee to contribute any money to the wedding of Leocadie and Modeste. She would have to try her luck with Mr Mukherjee.

Getting up and walking towards the window, she said, 'Shall we call the boys up for some cake?'

8. An Escape

As ANGEL SAT in the unfamiliar lounge sipping at a cup of tea made the bland, English way, she prayed silently for forgiveness. There were a number of things for which she hoped to be forgiven. Above all, it was a Sunday morning, and on a Sunday morning she should, of course, be in church with her family. Today her family had gone to a Pentecostal service in the big blue-and-white striped tent that was home to the Christian Life Assembly Church. Right now they would be singing hymns and praising the Lord, while Angel was sitting here, in this house that she did not know, aiding and abetting a deception. Well, three deceptions, really—one of which might possibly cancel out the sin of the second, though she was not entirely sure about that.

First, while not actually *lying* to Jenna's husband, she had participated in allowing him to believe that, this morning, his wife would be safely at St Michael's Catholic Church—near the American embassy— with the Tungaraza family; and yet, here was Jenna in this unfamiliar lounge with Angel and two strangers instead. But perhaps it was not wrong to lie to the CIA about his wife being at church, because he himself was lying to his wife and was—in all probability—lying in bed with his neighbour Linda at this very moment.

Of course, by providing somewhere else for his wife to be, Angel was aiding that deception; and that was the second reason why she needed forgiving—although deceiving a deceiver was perhaps not so much of a sin. Thirdly, there was the extremely troubling matter for which Angel asked forgiveness every Sunday: the matter of not telling Jenna about her husband's infidelity—although Angel felt sure that if she were to tell Jenna, that would also be something for which she would need to ask forgiveness. It was a very complicated situation indeed.

So Angel prayed for forgiveness; but prayer was also a time to give thanks, and she gave silent thanks now for a number of things as she took another sip of the rather insipid tea. As always, she was grateful for a new customer—in this case Kwame, the man in whose lounge she now sat. A few days earlier, Pius's Ghanaian colleague, Dr Sembene, had come to see Angel to order a cake on behalf of Kwame, who would be hosting a small gathering that Sunday afternoon. Kwame's wife, Akosua, would be visiting from Accra, and a number of Ghanaians would be coming to greet her and to hear news from home. Of course, Angel had tried to get as much information as possible about Akosua from Dr Sembene in order to design the perfect cake for her—but, never having actually met Akosua, Dr Sembene was able to tell Angel only one fact about her. That had meant three things: that the cake Angel had brought with her this morning, while both colourful and much admired, was rather non-specific; that Angel and Jenna would have to pretend to be going to church while spending time with Kwame and Akosua instead; and that Angel had another reason to give thanks. Yes, the one piece of information that Dr Sembene had been able to give Angel was very important indeed: Akosua was a trainer of literacy teachers.

Jenna and Akosua were so caught up in their conversation that they had not noticed when Kwame's mobile phone had rung and he had stepped out into the garden—filled with colourful frangipanis and canna lilies—to take the call, apologising to Angel for interrupting their conversation. Kwame had been telling her about his work as an investigator for the trials that were taking place in Arusha, in Angel's country. The suspects awaiting trial there were accused of planning and leading the killings in Rwanda, and Kwame was part of the international team that was gathering evidence and witnesses against them.

Angel put down her cup of tea and reached down to the ground for the plastic bag at her feet. It contained two more reasons to give thanks. Akosua had brought with her from Accra a large number of lengths of beautiful cloth to sell, produced by a group of women who supported themselves by buying cheap cotton fabric, dying it, then printing special designs and patterns on it before selling it for a healthy profit. Akosua had told her that each of the patterns had a special meaning, and that in the past only men had been allowed to use those patterns, always printing them in black on a limited range of colours. What the group of women was doing was both traditional and modern.

Angel fingered and admired the two lengths that she had bought. The fabric of one was a light orange colour, printed in bright yellow and gold with a design that was about people cooperating with one another and depending on one another. Akosua had told her what that pattern said: *Help me and let me help you.* This was the cloth that would become her dress for Leocadie's wedding to Modeste.

'You have chosen two beautiful pieces,' said Kwame, who had come in from the garden and was easing himself back into the chair across from Angel.

'*Eh*, but it was difficult to choose! They're all so beautiful. At first I wanted to choose that green one, because Akosua told me that the pattern on there said: *What I hear, I keep*. I like that, because I'm a professional somebody and I know about confidentiality. But I'm sure you know about that in your work, too.'

'Absolutely. No witness wants to come forward without some kind of guarantee of confidentiality. But it's very difficult here, because if somebody sees somebody talking to me, then automatically they assume that person has revealed something to me about somebody else, and then there can be threats of reprisals. Although, of course, many people feel more comfortable talking to an investigator who belongs to neither this group nor that. Still, confidentiality remains a very big problem. By the way, if you *had* taken that green piece with the confidentiality pattern, it would have given you two very different outfits. Those pieces you have chosen are quite similar.'

'Yes. But as soon as Akosua explained this other one to me, I knew I had to have it.' Angel indicated the second of her two pieces, a pale lemon yellow printed with gold and bright orange. 'This pattern talks about reconciling and making peace. As soon as I heard that, I knew that I must buy it for a special wedding dress, and then I must have this other one that is like it, rather than the green one, because I'm going to be the bride's mother at that wedding.'

'Oh, your daughter is getting married? Congratulations.'

'Thank you, Kwame. She's not my daughter; my daughter is unfortunately late. But I'm the bride's mother for the wedding. It will be a special wedding, an example of this reconciliation that everybody is talking about here.'

Kwame shook his head sadly. 'Oh, Angel, that is a wedding that I need to witness! My job makes it very difficult for me to believe in reconciliation, even though I fully want to believe in it. I *need* to believe in it.' Kwame glanced towards his wife, who was talking animatedly with Jenna, and lowered his voice a little. 'I was here before, you know.'

'Before?'

'In 1994. I was one of the UN blue berets. Our job was to keep the peace, but of course there was no peace to keep. And we had no mandate to *create* peace by preventing or stopping the killing because we could not use force. In effect, we were here simply as witnesses. That's why I've come back here now to do this job. I want to find a way to put things right, to contribute, to make up for my powerlessness, my uselessness before. I feel for these witnesses. I know that their silence might protect them from harm by others, but it can also destroy them from the inside. The counsellor who helped me afterwards told me that sometimes you need to dig deep into a wound to remove all the poison before it can heal. These people need to tell what happened; they need to get it all out. Of course it wasn't my own people's slaughter, my own family's slaughter, that I witnessed—so there's no way I can claim that I was a witness in the same way that these people were.' Again Kwame glanced towards Akosua to make sure that she was not listening. 'Actually, I've never told my wife about the things I witnessed here.'

Angel spoke in a low voice, too. 'Not even when you first got back home?'

'No. I didn't know her then. We've only been married a short while. If she had known me then, she would never have married me. I was a mess. And if she knew what I'd seen, she'd never have let me come back here. Absolutely not. She would have worried too much about me.'

Angel was quiet for a moment. She wanted to say that it was important to tell the truth, but then she remembered her own lies, the ones for which she had been asking forgiveness just moments earlier. Then she thought of her daughter, who had concealed from her the truth that her marriage was over, leaving Angel to discover by accident from the household help over the phone that Baba-Faith had not lived there for months, and she thought about what other truths Vinas may have concealed, and about what Thérèse had said about a lie holding love in its heart. Then she thought about Odile, and what she might have witnessed and experienced. And then she did not want to think any more.

'Sometimes,' she said with a sigh, 'life can be too complicated. But, Kwame, you must come to this special wedding that I'm organising. I'll be sure to give you an invitation. Perhaps what you'll witness there will help your own wound to heal.'

'I hope so, Angel. Thank you.'

A loud hoot sounded on the other side of the gate. Pius was on his way back from church with the red Microbus full of happy and excited children, and it was time to go home. On the way, Jenna was more animated than Angel had ever seen her.

'Oh, Angel, thank you so much!' she kept declaring. 'Akosua's helped me to see where I've been going wrong with my literacy class, and how to put it right. And it's great to know that I've been doing at least *some* things right!'

'Jenna, you need to calm down,' Angel warned. 'Remember that when you get home, you need to look like somebody who has been talking to God. You need to look like you have peace in your heart.'

After a satisfying lunch of spicy beans cooked with coconut and served with sweet potato and cabbage, Pius retired to the bedroom for an afternoon nap, and Angel settled with Titi, the children and Safiya in front of the television. Ken Akimoto had recently returned from one of his trips home to America, bringing with him a new collection of films that his family had taped for him. Angel had chosen one of them that Sophie had said would be fine for the children to watch.

Less than half an hour into the film, someone knocked on the door. Not welcoming the interruption, Angel went to the door instead of simply calling for the visitor to come in. It was Linda, saying that she wanted to order a cake.

'I can see that you're busy, though, Angel, so maybe I should come back another time.'

'No, no, Linda, I'm never too busy for business. But we can't talk in here. Would you like to go out into the yard?'

'Not a good idea with these sudden rainstorms—and it's probably still muddy out there from the last one. Come upstairs to mine.'

'OK, let me just get what I need and tell my family where I'll be, and I'll see you up there in a minute.'

Angel gathered a Cake Order Form, her photo album, her diary and a pen, and set off up the stairs to Linda's apartment, trying very hard not to think about what Linda might have been doing in her apartment that morning while Jenna had been out. As she ascended the final flight of stairs, she decided that it would be easier to focus instead on Bosco, and the desperate love he had once felt for Linda; there was nothing awkward or unethical in that story to make her feel uncomfortable. In fact it was a happy story now, because Bosco had decided to love Alice instead.

She found the door open and Linda inside opening a bottle of Amstel. A sleeveless black T-shirt stretched tightly across her full breasts, ending about ten centimetres above where her short denim skirt began, and exposing a silver stud in her navel. Her long dark hair was tied back loosely in a ponytail.

'Come in, Angel, have a seat. Would you like a beer? Not that local

Primus or Mützig rubbish. They say Amstel's illegally imported from Burundi so they're cracking down on it. It's really hard to get now, but somehow Leocadie still manages to find it.'

'No, thank you, Linda. I don't drink.'

'You're not a Muslim, are you?'

'No, I'm not a Muslim; I'm just somebody who doesn't drink.' Angel settled herself into a familiar-looking chair.

'You don't know what you're missing, Angel. This place is so much easier to take when you're not stone-cold sober all the time, believe you me! Can I make you some tea instead?'

'That would be very nice, thank you.'

Linda moved across to the far end of the lounge, which served as the kitchen area, and switched on an electric kettle. Her apartment had only one bedroom, and Angel was relieved that the door to it was shut. She did not want to be faced with the sight of an unmade bed or any other evidence of the morning's activities—sinful activities that Angel herself had made possible.

'I've just come from having lunch with friends at Flamingo. Have you eaten there?'

'The Chinese? No, it's too expensive for us to eat out. We're a family of eight. *Eight!*'

'Oh, but you should go out sometime just with your husband. Leave the kids with your Titi and get him to take you to the Turtle Café one Friday night. Great live music, sexy Congolese dancing.' Linda swivelled her hips provocatively.

'*Eh*, Linda, I'm a *grandmother!*' Angel laughed. 'That is not a place for people as old as Pius and me.'

Linda smiled as she poured boiling water onto a tea bag. 'Maybe not. But I'd go mad if I had to eat at home all the time. Milk? Sugar?'

'Yes, please. Just three sugars. But I've been with Pius to functions at a few places here: Jali Club is very nice, and Baobab. A friend of mine has a restaurant in Remera called Chez Françoise. Do you know it?'

'No, I don't. What kind of food do they serve?'

'Barbecued fish and chicken, brochettes, chips, that kind of thing. And if you want to hold a party there, Françoise can order one of my cakes for dessert.'

'Oh,' said Linda, handing Angel the mug of tea and sitting down opposite her with her bottle of beer. 'Now that sounds interesting. What kind of place is it?'

'It's like a garden, with tables and chairs under shelters made of grass. And the cooking is done there outside as well, over a fire.'

'That sounds like just the sort of place I'm looking for. I want to throw a small party next weekend, but this flat's too poky and I don't want to cook. I thought of asking Ken if I could use his place, but it'd be nice to go somewhere different for once.' Linda lit a cigarette and inhaled deeply.

'Go and have a look at Chez Françoise and see if you like it. Bosco knows the place; he can take you there.'

'Bosco? Who's Bosco?'

Eh! thought Angel, and she knew at once that she could never, ever tell Bosco that Linda, who he had loved with all his heart, did not know who he was. Aloud she said, 'Bosco is Ken's driver.'

'Oh, right. But I've got my own car; I'll just get directions from you.'

'OK.' Angel took a sip of her tea, the second time she had had to drink English tea that day. At least she had had a good cup of properly made tea when her family had got home that morning. 'Is it a party for your birthday, Linda?'

'God no, it's a much more important celebration than that. I just heard yesterday that my divorce is now final.' Linda raised her bottle in the gesture of a toast and took a large gulp of beer.

Angel did not know what to say. *Wazungu* these days did not take their marriages seriously. Divorce meant that you had failed in your marriage, and to fail was never a good thing. How could failure be a reason for celebration? Really, it should be a reason for shame.

'Oh, don't look at me like that, Angel. My marriage was a bloody disaster. Mum and Dad bullied me into it. They wanted their daughter to marry a nice conservative career diplomat, the son of their nice conservative friends. Trouble was, he was as boring as hell, so I rebelled and got involved in human rights work, which of course was an embarrassment to his precious career.'

Angel wondered if Linda's human rights work could not also be an embarrassment to the CIA. But perhaps it did not matter if they were not actually married. Certainly Jenna's work as a literacy teacher could not embarrass him—although of course it would embarrass him if his bosses ever discovered that one of their agents was not able even to detect a covert operation that was under way in his own home.

'So, do you think your husband is also going to celebrate this divorce?'

'God yes. He certainly won't be crying into his sherry, that's for sure. Now he can find himself a wife who'll keep her mouth shut and be totally uncontroversial, a sweet hostess for embassy functions.'

Angel thought of Mrs Margaret Wanyika, who was exactly the kind of wife that an ambassador needed: well groomed, unfailingly polite and always in agreement with her husband and her government's policies.

'I can see that you two were not a good match.'

'We were a bloody disaster.' Linda lit another cigarette. 'So this party, Angel. It's to celebrate my escape, so I want a cake that suggests escape or freedom in some way.'

'Do you want to look through this to get some ideas?' Angel offered her photo album, but Linda waved it away.

'I've seen loads of your cakes at Ken's. I'll leave the design up to you. I'm sure you're much more creative than I am.'

'OK, I'll think about it very carefully so that I don't disappoint you. But I'll need to know how many people will be at the party so that I know how big to make the cake, and then we can work out the cost.'

'Fine. Whatever.'

Linda opened another bottle of Amstel as they filled out a Cake Order Form, and then she opened her purse and counted out the total price. Angel saw that her purse was extremely full of banknotes.

'I couldn't be bothered with deposits, Angel. Now I know I've paid you and I don't owe you anything.'

'Thank you, Linda.' Angel folded the proffered banknotes and tucked them into her brassiere. 'You know, it's interesting that you've told me about a divorce today, because I was planning to come and tell you about a wedding.'

'Oh? Whose wedding?'

'A wedding of two people that everybody in this compound knows.'

'Oh God, don't tell me. Let me guess. Omar's going to marry Eugenia? Prosper's going to marry your Titi? Dave the Canadian is going to forgive Jeanne d'Arc and marry her?'

Linda collapsed into laughter and Angel joined her, laughing harder than she had in a long time. Her laughter forced tears from her eyes, and she had to delve into her brassiere for a tissue. It was quite a while before she was able to speak.

'No, none of those, Linda. No, Modeste is going to marry Leocadie.'

'Oh, great. Doesn't she already have his baby?'

'Yes. Beckham. But they're not people with family; they're alone. So I'm going to be the mother of the wedding and I'm asking everyone in this compound and this street to help out with a contribution, because all of us are their family.'

'Of course I'll contribute.' Linda stubbed out her cigarette and reached for her purse again. 'Do we get an invitation to the wedding if we make a donation?'

'Yes, of course.' Angel could see that Linda was deciding how much to give. 'You *Wazungu* who are earning dollars are able to contribute very well. It's nothing to you, but it's everything to people who have nothing.'

Linda reconsidered and fingered an additional note.

'And let us not forget that even now, on a Sunday afternoon, it is Modeste who is outside guarding your vehicle from thieves.'

Linda took another note from her purse.

'And Leocadie is the one who is able to find Amstel for you when it is very difficult.'

Linda took two more notes from her purse and handed the money to Angel, who tucked it into her diary to keep it separate from the cake money that was in her brassiere.

'Thank you, Linda. You're a very generous somebody.'

Later that evening, Angel found herself seated in another of the compound's one-bedroom apartments, this time on the top floor of Ken Akimoto's side of the building. So far she had visited all of the people in the compound whom she already knew well, and she had collected a sizeable amount of money from them for the wedding. Sophie had given her a big brown envelope in which to keep it all so that she did not have to walk around with banknotes bulging out of her diary. But Sophie and Catherine had surprised her with their reluctance to contribute money—and their reason was not that they were volunteers with little money to give.

'How can you ask us to contribute to *bride-price*, Angel?' Catherine had asked, looking appalled. 'Why should we contribute to the purchase of a woman by a man?'

'Or at least, the purchase of her womb and her labour,' Sophie had clarified.

'No, no, that's not how it is,' Angel had hastily explained. She had forgotten about the sensitivities of *Wazungu*, especially *Wazungu* who were feminists. 'I'm just saying bride-price because that's what people here understand. But Modeste has no family who want to buy Leocadie for their son, and Leocadie has no family who want to sell her. This money that I'm collecting is for Leocadie and Modeste and Beckham, to pay for a nice wedding and to give them a good start as a family.'

Satisfied, Catherine and Sophie had contributed generously.

Then Angel had called upon several of the families she knew who lived in the houses lining the dirt road on which the compound—and Leocadie's shop—stood. Starting at the far end and working her way back towards the compound, she had avoided the homes where she did not know the people; those she would tackle during the day rather than in the gathering darkness of evening when people might be suspicious of somebody they did not know asking for money. She would also wait a few days before approaching them so that news of her collection for the wedding could have time to reach them from the neighbours who knew Angel and had already contributed. Of course, some of the people she knew had been out that evening, and she would have to remember who they were so that she could call on them another time.

As she went from house to house in the street, she thought about what Catherine and Sophie had said about bride-price. She had never felt that Pius had *bought* her—or her womb, or her labour—in any way. He had simply approached her parents in the traditional, respectful way to ask for her hand in marriage; and he had compensated them for the expenses that they had incurred in raising her. But she did have a cousin in Bukoba who had not been able to conceive, and the girl's husband had returned her to Angel's uncle and demanded the return of the cows that he had paid. Angel could see that that had been no different from buying a radio that does not work and then taking it back to the shop for a refund.

The Tungarazas' own children had been both traditional and modern when it came to bride-price. Pius had handed over the cash equivalent of a reasonably sized herd to the parents of their daughter-in-law, Evelina. Vinas, on the other hand, had said she could not be bothered with anything like that; she was happy enough to be marrying a man she loved, whose family had already invested everything they had in helping him to qualify as a teacher-trainer, and whose father was in any case already late. Angel and Pius had been satisfied enough with both of these arrangements—and although they had never discussed it, Angel felt that they would be glad if their three grandsons grew up to be more modern; they could certainly not afford high sums to be negotiated for the wives of three more boys.

As she had emerged from the yard next door to the Mukherjees with yet another contribution tucked into her envelope, she had met two men ambling towards her in what would now be total darkness were it not for a small sliver of moon. They wore long white Indian shirts over trousers and sandals, and their smiles glowed whitely as they greeted her.

'Mrs Tungaraza, hello!'

'Hello, Mr Mukherjee, Dr Manavendra. Have you been for your evening walk?'

'Yes, indeed,' said Mr Mukherjee. 'But we do not normally see you out walking in the evenings. Are you alone? Is Tungaraza not with you?'

'I'm alone, Mr Mukherjee, but I'm on my way home to my husband. I usually see you walking in the evenings with your wives. Where are they this evening?'

'Ebola!' declared Dr Manavendra. 'Our wives won't leave the house until the scare is over.'

'But that's in Uganda,' said Angel, 'far from here. And yesterday in *New Vision* it said that nobody had died from it there for twelve days.'

'Yes, it's nearly over in Uganda,' said Mr Mukherjee with a laugh. 'Soon the hysteria in our house will be over, too. At least I managed to insist that the boys should go back to school. By the way, Mrs Tungaraza, the cake you made for my cousin was excellent.'

'Excellent,' agreed Dr Manavendra.

'I'm so happy that you liked it.' Angel's smile gleamed in the moonlight. 'I'm happy that I met you here on the road this evening so that I don't need to disturb you at home. I'm collecting dowry contributions for Leocadie, who works here in the shop. She wants to get married but she has no family to help her. I'm acting as her mother for the negotiations and the wedding.'

'Oh, very good,' said Mr Mukherjee, reaching for his wallet in the back pocket of his trousers.

'Yes, yes,' said Dr Manavendra, mirroring his colleague.

Angel held out the envelope with the mouth of it open so that the two men could place their contributions directly inside it.

'Thank you very much. It's very difficult for people who have nothing and no family, especially when those around them are earning dollars.'

'Very difficult,' agreed Mr Mukherjee, closing his wallet and replacing it firmly in his back pocket. 'But, Mrs Tungaraza, you must go home now. It's not safe for a lady to be out on her own at night; there's always a possibility that eve-teasing can occur.'

'Always a possibility,' agreed Dr Manavendra. 'Let us escort you home.'

'Oh, I'll be fine, really.'

'No, we insist. Come along.'

The two men walked with Angel past Leocadie's shop and past the big green skip that was already filled to overflowing again with the neighbourhood's rubbish.

'*Oof*, this is smelling very badly,' said Mr Mukherjee.

'Very badly,' agreed Dr Manavendra. 'And there's nowhere for us to put our rubbish without making mess.'

They left Angel within a few feet of the entrance to her building, when Patrice and Kalisa had greeted her and it was clear that she was safe, and turned back towards the home that their families shared.

Despite the cool night air, Angel's head was feeling very hot, so instead of going inside immediately, she sat herself down on one of the large rocks that lined the walkway to the entrance and fanned her face with the envelope of money, careful to hold it closed so that she did not shower banknotes out into the night as she did so.

The compound's owner had recently made an attempt at beautifying the front of the building with a few shrubs and some plants in enormous clay containers. Just next to the entrance was a large bush of a plant that flowered only at night, small white blossoms with a very strong perfume. The plant exhaled its perfume as Angel sat on the rock beside it, and her fanning brought its scent right to her nostrils.

Immediately—almost violently—the smell brought back a flood of memories: Vinas phoning to say she was too busy to come to Dar with the children for the school holidays, she would send them alone on the plane; Vinas phoning to check that they had arrived safely, to hear Pius's and Angel's assurances that no, her two were not too much for them on top of Joseph's three, who already lived with them; Vinas's friend phoning in a panic to tell them about the headache that no number of painkillers would take away, about using her key because Vinas had not answered her knock, about rushing her to Mount Meru Hospital, where the doctors had shaken their heads and told her to summon the family urgently; finding Vinas already cold in the morgue when they arrived; gathering the children's things to take back with them to Dar; sitting on the edge of Vinas's bed, trying to imagine the intensity of the pain that had pushed so many tablets out of the empty bubble-packs on her bedside table; needing fresh air, going out into Vinas's night-time garden, sitting under just such a night-blooming bush, gulping in the same perfume, sobbing because God had not felt it enough to take only their son.

'Madame? *Vous êtes malade?*' Patrice stood before her, peering into her face with concern.

'*Non, non, Patrice, ça va. Merci.*' Angel reached into her brassiere for a tissue and dabbed at her eyes and her hot face.

She gave a reassuring smile and Patrice retreated. Really, she must pull herself together. All of that was well over a year ago now, and dwelling on it was not going to bring her daughter back. It was not helpful to be sad when she needed to be strong. There were five children—*five!*—in her care now, and that was where her attention should be.

And she had a wedding to organise. Leocadie and Modeste were going to have a perfect day. There was so much to do! It was time to make a start on the residents of the compound whom she did not know well, and that was going to be a challenge.

And so it was that she found herself sitting in the Canadian's one-bedroom apartment, watching him enjoy one of the cupcakes that she had brought with her to sweeten her request. He was a tall man, somewhere in his late thirties, with very short brown hair and rimless spectacles. Angel noticed a gold band on his wedding finger.

'I'm not even going to be here for this wedding,' he said, his mouth still full, 'so it's hardly my responsibility to help pay for it. I'm only here on a short-term consultancy.'

'What exactly is it that you are consulting about, Dave?'

'I'm helping the government to prepare its interim poverty-reduction strategy paper for the IMF.'

'*Eh*, that is very interesting. Do you have some good ideas for reducing poverty here?'

He laughed and shook his head. 'That's not my job. I just have to make sure these guys write the paper the way they're supposed to write it. *Their* job is content, *my* job is form—although I'm finding myself having to assist with the sections on frontloading priority actions and mechanisms for channelling donor resources to priority programmes.'

Angel thought for a moment. 'Is that a way of talking about how to give money where it's most needed?'

His smile was condescending. 'In a way.'

'And tell me, does it ever happen that a donor gives money for one thing only to find that the money is used for something else instead?'

'All the time. It's expected—or, at least, it's not unexpected.'

'It's expected? Then why does the IMF give the money if it expects that it will not be used for the right thing?'

'Ah, but the IMF doesn't *give* money. It *lends* money. Ultimately all that matters is that it gets the money back, with interest. If the country doesn't use it the way it said it would, or if it uses it the right way but the project turns out to be a failure, that's not our concern; it's not our responsibility.'

'I see.'

'So anyway, Angel, I'm meeting some people for dinner tonight at Aux Caprices du Palais, and I need to get showered and dressed. This wedding you're organising doesn't concern me, so I don't think it's right to expect me to contribute. Rwandans are always holding their hands out asking for money.' He stood up.

Angel remained seated. She spoke without looking up at him. 'Yes, there are many beggars here. It's unfortunate that their poverty has not yet been reduced so that they can stop doing that. Those beggars are very inconvenient for visitors, especially for visitors who can afford to eat their dinner at the most expensive restaurant in the city. But those who have jobs are not begging, and this is a marriage of two people with jobs. The job of a security guard for this compound is very important. If something bad happens here, it's the security guards who will protect us. For example, if somebody steals money from us, it's the security guards who will stop that thief in the street outside and prevent that thief from running away with our money. They are the ones who will make sure that we will get our money back, who will solve our problem for us before the police become involved and before there is any embarrassment to our families.'

The Canadian stared hard at Angel. Then he threw his head back and laughed out loud, clapping his hands together.

'Bravo, Angel! You really are good! You know, I don't feel I owe anybody anything, certainly not the money that I work damn hard for. But I do admire your tactics, I really do.' He turned and went into his bedroom. Angel watched him go to the wardrobe and take out a box. He removed a banknote and then replaced the box in the wardrobe and came back into the lounge. Angel stood up.

'I don't suppose you've got change for a hundred-dollar bill?'

'Of course not,' said Angel, taking the note and tucking it into her brassiere.

'Of course not,' echoed the Canadian.

'Thank you, Dave. I hope you enjoy your dinner at Caprices.' Angel put her hand out. Reluctantly, the Canadian shook it.

As she walked down the stairs Angel put that same hand over her breast and felt the shape of the money in her brassiere. She had not put it with the rest of the money in her envelope because it was not going to go towards the wedding. She was going to give it to Jeanne d'Arc, one Rwandan to whom the Canadian most certainly *did* owe his money.

Of course, she had asked for the money for one thing and was going to use it for something else. But that was not unexpected.

Still, it was undoubtedly a lie. Silently, she offered up another prayer for forgiveness.

9. A Welcome

THE DRIVER of the taxi-voiture opened the back door and carefully took the cake-board that his passenger handed to him to hold while she got out of the car. He looked at the cake admiringly. It seemed to have been built up out of red-earth bricks sealed together with grey cement. On the upper surface of the cake was a large window giving a view into a dark grey interior. Thick vertical bars in light grey blocked the window, but the central bar had been broken and the bars on either side of it had been bent. Tied to the lower edge of one of the bars was a thick plait of powder-pink marzipan that looked like fabric; it hung out of the window and down over the edge of the cake, settling into a pool of plaited fabric on the cake-board.

'What does this cake say to you?' Angel asked the driver, paying him the agreed fare and relieving him of the board.

The driver pocketed Angel's fare as he spoke. '*Bibi*, it says to me that somebody has escaped from prison. He has broken the bars on the window, and climbed out on a rope that he has made from his prison uniform.'

'*Eh*, that is exactly what I want this cake to say! Thank you.'

The taxi driver furrowed his brow. '*Bibi*, is this a cake for somebody who has escaped from prison?'

'No, no. It's a cake for a *Mzungu* who has divorced her husband. She's having a party tonight here at Chez Françoise because her marriage was like a prison and now she's celebrating because she has escaped.'

'Eh, *Wazungu*!' said the taxi driver, shaking his head.

'Uh-uh,' agreed Angel, shaking her head, too.

'Angel! Are you going to stand there all morning talking to the taxi driver, or are you going to come inside and drink a soda with me?' Françoise had appeared at the gate leading into her garden, with blue plastic rollers in her hair and a green and yellow *kanga* tied round her short, stocky frame. She led Angel through the garden that constituted Chez Françoise, shouting instructions along the way to a woman who was wiping down the white plastic tables and chairs with a cloth.

'*Eh*, that cake is beautiful!' declared Françoise, as Angel placed it carefully on the counter of the small bar just inside the entrance to the house. 'This Linda is a very strange *Mzungu*, but thank you for sending her to me. It's not often that *Wazungu* come here, and tonight there'll be a party of sixteen. Tell me, Angel, is that girl always only halfway dressed?'

Angel laughed as she endeavoured to balance her buttocks—tightly encased in a smart long skirt—on a high wooden bar stool that rocked slightly on the uneven floor surface. She held on to the edge of the bartop to prevent herself from toppling over.

'*Eh*, Françoise, I hope she dresses more modestly when she talks with big men about human rights being violated. How is a minister going to listen to what she is saying about rape, meanwhile she is showing him her breasts and her stomach and her thighs?'

'At least he'll be *thinking* about rape!' said Françoise, laughing and shaking her head. 'Fanta *citron*?'

'Thank you.'

Françoise retrieved two bottles of lemon Fanta from one of the two large fridges that stood against the wall behind the bar, and levered off their tops. She placed two glasses on the counter before climbing onto a bar stool on the other side of the counter, opposite Angel.

'But seriously, Angel, even if she covers up her body, she's still too young. Big people cannot take a young person seriously.'

'Exactly. It's only with age that a person becomes wise.'

'Yes.' Françoise drank some of the soda that she had poured into her glass. 'Whoever is paying her big *Mzungu* salary, they are wasting their money, because what can she achieve here? Nobody will listen to her.'

'But still, they're *spending* their money; sometimes that's all that matters to some organisations. They can say to everybody, "Look how many dollars we are spending in Rwanda; look how much we care about that country."' Angel sipped her soda before continuing. 'But let us not complain too much, Françoise. Tonight her *Wazungu* friends will be spending their *Wazungu* salaries here at Chez Françoise.'

'Yes.' Françoise smiled. 'I'm going to make everything perfect for them so that all of them will want to come back again.'

'A good way to impress them tonight will be to serve Amstel.'

'Yes, thank you for giving me that tip earlier. I phoned a friend in Bujumbura and she was able to get two cases to me. Well, there *were* four cases, but the customs officials on both sides of the border had to be taken care of. But I think that will be enough to please these *Wazungu*. I do need more customers.'

'Is business still not good?'

'It can always be better. A lot of customers come just to drink, and then they go home to eat. Or they come here with their stomachs already full. It's only when they eat here that I can make a good profit.' Françoise sighed. 'It's not easy to raise a child alone.'

'*Eh*, it must be very difficult,' said Angel. 'I'm lucky that I still have Pius; I don't know what I would do without him. I'm not an educated somebody who can get a good job with a good salary.'

'Me neither,' said Françoise. 'I thank God that my husband built this business in our garden many years ago. After they killed him and our first-born, all I had to do was keep it going.'

'*Eh*, Françoise! I knew that your husband was late, but I didn't know that they had killed your first-born, too!'

'You didn't know?' Françoise looked surprised.

Angel shook her head. 'You never told me, Françoise. How can I know something that I'm not told?'

'I'm sorry, Angel. I thought you knew because everybody knows. Everybody round here.' The circular gesture that she made with her right arm to indicate everybody in the vicinity—perhaps even everybody in Kigali—triggered a serious wobble of her stool. Steadying herself by clutching at the counter, she went on, 'But really, when I think about it, how can somebody from outside this place know without being told? So let me tell you now, Angel.' She took a sip of soda, and when she spoke again there was no sadness in her voice; there was no emotion at all. 'They killed my first-born as well as my husband.' Her words seemed to come from a barren hardness deep inside her, a place of cold volcanic rock where no life could take root and thrive.

'I'm very sorry, Françoise,' said Angel, sorry for Françoise's loss but also sorry for having made her friend tell her that she had lost a child.

'It happened right there,' she said, pointing towards the gate that opened on to the street from the garden. 'I watched it.'

'*Eh!* You watched it?' Angel clapped her hand over her mouth and looked at Françoise with wide eyes.

'Yes. I'd gone to check on my mother-in-law because she wasn't well. Gérard was still a small baby, so I strapped him to my back and took him with me. I was still breastfeeding. When I came back in the evening the darkness was already coming. I saw from the end of the road that there were many people near our gate, and I thought that they were customers. But as I got closer I saw that they were young men with machetes and soldiers with guns. I knew at once that they had found out.'

'Found out what?'

'We'd been hiding people here, protecting them from the killers. There's a space in this house between the ceiling and the roof; I don't know how many we put in there. And round the back there's a lean-to where we keep the wood for the cooking fire. Some hid in there, behind the wood.'

'*Eh!* Were these people your friends?'

'Some were friends; some were neighbours; some we didn't know.'

'But you risked your lives for them?'

'Angel, you have to understand what was happening. Every day the radio told us that it was our duty to kill these people; they said that they were *inyenzi*, cockroaches, not human beings. But if we had killed them, we would not have felt like human beings ourselves. How could we live with the blood of our friends and our neighbours on our hands? There were thousands who did what they were told to do, thousands who had no choice because it was kill or be killed. But we felt that we had a choice because we had this bar.'

Angel was confused. 'I don't understand. What does this bar have to do with it?'

'We'd heard about what was happening at Mille Collines. Thousands were hiding there from the killers. Whenever the soldiers went to that hotel looking for *inyenzi*, the manager gave them beer to drink and they went away.'

'So you thought you could do the same?'

'Yes—but of course on a much smaller scale. And it worked for a while. Until that evening when I hid behind the wall of a garden across the road with my baby on my back and I watched them hacking his brother and his father to death, along with the people from in the ceiling and from behind the wood.' Françoise took a sip of her soda. She seemed unmoved by her own story, as if she had just spoken about buying potatoes at the market.

'*Eh!*' Angel found the horror too difficult to imagine. Yes, she had lost her own children, unexpectedly, and her son's death had been violent, but she had not watched either of them die. She and Pius had begun to prepare themselves to lose Joseph from the moment he had told them that he was positive, even though he was still fit and well. Even so, when the police had come to their door in Dar es Salaam to tell them what they had learned from their colleagues in Mwanza, the shock of his loss had been devastating, and it had taken them a long time to learn to cope with it. Then they had lost Vinas, too, and they had still not even begun to cope with that. They had not even spoken—really spoken—to each other about it yet. When they did, would Angel be able to do it in the way that Françoise did, without showing any emotion? Perhaps Françoise simply had no emotion left to show.

'What did you do after that, Françoise?'

'I sat behind that wall for a long time, praying to God to keep my baby quiet until the killers had moved on. Then I spent the whole night making my way slowly back to my mother-in-law's house—because where else did I have to go? But when I got there at dawn, I found that the killers had already been there before us.'

'Eh!'

'Yes. So I fled up north to where a relative worked on a pyrethrum farm. I was safe there; nobody was going to try to kill me, because nobody there knew that I was guilty of trying to save lives. It wasn't long before Kagame's forces came and put an end to the killings. When it was safe enough to come back, I expected to find the bodies still here, but they had all been taken and buried in a mass grave somewhere. All I could do was clean up this place and begin again.'

'Eh, Françoise, you have told me a very sad story,' said Angel, shaking her head. 'But at least you survived.'

Francoise rolled her eyes up in her head, slid down from her bar stool, and drained her glass. Then she took a deep breath, and said, 'Let me tell you something about surviving, Angel. People talk about survival as if it's always a good thing, like it's some kind of a blessing. But ask around among survivors and you'll find that many will admit that survival is not always the better choice. There are many of us who wish every day that we had *not* survived. Do you think I feel blessed to go in and out through that gate where my husband and my child were killed? Do you think I feel blessed to see what I saw that night every time I close my eyes and try to sleep? Do you think I feel blessed not knowing where the bodies of my husband and my first-born lie?'

Angel looked at her friend. For the first time ever, Françoise had shown emotion—and that emotion was anger. 'No, I'm sure you don't feel blessed. Survival must be a very difficult thing, Françoise.'

'I tell you, Angel, if I'd been alone that night, if I hadn't had Gérard on my back, I would have come out from behind that wall and said to the soldiers, "I am that man's wife. I too am guilty of protecting *inyenzi*; I too must die." I did not do that. But there are many, many times when I wish I had.'

'Eh! It's a very sad thing that you're telling me, Françoise.' Angel reached into her brassiere for a tissue, removed her glasses, and dabbed at her eyes.

'I'm telling you because you're my friend, Angel—and because you're not from here, so I can be honest with you. But what I'm telling you is not something unusual.'

Angel shook her head and was silent for a while before she spoke. She put her glasses back on. 'Françoise, my friend, you have educated me today. These things have not been easy for me to hear, but now I understand better. Thank you for telling me.'

'No, Angel, I am the one who must thank you. Thank you for being someone who has ears that want to hear my story and a heart that wants to understand it. And thank you for sending a big group of *Wazungu* to Chez Françoise.' Françoise flashed her teeth in a wide smile, and Angel found herself smiling back. What they had spoken about had already been put away, like potatoes that have been brought home from the market and placed inside a cupboard in the kitchen.

'I'm sure it will be a very good party, Françoise. Those *Wazungu* will enjoy themselves, and they'll tell others to come here.'

'*Eh*, and when they see your beautiful cake they'll tell others to come to you.'

'Let us hope.'

'Yes. Let us hope.'

It was shortly before noon when Angel eased herself out of a packed minibus-taxi at Kigali's central station. The sun was extremely hot now, but Angel did not have to meet Odile until 12.45, so there was no need to make herself any hotter by hurrying. She walked slowly up to the traffic circle at Place de la Constitution and headed in the direction of the post office, looking for a place where the road was safe to cross. She passed the row of men who sat on chairs placed on the unsurfaced roadside, each behind a small desk and typewriter, preparing documents for the clients who stood over them dictating or issuing instructions. Beyond them she was approached by a few money-changers, the overflow of the large crowd who operated outside the post office.

'*Change*, madame?'

'*Non, merci.*' Actually, she did want to change some money—the hundred-dollar note that the Canadian had given her—but she wanted to do that at the bank, even though she would get a much better rate from the money-changers on the street.

She crossed the road and made her way back around another section of the outer perimeter of the traffic circle, turning right into Boulevard de la Révolution. On the corner was the Office Rwandais du Tourisme et des Parcs Nationaux, where people went for permits to visit the gorillas in the rainforest in the north. She was not sure why anybody would want to do that, but it was popular enough among *Wazungu*.

The boulevard was wide and shady, lined with tall eucalyptus trees, and Angel appreciated its coolness as she approached another, smaller traffic circle, the Place de l'Indépendence. Here she found a young man sitting at the roadside selling secondhand shoes. She greeted him in Swahili and he returned her greeting, jumping to his feet. The shoes were laid out neatly in pairs on the ground. Angel scanned them keenly, searching for the perfect shoe to complement her dress for Leocadie's wedding. Alas, there was nothing here that would do.

'Are you looking for something special, Auntie?'

'Yes, but I don't see it here. It must be yellow or orange, or at least white. Smart-smart.'

'Wait here, Auntie,' instructed the young man. Shouting instructions in Kinyarwanda to a boy who stood on the other side of the road, he raced up the road on his bare feet.

The boy on the other side of the road eyed Angel and then, bending to pick up what lay at his feet, he crossed to where she stood. He bent again, and placed his bathroom scale at her feet.

'*Deux cents francs*, madame,' he said.

'*Non, merci*,' said Angel.

'*Cent francs*, madame.'

Angel shook her head. '*Non, merci. Non.*' The degree to which her skirt strained across her buttocks and thighs already told her as much as she wanted to know. The boy moved his scale away and squatted down sulkily next to it, eyeing Angel to make sure she did not try to make off with any of his friend's shoes.

Within minutes, the shoe-seller was back, panting towards her with two other men in pursuit, each carrying a large sack over one shoulder. They rushed towards her, each desperate to be the first to reach her, and spilled the contents of their sacks at her feet, talking nonstop in Kinyarwanda. Scrabbling among his wares, one retrieved a white shoe with a high heel and a strap across the top secured at the side with a gold buckle. Angel could see at once that it would be too small for her. She shook her head.

The other man produced a bright yellow sandal that would fit Angel well enough. She took it from him and examined it thoughtfully. The colour was good, but the heel was very flat, making it too casual for the wedding. She handed it back, shaking her head.

As both men continued to scrabble about for the perfect shoe for her, Angel became aware of a child's high-pitched shouting, rapidly gaining in volume. Looking to her right, she saw a very small boy hurtling towards her, clutching something gold and shiny to his chest. Reaching her, the boy drew to a halt and, gasping for breath, held up what he had been carrying. It was a pair of gold court shoes, clearly secondhand but still smart, with a heel that was not too high and not too flat, in a size that would fit Angel. The shoes would look beautiful with her wedding outfit. Having regained his breath, the small boy was now babbling ceaselessly up at her in Kinyarwanda.

'What is he saying?' she asked the original shoe-seller in Swahili.

'He says his mother is selling that shoe for a very good price, Auntie. He wants you to go with him to pay his mother. She is selling on the street just before the pharmacy.'

'Thank you. Please thank these other gentlemen for me and tell them that this boy has brought me exactly what I'm looking for. I'm sorry that I cannot buy from all of you.'

The young man smiled. 'No problem, Auntie. Maybe next time.'

Angel took the small boy's hand and allowed herself to be led to where a woman sat at the side of the road with a few pairs of shoes laid out before her. They negotiated a reasonable price, and Angel handed over some money from her brassiere while the woman placed the shoes in an old plastic bag. Seeing somebody with money to make a purchase, several sellers of pirated music cassettes approached Angel, but she waved them off with a smile and crossed the road to the entrance of the Banque Commerciale du Rwanda, where a bored security guard checked that her plastic bag did not contain a gun before allowing her to enter.

Once inside the plush, modern building, she made her way round to the foreign-currency section of the bank. She stood behind the stripe on the floor where people were supposed to wait until the cashier was free. There was just one customer busy at the window ahead of her, a large man in West African attire who was waiting patiently for paperwork to be completed. At last he signed, took his own copy, and, thanking the cashier, walked away.

Angel approached the window, removing the hundred-dollar note from its place of safety inside her brassiere. The cashier was still busy putting the previous client's paperwork together with a paperclip and had not yet looked up at her. When he did, his eyes lit up above his reading glasses and a large smile spread across his face.

'Angel!'

'Hello, Dieudonné. How are you?'

'*Eh*, I'm very well, Angel. And how are you?'

'Fine, fine. How are your mother and your sister?'

'Oh, everybody is very well, thank you. And how are your children and your husband?'

'Everybody is well, thank you, Dieudonné.'

'*Eh*, I'm happy to see you. You're lucky that you came just at this time, because in a few minutes I'll be on lunch.'

'Yes, I thought so. I've just brought some dollars to change into francs, and then I'm meeting a very good friend for lunch, a lovely Rwandan girl.'

'That is very nice.' Dieudonné took Angel's single banknote and began counting out a large pile of Rwandan francs.

'Dieudonné, it would make me very happy if you would join us for lunch. I like my friends to know one another, and I'm sure that you two will like each other.'

Dieudonné laughed as he handed the money over to Angel. 'Then I would like to meet her! But I have only one hour for lunch.'

'No problem. I'm meeting her nearby, at Terra Nova, opposite the post office. They have a buffet, so we can get our lunch quickly.'

'In fact I go there quite often. Shall I meet you there in ten minutes?'

'Perfect.'

Angel tucked the wad of francs into her brassiere and headed out of the bank with her gold shoes in their plastic bag. She made her way back down the shady boulevard, greeting the shoe-seller with a smile as she passed him, and then round into Avenue de la Paix before crossing the road at the post office. She entered the yard of the outdoor restaurant, where a waiter was settling Odile at a white plastic table in the shade. The young woman smiled when she saw Angel, standing up to kiss her left cheek, then her right, then her left again.

'How are you, my dear?'

'I'm well, Angel. Thank you for suggesting that we meet here for lunch. Usually I just eat at the restaurant at work, but it's nice to take a break like this, especially at the end of the week.'

'It's nice for me, too. Usually I eat at home with the children, but I thought it would be good to spend some time with my friend away from her work—and away from my work, too. The children are safe without me because Titi is there.'

A waiter brought a cold Coke for Odile, levered open the bottle, and poured it into a glass. Angel asked him for a cold Fanta *citron*.

'Odile, I hope you don't mind. I've just bumped into another friend of mine and I invited him to join us for lunch. He's a very nice young man. Very nice indeed.'

Odile smiled nervously. 'Angel! What are you trying to do?'

Angel smiled back. 'I'm trying to introduce two of my friends to each other. I want them to know each other; that's all. They are under no obligation to like each other.'

In the event, though, Odile and Dieudonné *had* liked each other, and Angel found that extremely satisfying as she sat in her cool lounge later that afternoon, fanning her face with a Cake Order Form and appreciating the looseness of her *kanga* and T-shirt. Her bare feet were up on the coffee table, her ankles swollen from the heat and the busyness of her day. The girls were working on their homework with Safiya upstairs, while the boys were out in the yard with Titi, kicking their ball around halfheartedly in the heat.

Half dozing, Angel assessed that, overall, it had been a successful day: people had admired her prison-escape cake; she had gained a new perspective on the matter of survival; she had found exactly the right pair of shoes for Leocadie's wedding; and, best of all, Odile and Dieudonné had found plenty to talk about over their plates of delicious *matoke*, rice, fried potatoes, cassava leaves, carrots, beef and chicken.

Beginning to drop off to sleep, Angel was roused by a heavy knock on the open door of her apartment.

'Hello?' called a deep male voice. 'Angel?'

Angel took her feet off the coffee table and stood up, calling as she did so for the visitor to come in. The head that looked round the open door was bald on top with a band of black hair from ear to ear at the back and a neatly trimmed black beard from ear to ear at the front.

'Hello, Angel,' said the Egyptian, talking through his alarmingly big, hooked nose.

'Mr Omar!' said Angel.

'Just Omar,' he said, shaking Angel's hand. 'I hope I'm not disturbing you?'

'Not at all, Omar. Please come and sit. You know, I've called at your apartment a few times this week, but you've always been out.'

'Yes, Eugenia told me.' Omar sat down heavily opposite Angel. 'I believe you're collecting money for a special wedding?'

'Yes. One of our security guards is going to marry the girl who runs the shop in our street. I'm organising the wedding for them because they have no family except for us in this compound.'

'Of course I'll contribute.' Omar stood to retrieve his wallet from the back pocket of his trousers and then sat down heavily again. He took a few notes from his wallet and handed them to Angel, then left his wallet on the coffee table. 'And I'd like you to make a cake for me, Angel.'

Angel smiled as she stood up. 'Then I'll give you my album of cakes to look through while I make tea for us to drink. We cannot discuss business without tea!'

Angel gave Omar her photo album and went into her bedroom to put his contribution with the rest of the wedding money in the envelope that she was keeping on the top of the wardrobe for safety. Then she went into the kitchen to make tea.

When she came back into the lounge carrying two steaming mugs, Omar was admiring her photos.

'You're very clever, Angel. Something of an artist, in fact.'

'Thank you, Omar.' Angel put the mugs on the coffee table and sat down, patting her hair with her hand. 'I'm sorry I can't offer you cake to eat with your tea. I wasn't here at lunchtime, and the children ate all the cake instead of eating their rice and beans.'

Omar suddenly made an alarming sound through his enormous nose, rather like the sound of hippos mating in the shallows of Lake Victoria. But he was smiling and his belly was moving up and down. Angel smiled nervously.

'That's children for you,' he said. 'Mine would do just the same.'

'Oh, you have children?'

'Yes, yes. A son of sixteen and a daughter of thirteen. They're both in Paris with their mother. My daughter, Efra, she's coming to visit me here next week. That's why I want a cake. She's been angry with me, but I think we've negotiated a kind of peace.' Omar took a sip of tea. 'Oh, this is very good, Angel. What's the spice?'

'Cardamom. It's how we make tea in my home country.'

'Cardamom?'

'Yes.'

Omar put down his tea and sank his head into his hands.

'Omar?'

When he looked up, his pale brown complexion had turned slightly red. He shook his head.

'This will not do,' he said. 'I've been trying to forget an unfortunate incident, but it seems I cannot.'

'Omar, you're not making sense to me. Please tell me what's bothering you. It may be that I can help you.'

Omar made the alarming sound of mating hippos again, but this time it was much quieter, as if the hippos were in the distance, and he looked embarrassed. 'Perhaps you can, Angel. Some time back I was preparing *fattah* . . .'

'What is *fattah*?'

'It's a dish that we cook in Egypt, very well known. I'll cook it for you one day. Anyway, I had just started when I realised that I had no cardamoms left. So I sent Eugenia to my upstairs neighbours to ask for some.' Omar stopped talking and took a sip of tea. He put the mug down on the coffee table. 'But she came back with *condoms* instead.'

Angel could not stop herself from laughing. Omar looked at her and began to laugh as well, great blasts of mating grunts exploding from his nose. The more he made his hippo noise, the more Angel laughed, and the more she laughed, the more he did, too.

Several minutes passed before either was capable of speech.

'I suppose it *is* quite funny,' said Omar, wiping tears from his eyes with the handkerchief that he had retrieved from the pocket of his trousers. 'But I've been so very embarrassed about it.'

Angel was dabbing at her eyes with a tissue. '*Eh*, Omar, your story is very funny to me—more so because I've already heard part of it from Sophie.'

'Oh, no! Please tell me, Angel, what does she think of me that I send my servant to get condoms from her?'

'She's very embarrassed, Omar. In fact, she's been trying to avoid meeting you on the stairs.'

'I've been doing the same! I don't understand why Eugenia got it so wrong! All right, her English *is* limited, but we were in the kitchen, I was cooking, I needed cardamoms. How could she think I wanted condoms?'

Angel was still battling to control her laughter. 'I suppose a condom is more familiar to her than a cardamom,' she suggested. 'But tell me, Omar, how did this *fattah* of yours taste when you added the condoms?'

Again the mating bellow blasted from Omar's nose, and Angel doubled up with laughter.

'No,' said Omar, struggling to get his breath, 'I had to go out to buy some cardamoms. I didn't want to risk sending Eugenia to any other neighbours. I wish I'd known that you had some here.'

'Always,' said Angel, dabbing her eyes again. 'You can always get them from me. But I think that is one spice that you will not run out of again.'

'True, true. But, Angel, what should I do about Sophie? How should I explain the mistake to her?'

'I can explain it to her if you like,' Angel offered. 'Then perhaps you can talk about it together afterwards. I think she'll be nervous if you go and knock on her door before she understands what happened.'

Omar looked as though a weight had been lifted from his shoulders. 'I'd be very grateful if you'd do that for me, Angel. Thank you.'

'No problem. I'll tell you as soon as I've explained what happened, and then you can go and talk to her.' Angel sipped her tea. 'Now. You said that you want a cake for your daughter.'

'Yes. She'll be here for just over a week and I want to make her feel welcome, because things have been difficult between us since her mother and I split up.'

'And do you have an idea of how you want the cake to look or what you want it to say?'

'Yes. I saw one in your album shaped like a heart. I think it should be like that.'

'That's a very good shape for a situation like this,' agreed Angel. 'What colour do you think it should be?'

'Oh, red, definitely. It's her favourite colour. And perhaps it can have her name on the top. Efra. I'll show you how it's written in Arabic and you can copy it.'

'That would be good,' said Angel.

They spent a few minutes completing the formalities of the Cake Order Form and making arrangements for delivery before sitting back to finish their tea.

'You know, Omar, I've heard that some of the first *Wazungu* that came here thought that the Tutsi people had originally come from Egypt.'

'Oh, that's a misconception that's driving us mad! I think you know I'm a lawyer for the genocide trials here?' Angel nodded. 'Many of the accused try to use that as an excuse. Some half-brained colonial explorer thought the Tutsis looked more Arab than African, so he speculated that they must have come from down the Nile. That gave the *génocidaires* a perfect excuse to get rid of them.' Omar hooked the index and middle fingers of each hand and waved them in the air to indicate quotation marks. '*They don't belong here so let's send them back down the Nile to where they came from!*'

'Yes, they put all those bodies into the Kagera River and the river carried them to Lake Victoria.'

'The source of the Nile.'

'But they look nothing like somebody from Egypt!'

Omar pointed to himself with both hands. 'How many Tutsis have you seen who look like me?' A loud snort of derision blasted from his nose. 'Whoever the half-blind colonial was who made that observation should be charged with genocide, even though he's long dead. His words lit the fire in which the genocide would be cooked up—and the Belgian administration added fuel to the flames by exaggerating the differences.' Again Omar made quotation marks in the air. '*Tutsis are superior, so let's privilege them. And let's make everyone carry a card saying if they're Hutu or Tutsi—just so that we can tell the difference.* But of course the very perpetrators who are using what the colonials said as an excuse for their killing, they are the ones who are quick to reject everything else that the colonials ever said.'

Angel thought for a minute. 'I wonder if those colonials had any idea back then what the consequences of their actions would be today.'

'Oh, I'm sure they couldn't have known. I doubt if they would have cared, either.' Omar drained his mug and cradled it in his large hands. 'It's the same today. Government leaders don't think twice about borrowing money from the big financial institutions because they'll only have to pay it back in forty years' time—and in forty years' time it'll no longer be *their* responsibility because a different government will be in power. And how many of us ever stop to think about the consequences of our own actions on a daily basis? Look at me. I fooled around. It was fun. So I fooled around some more. Now my marriage is over and my son refuses to speak to me, and my daughter and I are struggling to be friends.'

Angel tried not to think about struggling to be friends with her own daughter. 'I suppose you're right, Omar. Perhaps it isn't human nature to think very far ahead.'

The two said nothing for a while as they contemplated this. It was Angel who broke the silence.

'But now you have an opportunity to make things better with your daughter, Omar. What do you plan to do while she's here?'

'Oh, I've deliberately not made any plans. I don't want her to accuse me of making decisions without consulting her; whenever I do something like that she shouts: *Objection!*' Omar's quotation marks shot up into the air around this word. 'I'll put a few options to her and then she can make up her own mind.'

'That'll be good. You know, Efra is not much older than my girls. Perhaps they can spend some time together while she's here.'

'Good idea. Thank you, Angel.' Omar put his empty mug down on the coffee table and stood up, tucking his wallet into his back pocket. 'And thank you in advance for speaking to Sophie for me.'

'No problem,' said Angel, beginning to laugh again.

10. A Confirmation

BOSCO SIGHED HEAVILY and banged the palm of his right hand down hard on the steering wheel of Ken Akimoto's Pajero. Angel was right: it was good for Alice that her father was trying to secure a scholarship for her to study in America. But it was certainly not good for Bosco.

'Auntie, what am I supposed to do while she's in America for her degree? For three years, Auntie. Three years is a very, very long time!'

'I'm sure she'll come home for holidays during that time, Bosco. *Eh,* Bosco! Be careful of these potholes! I don't want my teapot to break.'

In her lap, Angel cradled a beautiful blue-grey teapot, handmade by Batwa potters at the workshop outside Kigali that she had just visited with Bosco. She had thought long and hard about what to give Leocadie and Modeste as a wedding present, and at last she had decided that the most appropriate gift would be some of this pottery. The Batwa were a tiny minority in Rwanda, small not just in number but also in stature, and Angel had not heard about them before she came to live in Kigali. Of course she had heard about Hutus and Tutsis—in 1994 the whole world had heard about them—but she had not heard about this third group of tiny people who, long ago, used to live in the forests. They, too, had suffered terrible violence and discrimination, but Angel could not remember hearing about them in any of the news reports. It was only right, she thought, to commemorate the union of two of the three groups with a gift made by the third.

She had gone to the pottery workshop with no clear idea of exactly what she was looking for. It was Bosco who had pointed the teapot out to her. He had said that it was a good gift for Angel to give because she was always giving people tea to drink; it was something that would remind Leocadie of her wedding-mother. And he was right.

'Sorry, Auntie,' he said now, slowing down the Pajero. 'Auntie, it's not just that Alice will be away for three years. You know that since I got Perfect as my niece, I've wanted a baby of my own. Now, how can I wait three years for that?'

'But, Bosco, you knew when you met Alice that she intended to study at university. She was not one of the Girls Who Mean Business.'

'Yes, Auntie. But I thought she would attend classses here, at KIST.'

'And how was she going to attend classes *and* have a baby?'

'There are classes in the evenings, Auntie. She could look after the baby in the day while I'm at work, and then in the evening I could look after the baby while she attends classes.'

'That's a good plan, Bosco. But is it a plan that you and Alice made together?'

'No, Auntie,' said Bosco, slowing down further as he navigated his way around two cyclists.

'These days a man cannot make decisions on his own, Bosco. It was different before—when I was your age—but these days a man cannot just tell a girl what to do. There has to be consultation, negotiation. I'm sure Alice knows about these things, because Sophie is her teacher.'

Bosco was quiet for a while before he said, 'Then, Auntie, is it OK for me to ask her not to go to America?'

Angel looked at him. 'What do you think my answer to that question is going to be?'

He made a tutting sound with his tongue against the roof of his mouth and sighed heavily. 'It's not OK, Auntie.'

'Yes. If she gets the opportunity to go, then of course she must. She's still young, Bosco.'

'I know that, Auntie. If she goes, then I think I must love somebody else instead. Somebody who is not so young.'

'*Eh*, Bosco, the way you say that makes me think that you already know this somebody else that you're going to love.'

'No, Auntie.'

'Are you sure, Bosco?'

'*Eh*, Auntie!' Bosco gave an embarrassed smile. 'OK, I thought for a while of loving Odile. But Odile cannot bear children.'

'*Eh*? She cannot?' This was something that Angel had suspected, because it explained why Odile had never married. The purpose of marrying was to have children, and a woman who could not bear children was of little use to a man.

'Uh-uh. In the genocide they cut her with a machete in her parts, her woman's parts. I like Odile very, very much, she is very, very nice. But I want to have babies, so I'm not going to love her. No, Auntie, there is nobody else that I'm going to love. Not yet.'

'That's good. Because Alice has not gone to America yet, and maybe she won't go at all. It's not easy to get a scholarship.'

'I know, Auntie. I'm just trying to plan ahead.'

They drove in silence for a few moments. Angel ran her hands over the shiny roundness of the teapot in her lap, feeling very happy with her purchase. She was happy, too, that Ken had agreed to let Bosco drive her to the Batwa pottery workshop. And of course she was happy that Bosco was her friend.

'*Eh*, Auntie!' said Bosco suddenly. 'I forgot to tell you! Alice told me that her friend, the one who is the sister of Odile's brother's wife, that friend told Alice that Odile has a boyfriend now!'

'A boyfriend? Odile? Are you sure?'

'Very, very sure, Auntie.'

'*Eh!* Do you know this boyfriend's name, Bosco?'

'No, Auntie. But Odile's brother's wife told her sister, and then her sister told Alice, that he works in a bank.'

A wide smile lit up Angel's face. She was very happy indeed.

Later that afternoon, as she finished decorating a cake that had been ordered for a retirement party the following day, Angel received a visit from Jeanne d'Arc. The children had just settled down to do their homework in the lounge, so Angel made tea and took her guest down to the compound's yard, where they sat on *kangas* spread out in the shade.

Jeanne d'Arc was an extremely beautiful young girl, and it was easy to see why men were attracted to her—even though she dressed much more modestly than many of the other girls in her profession. Today she wore a long maroon skirt over low-heeled black sandals that revealed toenails painted in a dark red colour. The same colour adorned the nails on her long, slim fingers. Draped around her shoulders and secured with a small gold brooch at one shoulder was a thin black shawl that hung in soft folds to her knees. Long, thin extensions fell down her back from neat rows radiating back from her forehead.

'I'm happy that you came to see me, Jeanne d'Arc,' began Angel. 'I have something for you.'

'For me, Auntie?' Jeanne d'Arc looked confused.

'Yes.' Angel reached into her brassiere where she had slipped the money when she had left Jeanne d'Arc in the kitchen to watch that the milk did not boil over. She held the roll of Rwandan francs out to her guest. Jeanne d'Arc looked at the money but did not take it.

With a furrowed brow she said, 'What is it that you want me to do, Auntie?'

Angel gave her what she hoped was a reassuring smile. 'This is your money, Jeanne d'Arc. I got it for you from the Canadian.'

'*Eh?*' Jeanne d'Arc still did not take the money.

'Yes. I know that he took back from you the money that he owed you, and also some other money that was already yours. I don't know how much that was, but this is what I got from him.' Angel took Jeanne d'Arc's right hand and placed the money in it, closing her fingers around it.

'Oh, Auntie,' said Jeanne d'Arc, 'I am so ashamed! I tried to steal from that man. I should not have done that.' She tried to hand the money back to Angel, but Angel raised both her hands with the palms facing forward and would not take it. 'Please, Auntie, I cannot have this.'

'Jeanne d'Arc, did you not do sex with the Canadian?'

'Yes, Auntie, I did, but . . .'

Angel gave her no time to continue. 'So did you not earn that money?'

'Yes, Auntie, but . . .'

'And did he not take from you money that you had already earned?'

'Yes, Auntie, but . . .'

'But nothing, Jeanne d'Arc! OK, you tried to steal some money from him. But he took that money back, so that matter is finished. And in fact *he* stole that money from *you*. That money is rightfully yours and you must have it. Do you not want the money that you earned? Do you not need it?'

'*Eh*, I need it, Auntie.'

'Then you must have it. I insist. I will not take it back, Jeanne d'Arc.'

Angel sipped at her tea for a while to give the girl time to think, and watched her taking deep breaths and turning the roll of banknotes over and over in her hand. At last she looked up at Angel.

'Thank you, Auntie, I will take it. Thank you for getting it for me.'

'No problem.'

Then Jeanne d'Arc peeled off one of the notes and handed it to Angel. 'Auntie, I would like to contribute to the bride-price for Modeste and Leocadie. I was going to contribute only a small amount, but now I can give more.'

Angel accepted the note and tucked it into her brassiere, watching as the girl placed the rest of the notes inside a small black handbag.

'Thank you, Jeanne d'Arc. The herd of cows is becoming big now.'

'I'm glad, Auntie. *Eh*, I'm happy to have my money; thank you again.' Her beautiful face broke into a smile. 'It has saved me from having to pay for our room with sex.'

'Good. You said *our* room, Jeanne d'Arc. Do you share a room with another girl?'

'No, Auntie, I have my two young sisters and a small boy. I've been their mother since 1994.'

'But you look like you still need a mother yourself! How old are you now?'

'I think I'm seventeen, Auntie.'

'Seventeen?'

'Yes, Auntie.'

'So you were eleven when you became their mother?'

'Yes, Auntie.' She shrugged. 'I was the oldest one left. Our parents were late, and also our brothers.' She shrugged again.

'And the small boy?'

'After we fled into the forest, we found him there by himself. We couldn't just leave him; he was very small then.' Another shrug.

'And how have you been taking care of these children, Jeanne d'Arc?'

'At first—afterwards—we went back to our family's farm. We grew potatoes and cassava there, and some bananas. But it was very difficult for us because the men that we had seen kill our family, they were still there: they were our neighbours on the other hills. Some people came from an organisation, some *Wazungu*, and they tried to help us, but they could not find anybody from the boy's family who was still alive. Really, we could not stay there. Then we all came to Kigali.'

'And have you been prostituting yourself since then?'

'Yes, Auntie. Those men had already violated me. I was already spoiled, so it didn't matter. But my sisters were not spoiled, so I wouldn't let them work. My work pays for their schooling and our clothes and food, and also our rent.' She flashed a beautiful, shy smile at Angel.

'*Eh*, I'm proud of you, Jeanne d'Arc.'

'Thank you, Auntie. Now my first sister, Solange, she's going for her confirmation in the church, and I want her to have a party with her friends to celebrate. I've come to ask Auntie to make a cake for her party.'

'*Eh!* I will be honoured to make that cake!'

'Thank you, Auntie. Just something small and simple, please.'

'It will be a beautiful confirmation cake, Jeanne d'Arc. I'll give you a very good price. Tell me, how old is Solange?'

'At her school they say she's eleven. I think she's twelve or thirteen, but she's very small. I think the reason she's small isn't because she's young; I think it's because she didn't get enough food for a long time.'

'Is she about the same size as Grace, or as Faith?'

Jeanne d'Arc thought for a while. 'Maybe she's like Faith, but I'm not sure. Maybe she's smaller.' She shrugged.

'OK. Both of my girls have already been confirmed. Grace had her own confirmation dress, and then it was altered for Faith. Why don't you bring Solange to visit us? Then we can see if the dress fits her. If it needs altering in any way, you can take it to a place in Biryogo where there are some ladies who are learning to sew. They do good work and they're very cheap. I'll tell you where the place is. Solange will have a nice dress for her confirmation. She'll feel very proud.'

Tears began to well in Jeanne d'Arc's eyes. 'Auntie, you are very kind. It hasn't been easy for me to be a mother to children who are not my children, and now you are being a mother to me when I'm not your child. You are Leocadie's mother for the wedding, too. And I know that your children here are not your children but your grandchildren. I'm sorry that your own children are late. They were very lucky to have you as their mother.'

'*Eh*, Jeanne d'Arc. *Eh!*' Tears welled in Angel's eyes, too, now.

'Auntie?'

Angel delved into her brassiere for a tissue. '*Eh*, I'm sorry, Jeanne d'Arc.' She took off her glasses, put them in her lap and dabbed at her eyes. 'It's only that I wasn't a good mother to my own daughter.'

Jeanne d'Arc took Angel's hand that was not busy with the tissue and held it. 'No, Auntie, I don't believe that. You were a good mother to her.'

Angel's sigh was deep as she shook her head. 'No, Jeanne d'Arc. A good mother does not let her daughter marry a man who is going to disappoint her, to hurt her.'

Still holding Angel's hand, Jeanne d'Arc sipped at her tea. 'Was she in love with him, Auntie?'

'*Eh!* Very much!'

'Girls have told me that to be in love is a very nice thing, a happy thing. Did you not want her to be happy, Auntie?'

'Well, yes, of course I did.'

'Then I think you were a good mother, because you let her be happy, even if you were not. Now, say you didn't let her marry him, then you would be happy but she would be unhappy. Does a good mother not put her daughter's happiness before her own?'

Angel managed a smile despite her tears. 'That is true, Jeanne d'Arc. But somehow things were never the same between us after her wedding. She was far from us in Arusha; meanwhile we were in Dar es Salaam. But there was another kind of distance between us, too. We spoke often on the phone, and always she told me that everything was OK, but later I found out that it wasn't. She had another baby some time after Faith and Daniel, but he was weak, Jeanne d'Arc. Late within some few months.'

'I'm sorry, Auntie.'

'*Eh!* That was a bad year for all of us, because my son was shot by robbers at his house.'

'*Eh!* I'm sorry, Auntie.'

'And then my daughter's husband left her, and she didn't tell me. It was only by mistake that I heard it from her helper.' Angel clicked the tip of her tongue against the back of her teeth.

'You're confusing me now, Auntie. First you told me that you were a bad mother. Now I think you're telling me that she was a bad daughter. Now I'm not sure who it is that Auntie feels she needs to forgive.'

'Now *you're* confusing *me*, Jeanne d'Arc!'

'What you have told me is this, Auntie. You think you made a mistake because you let her marry a man who was not good. But that man made her happy for some time. And, Auntie, what we know here, in this country, is that our lives can be short. If we have the chance to be happy, we must take it. Even if it is a short happiness, we are glad to have it. Now your daughter, when she was no longer happy, she kept it secret. Why, Auntie? Because she loved you. She didn't want you to be more unhappy; you were already unhappy because of your son.'

'*Eh*, Jeanne d'Arc!' Angel squeezed the girl's hand, remembering Thérèse's words about a lie holding love in its heart. 'Part of my head is telling me that you're right; meanwhile the other part is still confused. That is something that I will think about later. But there's also another secret that she didn't tell me, a secret that I haven't yet told myself . . .' She put down her wet tissue, picked up her mug and drained it.

'Auntie, in Kinyarwanda we say that a hoe cannot be damaged by a stone that is exposed. I think it means that the truth will hurt us only if it remains hidden.'

'That is a good saying, Jeanne d'Arc, and I'm going to tell you the truth now, because I feel it is time for me to tell it. I will be hearing it for the first time myself as I tell it to you. It is what I've come to suspect, and now, right now at this minute, I'm accepting that it's true.' She swallowed hard. Then she took a deep breath, and spoke rapidly as she exhaled, anxious to say it, to hear it. 'My daughter was sick, Jeanne d'Arc. She found out that she was positive when her baby was sick. That's why their marriage broke up, because AIDS came to their house.' She had no more breath to exhale.

Jeanne d'Arc finished her tea, waiting quietly as Angel gulped in air and swallowed hard.

'But that is just a small secret. It's not something that I'll be ashamed to tell others, now that I've told myself, even though many of us are still not comfortable to talk about that disease. To catch such a disease does not make a person a sinner. A foolish somebody, yes. A careless some-body, yes. An unfortunate somebody, yes. But a sinner? No.'

Jeanne d'Arc nodded her head to every yes, and shook it to the no.

'That disease is just a small pebble, Jeanne d'Arc; it is not the stone that will break the hoe. You know, I'm going to stop being angry at Vinas for lying to me, because I've been lying to myself. I've told myself stories about stress, about blood pressure, about headaches. But the hoe has sliced straight through those stories now. I have another story, I have it ready to tell, but I know now that the hoe will not even notice it. That story is that it was an accident that Vinas took so many painkillers, that she was confused by her headache, that she failed to count.' Nothing could stop Angel now. 'Jeanne d'Arc, the stone that I need to dig up, the truth that I need to expose is this: my daughter wanted to die. She took those pills to suicide herself.'

When Angel stopped speaking, she was surprised to notice that she was no longer crying; she realised that she had in fact stopped crying as soon as she had decided to tell the truth. She felt empty of emotion, the way that Françoise had seemed when she had told her own story. Telling it had shifted something in her. Putting her glasses back on, she looked at Jeanne d'Arc and saw that there were tears in the girl's eyes.

'*Eh*, Jeanne d'Arc! I didn't mean to upset you. How can you weep for my story when your own is so much worse than mine?'

Jeanne d'Arc let go of Angel's hand, removed a length of pink toilet paper from her handbag and blew her nose delicately. Then she breathed in deeply before saying, 'Auntie, I'm weeping for *you*, not for your story, because the pain of loss is heavy in your heart.'

'There is a heavier weight than loss in my heart, Jeanne d'Arc. Everybody knows that suicide is a sin, that it sends a soul to Hell. *Eh*, it's very hard for me to know that Vinas is there.'

'Yes.' Jeanne d'Arc was silent for a few moments, then continued.

'But I think that Vinas chose to do what she did in order to save others, Auntie. When she suicided herself, did she not save her parents from the pain of watching her suffer? Did she not save her children from the pain of watching her die? I think that when a person dies to save others, Hell is not the place for her soul. I think the Bible tells us that such a soul belongs in Heaven.'

Angel looked at Jeanne d'Arc. How could someone so young be so wise? 'That is true, Jeanne d'Arc. After all, Jesus died to save others. Do you think that God—'

Angel's question was interrupted by a thumping sound and a loud *eh!* echoing in the stairwell, and then Prosper came tumbling out into the yard, landing spreadeagled in the dust.

'*Merde!*' he shouted, standing up and dusting himself down.

'Prosper?' said Angel. 'Are you OK?'

Prosper observed Angel and Jeanne d'Arc through eyes that were very red. 'I'm fine, madame. I just fell over something on the stairs on my way down. Modeste and Gaspard must take better care with the cleaning.' He swayed slightly on his feet. 'Madame, I could not help overhearing before I fell that you were talking to this girl about God and Jesus. That is very good. The Bible tells us much about the sin of prostitution.'

'Yes,' said Angel. 'It tells us that Jesus forgave prostitutes and allowed them to enter the Kingdom of Heaven.'

'*Eh*, madame! I hope that you have not been forgiving this sinner!'

'Actually, Prosper,' said Angel, smiling now, 'she is the one who has been forgiving a sinner.'

'*Eh!*' Prosper shook his head and moved unsteadily towards the door of his office. 'You ladies are very confused. I myself will find some verses in the Bible for you to read.'

They watched him struggle with the key and then enter his office, and they waited for him to emerge with his Bible. But he did not come. Then, softly at first but growing louder, came the sound of snoring.

Angel and Jeanne d'Arc looked at each other and began to giggle.

That evening, as Titi and Angel were busy preparing the family's supper in the kitchen, Pius settled down in the lounge to read the copy of *New Vision* that Dr Binaisa had passed on to him. The Ebola scare was well over now, and the boys were with the Mukherjee boys down the road, playing under the watchful eye of Miremba. In their bedroom, the girls and Safiya were styling one another's hair.

Pius was halfway through reading about new allegations concerning the smuggling of diamonds and coltan out of DRC when his concentration was broken by a knock at the door.

'*Karibu!*' he called, but nobody came in. Putting his newspaper down on the coffee table and grumbling to himself, he got up and went to open the door. Standing there were two young men who were clearly not from this part of Africa.

'Good evening, sir,' said the one who was wearing smart grey suit-trousers, a white shirt and a tie. 'I hope we're not disturbing you. We're looking for a Mrs Angel.'

'Oh, Angel is my wife,' said Pius, assuming that these must be customers for cakes. 'Please come in. Angel!' he called. 'You have visitors.'

Angel came out of the kitchen, wiping her hands on a cloth. 'Hello,' she said with a smile.

'Hello, Angel,' answered the young man in the tie. 'Omar upstairs sent us to talk to you. I hope this isn't an inconvenient time?'

'Not at all,' Angel lied. Emotionally drained after her talk with Jeanne d'Arc, she was in no mood at all for business, but as a businesswoman she was obliged to remain professional at all times.

'I'm Welcome Mabizela, and this is my friend Elvis Khumalo.'

Angel shook hands with them and introduced them to Pius, who shook hands with them, too.

'Please come and sit,' said Angel, and the four of them sat down around the coffee table. 'I think that Mabizela and Khumalo are South African names?'

'*Ja,*' said Welcome with a smile, 'we're from Johannesburg. I've come up here to facilitate workshops on reconciliation, based on my experience working with the Truth and Reconciliation Commission in South Africa.'

'*Eh!*' said Pius, sitting forward with interest. 'I'm sure you have many interesting stories to tell.'

'Don't say that to him, Pius: he'll never shut up.' Elvis shook his head and laughed. '*Eish*, he'll be telling his stories all night!'

Angel looked at Elvis, who was dressed far less conservatively than his friend in a smart red T-shirt and tight black denim jeans. Short extensions hung loosely around his head.

'And what is it that *you* do, Elvis?' she asked.

'I'm a journalist, mostly freelance, always looking for a story I can sell.' The smile that he flashed was brilliant white. 'In fact that's why Omar suggested we come and see you. He said you're organising a wedding, and I want to find out more about it. Maybe it's worth a story.'

'Angel,' said Pius, 'I want Welcome to tell me his stories about South Africa, and Elvis wants to talk to you about the wedding. Why don't we invite our visitors to join us for supper?'

'Of course,' said Angel, clapping her hands together. 'Please say you'll eat with us.'

'Oh, we can't impose on you like that . . .' began Welcome.

'Nonsense!' declared Angel. 'There's plenty of food for everyone. Really, we insist that you stay.'

Elvis glanced at Welcome before saying, 'In that case, we can't refuse. Thank you, Angel, we'd love to.'

Angel went into the kitchen to redirect the dinner preparations to satisfy two more mouths. Both of their guests were thin—but healthy young men usually had big appetites whatever size they were. The chicken pieces that were roasting in the oven would have to be removed from the bone when they were cooked, and chopped into smaller pieces. She would make a stew of peas and carrots in peanut sauce, and add the chicken to that. The rice that was already cooking was not going to be enough, and it was too late to add to it—but it could finish cooking and the family would eat it tomorrow. Instead, she would make a big pot of *ugali* to have with the chicken stew.

As she and Titi busied themselves in the kitchen, Angel listened to snatches of conversation from the lounge. Pius was questioning Welcome on the significance of the distinction between what South Africa called '*truth* and reconciliation' and what Rwanda called '*unity* and reconciliation'. Could truth not make reconciliation impossible? he was asking. Was unity a possibility in the absence of truth?

When the *ugali* was just a few minutes from being ready, Angel and Titi emerged from the kitchen, and Titi was introduced to the guests before being sent to fetch the boys from the Mukherjees'.

Angel accompanied Safiya upstairs so that she could have a quick word with the girl's mother.

'Amina, we have unexpected guests for supper, and you know that we have very little space. Can I send the girls up here with their plates of food?'

'Of course, Angel,' said Amina. 'We'll be ready to eat our own meal as soon as Vincenzo has finished washing.'

'Thank you, Amina. They'll come in a few minutes.'

Back downstairs, Angel had Grace and Faith wash their hands, then sent them upstairs with a plate each of *ugali* with the sauce of chicken stew. The boys arrived home with Titi, washed their hands, and were dispatched to their bedroom with their plates of food, where Titi would join them soon. Then Titi brought a big plastic bowl into the lounge, and as each of the guests and Pius in turn held their hands over it, Angel poured warm water from a jug over their hands while they washed them. Titi dished up for herself in the kitchen and retired to the bedroom with her plate.

Angel, Pius and their guests sat around the coffee table, forming balls of *ugali* in their fingers and dipping them into the large bowl of chicken stew. As they ate, Pius and Welcome discussed the theoretical and philosophical aspects of reconciliation, while Angel and Elvis concentrated on one practical example: the wedding of Leocadie and Modeste.

'I think this is a story for a magazine rather than a newspaper,' suggested Angel. 'There must be photographs of the wedding so that readers can see that these are real people, and that reconciliation is not just an idea.'

'I agree one hundred per cent,' said Elvis. 'It'll need to be much longer than the average newspaper story anyway. Both parties will need to tell their story.'

'That's true,' said Angel, reaching for the bowl of *ugali* and beginning to shape another ball with a dip in it to hold the sauce. 'But, Elvis, I must tell you that this is a story that will interest many journalists. Very many. From all over Africa, and even from Europe and America. Magazines like *Hello!* and Oprah's new *O* magazine will be interested.'

'Absolutely,' agreed Elvis. 'Of course I would want exclusive rights to the story, and exclusive access to everyone involved.'

'Yes, and I am the one who will decide who gets exclusive access, because I am the wedding mother and I am the one who can advise the two parties whether to talk to a journalist or not.'

'I understand,' said Elvis, smiling. 'So let's cut to the chase, Angel. What is it that will persuade you to grant a particular journalist exclusive rights to the story?'

She was ready with her answer: 'The magazine that is going to tell this story must sponsor a small piece of the wedding.'

'I see. And what small piece of the wedding are we talking about?'

'The cake.'

'The cake?' Elvis looked at Angel with a mixture of relief and surprise. 'Just the cake?'

'Yes. It's going to be a very beautiful cake that I'm going to make myself. When we've finished eating I'll show you photographs of other cakes that I've made.'

'OK. Let me make a few calls tomorrow and I'll let you know in the next day or two if that's going to be possible.'

'OK, Elvis. I won't give anybody else exclusive rights until I've heard from you.'

The meal progressed with a mix of political debate, storytelling and happy laughter, and afterwards Elvis made appreciative noises as he looked through Angel's photo album.

The guests expressed reluctance at having to go, but felt that they must because there were young children in the house who needed to get to sleep.

'Where are you staying?' asked Pius. 'Can I give you a lift?'

'Oh, thank you, no, we're close by,' said Welcome. 'At the Presbyterian Guesthouse. It's less than ten minutes' walk from here.'

'*Eh*, but you cannot walk tonight,' declared Pius. 'There's no moon, and there are no streetlights along this road. You won't find your way, I guarantee. No, I'll take you there in the Microbus. I insist.'

As soon as Pius had left with the South Africans, Angel and Titi began cleaning up in the kitchen and Benedict was sent upstairs to fetch the girls. Titi took the chicken bones, carrot peelings and other rubbish out to the skip in the street so that they would not attract cockroaches or make the kitchen smell in the night, leaving Angel to transfer the uneaten rice from the pot in which it had cooked to a plastic bowl to store in the fridge. As she occupied herself with this task, Angel thought about the two young men who had just shared dinner with them. Unless she was very much mistaken—which she was sure she was not—they were more than just friends. South Africa was truly a very modern country indeed.

Suddenly the door of the apartment flew open and Titi came rushing into the lounge, trembling and whimpering, with tears running down her face.

'*Eh*, Titi!' said Angel, coming out of the kitchen. 'What's happened?' She went over to Titi, put her arm round her shoulders and led her to the sofa, where she sat down beside her. The children gathered round and looked at Titi with big eyes as she struggled to control her breathing.

'Grace, bring Titi a glass of water,' commanded Angel. 'Faith, bring tissues. *Eh*, Titi, whatever has happened you are safe now. There's no need to cry. Nothing bad will happen to you in here.'

Titi wiped away her tears with the tissue that Faith had brought and took a sip from the glass of water that Grace had handed to her.

'*Eh*, Auntie!' she said, shaking her head. '*Eh!* I was not thinking when I took the rubbish to the skip. I forgot that it had been emptied.' She took another sip of water. 'When I opened the lid to put the rubbish inside, a voice in there spoke to me and hands grabbed the rubbish from me.'

'*Eh*, the *mayibobo* are back,' said Angel. A group of street children sometimes slept in the skip at night when there was enough space inside. It provided warmth and shelter and—perhaps most importantly— instant access to anything that the neighbourhood was discarding, some of which might pass for food.

'It was very dark, Auntie,' said Titi. 'It frightened me!'

'Of course it did, Titi. You've had a very bad fright. But you're fine now. Why don't you go and wash and prepare yourself for bed, and I'll make some hot milk and honey for you.'

'Thank you, Auntie.'

While she waited for the milk to boil, Angel checked that all the children had washed their feet and brushed their teeth, and settled them into their beds with the promise that Baba would come to say good night in a few minutes. After taking Titi her warm milk in bed, she went back into the kitchen and filled the rice-pot with water to soak overnight, thinking as she did so that the few grains of rice that clung obstinately to the bottom and sides of the pot would probably seem like a big meal to one of the *mayibobo* outside in the skip. Then she thought about the small boy who was living with Jeanne d'Arc, and about Jeanne d'Arc's younger sisters. If Jeanne d'Arc were not willing to do what she was probably doing at that very moment—perhaps even in this very compound—to keep them off the street, those children could well be in that very skip.

When Pius came back from delivering their visitors to their guest-house, he found Angel frying onions in a big pot.

'*Eh*, why are you cooking at this time of night?'

'There are *mayibobo* in the skip. I just want to take them something to eat.'

'I see. And have you forgotten the reason why I uprooted us all and left my comfortable job in Dar to come and work here in Kigali as a special consultant?'

'No, Pius, I haven't forgotten.'

'It was because I need to earn more money so that we can give our grandchildren a good life.'

'I know that.'

'But now it looks to me like you intend to use my salary to feed the entire world.'

Angel emptied the rice from the plastic bowl into the pot with the onions and gave it a good stir. 'No, Pius, I just intend to use a bit of my money from my cake business to put a bit of food into those homeless children's bellies before they fall asleep on everybody's stinking rubbish.' She silenced her husband with a look. 'Our children are waiting in their warm beds for their baba to come and say good night.'

Angel added a small amount of *pilipili* to the rice and onions to give the dish some flavour and warmth, and stirred until the rice had heated through. Then she spooned the food back into the plastic bowl.

Pius was coming out of the children's room as she carried the bowl towards the door of the apartment. She hesitated for a brief moment before speaking.

'Pius, when I come back, I want us to talk.'

'What about?'

'About something that I told myself today.'

'*Eh?*'

'Oh, Pius, is it not time for truth and unity and reconciliation to stop being just theories in our house?'

'What do you mean, Angel?'

'I mean . . .' She lowered her voice to a whisper, conscious that the children were not yet fully asleep. 'It wasn't an accident, was it?'

Pius's eyes widened, and he stared at his wife for almost a full minute without blinking. It was the way that a small animal on a bush road might stare at the headlights of a car coming towards it at night.

'I mean, Vinas,' she whispered. 'The pills . . .'

He shook his head, exhaling strongly as if he had been holding his breath for a very, very long time. 'No. It was no accident.' His eyes were damp as he reached out a hand and squeezed Angel's shoulder gently. 'Come back quickly, Angel. It really is time we faced the truth together.'

Outside, Angel found Kalisa sitting on one of the big rocks that lined the path to the building's entrance. She asked him to take the food to the *mayibobo* in the skip.

'When they've finished, the bowl must come back to me. I'll wait here.'

'Yes, madame.'

Angel took Kalisa's place on the rock and stared up at the stars in the very black sky. She thought of the cake she was going to make for Solange's confirmation. She and Jeanne d'Arc had agreed on a vanilla cake in the shape of a Christian cross, white on top to convey purity and with a turquoise and white basket-weave design piped around the sides to match the confirmation dress, which was white with turquoise ribbons threaded through it. Solange's name would be piped in turquoise across the top.

Then Angel became aware that something very important had happened. She had been sitting out here next to the same night-blooming plant that grew in Vinas's garden in Arusha, and she had not been thinking about her daughter. She had not felt overwhelmed by her death. She sniffed the air. Yes, the plant had indeed been exhaling its perfume as she sat there, but the scent had not undone her.

Eh! she said to herself, unsure if it was right or wrong to have let go of some of her grief. She took off her glasses to give them a clean, but saw that they did not need it, and put them back on again. She closed her eyes to get a better sense of what she was feeling. Yes, she was still very sad, but somehow, in a small way, part of her despair had changed. It had turned to hope.

When she opened her eyes, Kalisa was emerging from the total darkness and approaching her with a small child dressed in reeking rags. The little girl was running her fingers round the inside of the bowl before licking them clean. She handed the bowl to Angel with a big smile.

'*Murakoze cyane*. Thank you very much,' she said.

11. A Wedding

ON THE MORNING of the day before the wedding, Angel stood at her work table decorating the wedding cake. There were six pieces: one very large and five smaller, all of them round. Thérèse had come the day before to help her with all the mixing and beating, and that had given her the time she had needed to finish making the scores of sugar-paste flowers—bright yellow petals with orange centres—that she had been working on all week. Now she concentrated on positioning those flowers perfectly on the white tops of the five smaller cakes. The sides were iced in the same bright orange colour as the flowers' centres, and pale lemon-yellow piped stars surrounded the rim of each cake where the white tops met the orange sides.

She had already finished decorating the larger cake. The top was the same bright orange as the sides of the smaller cakes, and its sides were decorated in a basket-weave design of white and the same bright yellow as the petals of the flowers. To match the smaller cakes, the rim where the top met the sides was studded with pale lemon-yellow stars. Towards the outer edges of the orange surface circled a pattern that Angel had created by repeating the knot-of-reconciliation design from the fabric of Leocadie's dress, in lemon yellow outlined with bright yellow. And right in the centre of the cake stood the plastic figures of a bride and groom, the pink of their skin coloured dark brown with one of the children's watercolour paints.

The next day, Angel would assemble the six pieces on the special metal stand that had been manufactured to her specifications by one of Pius's colleagues, a professor of appropriate technology. From the heavy base rose a central rod about half a metre high, on top of which was a round metal platform with a small spike in the middle. This would hold the board on which the large cake would stand. Fanning out round the central rod, angled down at about forty-five degrees, were five more rods of the same length, each ending in a horizontal platform with a small spike in the middle. The five smaller cakes would go on those.

Angel glanced out towards the balcony where the cake stand stood. As soon as she had finished positioning the flowers on the smaller cakes, she would go out there and check if it was dry yet. Bosco had managed to find some tiny tins of gold paint at an Indian shop on Avenue de la Paix, and he had spent an hour or so the previous afternoon transforming the dull grey aluminium of the stand into glistening gold.

Angel smiled to herself as she worked, sure that this wedding cake was going to look spectacular—and that she was going to look equally spectacular standing next to it—in the photographs that Elvis would take for *True Love* magazine in South Africa. Noëlla had done her hair for her earlier in the week: black extensions braided back from her forehead to the crown of her head, from where black and gold extensions hung loosely to her shoulders. The style was glamorous, without being inappropriate for a grandmother, and was similar to the looser, longer, more youthful style that Agathe had braided for Leocadie. Angel had been reluctant to spend any money on having her hair styled, because she had been planning to wear an elaborate headdress, but Leocadie had persuaded her to opt for a smaller head-covering beneath which braids could hang that would echo her own.

'I want people to see that we are mother and daughter,' Leocadie had said—and of course it had been impossible for Angel to object to that.

In Angel's wardrobe hung the dress that Youssou had created for her from the soft Ghanaian fabric with the pattern that said, *Help me and let me help you*. Titi had gone with her for the taking of the measurements, and had stood behind her, secretly inserting two fingers between Angel's body and the tape measure at every point where Youssou had measured. The result was a dress that fitted perfectly: a well-tailored, fitted bodice with cap sleeves tapered out over her hips and continued to flare out to create a wide, flowing skirt that fell softly to her feet. A strip of the same fabric tied ornately round her head, plus the gold court shoes that she had bought on the street, would complete the ensemble.

It had been a hectic week for Angel: a week of organising caterers and florists and what seemed like a hundred other people, each of whom would be required to perform a particular function to ensure that the wedding and the reception went smoothly. The florist and the people who hired out tables, chairs and marquees had tried to charge her inflated prices—until she had returned to their premises with Françoise.

'Does this woman look like a *Mzungu* to you?' Françoise had demanded of them in Kinyarwanda, her left hand firmly on her hip as she gestured with her right. 'Of course not! Our sister here is from Bukoba, just the other side of the border, a border that is only there because, long ago, *Wazungu* drew a line and said, "Here is Rwanda and here is Tanzania." Now, if you want to say that people from that side of the line must pay more, then you are saying that you are happy that those *Wazungu* drew those lines all over Africa long ago, that they were right to take our land and cut it up however they wanted. Is that what you want to say? *Is it?* Of course not! No, our sister will pay what *Banyarwanda* pay.'

And every night, at the end of each hectic day, Angel and Pius had talked in the way they always used to talk before the circumstances of their daughter's death had given them something not to talk about. AIDS had been a difficult word to speak about their son, but the bullet that had taken him had taken away their need to speak it. Now they spoke it about their daughter, together with another word: suicide. During the past week, both of those words had passed between them so often that they had lost their power, in the way that an old coin that has lost its shine seems to have less value. They were just words now, words they were able to speak with understanding rather than dread.

It had hurt them both that Vinas had not felt able to tell them she was ill—although, in truth, they did understand her motives. After all, Joseph had waited to tell them until his wife was very ill and he needed their help with the children. He had done that to spare them the worry, just as Vinas had. And both Pius and Angel had to admit that, should either of them—God forbid—find themselves with frightening or devastating news about their own health, love might well persuade them to put it away at the back of the top shelf of the highest cupboard for some time before fetching it down and showing it to each other. Really, it was not too hard to understand.

'But I still wish that Vinas had let me be closer to her after her marriage, Pius.'

'And *I* still wish that Joseph had chosen to follow an academic career. But each bird must fly on its own wings, Angel.'

Pius was still not fully convinced that Vinas had not condemned herself to an eternity in Hell. It was a complicated muddle of doctrine and ethics, he felt, a muddle that he needed to work through and clarify in his own mind even though he longed to be able to accept the more straightforward conviction at which Jeanne d'Arc had helped Angel to arrive.

Last night, Pius had come home from work looking more at peace than he had in a long while. Instead of eating lunch in the staff canteen, he had joined Dr Binaisa in his fast and told him the full story of what had happened to Vinas.

'One of my brothers did the same thing,' Dr Binaisa had said matter-of-factly. 'Soon after he was diagnosed, he drove his car into the back of a truck full of *matoke*. People said it was a tragic accident, but of course we knew it wasn't. And another brother simply disappeared when he began to get sick. *Eh*, we suspect the fish in Lake Victoria have eaten well off him!'

Pius had been shocked by this attitude. 'But what does Islam say about suicide?'

'*Eh*, it's a terrible sin! If you suicide yourself, you'll be roasted in the fires of Hell.'

'Then do you not worry yourself about those brothers of yours who are roasting in Hell?'

'Tungaraza, there are more important things on this earth to worry myself about. My worry will not change what anybody else has already done. I'm alive and I have children to raise, and that is where I need to focus my attention.'

On the afternoon of the day before the wedding, Angel sat at her work table and went through her list of things to do, checking and rechecking for anything that might not have been confirmed and reconfirmed. The ceremony itself had been arranged: a short and simple Catholic service in the Sainte Famille Church. Angel would walk down the aisle with Leocadie and present her to Modeste, who would be waiting at the altar in his brown suit that had been made for him by a tailor in Remera, and his tie that the women at the centre in Biryogo had sewn for him from the same fabric as Leocadie's dress. Next to Modeste would be his best friend and fellow security guard, Gaspard. Their guard duties at the compound would be performed tomorrow by two KIST security guards who were happy to make some extra money on their day off.

Ken Akimoto had offered his Pajero as the wedding car; Bosco would take it to the florist tomorrow morning to have it adorned with flowers and ribbons, and in the afternoon he would drive Leocadie and Angel to the church. After the ceremony he would drive them, together with Modeste and Gaspard, to the reception in the compound's yard.

Early tomorrow morning, people would come and protect the yard from any possible rain showers by securing an enormous tarpaulin to the railings of the first-floor balconies at one side, and to the top of the boundary wall at the other. Patrice and Kalisa had already removed the last of the builder's rubble from the corner of the yard by taking a small wheelbarrow-load each night to a building site a few streets away, where they had come to an arrangement with the night security guard. The Tungarazas' trailer had been taken away and left for safekeeping in Dr Binaisa's yard. Tomorrow, people would deliver round plastic tables and chairs for the guests, as well as a long, high table to go under the washing lines for the bride and groom; the lines themselves would be draped with loose folds of white muslin, and the posts supporting them would be adorned with flowers and ribbons. Angel had reconfirmed all of those arrangements.

She had also reconfirmed with the students from KIST who would be helping out: Idi-Amini, an earnest young returnee from Uganda who owned a PA system, would be in charge of sound and music; Pacifique, who was using his camera to pay for his studies, would be the official photographer at the service and the reception; and the institution's troupe of traditional dancers would perform for the guests' entertainment.

Goats had already been slaughtered, and their meat would be cooked over open fires by the women from the restaurant at the centre in Biryogo, who would also cook huge pots of rice and vegetables. Beer and sodas would be supplied by Françoise, who would keep them cool in large aluminium tubs filled with iced water. Several of the Girls Who Mean Business would be on hand to serve the drinks and food, and Thérèse, Miremba, Eugenia, Titi and Jeanne d'Arc would wash guests' hands and help with serving. The food would not be served until the sun had set, so that Muslims and non-Muslims could eat together.

In the evening of the day before the wedding, Pius came home from work exhausted. Over dinner he explained that he and a small team of colleagues had just finished putting together an important application for a prestigious—and generous—new award for innovations in renewable-energy technologies. Their entry was a bread oven that the university had developed and manufactured, capable of baking 320 bread rolls every twenty minutes using only a quarter of the wood that a conventional oven used.

'So it will save the forests here, Baba?' Benedict asked.

'It will help, certainly.'

'Then I'm sure it will win the prize.' Benedict was confident.

Pius laughed. 'How can you be so sure?'

'Because the oven will make bread to feed people so that they don't die, and it will also save the forest so that the gorillas don't die. That is a very important oven, Baba.'

'I hope you're right,' said Pius. 'You know that my job here is to help the university to generate income, to make its own money so that it can keep itself running. Publicity from the award would help a great deal. But the winner will only be announced next year. What's more important is that we'll know soon if they want me to stay here for another year.'

'How soon will we know?' asked Angel.

'They've promised to let us know by the end of next week. You know that expatriates are only here until Rwandans have qualified to fill the positions that we're filling now. Apparently, every year at this time the expatriate staff become very nervous and start to whisper about who will have their contracts renewed and who will go home.'

'Are you nervous, Baba?' asked Grace.

Pius laughed. 'No, Grace, I'm not nervous. But I'd like to know soon so that I can start to make arrangements. If we're going back to Dar es Salaam, then we must contact your school there; and if we are going somewhere else, then I need to start researching that somewhere else on the internet.'

'We can go somewhere else, Uncle?' asked Titi.

'Possibly, Titi. The University of Dar es Salaam gave me extended leave, so I can still be away for another couple of years after this one. If they don't renew my contract here, I'm not obliged to go back there immediately. I'm sure there'll be other options.'

'What about us, Baba?' asked Daniel. 'Where will we go?'

'You'll come with me wherever I go,' assured Pius. 'We're a family. And, Titi, that includes you.'

Titi beamed. Grace and Faith had styled the section of her hair from her forehead to the crown of her head in neat cornrows, leaving her hair behind that to stand tall and natural in a halo effect round her head. Grace's long hair had been cornrowed all over, and Faith's shorter hair had been parted into neat, small squares and tied into little bunches with elastic bands.

'Rajesh and Kamal are going to live in India next year with Mama-Rajesh,' said Daniel, 'even if Baba-Rajesh lives here.'

'That's not going to happen to this family, Daniel,' said Angel. 'We're going to be together, wherever we are.'

Angel cried at the wedding. The entire service was in Kinyarwanda, so she did not understand all of it—although she did understand a lot more of it than she would have at the beginning of the year. But her tears had nothing to do with her frustration at not following the language; they were caused in part by memories of the wedding of her own daughter, Vinas, and in part by the obligations of her role at this wedding. The mother of the bride was fully expected to shed tears of joy, especially when her daughter looked as beautiful as Leocadie did. Youssou had stitched the pale lemon-yellow fabric with its gold and orange pattern into a separate blouse and skirt. The skirt fitted snugly over Leocadie's hips, then flared out and flowed softly around her gold sandals, and the sleeveless blouse had been tailored to her shape with a scoop neck and with small gold buttons running down the front. The white net veil that had been made by the women at the centre in Biryogo flowed down from a gold Alice-band around her shoulders and as far as her waist.

Throughout the ceremony, Beckham sat on Titi's lap in the front pew, kicking his legs and sucking at a corner of the shirt that the Biryogo women had stitched for him from the remnants of Leocadie's pale lemon-yellow fabric.

Afterwards, after Pacifique had made them pose at the entrance of the church for photographs, an alarming number of the guests crowded into the red Microbus with Pius, Titi and the children, and the wedding party got into Ken Akimoto's Pajero with Bosco at the wheel and Angel sitting next to him in the front. Angel noticed again—as she had done on the way to the church—that it was very easy to climb up into a big vehicle in a skirt that was voluminous rather than straight and tight. Perhaps this was the answer she had been searching for. She also noticed that Bosco was rather quiet.

'Is everything OK, Bosco?'

'*Eh*, Auntie, Alice's father has found a scholarship for her in America.'

'*Eh!*'

'He spent a very, very long time on the internet looking at American universities. Now he's found a university that will accept Alice and pay her fees and books and everything. That university is very excited about Alice, because they've never had a student from Rwanda before.'

'*Eh*, that is exciting news for Alice, Bosco!'

'Yes, Auntie, for Alice. But now I must find somebody else to love.'

'I'm sorry, Bosco. That is very sad.'

'Very, very sad, Auntie,' said Bosco, as he pressed his hand down on the Pajero's horn to tell the neighbourhood the happy news that he was driving a new bride and groom.

The wedding reception in the yard of the compound was a joyous occasion. Prosper fulfilled the role of master of ceremonies with the zeal of a man proclaiming from the pulpit, peppering his speech with quotations from the Bible and even managing—every now and then—to say something light-hearted enough to raise a laugh and a smattering of applause. There was thunderous applause for Angel, though, when Prosper announced how much money was in the bride-price envelope. Of course, in the absence of Leocadie's parents, that money belonged to the bride and groom—and it was enough to buy them a small two-roomed house. The house would have no electricity or water, but it would be their own. There were not many young couples who could start their married life so blessed, and throughout the party people continued to approach Angel to congratulate her.

'That is a very fine herd of cows, Mama-Leocadie!'

'*Eh*, Angel! Those cows have very big horns.'

'Mrs Tungaraza, when our daughters are ready to marry, you are the one who will negotiate bride-price for us!'

It was only much later, after all the speeches had been made and the tables and chairs had been pushed back so that the dancing could begin, that Prosper succumbed to an overindulgence in Primus and slid quietly from his chair onto the ground beneath the high table. Angel considered simply leaving him there, but in the end she fetched Gaspard, who fetched Kalisa, and together they carried Prosper to the seclusion of his office, where it would be safe for him to remain until morning.

Long before that, just after the sun had set and the guests who were fasting had arrived and the food could be served, Angel's heart was warmed by the sight of Odile entering the yard with Dieudonné, who was carrying a small boy on his shoulders. She rushed to greet them.

'Hello, Angel,' said Odile. 'Don't worry, we're not bringing extra hungry mouths to your party! We've just come to speak to Jeanne d'Arc.'

'There's food here for many hungry mouths,' assured Angel. 'You're very welcome. But tell me, Dieudonné, who is this handsome young boy on your shoulders?'

'This is Muto, the boy Jeanne d'Arc has raised. Muto, greet Auntie.'

Clinging on to Dieudonné's head with his left hand, Muto leaned down and shook Angel's hand with his right.

'Good boy,' said Dieudonné. 'We took him swimming with us at Cercle Sportif this afternoon. Now we want to check with Jeanne d'Arc if it would be OK for him to sleep over at Odile's tonight.'

Odile smiled at Angel. 'He's made friends with Emmanuel's children. They taught him how to swim.'

Angel's heart was ready to burst. Would the next wedding cake she made be for this couple? Would they adopt Muto? She pointed to the far end of the yard where Jeanne d'Arc was pouring water from a jug onto Omar's hands as he rinsed them over the plastic bowl held by Titi. 'There she is. I'm sure she'll be very happy for you to have Muto.'

She watched them weaving their way towards Jeanne d'Arc, stopping to greet guests whom they knew and to introduce Muto to them.

After the empty plates had been cleared away, and the leftovers sent to the *mayibobo* in the skip, the traditional dancers performed again to get the guests in the mood for dancing, and encouraged Leocadie and Modeste to join them. Beckham remained strapped to Leocadie's back all the time. Amina slipped into Leocadie's empty seat next to Angel.

'Our girls are growing up,' she said, indicating with a nod of her head for Angel to look at Grace and Safiya. Ignoring the dancers, the two girls were focusing all their attention on the young man who was beating the drum. Tall and bare-chested, he stood apart from the dancers, beating out a rhythm for them on a large drum that hung from a strap round his neck to the level of his groin. Without taking their eyes off him for a second, Grace and Safiya exchanged comments and giggled.

'*Eh!*' said Angel, shaking her head. 'Trouble is going to come knocking on our doors very, very soon!'

Later, when the guests had begun to dance to the music that Idi-Amini was selecting carefully and playing through his PA system, Angel observed two other girls looking at another young man in exactly the same way. She went over to join them.

'Thank you for performing here today,' she began, speaking to them in Swahili. 'Your traditional dancing is very, very beautiful.'

The girls surprised her by answering in English. 'Oh, thank you, Mrs Tungaraza. Thank you for the work. It's just a pity that not much of our fee comes to us after we've paid to hire our costumes and drums.'

'*Eh?* You don't have your own costumes?' The girls shook their heads. 'That is not good,' said Angel, shaking her head with them. 'But I have an idea. You must speak to my husband, because he is the one who is helping KIST to raise money. Perhaps you can persuade him that KIST should buy costumes for you, because you are the university's official dance troupe. Then when you perform at occasions like this, KIST can keep some of the money and the rest can come to you.'

'That is a very good idea, Mrs Tungaraza. KIST will soon recover the cost of the costumes and start to earn a profit; and without having to pay for costume hire, we'll be in a win-win situation.'

'*Eh*, you're speaking like a business student!' observed Angel.

The girl laughed. 'Yes, I'm doing management. But I'm sorry, Mrs Tungaraza, we have not introduced ourselves. I am Véronique, and my friend is Marie.'

Angel shook hands with both of them. 'Are you also studying management, Marie?'

'No, I'm doing civil engineering. We'll both graduate next year; then I'm hoping to go to Johannesburg for my Master's.'

'Well, your English is very good. I'm sure you'll be able to study there very easily.'

'Thank you, Mrs Tungaraza. At KIST we follow the government's policy of bilingualism.'

'Don't underestimate yourselves, girls,' said Angel. 'Actually, you're multilingual, because you know Kinyarwanda and Swahili as well as French and English. Please, girls, let us not think as Africans that it is only European things that are important. When you two become ministers of what-what-what in your government, you must set an example to others by saying that you are multilingual.'

'*Eh*, Mrs Tungaraza!' said Véronique, laughing. 'We are not going to become ministers of what-what-what!'

'Somebody is going to become those ministers,' assured Angel.

'Somebody who has studied at KIST or the National University in Butare. Why not you?'

Véronique and Marie exchanged glances.

'Mrs Tungaraza, you have given us a new idea,' said Véronique. 'I have only thought as far as graduating and getting a job in Kigali as an accountant. Now I will think about the possibility of bigger things.'

'That is good,' said Angel. 'But the reason I came to talk to you was not to turn you into government ministers. I came to talk to you because I saw you looking at that young man.' Angel nodded her head in the direction of Elvis Khumalo, who was deep in conversation with Kwame.

Once again, Véronique and Marie exchanged glances, this time looking embarrassed.

'He looks nice,' said Marie shyly.

'Oh, he is a very, very nice young man,' assured Angel, 'and I will introduce you to him in a moment. But first I must tell you that he is not a man who likes girls.'

'Mrs Tungaraza?'

'He's from South Africa,' explained Angel. 'I have even met his boyfriend.'

'*Eh!* He has a boyfriend?' asked Véronique. She looked at Angel with big eyes.

'That is a fashion in America,' said Marie, disappointed. 'I didn't know it had come to South Africa, too.'

'South Africa is very modern,' said Angel. 'But let me introduce you to him, Marie. He lives in Johannesburg and he can tell you all about studying there.'

Angel took the girls over to Elvis and introduced them, leaving them to talk. Earlier, Elvis had photographed the wedding cake from many different angles, including from a first-floor balcony, where he had lain on the ground and angled the camera through the railings, under the ropes of the massive tarpaulin that covered the yard. From above, the cake had looked like a giant sunflower. Elvis had taken other photographs during the wedding, of course—photos of the bride and groom, the dancers, the women cooking in the street outside the compound, Angel and Leocadie in their beautiful dresses—but he had concentrated particularly on the cake because that was the part of the wedding that *True Love* had sponsored. Angel could not wait to receive a copy of the magazine with her cake featured in it. She would be sure to show it to Mrs Margaret Wanyika so that the Tanzanian ambassador to Rwanda would know that a Tanzanian living in Kigali was famous in

South Africa—and also, if the truth be told, so that Mrs Wanyika could see how beautiful a wedding cake could be when it was not white. Of course, Angel would not mention to Mrs Wanyika that the man who had taken the photographs and written the article had a boyfriend.

'Thank you for inviting me, Angel,' said Kwame, whose conversation with Elvis had been interrupted by the introduction of the girls.

'It's my pleasure, Kwame. I hope this wedding has helped you to believe in reconciliation.'

'Oh, it will take a lot to make me believe in that, Angel.' He smiled broadly. 'But I'm pretending to believe in it, just for tonight.'

Angel smiled back at him. 'And how does it feel to pretend to believe?'

Kwame considered his answer before he spoke. 'It feels good,' he said. 'Peaceful. Perhaps that's how people here get through each day.'

'Eh, Kwame! You just concentrate on feeling good and peaceful. Don't worry yourself tonight about whether people believe in reconciliation in their hearts or just pretend in their heads to believe in it. Tonight you're going to be happy! By the way, have you seen what Leocadie and I did with Akosua's fabric?' Angel gestured at her dress.

'It's beautiful. Elvis has promised to send me copies of his photos so that I can send them to Akosua. She'll show them to the ladies who printed the fabric and I'm sure they'll be very excited.'

'Make sure that Elvis writes down in his notebook the name of that group of ladies. That must be in his article for the magazine. Eh, this is a truly pan-African celebration today! A wedding in Central Africa, organised by somebody from East Africa, cloth from West Africa, a magazine from South Africa. Eh!'

'Ah, pan-Africanism!' said the CIA, who had appeared silently at Angel's elbow. 'That sounds like an interesting conversation.'

Angel introduced Kwame and the CIA, and left them to talk while she steered Véronique away from Elvis and Marie, who were discussing Johannesburg's nightlife.

'I'd like to introduce you to a very nice young man, Véronique. He is like a son to me.'

'Does he like girls?' asked Véronique.

Angel laughed. 'Very much! Now, where is he? I saw him dancing just a moment ago.' Angel scanned the dancers. There was Modeste, dancing with Leocadie, and Catherine's boyfriend with Sophie. Gaspard was with one of the Girls Who Mean Business, and Ken Akimoto was with another. The drummer from the dancing troupe had attached himself to Linda, who was wearing something very small and very tight. Omar was dancing with Jenna, and Pius was doing his best with Grace. At last Angel spotted the young man she was looking for, and as the song faded, she grabbed him away from Catherine.

'Bosco, I want you to meet Véronique. Véronique, this is my dear friend Bosco.'

The two shook hands, assessing each other shyly with fleeting glances from downcast eyes.

'Véronique will graduate from KIST next year,' said Angel. 'She is not one of those girls who want to study overseas. She is going to work in Kigali as an accountant.'

'That is very, very good,' said Bosco.

'Bosco works for the United Nations,' continued Angel. 'He has a very good job there as a driver.'

'*Eh*, the United Nations?' Véronique sounded impressed: it was well known that a driver for the UN earned more than she could hope to earn as an accountant for any Rwandan business.

Angel left the two alone and moved off to where she recognised two men standing at the edge of the party, sipping sodas.

'Mr Mukherjee! Dr Manavendra! Welcome! Are your wives not with you?'

'Hello, Mrs Tungaraza,' said Mr Mukherjee. 'No, my wife is at home with Rajesh and Kamal. There is no one to look after them.'

'Ah, yes,' said Angel. 'Miremba is working here tonight. And where is Mrs Manavendra?'

'At home, too,' said Dr Manavendra. 'She is fearing germs.'

'Too many germs from shaking hands,' explained Mr Mukherjee. 'Very dangerous habit in Rwanda.'

'Very dangerous habit,' agreed Dr Manavendra. 'But we came to greet the couple. They look very happy.'

'Very happy,' agreed Mr Mukherjee. 'It's a lovely party, Mrs Tungaraza.'

'Lovely,' agreed Dr Manavendra.

Angel excused herself from the two Indians and went to look for Jenna. She found her chatting to Ken, who was rather full of Primus.

'When this party's finished, you must come to my apartment for karaoke,' he said to Angel, rather more loudly than was necessary.

'Thank you, Ken, but I think I'll be too tired. It's been a long day!'

'Everything's been beautiful, Angel,' assured Jenna. 'Ken, I hope you're going to invite that young man who's been doing the music to come for karaoke. He's been singing along, and his voice is great.'

'Good idea,' declared Ken. 'Maybe we can use his mikes so that more people can sing.' He moved off rather unsteadily towards Idi-Amini.

'I'm glad I have a moment alone with you, Angel,' said Jenna. 'I want to tell you that I've made a very big decision.' She looked around her before leaning closer to Angel. 'I'm going to leave my husband.'

Angel was surprised—and she was also confused by her own reaction: the end of a marriage was sad, but this news made her feel happy.

'When we go home for the vacation, I'm not going to come back.'

'*Eh*, Jenna, I'll miss you! And what about your students?'

'They can read now—enough to carry on without me, anyway. I've kept in touch with Akosua by email, and she's been encouraging me to go back to college and train in adult literacy. When I'm qualified, I'll come back to Africa—but I'll come back alone. Don't tell a soul, Angel. I'm not going to say anything to Rob until we're back in the States.'

'Of course I won't tell.'

'Oh, look,' said Jenna, pointing towards the high table. 'It looks like Leocadie and Modeste are preparing to leave.'

Angel made her way towards them.

'Thank you so much, Mama-Grace,' said Leocadie, tears beginning to well in her eyes. 'I never believed that somebody like me could have such a beautiful wedding.'

Modeste pumped Angel's hand vigorously. '*Eh*, madame!' he said, '*Muracoze cyane! Asante sana! Merci beaucoup!*'

Angel fetched Bosco—who was no longer talking to Véronique, but assured Angel that he had got her mobile-phone number—and organised the guests into a line for the couple to greet them all on their way to the Pajero, where Bosco waited to drive them to the house in Remera where Modeste rented a room.

Most of the guests left soon after that, and the stragglers took up Ken Akimoto's invitation to end the party in his apartment with the karaoke machine. Angel did not even think about clearing up the yard; there was the whole of Sunday to do that, and several women had volunteered to come and help. With the gate at the end of the compound's driveway firmly shut, and with Patrice and Kalisa on duty in the street—and Prosper still asleep in his office—everything would still be there in the morning.

She checked on the children and Titi in their bedroom and then slipped out of her smart wedding clothes, wrapping a *kanga* round her waist and pulling a T-shirt over her head. She made two mugs of sweet, milky tea in the kitchen. Covering one with a plate, she carried both of them out through the entrance to the building and sat down on one of the large rocks next to the bush that bloomed in the dark, filling the night with its perfume. She placed the mug with the plate on the ground and took a few sips from the other.

A group of women's voices blared from Ken's windows. Angel caught some of the words: *for sure . . . that's what friends are for . . .*

Next week she would go with Pius and a group of students on an outing to the Akagera National Park, a game reserve in the eastern part of Rwanda where it bordered with Tanzania. At the end of the following week the entire family would go in the red Microbus to Bukoba, where they would spend Christmas with various members of Angel's and Pius's families. From there, Titi would go by ferry across Lake Victoria to Mwanza, to visit a cousin and some friends. After that, in the new year, who knew where they would go? Angel thought that she could feel at home wherever they went.

A few minutes later, the lights of a vehicle shone into Angel's eyes, and the red Microbus pulled up outside the building. Pius was back from giving some of the wedding guests a ride home. As the sound of the engine died, she heard a new song in the air: *Ah, ah, ah, ah, staying alive, staying alive . . .*

She shifted to the edge of the large rock and patted at the space beside her. 'Sit with me here,' she said to her husband. 'I made you some tea.'

'Oh, that is exactly what I need,' said Pius, settling down on the rock next to Angel and picking up the mug of tea that had been kept warm by the plate.

Sitting in the cool Rwandan night, the quiet of the city interrupted by song and laughter, they sipped their tea together.

Gaile Parkin

Tell me a little about yourself and your life in Africa?

I was born in the small town of Kitwe in Zambia, and I've lived and worked in various parts of the continent. Rather than having a set base, I just go wherever the work takes me—and I'm single, so I have that freedom. It can be tough living sometimes without power or clean water, but I never have to do that for ever as thousands upon thousands of Africans do. It certainly makes me appreciate the luxury of everyday convenience that so many take for granted.

You have worked in Rwanda, counselling women who have survived the genocide. Do you think that they can now start to take control over their lives?

Rwandan women show the most incredible strength and resilience, and they are well on their way to claiming their place in the world. Rwanda has a higher percentage of female MPs than any other country in the world.

In the novel, you write very movingly about how AIDS affects families. Do you think the grip of the disease will ever lessen on the African continent?

Unfortunately, knowledge doesn't necessarily translate into behaviour—look at how people still smoke—nor is knowledge always power. In many parts of the continent the gender power differential is such that women and girls have no say at all in sexual relations, and insistence on safe behaviour can provoke a beating. As women gain more power in this arena, it can unfortunately trigger a backlash that sees rape statistics soaring. And in countries beset by war and conflict, how can people focus on the long-term effects of their behaviour choices when anything long-term appears unthinkable?

Where did the idea for *Baking Cakes in Kigali* come from?

I knew I wanted to write something positive, light and funny, rather than focusing on the darkness of Rwanda's recent past. That darkness is there— but it's by no means all that's there. The idea came to me that cakes for celebrations would be a good vehicle for highlighting the joys of the place, and Angel more or less stepped forward with the cakes.

This is your first novel. Have you always wanted to be a writer?

I've been writing for over twenty years, mostly educational materials and things I've never felt like putting my name on, so this novel was a major departure.

What research did you do?

I lived in Kigali for two years, teaching and mentoring at the new university there, Kigali Institute of Science and Technology (KIST), working with the student anti-AIDS club, counselling women and girls, writing speeches for politicians, being an activist for gender empowerment, and generally getting involved in a wide range of circles and activities. I had no idea at the time that in doing all of that, I was doing research for this book!

Do you make cakes yourself?

I do make cakes, but not very well—so I only bake them when I'm living in places where there isn't much competition. I pretty much make the recipe up as I go along and hope that I'm getting the quantities more or less right. Somehow, it always works.

Are you as creative as Angel?

I certainly don't have Angel's patience, attention to detail or sense of colour—though I have decorated a number of cakes as national flags, which is easy to do. The Ghanaian flag cake I created in Rwanda for Ghana's Independence Day celebrations was such a hit that they declared me an honorary Ghanaian.

Are you as good a listener as Angel?

In my counselling I listen not just to what people say, but how they say it—and of course I'm equally interested in hearing what they don't say. I'm very curious about people, and I'm happy to strike up a conversation with just about anybody. Eavesdropping is one of my favourite activities!

Will Angel appear in future novels?

Possibly. Stay tuned . . .

When it comes to taking time off, what do you like to do?

I love spending time with animals, whether it's a neighbourhood cat or a family of gorillas in the rainforest. And I'm a course junkie—I love attending courses in a broad range of fields, just for the thrill of learning something new.

Do you have any particular ambitions you'd still like to fulfil?

Of course! I've been wanting for the longest time to do some work with the displaced and traumatised of Darfur—either in Sudan itself or in neighbouring Chad. And I'd like to work on developing a rehabilitation programme for girls recovering from childhoods hijacked by soldiers. And I want to work towards getting dedicated children's hospitals set up in East and West Africa—at the moment the only one on the entire continent is in Cape Town. And . . .

If you could change one thing about yourself, what would it be?

I'd love to have more energy to ensure that I fulfil all my ambitions!